On One Side

Four impoverished native youths accused of savage rape. The untried young Hawaiian lawyer defending them. And the beautiful girl who became his best friend and lover.

On The Other Side

The assaulted woman. Her enraged husband and handsome, ruthless lover. Her imperious socialite mother. And the secret they concealed through the power of wealth and privilege, the clout of the U.S. Navy, the surgical skill of an alcoholic doctor, and the legal magic of a famous criminal attorney from the mainland.

And In The Middle

Curt Maddox, the hard-as-nails police officer investigating the crime, who had to discover who he was and where he stood as an island volcano of shame and scandal began to erupt. . . .

BLOOD AND ORCHIDS

"The characters are so finely depicted that the reader is compelled to follow their destinies."—*The New York Times*

"GRIPPING, SKILLFULLY TOLD."—*Best Sellers*

"VIVID, AWESOME, ENGROSSING."—*Publishers Weekly*

"EXPLOSIVE . . . THE PLOT REALLY MOVES."
—*Library Journal*

Thrilling Reading from SIGNET

BLOOD & ORCHIDS

NORMAN KATKOV

A SIGNET BOOK

NEW AMERICAN LIBRARY

NAL BOOKS ARE AVAILABLE AT QUANTITY DISCOUNTS WHEN USED
TO PROMOTE PRODUCTS OR SERVICES. FOR INFORMATION PLEASE
WRITE TO PREMIUM MARKETING DIVISION, NEW AMERICAN LIBRARY,
1633 BROADWAY, NEW YORK, NEW YORK 10019.

SIGNET TRADEMARK REG. U.S. PAT. OFF. AND FOREIGN COUNTRIES
REGISTERED TRADEMARK—MARCA REGISTRADA
HECHO EN CHICAGO, U.S.A.

SIGNET, SIGNET CLASSIC, MENTOR, PLUME, MERIDIAN and NAL BOOKS
are published by New American Library,
1633 Broadway, New York, New York 10019

First Signet Printing, October, 1984

6 7 8 9 10 11 12 13 14

PRINTED IN THE UNITED STATES OF AMERICA

To
MERVYN NELSON

Who set the course for this voyage

"My grandfather told me that when the first missionaries came, the islands emptied into the sea to greet them. Mothers swam with babies, and the old people were taken to the ships in outriggers. My grandfather told me the people covered the missionaries with so many flowers you could barely see their faces. When the missionaries came ashore with their children, they were like new brothers and sisters. All of them, without exception. My grandfather said the people of the islands treated the missionaries like a great big wonderful prize that had come out of the ocean. But the missionaries weren't happy. They saw too much evil in these smiling islands. All that naked skin. All that laughter. All that eating and singing and chasing around. The missionaries had to remove the evil. First they took away our gods and substituted their gods. Then they took away our land. They took away our queen and our palace. They made us dress like them and act like them. But they won't let us be like them. Or be with them, except to work in their fields or in their kitchens. They have ruined us. We were a free and easy people on these islands who didn't know any other way except to love. They outlawed love. The missionaries' sons brought the guns and the police, and the Navy did the rest."

—Princess Luahine

PART
1

IN HONOLULU early one Saturday night in September 1930, Maddox swung off Beretania Street and stopped in front of Iolani Palace. He was alone in a small black sedan registered to the Honolulu Police Department. Curt Maddox was a captain of detectives but he ranged all through the department. He was always downtown on Saturday night, always before the sailors and soldiers and merchant seamen from the freighters in the harbor filled up with okolehao, the bootleg whiskey made everywhere in the Territory. The weekend trouble began later, on the way to or from the girls, or when it was bad, in the parlors with the girls. Maddox liked certain places, all of them old, and Iolani Palace was a favorite. It hadn't changed.

Maddox was interested in the building, not its history. He was thirty-six, and the last monarch, Queen Liliuokalani, had been removed from the palace, forcibly, by the United States Navy in January 1893, the year before Maddox was born. Martin Snelling, the Territorial Governor, was the current tenant, but Maddox never thought of him sitting in the palace. Martin Snelling had been an accountant when he was appointed. To Maddox he was still an accountant.

In the darkness Maddox opened the car door wide and put his foot on the running board, hoping the sedan would become cooler. The night was warm. Maddox removed his hat, a dark gray felt that was too heavy for the evening. He sat back, looking through the open door at the two-story palace with the columned portico on each floor. Maddox liked the symmetry of the palace: the wide staircase in the center, the arched entrance with two columns on either side, the motif repeated directly above on the second floor, and the expansive cupola that crowned the building.

He had barely started to relax when he heard a car horn blasting in a series of short bursts. Headlights made a wide arc as the driver turned, followed by more headlights. The first car was leading the second, issuing directions with its horn. The two cars

3

went past Maddox, moving slowly. Maddox heard giggling and then a woman's shriek followed by much laughter. They were all innocents but they had ruined Maddox's respite. He moved his leg and closed the door. The Iolani Palace grounds had become too crowded.

For Maddox Honolulu had become too crowded. He was a native like any Hawaiian, like any Chinese or Japanese, or Tahitian, or Samoan, or Portuguese, or Filipino, or Korean, or Fijian, born in the Territory, and he resented, strongly and constantly, the enormous immigration of the last ten years that he believed had made Honolulu the stinkpot town it had become.

In those ten years Honolulu's population had increased by more than 50,000. Maddox knew the figure for 1920: 81,820. He had been in uniform and had thought the town too big even then. Now there were about 138,000 persons living right here in the same place. Each time someone came off a ship, someone already there was pushed back. Maddox turned into King Street, skirting the palace. Maddox wanted to drop a net into the ocean from Koko Head to Kaena Point.

There were lights everywhere now. Honolulu was as bright at night as at noon. In the *Outpost-Dispatch*, the morning newspaper, Maddox had learned Honolulu was about the same size as Tulsa, and Salt Lake City, and Paterson, New Jersey. But none of those towns had to worry about sailors and soldiers on top of the ordinary thieves working the wrong side of the street twenty-four hours a day. Maddox turned again, into Bishop Street, which ran down to the sea and to Aloha Tower standing over the pier where the luxury ships docked.

As Maddox approached the waterfront, the night became even brighter. Arrivals and departures were always galas in 1930, whether at midnight or morning. The ukuleles were ubiquitous, the leis were scattered like falling leaves, passengers were laden with souvenirs, and more were for sale around Aloha Tower and on the pier itself. The ship was always flying flags from the bow to the stern. Maddox wasn't sure whether a ship had docked or was sailing. He had spent his entire life within sight and sound of the Pacific, and yet he was a stranger to the sea. He avoided the ocean. He had, almost from the time he could remember, lived in the streets of Honolulu and in the city's alleys. This was his real residence.

He came to the piers because he liked Aloha Tower, Honolulu's welcoming gate. Maddox thought the stunted obelisk with its four clocks was beautiful, as imposing and majestic here in Honolulu as in the pyramids of Egypt's desert. Unlike Iolani

Palace, the tower was a part of Maddox's life. He had grown up telling the time by the tower's clocks, and he had, illogically, a private sense of proprietary pride for the guardian of the harbor.

They were sailing, all right. Maddox could see the taxis approaching, loaded with luggage. Closer, he could see passengers leaving other taxis, women counting suitcases, vendors crowding in, selling everything, two cops in uniform, both Hawaiian, trying to keep a double traffic lane clear. Maddox was driving slowly, watching the doings, and he heard but did not consider the clop-clop, clop-clop, clop-clop until he was almost on top of the horses. Maddox jammed down on the brake pedal to keep from slamming into the animals, and grabbed the wheel with both hands as the car rocked.

Directly ahead and crossing in front of him was an elegant, exquisite phaeton drawn by two matched bays. The horses were splendid, superbly trained. The animals' harness was extensively trimmed with silver, and they wore tiny bells that pealed softly as they moved. But the sound of the bells was smothered by the festive shouts and cries, the gaiety of the phaeton's occupants, men and women alike. They were all part of a bon voyage party, and they turned on Maddox en masse. "Get a horse!" a man shouted, and, "One side or a leg off!" cried another. "Hold your horses!" someone yelled, and this last demand convulsed them all. Maddox grinned. Their high spirits were infectious.

The driver whistled sharply and the horses moved forward. In his headlights Maddox recognized Hugh Osgood holding the reins. It was Osgood's phaeton. Maddox caught a glimpse of his wife. They were both about the same age as Maddox. He remembered being assigned to the church when they were married. Maddox had still been a rookie, and there was an army of cops working that afternoon. *Everyone* was at that wedding, from Hawaii, the big island, from Maui, from Kauai, from all over the States. Maddox watch them, still smiling, enjoying their enjoyment. He saw the horses wheel sharply, heading straight for the tower. Maddox laughed. Osgood was taking the carriage onto the pier, delivering his passengers right to the gangplank. If it was wide enough, Hugh Osgood would probably run the carriage up on deck. Maddox reached for his hat and turned the wheel, driving slowly, threading his way through the jumble of vehicles, private cars, taxis, and trucks around the tower. He made a wide circle and drove slowly toward the commercial heart of the city, thinking of Hugh Osgood.

Hugh Osgood was like a king himself, Maddox thought. He and his wife were like a king and queen. They *lived* like a king and queen. Everyone knew their mansion. You could put Iolani Palace in one wing of their place. Their servants alone would fill the palace. Maddox didn't know for sure, but he would have bet Osgood lived better than any of the Hawaiian kings. There were other people in the Territory who were in the same boat as Hugh Osgood. Nobody was wearing a crown in Hawaii now, but in a way one set of royalty had replaced another. The new rulers were a hell of a lot stronger, too. They had all the land *and* the money. There wasn't *one* king in Hawaii now—there were at least five, and each monarch had his own kingdom. *They* decided who ran the kingdoms. Martin Snelling was sitting in what had been King Kalakaua's bedroom in Iolani Palace because Harvey Koster had chosen the accountant for governor.

Leonard Fairly, who was too short to pass the physical examination for the Honolulu Police Department, was now chief of police because Hugh Osgood's father wanted him. Leonard Fairly had been a civilian clerk in the missing persons bureau when Jay Osgood made him a cop. Leonard Fairly had looked silly in uniform so he was kept inside. He had never walked a beat, never rode a squad car, never in his career used the .38 Police Positive. Maddox knew for a fact that Fairly had never made a pinch, not even a traffic arrest for running a light, but he was up on the third floor now, a little man in a big chair, giving the orders. Maddox tried to stay clear of Fairly and as long as it was mutual he didn't complain.

There were 284 cops in the department, including the chief and Maddox, and 138 of those were 100 percent Hawaiian. Most of the others had Hawaiian or Chinese blood. Only twenty-three were haoles, were white, but they were in charge. Maddox knew he would never see a Hawaiian in the chief's office. Maddoz had only one complaint to level against the Osgoods and the Kosters. He didn't care how many Japanese and Chinese they had imported to work the ranches and the plantations, especially on the other islands. He only cared about Honolulu. He wanted them to stop the crowds from settling down right here. Sometimes it looked like the whole world was on the way, figuring they could sit under a tree, fanning themselves with palm fronds for the rest of their lives and watching the hula.

Maddox was almost at the Punchbowl, the massive flattop mound that rose from the edge of the business district. He was only a few blocks away from Papakolea, a large Hawaiian section, but he rarely drove into the area. There were families living in places made of packing boxes, cooking outside, using oil drums for stoves in Papakolea that Saturday night. There were shacks with two and three families in a few rooms. The death rate in Papakolea was twice as high as it was among Hawaiians on the other islands. None of this was Maddox's concern. He was only interested in a Hawaiian if the fellow made trouble.

His sightseeing was over for the night. Maddox swung back, on his way to the saloons and the girls. He stopped along Merchant Street, turning into the curb near a movie theater. Two sailors of the Shore Patrol passed the sedan, swinging their nightsticks. They were in white and wore leggings. Each had a webbed belt around his middle, and each wore a holster on his hip with a .45 automatic. As they reached the corner and crossed the intersection, two military policemen appeared on Maddox's left. They wore brassards on their sleeves like the Shore Patrol, and they had leggings and webbed belts and holsters on their hips with the big blue steel .45 automatics. The two soldiers were swinging their nightsticks. "Going to Jerusalem," Maddox said, aloud. He didn't notice the slim, slight young man in the dark suit who walked with a limp, his left shoe scraping the pavement as he followed the soldiers and stopped to drop some letters into the mailbox on the corner in front of the movie theater.

The young man with the limp was Tom Halehone. He was twenty-three years old and lived in Papakolea, where he had been born. He was a lawyer who had been in practice for less than two months. Tom Halehone had an office with a desk and chairs and a telephone. On the door, in Gothic lettering, were the words THOMAS HALEHONE and below his name ATTORNEY AND COUNSELOR-AT-LAW. Tom Halehone read the words, entering and leaving his office, with a secret and embarrassing pleasure.

Tom came to the office on Saturday because he had no other place to go, and because it was a refuge, a sanctuary. His limp was a birthright that had made Tom an exile from early childhood. He had heard the rough, abrasive, humiliating sound of his shoe all his life. But it was as clear and demoralizing, as much an affront and abasement, and provoked as much anguish and loathing for himself today as when he had first realized that he could not walk like his playmates, when he had looked up, bewildered and frightened, at his mother and father and known, in the silence, that he was flawed. He was a cripple; it was as irreversible as the self-respect he had forfeited at birth.

He had spent the afternoon and early evening writing letters to law school classmates in San Francisco. Tom remained at the mailbox for a little while. He was without a destination. He had eaten a late lunch and wasn't hungry. It was too early to go home. Tom had returned to his parents' house from law school, but the years in San Francisco had changed him. The insularity of Papakolea, the narrow world in which his parents lived, was behind him, and he was awkward and ill at ease with his mother and father. Tom walked to the theater, looking at the huge advertisements under the marquee. He dug into his pocket for money as he approached the box office.

Maddox reached for the radio telephone hanging from a metal sleeve on the dashboard and depressed the Talk button. "Maddox."

"Nothing much, Captain," said the dispatcher in the radio room at police headquarters. "Little while ago there was some hassling down on Nuuanu Street. Sailors off a Chinese freighter banging heads. So far that's the story."

"I'm downtown," Maddox said, and replaced the radio telephone. He saw a kid scooping up change at the box office, turning to enter the theater. The kid had a bad leg. He walked like he was bouncing.

About three miles away, beyond Waikiki, on the beach, was the ramshackle, jerry-built Whispering Inn set up on pilings fifty yards from the water. To approach it cars turned onto a one-lane dirt road. There was no defined parking area. Cars were scattered all around the wooden building, some parked beneath the pilings that had no practical purpose. High tide never came close to the Whispering Inn. The first owner had decreed pilings as a gesture to the exotic.

Japanese lanterns were everywhere. There was a large room with tables set around an open space for dancing. The bandstand, used only on Saturday night, was against the kitchen wall, with lights and colored squares of glass above it moving continually in a circle in what was considered a theatrical effect.

Tonight the Whispering Inn had been taken over by a group of young Navy officers stationed at Pearl Harbor. No officer present held a rank higher than lieutenant, and many were ensigns on their first tour of duty. The group in charge of the night had guaranteed the Whispering Inn owner a certain amount of money, and each officer attending had paid in advance for the dinner and the dancing. All the liquor—moonshine—had been brought to the Whispering Inn by the guests, either okolehao purchased from bootleggers or gin manufactured by the officers, and in some cases by the officers' wives. Drinking had begun in daylight, either at several homes where caravans had formed for the drive to the inn, or at the roadhouse immediately upon arrival. Thus, although dinner was still being served, there were very few altogether sober men and women at the party.

Two of the guests were temporarily absent. They had left separately by an urgent prearrangement demanded by one, and they now stood well to the rear of the inn, beyond the last random cluster of parked cars.

They could not be seen, and because of the blaring band music, they could not be heard although they were talking with vehemence and with passion, with outrage and longing, with fear and fury and disgust. As the band stopped playing, they became silent, and the man, Lieutenant Bryce Partridge, hit the woman as hard as he could with his open hand, so hard he was almost thrown off balance by his own swing. The sound was like a gunshot.

The woman was Hester Anne Ashley Murdoch. She was twenty-one years old, and she had never in all of her life been struck by anyone. She had never been hurt. She had never seen an act of violence. She had never heard a slamming door.

"What kind of bilge are you handing out?" Bryce Partridge said. Both had been drinking, but Hester much less, and only to avoid censure. "You want to tell me it was the big romance of your life?"

Hester's face seemed on fire from the force of his blow. The night became darker. She reeled from the pain and the devastation he had wreaked upon her. Bryce had become someone else. "I love you," she said. "You said you love me."

"Sure, we love each other," Bryce said. "No threats, though." He raised his arm and she flinched, but he only pointed at her. "No threats."

"But I'm pregnant!" Hester said. She had to make him understand. They were tied together now. They had to face everything together. They had to tell Gerald and Ginny, tell the world. They had to face the world. Hester was not afraid so long as Bryce was with her. "You have to do something!"

She heard Bryce take a deep breath. "It's not my line of work, Hester. All I can do is pay and I will."

She was with a stranger. All that summer Bryce had been gentle and tender. He had made every day joyous, and every night ecstatic. "You promised!" she cried.

He whirled around to look for witnesses, and swung back to confront her. "I didn't promise anything," Bryce said. "I never promised. We were talking. I said if things were different it could have been us, you and me. Could have been." Bryce shook his head. "All you can do now is lose it fast."

Hester wanted to cover her ears. His words were like knife thrusts. She was in agony. "I love you," she said. "I don't love Gerald, I love you. I've never loved anyone but you. I don't want an abortion. I want you. I want your . . ."

He interrupted her. "You're not sticking me with this, Hester," Bryce said. "I won't let anyone deep-six me, not with the promotion lists four weeks away!"

"You were never honest, were you?" Hester said. "It wasn't only Ginny, it was the Navy."

"Of course it's the Navy!" Bryce said. "Haven't you learned anything about me? That's what I am! That's *all* I am! I'm the Navy!"

"You make everything dirty," Hester said. "You make me feel dirty." She reached for him, but he hit her hand with the back of his hand, hurting her.

"You're not ruining my life," Bryce said. He came even closer. "Don't make trouble, Hester. Don't do it. You haven't blundered into the gentlemen's corner of this world. Believe that."

He moved away, taking her by surprise, heading back toward the Whispering Inn. He was leaving her! She was losing him! He would be gone forever! She could not bear it! He had awakened her in those few short months. He had made her new. She was transformed, welcoming each day with glee, with passion. Hester was an only child. Her father, whom she had adored, died before she was six, and she was raised by a mother who expected a performance from Hester. She was forced into a private world by the behavior, the ritual her mother demanded. Hester's father had loved books, and had read to her from the time of her infancy. So she found her escape, becoming an omniverous, an insatiable reader. The addiction was permanent. She was really at peace only when she was alone with a book. She was slim and had a pleasing face with a full mouth and bright blue eyes. She might have been attractive, but she had no confidence and she believed herself awkward. Her mother equated beauty with chic, and her constant corrections and suggestions produced in Hester a quiet rebellion that endured. Hester was forced into a kind of slavery by a mother who needed the safety of companionship even when she woke. Hester had tried to escape. She had believed Gerald would rescue her, but he had failed, they had failed each other. Hester knew she was condemned within weeks of the marriage.

Bryce changed everything. All that summer she lived in a glow. His voice thrilled her. The sight of him made her tremble.

His hands, his mouth, his body against hers, his body in her, made her rapturous. She felt more than human. She believed she had become immortal. He made every hour, everything they did, an act of daring, of melodrama. She could not return to dreariness. She could not forfeit Bryce. He was her only chance. "Bryce, wait."

Hester hurried after him, moving awkwardly in the high heels she had always avoided. "Bryce, you can't go!" He didn't stop. He didn't *care!* A lifetime's sullen acquiescence suddenly turned into a mindless fury. "I'll give your precious Ginny my own welcoming present!" Hester said. As she caught up with him, he was upon her, one arm around Hester's middle, the other holding her wrist.

"Oh, no," Bryce said. "Oh, no, you don't. You stay away from Ginny." Bryce bent his head, looking down on her, blotting out the world. "Stay away, Hester. I told you I'd pay. You can't negotiate, Hester."

"But you're not paying!" she cried, her heart breaking. She twisted and turned, fighting him. She had become someone else, a different person. She kicked at him. "I'm paying. Only I am paying, and I want you both to pay, as well."

Bryce held on to her. She hurt him, kicking him again and again, scratching, swinging her free arm to hit him. She was possessed. An entire lifetime of frustration had turned her into a madwoman who wanted revenge from a stranger, from Ginny Partridge. "Ginny!" Hester shouted. "Ginny!" she yelled, as loud as she could. "Ginny!"

With his left arm around her, Bryce pulled back his fist and hit her in the face. Her head snapped back and blood appeared immediately. She said "Ah-h-h-h-h-h-h-h," and he hit her again. She staggered and began to run toward the Whispering Inn. Bryce caught her, holding her arm as if she were a dancing partner, swinging her wide, and as she came around, he hit her again, in the face. She started to fall but managed to stay on her feet. With her hands over her face, blood spurting from her wounds, she ran, away from the inn now.

Bryce Partridge followed her. He was beyond reason. He hit her in the back, using his arm and fist like a hammer. He drove her to her knees. She was on all fours, bleeding, feeling needles in her face. She started to crawl but he would not let her escape. He bent to lift her, using both hands, pulling her up from the dirt so he could hit her again, and again, with both fists. Her presence was a goad. He had to eliminate her. Only the appearance of headlights far to his left, a car coming from Waikiki, saved Hester. Bryce let her fall and left her, panting, his arms weary, wiping the sweat from his forehead as he lurched exhausted toward the inn. Bryce Partridge knew he was in great and imminent danger. He had again succumbed to the rage that turned him into a mindless savage, which he had, since childhood, tried to keep suppressed.

For almost two years, since a night in Newport News when two toughs had taunted him and he had left both in the street in the sleet, Bryce had kept his demon locked away. Now the woman he had just abandoned threatened to destroy him.

As his vigor returned, his breath came easier, and the trembling in his body receded, as the madness itself abated, Bryce journeyed steadily back into sanity. The band began to play once more. He could hear voices from the inn. Ahead, he saw a couple, close and looking for an unobserved pocket. Bryce veered sharply so he could not be seen, before realizing they were walking away from him, walking toward the sea. He had to examine himself, clothes, hands, hair, shoes. Hester had been bleeding. Bryce stayed in the shadows, circling the inn as he went to his car. He could use the dome light to correct himself. "Straighten out," he said, aloud. "Straighten out."

There was blood on Bryce's hands, fingers, and knuckles. He used his handkerchief, wetting it with his tongue and lips. He wiped the large class ring on his left hand. He combed his hair, craning his neck to look into the rearview mirror. "You can't run," he said to himself. *"You can't run!"*

He left the car. Bryce needed Ginny, he *needed* her. He had to be with his wife now, before Hester showed up. He had only one chance, *one!* He had to deny everything, every word Hester said, every accusation she made. He had never left the inn. He had been inside since his arrival. He had been in the head. He had left Ginny only for a few minutes. Bryce waited in the darkness, hidden by the pilings. The band wasn't playing. He couldn't walk in with the dance floor empty and everyone at the tables watching him. When he heard the music, Bryce hurried inside.

Everyone was dancing. The floor was jammed. Bryce moved straight ahead, into the dancers, looking for Ginny. He said, "Sorry," and, " 'Scuse me," and, "Passing through," and almost bumped into Ginny. She was directly ahead, her back to him. He touched her partner. "My turn, sport," he said, smiling. As she came into his arms, he felt her familiar body and wanted to close his eyes. He had his story now. He had been with his wife. "The head," he said, answering her question.

Ginny said, "Welcome back," into his ear, and kissed his

ear. He felt her tongue. Ginny Partridge could not get close enough. She pressed herself against Bryce. The last seven months, until the day before, had been a nightmare. She had been desolate. Their separation had made her as helpless, in her way, as her mother who had been dying of cancer. When Bryce received orders for Pearl Harbor, Ginny returned to Duluth, to her parents' home and her own bedroom. Her father was also sick and old, and she could not refuse his request. "It will only be temporary, Virginia," her father had said. "It won't be long." Ginny could not wait for her mother to die. She felt no guilt for leaving Duluth. Life had finished for her mother, and it was starting for Ginny. She belonged with Bryce.

Ginny Partridge was a large, full-bodied woman who was not really attractive. Her features were plain and pronounced. Her lips were full. Her nose was almost Roman. Her hands were big. Her hair was long and she wore it combed straight back and in a bun. But she was physically graceful. She had style, so that when she walked, when she was in motion, she was sexually desirable. Men watched her, and wanted her.

Ginny and Bryce were in the center of the floor and the band in the middle of a song when Ginny stopped dancing. She took his hand, leading him to their table. "Tired?" Bryce asked, alert and on the lookout, watching the entrance, waiting for Hester, ready for Hester who would be confronting him and his wife whom he had never left.

"I can't stand being this close to you," Ginny whispered.

"That'll pass," Bryce said, but both knew the truth. Bryce knew Ginny's secrets, her keen pleasure in the dark in his arms. With her, because he accommodated himself to her, he was rough and crude and demanding, and Ginny was his match. She often woke him afterward, woke him with her fingers, whispering, choosing her words for effect, joining him in crudities. She whispered to him now. He said, "Greetings," to someone, and to her, "Having fun?" She nodded, holding him. "It's your clambake," he said. "You're the name of the party: 'Welcome, Ginny.' "

"Bryce, I love it all," she said. "You and Hawaii and our little house and the party." They reached their table, which was set for six and was deserted. She looked out at the young people on the dance floor. "They're all so nice," she said. He held her chair.

"That they are," Bryce said, offering a testament. He knew every man in the Whispering Inn. He knew the capabilities of most. He had sailed with many, men he ranked and men who ranked him. He could grade each of those on sight, and he did not need a fitness report. They were all good men. They were Navy officers, from the Academy, and Bryce Partridge believed that single indentifying element to be the most worthwhile, the most distinctive and illustrious a man could claim.

"It's a marvelous party," Ginny said. She raised his hand and kissed it, but did not release him. Her thumb covered his ring. "I just noticed your knuckles," she said. "You've hurt yourself."

"It's nothing," Bryce said, pulling his hand. But Ginny held on to him.

"What happened, Bryce?"

He pulled sharply, pulling free. "I said nothing happened." He hid both hands, smiling at his wife. "I've been pounding the walls in frustration."

"That's over," Ginny said. "Forever."

"Anyone seen Hester? M' wife?" Ginny looked across the table at the slender man in the dark business suit who was drunk. Bryce put his arm around Ginny. "You met this bloke earlier," he said, "Gerald Murdoch."

"Delighted have you aboard," Gerald said. He was one of two men at the party in a suit and wearing a tie. He bowed over the chair. "Your husband's fine officer."

"I'll drink to that," Bryce said, reaching for the bottle of okolehao on the table. He didn't like alcohol, didn't trust it. "Gerald?"

Gerald nodded, swaying a little. Bryce poured the drinks. Gerald raised his glass. "Your health," he said. They drank, after which Gerald stepped back, holding the glass while he brought his heels together. "To the admiral," Gerald said.

"Bet your boots, Gerald," Bryce said, smiling indulgently at Ginny. "To the admiral."

Gerald finished his drink. "Seen Hester?" Bryce shrugged, using both hands in an aimless gesture. "Hester's vanishing American," Gerald said, and bowed to Ginny. " 'M have this dance, Mrs. Partridge?"

"Are you sure I can trust you with my wife?" Bryce asked, still smiling, watching them dancing away. Bryce turned his back. He raised both hands, holding them against his belly, and examined his knuckles. He then came out of the chair, facing the entrance. *Where was she?*

About a half-hour later a carful of young men reached the dirt road that ended in the beach. Ahead and to the right was the Whispering Inn. The car was a yellow and black 1929 Ford convertible, bright and glistening, polished to a high shine, the nickel-plate bumpers and headlights gleaming. Joe Liliuohe, who was twenty-five, was driving but the car belonged to his sister. She had owned it for a month and tonight, for the first time, she had allowed another human being, allowed Joe Liliuohe to drive it. Joe and his three companions had chipped in to fill the convertible with gasoline, and the deal, his deal, imposed on the others, was that the tank would be full when the car was returned to his sister. Joe knew how she felt about the convertible. She had saved ever since high school for the car. The top of the convertible was down. Harry Pohukaina and Mike Yoshida were in the backseat, and David Kwan was beside Joe Liliuohe. None of the four had ever owned a car. No one in their families, excepting Joe's sister, had ever owned a car, although Mike Yoshida's father, a truck driver, brought his employer's van home overnight on occasion.

They had been riding steadily since six-thirty. They had been seen by all their envious friends and acquaintances. They had been everywhere. Joe Liliuohe was here, near the Whispering Inn, on the edge of nowhere, out of desperation. He had no other destination and he was preparing to turn when David Kwan yelled, "Stop!" Although Joe had the wheel, David Kwan grabbed it. "Joe, stop!" he yelled. "Stop!"

All in one motion Joe knocked David's hand away and hit the brake, and finally saw, in the headlights but some distance ahead, the crumpled woman, one stark white arm extended above the mass of her hair like a plea for help. "Jesus Christ!" Joe said, and he was out of the convertible.

David Kwan stood up, grabbing the top of the windshield. Mike Yoshida and Harry Pohukaina were up. "It's a haole," Harry said. They had stopped for a white woman. "Let's get out of here," Harry said. He was scared. All three were scared.

Joe Liliuohe was scared himself but, Jesus, she was lying there. She could be dead or something. He'd never seen anyone dead. Joe moved around her, trying to see her face. He had a queasy feeling, but he had to do something. Joe wondered if she was breathing.

"Is she breathing?" asked David, stopping about ten feet back.

"Joe, we'd better beat it," said Harry Pohukaina, who was behind David with Mike Yoshida.

"We can call," Mike said.

"But don't give our names," said Harry Pohukaina.

"Shut your goddamn mouths," said Joe, mad at all of them,

although he felt like they did, like running. He couldn't run; couldn't leave her lying there. Queasy and shaking inside, he squatted and reached for the outstretched white arm and took the woman's wrist. He heard someone behind him and saw David's legs. "Do you know when someone's dead?" Joe asked.

"Let's beat it, Harry," said Mike Yoshida. Harry didn't move and Mike didn't move.

"I have to turn her," Joe said. "Help me turn her." David stepped straight back until he bumped into Mike Yoshida. Joe put one arm under the woman's head. He pushed his other arm under her knees. Slowly, slowly, he turned the woman.

"Oh, Jesus, look at her face," said David.

Mike Yoshida came closer to look, bending forward like he was on the edge of a cliff. Harry joined him on the edge of the cliff. "What did they do to her?" Mike asked, horrified. When Harry saw the woman, he felt like he was freezing.

"It's Hester Ashley!" Harry said, cursing his luck for being with Joe and his sister's goddamn car. "I'm going!"

"Hester Ashley?" Mike couldn't believe it. He bent over the edge of the cliff once more. "It's her! Joe, I'm telling you we gotta beat it!"

"Beat it," Joe said, "and at least shut your goddamn mouth." Her head moved against his arm. Joe looked down and heard a sound from her.

"Her leg moved!" said David. "I saw her leg move!"

"We have to take her to a hospital," Joe said.

"We can call an ambulance," said Harry Pohukaina.

"Do any goddamn thing you want," Joe said. "Help me, Dave."

"Joe, it's Hester Ashley," David said.

"I'll do it myself," Joe said. "I'll take her to the hospital and come back. Hester Ashley. I don't care who it is, you can't drive away and leave someone laying here like this." He brought her close, right up against him so he could lift her, and lifted her. He was scared stiff. "Open the goddamn car door, Dave."

David ran ahead and Joe carried Hester to the car. He bent with Hester, scratching his arm on some goddamn thing on the car, but he held her close so as not to hurt her, and set her on the front seat. "I'll be back," he told the others.

"I'm coming with you," said David.

"We're not staying out here," said Mike.

"Hurry up," Joe said. "Over here through my door." He pushed the driver's seat. "Will you for Christ's sake hurry up!"

He wanted to finish this thing. He didn't want Doris Ashley's daughter next to him for the rest of the goddamn night!

When all three were in the backseat, someone said, "Put up the top, Joe." Someone said, "Christ, yes, before they spot us." By that time Joe was making his horseshoe, heading for Mercy Hospital. He could hear music from the Whispering Inn.

"I'm not putting up the top. My sister wants it this way." He glanced at Hester Ashley. Her face made him gag. "Besides, she could die while I was still futzing around with the goddamn top."

David Kwan leaned forward. He couldn't stand to look at Hester but he had to look. "What do you think happened?"

"Fists did that," Joe said.

"Fists!" Harry Pohukaina wanted to jump. "Step on it!" he said. "Will you please step on it!"

Joe was speeding already..He couldn't take a chance on going much faster. He was turning every which way, taking all the streets without traffic, weaving his way toward Mercy Hospital. "I see it," said Mike Yoshida, who was half-standing in the backseat. "Do you see it, Joe?"

Joe didn't answer. He came in behind the hospital, riding along a border of towering oleander. They saw the broad carpet of light ahead extending halfway across the breadth of the street. A big sign said EMERGENCY ENTRANCE. Joe touched the brake. He reached the sign and turned. A police car, black and white, was parked beside the double swinging doors to the emergency room. "Let me out right here," said Harry Pohukaina. "Holy mackerel! Cops!" said Mike Yoshida.

None of the four saw Hester sit up in the front seat. She felt the rush of cool air against her battered face. In the first moment of consciousness she did not remember anything. She did not remember Bryce Partridge. She was in severe, in throbbing, pulsating, excruciating pain. Her face burned as though she were in flames. Her cheeks felt like pins were being driven into the flesh, thousands of stinging pins. Her teeth ached. Her lips felt puffed. She tried to open her mouth; when she did, she wanted to scream in agony. She saw the stranger beside her and heard someone say, "Quick, before the cops see us!" Hester turned and saw the three dark faces in the rear, and heard David Kwan say, "She's awake, Joe!"

Harry Pohukaina was immobilized with fear, with terror. He saw Joe reach for Hester. "I'll help you," Joe said. Hester tried to scream. She pawed at the door. She had to escape before he started hitting her. "You're hurt," Joe said. "We're at Mercy Hospital. I'll help you inside."

"Stay away!" she cried. She had to open the door. "Stay away!" She was wild. She made it out of the car, holding on to the open door, too weak to move.

"Oh, Jesus, Joe, will you please, please beat it?" Harry pleaded. "She's crazy."

"Wouldn't you be if someone did that to you? I'll help her to the door of the hospital," Joe said. He slid across the seat and Hester moved away from the convertible, swaying and screaming.

"Help!" Someone had to help her. "Help!" she screamed. He would beat her. She took a step. He would kill her. Hester was sure she was about to die until she saw him clearly and knew he hadn't hurt her. Bryce had beaten her. Hester remembered everything including the baby inside her.

David Kwan saw the emergency room door open. He saw an orderly, in white, holding the door. He saw the cop with the orderly, and behind both, a doctor, also in white, working on a guy on a table in the emergency room. David leaped on Joe, throwing both arms around him. "A cop's coming!" he said. Joe shook him off. David jumped into the car with Joe behind him. The orderly came away from the emergency room. "Quick, quick!" David said. "Back straight out!" The cop was behind the orderly watching the yellow and black convertible. The orderly reached Hester as the snazzy Ford backed out into the street, into the darkness.

"Don't hit me!" Hester cried, and lost consciousness. The orderly, whose name was Peter Monji, grabbed her as she started to drop.

"Give me a hand!" he said, and louder, "Will you give me a hand?" The cop saw the Ford making tracks. He reached Peter Monji and put out his hands for the broad. Both men moved awkwardly, holding Hester. "Do you see what they did to her?" asked Peter Monji. The cop looked. Her face was mincemeat. He looked again. She was a white woman. They reached the open emergency room door and in the strong lights the cop said, "Wait . . ." and stopped. It was Hester Ashley. "Where do we put her?" the cop asked. He had to call headquarters so they could tell Curt Maddox.

Five blocks away David Kwan said, "Let's head for home, Joe, okay?" Joe nodded but David could not see him in the darkness. "Joe?"

"How about you guys?" Joe asked. He heard the grunts of

assent from the backseat. The evening had turned into a total loss. Joe couldn't wait to give the convertible back to Sarah. He headed for the Punchbowl. All four lived in Papakolea. They rode in silence, each thinking of Hester Ashley, of her face, of the strange world, incomprehensible to them, in which a man could mutilate a woman.

"I try and block out her face but she's right there in front of me," said Mike Yoshida.

"Yeah, all right. So shut up," said Harry Pohukaina, and he tried not to see the woman's face but failed. Harry pushed himself back and erect, dropping his arm over the door, and spotted the drunk who teetered out from the curb. David touched Joe, alerting him.

"I see him," Joe said.

He was certain he would pass the drunk easily, but an instant later the man veered, aiming straight at the convertible. The drunk was off balance, trying not to fall. Joe turned hard, moving far over into the opposite lane. They were only a few feet from the intersection. Before Joe could swing back into his lane, a black Oakland sedan, as big as a barn, turned into the intersection and onto a collision course with the convertible.

Both cars stopped hard, throwing the occupants around. The Oakland was full of sailors in civilian clothes, and the driver leaned far out of the window to curse Joe, who rose, pointing at the drunk he had avoided. But the sailor wouldn't stop. He included Joe's mother. Joe came over the closed door of the convertible and Harry Pohukaina was right behind, wrapping a handkerchief around his hand.

The four doors of the Oakland flew open. Seven sailors came out, but the convertible was already empty. Joe led his gang, carrying the fight. "Keep them away from the car," he said, heading for the Oakland's driver.

The driver could fight. He hit Joe three times before Joe could swing. But the sailors had been drinking for hours, and Joe and his guys never drank. The four young natives would have had no problems despite the head counts but for the unfortunate circumstance of time and place. It was Saturday night and they were in downtown Honolulu. The streets were choked with sailors and soldiers. Garbled news of battle spread instantly: beach boys were attacking servicemen.

Shrill whistles sounded as the Military Police and the Shore Patrol converged on the fighting. Uniformed police, on foot or in pairs in black and white squad cars, headed for the trouble.

On his radio Maddox heard the dispatcher in police headquarters repeat the location of the brawl. But Maddox had already been told of Hester and was on his way to Mercy Hospital.

Most of the combatants ran. Joe and his pals were trapped, surrounded by servicemen, by Shore Patrol, by Military Police, and by the cops who kept coming into the intersection. The procedure that followed was standard. Those in the roundup who displayed I.D. cards were thrown into Army and Navy vehicles on their way to the brig and the stockade. For the civilians there were Black Marias from the Honolulu Police Department.

Joe Liliuohe had a single, overriding worry: his sister's car. He had to protect her car. Turning, twisting, bending, trying to hide, he reached the convertible. Mike Yoshida joined him. "They grabbed Harry and David," Mike said. Joe had the car started and was in reverse, praying he could move back far enough to swing around the Oakland. He almost made it. He was on his way when one of the sailors from the Oakland saw him. The sailor pointed and yelled, "He started it!" Three cops reached the convertible at the same time. "I'll drive," said one cop.

One block away Tom Halehone came out of the movie theater to the sounds of motors racing and gears grinding, of shouts and whistles. A policeman leaped out of a black and white that had just arrived. He saw Tom and grabbed him near the mailbox. The cop pushed his club behind Tom's arms and turned it slightly. "Move and I'll break your arm," said the cop. He was telling the absolute truth.

"I was in the movie. I just came out," Tom said.

"Everybody just came out," the cop said, moving the club and thrusting Tom into agony.

Tom heard a woman shout, "Let him go!" The cop was pushing Tom toward a Black Maria in the street. "Let him go!" the woman shouted. A tiny woman wearing extraordinarily high heels ran in front of Tom and the cop. She was the cashier from the box office of the theater. "He was in the movie like he said," the young woman declared.

"I'm supposed to believe *you!*"

"You better believe me. You better take your hands off him."

"Beat it or you're coming with him," the cop said.

"Do it!" she said. "I see your badge. Three-eight-two. You're three-eight-two. Take me in and by the time I'm finished you'll wish you were dead." She waited. "You said you were taking me in." The cop moved his nightstick, releasing Tom, and left them. "Animals," she said. She started for the box office. Tom was beside her and when she heard the rasping sound of his left shoe against the stone, she looked down. And looked up, looking straight ahead, but nothing the cop had done to Tom hurt as much as her glance.

"Thanks," Tom said. "I was on my way to jail." They reached the box office. She went inside, locking the door before climbing up on the stool. "Wow! I left all this money."

"Will you have any trouble?" Tom asked, and hated himself for speaking. She had saved him, and there was nothing he could do to help her. Tom knew she had learned everything when she had glanced down at his foot.

"I'm okay. You watch yourself," she said. So he had to make a smile and leave the box office, feeling her eyes as he crossed the glaring theater entrance and listened to the sound of his shoe on the concrete.

"Someone *did* that to her," said Dr. Frank Puana. Hester was on the table in the emergency room, in her clothes and unconscious. Dr. Puana, the emergency room physician who was on duty from six P.M. on, had given Hester a local anesthetic, procaine, with a 25-gauge needle to infiltrate the lacerations in her face before he began to cleanse her wounds. His patient was in great pain and he wanted to spare her, and he wanted no interference, involuntary or otherwise, when he began to suture. Frank Puana was determined to prevent scarring. He knew he had a flair and he would have been as devoted if Hester Anne Ashley Murdoch had been a charwoman.

His patient had drifted in and out of consciousness since Frank had first seen her. He had begun by cleansing the wounds, using saline in a bulb syringe to irrigate the torn and bleeding flesh. By some miracle nothing was broken. But her face was a mass of contusions and abrasions. The lacerations were everywhere, from her ear to her nose, in her chin, along both jaws, along her mouth, vertical, horizontal, and all jagged, deep slashes.

"She looks like someone went after her with a can opener," Maddox said.

"A ring could have done it," Frank said. "A man's ring." The orderly, Peter Monji, joined him with a suturing needle freshly threaded with black silk. Frank had already taken thirty sutures and he expected to take at least thirty more. He was sewing in two layers, first a line of subcutaneous sutures, and then another row, subcuticular, just below the skin. Frank had to be certain that when the skin was closed on the surface it did not bow open below.

"How many were in the car? The convertible?" Maddox asked.

"Three or four. At least three," said Peter Monji, and added hastily, "I couldn't tell for sure. It was dark and all."

Maddox looked down at Hester once more. Her eyes were two big blue-black discs, the flesh swollen into ridges that obliterated the eyelids. Her lips protruded; the lower lip hung loosely. "A man's ring," Maddox said. "How about a purse? Did she have a purse?"

"This is how she came, Captain," Frank said. "Will you step back now, please?" He was anxious to resume suturing, to finish quickly so he could give the patient the two grains, sixty milligrams, of phenobarbital that would sedate her and offer her some relief from the burning discomfort caused by her wounds.

Frank bent over Hester, the black silk trailing from the needle in his hand, and Peter took Maddox's place on the other side of the table.

"No word from her husband?" Maddox asked.

"No word from anyone," Frank said. He straightened up, holding the threaded needle, looking at the captain and waiting. Frank couldn't work and talk, and this wasn't police headquarters, this was his emergency room. "Anything else?"

Maddox didn't answer. He left the emergency room. His car was in front of the entrance, facing the door. Inside, Maddox picked up the radio telephone. "Maddox. I'm on my way to the Ashley place."

Windward, the Ashley home, was a monument in Honolulu. Everyone had seen pictures of it in the newspapers, but very few residents of Honolulu had ever been inside. An iron fence, eight feet high, ran along Kahala Avenue for more than a mile. Behind the fence was a border of hibiscus reaching above the spikes of the fence. The house was on a plateau, facing the East, the Mainland, a citadel high above the sea.

Doris Ashley always chose a motif, a theme for her dinner parties. She devoted much time and attention to an evening. A party at Windward was always intimate and always a surprise. Doris enjoyed the delighted reactions of her guests. From the time Preston Lord Ashley died, Doris Ashley had never entertained as many as twelve guests at once. Tonight there were eight.

Two of the four men in Windward that Saturday night owned, between them, more than 250,000 acres of land, arable, productive, rich with sugarcane and pineapple. There were, in 1930, over two and a half million acres of farming land in the Territory owned by haoles, by white men, sixteen times more than were held by Hawaiians, who had owned it all when Captain James Cook sighted the islands in 1778.

The subject at Windward was, as always, the land and the urgent need for labor to work the plantations and the farms. The Hawaiians as a source of labor had long ago been decimated, the supply of able-bodied, uncomplaining, and tractable men exhausted. They had been killed by disease, including venereal disease, influenza, and pneumonia, all brought by the white man's ships and those who came ashore from the ships.

This threat to production was quickly recognized by the large landowners and their plantation managers, and long before 1920, they had turned to Japan for new and healthy farm workers. Japanese had come by the thousands, but the haoles had learned, quickly, that the immigrants were a different breed. The Japanese were independent. They were recalcitrant. They balked at the harsh conditions of work and housing imposed by the owners and the plantation managers. They organized and became a united, defiant unit, demanding higher wages and more humane treatment from the plantation managers. And when these requests were refused, the Japanese left the fields. They went on strike. These became frequent until, in 1920, the Japanese mutinied, en masse. The 1920 strike was a long, bitter, costly episode. The owners believed themselves threatened. Their plantations and ranches had been private fiefs, and the newcomers had, successfully, laid seige to their dominance. The owners needed fresh, compliant, tractable laborers.

So they looked to the Orient once more. But the Chinese Exclusion Act had been passed by the Unites States Congress. Nevertheless the haoles were determined to rid themselves of what they called "the Japanese menace."

The campaign to bring Chinese labor to the islands was a unanimous, official undertaking by the Territory. The Territorial Legislature appropriated $21,000 to send a group to Washington. These men were to persuade Congress of the critical need for a Chinese work force in the Territory despite the law barring such immigration. The men who came to Washington proposed a compromise: The Chinese would be allowed to emigrate for five years. They would be used only for agriculture and as domestics. They would not exceed 21 percent of the population, and they would not be permitted to leave the Territory for the continental United States.

Members of the delegation from the Territory appeared before a committee of the House of Representatives to plead their case.

A congressman posed a question: Suppose a Chinese, during his five years in Hawaii, married an American citizen and refused to go home?

"Then we take him home," was the answer.

"By force?"

"By force if necessary."

Representative John E. Raker of California said, "If to that union there should be born a child, could you tear him away from that child, born in that country, tear him away by force and send him home, would you? Do you want that kind of law to be passed by Congress, to become effective in the Hawaiian Islands?"

"Yes, I do want it," was the answer.

The delegation lost. It was rebuffed, but neither they nor the men they represented were defeated. They accommodated themselves to the Japanese, sitting down with their leaders, giving ground minimally. The Japanese had won the right to bargain collectively, but the men across the table were as united, and they controlled the jobs.

Now, in 1930, they remained supreme. Sugar ruled the Territory, and the influence of the plantation owners was compounded and buttressed by those who led the industrial and the business communities of the islands.

It was an omniscient and impenetrable oligarchy, perpetuating itself through its vast wealth and centering its power in three decisive institutions: the Territorial Delegate to the United States Congress, the Territorial Governor, and the Territorial Legislature. By controlling these men, the oligarchy controlled Hawaii.

Ten years earlier, in 1920, Royal M. Mead of the Hawaiian Sugar Planters Association had told another committee of the House of Representatives in Washington, "I do not think there is any contest as to who shall dominate; the white race, the white people, the Americans in Hawaii are going to dominate and will continue to dominate . . . there is no question about it."

The eight guests Doris Ashley had invited to dinner that Saturday night in September 1930 would have raised their glasses to Royal Mead's testimony. Doris Ashley would have raised hers with them.

Guests always dined late at Windward since Doris Ashley preferred the continental mode. Long after eight P.M. she came to the center of her living room. "Attention! Attention!"

She led them through the dining room directly into the kitchen, where a bare table was set for nine. The smell of corned beef and cabbage, of simmering vegetables, was heady, irresistible. Amelia and Theresa, Doris Ashley's Hawaiian maids, had been banished.

Taking an apron from her chair and slipping it over her formal gown, Doris Ashley announced she was personally serving the meal she had cooked. "We're having a real old-fashioned New England boiled dinner exactly the way we did when I was growing up!"

Doris Moeller Ashley was born in the Bronx, and until she was twenty-three had never been farther north than Yonkers. But Boston, Back Bay, the Cape, the Vineyard, Nantucket, were all favorite and frequent allusions in the biography she had carefully crafted for herself.

Her guests were enchanted. They clustered around Doris Ashley as she raised the pot lids on the stove to permit quick previews of the feast. The steam escaping from the pots, the delicious odors, the large, sparkling kitchen, the inviting table, produced a gay mood. Doris Ashley had outdone herself. They were all seated, Doris Ashley at one end of the table, when someone pointed at the orchid in the center. "A secret admirer, Doris?"

The orchid was spectacular, all white and all grace. Someone said he thought of angel's wings; another that she thought of a horse's mane. Doris Ashley believed flowers were utilitarian, like rugs or chairs. She used flowers only for color. She waited for a pause. She took the envelope she had propped against the vase and removed the card inside, waving it slowly over her head for attention. "You are looking at my very own personal orchid," she said and read, aloud, *"Cattleya warneri alba variety Doris A."* Doris Ashley slipped the card into the envelope. "I'm being entered in the Territorial Sweeps," she said. "Courtesy of Delphine Lansing."

Everyone in the kitchen knew Delphine Lansing, and her name produced a chorus of amused, patronizing comments: on her height, on her hapless social yearning, on her sot of a husband. "No wonder she raises flowers," someone said. Delphine Lansing, whose father had left her a fortune, maintained the most extensive private gardens and greenhouses in Honolulu.

They were still in the kitchen, chattering over the coffee and fruit, when Doris Ashley heard the doorbell. She did not like surprises. She could not imagine who could be calling now, uninvited. Hester and Gerald could have left the party early, or Hester could have left alone. But Hester would never ring; the door was never locked. Doris Ashley rose to fill everyone's cup. She was at the other end of the table when she saw Amelia. "Carry on! Carry on!" Doris Ashley said. She left the kitchen and paused beside the maid. "It's the police," Amelia whispered.

Doris Ashley saw a big man in a dark suit standing in the entrance hall. He was lean and had black hair like a Hawaiian. He heard her coming and turned. Mrs. Ashley stopped in her tracks. The man she faced was neat. His suit was clean and freshly pressed; his hair was combed. And his stomach was flat; there was no trace of the flabby belly that was Doris Ashley's enduring memory of her father. But her visitor brought Herman Moeller back with abhorrent vividness, waiting at the door each Saturday night for half her wages. "I'm Curt Maddox, Mrs. Ashley," the man said. "I'm sorry to disturb you, but I didn't want to telephone and I didn't want to send anyone else." Doris Ashley came forward, trying to forget her father. She stopped at the foot of the staircase. "It's your daughter," Maddox said. "She's been hurt. Hurt bad." Maddox saw Doris Ashley turn white. "Maybe you'd like to sit down."

She was very frightened. She abandoned all disguise. "Tell me the worst." Maddox watched her in case she started to slip away.

"I said it's bad, but she's all right. She'll be all right," Maddox said. "Your daughter's been beaten."

"*Beaten?*" Doris Ashley held onto the banister. Maddox was close enough to catch her.

"Yes, ma'am. She's at Mercy Hospital. I've seen her. I've seen things like that. She was beaten. Her face . . ." he said, and stopped. Mrs. Ashley had enough to handle already.

Neither spoke. Doris Ashley pushed herself away from the staircase as if she were apologizing for her behavior. Maddox saw her coming back, saw the color in her face. "She left here with her husband."

"She's alone," Maddox said. "A police officer happened to be at the hospital when she came. She was . . . dropped off, you could say, left at the emergency entrance. The police officer saw some men in a car. I'll know more when I start moving on it, but I wanted to tell you."

"Thank you for coming, Mr. . . ."

"It's Captain, Mrs. Ashley. Captain Maddox. If you want, I'll drive you to the hospital."

"Yes, no. I have guests," Doris Ashley said, all in one breath. She had to think, she had to think.

"Suppose I handle them," Maddox said.

"No, no, no, no," Doris Ashley said. She was in her home. She couldn't hide. She refused to hide. But she needed help. She lowered her voice, speaking almost in a whisper. "What shall I say?"

"Your daughter had an accident. You stop right there," Maddox said. "My daughter had an accident." Doris Ashley was silent as though she was repeating the words. She left Maddox without replying.

Maddox saw the gang coming into the living room on their way home. He had never met any of Doris Ashley's guests, but he recognized all the men and most of the women. The women huddled around Doris but Maddox could see her shaking them off, leading everyone out. She opened the door. They went past Maddox like he wasn't there. When they were gone, she said, "Please wait."

She went up the stairs. Maddox looked into the living room, which ran the width of the house. The far wall was a succession of glass doors leading onto a deep terrace. There was moonlight on the terrace and a maid in uniform was cleaning up, moving around without a sound. Maddox thought of sitting in the living room for a few days with no telephone in the house. He heard footsteps.

She was coming down the stairs, wearing a cloth coat over a different dress. She had a purse and he could see gloves in one hand. Maddox knew how old Doris Ashley was because Harvey Koster, who had been Preston Lord Ashley's best man, had told him. Doris Ashley was forty-nine years old. She was thin, and he liked that about her. She was straight as a rail. Her head was up, and maybe that was why her skin was smooth. He had always thought she was taller but she probably gave that impression from the way she held herself. She sure knew how to dress. "I'm ready," she said.

Outside Maddox opened the front door of his car, holding it for her. Doris Ashley opened the rear door and stepped into the backseat. Maddox felt like she had kicked him. When his work put him in with any of the society people, he was always on guard. He had learned to slip and slide past their comments and slurs. He tried to remember they were in trouble, not he. But Doris had reached him. She made him feel he smelled.

Sitting behind Maddox as he drove through the gates of Windward, Doris Ashley could no longer keep Herman Moeller from her mind. Her father, the fetid Bronx apartment with its rancid smell of sausages and stews, of sauerkraut and beer, her mother of whom she had early become contemptuous for enduring Herman Moeller's tyranny, her two older brothers, hating him but growing daily like him, all converged, submerging her in the past as she rode to her ordeal in Mercy Hospital.

Herman Moeller worked and ate and slept, and never spoke

without a reference to money. He believed disaster was always on the threshold, and his purse, which was under his pillow when he lay in bed, was the enduring obsession of his life. He allowed each of Doris Moeller's brothers to finish the eighth grade before sending him into the street for a job, but he would not extend such privileges to a woman, a girl. When she was ten, Doris Moeller began to work every Saturday in the neighborhood grocery store. That summer she worked through the entire school vacation. Herman Moeller wanted her to remain in the grocery store, but Doris Moeller refused. If she could not return to school, she would not work. Herman Moeller persecuted her for two years, greeting her daily with threats and warnings, and when she was twelve, he issued an ultimatum. Either Doris Moeller left school or his home. When the girl ran into the kitchen, her mother whispered, "We're from the old country." Doris lived under her father's heel until she was sixteen.

Doris Moeller carefully planned her escape. First she found a job in a dress factory on 14th Street in Manhattan. She was an excellent seamstress; her mother had taught her well. She rented a room in a private house in Chelsea near the Hudson River. One Saturday night, after she had given her father half her earnings from the grocery store, she waited until her parents were asleep. She packed her clothes in two cardboard suitcases she had hidden, and she wrote, without a salutation, a note to Herman Moeller. "I am leaving and I won't be back."

In the month after her departure, Doris Moeller enrolled in night school to study shorthand and typing. She went from the factory to her classes, and when she returned to her room, practiced her shorthand. There were two typewriters in her employer's office, and he agreed to let her use them. She spent her lunch hours at the machine, ignoring the other employees who were like the people she had left behind. She was the best student in her classes, and when she had completed the course, her shorthand teacher recommended her for a job.

Doris Moeller was sent to a law firm on Wall Street. For the girl from the Bronx, the first glimpse of the expansive suites, the muted voices, the paneled walls, the private dining room, the elegantly dressed men, the chic women under the supervision of Miss Whaley, the executive secretary, was a revelation. Doris Moeller had found her world.

She was, from the start, excellent at her work. She began in the typing pool, sitting at the machine with briefs, contracts, legal forms of every variety. Unlike the other girls, however, she read and absorbed what she was typing. She was as diligent in her search for a social side to her new life. Doris Moeller cultivated the secretaries of the partners in the law firm. Some were women of style and sophistication and from them she learned how to dress, how to comport herself, even what to order in restaurants. With these new friends, Doris began to fashion an autobiography. She said she had been born and raised in Boston, a member of an old family that had come upon financial reverses, forcing her to earn a living. She was a superb fictioneer because she wanted to believe everything she said of herself.

She brought a Teutonic thoroughness to her work, and she caught the eye of Miss Whaley. Within a year she had moved from Chelsea to Murray Hill, near Miss Whaley's apartment, and shortly thereafter she became secretary to one of the firm's partners. Doris Moeller was a success.

There were men. She was a tall, svelte, handsome woman, and she never lacked for escorts. But they were not the type she had come to fancy, not like her employer and the other lawyers in the office, not like the clients with whom she came in contact daily.

So Doris Moeller remained free and unattached. Her salary rose. She took a larger apartment. Clothes became important, and in time she set the standard in the office. She established friendships but they were female friendships, women like herself, single and independent.

The years passed. Doris Moeller was not unhappy. She had won, through determination and dedication, a major triumph, escaping from her squalid, mean beginnings and transforming herself into a person of substance and accomplishment. She was twenty-six when Miss Whaley shared the great secret. The executive secretary planned to retire and would recommend Doris Moeller to succeed her. The girl from the Bronx had reached the heights. In that same week Preston Lord Ashley, of Honolulu, Hawaii, entered the law office and her life.

Preston Lord Ashley was forty-six, almost exactly twenty years older than Doris Moeller. Like so many others, he was the son and grandson of men who had taken fortunes from the islands. He had come to the Mainland on an extended business trip and, as Doris Moeller learned, it was a journey on which he had embarked reluctantly. Preston Ashley was at ease only in Honolulu.

Doris Moeller's employers were the New York correspondents of Preston Ashley's attorneys in Honolulu. He was anxious to finish his business and return home, and he was in the office constantly. Doris Moeller was with him and her employer constantly, and because she saw, quickly, that Preston Ashley was a shy, a sensitive man, she was considerate and helpful to the visitor. Three days after his arrival in New York, he asked her to dine with him. He said the city was so big, the pace so breakneck, he was cowed by it. Perhaps Doris Moeller could, in a way, introduce him to New York.

She had heard such stories for ten years. They were always from the hinterland, they were always alone, and they were always lonely. And they were always married. But something about Preston Ashley, some quality of wistfulness, made her break her own rule, and she accepted.

That first night she learned Preston Ashley had never married. She learned something of Hawaii, because he spoke of nothing else. But she also learned something of him. He was a true gentleman. He was cultured. He was a voracious reader. And he was, actually, a lonely man. They were together every night for the last ten nights of his stay in New York. He never kissed her, and when he said good-bye, at her desk in the office, he shook hands. Doris Moeller was bereft. She had glimpsed paradise, but it had been denied her. Four days later she received a telegram from San Francisco.

MY DEAR DORIS. YOU HAVE BEEN CONSTANTLY IN MY THOUGHTS. AS I CROSSED THE COUNTRY THE CLICKING WHEELS BENEATH SEEMED TO RE-PEAT YOUR NAME AS THOUGH CALLING TO YOU. BUT IT WAS I CALLING. I CANNOT FORGET YOU NOR WILL I EVER FORGET. I KNOW I AM MUCH OLDER BUT I MUST SPEAK. I LOVE YOU. WILL YOU MARRY ME?

She joined him in San Francisco. They sailed for Hawaii occupying separate cabins, and they were married within the week after their arrival in Honolulu.

Doris Ashley's place in society was assured. She started at the top. They were sought after. With Doris at his side, Preston became less retiring. They built Windward together. When it was finished, when they were settled, Doris said she wanted a child.

She wanted a daughter. She wanted a little girl to whom she could give everything that had been denied her. She wanted to create a princess. And she wanted a companion for her later years. Doris Ashley was a sensible and pragmatic woman. Her husband was twenty years older than she. She had been alone for most of her life. She did not intend to be alone in the end.

Preston Ashley was reluctant. He spoke of his age. He was a man totally lacking in ardor. Doris Ashley had accepted and reconciled herself to his crucial deficiency. She would not accept his protests. Hester Anne Ashley was born when Doris Ashley was twenty-eight years old

Hester was an adored child. Her father was enchanted with her, and Doris Ashley could not stay away from her baby. The nanny was helpless in the face of the infatuated parents. Hester Anne Ashley was born into a fairyland of indulgence from her father and confident, loving, authoritarian instruction from her mother.

Now, twenty-one years later, in the car with Maddox, it seemed to Doris Ashley that she had, since leaving Windward, lived through her entire life. "Beaten," the detective had said. "Beaten, beaten, beaten," the word echoed in her mind. She had to be strong, for her sake and for her baby's.

When Maddox stopped in front of the emergency entrance, Doris Ashley said, "I'll find my way. My son-in-law is, should be, at the Whispering Inn. You must know it. There was a Navy party. Navy people, officers and wives. Will you tell him yourself? Lieutenant Murdoch."

A young man in a Hawaiian shirt and white trousers who had sent a waiter after Lieutenant Murdoch was in the kitchen of the Whispering Inn. He was a little, thin, wiry man with curly blond hair cut short. When he saw Gerald Murdoch, he grinned. "Guess you're surprised, huh, Lieutenant?"

"Duane?" Gerald came through the bat wing doors into the kitchen. "Something wrong?" Duane York was a seaman second on the *Bluegill*, Gerald's submarine, and a member of his torpedo room section.

"Everything's fine, Lieutenant," Duane said. "Copacetic." He grinned again. "Almost."

"Fix that," said Gerald, and pawed at his jacket, trying to reach his pocket.

"No money, Lieutenant," Duane said. "I'm okay on money. Why I came, I was wondering if maybe I could use your car."

"Certainly use my car," Gerald said. He began to feel in his pockets. Duane York had often asked for and received the coupe. "Big date tonight, Duane?"

"Sure hope so," Duane said. The little man winked. Gerald's hands moved from pocket to pocket. "Lieutenant," Duane said, and pointed at the keys in Gerald's right hand.

"Right you are," said Gerald, handing over the keys. "Now wait a minute. Stay right there." Gerald reached into his pocket again.

"Nothing doing, Lieutenant," Duane said. Gerald had the folded bills in his hand. "Thanks, anyway."

"Good hunting," Gerald said. He clapped Duane on the shoulder. Gerald made a tottering about-face and marched unsteadily out of the kitchen. Duane York watched him

"Best flogging officer in the Navy," said Duane, aloud. He didn't care who heard him. He followed Gerald out through the bat wing doors as the band began playing.

Because the Whispering Inn was built on pilings, a wide wooden flight of stairs led to the entrance. Maddox parked in front of and parallel to the wooden stairs. Maddox saw a skinny little runt the size of a dime come out. He wasn't Maddox's idea of a Navy officer. Duane York was in too much of a hurry to notice anyone. He jumped over the last five steps. Maddox walked up the stairs to the double doors. This time he did not remove his hat. Maddox was in his territory.

He came in out of the darkness into the colored lights and the pounding music. The place was filled. He could smell the moonshine and the near beer. Maddox saw a pair of young folks stop dancing and head for the doors and the darkness. He stood in their path. "Point at Gerald Murdoch, will you?"

Gerald was standing at the far end of the inn, facing the sea. He had picked up someone's glass from someone's table, but he didn't want more to drink. He wanted to stretch out and close his eyes. But he couldn't leave without a ride. He didn't have a car. He didn't even have a wife. Hester was somewhere out on the beach reciting poetry to the porpoises. He wanted to throw the glass. When he turned to set it down, Maddox reached him. "Lieutenant Murdoch?"

Maddox extended his hand. "Curt Maddox," he said, watching Gerald's hands, looking for a ring. "I'm a cop."

Bryce Partridge was playing with the hair at the back of Ginny's neck when he saw Gerald with a big man wearing a hat. They were headed straight for him. Bryce said, "Ginny," and lifted her out of the chair, pulling her to him. She was startled, feeling his hands on her arms, imprisoning her. "Listen to me, Ginny." She opened her mouth, and he said, low and hard, "Listen. I have to tell you something." She was his only hope. She was all he had. If she didn't help him, he was finished. He had no idea which way she would swing when he told her, but he had no choice. "Don't ask questions. Don't answer. Don't stop me. This is life and death. My whole life, my career." They were almost at the table. "It could be all over, angel. Everything depends on you. While you were in the States . . ."

"Bryce," said Gerald. "Ginny." Bryce stood beside his wife, waiting for it. If Gerald swung, Bryce would act surprised; he would treat Gerald like a drunken pal. Gerald and the big man stopped. Gerald stepped out in front. " 'M very sorry but must leave," he said. He extended his hand to Ginny, and when she took it, he bowed slightly. "Want to wish you best of luck 'n' happiness here," Gerald said. He shook hands with Bryce. " 'Night, old friend," Gerald said.

Bryce's back was wet. "Leaving already?" he asked. "Anything wrong?"

" 'S Hester," Gerald said. "Nothing serious." He could not inflict his personal problems on his friends.

"Give her our love," Bryce said. "Will you do that, old man?"

"Certainly will, Bryce." Gerald bowed once more, and he and the big man wearing the hat started for the doors. Ginny pulled Bryce's arm, pulling him to her.

"Now, *old man*, you finish what you started," Ginny said.

"I love you more than anything on this sweet earth," Bryce said.

"You said life and death." He shifted until he was against her thigh.

"I was dead without you, angel," he said, his hand moving up her spine.

In Maddox's car Gerald said, "Now we're alone, Captain. No audience now. What kind of accident? Where is she? You're talking about my wife!"

"She's in Mercy Hospital," Maddox said. "She's hurt bad but she'll be all right, she'll recover. She was beaten."

"Beaten!"

"So far all I can tell you is that a carful of men brought her to the hospital. They let her out in front of the emergency room and made tracks."

"A carful!" Gerald saw faceless men in front of him, huge, hulking, unshaven, unwashed, with gaps in their teeth and hands like clubs. Where had they found her? Where had Hester gone? Why had she left the party, left the inn? She was always going off, with a book, with a bag of raisins and nut meats, with a basket to pick wild flowers. She was always alone, always late, always apologizing. Gerald hated her for what she had done, and in the next instant hated himself. He was overcome with shame, with guilt. Hester was in a *hospital*. Men had *mauled* her. He believed himself to blame. She disliked parties. He should not

have brought her. He should have come alone, or not at all. Gerald was merciless with himself. "Tell me the truth, please."

"I have, Lieutenant," Maddox said. "She'll be all right. That's not me talking, that's the doctor at Mercy Hospital talking." He looked at the Navy officer who sat straight up as though he were bound. "She'll be all right."

"I suppose you don't know who did this to her," Gerald said.

"Give us a chance, Lieutenant," Maddox said. "It just happened."

As Doris Ashley left Maddox's car and he drove past the emergency room door, she raised her right hand and pulled her coat over her left shoulder. She was not cold. The gesture was a lifelong response, almost a reflex. She was losing control of herself, and it was a condition she could not endure. She fought with all her will, all her resources, all her being. Doris Ashley had to win over her weakness. She had to be ready. She waited near the emergency room until Maddox was gone and the sound of the sedan had faded, until she was ready. She said, "You must," to herself, and opened the door.

She was blinded by the dazzling light. She closed her eyes. She heard, "Minute," from a man. When she could see, a figure in white was bent over the examining table, wiping the surface. He said, "Okay," making a ball of the towel and lobbing it into the wastebasket. Peter Monji, the orderly, said, "The doctor'll be right back," took a step, and stopped.

Peter turned like someone in a haunted house. "I guess you're here about your daughter," Peter said. "She's been moved, Mrs. Ashley. I'll show you, take you." He stepped back so she could pass and banged into the examining table. While he waited, Dr. Frank Puana came through an open arch. Frank recognized her on sight but before he could greet her, Peter said, "This is Mrs. Ashley, Doctor. I'm taking her upstairs."

"I'll take her," Frank said. "I'm Dr. Puana, Mrs. Ashley. I treated your daughter. I've just left her." He stepped back. "We can use this elevator." Doris Ashley crossed the emergency room and rode to the third floor with the doctor, listening as he spoke without pausing, telling her everything he had done for Hester. They reached a door with a NO VISITORS sign below the numbers 346. "Naturally, that doesn't include the family," Frank said. "I want her to have as much rest as possible."

He reached for the door but Doris said, "I'd like to be alone with my daughter." She had been on display long enough.

Mercy Hospital was old. The rooms were large and barren

with high ceilings. The single iron bed, painted white, was in the middle of the room, against the wall facing the door. Beside the bed was a high white gooseneck lamp, and flanking it a chair and a table against the bed. The metal shade around the light bulb was turned away from the bed, making a circle of light on the floor and wall. Hester was in the dark.

Doris Ashley came forward slowly, on Hester's right, straining to see. She reached the foot of the bed and said, "Oh-h-h-h-h-h," raising her hand like a shield and turning her head. Then she lowered her arm, forcing herself to face the bed.

Hester's arms were atop the covers. She had crawled for several yards, afraid Bryce would come back to resume his attack, crawling to the dirt road where she had fallen unconscious. Her fingernails were torn. Her arms were raw from her elbows to her wrists. Doris Ashley could see what had been done to Hester's face. Doris Ashley tried to hold on but she whimpered, like a child in the night.

Hester heard something and opened her eyes. Someone was there, a hulk there above her, and she tried to cry out but the effort was agony. She could hardly see. There were constant skyrockets in her eyes. She heard someone. "No . . . please," Hester said. "Please."

"Baby, it's me. It's Mother. Mother's here," said Doris Ashley. "I'm here with you, baby."

"Mother? *Mother?*" Doris Ashley heard Hester sob. "Don't let 'm . . . please . . ." Hester said.

"I won't, child. I'm here now." Doris Ashley lowered herself to the bed. She spoke softly. She used words from the nursery. Hester's eyes closed, and opened again in terror. "Yes, baby," said Doris Ashley, slipping her hand under Hester's as though she were lifting a fallen flower. She felt Hester's fingers close around hers. "I won't leave you," Doris said. She looked at Hester's face, forcing herself to see what they had done to her baby. She was overcome with hatred. She shook with hatred and rage. "Some *men!*" were the words the police officer, the captain, had used. "*Men!*" Doris Ashley said to herself. "They were *animals!* They were beasts!" They had destroyed everything! They had come like a typhoon, like a tidal wave or an earthquake, to ruin Doris Ashley's life. She had been in her home, in Windward, with her friends, in her kitchen with her friends, jolly and laughing. Everyone had been laughing. Everyone had loved her boiled dinner. A policeman had walked into her home, into *Windward! A policeman!* In front of her *friends!* She had been forced to dismiss her friends, to send them home. She remem-

bered their silence, their withdrawn, blank faces. They were all
talking about her now, about the policeman who had walked into
Windward, ending the party. Everyone would be talking about
her now, all over Honolulu, all over the Territory. Doris Ashley
wanted to cry out in protest. She spoke to herself. She warned
herself. She had to be in control of herself. If she lost control,
she was lost, they were lost. She watched Hester, her poor,
mutilated daugher. She put her other hand over Hester's. "Can
you talk to me, baby? Hester? Child? Would you like something?
Water?"

Hester could barely see her mother. Her mother seemed to be
behind smoke. She held tight to her mother's hand. "Stay
here."

"I'm here, baby," Doris Ashley said. "Mother is with you.
Mother won't leave you. Hester? Tell me what happened. How
did this happen? Where were you? You were with Gerald. You
went to a party with Gerald. Who are these *men?*" Hester said
something, but Doris Ashley didn't hear clearly, understandably.
"Say it again, baby. Tell me why these men had you in a car,
these men who did this."

"Didn't do anything," Hester said. When she spoke, the pain
mounted. Her skin felt like it was being pulled, like it would
crack in two. "Face . . ." Hester said, and groaned in pain.

"I see what they've done, baby," Doris Ashley said. "You
must tell me everything so they can be punished." She waited.
"The men in the car, baby. The men who brought you to the
hospital and threw you out like . . . rubbish."

"They didn't . . . they found me," Hester said. "Must've
found me," she said, and stopped.

"Where, child? I know it hurts, but you must help so the
police can catch them," Doris Ashley said. She waited. "Hester,
they are criminals. They're guilty of a criminal act."

"No, no . . ." Hester said, and stopped. She looked straight
up, hoping the pain would abate. "Not guilty." The pain was
like a knife. She moved, seeing her mother through the smoke
screen. "They didn't touch me, hit me. They didn't harm me."

"But they . . ." said Doris Ashley. "You were . . ." she
said, and stopped again. She believed now her horrors were only
beginning. She was uncomfortable on the bed and shifted her
legs, but began to slip and had to push hard on the mattress.
"Hester."

"I crawled away," Hester said. "Must've crawled away.
Must've been unconscious. Where's doctor? Please ask the doctor for something, a pill or something."

"I will, child, I will," Doris said. She could not hide. She had to listen. She could not defend herself unless she learned the truth. She already suspected the truth. Gerald Murdoch was really a total stranger.

Hester had tried to be secretive from the beginning. Doris Ashley remembered that Hester had met Gerald at the admiral's party. Although Gerald began to appear regularly at Windward, Hester was always ready and waiting; they always left immediately. Hester spoke very little of Gerald until, determined to escape from Doris Ashley, she announced they were being married.

"Hester, you must tell me so I can protect you," Doris said. "Did Gerald do this?"

"Poor Gerald," Hester said. "No, never."

Doris had to be positive. "It wasn't Gerald? Are you saying Gerald is not the one?" Doris waited. "Baby, answer me."

"I answered you." She moved her hand out from her mother's. "My face. Call the doctor, please."

"I will, child. I promise I will call the doctor. Just tell me who did this. Not those men, not Gerald. Who did this? Why would anyone do this? Who is the guilty one?"

"I'm guilty," Hester said. "I'm the guilty one because I'm the pregnant one."

"Pregnant," Doris Ashley said, quietly, as though she were repeating an ingredient of a recipe. She rose from the bed, raising her right hand to tug at her coat. For a moment she was somewhere by herself. Doris Ashley was like a person who has suffered a massive injury from a gun or a knife, or a terrible fall. The force of the trauma had not yet set in. She knew Hester was pregnant, knew Hester had been mauled. Doris Ashley went to the foot of the bed and faced the door. Her mind was blank until she suddenly understood that Gerald was not the father. She was positive. Hester had brought this upon her. Hester was to blame! The door opened, and a nurse appeared, determined to see the famous patient, towels over her arm. "Get out!"

Doris Ashley sprang at the door. The nurse jumped back, into the corridor. Doris Ashley followed, pulling at the door and closing it firmly, fumbling with the latch to lock it. She turned, looking at the bed, looking at her nemesis in the bed. She crossed the room, stopping beside the gooseneck lamp. "Did you say you were pregnant? *Pregnant?*" Hester's lips moved. "Yes, I heard you," Doris Ashley said, her voice rising. "I heard you! You're pregnant, but it's not Gerald's, is it? Naturally not. Naturally your husband wouldn't be the father! Naturally you've tired of your husband. After all, you've been married for more than a year. You were roaming in greener pastures. One man wasn't enough for Hester. You needed more. You needed a stableful.'' Doris Ashley was panting. She became weak. She needed help but there was no one in the world to help her. She was all alone. After tonight, she would always be alone. Everyone would know about Hester. Everyone would drop Doris Ashley, drop her flat. Honolulu would shun her. If she invited guests to Windward, they would make excuses. No one would come. Doris Ashley would be an outcast. Windward would become a mausoleum. Doris Ashley wanted to cry out in protest, wanted to tell the world she was not at fault, but she was exhausted. Hester's announcement had left her spent. Doris Ashley remembered the chair beside the bed and looked around as though she were lost. She was standing beside it. Gathering her coat, Doris Ashley sat down as though she had been thrown into the chair.

"You've ruined us," she said. "Well, who is it? Who is the man?" She thought she heard Hester. "Who?" Doris came out of the chair so she could hear.

"Bryce Partridge," Hester said. "Name's Bryce Partridge." Her mother was standing over her. "He's on the *Bluegill,* on the submarine with Gerald. Please stop now." Hester shut her eyes.

Doris Ashley was silent because she was trying to recover from catastrophe. She saw, in her head, two Geralds, two officers, two minor, inconsequential figures. Someone like Gerald had brought Doris Ashley to the edge of disaster. A Navy officer, one of faceless thousands, had made her run through this room like a chicken with its head cut off. She had behaved like a shrew, like her mother whom she had been trying for more than half her life to erase from memory. Doris Ashley was grateful that only the nurse had seen her. She had to be prepared now. Her future was at stake. She lowered herself to the bed. "Why did he beat you, baby?"

Doris Ashley asked questions until she had the whole story. Bryce Partridge deserved to die. He didn't belong with other people. Bryce Partridge should be thrown in front of a firing squad. She was ready to call the admiral. She could never, *ever,* tell the admiral, tell anyone on earth. From this moment forward, her own life, the rest of her life, depended on the secret she and Hester shared. "We have one hope, baby." When Hester heard her mother's proposal, she wanted to escape. She wanted to disappear, forever. "They're innocent!" Hester said.

"How can you be sure? You were unconscious. They could have done everything while you were unconscious."

"They didn't!" Hester said. "It's not true!"

"They could have taken you somewhere . . . abandoned before bringing you here." Doris Ashley put her hand over Hester's. "I'll help you, child," Doris Ashley said. "I'm the only human being on earth who can help you, baby. I'll protect you. I'll be facing everyone for you. Remember, *I'm* the one who is innocent. I am *totally innocent*. And I'll be with you. I'll be at your side. Mother will handle whatever comes if you help us now. You must help us now."

"I can't . . ." Hester said, and stopped. She was sinking, sinking.

"It's our only chance, baby," Doris Ashley said. "Unless we are together now, like one person now, we'll never live through this."

"They only drove me to the hospital," Hester said. "They saved me."

"No!" said Doris Ashley, and stronger, "*No!* I'm saving you! I'm facing the world for you! Your mother isn't pregnant by some . . . sailor. But I won't desert you! I'll be with you, speaking for you. I'll be speaking for you, baby." Doris Ashley looked down at her daughter. "Whatever I say will be coming from you." She rose. Hester raised her arm and Doris Ashley felt it against her, and then it fell away.

"Wait," Hester said. Mrs. Ashley left the bed. Behind her Hester said, "They didn't do anything." Doris crossed the room, and as she reached for the doorknob, Hester said, "They're innocent." Doris Ashley left the room. She stood in front of the door until she saw Gerald and the detective, the captain, come out of the elevator. "How is she?" Gerald asked.

"Sleeping, finally," she said.

"Did she tell you anything?" Gerald asked.

"It's terrible, Gerald. It seems unbelievable. This is 1930." She looked at the captain. "My daughter was raped."

"Is that what the doctor said?" Maddox asked.

"It is what I say, what Hester says. Those four men raped my daughter," said Doris Ashley.

In his car beside the emergency room door, Maddox lifted his radio telephone out of the sleeve on the dashboard and put his thumb over the Talk button. "Maddox. What's his name who was at Mercy Hospital earlier . . ."

"Roy Pabst," said the dispatcher.

"Roy Pabst," Maddox said. "Bring him in. I want to talk to him. I'm on my way."

"Captain, if this is about the Ashley woman, we've got those guys."

"You *what?*" Maddox frowned.

"They're here. And their car. They're in the tank," said the dispatcher. "They were in a fight with some sailors. Captain?"

"Yeah. Have someone put the arrest reports on my desk," Maddox said. He slipped the radio telephone into the sleeve. "In the tank," he said, aloud. "Funny."

Maddox drove downtown and turned into Merchant Street to police headquarters on the corner of Bethel. The convertible was in the parking area. He took his flashlight out of the sedan and examined the Ford. The car looked like it had just been driven out of the showroom. There were no stains on the upholstery. Everything looked brand-new.

Maddox walked to the property room. When a prisoner was booked, he was stripped: money, cigarettes, jewelry, including a wristwatch. These were stuffed into a nine-by-twelve-inch manila envelope with an inventory of the contents. Maddox examined the envelopes with the belongings of the four young men. None of the four had a ring.

Maddox rode up to the second floor in the elevator. He came into his office, reaching inside to press the light switch. The room was as gray and cold as a jail cell. Maddox had a steel desk and steel swivel chair. There were two windows behind the desk covered with venetian blinds. There was an upright telephone on the desk, which was usually clean. Maddox saw the arrest reports he had ordered from the dispatcher. Beside the desk was another steel chair, and to one side, at right angles to the door, was a rectangular wooden table with four more chairs. A large, round electric clock was on the wall over the door. He read the four arrest reports. He shuffled the reports, looking at the names of the four prisoners. "Joe Liliuohe," Maddox said, aloud. He bent forward, raising the telephone receiver. "Maddox. There's a man named Joe Liliuohe in the tank," Maddox said. "Bring him up."

Maddox took off his jacket and draped it over the back of his chair. He dropped his hat on the chair and unbuttoned his vest. When the turnkey brought in Joe Liliuohe, Maddox was in front of the desk, leaning against it. "All right," Maddox said to the turnkey.

The turnkey left. Maddox shook his head, wearily, and rubbed his face with his right hand. "Man, oh, man, you guys give me a hard time," Maddox said. Joe stood a few feet from the door in the center of the office. "If you guys would only go to bed like other people, I could go to bed." Maddox had turned into a patient, long-suffering, overworked friend of all humanity. "You're Joe . . ." Maddox said, and paused, and added, "Liliuohe. Do you know who I am?"

"I saw it on the door," Joe said. "Captain Curtis Maddox."

"Curt Maddox." Joe saw the big man push himself away from the desk and walk toward the rectangular table. He put out his left arm as though to embrace Joe. "Take a load off," Maddox said. Maddox reached the table and stopped, raising both arms high. "Man, I am tired," Maddox moved a chair out parallel from the table and sat down, stretching his legs and crossing his ankles. He pointed at another chair. Joe didn't move. "All right, you're tough," Maddox said.

"No, I'm not, Lieut . . . Captain," Joe said. "I'm plenty scared. I'm shaking inside. I heard one thing all my life ever since I can remember: Stay away from the police. I did. I never did anything wrong in my whole life. But I'm arrested now. I'm here."

Maddox pointed at Joe. "Hey, I just remembered you!" Maddox said, lying. He slapped the tabletop. "You played football!" Joe nodded. "I knew I'd seen you," Maddox said, triumphantly. He had identified Joe Liliuohe when he saw the name on the arrest report. "Look, Joe, I'll be straight with you. We have to talk. I have to ask you some questions. Will you for Pete's sake sit down?" Maddox moved one foot and nudged a chair leg until Joe came to the table and sat down facing Maddox, who laced his fingers over his belly. "The fight with the sailors was the end of the night for you guys," Maddox said. "Where were you tonight?"

"Why? We didn't do anything wrong," Joe said. Maddox was silent. "We were riding around," Joe said. Maddox was silent. Joe twisted in the chair. "We chipped in for gas and were riding," Joe said. "Downtown, out the Pali, back down, over to Waikiki, Diamond Head." He pointed at the window. "That's my sister's car down there. She saved more than three years for that car. The worst part is I kept nagging her to let me use it. This is the first time and I end up here, me and the car both."

"Have any girls with you tonight, Joe?" Maddox asked.

"Girls? No," Joe said. "We were alone, the four of us."

"Four young guys with a convertible ducking girls." Maddox shrugged. "Doesn't sound right."

"We weren't *ducking* anyone," Joe said.

"Things must've changed since I was your age," Maddox said. "You're telling me you didn't even *think* of girls?"

"I told you, this is the first time my sister let me use the car," Joe said. "I was real careful not to hurt anything in the car." He stopped. Joe felt as if he were in an icebox. "Are you talking about that woman we found?"

"A woman? Found?"

"Out near the Whispering Inn. A woman was laying in the middle of the road. She was right in front of us, out cold. Her face. It was . . . mush. Someone had punched up on her. I never saw anything like it in my life. I couldn't leave her laying there. So we . . . I took her to the hospital, to Mercy Hospital."

"So there were girls with you tonight," Maddox said. "Girl. One."

Joe came forward in the chair. "Not the way you mean it, no," Joe said. "I told you, she was laying in the road like a dog that had been run over."

"So you took pity on her," Maddox said.

"Anyone would've," Joe said. "You should've seen her."

"I have seen her," Maddox said. "I've been at the hospital. You're right, Joe. She looks like she went through a sausage grinder. Why would someone do that to a woman?"

"I've told you everything," Joe said, and, quickly, "Wait! I recognized her from her picture in the papers. Hester Ashley."

"Hester Ashley Murdoch," Maddox said. "Think back, Joe. What else went on tonight?"

Joe jumped up from the chair. "Nothing else went on! She was in the road! I couldn't leave her laying in the road! I drove her to the hospital!"

"You and your three pals," said Maddox.

"Yes, me and my three pals!" Joe said. "She came to at the hospital and jumped out of the car and that was the end of it!"

"I wish it was," Maddox said. "I wish to God it was the end, Joe." He sat up in the chair and crossed his legs. "But there's more. She was raped."

"She . . ." Joe's voice was hollow. He was shivering inside. He looked around, as though he wanted to bolt, but he sank down into the chair. "It's a lie."

Maddox watched the football player. He was scared enough now. He wasn't very tough. "I'll tell you this much, Joe. It's always better for someone when he admits what he did."

"We didn't do anything. We found her in the road out cold. She was unconscious." Joe's voice was a monotone.

"Is that your story?" Maddox asked. "Do you want to stick with that?"

"It's not a story," Joe said. He was pleading. "I'm telling you the truth."

"Could be you left out some of it," Maddox said. "Some of the truth."

"I didn't!" Joe said, turning from side to side, his entire body swinging right to left, right to left. The chair had become his cell.

"Maybe *you* didn't. Maybe your three pals had hot pants tonight. Maybe they—"

"That's not true!"

"—needed a hand from the left halfback, the big strong fellow who could tear up a whole line even without interference. Maybe you held her while—"

"That's crazy!"

"—they did the raping. The raping and the beating because even though you were holding her down, she kept—"

"Nobody touched her! None of us."

"—fighting, interfering with what your buddies had in mind so they had to hit her to keep her still, hit her a lot."

Joe sat quietly. He had stopped rocking. He was through, like an animal defeated by a maze. He seemed to be shrinking in the chair. "We didn't," he said, almost inaudibly.

Maddox uncrossed his legs and leaned forward, coming close to Joe. "Sometimes an accessory can make it easy on himself," Maddox said. "But he has to tell us everything, and hold nothing back."

"Told you everything."

Maddox continued as though Joe hadn't spoken. "If you swore to it, Joe boy, you could even walk out of here a free man."

Joe was looking at the floor, at his shoes and the floor, at his shoelaces and shoes, and the floor. "Joe?"

"We never touched her," Joe said to the floor. "I didn't. Harry didn't. Mike didn't. David didn't."

"You put her in that car of yours."

Joe looked up. "That's all we did. I did. I'm the one who did it. They were afraid to come near her, even look at her, because she was Hester Ashley. They wanted to leave, wanted me to leave. I wouldn't, couldn't. She was unconscious. You can't make me say more because there wasn't, isn't anymore to say."

"Maybe I was wrong about you," Maddox said. "Maybe you were as horny as your pals." Joe's head sank. He wanted to put his hands over his ears. "How many of you hit her?" Maddox asked.

"None of us," Joe said. He looked at Maddox. "Honest to God, we didn't touch her."

"But when you reached the hospital, you threw her out of the car and hauled ass," Maddox said.

"I told you when we came to the hospital, she was awake," Joe said. "She started yelling to let her out. She opened the door and jumped out before I could move. And a cop, policeman, and a guy in white came out of the hospital. We were all scared. That's why we left."

"But you're innocent," Maddox said. "You're all clean as a whistle." Maddox leaned back in his chair. "We've been sparring around in here ever since you showed up," Maddox said. "Suppose we play straight, Joe. If you play straight with me, maybe I can help you. I'll tell you this: I'll try and help you, and I mean it."

"What do you want me to do?"

"Tell me the truth," Maddox said.

"I've *told* you the truth, Captain. I swear it's the truth," Joe said. "I swear to God it's the honest to God's truth."

Maddox came out of his chair. "If this is the way you want it, this is the way it'll be." He went to his desk, dismissing Joe Liliuohe. Joe followed him.

"I told you everything exactly the way it happened!" Joe said.

Maddox pressed a button under his desk top. "The way what happened?"

"*Nothing!*" This guy behaved like he couldn't hear! "*Nothing happened!*" A detective opened the door.

"Take Joe down the hall for some coffee," Maddox said, instructing the detective to keep Joe Liliuohe separated from his three companions in the tank.

Maddox's back ached. He crossed his arms, rubbing his shoulders. He buttoned his vest and put on his jacket. Maddox stood beside his desk and spread apart the four arrest reports. He sat down, reaching for the upright telephone to call the turnkey.

Maddox brought the remaining three prisoners up one at a time, keeping the youngest, David Kwan, for last. He kept them all separated so none could communicate. He examined their hands while he questioned them. He lied. He wore a different disguise for each of the three. He was Simon Legree, a rabid bigot, like the plantation and ranch managers who had kept their own jails on Maui and Kauai. He was a cold, precise police officer, proceeding by the rules and regulations. And with David Kwan he was a minister, forgiving and sympathetic.

None of the three wavered, even when he warned Mike Yoshida that the first two had named him as the sole rapist, even when he offered to help David Kwan with his confession as he had helped all the others.

David Kwan began to cry. He covered his face with his hands, facing Maddox, weeping like a woman, softly, his shoulders shaking. But when he had wiped away the tears, and regained his composure, David told the same story Maddox had heard from each of the other three prisoners. Maddox pressed the button under his desk.

Alone in his office Maddox sat quietly, so still the only sound in the room was the *click* of the minute hand moving on the clock above the door. Maddox looked up at the clock. Twenty minutes after one. He was tired but not sleepy, and he knew he would not sleep. He used both hands to push together the four arrest reports. He rose, turning to the windows, spreading the venetian blinds apart with his fingers and looking down on Merchant Street, empty and shiny under the lights. He lowered his hand but stayed at the window looking at nothing. Maddox turned once more and picked up his hat, staring at the crown. He put on his hat. "She says they did it," Maddox said in the empty office.

A girl hurried through the streets and alleys and littered open spaces of Papakolea Sunday morning. She passed children playing in the dirt and women at work beside their homes. The girl was pale with anguish and fear. Whenever she was greeted or hailed, she acknowledged the salutation with a wave or a spoken reply, or both. She was a polite and well-mannered girl and she could not willingly offend, here among her own, or beyond, in the world of the haole. Yet she carried within her a fierce, almost a combative pride. She was a handsome girl, tall for a Hawaiian. Her black hair was cut like blond Carole Lombard's, parted on one side and curling around her neck. She had large brown eyes. She looked as if she belonged in a grass skirt at Aloha Tower, welcoming ship passengers with leis. But she was dressed in the Western fashion, in a white blouse and dark skirt, wearing stockings and saddle shoes.

Sometimes she ran for several yards until she was winded and had to slow to a walk once more. She reached a cross street and ran diagonally through the intersection, running around a man pushing a wheelbarrow. She reached the opposite side and started walking again, walking fast despite the sharp stitch in her side from her exertion. Sarah Liliuohe was almost at her destination.

A quarter mile to the west Tom Halehone was in the kitchen sitting sideways to the table, making his way slowly, thoroughly, through the Sunday edition of the *Outpost-Dispatch*. He wore old cotton pants and a T-shirt and his only pair of shoes. His parents were always barefoot in the house but Tom could not follow suit. His mother was gone, visiting a sick friend, and his father always fished on Sunday, leaving with first light, so Tom was alone, and after the night before, grateful for the luxury.

He had come home from the movie theater, from the cop's manhandling. There was a single light, in the kitchen, when he returned. He walked past it to the porch behind and heard his mother say, "It's Tom." The kitchen door was always open, set back against the porch wall so that Tom was almost immediately in the light. "I expected you for supper," his mother said. "I had—" she said, and broke off, rushing at him as he entered. "What happened?"

"Nothing. Nothing," Tom said, knowing he was in for it and angry with her already. His father was sitting sideways at the kitchen table with a cup of tea at his elbow. "Aren't you fishing tomorrow?" Tom asked.

"I was sleeping and woke up," said Sam Halehone.

"Look at your clothes!" said Tom's mother. Clara Halehone examined him for injuries. "Were you in an accident? Did you fall?" Tom had heard that question, that searing question, for as long as he could remember. She pawed at him. "Your jacket's torn!" she said, discovering the tear in the seam. "Did you fall?"

He had never fallen, even as a child, but she considered him, from birth, a broken wing, a frail and insubstantial creature who was in constant peril because of his short left leg. She had protected him from birth, beating down Sam Halehone's demands that Tom be set free to live like his playmates in the street. When Clara Halehone learned she could bear no more children, her devotion, her protectiveness, turned to obsession. She lived with the certain belief that her son was in constant danger.

"I didn't fall," Tom said, holding himself in check. "I'm all right. Do I *look* like I'm hurt? There was a fight downtown and . . ."

"You were in a *fight?*" his mother asked, interrupting.

"Let him talk," said Tom's father.

"Look at your tie, your hair," his mother said.

"You won't let him talk," his father said. Tom took his mother's arm and led her to the table. He made her sit.

"A cop thought I was in the fight and grabbed me. That's the whole story, so please, tonight only, don't play a scene."

"Like you're a thief," his mother said. "You're a *lawyer*. Did you tell him you're a lawyer?"

Tom looked at Clara and Sam Halehone sitting at their table. They seemed almost indistinguishable, two small, square persons with the same black hair and short, thick fingers. Tom smiled at his mother. "Did I tell him I was a lawyer? No, I didn't."

"Look what they did to you," his mother said. "Give me the jacket. I'll sew the jacket."

"There's no rush," Tom said, but he removed his jacket, hoping it would end the always endless postmortem. Clara held the jacket at the shoulders. "This is your suit from San Francisco," she said. "Those devils! Devils!"

Tom had graduated from law school in the suit. The money order from his parents came a month before commencement, and the note attached said it was for a new suit. The note was signed, "Your Mother," and beside those words, in his father's writing, "Father." He remembered opening the envelope in the vestibule of the rooming house. He remembered holding the money order and seeing them at the kitchen table, his father with the tea while his mother wrote on the lined paper, signed it, and gave the pencil to her husband. He remembered the steady appearance of all the money orders for three years. There was no law school in the Territory and the Mainland was Tom's only choice. Tom had talked of the law from the time he was in high school. He had hoped for a scholarship but none for which he applied was granted. Tom gave up his dream. In the States he would need lodging and food in addition to tuition and texts. "I'll get a job," he said.

Clara Halehone did not fight him. She retreated. The kitchen became silent. She knew her life was over. Her hopes had been smashed. Sam Halehone watched her mourn for almost a month. One evening he motioned to Tom and led his son outside. "You have to do what she wants," Sam said.

San Francisco was a fantasy. Tom was happy from the first. Classes were over by one o'clock but the students' day was only starting. There were cases to read for as long as a student's mind could focus. Tom was with his classmates. He was rarely alone. San Francisco never disappointed him. He was never accosted, never challenged. In three years he did not endure an indignity.

Yet he returned to Honolulu to take the Territory bar

examination. His mother wanted him back. She was fulfilled when he returned. Tom never spoke of his return. He was a young man with many secrets, and deepest among these was the reason for his departure from San Francisco. Tom was safe here, in his parents' home

The night before Sam Halehone had pushed aside his cup of tea. "I told you ten times stay in San Francisco," he said to Tom. "Why didn't you stay? You had a chance. Why did you come back? Now you're like me. You're dirt like me."

At the kitchen table with the Sunday paper, Tom turned a page, his arms spread wide, and saw a figure pass the window. He thought it was his mother returning from her sick friend but the footsteps on the porch steps were too brisk, and as he folded the newspaper, lowering it to look across the kitchen, he saw a girl in the open doorway. She wasn't dressed for Papakolea. As he rose, she said, "Excuse me. I'm sorry to come like this. Tom, can I talk to you?" He nodded. Who was she?

The girl came into the kitchen. She was almost at the table when he recognized her. "Sarah!" She was Sarah Liliuohe, Joe's kid sister. "I didn't know you!" Tom said. "I didn't connect Sarah with you!" She was so pretty. She reminded him of the girls in San Francisco. She dressed like the girls in the States. Tom couldn't remember when he had seen her last. He had run across Joe, once, downtown, since his return from law school. "Here," he said, taking a chair out from the table.

She didn't move. "Joe's in jail," she said. "They say he and three other boys raped a Navy officer's wife." Tom stared at her. He *knew* Joe. "They didn't do it!" Sarah said. "They didn't do anything! Joe swore to me! He *didn't!* He *didn't!*"

Tom wanted to comfort her. She seemed all alone in the world. "You don't have to convince me," Tom said.

"Will you help him? You're a lawyer now. Will you do something? Today?"

"I'll try," Tom said. "I haven't been a lawyer very long, though." So far Tom's practice, meager and spasmodic, came from people he had known all his life, older people here in Papakolea who needed a lease, or representation at a Territorial agency for a license or a permit. "This is a criminal case, Sarah. I've never handled a criminal case."

"You can try, can't you?" She was angry, looking at him as though he had failed her. "You're Joe's friend. Were. Where else should I have gone? There isn't anyone else."

Tom wanted to take back everything he had said. She made

him feel like a quitter. "I'll do my best," Tom said. "I'll do everything I can."

"Can you get him out of jail?" Sarah asked. "Do you need money? We don't have money. I spent everything on my car. Listen to me talking. I can't stop talking. If I stop, I'll think terrible thoughts of what could happen to Joe, to all four of them. This all happened because of my car. Joe had my car last night. They found this woman unconscious . . ." Sarah stopped, and put both hands over her mouth.

"Sarah?" Tom came toward her. "Sarah?" She lowered her hands.

"I didn't tell you the worst part," Sarah said. Tom saw her eyes wide with fear. "Joe told me the name of the woman. I don't remember her married name. It's Hester Ashley."

Tom said, "Ashley," short and flat. He looked away. Sarah watched him, and waited, and then started for the porch, on her way. Tom said, "Hey!" and, "Sarah!" and came after her, trying to forget his scraping shoe. Tom took her arm. She tried to shake him off and couldn't.

"I'll find someone!" Sarah said.

"You have someone!" He held onto her. "Sarah! *Sarah!*" he said, pulling her arm until she faced him. "I have to talk to Joe. I'll get dressed. Will you drive me downtown?"

"I can't," Sarah said. "The police kept my car." She pressed her knuckles against her lips.

"I'll get your car for you," Tom said. "First, I'll talk to Joe, and then I'll get your car back."

When Bryce Partridge woke Sunday morning, he was instantly back in the Whispering Inn, watching the big man who had come for Gerald Murdoch. The big man was a cop, or he worked for Doris Ashley somewhere, in some capacity, or he was a private citizen. The big man had moved with too much authority to be a private citizen. *Where was Hester?*

Ginny moved and touched him, saying, "Yum yum," coming closer, naked and warm and sticky. Bryce wanted to throw her through the window. He moved apart carefully so she wouldn't wake, left the bed, and, gathering clothes silently, walked out of the bedroom barefoot.

He needed a newspaper. In all his preparations for Ginny's arrival, renting the house, arranging for electricity and gas and water, installing a telephone, carting the endless cartons she had shipped over, he had forgotten to subscribe to a newspaper. He had to see a newspaper. *Somebody* had found Hester.

Directly across the street as he came out of the house Bryce saw the thick cylinder on the sidewalk. He looked around. There was a paper on the lawn to his left. If someone came out he would say he had made a small bet on the Navy game the day before and was checking the score. *She wasn't in the paper.*

Bryce put the newspaper together and dropped it on the lawn. He went back to his house and stopped in front of his door. Bryce remembered looking at his wristwatch before slipping out of the Whispering Inn to meet Hester. It was a few minutes before nine. His neighbor's newspaper had probably been printed by nine o'clock the night before. Bryce had to find a final edition of the *Outpost-Dispatch.*

He drove downtown, driving fast in the empty streets, directly to the *Outpost-Dispatch* building. On the first floor, the middle-aged woman at the classified advertising counter sold him the final edition. Bryce went back to his car and began with page one. He ran his forefinger down each column starting with column one. *She's dead!*

He hit the steering wheel with his fist. "She's not *dead*," he said, aloud. He looked down at the Sunday paper on the seat. She . . . could . . . be . . . dead, he thought. You've known what could happen for a long time. Don't pray and make your deals with God this time. She could be lying out there somewhere. *Where?* He started the engine and turned into the street.

Bryce parked in front of his house, and saw his neighbor's newspaper still on the lawn. He made himself ready for Ginny, who was probably awake. Bryce smelled coffee as he came into the house. "Howdy. I brought the Sunday paper."

He heard Ginny say, "The *poor girl!*" and he stopped. He was rigid. Ginny said, "The *poor, poor* girl." Bryce waited for his wife to come screaming at him. He heard Ginny say, "I'm so sorry. I wish . . . I'm very, very sorry." Bryce dropped the newspaper on a chair, watching the open entrance to the living room, but he had dismissed Ginny. He didn't care what Ginny said or did. He thought only of the admiral. If there was a court-martial, he'd take it. He wasn't running. He'd swear to . . . anything. Hester had threatened him. She had a gun. He strode forward, defiantly.

Ginny was beside the taboret that held the telephone. She was slumped against the wall. She seemed dazed. "Hester was raped last night," she said.

The crazy lying bitch! "She was *what?*"

"I can't believe it either," Ginny said.

"Ginny! You said she was raped." Ginny nodded. "Who raped her?" Bryce asked. "Ginny, who did it?"

"They don't know," Ginny said.

"Who are *they*?" He pointed at the telephone. "Who was on the phone?"

Her lips barely moved. "Gerald," she said. "It's so awful." She rubbed her hands over herself, fingers spread, as though she were trying to wipe away something filthy. "Somebody on top of you and in you." Her face contorted. She pulled her robe tight. "I have to put on clothes."

"Wait," Bryce said, and came to her, standing in front of her. She pushed back into the wall.

"I want to get dressed."

"Tell me what Gerald told you. Start at the beginning."

"I feel sick," she said. Bryce took her chin in his hand. She jerked her head, her arms folded across her chest, pressing her breasts.

"Ginny, I want you to talk to me," Bryce said. Then he said, "Angel, we've been apart so long we've forgotten we're married. We share. Good *and* bad."

She looked past him. "I called their home to thank Gerald for the party," she said. "Her mother's home. I couldn't find *their* number. The maid told me Hester was in the hospital and Gerald was with her. Mercy Hospital. I couldn't imagine why she was in the hospital. Remember, she disappeared last night. She didn't come back."

"Go on."

"I was very worried," Ginny said. "I was almost afraid to call the hospital. But I felt cowardly. I called and asked for Gerald. Hester was raped by four men."

"Four!"

"Why do you keep repeating everything?" Ginny flung her arms apart, hitting Bryce with the back of her hands. "Yes, four! Some natives! They grabbed her near the Whispering Inn. Now we know why she never came back to the party. *They* had her. Remember when Gerald was looking for Hester? He asked if we'd seen her? They probably had her already, those . . ." Ginny stopped.

"Where did they come from? If it was right outside the inn, we would have heard something," Bryce said. "What else did Gerald say?"

"Isn't that enough? Four of them," Ginny said. Ginny thought of eight hairy, filthy arms reaching for her. "Hester probably never had a chance to even call for help." She thought of eight hands over her mouth. "I'm going to the hospital," Ginny said.

"Now? Don't you think you ought to wait?"

"Wait for *what?*" Ginny asked. "What else can happen to her? Nothing worse on earth could happen to her."

"But after what did happen you ought to give her a chance to rest," Bryce said. "Gerald's with her. Besides, you've just met her. You're really not a friend."

"*You* are," Ginny said.

"Gerald's friend, yes. I'll call him. What's the name of the hospital again?"

"You don't have to call. You can see him when we get there."

"Angel, hold up a sec." He reached for her but she thrust his hand aside.

"Why are we standing here arguing? If you're a friend, you belong with a friend who's in trouble," Ginny said. "I want Hester and her mother to know they're not alone. If you want to stay, you can stay." Ginny took a step toward the bedroom but Bryce was blocking her.

"You're being pretty tough on me," he said. "Someone listening would think I was the ogre of the islands."

"Cut it out, Bryce," Ginny said. "You're still arguing about us. This isn't *about* us. This is about a girl whose life was probably ruined last night. I want to see Hester. I need to dress and you're stopping me."

Bryce stepped aside. He watched her walking into the corridor leading to the bedroom. "*Raped?*" Bryce said to himself. "When?" So the big man who had come for Gerald at the inn *was* a cop. But the cop showed up more than an hour after Bryce left Hester. "How do you know it was an hour? You didn't check the time," Bryce said to himself. "But there was no one around," he said. He had looked; they had been alone. "You were wrong," he said. They must have been watching him and Hester, lying low in the dark and waiting. Those four guys must have seen him, seen everything. They could deny everything! They could tell the cops they'd seen someone with Hester, seen someone hitting her. They were four against one now. They were *five* against one. "What will the bitch say? What will she tell Ginny? She'll see Ginny come through the door and start talking," Bryce said to himself. "Ginny!" he shouted, hurrying after his wife. Bryce wasn't sitting here waiting for the Shore Patrol to come after him.

* * *

While Bryce was dressing, a gray Navy car reached the admiral's quarters at Pearl Harbor. The house was alone, far out on a point, its veranda facing the sea like a prow. A heavy man in his thirties came out of the car. Commander James Saunders had been an All-American at the Navy Academy so he was a hero when he was commissioned. He was a hero again less than a year later when he saved four enlisted men during a fire on the destroyer to which he had been posted. Jimmy Saunders was the admiral's aide. He started up the wooden steps to the admiral's home and stopped with one foot on the first stair. A Filipino enlisted man in a white mess jacket was in the doorway pointing. "He's out there, sir."

Jimmy Saunders walked onto the beach. He saw the admiral's other mess boy ahead of him. The Filipino was holding a robe and slippers and a folded bath towel. "Is he about due back?"

"Mister, you lost your way . . . *Commander!* Excuse me, sir, I didn't recognize you, sorry. Sorry," said the Filipino. "He'll be back pretty soon, maybe. Can't be sure on Sunday."

Saunders used both hands to shade his eyes. He couldn't find a swimmer. The sea was clean to the horizon. He looked again, sweeping the ocean from left to right. As he dropped his arms, the Filipino said, "Straight ahead, Commander." Saunders thought he saw a flash of an arm far, far out. "He's on his way," said the Filipino.

Admiral Glenn Langdon came out of the water like he was approaching his throne. He was of middle height, five feet eight inches tall, but he looked much taller. He walked as though insisting he were taller. It was not an acquired characteristic. Glenn Langdon had arrived at the United States Navy Academy with that posture, and it was as much mental as physical. In his four years at the Acadeny, Glenn Langdon had accumulated more hours of E.M.I.—extra military instruction—than any midshipman in Annapolis history. His gig record remained. Glenn Langdon did not question authority unless it appeared unreasonable to him. A midshipman always loses, but Glenn Langdon was undefeated. While he was constantly gigged, the admiral remained unrepentant.

The admiral had served everywhere: the Mediterranean, the South Atlantic, the North Atlantic, Scapa Flow, the Yangtze, the Canal Zone. He had been, briefly, at an important desk in the American embassy in London, but the ambassador personally had demanded his removal.

He was a widower whose two daughters were married to Navy officers. He lived alone in the rambling quarters provided for the admiral commanding the Fourteenth Naval District. The admiral took the folded bath towel from the Filipino. "Jimmy, we must be in trouble if you're out here on Sunday morning waiting for me."

"Not on the base, sir, but trouble all the same," Saunders said. "A woman was raped last night. A Navy officer's wife. Doris Ashley's daughter." The Filipino dropped a slipper and in bending to retrieve it let the robe slip off his arm. When he came erect, the admiral was gone.

"Tell me the rest," the admiral said, marching to his quarters, the towel over his head and shoulders like a burnoose. Saunders' shoes filled with sand as he accompanied the admiral, who stopped at the wooden steps. The admiral lowered the towel, raising one leg to wipe the sand from his foot. "*Four* of them!" he said, his voice booming. "In *jail?*"

"It was just coincidence, sir," Saunders said. "They mixed it up with some of our boys downtown." The Filipino reached them with the admiral's robe and slippers.

"Drop them, drop them," the admiral said, thrusting his arm into a sleeve as the Filipino kneeled to set down the slippers. "Come on in, Jimmy." The admiral led Saunders into his quarters. "Send Hester. . . . Whom did she marry?"

"A submariner, sir," Saunders said. "A j.g. on the *Bluegill*. Gerald Murdoch."

"Send her flowers," the admiral said. "And send Doris flowers, send those to Windward." Saunders went to the telephone, and the admiral began to pace. "Godforsaken zoo," he said, including the entire Territory. The other Filipino entered with a sterling silver coffee service. He filled a cup for the admiral, who took it out of the saucer, holding it with both hands. "If she identified them, they're going to prison," the admiral said, loud, as Saunders spoke to the florist. "They'd better go to prison or every beach boy in Honolulu will be out on the hunt."

Around noon, Dr. Frank Puana, the emergency room physician who had treated Hester the night before, came out of his bedroom, barefoot and in shorts. The baby's crying had roused him and although the house was quiet again, he could no longer sleep.

In the kitchen Mary Sue was sitting beside the high chair feeding Jonathan, the baby, who was fourteen months old. Jonathan was unmistakably Mary Sue's child, light-skinned like his mother, with her blond hair. Frank's older boy, Eric, who was five, was his son in every way. "I was afraid he'd wake you," Mary Sue said. She was wearing shorts and one of Frank's old shirts. Her hair was bleached from the sun and her arms and legs were brown. She was a slender, attractive woman of twenty-nine, a year younger than Frank. Mary Sue, who was from Green Bay, Wisconsin, had been a nurse at Mercy Hospital. Frank thought she was the most beautiful woman on earth.

"Did you see the papers?" he asked.

"Sort of. In between," Mary Sue said. "Why?"

"I guess there was nothing in the papers or you wouldn't have asked," Frank said. "Doris Ashley's daughter was raped last night."

Mary Sue's eyes opened wide. "I don't believe it," she said. She set down the spoon. "Hester Ashley. Never, Frank."

"Hester Murdoch," Frank said. "It's true. Four men picked her up." He made a face. "They beat her," he said, and told Mary Sue of Hester's arrival at Mercy Hospital, of treating her in the emergency room.

"Frank, no one would come near Hester Ashley or whatever her name is now," said Mary Sue.

"There've been rapes all over Honolulu," Frank said.

"Not of white women," Mary Sue said. "Wait! Did you do a pelvic?"

"How could I do a pelvic? I treated her, and then she was admitted, and went upstairs. The rape came out later, when her mother arrived."

Mary Sue swung around in her chair like a stubborn child. "I can't stand it anymore!" she said. "She was *your* patient! Doris Ashley's daughter!"

"Mary Sue, I'm the emergency room physician," Frank said. "It's my job."

"It's your *punishment!*" said Mary Sue. "For being a Hawaiian." Frank smiled at her.

"Hawaiian and Japanese," Frank said. The attending physicians at Mercy Hospital, those who could admit patients, were all haoles. Even the emergency room post was unusual for someone with a Hawaiian background. Frank had been given the job with the understanding that he worked nights, and every night of every weekend in the year.

"You're still trying to joke," Mary Sue said. "Frank, we're leaving. I can't take it anymore. I won't let you take it anymore. It has to stop. I'm stopping it."

"Because Hester . . . Murdoch was raped?"

"Because you're being cheated," said Mary Sue. "You're the best, Frank." He grinned, and she said, "I'm not prejudiced. Remember, Doctor, I was a scrub nurse. I saw all those butterfingers in the O.R. They couldn't come near you. I never saw anyone with hands like yours. You shouldn't be sewing up drunks. You should be upstairs doing major surgery.''

"One of these days," Frank said. He spoke lightly, but he believed, secretly, that his ability would be recognized, would be finally rewarded, that he would be allowed on the attending physicians staff, that he would be able to open a practice because he had a hospital to which he could send his sick patients.

"You're dreaming again," Mary Sue said. She leaped up from the chair. "Do you want your sons to grow up and see the way their father is treated? Do you want your sons to live the way you have to live?" Frank rose and came to her. Mary Sue clung to him. "Frank, let's leave." He kissed her cheek and turned away. He hated what he was doing to her, hated himself for submitting to the onerous and degrading position he held at Mercy Hospital. Frank Puana knew he should leave Honolulu, leave the Territory, but something kept him, some deep mysterious need for the familiar, safe place where he had spent his life.

The years in Seattle, at the University of Washington School of Medicine, and, later, during his internship, had been a long, sustained, gnawing tenancy of loneliness. He had been homesick from the first day to the last. His love of medicine, his passion for his work, had kept him in Seattle. During the first two preclinical years, he left the campus only to sleep. From the start of his third year, from his first day on the wards with patients, he went back to his room only to change clothes. There was always an empty bed somewhere in the hospital. When he was not on call, he remained on the wards, following faculty physicians, watching them with patients. He never tired of medicine. The world beyond the hospital was alien, was foreign. He sailed for home three days after he finished interning.

In the kitchen Mary Sue said, "I loved this place when I came. I thought it was the most beautiful place in the world. When I met you, I felt like I was dreaming. No. I felt like it was a dream come true. I wanted to pinch myself. Everything was perfect. Too perfect. I wanted Eric to be a boy. I wanted him to look like you so I could have two of you. I *was* dreaming, though. This is your home, Frank. You were born here. Your sons were born here, but you're only a guest. All four of us are guests. Unwelcome guests. They don't want us, but since they can't deport us, they find ways to keep us out. Frank, let's leave."

He smiled at her again. "Pack up and move, just like that." He took Jonathan out of the high chair, holding the warm, fresh, sweet-smelling body close. "Let's explore it, Mary Sue. Where's Eric?"

A Black Maria turned into the long, gradual hill leading to Mercy Hospital from the east. Maddox was in the front seat beside the driver, a redheaded man in his late twenties wearing a suit. Maddox had left the regular driver at headquarters. "We'll come in the back way, Al," Maddox said. Although there were no openings, Maddox had taken Albert Keller out of uniform and assigned him to the detective division. Maddox had watched the redhead's work. He was too good to waste on drunks and speeding cars.

There was a metal panel above the sea. A rectangular window of shatterproof glass was set into the center of the panel. The window was on a track and an hour ago, in the empty van, Maddox had moved it a few inches. He and Al Keller had listened to the four handcuffed young men behind them since they had been loaded in the Black Maria. He heard only what he had been told in his office the night before. "There's a door at the end of the building they use for deliveries and laundry bins," Maddox said. "The stairwell is on the left. We'll take them up that way."

Al Keller backed up to the door. As he and Maddox left the Black Maria, Al stopped. He wore an open holster on his hip and he reached for the .38 Police Positive, shoving it into his waistband behind his belt buckle. Someone could come at him unseen, behind and on his right, to grab the piece. No one he could see was taking it away from him. "Al?" The redhead hurried to the rear of the Black Maria where Maddox waited. "Let them out."

Keller unlocked the doors, opening them wide. Joe Liliuohe led the others, moving awkwardly, bent forward so he wouldn't bang his head, his handcuffed wrists in front of him. The sunlight hurt for a minute. He lowered his right leg until he felt the single step. "Over here with me, Joe," Maddox said.

"Why can't you tell us anything? We're entitled to know something," Joe said.

There was no answer. As David Kwan appeared, head bent, Keller moved back and away from Maddox, keeping Joe between them. "Over here," Maddox said, pointing at Joe. Harry Pohukaina was next and Mike Yoshida followed him. Maddox had briefed Keller before they took the four prisoners out of the cells. "Let's start," Maddox said. Keller went ahead. "You follow him, Joe," Maddox said. "The rest of you, single file."

Maddox remained behind David Kwan, who was the last of the four in line.

When they were all in the third-floor corridor, Maddox stopped them. "We're in a hospital. Act like you're in a hospital." He pointed. "It's this way, Al." They came down the corridor to the visitors' room. "Take a load off," Maddox said. "I'll be back." Maddox left them, and Keller took a station in the entrance facing the four handcuffed prisoners.

Maddox stopped in front of 346, knocked, and, remembering his hat, raised his hand to remove it as the door opened out into the corridor. Doris Ashley held it. She looked like she was on her way to tea, although she had not slept. She had persuaded Gerald to spend the night at Windward instead of the carriage house she had converted for Hester and him. In her suite Doris had bathed and changed clothes, and returned alone to Mercy Hospital as she had planned, driving the Pierce-Arrow limousine, to take up her vigil beside Hester.

In the night Hester had slept and come awake and slept again, and come awake again. She was not really conscious. Once she said, "Voted most unpopular," and once, much later, "Daddy." Doris Ashley leaned forward in the chair beside the bed. Hester's eyes were closed, and she did not speak again, but Doris Ashley remembered, clearly, issuing an ultimatum when Hester was eight years old. "Daddy was my only friend," Hester said.

It was so rare a sign of candor, of rebellion, that Mrs. Ashley was stunned. She drew Hester to her, holding her daughter close. "I'm your friend, baby," Doris Ashley said. "I'm your best friend," she said, but she did not withdraw her ultimatum, and she could not, now, beside her battered daughter, remember what she had demanded of Hester that day so far in the past.

Hester Anne Ashley had succumbed, was defeated, long before she was eight years old. She was almost six on the night Preston Lord Ashley slumped down in his chair in the library at Windward, a book falling to the floor. Doris Ashley was bringing Hester in to say good night. Doris knew immediately but she ran to him. "Daddy's asleep," Hester said. Doris Ashley kept the truth from the child until it was time for the funeral.

That night Doris took Hester out of the library, calling for the nanny. She sent her baby to bed and returned for a last look at her husband. "Now I'm alone again," she said, aloud. The week after the funeral, Doris Ashley gave the nanny two months' salary and sent her away from Windward. Doris had Hester to herself.

Her father's death was the crucial event in Hester's life. In those first six years her only memories were of happy times, of *occasions* decreed as holidays by her father: Silly Saturday; Read a Book Week: Night of the Full Moon. Her father's fertile imagination kept Hester in attendance at a continuing fete. Because he loved the library, Hester loved it, and with his help she was reading, but barely, before she was four. Preston Lord Ashley encouraged her, and under his delighted guidance, she soon shared his addiction to books, all books.

Doris Ashley adored her daughter, adored the woman who would emerge from her loving devotion and tutelage. Once she was alone with Hester, Doris Ashley instituted her regimen. Windward became an academy. Hester went to school every day, and she went to dancing class and riding class, and to all of these pursuits Doris Ashley provided tutorial assistance. She never wearied. She was omnipresent. And she failed because Hester failed.

Hester was a small child with small bones. Her arms and legs were almost reedy. She was physically awkward like another is endowed with natural grace. With her fine, sand-colored hair and wan complexion she seemed like a child recovering from a long illness. The clothes Doris Ashley bought in wholesale lots didn't help. Doris Ashley persevered.

She hid her frustrations. She was never angry with Hester for the child's, the girl's, the young woman's lackluster performance. Doris Ashley knew she was right, and while there was no trace of her father's tyranny in her relationship with Hester, she had, unwittingly, inherited Herman Moeller's self-righteous fanaticism. Doris Ashley thought she was Hester's best friend when in fact her daughter, from childhood, never confided in her, never.

Hester was eighteen when she overheard two giggling classmates suggest a Most Unpopular prize for the yearbook. She heard herself declared the winner. Hester was not surprised, nor did she enjoy her two classmates' discomfiture when they discovered she had overheard them. Her alienation was an old and weary condition.

Yet the girls spurred Hester to action. She had for a long time known her life's work, and now, having reached eighteen, she acted, writing several hospitals in San Francisco to inquire about nurse's training. She kept her secret until she had chosen her hospital, returned the application forms, and been accepted for the fall class. Doris Ashley knew she could not survive Hester's absence, and she knew she could not openly object or forbid her daughter's departure. So Doris Ashley begged.

She pleaded for time to accept Hester's decision. "I've been a woman alone since your father died, baby," Doris Ashley said. She was relentless. She followed Hester through the rooms of Windward asking for mercy. Doris Ashley won a delay. Hester agreed to wait until she was twenty-one.

Now, in the doorway of Hester's room in Mercy Hospital, Doris Ashley faced the detective who said, "They're all here, Mrs. Ashley."

"Spare her as much as you can," Doris Ashley said.

"This won't take long," Maddox said. He returned to the visitors' room, stopping beside Keller. He decided to start with Joe, with the football player. Hester had been in the front seat with him. If she had seen anyone, she had seen him. "Joe."

Joe rose, his handcuffed wrists in his belly. "Don't be afraid," said Harry Pohukaina. "You didn't do anything, remember that."

"Let's take a walk," Maddox said. He kept Joe beside the wall as they came down the corridor. As they reached Hester's room, Maddox took Joe's arm. "In here." He opened the door and followed the handcuffed young man.

Joe stopped, facing the bed, facing Hester. He saw the woman beside the chair at the bed, recognizing her instantly from her pictures in the newspapers. It was her mother, Doris Ashley. Behind him Maddox closed the door.

Joe looked at the woman he had found in the dirt the night before. She was clean now between the clean white sheets, but she looked awful. She had swelled up. Her face was round like a balloon and every different color. She didn't look young, she looked old, older than her mother standing next to her. Joe was plenty scared. " 'Lo. Hope you're feeling better."

She didn't answer. She looked at Doris Ashley, at her mother. Doris Ashley sat down and took Hester's left hand in hers. "Officer?"

"Is he one of them?" Maddox asked.

Doris squeezed Hester's hand. Hester looked at her and at Joe, and nodded. "It's a lie!" Joe said, yelling.

"Are you sure, Mrs. Murdoch?" Maddox asked.

"Hester," said Doris Ashley, holding tight to her hand.

"Yes," said Hester. "Yes."

"You're lying!" Joe yelled. He was dying, right here in this hospital room. They were as good as killing him. They were killing him. "We didn't touch you except to help you!" he yelled. He stepped forward, but Maddox had him. Joe tried to shake him off but couldn't. "You're making up a whole story!" Joe yelled.

Maddox moved him toward the door. Joe turned his head,

looking at Hester. "What did you tell him? Someone beat you up and left you out in the dirt! It wasn't us! You know it! Why are you lying?"

As they left and the door closed, Hester pushed aside Doris Ashley's hand and threw back the bed covers. She rolled away from her mother, crying out with pain. Doris Ashley said, "No!" and fell on the bed, her arms out to seize Hester. Hester rolled from side to side, crying and moaning with the pain, shaking back and forth to free herself. She made it to her feet and stood barefoot on the cold, cold floor, her head spinning and knives and pins in her face. Doris Ashley left the bed and ran across the room, standing with her back to the door. Hester shook her head slowly.

"I can't," she said. She came forward, teetered, and seized the iron uprights at the foot of the bed to keep from falling. By that time her mother had her.

"No, baby, no, child," Doris Ashley said, both arms around Hester. "You must be strong, for both of us. We're innocent, too. You and I are innocent. I wish I could do this for you. If only I could face these men instead of you. I can only be with you, baby. Everything depends on you. Our lives are in your hands. If you fail us, we're lost, baby. You're lost, alone and disgraced. And you'll take me down with you." She moved Hester away from the foot of the bed. "Save us, child. Gather your strength." Doris sat her down on the bed. She straightened the covers. She bent to raise Hester's legs and set them on the bed. She straightened the bedclothes, slipping them over Hester. "You can't fail us in our hour of need, baby."

The instant Maddox and Joe appeared in the visitors' room, Harry Pohukaina was on his feet. "Where were you, Joe? What're they doing to us?"

"Quiet down," Maddox said.

"You can't stop us from talking," Joe said. "We're entitled to certain things. I want to use the telephone. I want to call someone to help us."

"Soon as we're back in headquarters," Maddox said. He pointed at David Kwan. "Your turn, son."

David didn't want anyone to catch him shaking. He couldn't stop himself. He squeezed his fingertips together trying to stop his hands from shaking. The handcuffs made noise as metal rubbed metal. "Don't worry," Harry said. David was afraid he'd bust out crying if he looked at Harry, at anyone.

Maddox led David down the hall to 346. Maddox opened the door, and David stopped right in front of him. "We didn't do anything like he said we did, lady. I swear we didn't. We would never do anything like that. I told him last night. We stopped because you were unconscious." Maddox shoved him into the room.

"Is he one of them?" Maddox asked. Doris Ashley looked down at Hester.

"The captain spoke to you," said Doris Ashley. Hester was silent.

"Is he one of them?" Maddox asked.

"Yes, yes," Hester said.

David started to cry. "All we did was bring her here," he said. He could taste the tears. He raised his wrists to wipe his face but the metal scraped his skin.

Outside, an old green Durant coupe stopped beside the hospital entrance. Duane York, the enlisted man who had borrowed Gerald's car the night before, was driving. Gerald was beside him. Gerald had called Duane's barracks. "I'm sorry, Duane, but I need my car." An hour earlier when Theresa had brought Gerald his coffee following Doris Ashley's instructions, he had learned his mother-in-law was gone, with the Pierce-Arrow.

"She said not to wake you," Theresa told him. "She said you're tired."

In front of the hospital Gerald said, "I'm sorry to do this to you, Duane. I'll have to keep the car."

"I'm the last of your worries, Lieutenant," Duane said. "There's plenty for you to worry over in this hospital." Gerald had told him Hester had been hurt at the party. Duane took the keys from the ignition. "I just thought of something, Lieutenant," Duane said. "You might have a whole lot to do today. I'm free as the breeze till reveille tomorrow. Maybe you'll need some help. I can hang around. If you need to chase after something, I'll do it and you can be with Mrs. Murdoch."

"I won't argue with you, Duane," Gerald said. "I won't forget your generosity, either."

"My generosity," Duane said. "Excuse me, sir, you have to turn that around. How many times have I had this car? How many times have you loaned me . . . I'd need a list long as my arm." Duane followed the lieutenant. He finally had a chance to show the lieutenant how he felt.

In the hospital Mike Yoshida was the last of the four whom Hester identified as those who had beaten and attacked her. Maddox had Mike beside him as they returned to the visitors' room. "Al."

Al Keller gestured at the three handcuffed prisoners. "On your feet," he said. Maddox reached him.

"We'll leave the way we came," Maddox said. "You first, I'm last." He turned Mike Yoshida around. "Follow him. Joe, you too." Maddox waved them forward, and without warning, grabbed Harry Pohukaina. "Wait," he said, sharply, and louder, "Al. *Al!*" Gerald Murdoch had come out of the elevator and the stairwell lay beyond it. The redhead whirled around, his right hand over his gun butt and his left arm out to stop anyone who decided to run. Maddox was waving. "This way! Quick!" He pushed Harry Pohukaina toward the stairwell at the other end of the corridor. Maddox grabbed David Kwan, shoving him ahead. Keller was coming with Joe and Mike Yoshida. "Move it, move it," Maddox said. "The other stairs." As Maddox followed the rest, Gerald saw him.

"Captain Maddox?" Gerald started after the group. Duane had to hurry to keep up.

Keller was in front. He came to the stairwell door and opened it. Maddox waved at him. Keller went through the door with Joe and Mike Yoshida behind him. David was next, and Harry Pohukaina was in front of Maddox. "Why the rush all of a sudden?" Harry asked. Maddox took Harry's arm.

"Captain!" Gerald said, loud. He could see the handcuffed man the captain was holding.

Maddox was at the stairwell door. He pushed Harry through it, and yelled, "Al, hold it here until I'm with you." Maddox pulled the door shut, waiting for Murdoch.

Duane had seen the guy with handcuffs. He was right beside the lieutenant as they reached the big guy at the door. The lieutenant had called him captain, so Duane figured the big man was a cop, a deke. This was a hospital, and here were cops running around with beach boys in handcuffs. Duane hated to think what he was thinking. The lieutenant said, "Wait a minute, Captain. Who were those men?"

"All police work, Lieutenant," Maddox said. Gerald started for the door and stopped like he was on the end of a rope. Maddox's arm was hooked through Gerald's arm.

"I wouldn't like it if I was rough with you," Maddox said. "I can't let you square off with my prisoners."

"I only want to see them."

"You'll see them when the time comes," Maddox said. "You'll see more of them than you'll ever want to see." Maddox slowly released Gerald. "You're an officer yourself, you should understand. I have to follow the book like you follow yours."

"I deserve to be told what's going on." Maddox relaxed. Whenever a man asked for an explanation, he was through fighting. Maddox glanced at the little guy, and recognized him. The Whispering Inn last night. "You can say anything in front of Duane," Gerald said. When he heard the Lieutenant, Duane knew he was set for as long as he served aboard the *Bluegill*.

"Anyway, it won't be a secret long," Maddox said. "The newspapers will be all over this case. This case won't have any boundaries. It'll be everywhere." Maddox buttoned his jacket. "Your wife identified them. There were four all right."

Gerald felt as though the captain were blaming him, as though he, too, were guilty. The captain was probably wondering why Hester had been outside by herself in the dark. The captain probably believed Gerald should have been with Hester to protect her. He hadn't even seen her *leave* the inn. She was always by herself. She always said, "Reading," when Gerald asked about her. He didn't understand the first thing about her. Duane probably had as many questions as the captain. Everyone who learned about Hester would have questions.

"They're in my custody," Maddox said. "My responsibility. You won't prove anything if you come after me. I wouldn't let you near them." Maddox opened the stairwell door.

Duane watched the deke leave. He couldn't look at the lieutenant. Duane knew everything now. He thought he would gag. Just thinking of those four guys made him sick. The way the deke *protected* them made him sick. "Gerald?"

Someone back there was calling the lieutenant. "I'll be in here, sir," Duane said, pointing at the visitors' room. He saw the lieutenant heading toward a couple standing with the nurses and then Duane recognized the man. It was Lieutenant Partridge, the communications officer on the *Bluegill*. The woman with the flowers was probably his wife.

Beside Bryce at the nurses' station, Ginny whispered, "He looks terrible." Bryce watched him coming, in a suit and shirt and tie, shoulders back, head up, the Annapolis product in classic mold. The sharp sound of Gerald's heels, click, click, click, click, was for Bryce like the ticking of a time bomb rolling down the corridor directly at him. Bryce had seen, recognized, the big brute with Gerald. He was the cop who had come to the Whispering Inn for Gerald. Bryce said Pray for me to himself, and extended his hand. "I'm awfully sorry, Gerald. I wish there was something to say."

"You're here," Gerald said. "That says everything." Bryce

wanted to sit down. He held on to Gerald's hand. He had to be sure.

"Do they know who did it?" Bryce asked.

"Hester identified all four men," Gerald said. "I was talking to the detective." Bryce put his arm across Gerald's shoulders.

"I'm glad we came, old sport," Bryce said.

"How is she?" Ginny asked. "Gosh, I feel *stupid* saying that. Can we see her?"

"I was just going in myself," Gerald said. "I'll ask." He left them.

"He makes me want to cry," Ginny said. Bryce took her arm.

"We're in the line of fire, angel," Bryce said. He led her toward the visitors' room. Duane saw them coming and figured they wanted to be alone. He said, "Seaman York, sir, from the torpedo room. I'm with the lieutenant, sir." Duane ducked past them, heading for a bench at one end of the corridor. In the visitors' room, Bryce released Ginny, walking to the windows. Hester *identified* them. Bryce remembered, he could see, clearly, Hester the night before. He could see her face. Why would a man, *any* man go after someone whose face was like a Halloween mask? Even when she was ready for the ball, Hester looked like the mascot. All through the spring, at every rendezvous, before every tryst, Bryce wondered why he had chosen her.

Bryce had been the pursuer. He had come, alone, to a party one Friday night in March. Bryce was living in the bachelor officer's quarters while Ginny remained with her parents in the States, and his shipmates included him in every activity. Bryce had brought the required bottle of okolehao to the party, adding it to the cluster on the kitchen sideboard. Bryce never allowed himself to become drunk, to lose authority over his body. He had accepted the invitation because he was lonely and because, from his first days of duty aboard the *Bluegill,* he liked his fellow officers.

He was the last to arrive that Friday night, and the rest, wives with husbands, bachelors with their dates, were, as someone said, "Feeling no pain." Bryce accepted a drink to avoid protests, and sidestepped comradely arms and discordant quartets, wandering through the small leased house looking at the Academy mementoes he loved. For weeks afterward, Bryce remembered that he didn't see the girl. She was so completely neutral, so drab, that he almost walked into her where she stood at the glassed bookcase she had opened, holding the copy of *Jane Eyre* she had taken from the matched set of classics brought by the hostess from the Mainland. He said, "Hello," and as she looked up from the page, taken unaware, "Bryce Partridge reporting for duty." Then he said, "*Volunteering* for duty," instantly and inexplicably on the make. He wanted, there at the bookcase, to bite her, to make small nibbles as she lay, infinitely demanding, in his arms.

She said, weakly, "I'm Hester Murdoch." He had startled her. She had looked up to see, at her side, a lean, hard figure, someone strange, someone who might have been a Spartan warrior returning in triumph. He seemed unreal, here at the usual Navy party to which she had reluctantly accompanied Gerald.

"Why aren't you drunk and disorderly?" Bryce asked.

"I'm not a good . . . drinker," Hester said, apologizing. Bryce made a half-turn to set down his glass, and as he swung back, as though he were hitting through the ball with his backhand, took the book from Hester's hands, running his fingers over her fingers.

"Your secret is safe with me," he said, putting the book on the shelf. "There must be a garden," he said.

Hester felt as though they were alone in the house, as though the others had vanished. The strange man who seemed to have materialized from antiquity, who blotted out everything and everyone, had taken command. He was leading her through the room, through the doors, onto the terrace with its potted plants, past the bickering couple trying to keep their voices low, their sibilants crackling with venom. Bryce took her past the light from the house deep into the shadows. "Now we're safe," he said. "Now tell me why it seems as though we're not strangers, as though I've always known you?" he said, lying. He was careful not to touch her. Bryce was sure it was important not to touch her yet.

Hester didn't answer because she could not, because the figure from the Aegean who had materialized beside the bookcase had enchanted her. She was incapable of speech. "And you've felt it," Bryce said, speaking for her. Since he had found her holding a book, he adapted to the circumstances. "I want my lips against yours," he said, careful to keep his distance, and, whispering, "When?"

He chose Sunday so she would have all of the following day to concentrate on their meeting. She refused, but he was quietly, fervently steadfast. She protested, but he remained adamant. "I've never . . ." she began, but he interrupted.

"Neither have I," he lied. Bryce made the plans. He laid out her part in detail. He had not been at Pearl long enough to be familiar with Honolulu, but he had always been safe in crowds so he chose the entrance of the Western Sky Hotel on Kalakau Avenue. "Wear white," he said, low. And although Hester repeated, almost frantically, her protests, Bryce was certain she would be with him Sunday.

Bryce had always been successful with women, and he was successful that Sunday, but he was unprepared for the scale of his victory. Bryce's confidence, his intuitive patience, his skilled instruction, the touch and feel of his arms and mouth, the pressure of his body, made Hester his grateful prisoner. Bryce was the hero she had hoped to find in Gerald, the hero she had sought since her father's death, the heroes of Windward's library shelves. For Hester that Sunday afternoon he became the dashing, romantic leader of every gallant regiment and doomed squadron of which she had read and dreamed from childhood.

She would not release him that Sunday. She was galvanized by him. She became wanton. "Tell me what to do," she said, and did everything better than anyone. "Tell me what you want, what you like, what pleases you," she said, and anticipated every wish. She seemed to be with him only to tantalize, to delight, to prolong, to fulfill. She was everywhere. Hester engulfed him, and when she had to release him, when they had to part so she could return to the carriage house below Windward, Hester had become his slave.

While Bryce waited in the visitors' room at Mercy Hospital remembering his first meeting with Hester, Doris Ashley sat in the chair beside the bed. "Are you awake, child?" Hester was silent. Doris Ashley looked at her daughter whose eyes were closed. "There was no other way," Doris Ashley said. "There was nothing else we could do. What else could we have done? We were given no choice. We had no choice, baby. We had to protect ourselves. Everyone has a right to protect herself. It's a law of nature, a basic law of nature." Doris Ashley heard the door and looked up. "Hello, Gerald. Baby, here's Gerald." Doris rose quickly to stand guard beside the bed in case Hester tried to do something or say something.

Gerald went to the other side of the bed. Hester looked worse. Her face was swollen. Her face bulged, filled with lumps and bumps and totally discolored. The black silk stitches made short, random lines across her cheeks and jaw. Gerald couldn't recognize Hester. He couldn't understand the people who had hit her. Gerald had never known of a man hitting a woman, of men ganging up to maul a woman. They were four against one! He could barely speak. "Is there anything I can do for you, Hester?" She shook her head. "Ginny and Bryce are here."

As Hester's eyes opened, Doris Ashley was on her way to the door. "You saw the sign, Gerald," she said. "No visitors. Those are doctor's orders." Doris Ashley reached the door. "Do you want me to tell them?"

Gerald said, "Excuse me, Hester." He left the bed. She heard him say, "I didn't intend to upset anyone. Neither did Ginny and Bryce." Hester heard the door open and shut. She heard her mother returning to the bed, and closed her eyes. "He comes here with his *wife!*" Doris Ashley said, all in a single gasp. "What kind of person is he? He is a crazy person. This man is crazy, child. You were lucky to escape with your life. How could he dare to *appear!*" She turned the chair and sat down facing the door. She glanced at Hester. As soon as Hester was asleep, Doris Ashley would talk with the head nurse. She wanted the NO VISITORS sign strictly enforced until Hester left Mercy Hospital. Bryce Partridge could try again.

Hester moved her hands, putting one atop the other over her breasts. Her mother was wrong. Bryce Partridge wasn't crazy. He was . . . Bryce. He was unlike any other human being on earth, any other human being who had ever lived or of whom anyone had ever written. He had no feelings except for himself. Hester had learned quickly since Bryce hid nothing about himself. He was . . . Bryce. And he had, without effort, without an overt gesture after that first night at the bookcase, turned Hester into a person without a will, without the strength of choice. And because she had seen, at last, that she was like a leaf in the wind, a nonentity who had returned to molest him, and had threatened him, Hester had unleashed Bryce Partridge the night before. And because Doris Ashley was her first and enduring master, Hester had sent four innocent boys to be sacrificed in her place. She wanted to scream the truth, and she wanted, with all her being, to see Bryce burst through the doorway to enfold her. She was revolted by herself, by her treachery and by the longing for Bryce that remained and that she was unable to eradicate.

As Doris Ashley sat beside the bed watching the door, Hester's eyes filled and from each a tear escaped, rolling across her battered face.

"Here's my office," said Tom Halehone as he and Sarah Liliuohe reached the doorway. "Up above here."

"Will you hurry?" Sarah asked, and, quickly, "I talk as though we'll be late, as though Joe will be gone."

"I'll be right back," Tom said. He climbed the stairs and

unlocked his office door. Tom put a yellow legal-size pad and some pencils into his briefcase. When he reached Sarah, she was pressed against the wall of the building watching the rain.

"Now we have to wait," Sarah said, as though they were trapped by a conspiracy. The soft Hawaiian rain that falls like the perimeter of a lawn sprinkler is quickly over. They were pressed together in the doorway, and when their shoulders touched, Tom's body tensed. He became rigid. He had never been with a girl except through accident. He had never, long enough, been able to ignore his foot. He had tried. Thrown together with a woman he would, secretly, urge himself on, compose courtly invitations, edit and rewrite them in his head, but these were never delivered.

He did not move away from Sarah. He could feel her shoulder. She was as tall as he. Tom surrendered to fantasy, forgetting everything and everyone but Sarah and himself, alone, marooned, fated to remain together. But the rain ceased and Sarah said, "We can go."

When they reached police headquarters, there was a rainbow in the hills. There were small white clouds around the rainbow, like washed and bleached boulders in a clear and sparkling creek. "I've never been here," Sarah said.

"It's only a building, a public building," Tom said.

"No, it's different," Sarah said. "There's a difference. It's full of guns. Joe's in there, in a cell. He's a prisoner behind bars. I can't believe he's in jail, but it's true. I washed my hair this morning, and went outside to comb it in the sun. The telephone rang. I heard my mother scream. Our lives have changed. One telephone call changed our lives. I feel like we've all been poisoned."

"You can wait for me," Tom said

"I could have waited at home," Sarah said. "I could have *stayed* home, locked up safe. I can't. I can't run. I won't. Joe's inside. My brother is inside. And the others. David Kwan is *almost* like a brother. They're in jail, I'm not. I'm free. But if I stay out here, I won't be, not to myself."

They came into a long corridor with pale green walls and ceiling. There was a heavy smell of disinfectant. The lights that burned everywhere gave the corridor an eerie look. It was damp in the building as though they were far underground. Sarah touched Tom. "I'm so scared."

Tom saw her hand on his arm. Her fingers were delicate, thin and long, reminding him of hands in an ancient painting. He had to catch his breath. When her arm fell, Tom felt as though she had left him. "In this place everyone is scared," he said. "Besides, it looks scary."

They heard footsteps, heavy and measured. Ahead, a middle-aged cop in uniform turned toward a flight of stairs. "Officer!" Tom led Sarah toward the cop. "I represent—"

"In there," said the cop, interrupting and pointing.

They followed his directions, entering a shallow room with a low curved ceiling. Directly ahead was a counter, shoulder-high and running the width of the room. Behind it and sitting high up like a judge was a sergeant in uniform. Set into the wall at his left was a cell door. Arresting officers came into a narrow hall behind the sergeant, bringing their prisoners to the cell door where they could be booked. As Sarah and Tom approached the counter, the sergeant was eating a papaya, slicing the fruit with a pocket knife. "Excuse me. My name is Tom Halehone. I'm counsel for Joe—"

"You're what?"

"I'm a lawyer representing Joe Liliuohe, David Kwan, Harry—"

"Them guys."

"I'd like to see my clients, please." The sergeant took out his handkerchief and set down the papaya. He set down his knife and reached for the telephone receiver.

"Go ahead," he told Tom.

"Which way is it, please?"

"Which way is it?" The sergeant dropped the receiver into its cradle. "You're a lawyer, aren't you?"

"This is my first time here," Tom said.

The sergeant came out of his chair. Slowly, enunciating slowly and clearly, accenting all vowels, speaking like he was instructing a defective, making two words out of "staircase," he directed Tom to the counsel room in the basement near the cell block. Sarah couldn't look at the sergeant. She wanted to slap him. "We'll find it," she said

"We?" The sergeant looked down at the broad. She was a good-looking broad. "Are you a lawyer?"

"I'm Joe Liliuohe's sister."

"Come back during visiting hours," said the sergeant. He sat down, reaching for the knife. Sarah swung around, walking fast.

"Thank you." Tom, listening to his shoe against the stone floor, followed Sarah.

In the corridor Sarah said, "I hate them all! They're all the same! Treating us like we were servants." She was pale with anger.

"He's not important," Tom said. "Forget him. Why don't you wait outside?"

"I belong here as much as he does," Sarah said. "It'll take more than him to make me leave. You go ahead. You'll be late."

On the stairs leading to the basement Tom heard a man singing in a language he could neither understand nor identify. The melody was lilting and merry. Tom thought of men and women dancing in the moonlight in a cobblestone square with pennants flying and an amateur orchestra of elderly men sitting on the edge of the fountain in the center, an open bottle of wine between the legs of each musician. He saw the square clearly in his head, somewhere in a medieval European village. He was among the dancers, the rest colorfully dressed, while only Sarah and he were in Western clothing. Sarah and he were dancing. They were very graceful, and the onlookers commented on their verve. The song ended and Tom returned, apprehensive and unsure, to the rendezvous with the four young men.

The counsel room was large, with a table and chairs. Tom set his briefcase on the table and took out the pad and pencils. He went to the open door and looked out but the corridor was deserted. He returned to the table and stood beside a chair. He heard someone say, "In here," and saw the turnkey, in uniform, in the doorway.

Joe Liliuohe was the first to enter. Tom saw a cluster of men behind him. "Knock on the door when you're finished," the turnkey said.

"Tommy, look where we are," Joe said. "Did you ever think we'd be together in *police* headquarters? Where's Sarah?"

"Upstairs," Tom said. The turnkey closed the door. Tom didn't recognize the three others with Joe.

"Who's this?" asked Mike Yoshida.

"Tommy Halehone from around my house," Joe said. "You remember Tommy from high school."

"I never went to high school," Mike said. "You said your sister was bringing a lawyer."

"Tommy's a lawyer," Joe said. "He went to the States and became a lawyer."

Harry Pohukaina came close, facing Tom. "You want to send him up against them?" He swung his arm in a wide arc as though he were throwing a discus. "Why don't we just confess?"

"Why . . ." Tom said, and stopped. He was a lawyer. He had been trained. And he was *free*. He said, "Joe, I'll tell the turnkey I want to see you alone."

"Hold it," Joe said, putting one hand in front of Tom as though he were breaking up a fight. "Shut up, Harry, or I'll shut you up."

"Try it," Harry said, and lunged to his left, picking up a chair and raising it over his shoulder. "I'll break this right over your head, goddamn you. I've been listening to you ever since last night, and look where I am. You're the one who had to stop for her. I wouldn't come near a haole woman if she was six feet under in a casket. But you wouldn't listen to anyone. I haven't even been near a woman for a month and now I'm in jail for rape." He backed away, ready with the chair. "You'll shut *me* up! I'll break your head open!"

Joe shoved Mike Yoshida aside, giving Tom a chance to reach him. "Joe! *Joe!* You're ready to prove the cops were right!"

"Harry, put the chair down," said David Kwan.

"Put it down," said Mike Yoshida. He dropped into a chair at the end of the table, bending forward. "Oh, Christ, what'll happen to us?"

Harry lowered the chair. He carried it to the end of the table and sat down beside Mike. Joe sat down, and David, the youngest in the room, moved to the wall, pressing against it as though there, somehow, he would find an escape.

"We're some gang, huh, Tom? Don't listen to them," Joe said.

"I must listen to them, to you, to all of you," Tom said. "First, you'd better listen to me. I'm new. I'm starting out, barely beginning. I'm not a criminal lawyer. You're entitled to the best counsel you can find. You can't and shouldn't worry about hurting my feelings."

"Now you know what kind of a guy Tom is," Joe said. "We're lucky he's still here after the welcome we gave him. I feel like kissing his hand. Guess why. Because I don't have money for a tank of gas, forget about a lawyer." He looked at Tom. "You knew I didn't have any dough, didn't you?"

"That's not why we're here," Tom said.

"Maybe you guys should apologize, too," Joe said. "But I'm only talking for myself. Will you help me, Tom?" David came away from the wall.

"None of us have money," David said. Tom took the legal pad and raised the cover. He reached for the pencils. He was ill at ease.

"Let's start with last night," Tom said. "Tell me everything. *Everything*. Begin with where you met each other. If you can remember the time, *whenever* you remember time, mention it.

One of you can start, and if any of the rest of you remembers something he forgot, bust in." Tom pointed a pencil. "Joe, it was your sister's car."

Joe began to talk. Tom wrote constantly. Often he asked Joe to repeat something. Often Tom stopped him to ask questions. Joe's account was detailed and complete. He looked at the others. "Did I skip anything?"

"I wish you'd skipped it all," said Harry. He pointed at Tom. "You heard the story. Where do we go from here?"

"Tomorrow the district attorney will probably file a felony complaint," Tom said. "Bail will be assigned and . . ."

"Are you deaf?" Mike Yoshida shouted, coming out of his chair. "We chipped in for *gas* and you're talking about *bail!*"

"Take it easy, Mike," said David.

Mike Yoshida whirled around, his fists clenched, his eyes wild. "Take it easy! Look at where we are! Look at what they're doing to us! I can't stay still! I want to run all the time!" He waved his arm. "I want to go headfirst into the wall." Tom saw the veins in the young man's neck, thick as pencils against his skin. "You expect me to behave like I sprained my ankle or lost a job? She says we *raped* her! What if they don't believe us? Nobody believes us so far! Four young punks against Hester Ashley! They'll send us away! We'll be in prison! We'll rot in prison! How many years will we be in prison?" He lunged at Tom, grabbing the tabletop with both hands. "You're a lawyer. How long will we be in prison?"

"Everything I've heard tells me you're innocent," Tom said. "You're all innocent."

Mike held onto the table. His face was red. "Suppose you're wrong," Mike said. "How many years? Pick the lowest. Take the least number of years. You have to tell me! I have to tell my mother so she can buy me calendars! How many calendars? Five? Ten? Twenty? A hundred?"

Tom wanted to reply but he could not. He had no answer for the hysterical young man. Tom didn't even know the Territory's punishment for rape. He would have to examine the Penal Code. Mike stepped back from the table. "It's no use," he said, quietly. "I'm dead. They're ending my life right in front of me."

Now Tom came out of his chair. "I won't think that way," he said. "I believe if you go to trial, the court will be convinced you're innocent, the court and the jury."

"How long before the trial?" Joe asked.

"It depends on the calendar, the court calendar," Tom said. "It depends on how many cases are ahead of yours."

"So we lay here in this pigsty rotting away," said Harry.

"You do not *lie* here," Tom said, loud. "They can't hold you without bail!"

"Bail means money," Joe said. "Tom, there's no money."

"You'll make bail," Tom said. He had to convince them. He refused to face his empty promise. Tom could not leave them without hope.

He stood alone beside the table later as the turnkey took the four back to the cell block. Alone and confronted with the mountainous fact of Hester Murdoch's accusation, Tom was numb. He picked up his pad and started to read the notes he had made, then abruptly shoved it into the open briefcase. He grabbed his pencils, dropping them into the briefcase. A single, blinding question repeated itself endlessly, pummeling him with almost physical force. Why had she identified the four? "They're innocent!" Tom said, aloud. He closed the briefcase, walking across the room as though he were in chains.

Tom came up the stairs to the first floor. Ahead of him, on a line with the entrance doors to the building, he saw Sarah Liliuohe. She was standing in the corridor. The sunlight coming through the windows seemed to form a nimbus around her. Tom was certain she had heard the scraping sound of his shoe and had risen from the bench behind her but this time, for the first time in his life, he was untouched. He ignored it. He forgot his heroic promise to produce bail, forgot everything.

He was light-headed. He wanted to smile. He did smile, was unable to stop smiling. He was suddenly happier than he had ever been in his life, happy, really, for the first time in his life. Something strange and mysterious, something unknown, had brushed him at the sight of the young woman in the sunlight. Her presence, the outlines of her face that became more distinct, more enchanting with every step he took, made him giddy. He wanted to touch her. He wanted to listen to her. He wanted to tell her everything, everything he had learned, discovered, embraced, adopted, solved, questioned; every failure that marked every day of his life, every dream, every hope, all of his ambitions. He was no longer ashamed. He could not contain himself. He had to tell her all this all at one time. He could see her clearly, see her hair and her eyes, her slim body and her skin. Tom knew he had never seen anyone, anywhere, as beautiful. She was ravishing. She was radiant. In those few wondrous and sacred seconds that elapsed between his first glimpse of her at the staircase and the time he joined Sarah his life changed. He wanted to share the magic, but when he stopped beside her and looked at the young woman who had been a stranger less than two hours ago and was now the most familiar, the most important human being in the world, he said only, "Hello." He no longer needed to speak. He was, for the first time ever, safe.

"You saw them, didn't you?" Sarah asked, wanting a miracle, wanting her brother and the others to appear from the stairs Tom had climbed.

Tom told her of the meeting in the counsel room. Sarah listened, all hope fading from her eyes. When he finished, Sarah said, "I make more than anyone in the family. Without me we wouldn't always eat." Sarah worked in a drugstore on King Street. She had started part-time while she was still in high school. "I know one hundred houses like ours," she said. "Where will we get the money for bail?" She took a key case from her purse and stopped, her arm raised. "My car key," she said. "I don't even have my car."

The convertible was Sarah Liliuohe's triumph. She had chosen the gaudy yellow and black runabout deliberately. It was an act of daring for Sarah, proof to the haole that she could be as frivolous as any of them.

"You'll have your car!" Tom said. "I'll get it released right now. You can come with me." Tom was for the first time ever showing off. "You'll have the bail, too," he said, and was so intoxicated by her presence that he managed to convince himself, for a little while, that he could breach the impossible.

Maddox stopped beside the dirt road and on a line with the Whispering Inn. He left his car and looked over the top at the roadhouse on the pilings. In daylight the inn was like a shipwreck driven onto the rocks by a savage and merciless storm. It seemed abandoned. There were no other cars. Maddox turned to the dirt road.

Two deep trenches had been worn into the road by cars coming and going from this open area near Waikiki. Maddox walked between the trenches, slowly as a beachcomber, looking for anything. He was after some tangible, some dimensional real object or part of an object, something he could hold and heft and examine, on which he could focus the entire weight of his experience and knowledge. "She identified them," Maddox said, aloud. He was after anything that would buttress or invalidate Hester's claim. Maddox continued for about a quarter of a mile. He turned and came back. The dirt between the trenches was flat. It was smooth. She could have been here. They could have left the convertible to lift her out of the dirt, moving around and tamping it down flat. Maddox arched his back, feeling the ache across his shoulders. He had slept for a few hours on the table in his office. He felt gritty. He needed a bath and a shave. He was hungry. Maddox pulled his hat brim down over his eyes and stood in the road looking at the Whispering Inn. "They didn't grab her off the dance floor," he said, aloud. Why was she out here alone?

Maddox left the road, still heel and toe, still looking. He was in brush now, low and scraggly, clumps of beach growth. He went almost to the Whispering Inn before making a wide turn and starting back toward the dirt road, feeling hot and puffy in the open under the sun. There were tire tracks here, in every direction and crisscrossing, made by cars coming to and from the roadhouse. Maddox continued, like someone on a high wire, looking for anything. He was far beyond the parking area when he said, exhaling, "Yeah . . ." Maddox was standing over the clear outlines made by the heels of a woman's shoes.

He found a man's footprints. And more of the woman's heels. He squatted, looking for more, for something left behind, for a brown stain that could be dried blood, for proof Hester had been here the night before, and not an officer with a dame with the hots. Maddox hurt. He came erect, looking, and waited until the pain was gone before squatting once more. Something glittered somewhere. Maddox dug, using both hands. "You buried it," he said aloud, berating himself, digging his fingers into the sand. He let the sand escape in a steady jet as though from an hourglass. Maddox stopped and threw the sand to one side. Below him was a man's shirt button, shreds of thread in the holes. Maddox used his handkerchief for the button and came erect, grunting. He was closer to the road than to the Whispering Inn. He tried to follow the footprints, the woman's and the man's, but there were none to lead him. Maddox remembered the number of cars parked every which way around the roadhouse when he had arrived the night before. He had come upon an untouched pocket. The departing cars could have obliterated any trace of a herd of elephants. Maddox put away his handkerchief. "You're holding a big piece of nothing," he said to himself as he heard a car.

Maddox almost rubbed his eyes. The yellow and black convertible was coming down the dirt road. Someone had raised the top so he couldn't see who was inside. The convertible stopped as Maddox approached it. He saw a girl come out. "The sister," Maddox said, aloud. A guy was with her, a guy with a limp. They stood in front of the convertible. Maddox frowned, trying to place the sister's friend. Something about him stopped Maddox.

When he was closer, he could see them working hard to ignore him. The fellow with the limp was no older than the four downtown in the tank. Maddox thought he might be the dame's minister. A lot of them went to church these days. Maddox could have sworn he had seen the minister but could not connect him with the young man who had walked in front of his car on the way to the movie house fifteen hours earlier. "I suppose you can prove it's your car."

"I suppose you can prove it's any of your business," Sarah said. She wanted to kick the big man.

"Can try," Maddox said, taking his hand out of his pocket to show them the gold badge.

"You don't have any right to stop people this way," Sarah said. Tom said, low, "Sarah," touching her. She didn't hear him. She pulled her arm away, alone with Maddox. "I'd like to see you stopping anyone on Merchant Street. I haven't done anything wrong but that's no excuse, is it?" Maddox saw her step clear of the minister to leave him out. Joe Liliuohe had some sister.

"It's her car, Officer," Tom said. "This is Sarah Liliuohe. You must have seen the car at headquarters. It was impounded but it was just released. Sarah Liliuohe is the owner of record. She can show you the registration." So Maddox knew the minister wasn't a minister; he was a lawyer. That young, he was just starting out, just back from the States, probably. He probably lived in Papakolea, was probably a pal of all four of the kids in the tank, probably lived down the street. They were sending this kid, this gimp, in against Phil Murray. Christ, it was pathetic.

"That leaves you," Maddox said. The girl swung around, reaching for the car door.

"I'm Tom Halehone." Maddox saw her reach into the glove compartment. "I'm representing the suspects you took into custody last night," Tom said.

"Don't talk to him!" Sarah said. She waved the car registration. "He asked whether I own this car! I own this car! You don't have to talk to him!"

Maddox wanted to stretch. His back was tied in knots. "You ought to straighten out your girl friend, Counselor," Maddox said. "I'm investigating a crime. You keep it in mind, too. If you come into possession of anything that might be considered evidence in the solution of this crime, it's your duty to so inform the police. I wouldn't like to be in court and have you showing the jury something brand-new to me. You'd be a disbarred lawyer before you began.'' Maddox raised his hat and wiped his forehead. ''Aloha.''

''I hate him!'' Sarah said, low but not low enough. Maddox kept walking toward his car.

''He was following the rules,'' Tom said.

''You know what I mean,'' Sarah said, watching Maddox, hoping he would trip or fall or hit his head. Tom looked away. He knew exactly what Sarah meant. He thought now of a hundred responses to the captain's insolence and contempt but he was too late, too late.

''. . . also ask for your encompassing blessing on each and all members of this noble chamber, the most hallowed hall of the Republic,'' said Rabbi Sidney Ellis Applebaum, delivering the invocation in the United States Senate Monday at noon.

Rabbi Applebaum stood beside the Vice-President, who was presiding. ''We beseech you,'' said the rabbi, ''to guide these dedicated men in their deliberations so they may continue to lead our glorious land to the destiny You have chosen for all of Your children who live in such harmony on its shores. Let all who are gathered here take sustenance from Your protection and let each receive, in equal measure, Your wisdom. Amen.''

Senator Floyd Rasmussen was standing before the rabbi raised his head. ''Mr. President.''

Floyd Rasmussen, the junior senator from Idaho, was in the second year of his first term. He was the founder and publisher of a weekly newspaper who had made the biblical editorials he wrote the winning issue of his campaign. Rasmussen was a large, rotund man with white, puffy skin. His chin lay over his shirt collar and his belly began at this chest. His vest was buttoned but his jacket was always open. He had a powerful voice and he enjoyed speaking. Like all freshman senators, he had spoken very little. ''Mr. President!'' This time Rasmussen could be heard in the cloakroom and beyond.

Rabbi Applebaum left the podium. The Vice-President studied the junior senator from Idaho. ''For what purpose does the senator rise?''

''I rise to address a crisis that demands the immediate and total attention of the United States of America.''

The Vice-President set down his gavel, took out his handkerchief, and blew his nose. He did it again. The Vice-President didn't like Floyd Rasmussen: his clothes, his mealy-mouthed pieties, his lunch that he carried on the walk from his apartment to the Capitol. "Immediate and total attention of the United States of America," said the Vice-President. "Are we at war?"

Even Rabbi Applebaum, reaching the cloakroom entrance, began to laugh as he left. Even the pages laughed, ducking their heads. Floyd Rasmussen was submerged in laughter. He listened, his left hand on a folded newspaper on his desk. Rasmussen was silent until the Senate became silent. "As a matter of fact, Mr. President, we *are* at war. This country is at war. It's not the kind of war where two countries line up, army against army. It's not a formal war. All the same an enemy is attacking."

"I'm sure the senator from Idaho has an interesting mystery to unravel," said the Vice-President. "All he has to do is wait until the Chair can accommodate him. He probably remembers that when the Senate adjourned Friday, it was in the middle of a debate and the gentleman from Pennsylvania had the floor."

"Mr. President, I was here Friday when the Senate adjourned," said Rasmussen. "I'm out of order, no question about it." Rasmussen looked over his shoulder. "I apologize to the distinguished gentleman from Pennsylvania. I'm the last man in the world to forget a senator's prerogatives."

"In that case," said the Vice-President, "you can let your colleague from Pennsylvania have the floor, which is his *anyway*," said the Vice-President.

Rasmussen looked over his shoulder once more. "About the last thing I want to do is hurt the feelings of the illustrious senator from Pennsylvania," Rasmussen said. "He was a kind of model to me long before I ever dreamed I would be privileged to be here. He's gone out of his way to be nice from my first day." Rasmussen turned back to the dais. "If he would give me the chance to speak my piece, we'd learn fast enough whether I came here from Boise to make people laugh or be a senator of the United States."

The senator from Pennsylvania flicked his wrist, and Rasmussen picked up the newspaper, holding it against his knee. "A minute ago I told the Senate we had an enemy attacking our country," Rasmussen said. He raised his arm high above his head, holding the newspaper, which was folded once. Across the front in huge block type, black ink glistening, the banner headline read, "NATIVES RAVAGE NAVY WIFE!"

Rasmussen began to move in a circle, turning as slowly as a figure on a medieval cathedral. "Natives ravage Navy wife," he said, turning. "Natives ravage Navy wife," he repeated. Rasmussen quoted the headline a third time before completing his circle and dropping the newspaper on his desk, Daniel Webster's desk.

"No mystery about this war," Rasmussen said. "Everybody in the United States knows about it. Everybody in the Territory of Hawaii knows. They know something else out there, surrounded by thousands and thousands of aboriginals. They know that starting last Saturday night, no American woman is safe. They know every wife and mother in the Territory is in danger. She can be grabbed at any time of day or night. She can be carried away by a tribe of savages, attacked, abused, beaten, and dumped like a carcass as Hester Murdoch was discarded.

"Last Saturday evening Hester Murdoch, the young wife of a Navy Lieutenant, left her home for a social event. A few hours later she was in a hospital more dead than alive. It must have been an act of God Almighty that delivered these four natives into the hands of the police. My question is, how big is their army? How many more are in the jungle waiting to pounce?

"I won't sit silently while American women are in danger. I'm saying here and now I want every citizen of the United States protected wherever the flag flies. A war started out there in the Pacific Saturday night. We have to win it, and do it fast. So I'm asking the Secretary of the Navy and the Secretary of the Army to tell the people of this country how long it'll be before our women are safe.

"I'm asking those two Secretaries for a quick answer, because I don't want to stand here again, breaking the parliamentary rules of the Senate to report another one of these tragedies." Rasmussen stopped. They were all watching and waiting. He let them wait until he was good and ready. Then he looked over his shoulder. "I'd like to thank the distinguished senator from Pennsylvania for the courtesy he showed me here today," Rasmussen said, and sat down.

He heard the senator rise and thank *him*. He heard other senators asking to be recognized. Before the Vice-President let any of them speak, he spoke. The Vice-President called Rasmussen "the vigilant senator from Idaho, our lone sentry." Everyone behaved like he had made a real, lasting impresssion, but Floyd Rasmussen wasn't sure. As he heard himself congratulated, Rasmussen looked up, for the first time since entering the Senate, at the gallery.

Phoebe Rasmussen was approximately the size of the senator. She, too, was pasty white, with white puffy hands and fingers. Her black hat seemed a copy of Napoleon's, and her coat, open, covered the seats on either side of her. She had been watching

Floyd, expecting his silent question, and when he looked up, she neither smiled nor nodded, nor gave the slightest signal, but Senator Rasmussen knew he had won a giant victory. Phoebe Rasmussen was always right about her husband.

When Senator Rasmussen heard the last accolade, it was twelve-thirty in Washington, six-thirty in the morning in Honolulu. Four hours later Sarah parked the convertible a block from the courthouse. Beside her Tom reached for the briefcase between his legs. Sarah looked at him. "Are we early?" Tom shook his head. "I was hoping we were early," Sarah said.

On the sidewalk Tom said, "Shouldn't you lock up?"

"I forgot," Sarah said. Tom had helped her put up the canvas top and fasten it. They started for the courthouse across the street from police headquarters. Tom had his shoulders back and head up, trying to be taller than Sarah. "I'm so scared," she said. "I feel like I'm being sent to the principal's office for something I didn't do. Will it take long? Did I ask you that already?" Her leg brushed his. He nodded, making a smile for her. "I shouldn't have come," she said. "I shouldn't be bothering you."

"You mustn't say that, mustn't think it," Tom said. She had changed everything for him. He had fallen asleep seeing her face. He had wakened in a glow, hurrying, because Sarah was coming to drive him. "You're not bothering me," Tom said. "You . . . help me."

Municipal court was wide but shallow, with four rows of benches on each side of the aisle. When Sarah and Tom entered, they saw, immediately, to their right in the first two rows, a small group of men and women huddled together like castaways on a raft. They were neat and clean and they sat, with their black hair and dark faces, like dolls from a faraway island set in a store window. They were the families of the young men whom Hester had identified as her rapists.

When Sarah saw them, she said, "I should have made my mother come with me. She said she would die if she saw Joe this way. I should have tried harder. The others will see their mothers or sisters or someone. But there's nobody here for Joe."

"You're here," Tom said.

Sarah turned to him, "*You're* here," she said. "You're the most important person, the only person who can help Joe." She put her hand to her mouth like a naughty child. "All I can think of is Joe but the others are in the same trouble," she said. "Mike Yoshida sat behind me from the time we went to kindergarten. He yells a lot but he wouldn't hurt a fly. None of them would hurt a fly. You must be tired of hearing me talk.''

He wanted to listen forever but he said, ''We'd better sit down.''

In the second row they joined the others, who moved aside so Sarah and Tom were on the aisle. ''This is Tom Halehone,'' Sarah whispered. ''He's their lawyer.'' Everyone turned, making silent hellos, all of them afraid, afraid even to talk in the inactive courtroom.

Tom set his briefcase on the aisle. Sarah leaned close to him. ''What happens now?'' she whispered.

''You can talk,'' he said. ''Court isn't in session.''

''I can't help it,'' Sarah said. ''Please tell me.''

''They'll be arraigned,'' Tom said. ''That means they'll be charged with a crime, a felony. Someone from the district attorney's office will be here to represent the State, the prosecution. The judge will . . .''

''They're criminals already!'' Sarah said, interrupting him, her fear gone. ''They're being treated like they did it!''

''It's not true, Sarah,'' Tom said. ''They're innocent. That's why we're in this court—because they *are* innocent.'' He spoke quietly, steadily, trying to reassure her, surprised once more by her sudden combative outbursts.

Ahead of them, at the empty witness stand, a bailiff in uniform stood beside the court reporter. To the left, in the jury box, were a group of men, their hats in their laps or on the rail in front of the first row of six chairs. They were all newspapermen and most never came to municipal court, which was rarely a source of news. There were two Japanese from the Japanese language papers, and a Chinese. The Associated Press correspondent was in the first row, sitting beside Jeff Terwilliger of the *Outpost-Dispatch*, who always wrote his paper's lead local or territorial story.

The bailiff went to the light switch and the court reporter sat down at his table. The courtroom became bright. The bailiff crossed the courtroom to a door beside the stairs leading up to the bench. He opened the door and disappeared for a moment. When he emerged, he stopped in front of the bench. ''All rise.''

A man in judge's robes came through the door and went up the stairs to the bench. ''Municipal Court of the County of Honolulu, Territory of Hawaii, is now in session,'' said the bailiff. ''Honorable Fletcher Briggs, presiding.''

Judge Fletcher Briggs was sixty-three years old and had been on the municipal court bench for twenty years. He could have retired at sixty but he was a widower and, except for his cars, nothing interested him. And he liked his court. He liked the deference. He liked the bench, liked the activity guaranteed him daily by the daily police arrests. He liked reading his name in the newspapers; he was often quoted.

As Judge Briggs settled himself into his chair, two men carrying briefcases entered the courtroom. Tom recognized the older man. He was Philip Murray, the district attorney of Honolulu. Philip Murray was serving his third four-year term. Tom had expected an assistant district attorney to appear for the arraignment. His heart was pounding. The two went through the gate and into the well, setting down their briefcases on the prosecution table. As Philip Murray went to the bench, Maddox entered the courtroom.

He came down the aisle, pushing through the gate to join Leslie McAdams, the assistant district attorney. Maddox put his hat on the prosecution table, and pulled out a chair. "Why is he here?" Sarah whispered.

Tom was silent. He watched the bench. He knew Murray was with the judge, asking for the four prisoners to be arraigned first. Tom was in a countdown and he didn't want to talk, didn't want to deflect himself. He saw Judge Briggs crook his finger at the bailiff, who walked away from the prisoners' door. "Are they here?"

"Yes, they are, Your Honor," said the bailiff. The judge looked through the papers in front of him. "I clipped all four of them together," the bailiff said.

The judge found the paper clip and pulled the four forms from the stack. "Here they are, Phil," said the judge, and to the bailiff, "Bring them in."

Tom watched the district attorney return to the prosecution table and stand and open his briefcase as he talked to Maddox. Someone near Tom sobbed in a soft cry of anguish, and Tom turned to see the bailiff beside the open door near the jury box.

Harry Pohukaina was the first one into the courtroom. Joe, David Kwan, and Mike Yoshida followed. They were all handcuffed. Sarah took Tom's hand. He felt the warm, smooth skin against his, and the slender fingers, and the frightened pressure as she clung to him. He was emboldened by her touch. "Look what they've done," Sarah whispered.

The bailiff brought the four to the front of the bench. They were unshaven and unwashed. They had been in their clothes, cheap cottons, for two days and two nights, and they were dirty.

Their hair was uncombed. All four had been defeated by the last thirty-six hours.

"Joe Liliuohe," said the judge. "David Kwan. Harry Pohukaina. Michael Yoshida," he said, reading. "You are charged with suspicion of rape and aggravated assault. The police officer heading the investigation has presented evidence that links you with the commission of this serious crime. You have been identified by the victim. The district attorney believes there is sufficient evidence to bring you to trial. He will so notify the grand jury. This is a first arraignment. It is my duty to inform you of the charges against you. I have done so. All of you are entitled to counsel. If you do not have counsel, it is the duty of the court to appoint counsel who will represent you."

Tom rose. "Your Honor," he said, and moved out into the aisle, kicking his briefcase. It fell, hitting the floor with a loud smack. He bent, cursing himself for bringing the damn briefcase. "Your Honor, I represent the defendants," Tom said, coming through the gate to set the briefcase down on the defense counsel table.

Maddox watched the kid. His age, his limp, his appearance here, coming up against Phil Murray, made Maddox angry. He felt like kicking the kid's ass all the way up the aisle out of the courtroom. They were all sitting ducks, all of them, the four in front of the bench, and the Boy Scout they had found to defend them. Maddox was sorry he had come. "You have heard the charges against you," said the judge. "How do you plead?"

Tom joined the four, standing beside Joe. "My clients are innocent, Your Honor."

"The defendants have submitted a plea of innocent, they are hereby bound over for trial," said the judge.

"Your Honor, I ask that my clients be released on their own recognizance," Tom said.

"Your Honor!" The district attorney went past Tom and the four handcuffed young men, stopping at a right angle to the bench so he could see the judge and the defendants. "Your Honor, these defendants are charged with rape. There is no more loathsome crime. A man who seizes a woman against her will and forces himself upon her is committing the most repulsive act in any society. He is considered a criminal in every country in the world." Murray held up his hand, thumb bent and four fingers spread. "Multiply by four," he said. "These four were the hunting party Saturday night. They found their quarry. Hester Ashley Murdoch was a young woman in her early twenties, a married woman, newly married. She was a brave woman."

Murray looked at the defendants, speaking to them. "She fought these four . . . hunters. Look at them. Four against one. They beat her until she was unrecognizable. They beat her into the ground *before* they raped her." Murray looked up at Judge Briggs. "I ask that the defendants be held for trial without bail."

As Murray walked past the bench on his way to the prosecution table, Tom said, "Your Honor, I agree with the district attorney." Murray's head swung around. "No crime is worse than rape," Tom continued. "The man who rapes a woman shouldn't be allowed to walk free. He doesn't belong with decent people. He should be shut away so other people can walk free and safely. The district attorney is right in everything he says about such men." Tom pointed. "But *these* men didn't rape anyone. My clients have been *charged* with a crime but they haven't been *convicted* of a crime. They're innocent, Your Honor. They have never harmed anyone," Tom said, and then, "Any *living* thing. My clients have lived their whole lives in Honolulu. Their parents have lived their lives here. None of them, my clients, or their parents, or any member of any of their families, their four families, has ever been charged with any crime, has ever appeared in a court of law on a criminal indictment. That proves something about my clients, Your Honor. It proves they are decent people who were raised decently by decent parents. They did *not* commit the crime for which they have been held, Your Honor," Tom said. Maddox moved his chair so he could see more. The young guy had trouble walking, but he had no problems in the brain department.

"Your Honor," said the district attorney, standing beside the prosecution table. "With the court's permission, I'd like to go back to what I said earlier. I said, 'Hester Ashley Murdoch *was* a young woman.' I said, 'She *was* a brave woman.' Was, not *is*, Your Honor. Past tense. A big part of Hester Murdoch's life ended Saturday night." Murray took one long step toward the defendants, his arm out. "They ended it. Hester Murdoch will never be the same. She . . will . . . never . . . be . . . the . . . same. She's in Mercy Hospital now. Maybe she'll recover from the battering she received. Maybe. But she'll *never* recover from the sexual abuse. Never. Will Hester Murdoch ever be able to walk out in the moonlight? Will she ever be able to go anywhere alone? Will she ever be able to forget the four figures who surrounded her, and then one by one fell upon her? Your Honor, Hester Murdoch *was* in the prime of her life Saturday night. She lost everything in less than an hour. It's too late for her, Your Honor. But we have to protect the other wives, and daughters, and *mothers* in Honolulu. I'm asking the court again to keep these defendants away from our women!''

"Thank you, gentlemen," said Judge Briggs. "The court understands the gravity of this crime. The court agrees with the district attorney as well as defense counsel. There's nothing worse than the crime of rape. But the court also takes into consideration defense counsel's argument setting forth the characters of the defendants. We have four defendants in jail for the first time and in court for the first time. Also, the district attorney is aware that this is a first arraignment. It has only three functions: to acquaint the defendants with the charge against them; to be certain they are represented by counsel; to set bail if the court feels there should be bail. In this case the court holds there should be bail, so the district attorney's request that the defendants be held without bail is denied.''

"Your Honor, I ask that bail be set at twenty-five thousand dollars," Murray said.

"Can I respond, Your Honor?" Tom asked. The judge nodded. "Your Honor, bail of twenty-five thousand dollars might as well be twenty-five million. Every one of my clients is out of a job. Their families can barely earn a living. I humbly ask the court to take into account my clients' financial conditions.''

"I want to remind the court that our purpose here is to bring these defendants to trial," Murray said. "I ask the court to help the State by setting bail that will ensure the defendants' appearance when trial begins." Maddox watched the young guy, knowing he wasn't finished yet.

"Your Honor," Tom said, "I've already told the court that a large bail is like no bail for my clients. The district attorney wants to be sure my clients appear for trial. I'll *guarantee* they'll appear for trial!''

"Guarantee!" The district attorney wore his skepticism like a banner.

Tom whirled around. He seemed ready to leap at the district attorney. "Guarantee!" Tom said. He was positive, ready to lay his life on the line. "Guarantee!" he repeated, and faced the bench. "Your Honor, I would like to add one more word with the court's permission. These defendants are like my own brothers. One of them *treated* me like a brother. They swore to me they're innocent. They *are* innocent under the law, and are entitled to be treated like innocent people.''

"Gentlemen," said the judge, and paused to let counsel know they were finished. "We have exhausted this argument. I'll set bail at ten thousand dollars for each defendant.''

The reporters in the jury box all rose, following Jeff Terwilliger of the *Outpost-Dispatch*, who had been sitting in the foreman's chair. As they crossed the wall to the gate, Joe Liliuohe looked at Tom. "So we're headed back where we came from," Joe said.

"Only until we raise bail," Tom said. He had to look at Joe and couldn't.

"Yeah, sure," Joe said, as the bailiff stopped in front of him to herd the defendants toward the prisoners' door.

Sarah was in the aisle but she had to move back as the reporters came through the gate on their way out. At the prosecution table Maddox reached for his hat.

"Tell me about this Halehone, Phil," Maddox said.

"I can't, I never laid eyes on him," said the district attorney. "Have you, Les?" His assistant raised both hands and dropped them. "Ask me tomorrow, Curt," said the district attorney.

"Tomorrow I'll know," Maddox said.

Tom remained at the defense counsel table watching the four young men in handcuffs as they left the courtroom. He wanted to follow them, promising . . . something, but he could only turn away.

Sarah was at the gate. She was glowing. Her eyes were bright with hope. "You were wonderful!" she said. "You stood up like a . . . a hero! You weren't afraid of them!" She bent to pick up Tom's briefcase. "You showed them they couldn't walk all over us! I didn't understand what you were, what you could do, what it meant being a lawyer!" She was unmindful of the men and women in the first two rows who were gathering themselves to leave. Sarah stayed with Tom as they made their way to the doors. "When I came for you yesterday, I was like a wild person," Sarah said. "I was so scared. I was so scared here this morning. You changed everything. Now I believe everything will be all right."

No one, anywhere, had ever spoken to Tom as Sarah had. He could hear her, hear everything, again and again, as they came out of the courtroom. He knew it was all false, all unreal, but he could not, yet, face the truth. "The first thing is to get them out of jail," Sarah said.

Tom had to end her dream, end it fast. "I didn't win anything in there, Sarah," he said. "It's still impossible because ten thousand dollars is as bad as twenty-five thousand."

"But we don't have to pay the whole ten thousand, do we?"

"The bail bondsman usually takes ten percent of the bail," Tom said.

"There!" Sarah divided quickly. "It's . . . one thousand dollars!"

"Sarah." Tom stopped her. They moved to the side, near the wall. "It's one thousand for each, and the bail bondsman will want collateral for the rest of the money."

She said sadly, "Collateral." Then she said, "We'll collect money! We'll go from house to house! We'll ask children to help! I wish I didn't have to go to work! We'll start tonight, after work," Sarah said, enrolling him, and walking toward the entrance. "I'll pick you up. Will you be in your office?"

She had won again. Tom dismissed the truth once more, shutting his mind to the amount of bail. He could not resist her. "I'll pick *you* up," he said. "I'll come to the drugstore."

By that time the afternoon newspapers in Washington were on the street. In some of them Senator Rasmussen was on the front page, and in all of them the words RAPE and NAVY OFFICER'S WIFE were in the headlines.

The admiral liked to lunch alone in his office at headquarters during the week, and he had just been served a swordfish fillet when Jimmy Saunders knocked on his door and opened it. He was holding a cable. "Sorry to disturb you, sir," Saunders said. He stayed at the door, raising the cable. "I thought you'd better see this now." Saunders didn't move until the admiral waved him forward.

"Bring me my glasses, Jimmy," said the admiral, who refused to carry them, refused to be reminded he needed help now. Saunders went to the desk for the glasses. The admiral sat back, tilting his head back, holding the cable as though he were looking through a stereopticon.

"SECNAV TO COMFOURTEEN," began the message from the Secretary of the Navy in Washington to the commanding officer of the Fourteenth Naval District. "UNITED STATES SENATORS SHOCKED RAPE YOUR COMMAND. SUGGEST IMMEDIATE SAFETY PROGRAM PREVENT RECURRENCE. EXPECT DETAILS SOONEST."

The admiral removed his glasses. "You've disturbed me, all right," he said. He rose, carrying the cable and his glasses to his desk. "Do they expect me to round up every wife and daughter of every officer and enlisted man in Honolulu? Jimmy, work up something for my signature. General distribution."

"Yes, sir, I'll do it right away," Saunders said. The admiral waved at his lunch.

"And tell the chef to remove that. I've just lost my appetite." Saunders walked toward the door. The admiral looked down at the cable, which was a blur without his glasses. "Goddamnit, I didn't rape the girl!"

Maddox drove from the courthouse to the waterfront, turning his car into a narrow street between the warehouses. He turned again, into an alley, and stopped beside a three-story brick building. It was a hostile building, like a penitentiary, and it bore no identification. Maddox entered by a narrow door.

He was in a warehouse. Cartons, barrels, bales, crates, sacks, large and small machines shipped from everywhere covered the entire floor. Men with tractors and dollies moved through the aisles between the walls of goods. To Maddox's left, directly ahead, was a wooden staircase against the brick wall. Maddox climbed the steps to an unmarked door and came into a small room crowded with a desk and two chairs and filing cabinets. A middle-aged woman, short and fat, sat behind the desk. Although the day was warm, she wore a topcoat. "Hello, Isabel."

"Hello, Curt. He's waiting," said Isabel Dordell. "Some stinky doings, isn't it? They're beasts," Isabel said. "They're worse than beasts. A beast has a mate. He doesn't worry about other beasts raping her. The poor girl. She's scarred for life. I'd kill them all. They should get the electric chair."

"We don't have one," Maddox said. He knocked on a door and opened it.

Maddox came into a larger room. Four windows were spaced evenly in opposite walls. Between them was a large rolltop desk. On it was an upright telephone. In a corner was a coat tree with a hat and an umbrella, on the floor a pair of black rubbers and a large, rectangular, wrapped package. A single chair was beside the desk. Behind it sat a neat, compact man who was almost bald; his hair was completely gray. He was gray. Here, in the constant sun where he had lived his entire life, the man seemed never to have been outdoors. He seemed like no one at all. He looked like whatever his beholder imagined him to be: a bank clerk, a high school teacher, a public employee, a librarian, a fussy custodian, an office manager. His name was Harvey Koster, he was fifty-five years old, and he was the richest, the most powerful man in the Territory of Hawaii.

Maddox took off his hat before he was inside. "Hello, Mr. Koster."

"I expected you earlier, Curt."

"I've been moving around some since Saturday night," Maddox said. "This is a mess. We're not in Alabama or somewhere in the States. Nobody brought these people here. They *were* here.

They've been pushed far enough. All we can do now is shove them into the ocean.''

"I hope you haven't been repeating those words where you can be heard," Koster said.

"You should know me better."

"Now, Curt, nobody can hear me either," Koster said. "I depend on you for information. You help me. You're close to me. You're the only soul on this earth with whom I share certain matters. We're man to man in this office."

Maddox knew the last words would never be true, but he said, "Thanks, Mr. Koster."

"We're in real trouble," Koster said. "No woman is safe. Wild men are loose in Honolulu."

"That's bull," Maddox said.

"You won't face facts, Curt," Koster said. "You're a man of the islands, and your world stops in the islands. I'm worried about the Mainland. Everyone in the States is reading about us now, and talking about us. Every newspaper will splash us across the front page. The subject is sex. Sex unlocks the cellar doors of the soul. Men in Washington, the men who make the decisions, will believe the worst. How will they feel about statehood now? We could remain a Territory for another hundred years. Curt, those four natives must pay the penalty."

"Not for awhile," Maddox said. "They have to stand trial."

"I'd like to clear this up," Koster said. "They should be told they'll have a lighter sentence if they admit their guilt."

"I've been at them," Maddox said. "I tried to cross them up." He shook his head.

"Tell them it's hopeless," Koster said. "Who will believe them over Doris Ashley?"

"Doris Ashley wasn't there."

"She is the most important person in this," Koster said. "I've heard people talking already. They say Doris Ashley's daughter was raped."

"According to her daughter she was raped," Maddox said.

Koster sat up in his chair. "Finish it, Curt."

"Those kids were grabbed four miles from Mercy Hospital," Maddox said. "They were in a fight downtown with some sailors. They dropped the woman at Mercy Hospital and drove *downtown. Downtown.* If I raped someone, would I head for the lights, or would I sneak home and lock all the doors?"

"You've never studied them, Curt. They are not like us," Koster said. "They are primitive. They were here for hundreds, thousands of years, in this Garden of Eden, in the middle of billions of dollars. What did they produce? A surfboard and a roasted pig.''

Harvey Koster's attitude toward the islanders, his beliefs, were based entirely on the single fact that the Hawaiians before the arrival of the missionaries had squandered their gifts, the gifts of a provident nature. Koster was contemptuous of the islander, of those from all the islands of the Pacific. He was also vigilant and, with the Oriental, Chinese, and Japanese, wary and on guard. Harvey Koster was a private, almost a mysterious person, and yet he was a leader of the Territory, and a spokesman for the other leaders.

For his ranches and plantations Koster hired only the descendants of missionaries as managers. Koster wanted a labor force that expected nothing beyond a life in which it used a hoe and a sugarcane knife, and his managers recruited such hands for the fields. Koster insisted on low wages because he was convinced that an increase in salary quickly produced a decrease in efficiency. Other landowners followed suit, and Koster's practices became a watchword. By 1930, 25 percent of the plantation managers were grandsons and great-grandsons of the missionaries.

It was Harvey Koster who encouraged and urged an official educational policy for the public schools in the Territory. He believed that the male student should be taught agriculture and nothing else. He was enthusiastically supported. Koster believed he was acting in the public interest as well as his own. He was convinced that an attempt to educate anyone from anywhere in the Pacific would fail and be a costly error.

So the turmoil caused by Doris Ashley's daughter and her assailants was of concern to Harvey Koster only because it could threaten the performance of his employees in the warehouses, the inter-island steamers he owned, the Honolulu bus line he controlled, and the plantations. ''Those four are guilty, Curt,'' Koster said. ''Hester has identified them. The sooner they are punished, the sooner we'll be out of trouble.'' Koster stopped. Maddox always knew when to leave.

''I'll keep in touch, Mr. Koster,'' Maddox said. He went through the secretary's small office to the staircase that rose steeply from the warehouse floor. He reached for the two-by-four railing. There was a steady ache across his shoulders. He thought of food but wasn't hungry, although he couldn't remember when he had eaten. His mind could not go beyond sleep. Below him a workman set down a huge bale of hemp. Usually Maddox could handle the staircase. But he was tired now, he was weary all through him, and had no defenses. He was back in it before he could shut his mind to the past.

Harvey Koster had found Maddox asleep on some bales of hemp under the staircase. Maddox remembered Koster's umbrella prodding him and the words "This is private property." Curtis Maddox was twelve years old and had been living in the Honolulu streets since he was eight.

The boy wasn't frightened. Nothing on earth could frighten him again. "Where's your family?" Koster asked. "Where do you belong?" The boy jumped. He was almost at the door when he fell, skinning his hands and knees on the cement floor. He had not come fully awake and he was starving. He rose again to flee, and fell. He would not quit. He ran once more, but Koster was in front of the door. "Whose boy are you?" The boy was silent. Something in his eyes, something within him, a fierce and unyielding defiance, some basic and palpable determination, reached out to Koster. "Are you hungry?"

It was the beginning between the boy and the man, the most influential man in the Pacific Ocean, and it was the end of the lad's flight. Koster bought him the first complete and sensible meal he had eaten since he had stolen away from his mother's room before dawn one morning.

His mother had hated him before he was born. Maddox began with her hate. She tried to ignore him, leaving him in the kitchen with the cook for hours, and she hit him until the other girls in the house stopped her. His mother even refused to name him. Curtis was the name of the madam's father.

In the café to which Koster took him the man watched the boy eat. The boy's filthy hands, his open sores, the layers of dirt on his body revolted Harvey Koster. The boy held his knife and fork like sledges. Yet Koster sat silently in the cheap restaurant he had never before entered, waiting until the boy finished.

They left the table, and the boy, who had always run before, made no effort to escape. Koster hoped the boy would leave, but the silent, scarred urchin, almost feral in manner, remained at his side. Koster had to leave him and walk away from the café.

At five o'clock that afternoon, carrying his umbrella, Koster came out of the warehouse. The boy sat on the running board of Koster's car. "You can't stay with me," Koster said. "I have no place for you." He was not lying. There were eight rooms in Koster's house but even Sidney Akamura, his man, went home every night.

The boy rose and walked off. "Come back," Koster said.

"Come back, I say." Koster opened the car door and pointed with his umbrella.

He drove the boy to one of his plantations. "This is Curtis Maddox," Koster told the manager. "He'll be living here. He can work. But he's a boy, not a man. Let him do boy's work."

Once a month, on Sunday, Koster drove out to the ranch. The manager learned to have the boy ready. The boy always wore clean clothes. Koster always asked to see the boy's bank book. He always said, "Good, good."

In the week after he became twenty-one years old, Maddox told Harvey Koster he wanted to join the Honolulu Police Department. Maddox wanted to apply the next day. "You have a good job, Curt," Koster said.

"I think I'll like police work," Maddox said.

"Is there a woman?" Koster asked. "A woman can make terrible demands, Curt. Women are not sensible. They are not giving. They are selfish and cunning. A woman diminishes a man."

"There's no woman," Maddox said.

"You'll be in charge of all the help at the Koster ranches and plantations one day," said Maddox's benefactor.

Maddox knew Koster could stop him cold, could make a telephone call that would keep him from ever wearing the police uniform. If Koster stopped him, Maddox had decided he would emigrate to the States. He could not tell Koster that he had to find a place for himself. He could no longer owe anyone, Koster most of all. On the plantation and even in Honolulu, Maddox had heard stories about Koster and him. Everyone knew he was Harvey Koster's favorite, his *only* favorite. Everyone knew Koster was training Maddox. And twice, both times in Honolulu, Maddox had been told, by men he trusted, that many people were certain he was Harvey Koster's illegitimate son.

So Maddox believed he had no choice. He had to prove he could make it alone. And since he had trained for protective work on Harvey Koster's plantation, he chose the police. "I'm sorry you're leaving me, Curt," said Koster.

"I'll never leave you, Mr. Koster," Maddox said. "I'll never be farther away than your telephone."

Now, fifteen years later, Maddox left the warehouse, leaving behind the abandoned, homeless child whom Koster had found that day on the bales of hemp. Maddox drove from the warehouse to his home. He was sleeping when Koster left his office at exactly five o'clock, carrying the large wrapped package.

Koster's home was hidden from the street by a forest. The

house was covered with bougainvillea, with Burmese honeysuckle, with wisteria, with climbing roses that seemed never to end. There were flowers everywhere. He liked flowers. His two gardeners had orders to give flowers their first attention.

There were no flowers in the house. It was a serene, an ordered and exquisite house, completely Oriental. The wood floors were almost everywhere bare. The furniture was sparse, the colors bold and brilliant.

Sidney Akamura was gone for the day. Koster unlocked the front door and went directly up the stairs with his package. He opened the door of the master bedroom. To one side of his bed was the open dressing room. Inside, a full-length mirror faced the bedroom. Koster touched the wall beside the mirror. The mirror swung out into the dressing room, releasing blinding lights. The lights were everywhere beyond the dressing room. Koster had to lower his head and when he was erect once more, he was in an enormous room with white walls. The ceiling was full of lights. He stood with his package among thousands of dolls.

Harvey Koster was in a lilliputian world. He was engulfed by dolls. They stood, sat, climbed small ebony trees, swung on swings, were atop slides, played in sandboxes, ate at tables covered with linen and set with china and flatware. They slept in beds, singly or in pairs. They sat at desks in classrooms facing teachers at lecterns who stood in front of blackboards containing history lessons, arithmetic problems, musical scales. They were at home, cleaning kitchens, dusting furniture, using steam irons at ironing boards. They were on streets, residential or commercial, walking arm in arm, some with parasols, some at shop windows, some entering shops, some leaving. Harvey Koster had created a world behind his dressing room in his home, and not a single doll in his teeming community wore pants. His companions, his loved ones, his only confidantes, were all feminine.

Quickly, almost urgently, Koster tore the paper wrapping from the package he had coveted throughout the day. The box was ornate, manufactured to resemble wood. Through an isinglass window Koster could see a delicate, oval face with black hair worn in braids about the head and pink cheeks. Koster tried and could not raise the box cover. He went to his knees, hugging the box, pushing down with his fingertips, pushing up with his other hand, his starched, stiff shirt collar cutting into his neck, determined, combative, until he felt the cover yield. It came up and off, and, kneeling, Koster looked down into the face of the prima ballerina. He adored her.

She lay on white satin. She wore a white tutu and white silk stockings, and black grosgrain ballet slippers. Koster reached into the box with both hands to lift his new jewel.

He came up on one leg and set the ballerina on the floor so she faced their audience, hers and Koster's. She was in the fifth position. Koster was infatuated. She would be the star in the ballet company he would assemble on the stage of the theater already being built in Grand Rapids, Michigan. Koster had not yet decided where he would place his theater. He would have to plan carefully. He did not want to think of his monumental problem today. Koster pushed the box and cover and wrapping aside.

"Girls! Attention! Attention, girls!" Koster said. "I would like you all to meet . . ." Koster stopped. He had not thought of the prima ballerina's name. She had to have a special, an evocative name. "Camille!" he announced, in triumph. "I would like you all to meet Camille!" He smiled tenderly at her. "Camille, this is your audience," said Harvey Koster.

ABSOLUTELY NO VISITORS read the top line, ABSOLUTELY NO EXCEPTIONS was the bottom line across the large wooden sign on two steel legs at the end of the pier. The pier began at the cliff that rose from the sea along that section of Hawaii, the big island. On the deck of the inter-island steamer, Tom could see the narrow, serpentine path leading up from the water. As the steamer nudged the pier and crewmen jumped off to tie her up, Tom made his way aft. He was wearing his suit and a shirt and tie.

The gangplank went over the side and crewmen with large dollies began moving cartons and sacks onto the pier. One dolly was loaded with salt licks. Tom slipped in between two dollies. "Hey, you!"

The voice, hoarse and amplified as it issued from the megaphone, was the captain's. Tom didn't stop. "You, there!" Tom reached the pier. The captain was right behind him, at the rail beside the gangplank. "Are you deaf?" He pointed at the sign with the megaphone. *"And* blind?"

Tom climbed the gangplank. The captain stopped him as he returned to the steamer. "This isn't a tourist ship. She doesn't like tourists."

Tom limped past him, away from the phlegm-filled voice and the guffaws of the crewmen. He went forward, standing above the bowline that dropped from the prow. He thought of shinnying down the rope to the pier. They would see him. They would be waiting for him. He hit the rail with his hand, and felt his fingers tingling with pain.

The expedition to Hawaii was Tom's idea. He had known immediately that Sarah's plans to collect the bail bond money were fantasy. There was no money in Papakolea. But he had been unable to smash her hopes. In police headquarters during his first meeting with the four prisoners, Tom had spoken impulsively when he told them they would be released while they waited for trial. He felt himself responsible.

Sarah drove him to the docks early the morning he left. She said she would be waiting for him. "You're our only chance," she said. Tom couldn't quit without trying.

He saw the captain beside the gangplank. Tom moved back until he was hidden by the pilothouse. He was alone. All hands were unloading. "Quick, quick," he said to himself, removing his jacket. He pushed off his shoes, bending to tie the shoelaces together. He put the shoes around his neck and he was ready. Tom's hands were shaking but it was not from fear of the ocean, fear of the dive. The sea was his home.

Everyone in Honolulu could swim and the boys became the best swimmers. They grew up in the water. The ocean was another backyard. Yet there were other sports for which they forsook the sea, or a band would form for mischief downtown. Tom was excluded because he was a liability. If they had to run, he could not run with them. If he was caught, he could give their names, and they would be caught. If a team wanted to win, his presence would ensure a loss. Tom was cast out, and so he remained on the beach. The sea became his great friend.

With his shoes around his neck Tom climbed over the rail, holding on until a wave appeared. He dove like a hawk. His body slid into the water like a blade.

He surfaced instantly, swimming to the hull and heading for open sea. When he reached the stern, he dove again, swimming deep, trying to fix the pier in his head. He wanted to reach the pilings so he would be hidden when he surfaced. He swam until he could no longer remain below, and came up with his mouth open, gulping air. He was beyond the pier. He dove once more, swimming until he felt the rocks and rising instantly to hurry out of the water before a wave captured him and threw him into the boulders.

He crawled onto the muddy shore, his shoes banging against his body, clutching, slipping, digging with his feet. Someone yelled, "Captain!"; someone else, "Captain, look!"

"Hey, you!" came the captain's voice through the megaphone.

Tom reached the narrow path. The ground was hard. He couldn't stop to get into his shoes. Wet, muddy, scratched, his feet cut, the captain's booming threats following him, Tom came up the path, dragging his left foot along the pebbles and stones.

The captain's voice faded. Tom reached the top. He was at the edge of a mesa stretching to the horizon. About a city block ahead of him was a long, one-story home. A veranda ran the length of the house. To the left was a large barn and everywhere Tom saw cattle and horses. A man was driving a tractor toward the barn. There was pyracantha along the cliff, untended and thick. Standing behind it, Tom held his shoes upside down to empty them. He managed to separate the shoelaces. The shoes were wet and squishy on his feet, and he was cold as he came through the pyracantha and heard a woman: "Jack Manakula, I'll kill you! Didn't I say stay close today?"

"For your information I can't be ten places at the same time," a man said. "I'm not smart like you."

Tom saw the tractor beside a corral. A man about his father's age was climbing through the fence. In the center of the corral, on her knees in the dirt beside a cow who was down with her hind legs spread wide, was a woman.

She was enormous. She was big even down in the dirt. She had big arms and big hands. Her hair was black, wound in braids around her head. She wore a man's clothes. She was filthy with dirt and dust and amniotic fluid, and she was between the cow's spread legs in the slimy, wet, membranous placenta.

A calf's legs protruded from the cow, and the woman held them tightly, the cow's leg over her head brushing her hair. The woman ignored it, ignoring everything. She was talking to the cow, cooing to the animal in an endless, soothing, encouraging monologue. "You'll be fine," the woman said. "It'll be over soon. You're doing swell. Give me another push, there's my good girl." She glanced up at the man. "For the sweet Lord's sake, Jack, help me turn this calf!"

Jack Manakula pulled his hat down low on his head and went to his knees beside the woman. "Move over."

Tom watched them in the dirt. She was twice as big. They began to turn the unborn calf. "Don't rush it," the woman said. "Jack, don't rush it!"

"Keep gabbing," Jack said, "and you'll scare her and she'll kick us both into the middle of next July." The woman didn't reply. Working together, each holding a leg of the unborn calf, steadily and slowly turning the animal within the uterine walls, the man and the woman on their knees guaranteed the birth. The calf began to move out of the uterus. The woman talked to the cow. The man's hat fell. "It's coming, it's coming," the woman said, and in one final, convulsive shudder, the cow delivered.

"Hold it now while I get up," the woman said. "Let me up first." She set her hands flat into the dirt to push herself erect. She was puffing. "Let me have it now."

Jack rose to a squatting position, his hands under the newborn, cowled with shreds and tatters of the placenta. He lifted the wet, quivering, blinking, bewildered creature, one minute old, until its feet dangled. But it could not stand. The woman took the calf, her arms around the animal, murmuring to the creature. Jack picked up his hat and rose. "You've won yourself a bull," he said.

"About time my luck changed," the woman said. She was holding the calf, snuggling the animal against her, unmindful of the wet fur and the trailing placenta. "He's a good one, huh, Jack?"

"Have to wait a year to find out," Jack said, slapping the dirt from his hat.

The cow lumbered to its feet. "Here's your baby," said the big woman. She held on to the calf as the cow began to lick and swallow the placenta that would stimulate the flow of milk. "Look at him!" the woman said. "He's ready already!" She released the calf, which was wobbly and swayed against the warm flanks of the cow, but was standing independently. The woman began to smile. She stood with her legs spread, her knuckles pressing into her hips. Tom had never seen a more authoritative, more imposing figure. He had never met the Princess Luahine.

She was fifty-five years old, the last remaining member of the Queen Liliuokalani's family, the deposed queen. She had been second in line to the throne. She was eighteen when the monarchy surrendered, when the invaders, as she called them, became supreme. The princess left Honolulu forever, coming to Hawaii, to the big island, to thousands of acres that had neither been sold nor stolen.

The princess remained alone on her vast ranch, working the ranch, riding out for the roundup twice every year with Jack Manakula, sleeping on the ground with the other hands.

Today the princess was happy. She had a new bull. She was smiling until a flash of white caught her eye and she saw the skinned cat with the limp heading for the corral. "Jack, what does 'no visitors' mean?"

Jack squinted. "Where'd he come from?"

"Look at him," said the princess. "He swam. They're coming out of the water now."

"Well, you could sow mines along the coast."

"I'll do it, too," said the princess. Tom was out of earshot. He saw the princess bend double to make her way, laboriously, out of the corral. "Send him away, Jack."

"You have to leave," Jack said. "So long."

Tom didn't stop. When he was close enough, he spoke to the princess, speaking in their language, not the invader's. "I'm sorry," he said. "I know your rules. This is an emergency."

"Speak English," said the princess. "The Hawaiian language is dead, gone, and buried."

So in English Tom said, "Princess Luahine, my name is Tom Halehone. I . . ."

She stopped him. "There's no princess," she said. "I'm a rancher." She pointed at the corral. "Those are my subjects. I don't have two-legged subjects."

"I have to talk to you," Tom said.

"You can't talk to me. I'm not interested," said the princess. "Now you can swim back."

"I came on the inter-island," Tom said.

"I didn't think you walked over," said the princess. "I'm tired. Don't make me throw you off."

"They wouldn't let me on the dock," Tom said. "I had to swim. I had to see you."

"Jack," she said. Jack went for Tom, who moved back.

"No, wait," Tom said. "There's serious trouble in Honolulu. I'm a lawyer, Princess . . . ma'am. You have to listen."

"You're wrong," the princess said. "Jack, will you?" The princess started for the house and Tom followed her. Jack reached for him, but Tom shook him off. "You have to listen to me!" Tom said, his voice rising. He made an arc around the princess until he was facing her and walking backward. "There's been a rape."

"That's the new sport over there," the princess said.

"This is different. It was a white woman, a haole," Tom said. "A Navy officer's wife. They arrested four men. I know them. I've known them all my life. They didn't do it."

"Do you expect them to confess?"

Tom was frantic. He couldn't reach her. He had made it this far, and it was useless. "I know they're innocent!"

"Excuse me," said the captain. He was behind them, breathing hard after the climb from the pier. He pointed at Tom. "Come on, you."

Tom hated the princess. "What kind of person are you? Don't you have feelings for anything but *cows?* Do you think this is fun for me, hiding and sneaking, diving overboard, swimming into rocks? I had to do this! There's no one else! I *had* to come here! You have to *listen!*"

The captain was close but Tom saw Jack Manakula wave him off and shake his head. Speaking rapidly, the words almost jumbled, Tom told the princess the entire wretched story. "The judge could have set bail at one thousand dollars, at five hundred instead of ten thousand, and it wouldn't have made any difference," Tom said. "We can't raise the money. There's no collateral. They'll be sitting in their cells until the trial unless someone helps them."

The princess looked at Jack. "I saw you wave off the captain. Suppose you take the steamer, too."

"All he asked you to do was listen," Jack said.

"Maybe I'll run my life without you," said the princess. She turned back to Tom. "Do you know how many stories I get around here? An average of one hundred letters a month come up here," said the princess. "Every one is an emergency. Everyone needs money. They need an operation. They need steamship tickets to the States. They want to buy a ranch, a store, a restaurant. They want to send their son to school, their daughter to school. They want five dollars, five thousand, fifty thousand. They're like vultures over there in Honolulu. There's no one in Oahu without a crisis."

"They're innocent," Tom said. "They didn't rape that woman."

"How about me?" asked the princess. "I'm innocent, too," she said, and ended the audience. She walked past Tom without looking at him, without looking at any of the men.

"But you're not in trouble!" Tom said. His voice rose. "You can walk away! You're *safe!*"

The princess stopped. She turned to look at the skinny, wet kid with the limp who had dived off the steamer, swimming into the rocks, all for someone else. He was a game little rooster. "What did you say your name was?"

"Tom Halehone."

"All right, Tom Halehone," said the princess. "You can tell them I'll pledge the bail. They'll take me for collateral."

Tom said, "I . . ." and stopped. He was cold and shivering. He said, "I . . . thank you."

"They'll need a lawyer," said the princess.

"I'm their lawyer."

"You!" said the princess. "You and those four kids would all be one big dark blob in court. The jury wouldn't be able to tell you apart. Doris Ashley's daughter. Of all the women in Honolulu, it had to be Doris Ashley's daughter. You need a haole lawyer.''

"A haole lawyer is a haole," Tom said. "They'll be a dark blob with or without me. I'm going to defend them.''

"At least it'll get you off the place," said the princess. She fell silent. She crossed her arms, holding her elbows, looking out at the silver, glistening ocean.

"My grandfather told me that when the first missionaries came, the islands emptied into the sea to greet them,'' the princess said. "Mothers swam with babies, and the old people were taken to the ships in outriggers. My grandfather told me the people covered the missionaries with so many flowers you could barely see their faces. When the missionaries came ashore with their children, they were like new brothers and sisters. All of them, without exception. My grandfather said the people of the islands treated the missionaries like a great big wonderful prize that had come out of the ocean. But the missionaries weren't happy. They saw too much evil in these smiling islands. All that naked skin. All that laughter. All that eating and singing and chasing around. The missionaries had to remove the evil. First they took away our gods and substituted their gods. Then they took away our land. They took away our queen and our palace. They made us dress like them and act like them. But they won't let us *be* like them. Or be *with* them, except to work in their fields or in their kitchens. They have ruined us. We were a free and easy people on these islands who didn't know any other way except to love. They outlawed love. The missionaries' sons brought the guns and the police, and the Navy did the rest.''

The princess dropped her arms. She rubbed her nose with the back of her hand. "See what you've done to me, boy,'' she said to Tom. "You wait. I'll give you a check.''

PART
2

In the dark in the convertible Sarah saw another set of running lights far out. She had been waiting so long, parked at the docks, she felt stiff. She tried to make herself comfortable. She said, "This won't be it," preparing herself for another disappointment, and as she spoke a slash of light hit the water. This boat was docking. Sarah watched the light make an arc until it was pointed at the shore. Sarah ran.

She reached the dock but could not see the boat; it was blacked out by the light. Sarah went to the far end. Another light blazed, from the stern, and then Sarah saw the outline of the inter-island. She saw figures on deck as the boat veered and slowed, heading into the dock to tie up. The boat was beside her and passing her, and Tom was at the rail waving. "Sarah!"

Sarah saw crewmen with ropes jumping onto the dock fore and aft. She lost Tom, and found him again, at the rail beside the gangplank. She saw him clearly. He was happy! She was positive! "Tom!" she cried, and saw him nodding. Sarah clapped her hands, jumping up and down. Tom was grinning and shaking his head. "Hey!"

He was the first one off the boat. They grabbed each other, kissing, both missing, her lips against his chin, and his lips brushing her cheek. "Did you really . . . ?" she began, and saw the check he took out of his inside pocket. Sarah hugged him again and Tom put his arm around her. They were like victorious teammates leaving the playing field, babbling as they walked along the dock.

At the convertible Sarah said, "Can I see it again?" Tom raised the check level with her eyes. "How did you . . . ?" Sarah began and stopped. "Will you tell me everything? Tell me everything." Tom nodded, opening the door for her. "You drive," Sarah said. "I want you to drive."

Sarah listened to Tom's account of the adventure, gasping, injecting asides of incredulity, promising not to interrupt again and interrupting. "You're the bravest person I ever met," Sarah said. He made a weak disclaimer. Tom luxuriated in her praise, and he was, now that he was home, very tired.

The wild exuberance of Tom's return, the long gamble they had shared, had tired both. They became silent until Tom said, "This time tomorrow Joe will be sleeping at home. They'll all be sleeping at home."

"Because of you," Sarah said.

"Anyway . . ." Tom said. They were quiet once more, approaching the Punchbowl and Papakolea.

"You probably want to go straight home," Sarah said, quietly. Tom's heart stopped, and started. He wanted to look at her but he watched the road.

"No, I don't have to . . . go home."

"You must be hungry," Sarah said.

"I'm not," Tom said. "Are you?"

"No, I'm not. I thought you . . . On the boat all that time . . . You must be tired out, seeing the princess and everything."

Sarah seemed to be talking from a distance. Tom's heart was beating fast. "I'm not tired," he said. His voice sounded strange, sounded hollow. His lips were dry and his throat. He wet his lips. "Sarah?" He had to look at her. She was sitting near the door, her hands in her lap. "Don't worry about me. If you really want to go somewhere . . . where do you want to go?"

"I thought," she said, low, and paused. "I suppose you're sick of the beach by now."

"No, the beach is fine," Tom said. "I'd like to go to the beach." His forehead was burning. He turned the wheel. "There's a place out near . . . I'll show you," Tom said. He swallowed. There was a huge chasm between them. Tom dropped his right hand and waited, and then moved it across the seat, silently. His fingers bumped Sarah's purse. His hand went around her purse, fingers out, while he watched the road, steering with his left hand, until he felt her thigh and stopped. Sarah was looking straight ahead as she lowered her hand over his hand, their fingers groping to interlock.

They reached the beach. Tom released her to shift gears. He drove toward the surf. "I always liked this part down here," he said. "Is this all right?" She didn't answer. Tom stopped and turned off the engine. He darkened the lights. He said, "Sarah?" and reached for her hand. He had her hand, moving across the seat, putting her purse aside, feeling her as she joined him. Carefully, delicately, gently, tentatively, Tom kissed her.

Sarah put her arm around him. Her lips were open. Her lips were soft and demanding, soft and yielding and demanding. She said, "I've thought of you so much. All I think of is you. I think of you wherever I am." He wanted to kiss her forever, feel her open lips welcoming him. "Tom?" Their faces touched. "Do you love me?"

"Yes, yes, I love you. Yes, I love you." He couldn't bring her close enough. He had to be closer. "I love you, Sarah. I love you, love you."

Her lips were hot. Her face was hot. Tom was holding her, over her, beside her, kissing her. "I love you," Sarah said. "I love you, Tom. I love you," she said. Holding him, Sarah lay back against the door and the seat, bringing Tom with her. Tom felt her moving, felt her legs moving and parting. She said, "Wait," moving once more until Tom's leg was between hers. When Tom kissed her, she made a sound, moving once more until she had him encircled, entwined. Her hands were busy in the dark, pulling and tugging until he felt her fingers trailing across his bare back, gentle trickles of suggestive, of maddening excitement. "Tom?" Her body rose to join his. "I never have. Have you ever?"

His hand was on her bare thigh, higher on her thigh. "Yes," he said. "A few . . . No." He looked into her eyes. "I never have, Sarah. Never."

"I promised, made a promise I wouldn't until I was married," Sarah said. "No one ever . . . I never did this much," she said, closer, warmer, softer beneath him. "I promised . . . Do you want to? I want you to. . . . Here," she said, and took his hand.

Windward was on a ridge, at the top of sloping hills that formed the western edge of Oahu. Below the big house and to the right was a garage and below it the old carriage house. When Gerald Murdoch had come to ask, formally, for Hester's hand, Doris Ashley had been panic-stricken. Hester was leaving! Doris Ashley would be alone with the wind and the echoes, dependent on Amelia and Theresa, those bovines. She had to save herself and quickly, before the marriage.

Doris Ashley worked in absolute secrecy. She told Hester the workmen were at Windward to keep the carriage house from collapsing. "Only the roof beam is intact," Doris Ashley said. She said she was preserving the carriage house for sentimental reasons.

She didn't rest. She paid premium wages, keeping the workmen late and bringing them to Windward on weekends. She had always been her own decorator and she shopped alone to furnish the carriage house. She arranged deliveries during Hester's absences. She kept Amelia and Theresa there for hours, lining kitchen cabinets, filling the linen closet, unpacking china and flatware. Doris Ashley won, finishing ahead of the marriage.

"I have a little surprise, Gerald," she said, meeting him at the entrance to Windward one day. Doris Ashley let him drive her down to the carriage house. She unlocked the new door with a gold key, one of two on a gold chain. Doris Ashley led him past the new flight of stairs into the living room. "Have you guessed?"

She dangled the chain. "You children are just beginning," Doris Ashley said. "You're starting the best time of your lives, and the most important. Finding, furnishing a home is a long, hard job. I tried to spare you. Please don't be angry." She waited for Gerald's reaction, waited desperately.

When he said, "How can I ever thank you for everything?" Doris Ashley clutched the back of a Queen Anne chair. She was safe, for a little while.

For a little while Hester and Gerald were happy. They were united, making the carriage house their own. Gerald remembered the first weeks of their marriage as he sat beside Hester's bed in Mercy Hospital. Seeing her in bed, her battered face so discolored as to be unrecognizable, Gerald was overcome with sorrow. He grieved for Hester.

Late in the week Gerald Murdoch woke early one morning. He had cleaned his white shoes the night before and he had a fresh white uniform. The day was still gray and damp when he left the carriage house and walked to the garage. The racing green Durant he had bought, used, in Honolulu, was beside Doris Ashley's massive Pierce-Arrow town car.

Gerald was in a hurry. He had deliberately risen early. He was determined to be out of Windward before Doris Ashley commandeered him once more. Gerald planned to call Hester from Pearl Harbor to tell her he would be at the hospital late in the afternoon. He could not sit beside Hester through another silent, unhappy day. Gerald was sure Hester would welcome his absence. They were equally miserable. Hours passed in which neither spoke.

He started the Durant and backed out of the garage. He couldn't wait to reach Pearl. He felt as though he had been gone for a year.

Gerald drove onto the Navy base at peace for the first time since the police detective had come for him Saturday night. He was finally back where he belonged. He slowed down as he approached the Shore Patrol station in the middle of the entrance.

"Lieutenant Murdoch," Gerald said, raising his I.D. and shifting gears to proceed.

"Oh, Lieutenant. *Lieutenant!*" said the S.P. He was an enlisted man, and he came out of the station, bending to look into the car. "I'm real sorry about Mrs. Murdoch, sir," said the S.P. One of his canines was missing, and the gap in his upper teeth gave Gerald the impression the enlisted man was grinning.

Gerald said, "Thank you," and drove onto the base. The enlisted man picked up the telephone. "Commander Saunders," he said, following orders.

Gerald drove directly to the bachelor officers' quarters. He parked beside the mess entrance. He had planned to be the first man in for breakfast but he saw two ensigns sitting together. Gerald took a tray and flatware, stopping first for coffee. He filled a cup and drank, and standing at the urns, drank a second time. Gerald felt the hot liquid inside. He was back home.

Gerald selected a larger than usual breakfast, eggs and potatoes, toast and butter and jam. He signed his chit and carried the tray to a far corner table where he could see without being seen. He was buttering toast when someone said, "Lieutenant Murdoch?" Gerald looked up. One of the ensigns was at the table. He introduced himself. "Please extend my sympathy to Mrs. Murdoch, sir," said the ensign. He made an about-face and returned to his companion. Gerald bent over his tray.

He was eating his eggs when he saw a lieutenant commander coming. "Lieutenant?" Gerald had to rise because the officer was his senior. The lieutenant commander shook hands. When he was gone, Gerald sat down. He counted to twenty slowly and left the mess.

Gerald was in the submarine pens, walking to the *Bluegill*, when someone threw an arm over his shoulders. "Glad you're back, old sport," said Bryce Partridge.

Gerald said "Thanks" quietly, but he was almost overcome with feeling. He had returned to duty hoping for exactly the welcome Bryce had offered. Bryce had changed everything. Submariners were different.

He was mistaken. Led by the captain, there was an actual lineup of officers, each one with his own damned speech. Gerald had to respond to every one of them. Bryce finally rescued him. "Lieutenant Murdoch isn't running for office, gentlemen, he's reporting for duty."

Before Gerald could remove his blouse to change into his working khakis, he was summoned by the captain. Gerald recognized the commander who was leaning against the periscope. It was Jimmy Saunders, the admiral's flag aide. "The admiral asked me to deliver his regrets, Lieutenant," said Saunders.

Gerald was at attention. "Thank you, sir."

"I'm sorry as hell, Lieutenant," Saunders said. He shook hands. "Please tell Mrs. Murdoch."

Gerald finally escaped. He finally went back to duty. He saw Duane York later in the morning and invited the enlisted man to join him for lunch. "Off the base somewhere," Gerald said. "Everyone around here behaves like I've been lost at sea."

As Duane accepted, proudly, Gerald's invitation, Hester pressed the call button on the rubber cord pinned to her bed in Mercy Hospital. In the corridor a red light over her door came up, and another light glowed in the nurses' station. Hester lay high up on the pillows. She had begun her preparations the day before, making a reminder list and putting an X beside each item as it was accomplished. She had left her mother for last, telephoning Windward just before calling for a nurse. Doris Ashley was still at home. She told Hester she would be leaving for the hospital soon. So Hester had plenty of time. She was very frightened.

A nurse opened the door, holding it open and remaining in the doorway. "Can I do something for you, Mrs. Murdoch?"

"Oh, no. *Yes!*" Hester said. "I want to nap. Will you tell everyone? Tell everyone I should not be disturbed?"

"Would you like me to lower the shades?" asked the nurse.

"No, thank you," Hester said. "Just tell everyone." Hester knew she had to do it quickly, do it *now*, before her fear made it impossible. As the door closed, Hester took the *Outpost-Dispatch* from under the covers. She had learned the lawyer's name when she read of the arraignment and the bail. Hester had underlined his name and the day before she had called Information and asked for his telephone number. "H . . . a . . . l . . . e . . . h . . . o . . . n . . . e," Hester said, spelling the name. "He's a lawyer, an attorney, an attorney at law," she said. Hester wrote the number in the newspaper margin beside Tom's name. So she was ready.

Hester took the telephone from the night table and set it beside her on the bed. She raised the receiver.

"Number, please," said the switchboard operator behind the admitting counter on the first floor. "Mrs. *Murdoch?*"

"Yes, yes, I'm here," Hester said. She had memorized the number, but now she could not remember. "Wait." Hester raised the *Outpost-Dispatch* and holding the newspaper close, read Tom's number aloud. Hester heard the ring. She wanted to drop the receiver and run out of the room. She heard another ring. Her heart leaped. He wasn't there! Hester wanted to slip the receiver into the cradle. "You promised!" she said, remembering her vow the day before. She remembered the four boys being led into her room one at a time. She saw them all through the day and night now, all four together at the foot of her bed, shoulder to shoulder and faceless. She heard another ring. She dropped her head into the pillows, weak with gratitude, and heard Tom say, "Hello."

She felt a crushing weight on her chest. She could hardly breathe. Tell him! "Hello," Tom said, standing beside his desk. He had heard his telephone ringing as he reached the head of the stairs and fumbled for his keys, hoping, *hoping* for a client. "Hello."

Hester was choking. She couldn't breathe. Tell him! Say, "They're innocent!" Say, "They're *innocent! They're all innocent!*" Tell him! Say, *"I'm* guilty!" Say it!

Tom said, *"Hello!"* and jiggled the receiver cradle. *"Hello!"*

Hester heard the clank! as Tom replaced the receiver. She turned her head as though she had been watched. Hester set the telephone on the night table. She pushed her head into the pillow. The movement of her tender, mutilated face against the harsh hospital pillowcase was agonizing. She wanted to cry out, but she remained silent, welcoming the pain, welcoming the punishment for her cowardice.

Six weeks later Dr. Frank Puana entered the emergency room at Mercy Hospital ready for the night's work. "Hello, Doc," said Peter Monji, the orderly. He pointed at the mail rack. Frank took an envelope out of his cubicle. Inside was a hand-written note. "Dear Frank," and, "Please come to my office when you arrive. This is confidential. Claude Lansing."

Frank had never received a communication, oral or written, from the chief of staff. Frank had to call Mary Sue. He turned away from the mail rack and stopped. The chief said it was confidential but Frank didn't hesitate for that reason. He and Mary Sue had no secrets. Frank decided to wait until he had something to tell her. The chief's summons had to mean good news because it couldn't be bad. Frank Puana was right down at the bottom. He hurried toward the lobby and the elevators.

Frank had never been in Claude Lansing's office. It was twice the size of the emergency room. Lansing walked toward Frank to greet him. Frank could see the spider angiomatosis in the older man's face, the red threads made by broken capillaries and ruptured arteries. He saw similar faces every night as the police began delivering injured and wounded drunks. Frank did not remember the angiomatosis. He felt as though he had invaded Lansing's privacy.

Lansing led him to a sofa and took a chair beside it. "I know you're wondering about this mysterious summons," Lansing said. "It's a patient, Frank. I sent for you because Hester Ashley . . . Murdoch is in the hospital. She missed her period, Frank. She's pregnant. A final souvenir of her horrible experience."

So Frank knew he would not be calling Mary Sue. He would not be moving out of the emergency room. He cursed himself for hoping. He wanted to leave. "Why did you ask me to come here, Doctor?"

"She needs a D. and C.," said Lansing, using the common abbreviation for a dilation of the cervix and curettage of the uterus. "It must be done discreetly for her sake," Lansing said. "No nurses means no gossip. I'd like you with me, Frank."

Lansing had not, really, answered Frank's question. Of the entire staff, which meant the ranking medical community in Honolulu, Lansing had picked him, the pariah. Frank crossed his legs, trying to look as though he belonged. "When are you doing her, Doctor?"

"I thought we'd wait until the hospital quiets down," Lansing said.

Frank had to say it. "There'll be nobody in the emergency room."

"You're being covered," said the chief. He came out of his chair. "Excuse me." He went into his bathroom and locked it. Lansing drank directly from the bottle and set it down, holding the sink with both hands before reaching for the mouthwash.

The events that resulted in Frank's summons by the chief of staff began that morning in the living room of Windward, where Gerald Murdoch had said, "I should be with you, Hester. My place is with you."

Gerald was in uniform. He was late but had called Pearl Harbor. Hester sat in a chair, dressed and wearing a coat, a small suitcase beside her. "You'd only be waiting," she said. "Hours and hours. You've done enough waiting." She looked up at him. "Thank you," she said, as though a passerby in a terminal had offered to assist her.

"The best help you can give, Gerald, is to follow your routine," said Doris Ashley. "Business as usual. The goal is not to be noticed. Haven't we had enough notice?"

He went to Hester, bending to kiss her cheek. "I'm very sorry, Hester. I'd give anything to make it easier for you."

When he was gone, Hester said, "Poor Gerald. Poor Hester. Poor Gerald and Hester."

"We're at the end," said Doris Ashley. "This will be the end. It'll be over in a few days."

"I want to keep the baby," Hester said. Doris Ashley rushed toward her.

"You can't! Hester! Child, it's impossible!" said Doris Ashley. "Why are you doing this now? We've settled this! Everything is settled!"

"I want him," Hester said. She had, for days, been talking to the baby, silently or aloud, trying to become acquainted with him. She had been telling him about herself, her true, secret self, but she had not spoken of his father. She could not tell him his father had beaten her, had left her in the dirt. She could not say his father didn't *care*, didn't have *any* feelings for *anyone*. And she could not say that even thinking, now, about his father, about Bryce, made her ache for the man she had come to loathe as she loathed herself.

"Stop! Stop this minute!" said Doris Ashley. "You cannot! Gerald would know! He would *know!*"

"I don't care," Hester said. "Gerald wouldn't care. He'd say, good riddance." She looked at the sea. "He would have a chance at a new life. Like the baby."

"Hester! *Hester!*" Doris Ashley wanted to shake her. "Why are you torturing me? Why do you insist on torturing me? You're trying to bring this house down on our heads! What you're saying will destroy us! Baby, we'd live in shame!" Doris Ashley leaned forward, arms out, lifting Hester from the chair and hugging her. "Be strong, child. We'll both be strong. Only one more day!" They heard a car in the driveway. Doris Ashley dropped her arms. "It's her!" She took the small suitcase. "Hester!" They heard the doorbell. "We'll do it together, baby."

Amelia went to the door. Doris Ashley had Hester's arm as they followed her. Amelia appeared. "Mrs. Lansing."

"Delphine! Come *in!* Come *in!*" said Doris Ashley. Delphine Lansing entered the living room and stopped, as though she were in a museum and waiting for someone in authority to instruct her.

Delphine Lansing was five feet nine inches tall and very thin. She was fifty-six years old, her hair shot through with gray. Her two married sons were both on the Mainland. She swam every morning and every afternoon and was in her garden all day. She was brown like a Hawaiian was brown.

"Good morning, dear," said Doris Ashley. She released Hester to take Delphine's hands in hers, standing on tiptoe to kiss the other woman's cheek. "How can I thank you? You and Claude?"

"I'm only driving you to the hospital," said Delphine.

"I know exactly what you're doing for us," said Doris Ashley. "Now. In our need." She turned to include Hester. "We'll never forget. Never, never. Hester and I have been talking about nothing else. We were so alone, Delphine. You've rescued us." She watched Hester.

"You're very kind, Mrs. Lansing," Hester said.

Delphine Lansing moved her hands aimlessly. "I suppose we should leave." She looked around the room.

"You'll come back one day soon," said Doris Ashley. "One day when this is behind us, you and I will sit here quietly and have tea and talk."

As Amelia opened the door, Delphine said, "I've brought you something, Doris. It's for Christmas, but it's not a Christmas present." She came out to stand over a deep clay pot. It held four cymbidium bulbs, bulging above the potting mix and bunched tightly together. "There are two spikes," Delphine said, pointing. "Here and here." She was smiling a little with pride, and embarrassed. "I didn't expect anything from them this year. I separated these in June, all my Bethlehems." She looked up at the sky. "They need filtered sun. I shouldn't keep you standing here while I carry on."

Claude Lansing had put a hold on room 333 the day before. Delphine and Doris Ashley had Hester between them as the three entered the lobby of Mercy Hospital. Hester's collar was turned up and she kept her head down. They used the stairs to the third floor. A NO VISITORS sign hung on 333. Inside Delphine said, "You can lock the door. You can keep it locked. I have to see Claude. I'll be back."

"Shall I come with you? I'm ready to come with you," Doris Ashley said.

"This way is better," Delphine said. She looked past Doris Ashley at Hester who was removing her coat. At that moment Delphine Lansing felt closer to the sad, remote girl than to anyone on earth. "Hester? Try not to worry. You have no reason to worry." Delphine opened the door and tripped the lock. "I'll knock."

Claude Lansing rose from behind his desk as his wife entered the office. Although Delphine hated herself for it, the sight of him could still affect her. He was an inch shorter than his wife. His head was perfectly formed. He had full lips and a nose like a statue's. His hair was russet-colored and full, combed straight back from his forehead. He was very handsome and had always known it. "Is she here?"

"She and Doris," said Delphine. She came to the desk.

"I don't understand this secrecy," Lansing said.

"These people have had enough publicity," Delphine said. "When will you do it?"

Lansing took a comb out of his breast pocket and ran it through his hair, patting the back of his head. "Tonight," he said. "After visiting hours."

"Good. That's good." She felt light-headed. She had not slept much. "You'll be alone," Delphine said.

"We went through that," Lansing said. "Why must you be mixed up in this?"

"We went through that, too," Delphine said. Her hands were trembling. She opened the purse for the folded sheet of paper Doris Ashley had given her. "This is for tomorrow," Delphine said. "Do this after Hester is home."

"Do what? *Now* what?" Lansing reached for his glasses. He read, "Hester Ashley Murdoch underwent surgery today at Mercy Hospital for termination of a pregnancy. Six weeks ago Mrs. Murdoch was seized, kidnapped, beaten, and sexually assaulted by a band of men. Mrs. Murdoch's pregnancy is the result." He dropped the sheet of paper. "Are you writing press releases now, too?"

"Doris Ashley wrote it," Delphine said. "She thought it should come from you."

"Then let her give it to the reporters," Lansing said. "Let her do the D. and C."

"Claude." Delphine's chest rose and fell as though she had been running to the limit of endurance. "There's more." He dropped his glasses, looking up at his wife. "Hester is three months pregnant," she said.

He said, low, "You must be mad." Delphine wanted to sit down but she believed he would win if she sank into a chair. "Get her out of here," Lansing said. "You brought her in, you get her out." He took his comb. "Twelve weeks into term," he said, combing his hair. "You're all mad. You and Doris Ashley and the girl."

"This is between us," Delphine said. "Between you and me, Claude. Omit Doris Ashley. Omit her daughter."

"*Omit!*" He pointed with the comb. "You want us to remove a fetus somewhere around twelve weeks into *term?*"

"Us?" Delphine was against the desk, facing him. "Us?"

"Us. We. It is the way we talk, the way all doctors talk," Lansing said.

"For quite a while now, Dr. Lansing, I haven't heard you talk at all," Delphine said. "Not in front of me. Not legibly. I mean intelligibly."

"This is intelligible," Lansing said. "I won't do it." He pushed back his chair.

"Oh, drink here," Delphine said. "Why do you keep up the act? Whom do you think you're fooling?"

"I am fooling myself," Lansing said. He went into the bathroom and closed the door. He took a bottle of pure alcohol from the medicine cabinet. He drank from a glass and afterward used mouthwash. Lansing washed his hands. "No, sir," he said, aloud, to the mirror. He opened the bathroom door to face her.

"You're fortified now so let's finish," Delphine said.

"It's finished," Lansing said. "I won't do it."

"You have to do it," Delphine said. "You must do it. Doris Ashley asked me for help. She came to me for help. Doris Ashley could pick up the telephone and have the entire United States Navy at her gate, but she asked me. She needed a friend and she chose me. Doris Ashley may be high and mighty but she is a woman alone. I know how she feels, Claude. I said I would help her. Hester cannot bear this baby, not now, not after what she's been through, the horror she's been through. Hester is a fragile, frail, delicate young woman. This pregnancy could send her over the edge."

Lansing put his arm across the back of the chair. "I'm telling you, Delphine. Take her home."

"I'm telling *you*," Delphine said, coming around the desk at him. "You'll help these people or you won't have a home. You won't. But you can't exist alone. You cannot. I can and will if I have to. I've been alone all my life. I'll do it starting now, starting tonight. I'll lock you out tonight, Claude. You'll never walk into the house you love, the house my father built for you."

"Must I listen to our autobiography?"

"You're feeling strong now because of the drink," Delphine said. "You can stroll back into your toilet for another drink, for ten drinks. You can have all the fortification you need because tonight you will do what I'm asking. Doris Ashley called me. She *called* me. Doris Ashley. She's making me her friend. I have nobody. I haven't heard from the boys since last Christmas, since the two Christmas cards. That's what I have for sons, Claude, the sons I raised. That leaves me with you, with you and the flowers and the fish in the ocean. Do you think I head for the water because I love it? I'm not Gertrude Ederle. I have nothing else to do. I'm a big, tall, homely woman who has lived with a drinker for thirty-five years and now I have a chance. I want to be Doris Ashley's friend and you won't spoil my chances. If you stop me, I'll stop you, Claude. I'll have you thrown out of this Taj Mahal of yours in two shakes. I bought you this office, my father did, and I'll yell drunk until the board fires you to shut me up.''

They were close enough to touch, but thirty-five years of unhappiness and despair and shattered hopes lay between them. Delphine was shaking. She was afraid she would faint. Only when she was certain, when she was positive he was finished, did she leave the office.

That night Lansing carried his own medical bag into the operating theater. From it he took several instruments and set them into the sterilizer. Lansing removed his jacket. He pushed a rectangular table, a Mayo stand, to the foot of the operating table and stationed it on the right. Lansing covered the Mayo stand with huck towels. He took a syringe from his medical bag and a vial, and drew five cubic centimeters of pentobarbital from it. He set the syringe on the huck towels.

Lansing took sterile rubber gloves from a drawer and pulled them over his hands. He watched the clock for several minutes, then opened the sterilizer and lifted the tray with the instruments. He arranged these carefully on the huck towels, and covered them with more towels. Lansing pulled off the rubber gloves and discarded them. He put on his jacket and leaned against the operating table as he combed his hair. He had to position the woman before returning to his office for Puana, and for the bottle in the bathroom.

In the scrub room later Lansing and Frank Puana undressed in front of lockers. Frank saw Lansing bend for the scrub suit on the bench, and sway. Frank thought he was falling, and lunged forward, but Lansing grabbed the open door locker. "I must have turned my ankle," Lansing said.

Frank was at the sinks, scrubbing, when Lansing pushed through the double swinging doors to the operating room. Hester was on the operating table, flat on her back. Lansing had draped her, covering her with a white sheet that fell over the sides of the table. Rising vertically from the corners at the foot of the table were two metal rods, each with a stirrup. A leather strap was attached to each stirrup, and Lansing had buckled these over

Hester's knees so that her legs hung over the rods. Lansing stopped beside Hester. "We're almost ready," he said, and then, responding instinctively, "I'm sorry you're so frightened. There's no danger. You can believe me."

Hester could feel the fear in her throat, choking her. She couldn't swallow. She couldn't move. He had chained her. "I'm going to give you something," Lansing said. "You'll be asleep in a moment, and by the time you wake, you'll be back in your room."

Lansing turned to the Mayo stand and lifted the huck towels, letting them drop to the floor. He took the syringe in his right hand. With his left, he turned Hester's wrist and bent over the operating table. As he lowered the syringe, his hand was shaking. Lansing put his right hand on Hester's forearm. Pressing down to steady himself, Lansing injected the five cc's of pentobarbital.

Hester felt the sting of the needle. She heard Lansing's footsteps as he left her. She was completely alone. She tried to say good-bye to the baby, and could not. He wasn't her baby any longer. She had lost him because she was evil. She was paying for her evil act, for sending four boys who had helped her into hell and damnation. She belonged in hell. She wanted to take their place. She wanted to go now and tell the truth, tell everyone the truth, but she was a prisoner. She was shackled. Hester's eyes closed and she began to slip away under the pentobarbital.

Frank was still scrubbing when Lansing returned, joining him at the sinks. "We're ready," Lansing said, taking a brush from the dispenser. Frank looked at the clock, and when twelve minutes had passed, came erect, arms raised in front of him and bent at the elbows. He pushed through the double doors into the operating room. Since they were working without a surgical nurse, Frank went to the sterile linen cabinet for a towel. Wiping his hands, he stopped beside the operating table to look at the patient.

He had not seen the patient since the night he had treated her six weeks earlier. Frank bent over the unconscious woman, examining the groups of linear dots left by his sutures. Even those would fade. Frank smiled, pleased with his results. He started to come erect and stopped, then bent once more, his smile gone.

Hester's lips were dark and full. Frank saw the shadows under her eyes and along her cheekbones. The patient wore the mask of pregnancy, the visible evidence of the large quantity of melanin that appears in women during gestation. Frank straightened up.

He couldn't believe he was wrong but he had to be sure. Frank put his hand on Hester's belly, pushing gently. He raised his hand and lowered it, at the pelvic area, pushing. Hester was around three months pregnant. So she had been pregnant the night Frank had first treated her, in the emergency room.

Lansing had lied. He had brought Frank upstairs to assist in an abortion, to commit a crime. Abortion was a crime in every state in the United States and in the Territory.

"Frank!" Lansing's voice would have carried across a field. He was at the sterile linen cabinet, wiping his hands with a huck towel. "I wanted to tell you myself," Lansing said.

"I'm leaving," Frank said.

Lansing moved, lurching, as Frank stepped away from the operating table. "Wait," Lansing said. "Wait." Frank wanted to call Lansing every name he could think of but a lifetime of obeisance stopped him beside the Mayo stand. "This is a therapeutic abortion," Lansing said, lying. "It is indicated. It's necessary. It is my professional judgment."

As Frank faced Lansing, the chief's face disappeared and was replaced by another face. Frank could not remember the man's name. Frank had been a senior in medical school, on the wards in University Hospital in Seattle, the night he helped treat the patient who was full of morphine. Frank and the intern saved the patient's life. In the evening following, the patient pleaded for morphine, offering Frank his gold wristwatch. Frank and the intern put the patient in restraint. Sitting with the patient, Frank learned he was a doctor, had been a doctor. He had lost his license in Boston when the police were called by the father of a girl who had hemorrhaged and died after an abortion.

The man, the former doctor, moved across the country. In his Seattle office he practiced podiatry, removing corns from toes during the day and performing abortions at night. He told Frank he had become addicted when he realized he could not kill himself.

"Frank, I am the surgeon of record," Lansing said. "I ordered the O.R. I've already filed the surgical report for the House Committee," he said, lying.

"I don't want to be involved, Doctor," Frank said.

"It's a simple procedure," Lansing said. "It's elementary! You're here because I'm following house rules! Two physicians!"

Frank had all the speeches in his head. House rules also demanded a scrub nurse. Where was the scrub nurse? Where was the sterile technique without her? Why was Hester here at eight o'clock in the evening? But Frank only said, "I'm leaving."

It was Claude Lansing's final defeat. Now even this *native* had spit on him. "Leave!" Lansing said. *"Leave!* You belong in the emergency room! The right man for the right job!"

Frank said, almost inaudibly, "That's nothing new," and started for the scrub room. But Lansing cut him off, guarding the swinging doors, arms out.

"Frank, no, listen," Lansing said, all in a rush. "I'm sorry. I apologize. I humbly apologize."

"The hell with you!" Frank said. "The hell with you!" He raised his fists for the first time in his life, not at Lansing but at a host of oppressors. He stood with his hands in front of him, unable to move.

"You don't belong in the emergency room," Lansing said. "No one knows it better than I. There. I've admitted it. Stay here, Frank. *Stay!* You'll have your reward! I'll deliver your reward myself. You'll get the next staff appointment at this hospital!"

Frank was revolted. He had waited so long, endured such indignities, that Lansing's promise, his disreputable offer, made him writhe with anger and self-pity. But he did not push Lansing aside, he made no move to reach the swinging doors of the scrub room. He did not want to return, forever, to the drunks and the bleeding combatants below, and when Lansing said, "You have my word, Frank," and returned to the sterile linen cabinet, Frank followed.

They gowned each other. They took sterile rubber gloves. They raised their masks. Lansing stopped behind the Mayo stand. "Take over for me, Frank," he said. "I haven't felt right all day."

So Lansing had finally offered the last condition of his deal. Frank could have pulled off his gloves, throwing them into Lansing's face. He could have told Lansing he wasn't risking his life, his *life*, for a drunk. He could have turned his back, leaving the O.R. without even looking at Lansing. Frank didn't move. He thought of Mary Sue, *saw* her, saw her face glow when he told her he was on staff. He would keep his secret until Lansing made the announcement. When Lansing said, "I'll assist, Frank," he took his position between the two metal uprights rising from the foot of the operating table.

Frank was facing the patient. He put his right hand over his left, pushing up on the rubber glove. He pushed up on the right glove. He waited until he was *with* the patient, until he and the patient were alone. When he was ready, Frank reached for the speculum, the first instrument in the row of instruments on the Mayo stand.

Frank held a slender tube with a tiny mirror at one end. He came under the drape, up to the operating table, bending to carefully insert the speculum and open the vagina. He had to reach the cervix. Frank switched hands, and extended his right. Lansing was ready with the cervical tanaculum, a long, slender instrument with a hook, thin as wire, on one end. Lansing slapped it into Frank's hand. Holding the vagina open with the speculum in his left hand, Frank used the hook to raise the lip of the cervix. He released the tenaculum, letting it lay on the patient's belly. He had exposed the uterus and was ready for the abortion.

The mouth of the uterus is always closed, opening slowly and with increasing pain when a woman reaches full term and labor begins. Frank had now, six months early, to open the patient's uterus so he could work inside. Lansing gave him a Haggard dilator.

Frank held a gleaming cylindrical instrument, smaller in circumference than a pencil. Using it, Frank began to push, slowly, methodically, with measured strokes, into the soft, muscular tissue of the mouth of the uterus. He had to be infinitely patient. He could only, barely, exert pressure. If he poked, he would invite disaster. His movements were rhythmic. "Frank?"

Frank didn't acknowledge Lansing. The drunk was not in Frank's world, his and Hester's. He continued without pause until at last the Haggard dilator moved through and into the uterus. Frank dropped the instrument on Hester's belly and extended his right hand. Lansing slipped another dilator into his palm, thicker than the first. Once again Frank began to push, barely, carefully. When he was into the uterus again, he dropped the dilator beside the first on Hester's belly, and Lansing gave him a third, thicker than the second. Frank proceeded until he was certain he had enough room for the curette. Frank extended his right hand for the curette. "I'm in."

A curette is a spoon with a long handle. The spoon is sharp. It is a surgical instrument. Against the wall of the uterus lay the placenta, the viscous mass that unites the growing fetus to its host, its mother, and provides the vascular transmission to the growing embryo, gives it blood. The fetus is joined to the placenta and develops from the placenta. Frank inserted the curette and began to remove the fetus, to clean the uterus, rid it of the intruder. He was performing an abortion.

Frank's only responsibility was to the patient, and paramount was his obligation to maintain her reproductive capability. He used the curette for fifteen minutes, and when he removed it, when he stepped back and out of the drape, standing erect, dropping the instrument, Hester was no longer pregnant, and she was neither injured, nor, Frank believed, would she be barren. "Let me have fifteen cc's of pitocin."

Lansing was ready with the syringe. Frank took it and came around to the middle of the table. He looked down at the patient, who was still asleep. Frank held her wrist and injected the drug. He was finished. By the time he turned to the Mayo stand with the empty syringe, Lansing had dropped his mask and was on his way to the scrub room, pulling off his gloves. Lansing had to change clothes and bring a wheeled stretcher into the operating room on which he would take Hester to 333. But he needed a drink quickly. "Good work, Frank," Lansing said, pushing into the swinging doors.

Frank followed him. He had to remind Lansing of their bargain. He had to say it. "The first staff opening is mine." No. "The first staff opening belongs to me, Doctor." No. "Doctor, you *promised* me the first opening." No. *Yes!* NO! This way: "I'm *joining* the staff, Doctor!" He said nothing. He stood before his locker, dropping the loose-fitting scrub suit to put on his usual whites. "She shouldn't have any trouble, Doctor," Frank said.

"I'm sure she won't," Lansing said, pushing his shirttails down into his trousers. "I still have a meeting to attend," he said, lying. Frank saw Lansing take his jacket and tie out of the locker. Lansing was leaving, he was leaving!

"Doctor!" The bastard wouldn't look at Frank. He was on his way. Frank stepped over the bench in front of the locker, hating himself for smiling. He hated Lansing. "I appreciate your offer, Doctor." He was chasing the bastard. Lansing nodded at him. Frank could not let him get away! He had to say it! "I mean the staff appointment."

Lansing hurried to his drink. Frank followed him into the corridor, smiling once more. "I'll be counting the days."

"You'll have to be patient," Lansing said. "Excuse me," he said, and was on his way.

"You are the voice of the people," said Phoebe Rasmussen in the senator's office in Washington. The senator's desk was covered with open cartons that had held No. 303 tins of canned vegetables and were now filled with letters and postcards. Floyd A. Rasmussen had told his staff to bring the mail to his desk. "Look, Floyd. *Look!*" She shoved her hands into a carton, digging with her fat fingers. She lifted a mass of mail from the box, using her hands like a shovel, letting the envelopes and postcards cascade over her wrists, her eyes glistening like a thief's at an open safe. "You've captured the country's heart!"

The senator dug with her and together, deliberately, they scattered letters over the desk and onto the floor around the desk. "America is speaking through your voice. Floyd, you are the chosen instrument of a divine order. Prepare yourself."

Floyd Rasmussen lowered his head as though he was praying. His wife went to a leather sofa beside the office door. She sat in the center of the sofa, opening her coat and spreading it out like someone saving seats in the theater. She removed her hat, watching her husband.

They had called the press conference for eleven o'clock so the senator would be covered in the home editions of the afternoon papers in the Eastern Time Zone, and the afternoon papers everywhere else in the country. All the morning newspapers would have the story. "Chosen instrument of a divine order," the senator said to himself. The proof lay on his desk. He waited, standing.

At ten minutes after eleven there were nine reporters around the senator's desk including men from the Associated Press, United Press, and International News Service. "Six weeks ago a horrible crime was committed on American soil," said the senator. "An innocent young woman, wife of an officer in the United States Navy, was raped in Honolulu. I rose in the Senate to demand protection for our women in Hawaii. My voice was not heard here in Washington. The Secretary of the Navy has not responded. The Secretary of War has not responded. My voice was not heard in Washington." The senator pushed his right hand into a carton and raised a handful of mail. "But it has been heard elsewhere in the Republic. Fargo, North Dakota," he said, reading a postmark. "Peoria, Illinois. Chicago, Illinois. Tupelo, Mississippi. Pensacola, Florida," he said, reading aloud. "New York, Yakima, Washington. Boise. Boise. Roswell, New Mexico." He dropped the letters as though scattering coins to beggars. "You can read for yourselves, gentlemen. My fellow Americans from every corner of the land share my feelings about the danger facing us. They're asking me to speak for them. It is a command. I will not fail these good people.

"Yesterday we all learned that Hester Murdoch, the victim of the assault in Honolulu, was forced to undergo surgery as a result of the assault on her. She will recover from the effects of the knife but who knows if she will ever regain the life she led? Who knows if Hester Murdoch will ever be young again?" The senator looked across his office at Phoebe. She urged him on.

"While this innocent woman lies in her hospital bed, her life shattered, these four men roam the streets of Honolulu, free as the wind," said the senator, spreading his arms wide to take in all the cartons on his desk. "All America demands that they be punished, that United States soil be cleansed of their dangerous presence. In less than an hour I shall rise again on the floor of the Senate, where I will convey the wishes of my fellow citizens, men and women, to their elected representatives. I shall ask the death penalty for these four carrion." The senator opened his desk drawer and took out copies of the speech Phoebe and he had written. He distributed the copies to the nine reporters. "I have a few minutes before I must leave for the Senate," he said. "Do you have any questions?" Phoebe Rasmussen reached for her hat.

On Daniel Webster's desk when Floyd Rasmussen rose in the Senate were the remaining copies of the speech. The senator knew every word. "Mr. President."

As he finished, he could see the senior senator from Virginia come to his feet. "Mr. President, I rise to add my name to that of the distinguished gentleman from the great state of Idaho. I wish to stand beside him in his valiant crusade for justice." Rasmussen rose again.

"Mr. President, my illustrious colleague, who has so nobly represented the Old Dominion in the greatest traditions of statesmanship, does me a special honor," Rasmussen said. "I welcome his membership in our ranks." To his left he saw Morris of Alabama, rising.

In all, four Senators joined Rasmussen's request that Joe Liliuohe, Harry Pohukaina, David Kwan, and Mike Yoshida be put to death. Later in the afternoon and the next morning, Rasmussen heard from five members of the House of Representatives who added their names to his. "You are leading a crusade," Phoebe said.

Early on the second morning after Hester's abortion, before nurses and patients had begun the day, when only the kitchen was active, Gerald led Hester out of Mercy Hospital to his car. "I told your mother we didn't need help," Gerald said. "I made it clear to her. I thought it would be easier for you with only the two of us."

Hester said, "Thank you," as though she had never seen Gerald before.

He drove slowly, in case he had to stop suddenly. Hester sat beside him like someone in mourning. Gerald felt very sorry for her. He wanted to help. "Would you like to stop for breakfast? I could find a coffee shop." Hester shook her head.

She was so sad, she seemed so lost, he tried again. "Do you remember the first time you were in the car with me?"

"The admiral's party," Hester said. The admiral's party always fell on the last Sunday in May, preceding Memorial Day. Every officer and every officer's wife was at the party. They were on view for the civilian guests of Honolulu, of Oahu, of the other islands. Each year the rulers of the Territory were the honored guests on the lawns of the admiral's quarters.

Doris Ashley pleaded with Hester to attend. "Your name is on the invitation. Let me be proud, too, baby. We're the only Ashleys now, you and I. Mother and daughter."

At Pearl Harbor the mass of white uniforms, like a field of daisies, was blinding. Doris Ashley and Hester were greeted by the admiral. Doris Ashley was among old friends, and Hester escaped quickly, walking toward the beach. The wind came off the ocean and Hester had to hold her hat. The wind pulled the brim down over her eyes and before she could raise it, Hester walked into someone. She felt someone's body, felt someone's hands, heard a man say, "I'm sorry. I hope I didn't hurt you." She removed her hat, facing the young officer. "You stumbled and I was afraid you might fall," he said. "I'm Gerald Murdoch."

"I'm Hester Ashley," she said. Hester saw him bow formally and reach for her hand, and believed he was responding to her name, to Ashley. Except in Windward everyone changed when they heard her name.

"Can I bring you anything?" Gerald asked. "Punch? The admiral says we're all hosts today." When Hester said no and stepped away, he followed. She heard the desperate ring in his voice. "May I walk along with you?" He was at attention as though waiting to be disciplined. Hester was puzzled. There were pretty girls all around them. She did not immediately reply, and Gerald thought she was about to refuse. "I don't know anyone," he said. "I'm alone." He said exactly the right thing to the right person. Hester had been, everywhere, always alone.

By the end of the afternoon Hester knew that Pike's Crossing, in Bayliss County, South Carolina, had a population of 3500, that Gerald had graduated from Robert E. Lee High School, that when he left home to enter the United States Naval Academy, the biggest town he had ever seen was Forsythe, the county seat. He lost his diffidence, his appealing shyness, only when he spoke of the Navy. She saw him glow. "My shipmates are the finest . . ." he said, and broke off. "There's one," he said, and introduced her to an ensign who was passing with a woman.

They walked to the end of a jetty surrounded by an iron fence, waist high. "Golly, I haven't stopped talking once," Gerald said. "You must be tired of listening." Hester's estimate of herself was identical, and when he asked her to have dinner with him, she accepted.

That night, Doris Ashley dined alone and was in the living room with her coffee when Hester and Gerald reached Windward. Hester introduced Gerald, who bowed over Doris Ashley's hand. "I'm honored to meet you, ma'am."

Doris Ashley approved of the lieutenant. She valued good manners. She left the young people alone and Hester took Gerald to the terrace. She expected him to talk about Windward like every visitor but he said, "I've never seen so many books. Have you read them all?" Hester had read many several times.

He was interested in her. He asked questions. Hester was flattered, and gave him a glimpse of herself, her private self. When they parted, Gerald said, "I think this is the best time I've had in . . . ever. May I see you again?"

Gerald saw her whenever he was free. He pursued Hester. He was courtly and attentive. Because he was new to Honolulu and Hester had always been alone, they were always alone. Gerald had never before been successful with women. He had found someone who liked being with him and he reveled in his luck. He refused to share her.

For the first time, Hester was not told what to do, was not instructed. Gerald asked for her suggestions; he insisted they follow her lead. Whenever he came for her, Gerald began by learning her preference for the day or evening. His flattery was narcotizing. Gerald seemed infinitely romantic.

Their marriage was a climax instead of a beginning. Doris Ashley betrayed the newlyweds when she shackled them to the carriage house. Their lovemaking was disastrous. Hester was innocent and Gerald was inept. He was instantly inflamed, instantly upon her, leaving her, hardly aroused, very quickly. At first he apologized, but within weeks they were like roommates. Once Gerald went to a Navy doctor at Pearl Harbor. Gerald was honest. The doctor gave him a book. It was a text. Gerald crammed, preparing himself as though he was studying for a test. Hester's bed and his were separated by a night table. One night Gerald left his bed to join her. He began to caress Hester, following the text's directions, unaware that he was, really, taking the exam. They were like two puppets, and after that night, Gerald stopped trying.

Hester took refuge in her only salvation, her books. She emptied Windward of her library. The carriage house was heaped high with books. Whenever Gerald returned from Pearl Harbor she was reading. Gerald began a campaign to woo her away from her addiction. He took her sailing but Hester was quickly and violently seasick. She disliked athletics of any kind, even as a spectator. They went to a few parties at the Officers' Club but Hester was not a good dancer and she was not gregarious. She could not enter into the hearty, raucous, alcoholic bantering.

Hester tried to cook but her meals were a botch. Gerald announced he would be the family chef. For the first few nights he was enthusiastic and good-natured. Predictably, he soon wearied of entering the kitchen to prepare a meal after a day of duty. They were dining around ten P.M. He quit.

They both quit. They withdrew, silently and with some dignity, sparing themselves recrimination and regret. They had both lost. Both had married creatures of their own creation, persons who did not exist. The carriage house was occupied by a pathetic pair who knew nothing of each other except their names.

In the car, bringing Hester home from Mercy Hospital, Gerald said, "I wish the admiral was giving his party this weekend. We could start all over again." After a moment, he said, "Hester?"

"I'm sorry, Gerald," she said. "I didn't hear you. I apologize."

"*I* apologize," he said, quietly. She had stopped *listening*. "I shouldn't be bothering you." A band tightened around his forehead.

"Oh, you're not . . ." Hester said, her voice trailing off. "Really," she said. "Really."

Their silence carried them to Windward. As Gerald stopped in front of the carriage house, he raised his arm, holding it across Hester's chest. "I'm not a very good navigator," he said. "Wait. I'll swing around so you'll be next to the door."

"I can walk," Hester said. She opened the car door, but Gerald leaned across her to close it. "I can walk!" Hester said, and fought him for the door handle. "Gerald! Let me out!" Months of agony coalesced into the struggle but it was short-lived. Hester said, "You're hurting me!" and Gerald lurched back, dropping his arm, scrambling away from her. Inflicting physical pain on a woman was anathema. To the man from Pike's Crossing, no single act was more heinous. He was no better than those four degenerates who had beaten Hester.

Gerald was out of the car before Hester could move, and hurrying around it. He kept at a distance as she emerged, ready to assist her if he was needed. When she passed him, Gerald ran ahead to open the door of the carriage house. Inside he said, "Can I do anything? Would you like some tea? Can I help you upstairs?"

Hester was beside the banister at the foot of the stairs leading to the bedrooms. To Gerald she seemed old, much older than he, and weak, frail and weak, like someone who has always been sick. Her coat hung on her like a shawl. He wanted to help her, wanted her to understand he would not abandon her. He tried to tell her but Hester said, "Poor Gerald. Poor, noble Gerald. You can report to duty." She held on to the banister as she climbed the stairs.

Gerald said, "Aye, aye, ma'am," and made a mock salute. He watched her, his head throbbing, until she reached the top of the stairs and moved out of sight. Gerald went into the kitchen and found the tin of tea, and stopped as though he had been caught stealing. He could hear Hester above him. She didn't *want* him with her. He set down the tin, hard, and rushed out to his car.

At Pearl Harbor late that afternoon, Gerald drove from the submarine pens to the Officers' Club. Hester was in no rush to see him so Gerald was in no rush. The bar was full and still filling. The male voices, the laughter, the good-natured, parochial teasing cheered Gerald. He was warmed, succored, in the midst of his peers. His quick well-being brought with it a flash of guilt. He thought of Hester, alone with the wounds inflicted on her in Mercy Hospital. Gerald went to a telephone at the end of the bar. "Hester?"

The telephone had wakened Hester. She was propped up in bed, the light from the night table in her face, an open book on her belly. She heard voices, men who seemed to be shouting. "Who is this?"

"It's Gerald," he said. "I may be a little late." He decided to have one drink and leave. As he replaced the telephone receiver, he heard a man say, "I've heard of women who like the dark meat."

A second man said, "*Four* of them?" Gerald was paralyzed. He was sick inside. He wanted to rest against the bar.

"Maybe she started with one or two," said the first man. Gerald had to turn. The man talking was a lieutenant junior grade. "Maybe two others came by for helpings, and wouldn't take no for an answer," he said to an ensign at the bar beside him.

"Have you *seen* her?" the ensign asked.

"Still waters run deep, Ensign," said the lieutenant. Gerald leaped. He bumped into someone and jabbed with his elbow, coming on to pull at the lieutenant, who was closest. He had the lieutenant with both hands, holding uniform and flesh beneath the uniform, pulling the man around and away from the bar. Gerald pulled back his arm and swung. He had never fought. His swing was awkward, his fist was flaccid, the lieutenant was bigger. Gerald's fist collapsed against the lieutenant's arm.

"What in the name of . . . ?" said the lieutenant, and he slapped Gerald's other fist aside as he swung. The ensign was ready then. He had a clear shot at Gerald, who was tied up by the lieutenant.

"Insult my wife, goddamn . . . !" Gerald said, and was stopped by the ensign's fist. The punch caught Gerald high in the face, on the cheekbone, sending him careening.

He didn't fall. He righted himself, but the ensign was after him and Gerald's arms were down. The lieutenant reprieved Gerald, taking the ensign's arm to push him back. "I fight my own battles," he said.

The entire bar was in on it then. Far down the bar Bryce Partridge identified Gerald as one of the combatants, and saw two against one. By the time the lieutenant had pushed the ensign away, raised his fists, and set himself to start punching, Bryce was there. "Let's make it even, sport," Bryce said.

"This isn't your fight," said the lieutenant. Bryce saw the ensign coming on his right.

"It's my fight," said Gerald. "My wife," he said, but nobody heard him. Warnings from all sides drowned him out. "They insulted my wife." The ensign swung first, and Bryce came into and under the swing, hooking with his left into the belly. The ensign let out a long, croaking grunt.

"Gentlemen!" A captain, a four-striper, whose appearance had started the warnings, reached them. "Where in the hell do you think you are?" The big room became silent except for the ensign's retching. "Get him into the head!" said the captain. Two officers grabbed the ensign, lifting him off his feet. Those three were the only men in motion. The rest were at attention, including the bartenders, who were enlisted men.

Gerald said, "Sir," and the captain, who was disgusted by the performance he had seen, faced the officer with the bloody cheek. The captain was ready for him.

"You speak when you're spoken to, mister," said the captain. "I want all of you to put yourselves on report," he said, and pointed at the men's room in the corner. "Including the ensign."

"Sir, I am entirely at fault here," Gerald said. The captain almost put Gerald under arrest. But the blood was trickling down Gerald's face onto his white collar and down across his shoulder boards. "Murdoch, Gerald," he said, and repeated his serial number. "Lieutenant, junior grade."

The captain heard "Murdoch," and his mind said "Ashley, Hester Ashley," giving him the answer to the only question he might have asked of the combatants. The captain looked at the other j.g., the bigger one, the man who was facing Murdoch. The captain was good at faces. He pointed at Gerald said "Take care of that cut," and went to the bar. He took off his cap, and when the bartender joined him, the men in the Officers' Club returned, cautiously, to their drinks and their companions.

"Let's take you over to the hospital," Bryce said, but Gerald was ahead of him. Bryce caught up, and Gerald almost ran.

"Leave me alone!" he said, almost in a sob. "Leave me alone!" As he reached the entrance, the door opened. Holding his handkerchief to his face, Gerald rushed past three men, head down. He did not want to be seen. Gerald reached his car and fell back against the seat. In his head he saw the bar of the club, saw the men lined up, end to end, heard them all discussing Hester. All of them said Hester had invited the men to join her, to help themselves to her. Gerald started the engine and drove away from the Officers' Club, toward the entrance to Pearl Harbor. They would ask his name if he went to the hospital. The medics would put down his name, waiting until he left to talk about Hester.

"Fifty!" Maddox dropped his hat on Leonard Fairly's desk, looking down at the chief of police. "You're putting *fifty* men out there tomorrow morning? Are we being invaded?"

"We need to be ready for anything," said the chief. The trial of the four young men accused of raping Hester began the next day.

"You can't believe there'll be trouble," Maddox said. "Most of those people can't even find the courthouse. Most of them, ninety-nine percent of them, have jobs. Tomorrow's no holiday." The chief picked up a brass letter opener. "Cancel it, Len."

"This thing has caused a lot of talk," the chief said. "Not only here, all over the Territory. I've heard it wherever I go. Men stop me wherever I go. They're worried."

"They're always worried," Maddox said. "Some kanaka somewhere takes off for a day and they're always convinced the ranch hands are ready to strike. It's the favorite sport in the Territory, worrying over what the natives will do. The *natives!*'' Maddox said. ''The natives are afraid to cross the street.''

''I'm not taking any chances.''

Maddox arched his back, hoping to ease the ache across his shoulders. It was almost six o'clock. He had been in and out of headquarters for ten hours. ''You'll have more cops than people in front of the courthouse,'' Maddox said. ''Don't do it.''

''I didn't bring you up here to argue,'' said the chief. He tossed the letter opener into the air, end over end, and caught it. The chief tried to stay in his chair when he was with Maddox. The big man made him feel even shorter.

''We'll look like we're expecting a riot,'' Maddox said. ''The reporters will think so. They'll see the small army and figure you know something they don't. They'll spread it all over the papers. 'Police Brace for Trouble,' '' Maddox said, forming a headline. ''Instead of the trial, we'll be on the front page, exactly where we shouldn't be. If there's one thing cops don't need, it's publicity. By tomorrow night the governor will be calling. He'll want *more* cops. For Christ's sake, Len, there won't be room left for anyone else. You'll have a street full of blue uniforms lined up for a parade.'' Maddox watched the chief playing with the letter opener.

''I'd rather be safe than sorry,'' the chief said. ''You'll be in charge, Curt.''

Maddox picked up his hat. ''I'm off tomorrow.'' The chief dropped the letter opener on the desk.

''Sunday is your day off.''

''I've got time coming,'' Maddox said. ''I'll show you my time sheet.'' Maddox had never kept a time sheet.

''I'm ordering you to command the courthouse detail tomorrow,'' the chief said. Curt Maddox's guardian angel, his secret father, didn't worry the chief this time. Harvey Koster would agree with him 100 percent.

By nine o'clock the next morning Maddox had deployed the fifty uniformed policemen in front of the courthouse. There were two files leading from both corners of the building and facing each other. The rest were in front of the courthouse in another line broken by the broad entrance, which was clear. Maddox stood beside one of the two iron upright NO PARKING signs on the sidewalk at the curb. He summoned the lieutenants and sergeants.

''Spread out,'' Maddox said. ''You'll be on the line with the rest. No rousting today. Nobody gets tough. No pinches for loitering. No *pinches*. I'll decide if someone is creating a disturbance. You come to me, you show me. Pass the word." He looked at the sergeants and lieutenants. "Do it now."

Maddox watched them disperse, taking up positions among the rows of cops, so he didn't see Jeff Terwilliger and the other man. "For Pete's sake, Maddox, this is a trial, not a revolution," Terwilliger said.

"Funny." A group of men came out of the alley, turning to the entrance. Two carried large, square newspaper cameras. Maddox saw the Associated Press correspondent beside the photographers.

"Seriously, why the army?" Terwilliger asked.

"Chief of Police Fairly is providing for the safety of the public," Maddox said. Terwilliger grinned.

"Great news source," he said to the New York reporter beside him.

Maddox gestured at the group of newspapermen and jabbed his finger at the courthouse doors. "Join the others," he said to Terwilliger, who stopped smiling.

"We're covering a story," Terwilliger said.

"Not here, you're not," Maddox said. "I'm not letting you guys jam me up when they come out of their cars." He pointed once more. "Beat it."

Walking toward the doors, the New York reporter looked back at Maddox. "Who the hell *is* he?"

"A sorehead," Terwilliger said. "He enjoys it."

The New York reporter stopped and raised his head to the sun. The morning was incandescent. Puffs of white clouds drifted across a sky so blue it seemed luminous. The lawn flanking the entrance had been watered early, and the smell, sweet and humid, rose from the clipped grass. In front of the courthouse was a solid border of birds of paradise. The brilliant orange and blue of the flowers, poised for flight, were spectacular. "I left New York in a blizzard," the reporter said. "I couldn't even *find* the ship in San Francisco with the rain and the fog. I sneezed halfway across." He turned in a slow circle as though he were following the sun. "You people are on vacation fifty-two weeks a year."

He and Terwilliger joined the newspapermen at the courthouse doors. Others appeared, including reporters and photographers from the Japanese language dailies.

A Filipino in white overalls spattered with paint stopped beside Maddox. "Trial begin?"

"Today's the day," Maddox said. "Join the fun."

"No work, no pay," said the Filipino. Maddox thought of

driving him to the chief's office. The Filipino crossed the street, breaking into a trot as the yellow and black convertible turned the corner. Maddox saw the car. The party was starting.

In the convertible Joe Liliuohe said, "Tom look!" Tom sat between him and Sarah. "What's he doing here?"

"He's probably in charge outside," Tom said. "He's not in this."

"He was in it that night," Joe said, "and the next morning. He was in it then, all right." Sarah stopped between the NO PARKING signs. "I never saw so many cops," Joe said. "I guess they're here to protect all the women from the rapists."

"Stop it," Sarah said. "*Stop!*" She was afraid. She had awakened afraid. Tom nudged Joe and the latter opened the door. As Joe left the car, Sarah took Tom's hand, squeezing. His hand was warm. "I'm so scared."

He raised her hand to his lips. "Everything will be all right," Tom said.

"I wish I didn't have to work," Sarah said. "I wish I could be with you."

Tom could feel her against him, feel her hand in his. He wanted to put his arms around her. He wanted to kiss her. He wanted to kiss her and kiss her and feel her bringing him close, closer, welcoming him. The courthouse was far away. "You're with me."

"Say it again."

"You're with me," Tom said. "You're always with me now. I'm never alone now." They heard the rapping on the windshield. Maddox was bent over the hood.

"Move it," Maddox said. She was a pretty girl.

Tom came out of the car and for a single terrifying moment he was immobilized. Joe was gone! But Maddox was there, leaning against the iron upright. Maddox wouldn't have let Joe run. Tom heard the engine as Sarah drove off, and then saw Joe near the corner, with David Kwan and his father. Joe and David waved. Tom stopped in the broad entrance, waiting for them.

Maddox saw the kid with his father, who was the size of a mouse. "Some trouble," he said to himself. The four of them walked toward the doors where the photographers waited with their cameras, holding the flash guns over their heads.

Around nine o'clock one of the police lieutenants left his post, joining Maddox. "Take a look, captain." Maddox turned. A line of men and women, Orientals and Hawaiians, stood on the sidewalk across the street, facing the courthouse. Maddox counted. There were eleven.

"Should we call for help?"

The lieutenant was uncomfortable. "Well, I figured I'd tell you." He walked off and Maddox saw the black and white police car turn into the alley. He saw the two cops in front and the man in the rear. The man looked familiar. Maddox followed. There was a door to the courthouse in the alley.

As Maddox reached the alley, the police car stopped beside the side entrance door. The two cops came out, opening both rear doors. Maddox saw Murdoch emerge from the back and reach in to help his wife. The driver helped Doris Ashley out of the other side. Maddox knew Harvey Koster hadn't sent the squad out to Windward. Harvey Koster would have called him. Len Fairly had ordered the police car to Windward, leaving Maddox with the troops. Maddox grinned, thinking of the chief and his petty secrets. He watched Doris Ashley holding her hat. She and the girl were dressed for a funeral.

He heard a rush behind him and turned to see reporters and photographers running toward the alley. Maddox spread his arms wide. "End of the road," he said.

"You can't stop us!" yelled a photographer. Maddox lowered his arms, walking into the group, facing the photographer.

"Wanna bet?" Maddox waited. Behind them he saw Mike Yoshida with another kid, probably his brother, wearing their best clothes. Jeff Terwilliger saw them and hurried back, and the others followed. Maddox looked across the street. The line of men and women was longer. Maddox stepped off the curb.

They didn't seem to be breathing. Nobody moved. Nobody coughed. Maddox stopped in the gutter. "This is a business street," he said. "People will be coming in and out of these stores. Cars will be parking here. There's nothing to see out here. You'd better move along." Nobody moved. Maddox stepped over the curb, stopping between two Chinese. "I don't care which way you go, but you're going," he said. "Right now." Maddox used both hands, nudging the men on each side of him.

"More rough stuff," someone said, but the line broke open, men and women moved in both directions, and Maddox was quickly alone. Watching them disperse, Maddox saw someone stop on the corner. He was a trim fellow in a sport shirt. Maddox figured he was in his twenties, a good-looking guy, built like an athlete. Bryce Partridge had detoured on his way to duty at Pearl Harbor, parking a block from the courthouse.

An hour earlier, while Bryce had been reading Jeff Terwilliger's story about the start of the trial in the *Outpost-Dispatch*, Ginny

Partridge had said, "I feel so sorry for her." He had flipped the front page to read below the fold. "Bryce!"

"I didn't hear you, angel," he said, lying.

"Hester," Ginny said. "I tried to call her but no one answered. They're probably on their way. It must be terrible for her. She'll be on display, in the pit, like a slave in the colosseum, with everyone ogling her." Bryce put down the newspaper.

"It won't last long."

"One day is too long," Ginny said. As he rose, taking the car keys out of his pocket, Ginny leaped up. "Wait. Can you wait while I change?"

"Ginny, I don't check in with a shop foreman," Bryce said. "I'm a Navy officer." She blocked his path.

"I'll be ready in a jiff," she said. "You can drop me off at the courthouse on your way to Pearl. I want to be with Hester. Someone should be with her."

"Angel, someone *is* with her. Gerald is with her, and her mother."

"Gerald's a man!" Ginny said. Color rose in her cheeks as her mind filled with the thought of Hester in the dirt, helpless and struggling while three of them held her down. "And her mother doesn't, can't understand!" Ginny said.

"Her mother doesn't understand?"

"She's old!" Ginny said, arguing. "You don't understand, either! It could have been me! They could have taken me!"

"Ginny." He tried to put his arms around her, but she pulled away. Bryce's fingers closed around the car keys, and opened instantly. The sight of his fist frightened him for a moment. He said, gently, "I didn't mean to upset you," and stepped aside to go around her. His voice and manner dissolved Ginny's temper.

"Was anyone ever as kind?" Ginny kissed him. "Will you wait?"

He put his forefinger to her lips and Ginny kissed it. He said, "I won't let you go." She looked at him. "I won't let you sit in court with those four . . . men in front of you, listening to that ugly story. You've put yourself in Hester's place. You'll be hearing the witnesses, listening to what happened to *you*." He made a small smile. "I'm your husband. I'm supposed to protect you. Gerald is protecting Hester. No courthouse. It's an order, puss."

Standing at the corner Bryce saw the newspapermen jostle for position as some guy, a Hawaiian, approached the doors. He was all slicked up. Suddenly Bryce recognized him, although he couldn't remember the Hawaiian's name. He had seen pictures of all four in the newspapers, day after day, seen their pictures in the *Outpost-Dispatch* an hour ago, but he could not put the right name with the right face. Bryce made an about-face and walked rapidly toward his car, swearing he would not return.

Maddox watched the reporters with Harry Pohukaina. The young guy charged into the reporters, plowing through them to the doors. The photographers loaded their cameras. The sun filled the street and the courthouse windows sparkled. Maddox was alone. "Fifty," he said, aloud, looking at the rows of cops in front of the courthouse.

"Hear ye, hear ye, hear ye, the District Court of the County of Honolulu, Oahu, Territory of Hawaii, Honorable Judge Samuel Walker presiding, is now in session," said the bailiff. He waited until the judge was comfortable on the bench. "Be seated," said the bailiff. "Number one-eight-four-seven. People versus Joseph Liliuohe, Harry Pohukaina, David Kwan, Michael Yoshida."

On the bench Judge Walker, who had celebrated his sixtieth birthday with his wife and children and grandchildren the previous Saturday, watched the courtroom settle. Judge Walker began each day with calisthenics. The discipline was lifelong. He had, by example, instilled his devotion to physical fitness in his sons and daughters. He was an avid outdoorsman, and he and his wife had camped with the children since the oldest was born.

The judge saw Doris Ashley immediately, in the first row, between her daughter and son-in-law. He did not know her. He had never met Preston Lord Ashley nor seen Windward. She seemed very confident, even defiant.

Doris Ashley was quaking. She had to be brave, for her sake and for Hester's. She had to infuse Hester with her strength. Doris Ashley had brought Hester to Windward the day before, brought the clothes she had chosen for Hester from the carriage house. She had kept Hester with her, in the master suite, but when she woke, she was alone. Doris found Hester on the terrace, barefoot, in her nightgown. "I can't go through with it," Hester said.

"Baby, you'll be . . ." Doris Ashley began, and stopped as Hester ran. Doris chased her to the entrance hall and blocked the door.

"If you make me go, I'll tell the truth," Hester said.

"Do you hear what you're saying? Listen to what you're saying. We'll be *criminals*."

"We are criminals," Hester said. "I'm a criminal. I belong in jail." She ran toward the kitchen and the door to the outside. Doris Ashley caught her. Hester didn't fight. "I'll tell them to put me in jail."

"I'll kill myself," Doris said, lying. "You'll kill me. You'll be killing me." They could hear Amelia and Theresa in the room beside the kitchen.

"Tell them I'm sick," Hester said. "I'll sign a statement. Let me sign a statement."

"Poor baby," Doris Ashley said. "If only I could take your place. I'll run you a bath, baby."

She dressed Hester. They were dressed alike, in dark clothes with dark hats. In the courtroom beside Hester Doris Ashley waited for her ordeal to begin.

At the prosecution table Judge Walker saw Philip Murray talking with Leslie McAdams, the new assistant district attorney. "Is the State ready for trial?"

Murray rose. "The State is ready, Your Honor." The judge looked down at the four defendants and their lawyer.

"Are the defendants present?" asked the judge. Tom rose.

"The defendants are present, Your Honor," Tom said.

"Is the defense ready for trial?"

Tom felt as though the judge was on top of him. Murray and McAdams were watching him. Everyone was watching him. He should have let the princess pick her lawyer. No! He should have brought someone in to help him. No! He should have asked for a continuance to complete his preparation. No! "The defense is ready, Your Honor."

Inside the well behind Tom were the reporters and newspaper artists, in a row of chairs reaching from one side of the courtroom to the other. Many were from the Mainland, and Judge Walker had decided to put them in the well, keeping the benches on both sides of the aisle for the public. Judge Walker believed the public was entitled to access in his court.

On the left, in the first rows behind the reporters, were the fifty men of the jury panel. "Gentlemen of the jury panel," the judge began, "this case has stirred up a whole lot of publicity. It's been all over the newspapers and on the radio. So the court can't expect, and counsel shouldn't expect, to seat a jury that doesn't have prior knowledge. But the court demands that the jury hasn't reached any *opinions*, hasn't decided on guilt or innocence. Now if any of you *has* decided, tell the court and you'll be excused. You can leave." The judge didn't see a single hand.

"If any of you are acquainted with the principals in this case, you'll be excused and you can leave," the judge said. He didn't see a hand. "The defendants in this case are of different racial backgrounds," the judge said. "If any of you has any prejudice concerning race, creed, or color, it disqualifies you." The judge waited. He had a bunch of liars in his court. "Bailiff."

The bailiff went to the jury box. Twelve men rose from the first two benches. They had been selected by lot and juror number one, George Maynard, took the first seat in the first row. The others took seats according to their numbers. "Mr. Murray."

The district attorney rose, holding the list with the names of the panel. "Mr. Maynard. How do you earn your living?"

"I'm a plumber."

"Are you a family man? Do you have any children?"

"One. I've got a daughter."

"How old is she?"

"Twelve. Twelve years old," answered Maynard.

"Acceptable to the State, Your Honor," Murray said.

"Mr. Halehone," said the judge. Tom rose, stepping back so Maynard could see all four defendants.

"Acceptable, Your Honor," Tom said. So the first juror had been chosen, and he would serve as foreman.

"Mr. Murray," said the judge. The district attorney studied the list, although he had decided before the judge was in the courtroom. "I challenge the juror," Murray said, and the bailiff gestured at Akira Hanato, who was excused.

The challenge was peremptory and not open or vulnerable to contradiction. Prosecution and defense counsel each had six peremptory challenges for each defendant. So Murray and Tom could, between them, refuse to seat forty-eight men of the panel. Each also shared the right to challenge for cause. Either Murray or Tom, after questioning a juror, could conclude that he would not be impartial, that his presence in the box would be detrimental to the prosecution or the defense. These challenges were unlimited in number, but no juror could be excused for cause without the consent of the judge.

Akiro Hanato passed Tom, who was bent over the table, holding the list with the names of the panel. Tom's heart was pounding. He could see Murray, who was sitting parallel to the prosecution table, his legs crossed, comfortable, as though he were watching a ball game. Tom knew already that Murray intended to fill the jury box with haoles. "Mr. Murray," said the judge.

The district attorney looked at Fred Hofstader, the man beside

Hanato's empty chair. "Mr. Hofstader, how long have you lived in Honolulu?"

"Twenty-some years."

"What do you do?" asked Murray.

"Not much. Little things around the house."

"I meant, how do you earn your living?"

"Oh, yeah. Yeah. I'm a painter, a house painter," Hofstader said.

"Acceptable, Your Honor," Murray said.

"Mr. Halehone," said the judge. Tom rose, facing the judge, but he was talking to the district attorney.

"I challenge the juror," Tom said. He saw McAdams lean forward, whispering to Murray, and then he saw Murray glance over his shoulder to look directly at him.

"You're excused," said the judge to Hofstader. "You can leave."

Tom used two more peremptory challenges on the next two men, Victor Pasket and Harley Moore. The sixth was Louis Elahi. Murray challenged him. George Maynard was alone in the first row of the jury box.

Tom looked at the list of names. Number seven, behind Maynard, was Edward Broderick, and beside him sat Herbert Iaukea. The other four men were haoles. Most of the panel were haoles. Tom would run out of peremptory challenges long before the district attorney. He would be challenging for cause and need the judge's approval. He would lose. He would be arguing before a haole jury by the end of the day. Tom heard Joe moving his chair. He could feel all four of them around him. Tom could see them, standing, when the jury came in. He could see them being taken from the courtroom on the way to prison.

"Mr. Broderick." Murray was on his feet. "You heard His Honor warn the panel about having any opinions in this case. Do you have any opinions?"

"No, sir, I don't," Broderick said.

"Do you know anyone in this case?"

"I don't know anyone," Broderick said.

"Do you carry any feelings for people because of their race?"

"No, sir, not me." Tom was sure he was lying. They were all lying, but he had no choice. When Murray said, "Acceptable," Tom rose.

"Acceptable to the defense, Your Honor," Tom said. By accepting this juror he was asking Murray for a truce.

Murray challenged Herbert Iaukea, so Tom had the district attorney's answer. Murray would never quit. Four of the first twelve men remained and Tom used peremptory challenges for all. The bailiff brought ten more men into the jury box, including Chester Lahaina. As the last of the nine was excused and the bailiff followed Lahaina to fill the jury box a third time, the judge said. "Hold it." He raised both hands, motioning Tom and Murray to the bench. "Counsel."

"Two out of twenty-two," said the judge. "You can add and subtract. We'll have four from the first panel, maybe. They only gave us two panels. We're not the only court in this county, counsel. I'll have to adjourn while the jury commissioner finds me another panel. Let me in on your secret."

"I'm using my peremptory challenges, Your Honor," Murray said.

"Thanks for nothing," said the judge. "Your turn," he said to Tom.

"I'm trying to seat an impartial jury, Your Honor."

"*My* turn," the judge said. "You'll be fresh out of your peremptory pretty quick, both of you. You'll be into cause, and you won't be running through the next panel like salts. This case is going to trial, understand?"

Murray looked up. "Is Your Honor threatening me?"

"No, and don't you threaten me, Mr. District Attorney," said the judge. "Not in my court. I'll match my reversals with any judge in the Territory." He waved at the bailiff. "Seat them," he said.

Tom went back to the defendants. They were watching him. His hands were damp. He rubbed his hands on his thighs. Murray could talk tough because he had Hester Murdoch to put on the stand. Harry nudged Tom. "What did he say?" Harry whispered. They were all hunched over the table. Tom shook his head. When the judge recessed for lunch, the same two jurors were in the box.

Gerald came to his feet, leaning against the rail. He saw the defendants rise, bunched around their lawyer. He saw the big one, Liliuohe, their chief. Liliuohe stepped away from the rest of the gang, standing by himself. He was enjoying himself. He was proud. "Gerald."

Doris Ashley was in the aisle with Hester. "I've reserved a table for us at the club," she said. Hester moved back, out of the aisle. Everyone in Honolulu went to the Hawaii Club for lunch. Everyone would tell her how sorry they were. They would file past the table like people at a wake. The women would kiss her. She would have to thank everyone, lying to everyone. "I'll wait here," Hester said.

"Baby, we can't hide," said Doris Ashley. "We must hold up our heads. Gerald." Damn her, she was celebrating. "We'll walk," said Doris Ashley. "We need the fresh air." Hester sat down, her legs under the bench. Someone bumped into Doris Ashley. "Gerald, help her." People were watching them. The district attorney came through the gate.

"Excuse me," Murray said. Doris Ashley had to step out of the aisle. "Something wrong?" he asked.

Doris Ashley wanted to kick him. "No, no. My daughter felt a little faint. You mustn't concern yourself." She moved into the aisle. "They're expecting us, baby." Hester lowered her head. "Gerald, help her."

Gerald sat down beside Hester. She thought he would save her. "Let's wait until the rest leave," he said. Bryce would have put his arm around her and laughed at Doris Ashley.

"Good," said Doris. "I agree, Gerald. We'll wait." Gerald saw the defendants come through the gate with their lawyer, saw them march up the aisle in triumph.

Outside the courthouse Mike Yoshida said they could eat cheaply at his uncle's restaurant nearby. To Tom eating seemed like a punishment. He needed to think. He had to stop Murray. How could he stop Murray? "I'm not very hungry."

He could not escape. They surrounded him. He was their bastion. They were safe with him. They had come to believe him, accept his promises of justice and freedom.

Mike ordered. They were gluttonous, four healthy young men gorging themselves on the restaurant owner's largesse. Tom didn't remember what he ate. The tea was scalding. The voices around him seemed deafening. The faces at the table faded and Tom saw only the two haoles in the jury box. "We should be starting back."

The courtroom was empty and dark when Tom entered, ahead of the others. At the defense table Tom took the list with the names of the men on the panel. He held it close so he could read. Tom looked up at the ceiling. The lights extended in two parallels from the bench to the courtroom doors. A surge of feeling, almost electric in force, swept through him. Tom left the table and stopped beside the witness box. He looked at the defendants sitting together and facing him. He heard their questions, demanding an explanation. "Nothing," he said, as the lights came up. Tom hadn't seen the bailiff enter, and he had forgotten the list in his hand. He read it again. Warren Kemahele would be the number-four juror when the bailiff brought in the next ten men from the panel.

Judge Walker came into the courtroom a few minutes before two o'clock. Tom watched the bailiff lead ten men to the jury box. Warren Kemahele was the second in line. He looked like everyone's grandfather. He wore a brand-new white shirt. The collar was still stiff and full of angles. "Counsel approach the bench."

Tom was there ahead of the district attorney. As Murray joined him, the judge said, "I expect us to do a lot better this afternoon."

Tom swallowed. His throat hurt. "Your Honor, the panel heard your instructions this morning." He had to believe in Warren Kamahele. One was better than nothing. "The defense is willing to have the jury sworn in right now."

"*You're* willing," Murray said. "You're not the district attorney."

"First good idea I've heard today," said the judge. "How about it, Mr. Murray?"

"I'm not here to let the defense pick a jury," Murray said.

"He's not picking it," said the judge. "He's asking you to agree."

"I disagree," Murray said. "Why the rush? We're in the first day, Your Honor."

"Thanks for reminding me," said the judge. "Good-bye."

Tom returned to the defense counsel table. He couldn't stop Murray. He heard Harry Pohukaina asking him questions. He couldn't reply. He couldn't look at Harry, at any of them. They didn't have a chance. "Mr. Murray."

Murray walked toward the jury box holding the panel list. Number three was Melvin Fielding. He wore a white suit with black and white shoes, and he had a flower in his lapel. "Mr. . . . . Fielding," said Murray, reading. "What is your profession, Mr. Fielding?"

"Insurance. I'm an insurance man," Fielding said. "I handle any and all coverage, cradle to grave."

"Are you a married man?"

"Wedded to my work, as the saying goes," Fielding said. "Never found the time, I guess."

"Are you a native of Hawaii, Mr. Fielding?" Murray asked.

"Born and bred, yes, sir."

"Acceptable to the State, Your Honor," Murray said.

"Mr. Halehone," said the judge. Tom waited until the district attorney was in his chair.

"Your Honor, I have the utmost respect for the district attorney. He is a leading member of the bar. If the juror is acceptable to the district attorney, he is acceptable to the defense.'' Tom was asking Murray to seat Warren Kamahele.

"Good, good,'' said the judge. "All right, Mr. Murray. How about number four?''

Murray remained in his chair. "The State challenges the juror.''

"You haven't even *looked* at him!'' Tom said, out of his chair and swinging around the defense counsel table. "You're challenging *names!*'' Tom stopped in front of the bench, waving the list over his head. "Why not excuse the rest of the panel, Your Honor!''

"Your Honor . . .'' Murray said, but Tom was shouting.

"Excuse the second panel!'' Tom shouted. "Why waste everybody's time?''

"Order!'' Judge Walker pounded the gavel. "Counsel! Both of you! Order!'' Murray came across the well like a torpedo.

"This man doesn't belong in a courtroom!'' Murray shouted.

"Hold it right now!'' the judge said, standing and leaning over the bench. "I'm warning you both!'' He pointed the gavel. "Back off, Mr. Murray. Back off, I said!'' The judge gestured, and as Murray stepped back, pointed at Tom. "You were spouting off about the bar a little while ago. You must've sneaked in! For your information the district attorney was using his peremptory challenges,'' the judge said. He reached behind him for his chair. "Suppose you both head for neutral corners.''

Tom returned to the defense counsel table. All four were grinning. Joe winked. They were proud of him. Tom wanted to scream, telling them to run for their lives. Tom stopped beside his chair. He had nothing more to lose. "Your Honor.''

"Watch yourself, counsel,'' the judge said.

"My clients are entitled to a jury of their peers,'' Tom said. "They won't get it in this court because the district attorney doesn't want a jury. He wants a cheering section.''

Murray jumped up, raising his arm to hit the chair with his fist. "I won't take any more of this!''

"That makes two of us,'' the judge said. "I've had enough from you, Mr. Halehone.''

"You can cite me for contempt,'' Tom said. He was shaking. "You can remove me. I can't represent my clients in this court. Not with the district attorney in this court. Nobody can represent them. The defendants don't have a chance. They'll never get a fair trial! It'll be over before it starts!''

"You got your wish!'' said the judge. "You're in contempt!''

"Putting me in jail won't change anything,'' Tom said. "My

clients are sunk! They're sunk!'' Tom swung around, lunging at the jury box, stopping beside Warren Kamahele, who shrank back as though Tom were about to hit him. ''Look at this juror!'' Tom said, shouting again. ''The district attorney challenged him for one reason! His *name!*''

''That's a lie!'' shouted Murray, lying. The judge was pounding the gavel.

''Bailiff!'' The judge kept hitting the bench with the gavel. Tom held on to the jury box, trying to stop shaking.

''His name is Warren Kamahele,'' Tom said. The bailiff was heading for him. ''He's a citizen or he wouldn't be here,'' Tom said. ''He doesn't look like a mass murderer. Are you a mass murderer, Mr. Kamahele?'' The bailiff reached the jury box.

''Don't give me any trouble,'' he said, low.

''I'm not trying to escape,'' Tom shouted. ''I only want to ask a few questions.''

''Can't Your Honor *stop* him?'' Murray strode to the bench. ''He's turning the court into a three-ring circus.''

''Bailiff!'' the judge said. Tom ducked under the bailiff's arm, darting past him to stop near the witness box.

''The juror's been excused,'' Tom said. ''Why is the district attorney afraid to let me question him?''

''You're a disgrace,'' Murray said. ''You've broken every rule of conduct in the book.''

''You're right,'' Tom said. ''I'm in contempt, you're not. I haven't seated any jurors, you have. I haven't served my clients, I've hurt them. I believed they would receive justice here. I *convinced* them they would receive justice and they finally believed me. They shouldn't have believed me. You're right, I've broken every rule. So you win, Mr. Murray. You stopped me.'' Tom walked toward the defense counsel table. He had to face all four of them.

Judge Walker saw the long row of reporters, their heads bent as though they were praying, their hands moving as they scribbled their notes. People everywhere, all over the Territory and all over the Mainland, would be reading the reporters' stories tomorrow, about the crippled kanaka who claimed he couldn't get a fair trial in Sam Walker's court. ''Mr. Halehone.'' The judge pointed the gavel. ''You wanted to question him, question him.''

''You can't do it!'' Murray shouted.

''I'm doing it!'' the judge said. ''Save your motions for the end of the trial, counsel,'' and to Tom, ''You were in an awful rush. Question him, question him.''

"Thank you, Your Honor," Tom said. He returned to the jury box, facing Warren Kamahele. "You mustn't be afraid," Tom said. "You'll be leaving here in a few minutes. You won't have to come back." Tom smiled at him. "How old are you, Mr. Kamahele?"

"I'm sixty-five," Kamahele said. "Almost sixty-six, pretty soon."

"Are you married?"

Gripping the chair arms, the elderly man said, "Yes, married."

"Do you have children?"

"Three children," Kamahele said.

"Tell us about your children," Tom said. "How old are they? How do they earn a living?"

"They're all grown up," said Kamahele. "Two boys and a girl. The oldest boy, Adam, he's a minister. Now *his* boy thinks he'll be a minister, too. My other boy, Luke, he's a teacher. Likes to teach. He even comes to Adam's church on Sunday to teach Sunday school."

Tom smiled. "Don't forget your daughter."

"She's home, home with us, me and my wife," Kamahele said. "Her husband died, so she came home with *her* boys. Two boys. She works, works hard. Her oldest boy is in the States, University of Colorado. He was always with the animals, her boy. He's studying so he can be a . . ." Kamahele shook his head.

"Veterinarian," Tom said.

"Veterinarian," Kamahele said. He almost told the lawyer about the goose that was still living in the backyard, but he decided not to take chances. The lawyer had said he could go home pretty soon.

"You have a nice family," Tom said. "You ought to be proud."

"All nice," Kamahele said. "Their children nice, too." Tom moved aside so Murray could see Kamahele. "Do you own your own home?" Tom asked.

"Almost. Couple more years and she's paid," Kamahele said.

"Do you have many debts?" Tom asked. Kamahele watched Tom until he said, "Do you owe much money?"

"Always pay cash," said Kamahele. "If we can't pay, we don't buy."

"Mr. Kamahele, have you ever been arrested?"

"*Arrested!*" Kamahele put his hand over his mouth, astonished by the question. "For *what?*"

"For anything," Tom said. "Have you ever been arrested for breaking the law?"

"No, no, no," Kamahele said, shaking his head for emphasis each time he spoke.

"Has anyone in your family ever been arrested?" Tom asked. "Your wife, or your children, or any of your grandchildren?"

"No, sir. Not one, no one in my family," Kamahele said. He moved forward in the chair for the first time since entering the jury box. "I never even knew one single policeman in all my life." He made a sound.

"I didn't hear you," Tom said.

"I remembered," Kamahele said. "My boy, Adam, the minister, when he was in school, he was a school policeman. So I knew *one* policeman in all my life."

"Thank you very much, Mr. Kamahele," Tom said. He gestured to the elderly man, who then pushed himself out of the chair. Tom looked at the bench. "Thank you, Your Honor." Tom waited beside the foreman for Kamahele and walked with him to the aisle beside the wall.

At the prosecution table Leslie McAdams leaned forward. "Walker doesn't belong on the bench," he whispered.

"Nobody belongs on the bench," Murray said. He scratched his arm. "My psoriasis is back."

"We can still stop him," McAdams said, of Tom.

"Nope. He stopped us," Murray said. McAdams sat up, staring at the district attorney. "The reporters aren't dumb, and some of them are Mainland reporters. Halehone put on his show for them. They'd say we filled the jury box with a lynching party. Wouldn't *that* look good in the States."

At four o'clock when Judge Walker adjourned, a fourth juror had been seated. His name was Tanoye Fujimoto. "Mr. Halehone, I'll see you in my chambers," said the judge.

A secretary said, "He's expecting you," and nodded at the closed door. Tom knocked. "I said he's *expecting* you." Tom opened the door. Judge Walker was behind his desk in shirt-sleeves. He lit a cigarette. The judge let Tom stand.

"I'm not sending you to jail," the judge said. "I should but I'm not." He didn't intend to turn the smart aleck into a hero. "I'm fining you. So you had a free ride today." He put his elbows on the desk. "Your last free ride, counsel. No more fireworks, understand?" He waved his hand in dismissal while Tom was thanking him.

Two days later, just before the lunch recess, the jury was complete. The last man seated was Andrew Lihilini.

* * *

Jeff Terwilliger wrote in the *Outpost-Dispatch:*

> "Never in my career, as a lawyer in private practice,
> and as district attorney, have I encountered a criminal case
> so heinous, so ugly, so wanton, so brutal."

With those words, Philip Murray began the State's opening statement yesterday in the rape trial of Hester Ashley
Murdoch.

"A young, vibrant sheltered woman, recently married,
an open-hearted, *trusting* woman with the innocence of a
child, has been maimed, perhaps permanently, as the result of an attack by four men whose savage assault leaves
all decent people reeling," said the district attorney.

Murray carefully outlined the State's case against the
four defendants, Joseph Liliuohe, Harry Pohukaina, Michael Yoshida, and David Kwan. The district attorney said
the evidence against the four is overwhelming and he
presented his argument in detail. Murray saved his most
damaging words for the end of his statement, telling the
jury that Hester Ashley Murdoch had identified the four
defendants on the day after they raped her.

In his office in headquarters at Pearl Harbor, the admiral read,
slowly, Terwilliger's story, which began on page one. Glenn
Langdon wore his reading glasses, bent over the story. The
admiral opened the newspaper to page fourteen, where the story
continued.

> By contrast, Tom Halehone, the defense counsel, pre-
> sented a brief opening statement. He told the jury that the
> defendants were innocent. He offered short biographical
> sketches of all four, none of whom had ever been involved
> with the police before the fateful night.

"Never *caught* before," the admiral said aloud. He put down
the newspaper, full length, on his desk, and reached for the
ruler. The admiral moved his hand over the desk. He removed
his glasses and lifted the newspaper. The ruler was gone. "Chief!"

A man as old as the admiral opened the door. The chief
yeoman wore a blue uniform with a foot-long array of red hash
marks on his right sleeve. "Where's my ruler?"

The ruler belonged to the chief, who had taken it at the end of the previous day. The admiral demanded a clean desk. "I'll bring it, sir."

Using the ruler, the admiral cut Terwilliger's story out of the newspaper. He took a file folder from a drawer of his desk. In it were Terwilliger's previous stories of the trial. The admiral read, again, the names of the jury. Over Tanoye Fujimoto and Andrew Lihilini the admiral had put, in ink, a question mark.

"Call your first witness," said Judge Walker on the morning after opening arguments.

"Call Peter Monji," said the district attorney. The slender young man, his black hair combed straight back and glistening with pomade, walked down the aisle. He wore a light suit and black and white shoes. He bent over the gate, fumbling with the latch before opening it. The district attorney was waiting at the witness box. Peter Monji sat down, tugging at each pants leg to preserve the crease.

When he was sworn in, Murray said, "State your name and your occupation."

"My name is Peter Monji and I'm an orderly in the emergency room at Mercy Hospital."

"Sum up your duties for the jury," Murray said. "Tell the jury what you do."

"I'm an orderly," Peter said. "I help with the patients, help the doc . . . doctor hold them down on the table so he can work. I bring him stuff, syringes, medicine, tape, sponges, bandages, whatever he needs."

"Mr. Monji, was Hester Murdoch a patient on the night of September twentieth?" Nobody had ever called him mister.

"Yes, sir. Hester Anne Ashley Murdoch was a patient."

"Now, Mr. Monji. Tell the court when you first saw Mrs. Murdoch."

"I first saw her outside . . . me and the cop."

At the defense table Mike Yoshida glared at Joe. "Because you had to hang around." He felt Tom's hand shaking him, and fell back in his chair, looking at the witness box.

"Outside the emergency room?" asked Murray.

"Yeah . . . yes."

"Tell us in your own words how you discovered Mrs. Murdoch," said the district attorney.

"I was in the emergency room. We were busy," Peter said. "You know, Saturday night. This cop . . . officer was there. He'd brought in this guy who was knifed . . . was cut up . . . stabbed. The patient was stabbed. And the doc . . . doctor, was working on him, suturing him, and I was helping, holding him down like I told you. All of a sudden we heard this noise, heard this woman screaming kind of. I went to take a look, me and the cop . . . officer. A car pulled out, shot out of the parking lot and there she was, staggering around. She looked like she was going down any second.''

"Going down?"

"Like she'd drop. Fall," Peter said. "So me and the . . . officer went after her.''

"You brought her into the emergency room?"

"Half-carried her in," Peter said. "She was hurt awful bad. Her face.'' Peter grimaced.

Sitting beside Hester, Gerald watched the four hulks with their lawyer. He couldn't see *their* faces. He wanted to see *them*, see the smirks on their faces as they sat comfortably listening.

"Describe her face," said the district attorney.

"Just a mess," said Peter. "Like someone had gone to work with a meat cleaver. Or a baseball bat.''

"Or fists?"

"Objection," said Tom. "The district attorney is leading the witness.'' But the jury had heard the question.

"Your Honor, the witness works in the emergency room of a hospital," said Murray. "He may not be an expert witness, but he has had wide experience with such cases.''

"I'll allow the question," said Judge Walker. "Overruled.''

"Mr. Monji, could Mrs. Murdoch's injuries have been caused by someone's fists?''

"Yeah . . . yes . . . Sure," Peter said. Murray continued to question the orderly, asking for specific responses.

Gerald leaned forward, hidden by the reporters sitting in front of the rail. He wanted to shut out Monji's voice. He wanted to leap up, demanding that Murray stop. Gerald's head was throbbing. He needed a drink of water, but he couldn't leave. He couldn't allow the world to think he was being chased out of the courtroom. "No further questions.''

"Tom!" Joe was leaning toward him, hands on the defense table, fingers spread. "They think we did it!'' Tom shook his head. *"Tom!"*

"Is counsel going to cross-examine or not?'' Judge Walker looked down.

"Excuse me, Your Honor," Tom said, pushing his chair aside and leaving the defense table. He walked to the witness box. "Mr. Monji, how long was Mrs. Murdoch in the emergency room?''

"An hour . . . maybe longer. She was hurt awful bad. Doc . . . Doctor Puana worked on her a long time."

"An hour or longer," Tom said. "You were with her all the time?"

"Yeah, sure. I was helping," said Peter.

"Did Mrs. Murdoch say she had been raped?"

"She didn't say anything."

"She didn't speak during the hour or more she was in the emergency room? Didn't say a single word?"

"Well, hardly. Her name, and every once in a while she'd say something like she was hurt real bad, something like that. Like, stop, or don't hurt me, something like that."

"Did she say she had been raped?" Tom asked.

"No, she didn't."

"Did she use the word *rape?*" Tom asked.

"Objection," Murray said. "Counsel is hectoring the witness."

"Overruled," said the judge. Take rape out of the case and they might all as well go home.

"I'll repeat the question," Tom said. "Did she use the word *rape?*"

"If she did, I didn't hear her," Peter said.

"Did you hear *anyone* use the word *rape?*" Tom asked.

"While she was in the emergency room?"

"While Hester Murdoch was in the emergency room," Tom said. "Did anyone use the word *rape?*"

"Not that night, no," Peter said.

"We're *talking* about that night," Tom said. "Did you hear the word *rape that . . . night.*"

"No," Peter said, and the judge leaned to his left.

"All right, Counsel," the judge said. "You've milked it dry."

The net tightened around the four defendants in the rape trial of Hester Anne Ashley Murdoch yesterday.

After four days of testimony before Judge Stanley Walker in District Court, the State's case against Joseph Liliuohe, Harry Pohukaina, Michael Yoshida, and David Kwan seems airtight. District Attorney Philip Murray continues to present a carefully constructed chain of evidence linking the defendants to the reprehensible crime that has shocked Hawaii and the Mainland.

Officer Roy Pabst of the Honolulu Police Department, the first witness called yesterday, corroborated previous testimony as Murray questioned him concerning Mrs.

Murdoch's condition when she appeared in the emergency room of Mercy Hospital, the night of September 20. Pabst had brought a man knifed in a downtown brawl to the emergency room for treatment.

The defense lawyer, Tom Halehone, followed the pattern of cross-examination he has pursued from the beginning, asking Pabst if Mrs. Murdoch said she had been raped. Although Pabst replied she had not, Halehone hammered away at the witness until Judge Walker, as he has previously, ordered the defense lawyer to change his line of questioning.

Gerald read every word of Terwilliger's story. He sat in the living room at Windward, wearing a light suit, waiting for Hester and Doris Ashley. Theresa had brought him a cup of coffee but Gerald had refused it. He had wakened, alone in the carriage house, and long before daylight he had been in the small kitchen, dressed and standing beside the stove as he drank the coffee he had made.

He was still reading when he heard the crunching sound of tires in the gravel driveway. Gerald went to the doors and saw the police car. He wanted to send it back. He wanted to drive to Pearl Harbor and ask the admiral for sea duty, anywhere, on any ship. He wanted to leave Honolulu forever. Gerald closed the door and walked through the dining room into the kitchen. "Tell them the car is here," he said to Theresa.

"My name is Frank Puana, I am a doctor of medicine," Frank said, in the witness box. He was wearing the suit and shoes in which he had been married. Mary Sue had shined the shoes while Frank shaved that morning. She had washed and ironed the white silk handkerchief, slipping it neatly into the jacket pocket. Even without the vest he was warm. He loathed being on display. The witness chair was slippery. Frank felt like he was sliding.

"Where do you practice, Doctor?" asked the district attorney.

"I'm at Mercy Hospital."

"You're on the staff at Mercy Hospital," Murray said. Frank cringed as though Murray had slapped him. He turned in the chair but there was no escape. The lawyer was forcing him to tell the whole world.

"I am employed in the emergency room," Frank said.

"What sort of illness do you handle in the emergency room?" Murray asked.

Frank looked straight at the district attorney. "I'm a doctor," Frank said. "A physician and surgeon, qualified to practice medicine. *Licensed* to practice medicine, in the Territory and in thirty-nine states of the United States. I treat the patient for the problem that brought him to me.'' Judge Walker looked down at the kanaka in the witness box who was behaving like the D.A. had called him a quack.

Murray smiled. ''Doctor, you're here as an expert witness,'' he said. ''Your credentials are beyond reproach. My question is directed at your work in the emergency room of Mercy Hospital.''

''I remember the question,'' Frank said, ''and I answered it. I see everything, injuries, fractures, knife wounds, bullet wounds, women in labor, inflamed gallbladders, acute appendixes, concussions, everything.''

''You *see* them,'' Murray said. ''You don't *treat* them all, do you, Doctor? You don't take out an appendix in the emergency room.''

''I treat mainly those patients who have been injured and need immediate care, primary care,'' Frank said.

''Injuries,'' Murray said. The judge looked down.

''You're treading water, counsel,'' the judge said. ''The witness is a doctor. *Licensed*. It's established.'' Murray scratched his arm.

''Dr. Puana, were you on duty the night of September twentieth?'' Murray asked.

''I was,'' Frank said.

''Did you treat Hester Murdoch that night?''

''Yes, I did,'' Frank said. He could see her in the front row between her husband and her mother. He had treated her *after* that night, too. He could have told the whole world that, too. He could have given those reporters in the row of chairs a story that would explode like a bomb. The four defendants were watching him. Frank wasn't afraid of them. He hadn't raped Hester Murdoch, they had raped her. He hadn't committed a crime. He had followed the orders of the chief of staff. Claude Lansing had told him it was a therapeutic abortion. Frank concentrated on Lansing. Frank would never again need to say he was *employed*. The next time he sat in the witness chair he would be on the staff.

''Please describe Mrs. Murdoch's condition when you first saw her,'' Murray said.

''The patient had multiple contusions, lacerations, and abrasions of the face and neck,'' Frank said.

''Caused by a person's fist?'' Murray asked. Tom came out of his chair.

"Objection, Your Honor. The district attorney is leading the witness."

"Sustained," said Judge Walker.

"I'll rephrase the question, Your Honor," Murray said. "I'd like to remind the court that we have been through this with a previous witness."

"You've reminded me," said the judge. "Move along, counsel."

"Doctor, in your professional opinion could Mrs. Murdoch's injuries have been caused by someone's fists?"

"Yes," Frank said.

"Could the injuries have been caused by more than one person?" Murray asked.

"Yes," Frank said.

"Thank you, Doctor," Murray said. "Please tell the court how you treated Mrs. Murdoch." Murray managed a smile. "Remember, we are laymen."

"I spend my career with laymen," Frank said. "Patients and their families." He sat back. The chair was no longer slippery. From his first day on the wards with patients, in his junior year of medical school, Frank had welcomed, had enjoyed, the dialogue with those in his care. He glanced at Hester. Her face was without a trace of blemish. His sutures had been textbook examples. Murray didn't interrupt. As Frank became silent, Murray said, "Thank you, Doctor. Cross-examine."

Tom left the defense counsel table. "Doctor Puana." He stopped at Frank's left, standing so that both could see Hester. "Did you talk to Mrs. Murdoch while you were treating her?"

"She was in no condition to talk," Frank said. "She was barely conscious."

"You didn't answer my question, Doctor," Tom said. "Did you talk to Mrs. Murdoch?"

"I didn't have time to talk," Frank said.

"Did you know whom you were treating?"

"Of course I knew," Frank said.

"You knew the patient's name was Hester Murdoch?"

"Yes, of course."

"How did you know?" Tom asked.

"She *told* me. I asked her and she told me," Frank said.

"So you *did* talk to Mrs. Murdoch."

"If you can call that talking," Frank said. Tom was silent for a time. The guy was so *mad*.

"Can you recall anything else you said or Mrs. Murdoch said?"

"The patient was anesthetized," Frank said. "I had anesthetized her."

"Was she conscious?" Tom asked.

"She slipped in and out," Frank said. "And I was busy. I had a severely injured patient."

"Please try and remember, Doctor," Tom said. "It's very important. Did Mrs. Murdoch tell you anything besides her name?"

"I've already told you . . ." Frank said, and stopped, shaking his head. "No."

"Did she say she had been raped?"

In the first row Hester whispered, "Let me out." She started to rise but Doris Ashley took her arm.

"She did not," Frank said.

Hester wrenched her arm free. "I need a drink of water," she said, rising. Doris Ashley came erect. She couldn't let Hester leave alone. Hester would disappear. Doris needed help. "Gerald."

Gerald didn't turn. He didn't look at them. He shook his head, watching the witness. Someone had to stay and face those four buggers.

Tom saw Hester and Doris Ashley in the aisle. He left the witness box, standing with his back to the bench. "Doctor, did you examine Mrs. Murdoch to learn whether she had been raped?"

"Did I . . . ? No!" Frank said. Tom watched Hester and Doris Ashley leave the courtroom. He turned to the witness box.

"Were there any signs that Mrs. Murdoch had been raped?" Tom asked. "Were her clothes torn?"

"Her dress was dirty," Frank said.

"Was it torn? Were there signs of a struggle?" Tom asked.

"I told you, her dress was dirty," Frank said.

"Were her undergarments torn?"

"I can't answer that question," Frank said. "I wasn't treating her for . . . I've already said I didn't examine her for evidence of sexual activity."

"Was Mrs. Murdoch wearing undergarments?" Tom asked.

Judge Walker waved his hand at Tom. "All right, counsel," said the judge. "You've used up the line of questioning. Next."

"I have one more question, Your Honor," Tom said. He moved to the witness box. "Speaking as a doctor, do you have any evidence to prove Mrs. Murdoch was raped?"

"I do not!"

"None?"

"None!" Frank said.

*   *   *

When the court convened after lunch, the district attorney called Doris Ashley to the witness box. In the first row Doris moved her gloves from one hand to the other. "Now is my time to be tested," she whispered to Hester. "I won't fail you, baby." Doris Ashley rose with her head high. She came through the gate, walking toward the bailiff with the Bible as though she were following an usher to her seat for the Sunday polo.

Murray's interrogation was brief. After establishing Doris Ashley as Hester's mother, Murray said, "I have only two more questions. One, how did you learn your daughter had been sexually assaulted by four men?"

"She told me," said Doris Ashley. "From her hospital bed, her bed of pain."

"Mrs. Ashley," said the judge. When she looked up at the bench, he said, "Confine yourself to answering the question." He sat back. "Strike, 'From her hospital bed, her bed of pain,' " the judge told the court stenographer.

"My final question, Mrs. Ashley," Murray said. "Has your daughter ever lied to you?"

"Never," answered Doris Ashley, lying.

"Your witness," Murray said, passing the defense counsel table.

"No questions," Tom said. He would only lose by cross-examination, creating sympathy for Doris Ashley, a widow thrust into the cruel glare of public attention. Tom remained standing as Mrs. Ashley crossed the well, remained beside his chair until she joined Hester in the first row.

"Call Dr. Claude Lansing," said the district attorney. The bailiff at the rear of the courtroom opened one of the doors.

"Doctor," he said. Lansing tugged at the hem of his jacket. He was wearing a plaid suit with a double-breasted vest. He was ready. He had been sucking lozenges for almost an hour and his breath was clear. Lansing fluffed the handkerchief in his jacket pocket and came through the doors.

The district attorney was as short as he had been with Doris Ashley. Lansing testified that Hester had undergone surgery to terminate a pregnancy six weeks after the night she was first admitted to Mercy Hospital beaten and dazed.

"How long had Mrs. Murdoch been pregnant, Doctor?" Murray asked.

Lansing took out his comb. "Between seven and eight weeks—the first day after the last menstrual period is judged as the first day of pregnancy," Lansing said.

"No more questions, Your Honor," Murray said. Tom rose, walking toward Lansing.

"Doctor, is there any way of proving who was responsible for *Mrs*. Murdoch's pregnancy?" Tom asked.

"There is no scientific method," Lansing said.

"Could it have been Mrs. Murdoch's husband?"

"Objection," Murray said, on his feet. "Counsel is asking for conjecture."

"Overruled," the judge said. "The witness will answer the question."

Lansing looked up at the bench. "I *have* responded," he said. "The question cannot be answered scientifically."

"In other words we'll never know who was the father of the unborn child," Tom said.

"Precisely!" said Lansing. He ran his hands over his hair. His throat was dry.

"Thank you, Doctor," Tom said, and turned away. Lansing looked up at the judge.

"You're excused, Doctor," the judge said. Lansing came out of the witness box. He tried to saunter as though he had all the time in the world. In his medical bag in his car downstairs was a bottle of alcohol. As Lansing started up the aisle, the district attorney came out of his chair.

Murray turned his back on the bench, skirting the reporters in their chairs and stopping at the gate to the well. "Call Hester Anne Ashley Murdoch," he said, as though he were talking to her alone. He bent to open the gate. His manner was like a footman's.

"I'm here with you, baby," Doris Ashley whispered.

Gerald said, "Good luck," and stood up, extending his hand to help Hester. Doris Ashley rose. Hester could hear the buzzing around her, like wasps circling to attack. She was all alone. Doris Ashley led her into the aisle and kissed her. "Be strong for both of us."

"Mrs. Murdoch," Murray said, holding the open gate. Hester entered the well and Murray moved around and behind her to be on Hester's right, between her and the defendants. But Hester could see them, see each one. She could see their lawyer.

Tom leaned far over the table, staring at the defendants. He had waited to rehearse them until they returned from lunch, stopping them in the courthouse lobby. "Take it easy," Joe said. "We're deaf, dumb, and blind, okay?"

Murray helped Hester into the witness box. He stepped aside while she was sworn in. When Hester was seated, Murray came forward, standing beside her. "Please tell the court your name and age."

"My name is Hester Murdoch. I am twenty-one." She saw the defendants in front of her and lowered her head.

"Where do you live?" Murray asked. Hester told him.

"You live in the home known as Windward," Murray said.

"Yes. No. I . . . we live in the carriage house," Hester said.

"The carriage house. Could you explain to the jury, Mrs. Murdoch?" His manner had changed. He was avuncular, like the trusted family doctor sitting beside the child in her bed.

"We live . . . my husband and I live in the carriage house," Hester said. "When we were married . . . before my marriage, my mother remodeled the carriage house for us."

"As a sort of wedding gift," said the district attorney. He waited. "Mrs. Murdoch?" Hester raised her head. She was looking at the defendants. She turned and saw the jury. They would pronounce the defendants guilty. Hester turned once more. Doris Ashley nodded, encouraging her.

"Yes, as a wedding gift," Hester said.

"How long have you been married, Mrs. Murdoch?"

"A year and a half," Hester said. "Almost a year and a half."

"A year and a half," Murray said. "Newlyweds." Murray put his hands on the witness box, watching Hester. "Are you feeling all right, Mrs. Murdoch?"

"Yes. Yes."

"Now-w-w-w-w-w-w," Murray said, letting the word drag to emphasize his reluctance. "I must ask you to go back to a certain night in September, a Saturday night, the night of September twentieth. Where were you that night?"

Hester could still feel the Bible on her hand. She could hear the oath she had repeated. She could hear the prison gates clanging, hear the huge key turning in the massive lock, closing on the four young men she was sending to their doom. "I must tell you the truth!" she said, loud. Hester saw her mother come out of the seat, saw her mother standing alone, saw her mother's face, like a death mask.

Tom came halfway out of his chair. He heard Murray say, gently, "Of course you'll tell us the truth, Mrs. Murdoch. The court doesn't doubt you. You mustn't be afraid. No one needs to be afraid of the truth."

Hester saw her mother return to her seat. "I'll repeat the question, Mrs. Murdoch," Murray said. "Where were you on the night of September twentieth?"

"I was at the Whispering Inn," Hester said, trying not to see anyone.

"With your husband?"

She wanted to say, "I was with Bryce. I was with Bryce Partridge, the father of my baby. He beat me."

"Mrs. Murdoch? Were you at the Whispering Inn with your husband?" Murray asked.

"Yes."

Slowly, patiently, meticulously, Murray led Hester through the early hours of the evening. "Why did you leave the party?"

She wanted to say, "I left because I was pregnant. I had to tell Bryce. I thought he would take me away with him."

"Why did you leave the party?" Murray asked, again.

"It was very warm and noisy," Hester said. "And smoky. I felt dizzy. I went out because I was dizzy."

"To clear your head," Murray said. "You left the party to clear your head."

"Yes, to clear my head," Hester said.

"You were alone, a young woman of twenty-one, who had recently been married and was beginning a new life," Murray said. "Please go on, Mrs. Murdoch. Tell the jury, in your own words, what happened when you left your husband for a few moments."

"I . . . I walked," Hester said. "I kept walking until I couldn't hear the music. I thought I would feel better if everything was still for a little while."

"You were alone, in the dark," Murray said. "Were you frightened?"

"No, not then."

"Not then," Murray said. "Did anything occur to frighten you?"

Hester said, "Yes," but she could not be heard.

"I'm sorry, Mrs. Murdoch. Could you speak louder? Did anything occur to frighten you?"

"The men in the car," Hester said, and saw her mother with Gerald, heard her mother telling her to be brave, to save her, save them.

"The men in the car," Murray said, and asked Hester to describe the car. He asked her how many men were in the car. His questions were framed to contain Hester's answers.

Tom didn't look at her. He watched the others at the defense table. In the lobby he had made them promise they would be silent, would not move. He heard Hester's lies, waited for her to complete her lies, tried not to be affected. "Do you see those four men who fell upon you and raped you here in this courtroom?"

"Yes." Murray left the witness box, walking to the defense table. He stopped behind Joe.

"Is Joseph Liliuohe one of those men?"

"Yes." Murray took a step, stopping behind David Kwan.

"Is David Kwan one of those men?"

"Yes." Murray moved to Mike Yoshida's chair, and afterward to Harry's chair. Hester identified both. Murray looked at the newspapermen along the rail making notes, and went back to the witness box.

"You have been very brave here today, Mrs. Murdoch," Murray said, and he was the doctor with the patient once more. "I'm only sorry I could not have spared you this ordeal." He turned away. "No further questions, Your Honor."

Tom picked up the sheaf of papers. Someone whispered, "Tom," but he didn't acknowledge the summons. They weren't in it. He was in it, alone. He should have brought Sarah to court, spoken to her boss. No! Sarah couldn't help. She was more scared than he was. No one could help. He went to the witness stand, still carrying the papers.

"Mrs. Murdoch, you've identified the *four* defendants as the *four* men who assaulted and beat you," Tom said. "You've testified it happened at night, is that correct?"

"Yes, that is correct."

"What time did this . . . incident take place?" Tom asked, and, quickly, "Approximately?"

"Approximately?" Tom saw her pulling at her fingers. "I can't say," Hester said.

"Would nine o'clock, approximately, be close to the time?" Tom asked.

"I really can't say."

Gerald watched the lawyer reading the papers in his hand. He was torturing Hester. He was no better than the four at the table. He was one of them. He stood there as though *he* were innocent and Hester was on trial. Tom raised his arm, displaying the papers he held.

"According to the records of the emergency room in Mercy Hospital, you were admitted at twenty minutes past ten on the night of September twentieth," Tom said. "How long before twenty minutes past ten would you say you encountered the *four* defendants?"

Hester looked up at the bench, begging for help. Murray

spoke as he left his chair. "Objection, Your Honor," Murray said. "Counsel is hectoring the witness."

"Overruled," said the judge. The next time Doris Ashley stood up like she was lording it over the peasants, he'd set the bailiff on her. Mrs. Ashley wasn't in Windward. The judge looked down at Hester. "The witness must answer the question. Approximately what time did the encounter take place?"

"I've said . . ." Hester stopped. "Nine o'clock," she said. "Approximately nine o'clock." The judge nodded at Tom.

"Mrs. Murdoch, you have testified that the defendants first saw you near the Whispering Inn," Tom said. Tom displayed the sheaf of papers. "The Weather Service report for the night of September twentieth shows overcast skies and a quarter moon." Tom left the witness box, returning to the defense table. He stopped behind the defendants, with two on either side of him. "You saw these *four* defendants at approximately nine o'clock at night, with overcast skies and a quarter moon. You identified these *four* defendants as the *four* men who assaulted you, beat you, and sexually attacked you. Is that correct?"

"Yes," Hester said. Why didn't he stop? "Yes, yes."

Tom left the defense table, stopping on a line with the gate, facing the judge. He pointed at the ceiling. "Your Honor, I would like to have the lights turned off in the courtroom." He pointed at the windows. "I would like to have the shades pulled down."

"Object, Your Honor," Murray said. "Counsel is trying to turn the court into a sideshow."

"Your Honor, I'm trying . . ." Tom said, and was stopped by the pounding gavel.

"No one turns *this* court into a sideshow, Mr. Murray," said the judge. "Your turn," he said to Tom. "What *are* you trying to do?"

"Your Honor, my clients are on trial for a serious crime," Tom said. "The punishment is severe. If the gentlemen of the jury find these *four* defendants guilty, their lives will be finished. They're young, *too*," Tom said, reminding the jury of Murray's dramatic asides when the district attorney had been questioning Hester. "One of the defendants is twenty-one. One is less than twenty-one. This entire case rests on the testimony of one witness, Hester Anne Ashley Murdoch. No other witness has incriminated or identified the defendants. Mrs. Murdoch says she saw her attackers in the dark, on a cloudy night in the dark. I'm asking the court for permission to have approximately the same conditions here."

"Your Honor!" Murray was standing and outraged. "Mrs. Murdoch has already identified the defendants!"

"I was here, counsel," the judge said. "Bailiff, turn off the lights and drop all the shades."

"Thank you, Your Honor," Tom said, walking to the defense table as the low, excited murmur from the spectators filled the courtroom. The judge rose and bent over the bench.

"Help him," the judge said to the court reporter. The lights darkened as the court reporter walked toward the windows. The bailiff followed him.

"I expect order in this court," the judge said. Sitting behind the defense table, Jeff Terwilliger pushed his pencil into his jacket pocket. He shoved the folded sheets of copy paper with his notes into another pocket.

Voices stopped and the sound of feet shuffling ended. Tom could hear the dry rustling sound of the shades being lowered. The bailiff and the court reporter returned to their places. Tom was standing. "Mrs. Murdoch."

Hester saw the figure standing in the shadows. She heard him say, "Let's go back to the night of September twentieth near the Whispering Inn. You have testified that at approximately nine P.M. that night you were seized by four men. Will the defendants rise?"

Hester heard the chairs against the floor. She saw other figures. She heard them moving, heard the chairs scraping. "Mrs. Murdoch, are these the four men you saw near the Whispering Inn?"

She saw the figures ahead of her. They were in a row facing her. She saw the big one, the one who had driven the car. She wanted to scream at them, scream, "Run, run, run, *run!*"

"Mrs. Murdoch. Are these the four men you saw near the Whispering Inn?"

"Yes. Yes. They are," Hester said. She dug her fingernails into her hands.

Tom heard her clearly. "I can't hear you."

"Yes. *Yes!*"

"You're absolutely positive?" Tom asked.

"Yes!"

"Without the slightest doubt?" Tom asked.

"Objection, Your Honor," Murray said. "Now counsel *is* hectoring the witness."

"The court is satisfied with the witness's answers," the judge said.

"Your Honor, I'm fighting to prove my clients are innocent," Tom said. "I'm asking the court to allow Mrs. Murdoch to answer the last question, *my* last question."

"Answer the question, Mrs. Murdoch," the Judge said.

"Will the court reporter repeat the question?" Tom asked. The court reporter bent over his pad, squinting.

"Without the slightest doubt?" he said.

"Yes," Hester said.

"Will the bailiff please turn on the lights?" Tom asked. The bailiff reached for the switch. As the lights came up, someone said, awed, "Look!" Someone else pointed and said, "*Look!*" Another said, "Over there, next to the jury!" Men in the jury box swung around, staring at Harry Pohukaina and Mike Yoshida, who were standing beside them.

Standing with Joe and David Kwan were Jeff Terwilliger and the New York reporter who had agreed to their roles during the lunch recess. Someone said, "They switched!" The judge pounded the gavel. Leslie McAdams grabbed Murray's arm. "*Phil!*" He pointed at Tom, who was sitting in Jeff Terwilliger's chair with the newspapermen.

Doris Ashley raised her arm as though she intended to strike someone. "That's not fair!" she said.

"Quiet! I said quiet!" Judge Walker was almost shouting as he looked down at the defense counsel and Jeff Terwilliger standing with the two defendants.

Hester sat on the edge of her chair as though she were being hazed. She saw the pair at the jury box. She saw the lawyer and a stranger with the other two at the table. She thought of being beheaded. She could see the guillotine. She could hear the cries of the mob demanding vengeance. She could hear the judge telling them to go back to their chairs, telling the people he would clear the court. Hester could see her mother, who was covering her face, and she could see Gerald, who seemed to be far, far away, who seemed frozen.

Four days later, sixty-four hours after the jury had been locked in the jury room, the foreman summoned the bailiff. He went directly to Judge Walker's chambers. The judge's new golf bag with his new set of clubs was on a chair beside the desk. He refused to leave them in his car. The judge figured he could play nine holes anyway after locking up the jury for the night. Riverside, a municipal course, was on his way home. "You'll be out on the course early," said the bailiff.

"I won't be out at all," said the judge. "Not after this." He ordered the bailiff to alert the principals. When he was alone, the judge telephoned police headquarters. "They're coming in, Len," he said to the chief.

Leonard Fairly called the dispatcher. "Maddox isn't in the building," the chief said. "Find him."

In his office Tom said, "Thank you," and replaced the receiver. "The jury's coming in," he said. Joe and David Kwan were on the other side of the desk. Mike Yoshida got up, and Harry Pohukaina came away from the windows, walking without a sound. They were all watching him. Tom felt hollow inside.

"What do you think?" Joe asked. Harry said, "Tom," and, "Tommy?" Mike pushed himself between Joe and David. "For Christ's sake, say something."

"You're innocent," Tom said. *"You're innocent!"*

"You're not on the goddamn jury!" Mike said, and lowered his head, and said, for the first time, "I'm sorry. After everything you've done."

"We can't stay here," Harry said. "We can't duck it." Tom rose and sat down.

"I have to tell Sarah," he said. Her employer had agreed to release her so she could be in court for the verdict.

"I want to call my father," David said.

"Maybe he's better off if you don't call him," Joe said.

"I have to call him."

"Do it!" Harry said, fiercely. "Let's get it over with!" He looked at Joe, and his voice fell. "I'm so goddamn scared."

While Tom talked with Sarah, Maddox was in the barbershop. He never shaved himself on the mornings he had a haircut. The barber shaved him and usually gave Maddox a shampoo. Maddox was in the chair for an hour, and when he emerged, he could hear, faintly, the police radio in his car. Inside, as he turned the ignition key, the dispatcher said, "Two-one-two, two-one-two." Maddox reached for the microphone on a cord beside the radio.

"Two-one-two."

"Two-one-two to the courthouse," said the dispatcher. "The chief sent down a whole detail. The jury's coming in." Maddox replaced the microphone.

"More waste," he said, and turned the wheel, making an illegal horseshoe turn.

In the courtroom Tom stood beside the defense counsel table, watching the doors, waiting for Sarah. His briefcase lay in the far corner of the first row, behind the defendants. Tom had told the bailiff he was saving the place. The courtroom was full. The reporters were in their chairs before the rail. Tom saw the district attorney and his assistant at the prosecution table. He could see

Doris Ashley and Hester and her husband in the first row beside the aisle. "Tom?"

Joe motioned to him. Tom wanted to yell, "Leave me alone!" He couldn't talk anymore. He had nothing left to say. He was out of it now. Everyone was out of it now. The twelve men in the jury room had Joe's answer. "Tom!" Joe motioned once more, and leaned back in his chair. Tom stopped beside him. Joe craned his neck and whispered, "If we're . . . do they take us straight to prison right here?" Harry heard him, looking at Tom, waiting.

Mike heard him. "Can't we even . . . ?" He stopped. "I never really believed it until today," he said.

Joe pulled at Tom's arm. "Tom." David Kwan saved him.

"There's my father!" David jumped up as though he were being rescued. "He needs a place to sit!" Tom saw the little man standing in front of the doors, holding his hat over his chest, looking from side to side, uncertain and frightened.

"I'll help him," Tom said, and as he left them gratefully, he saw Sarah enter the courtroom. He forgot Joe, forgot the others, forgot the jury. He passed the empty jury box and didn't know it. He didn't know he was smiling. He had been with Sarah less than two hours ago when she had driven him and Joe to his office, but he hurried toward her, waving, trying to be taller so she could find him across the massed spectators. He felt as though they were being reunited. "Sarah."

He had her, had her hand in his. "Mr. Kwan," Tom said. The frightened man stiffened, turning to face his accuser, waiting to be seized and punished. "You're with us, Mr. Kwan," Tom said. "This is Sarah, Joe's sister. Don't be afraid." He led them, single file, along the back wall of the courtroom to the far side.

Sarah's hand closed tightly over his. "I'm afraid," she whispered. "After you called, I was afraid to come, and I was afraid not to come. I'm afraid to see Joe, see any of them. I'm afraid to see the jury. I'm afraid to listen. I'm making it worse for you."

"No, never," Tom said. He turned his head to look at her. "Never, Sarah." They reached the first row and Tom took his briefcase. "You can sit here, Mr. Kwan. You can both sit here." Tom saw the bailiff crossing the well to the door beside the empty jury box. "I have to go." Sarah's hand slipped from his as though they were being separated forcibly.

Across the courtroom, on the other side of the aisle, Doris Ashley was completely alone. She was facing the flag but didn't see it. She saw Windward. She concentrated on Windward. She would be back soon, back safe very soon. Her ordeal would be over very soon. Tomorrow morning, early, she would take Theresa and Amelia in hand. Their holiday was ending. Their days of loafing were over. Doris Ashley intended to have Windward glowing by the end of the week. She would wait a reasonable period before accepting any invitations, before entertaining. She would be in seclusion for a little while, regaining her strength after her terrible experience. She needed a motif for her first social evening at home.

In front of her, at the prosecution table, Leslie McAdams said, "Here they come." Philip Murray saw the bailiff enter the courtroom and hold the door as the jury followed him. The district attorney scratched his arm.

"What the hell are they waiting for?" whispered Mike Yoshida. The bailiff crossed the courtroom, opening the door beside the bench.

"Shut up," Joe whispered. "For Jesus Christ's sake, shut up." He looked at the jury, trying to see inside their heads. He was praying. He heard the door and turned as the bailiff stopped, facing the courtroom.

"Hear ye, hear ye, hear ye, the District Court of the County of Honolulu, Oahu, Territory of Hawaii, Honorable Judge Samuel Walker presiding, is now in session," said the bailiff. The judge reached his chair. "Be seated. Number one-eight-four-seven, People versus Joseph Liliuohe, Harry Pohukaina, David Kwan, Michael Yoshida."

Judge Walker looked out at the courtroom. "In a minute I'll ask the jury for its verdict," the judge said. "You're here as guests of the court. There will be no disturbances in the court, no demonstrations. I'm warning the press, too. We'll do this in an orderly manner." The judge gave the courtroom time to let his words sink in. He waited for absolute silence. "Gentlemen of the jury, have you reached a verdict?"

The foreman rose. "Your Honor, we have not been able to agree on a verdict," said the foreman, telling the judge what he already knew.

"It's a hung jury," whispered the New York newspaperman to Jeff Terwilliger. "Halfway around the world for a hung jury!"

"*Tom!*" Joe was bent over the table. The others were bunched together, leaning forward.

"It's a mistrial," Tom whispered. They weren't going to prison! He had kept them from going to prison!

"Your Honor!" Murray was standing beside his chair, looking across the courtroom at the jury box. "Your Honor, I ask that the jury be polled."

"All right, Mr. Murray," the judge said. "Mr. Foreman, the district attorney has asked for a poll. You may tell the court the results of the last vote taken by the jury, *but*," the judge said, his voice ringing, "you may not tell the court whether the vote was for innocent or guilty."

"So I'm sure I got it straight, Your Honor, you're asking the number who voted one way and the number who voted the other way."

The judge pointed the gavel at the foreman. "Exactly," he said. "You're correct. The numbers. Only the numbers."

"Yes, sir," said the foreman. "Only the numbers. Ten to two." Almost everyone in the courtroom, including the newspapermen, looked at Tanoye Fujimoto and Andrew Lihilini sitting near the foreman in the jury box. Murray whirled around, turning his back and closing his briefcase. "The vote was ten to two," said the foreman.

The judge swung the gavel, hitting the bench once. "The jury having failed to reach a verdict, it is herewith dismissed," the judge said. He saw the defense lawyer standing. "A trial date will be fixed by the presiding judge. The defendants will be continued in bail pending their appearance in court," said the judge.

"Your Honor, I move that the charges against my clients be dismissed," Tom said.

"Denied," said Judge Walker. "This court is adjourned." Jeff Terwilliger was on his feet and running before the judge dropped the gavel. The reporters scattered, moving toward the gate and the aisles at each side of the courtroom.

The jury rose. Tom stood beside his chair, facing the jury box. The twelve men began to file out. Someone, Joe or Mike Yoshida, jostled Tom, but he pushed the intruder aside, watching the jury. Tanoye Fujimoto kept moving. But as Andrew Lihilini reached the foreman's chair, he stopped. He looked back, and for only an instant his eyes met Tom's.

Sarah was standing, trapped in the first row by the rush of reporters. She couldn't reach Tom or Joe, couldn't come out into the aisle. She saw Joe with Tom, saw David Kwan approaching to reach his father, saw Harry and Mike waving their arms and talking, but she couldn't hear them, couldn't hear anyone, although the courtroom was full of voices.

At the defense table Harry said, "Another goddamn trial." He kicked a chair.

"We're right back where we started," said Mike Yoshida.

Tom felt like punching him. "You're wrong!" he said. "You're dead wrong! You're not on your way to prison! You're on your way home! You're free!"

"We're free till the next time," Joe said.

"Next time the verdict will be innocent!" Tom said. "Next time you'll be free forever!" He was absolutely certain.

"Yeah, sure," said Mike, yanking at the knot of his tie to unbutton his shirt collar. He'd been choking since the first day of the trial.

Fifteen feet away, Gerald rose, buttoning his jacket, watching the gang at the defense table. "We won't leave just yet, Gerald," said Doris Ashley. "We'll wait until these cattle have finished stampeding." He didn't reply. "You can sit down." He was tired of her orders. He saw the girl with the gang, joining the celebration. They were ready for a hot time. They would pass around the okolehao tonight, laughing at the haoles they had whipped, at Hester Murdoch and her sap of a husband. Their crippled lawyer and the girl were coming toward the gate now with the others following. The big fellow, the leader, Joe, moved ahead, still running the show, opening the gate, letting the others pass him. They were close enough for Gerald to see their sweaty faces. They were like chimps, dressed in suits to show off their tricks, only they weren't behind bars, they weren't trapped. He was trapped. "Gerald."

Doris Ashley came to her feet. "We're ready," she said. "Hester? Baby, we're ready." The last spectators were leaving the courtroom. Gerald saw a man come through the doors. He went through the people as though they weren't there, and as he approached, Gerald recognized him. It was the detective who had come for him in the Whispering Inn, who had plunged Gerald into his nightmare.

"Mrs. Ashley, a small army is out in the alley," Maddox said. "Reporters and photographers. I've brought some officers with me, and maybe we can make it easier for you folks." He paused. "Captain Maddox."

"Of course," said Doris Ashley. "Thank you, Captain. I'll remember to mention your name to Chief Fairly."

They followed Maddox out of the courtroom. Six policemen in uniform formed a circle around them. On the first floor the police car was beside the door to the alley. The two cops were waiting. Gerald could see the mass of reporters. "Give us a minute," Maddox said, and to the officers, "Move them back."

The policemen went out into the alley, hands raised, walking into the newspapermen and pushing. "Now," Maddox said, opening the door wide. Doris Ashley took Hester's hand.

"Hurry, Gerald," Doris Ashley said. Gerald heard the reporters yelling their questions. The flash guns exploded. He blinked and bumped into Hester, and then they were in the back seat, and Maddox slammed the door, slapping the car roof.

"Move it, move it," Maddox said.

Squished in the middle of the back seat, Hester could see only the two garrison caps, the two necks, the two sets of shoulders in front of her. She could see the bulge of fat over the driver's shirt collar. Bryce's skin was like a drum. He was like David, like the pictures of Michelangelo's masterwork in her book of the Renaissance. After all these months, Hester could see him, see every inch of him as though he were alone with her. She closed her eyes and opened them, looking out of the window, studying everything she saw, concentrating to drive Bryce out of her mind. She made a sacred vow to destroy the Michelangelo immediately, the instant she reached the carriage house. She would tear the picture to pieces, but even as she made her oath, she saw Bryce once more. She wanted to weep. She wanted to cry out for help, because she was powerless to stop herself. She had to see him one last time. She swore it would be good-bye. She would send a letter to Pearl Harbor where it was safe.

In her corner beside Hester, Doris Ashley met her setback head-on. She had all her life refused to shrink from whatever obstacle lay in her path. She could not survive otherwise. She could not lock herself away, extracting the pity of her friends. She abhorred pity. The donor became, instantly, her superior. Doris Ashley refused to acknowledge anyone's superiority. She would face the new trial when the day came. She could not now consider the new trial in Hester's presence. She would allow Hester to recover from the punishment of the last weeks and months. She would maintain eternal vigilance, satisfying Hester's every wish, every demand. Meanwhile, she would, immediately, tomorrow morning, commence her plan. Amelia and Theresa would scour Windward, would bring Windward to a glow. In a few weeks, she would open her doors again. She would limit her entertaining to her closest friends. Tomorrow she would think of a motif for her first dinner.

Between the alley flanking the courthouse and the gates of Windward on Kahala Avenue, no one in the police car spoke.

They rode in silence. Both cops left the car to open the rear doors. Gerald thanked the police, and Doris Ashley thanked them. "We're home, baby," she said, but Hester was gone. Hester was running down the path, past Windward toward the carriage house. "Her clothes," Doris Ashley said to Gerald. "All her clothes are here." He left her as though she hadn't spoken.

Gerald could see Hester ahead until the land sloped sharply and she dropped from sight. For an insane moment he wanted to dash after her, catch her, ask why she was running from him, from her husband, shake an answer from her. The impulse passed, and Gerald almost stopped. He was exhausted. He felt as though his strength had been drained. He wanted to lie down. The trial was over but nothing was over. Nothing had changed. Those four apes were roaming the streets. He came to the carriage house as though the elegant, two-story structure was a hell-hole.

Inside, the air was stale. The rooms felt close. Gerald had lived alone all through the trial. He had kept the kitchen and the bedroom clean, making his own bed every morning before he went downstairs for coffee. He opened all the windows and listened for a sound from Hester. He felt as though he were in a tomb.

Gerald did not like whiskey, and the bootleg liquor was repugnant. He always kept a bottle for guests and now, in despair, he went into the kitchen for a drink. He took the bottle from the cupboard, and a glass, but he set both down. Gerald discovered, shamefully, that he had thought only of himself from the time the jury foreman announced they could not agree. He had not even considered Hester's feelings. Hester, not he, had been on trial. Hester would be on trial once more, forced to undergo a second inquisition. Gerald said, aloud, *"You . . ."* and paused, reviling himself. He was no better than the two men in the Officers' Club. He left the kitchen, climbing the stairs.

The bedroom door was open but Gerald stopped and knocked. Hester was on her bed, atop the bedspread that covered the pillows. She had slipped off her shoes, and she was curled up, eyes wide, looking at Gerald without a sign of recognition. She was in Bryce's arms. "I want to tell you how sorry I am," Gerald said.

"Thank you. Thank you, Gerald."

"Would you like me to open the windows?" He crossed the bedroom. "I've been closing them every morning to keep the

dust out," he said. He stopped between the beds. "Can I bring
you something?"

"No, thank you. Thank you, not now," Hester said. He felt
like a stranger, like a trespasser. "Thank you." She was back
with Bryce before he was out of the bedroom.

Gerald came down the stairs. The carriage house was still
stuffy. He removed his jacket and rolled up his sleeves. He stood
at the windows in the living room facing the sea, welcoming the
strong breeze from the Pacific. Gerald remembered that he had
not eaten lunch. He swung around, returning to the kitchen,
scooping up the bottle of bootleg to remove it from sight. Gerald
opened the refrigerator, studying the interior. Sometimes he
liked a snack before sleeping, and he had shopped while he was
alone in the carriage house. Gerald bent forward, like a child
geared for a feast. A trace of a smile creased his face.

When Gerald knocked on the bedroom door once more, he
was balancing a tray on his left hand. The tray was filled: sliced
hard-boiled eggs, sardines, abalone, liverwurst, a small bowl of
mustard and another of mayonnaise, crackers, cookies, milk,
napkins, plates, and flatware. "Fit for a king," Gerald said. "Or
a queen."

He set the tray on the night table. Hester turned on the bed
reluctantly, losing Bryce. She could not spoil Gerald's surprise.
She pushed herself up, and Gerald spread a napkin over her lap.
"A person has to eat, my grandmother always said." He took a
plate, and knife and fork, standing at attention, playing the
waiter. "Would madame care to choose?"

"Anything," Hester said, and quickly, "You choose, Gerald."

"Very good, madame." He took small portions, arranging the
food carefully. Gerald set the plate on the napkin and gave
Hester another napkin. "*Bon appetit*," he said, remembering his
Academy French. Gerald took the second plate, chose sparingly,
and sat down on his bed, knees together, straight as a ramrod. "I
hope you like everything."

Hester remembered Bryce's forays. They stole sugar cane or
pineapple and sped away, stopping miles beyond to gorge
themselves, eating like animals, hands and faces sticky and wet.
Their hands were full, and Bryce would kiss her, his lips soft
and hot. She could feel his lips, now, here on her bed. "Would
you like some milk?"

Gerald was holding the glass. She did not want to disappoint
him. He had been so patient, so considerate. He had saved her
from her mother. Hester could not have endured the weeks in
Windward if Gerald had not been there, through dinner and the

evening, and when she woke. She nodded and their hands touched as she took the glass. "Let me have your plate," he said.

Hester obeyed. She ate, dutifully, everything he had given her. She drank the milk. "Dessert!" He was standing over her with the tray. Hester took a cookie. Gerald set down the tray and watched her nibbling on the cookie. Her ankles were crossed. Her dress was bunched up, just covering her knees. "Feel better?" Hester nodded. She felt stuffed and drowsy. Gerald took the plate and the napkin from her. He stood over her for a moment, and then sat down on her bed. "Hello." He put his hand on her thigh and leaned forward, moving his hand until he touched her breast, and kissed her. He pushed his arm under her shoulders, kissing her. Holding Hester captive, Gerald lay down beside her. "Darling." He began to raise her dress. "Sweetheart." His hand dropped to her thigh, fumbling, pulling, insistent. "It's been so long."

Hester accepted him. She welcomed him, needing to obliterate Bryce, drive Bryce forever from her mind and body, but she was unprepared for Gerald's attack.

He thrust himself upon her. He began to groan, "Ah-ah-ah-ah," in short, harsh grunts. His chin dug into her shoulder. His fingers dug into her. He was clawing, hurting her. "Ah-ah-ah-ah." Hester raised her hands, pushing his face away from her.

"Stop! Stop!" She rolled from side to side, pushing his face, hitting him, writhing on the bed to rid herself of him. "Stop!" she cried, and turned once more, her entire body heaving until she was free. She rolled away, rolled out of the bed, ran as though he were after her, reached the bathroom, slammed the door and locked it. She fell against the door. She had to bathe. She had to scrub herself. She had to rid herself of him, but she was helpless. Sobbing, she slid to the floor, huddled against the door.

PART
3

"STANDEASY, Lieutenant," said the admiral in his office. The admiral's driver had appeared at the *Bluegill* around eleven o'clock the morning after the trial, bringing Gerald to headquarters. "You know Commander Saunders." Gerald exchanged greetings with Jimmy Saunders.

"Your trial would be a joke if it wasn't tragic," said the admiral. "Jimmy." Saunders gave Gerald an official Navy communications form. "Read it, Lieutenant," said the admiral.

"Comfourteen to Secnav," Gerald read. "A cunning native lawyer and two henchmen made a mockery of justice here yesterday. Jury unable reach verdict because two natives firmstood. Law here impotent. Intend to protect families of officers and men my command." The admiral had sent the cable to ward off another dispatch from Washington.

"Take my respects and sympathy to Hester, Lieutenant," said the admiral. "And to her mother. You've all had a bad time." He crossed the office with Gerald. "My door is always open to you, son."

The admiral returned to his desk. From the middle drawer he took a copy of his message to the Secretary of the Navy. Across the top he wrote, "For your information. Glenn Langdon, Admiral, U.S.N."

He folded the Navy form and slipped it into a long white business envelope and sealed it. The admiral addressed it to Senator Floyd Rasmussen in Washington. "Chief!"

In the corridor Gerald saw two officers approaching. He bent over a water fountain, grateful for the refuge, hoping they hadn't recognized him, keeping his head averted until they passed. He straightened up, walking swiftly to a stairwell. "My door is always open to you, son," Gerald said to himself. "*Son!*" He felt as though he carried a brand.

The admiral's driver saw the lieutenant approaching the doors in headquarters, and came out of the limousine, standing at attention. The lieutenant looked like he had just been released from solitary confinement. "About time for lunch, sir," said the driver. "Would the lieutenant like to be dropped off at the Officers' Club?"

Gerald stopped in front of the driver, facing the enlisted man. "I would *not* like to be dropped off at the Officers' Club. I would like to be returned to the *Bluegill*, do you understand? Is that simple enough English?"

"Yes, sir, the *Bluegill*, sir." The driver stared straight ahead at nothing. An enlisted man didn't look directly at an officer, and the driver didn't want any trouble. He had the best duty at Pearl. He remained at attention until he was sure the lieutenant was comfortable before closing the door.

Gerald couldn't keep his hands still. He drummed his fingers on the seat. The *Officers'* Club! He could still see, vividly, those two swine, still hear them saying Hester had invited, had welcomed the apes in the convertible. "You're not in a funeral procession, driver!"

The admiral must have really chewed his ass, the driver decided. He turned carefully, taking a shortcut.

As the driver stopped at the submarine pens, Gerald opened the door. "Stay put," he said, and stepped out of the limousine. He could see officers and men leaving the sub for chow. Someone hailed Gerald, but he continued walking, waving his arm to acknowledge the greeting. He couldn't listen to another expression of sympathy, couldn't shake another man's hand, couldn't bear to repeat his litany of gratitude. He felt logy from lack of sleep. His legs were heavy. He was sick with fatigue, with weariness. "Hi, Lieutenant."

Gerald hadn't seen Duane York. The short, slight torpedoman in faded work denims and white cap had come out of nowhere. "I didn't even see you."

"I guess I'm pretty easy to miss," Duane said. He grinned. For a single crazy instant Gerald wanted to throw his arms around the skinny enlisted man. It seemed to Gerald that Duane was the only real friend he had in the world.

"Do you have any plans, Duane? For lunch?" Duane's hunch had been right. The lieutenant looked like he was walking in his sleep when Duane had spotted him.

"Just hit the chow line," Duane said. "I can skip that anytime."

"I don't want you to skip lunch," Gerald said. "Why don't we drive off the base somewhere?"

"Okay with me, sir," Duane said. How many officers would ask an enlisted man to have lunch? None, zero. There weren't any like the lieutenant. Duane would have gone AWOL if the lieutenant had asked him.

The lieutenant didn't say another word all the way to his car. He was back walking in his sleep again. Duane almost said the lieutenant ought to make sick call. "Do you want me to drive, sir?"

Gerald nodded, giving Duane the keys. In the car he removed his cap, dropping it on the dashboard. Every now and then Duane would steal a look. The lieutenant sat there like he was hypnotized. He was in bad shape. All of a sudden he hit the door with his fist. "They're guilty!"

So Duane had the answer to the riddle. "Hell, I knew that from the start, Lieutenant," Duane said.

"You and I know it but nobody else does," Gerald said. He hit the door again. "Those bastards are out there, free as the breeze, *bragging!*"

Duane stopped at the entrance for the Shore Patrol to wave them on. He drove out of Pearl Harbor. He didn't care if they never ate. He'd let the lieutenant decide. "I'd like to round up those bastards and *beat* the truth out of them!" Gerald said.

The idea hit Duane like a ton of bricks. At first he felt winded, like he'd been charging uphill or something. He shifted in the seat, closer to the window for some air. He stole another look. The lieutenant sat beside him like he was on his way to the brig. Duane moved his hands, gripping the wheel high up. He felt like someone had sounded battle stations, and in a way he was right. Duane never thought of backing off because nobody had ever treated him like the lieutenant. The lieutenant had proved how he felt about one hundred times. It was Duane's turn now.

"I know how you feel, sir, for a fact," Duane said. "Beating the truth out of them and all. But you can't do it. Lieutenant?" When Gerald turned, Duane said, "I can."

"You!" Gerald began to shake his head.

"Me and some friends," Duane said. Gerald was shaking his head.

"You can't," Gerald said. "You can't. It's out of the question, Duane. It's out of the question." Duane turned off the road onto the shoulder and stopped.

"Sir, you said once I was a good friend. I remember the words," Duane said. " 'You're a good friend, Duane.' Up to now it's the other way around, Lieutenant. *You've* been a good friend to me, but I never had a chance to prove I'm a good friend to you. Here's my chance." Gerald began to shake his head.

"I couldn't let you take the risk," he said.

"Listen, Lieutenant. Okay? Just listen," Duane said. "They're guilty. The cops and the judge and the jury don't believe it. Only thing left is to show everyone the proof. Let me get it for you," Duane said. "I want to get it for you."

After inspection the following Saturday morning, the *Bluegill* emptied. Officers and men left the base for weekend liberty. Only the watch detail under the command of Ensign Denis Watrous remained. Ensign Watrous was forward, beside the conning tower ladder, when he saw Gerald. The ensign smiled. "Lieutenant, if you're that much in love with the boat, I can arrange for you to spend the weekend here."

"I wouldn't deprive you of the fun," Gerald said. "I forgot my tennis stuff." He made his way aft to the torpedo room. Gerald opened a tool locker and took out the small canvas bag he had bought earlier in the week. The neck of a tennis racquet protruded from the bag. Gerald walked slowly through the submarine, looking everywhere for signs of the crew. When he reached the armory, Gerald stopped in the gangway. He waited, listening. He didn't move. When he was certain he was alone, Gerald opened the canvas bag, holding it in his left hand. With his right he took a key from his pocket and unlocked the armory. The metal door creaked and Gerald moved quickly. He put two .45 caliber automatic revolvers into the bag. From the ammunition locker he took two .45 caliber clips. Gerald came erect, closing the armory and locking it. He closed the canvas bag and waited, listening. He was in the clear. He would be topside in less than a minute. He was on his way when Ensign Watrous came out of the wardroom with a cup of coffee. "I hope you bloody them up, Lieutenant."

"*What?*" Gerald stopped. "What did you say?"

Ensign Watrous pointed at the canvas bag. "Your tennis. I hope you win," he said.

"Oh . . . Sure, thanks," Gerald said. He hurried off the submarine, wiping the perspiration from his upper lip.

With the canvas bag on the front seat beside him Gerald left Pearl Harbor. He stopped on a deserted stretch of the road. Gerald opened the bag. He pushed a clip into one of the guns and set the safety. He loaded the other gun and set the safety on it. He picked up a nine-by-twelve-inch envelope from the seat and opened it. Inside were four sheets of typewritten paper. On each sheet Gerald had typed, "I ADMIT I RAPED HESTER MURDOCH." Below, on the first sheet, Gerald had typed, "JOSEPH LILIUOHE," with a line above the name. The other sheets were for Liliuohe's pals. Gerald looked through the typewritten pages.

Everything was in order. He pushed the paper back into the envelope and set it into the canvas bag.

Gerald drove to downtown Honolulu and stayed the rest of the day. Late in the afternoon he parked near Iolani Palace. He looked at his wristwatch. It was seventeen minutes after five. The canvas bag lay beside him. Gerald took out his wallet. In it, folded, was one hundred dollars. He removed the money and put it under the bag. Gerald's fingers drummed on the steering wheel. He could see the wristwatch in his head.

"Right on time," said Duane York, opening the car door. He was wearing a Hawaiian shirt that fell over his waist. Duane sat down beside Gerald. "Five-thirty." Duane touched the canvas bag. "I take this, right, sir?"

"Right, but you can't use it, Duane."

"*It?* Did you only bring one, Lieutenant?"

"I followed the plan," Gerald said. "You can't use *them*. That's part of the plan, too." He took the money from beneath the bag. "Did you rent the cars?"

"I gave the guy five bucks' deposit," Duane said. "He's holding two for me." Gerald gave him the money.

"I don't want this to cost you a cent," Gerald said.

"Lieutenant, I'm not *buying* those two cars," Duane said.

"You should be prepared for any emergency."

Duane stretched his right leg so he could shove the dough into his pocket. "Everything's on," he said. "See you Monday, Lieutenant." They had set a rendezvous before reveille on Monday so Gerald could return the weapons to the armory. Duane had the canvas bag, and Gerald put his hand over it.

"I want to thank your friends," he said.

Duane looked at him. "Sir, my advice is, you blow." He smiled. "This is a volunteer mission. You're out of it, sir." He opened the car door.

"Duane? Thanks." The slim little man in the loose sport shirt nodded, and left.

A few minutes after eight o'clock a car stopped in the dark near an intersection in Papakolea. Duane York was behind the wheel. Another car coming toward him stopped on the far side of the intersection. The driver blinked his lights and Duane responded. Forrest Kinselman was driving the other car and Wesley Trask was with him. Conrad Hensel was beside Duane. All four were enlisted men serving aboard the *Bluegill*. "Guess we're in it now," Connie said.

Duane studied him. "You want to leave, leave."

"I said I'm in, I'm in," Connie rolled down the window to spit. "I wish I had a snort."

"Why don't you just blow?"

Connie swung around, bumping the canvas bag on the seat. "Lay off, Duane. I said I'm with you, I'm with you."

"Okay, but forget the snorts," Duane said. "We made a battle plan and you never change a battle plan."

They watched the intersection. A man crossed the street. Another. Two women. A woman carrying an infant and holding a little girl by the hand. A man and a woman. Two boys in their early teens. "Don't the bastards ever come home?" Duane said.

Long afterward Connie leaned forward, his head almost touching the windshield. "Over there." Two elongated shadows moved into the intersection under the arc light.

They heard someone say. "I'm supposed to be out with my father in the morning."

"Sleep on the boat," someone said.

Duane reached into the canvas bag for the .45 automatic. It was like holding ice. "Get set."

"How do you know they're the guys?"

"I've seen them," Duane said. They were both whispering. Then he saw two of them but they were too far away to identify. He took the big gun from the canvas bag, leaning out of his window for a better look. Christ, he had two of them, the young kid and another one. "Quick!" Connie came out of the car and slammed the door. Duane's heart was going a mile a minute. He didn't think about it. His mouth was dry. He didn't think about it. He left the car with the automatic, waiting in the shadows while Connie came out after them.

"Hey, where the hell am I?" Connie asked. "How do I head back to town?" David Kwan and Harry Pohukaina stopped and Connie stopped.

"You have to turn around," David said, pointing directly at Duane.

"Show me, huh?" They were coming now, the young kid and the other one. Duane began to circle them, staying out of the light. "Which way is shortest? I'm low on gas," Connie said.

Duane's heart was coming through his shirt. He didn't think about it, walking straight out into the light, pointing the gun. "Suppose you show him? Both of you." Their mouths were open like fish on the beach. "Start walking! Move! Move!" They had to clear the intersection before someone showed up.

"You heard him," Connie said, shoving David. He shoved

Harry, herding them toward the other car. Wesley Trask jumped out and opened the back door, then returned to the front seat.

"Who are you? You're not cops," Harry said. Duane punched him.

"Shut up! Shut up!" Duane shoved him. Forrest had the motor running. "Inside," Duane said, and he jammed the gun into David's back. "Inside, inside." He was sweating to beat the band. Wes was sitting on his knees in the front seat, holding his .45 automatic, facing the rear. Connie shoved Harry into the back and Duane pushed David Kwan. "Beat it," Duane said to Forrest. The car shot forward.

"Two down and two to go," Connie said. He nudged Duane, nodding. "How do you like that operation?"

"We're only halfway there," Duane said.

Akura Yoshida, Mike's mother, was always awake and in her kitchen before dawn. For years she had cooked for the haoles, before and after her marriage, and the hours of service demanded of her had become a habit. Her kitchen light was always the first to glow in the neighborhood. She always started by cleaning the kitchen, which she always cleaned before she went to bed. She had the back door open, the dust pan angled against it, when she heard her son say, "Where the hell are you taking me?"

Akura Yoshida dropped the broom and ran out of the kitchen. She saw a car careen around the corner. She didn't see Mike. She screamed, "Mike!" She ran into the street screaming, "Mike, Mike! They took Mike!" She was a tiny woman with black hair down to her waist. "They took Mike!" she screamed, and began to pull at her cheeks.

Duane drove without his headlights until he was a long way away from Mike's house. Connie was on his knees beside Duane, facing Mike in the backseat, the big gun pointed at the prisoner. "Who are you? Where are you taking me?" Mike asked, looking at the gun, at the finger on the trigger.

"Shut up," Duane said. "All you do is shut up." He turned the key, killing the engine and coasting to a stop a half block from Joe Liliuohe's house. He saw lights come up in a house while he waited for the big one, the top guy, the one who had dumped Hester Murdoch at the hospital after they were done with her.

"He's probably asleep in there," Connie said. "He's probably been home since midnight."

"Where's your buddy?" Duane asked.

Mike was paralyzed. He could hardly breathe. The gun muzzle was as big as a cave, and moving in on him. "I don't know. Honest to God, I don't know." He was going to die. "I don't *know!*" The lights came up in another house.

"They're waking up all over," Connie said.

"Shut up!" Duane grabbed the gun and raised it, aiming at Mike. Duane wanted the head man. "Where is he? You talk or you'll never talk again."

"Honest to God," Mike said. "Honest to God." He felt like he was floating, like he didn't weigh anything, like he was dead already. "Honest to God."

"We better blow," Connie said. "Everyone heard her screaming back there. They'll be out looking for us. There's one!" Duane turned to see a man far ahead, walking toward the car. "He'll spot us and yell for help," Connie said.

"I should've come here first," Duane said.

"It's too late now," Connie said. "It's *too late!*"

"Okay, okay." Duane gave Connie the gun and started the motor. He shifted, releasing the clutch and moving out into the street, watching for the top guy, for Joe.

"Sarah! Sarah! Wake up!" Her mother was standing over the bed. "They took Mike Yoshida from in front of his house!" said Elizabeth Liliuohe. "Men in a car!"

"Where's Joe?"

"Gone! He's gone!" said her mother. Elizabeth Liliuohe dropped down on the bed, covering her face with her hands, rocking back and forth. Sarah grabbed her robe, pushing her feet into slippers. She drove to David Kwan's house. There were people outside so Sarah had her answer without stopping. David was gone. She drove to Harry Pohukaina's house. His brother said, "The cops took Harry."

"Joe's safe," Sarah said to herself, speeding home. "How do you know? He's with Becky Hanatani. You're guessing. You're hoping. They took him. He's safe with Becky!" Sarah didn't believe it.

Sarah ran into her house and called Tom. "I'll be right over," Tom said.

"No, I'll come for you," Sarah said, and hurried into her bedroom, pulling off her robe. Elizabeth Liliuohe was sitting on the bed, looking at the wall.

"I'll never see him," said Sarah's mother.

"Joe's safe," Sarah said, lying. "He's safe."

Tom was in the street walking toward her house when Sarah

drove into his block. "It wasn't the police," he said, opening the convertible door. "I called."

"I knew that right away," Sarah said, starting for Becky Hanatani's apartment. "The police don't have to come in the middle of the night. They can come anytime." Her voice rose. "They're being lynched! They'll be hung! It's what they do in the States!"

"Hawaii isn't the States," Tom said.

"It's worse." Sarah looked at him like he was the enemy. "You were in the States! You lived with people there in the same building! When did you live with any of them here? When did you eat with them here? They can do anything here to any of us! We're not people here!" A lifetime of denigration, of being totally ostracized, prodded her. "They can do anything to us! They do! If someone argues, they throw him out! They don't care if he starves! When the Japanese had their strike, they were thrown off the ranches." Sarah had been a little girl but she remembered the outcry. The Japanese had been treated like traitors. "We're worse than animals!" Sarah said, raging. She was wild with anger. "They *own* us! They own everything! It's their newspapers! You can't see the truth in the newspapers! Hawaii isn't the States," Sarah said, furious even with Tom. "Of course it isn't the States! This is a separate country, their country. They still have their own jails on the ranches. My uncle was put in jail for coming home without permission when my aunt had a baby. They put him in jail. They took away his pay until he came out and went back to work. My uncle heard the plantation manager say you had to keep wages low. He said if you paid higher wages the men worked less." Sarah bit her lip, refusing to cry. "I wish they'd been found guilty. At least they'd be alive." A red light ahead changed to green and Sarah put out her arm.

"Why are you turning? We have to tell the police," Tom said.

"I have to find Joe," Sarah said. "Unless they took him."

Sarah drove to Becky Hanatani's apartment. Becky lived on the second floor. Tom followed Sarah up the stairs to a balcony that ran the length of the building. Sarah pressed the doorbell. There was no answer. She knocked. Tom knocked. Sarah began to pound on the door with her fists. Tom tried to stop her. She fought him. Tom took her wrists, pulling her away from the door. "Sarah!" He held on to her until she quit.

"They took Becky, too," Sarah said, slumping against him, joining her mother in surrender.

Holding her, feeling her weak now and defenseless in his arms, Tom was filled with love. He could not let her sink into despair. "Sarah." He put his face into her hair. "There's another place," he said, and with his arm around her, led her to the stairs. She did not resist. She was dazed and broken by the agony of the last hour.

While he was walking to the convertible Tom said, "I'll drive." He helped her into the car. Tom drove toward the sea. He left Honolulu, reaching open country, continuing until he saw the unmarked road and turned into it toward the beach. Nothing had changed in the ten years since he had walked along it to the ocean. The road was part of the beach, sandy and soft.

The tide was out, almost at dead low. There was a wide, flat swath of glistening, packed sand at the water's edge. Tom stopped. "I'll be right back." By the time he was out of the car, Sarah was out of the car.

"I can't sit here," she said. "Why did you come here? We have to find Joe, *if* we can find him." She spread her arms wide, her voice rising once more. "There's nothing here! You wasted all this time!" She started back toward the convertible.

"Sarah!" He didn't follow her. "Joe might be here," Tom said. She stopped beside the convertible, opening the car door. Tom turned and began to walk away from her. He could see the curve of the cove far ahead.

Tom heard her close the car door. He kept going, listening for the sound of the motor. There was only the ripple of the wavelets on the beach. Then Sarah caught up with him. "No one's here," she said. "The beach is empty. We should be looking for him. Tom!"

He stopped and pointed. They were at one end of the cove. Far back the sea had dug a concave canopy out of the headland. The sea had brought large rocks up onto the beach and these were scattered throughout the cove. Beside a huge boulder, beyond the reach of high tide, was a bundle wrapped in a blanket. Sarah touched him. "Do you think . . . ?"

"Joe and I used to come out here," Tom said. "It's the best body surfing anywhere." He was in a hurry to reach the bundle but Sarah stopped him. She took his hand. They were touching, her hip against his hip, her shoulder against his. Tom could feel her all through him. He wanted to hold her forever.

"What would I do without you?" Sarah pressed his hand to her lips.

"You'll never be without me." He wanted to kiss her but,

holding hands, they continued, making their way through the big rocks.

Joe's head was visible above the hem of the blanket. They could see Becky's head pushed into Joe's shoulder. Tom shoved his shoe into the blanket. "Joe."

"Joe, wake up," Sarah said, bending and shaking him. He came awake, blinking and squinting, and seeing them, grinned.

"Where'd you come from?" He nudged Becky. "Wake up, sleepyhead."

"Ooh, I was in such a deep sleep," Becky said. She was a beautiful young woman with large black eyes and full red lips who would have been spectacular if she was not plump. Becky Hanatani loved food, all food. She loved to cook and eat and watch those with her eat. "Why'd you wake me, huh? Sarah!"

"Hey, Tom, how about some body surfing right now?" Joe asked.

"They took Mike Yoshida, and Harry, and David," Sarah said.

Joe came straight back out of the blanket, his legs thrashing as he kicked to come free. "*Who? Took?* Tom, what is she *talking* about?"

Tom told him of the abductions. Joe came to his feet, wearing shorts. "We have to find them," he said, reaching for his pants.

"Not you," Sarah said. "Joe, it's a lynching!"

"Christ, I don't know where to start looking," Joe said. He pulled on his pants as Becky rose with the blanket around her, turning her back to begin dressing.

"You're not looking for them," Sarah said. "They're looking for *you*."

"We'll take you home, and then I'll go call the police," Tom said.

"The *police!*" Joe was incredulous. "They're the enemies!"

"We're wasting time," Tom said. "You're going home, Joe. You're staying home. People have been kidnapped. So it's police. The police will handle this."

"I'm free, goddamnit," Joe said. "Even their goddamn judge said I'm free."

"Stop arguing," Sarah said. "We have to leave. You're not safe here. You're not safe outside."

Joe picked up the blanket. "I'm afraid to think of those three guys. Do you know how old David Kwan is? He's a *baby!*" Joe started for the convertible, walking ahead of the others. "This whole goddamn thing is my fault."

In the car Sarah said, "Becky, we'll take Joe home first."

"I want to stay with him," Becky said.

"Faster, Tom, faster," Sarah said.

Her mother heard the car and was out of the house before Tom stopped. "He's not here!" she cried, and saw Joe in the backseat. She grabbed Sarah, pulling her out of the convertible to reach Joe.

In the house Joe couldn't stop moving. "I'm supposed to stay here *hiding* while those other guys are out there somewhere?"

"Yes," Sarah said. "Yes, yes, yes."

"You can't help them," Tom said. "Only the police can help them. Sarah, will you drive me?"

Joe picked up the telephone as though he were about to throw it. "Call them for all the goddamn good it'll do."

"They have to start a search," Tom said. "That's why I'm going downtown. A crime has been committed. They can't act like nothing happened." Sarah left the house with him.

"You take the car," she said. "I'm afraid to leave, afraid Joe will get out. Tom?" She touched him. "I want to be here and I want to be with you."

"You're with me," he said. "I told you. You're always with me now. We're never apart now." She kissed Tom, following him to the convertible. "Be careful," she said. "Be careful for me."

Tom drove to police headquarters. The desk sergeant was reading the comics of the Sunday newspaper. "Sergeant?" The comics dropped. "I'd like to see Captain Maddox."

"Tomorrow." The desk sergeant raised the comics. Tom walked toward the corridor. The sound of the scraping shoe annoyed the sergeant. He lowered the comics once more to frown at the intruder.

Tom went to a pay telephone and opened the directory. He put his forefinger under Curtis Maddox and repeated the number silently. He put a nickel into the telephone and gave the operator the number. The ring lasted only a few seconds. "Maddox."

"Captain, my name is Tom Halehone. I . . ."

"The lawyer," Maddox said. He was on his belly beneath the covers. He looked at the clock beside his gun in the holster. It was barely eight o'clock.

"Yes, sir," Tom said. "Captain, three men have been kidnapped."

"Zip, zip, zip," Maddox said. He knew everything already, and nothing in his lifetime had been as bad. He was furious with himself for being in bed, as though he could have, somehow, blocked the kidnappers. Maddox threw back the covers, swinging his legs over the bed and sitting naked, holding the receiver. "What three men?" he asked, wondering about the fourth.

"Mike Yoshida, Harry Pohukaina, and David Kwan," Tom said.

So the halfback was loose. Why was he loose? Maddox cursed himself for wasting time. "Who says they were kidnapped? Who saw it?"

Tom told Maddox Mike Yoshida's mother had seen a car speeding off. "How about the other two?" Maddox asked.

"They're not home," Tom said. "They always come home."

"Everyone who runs away always comes home," Maddox said. What lunatics had grabbed those three?

"Captain, they didn't run away."

"But you decided they were kidnapped," Maddox said. "Go down to headquarters and file a missing persons report."

"I am at headquarters," Tom said. "Captain, I . . ."

"Room one-oh-three," Maddox said. "First door to the left of the trophy case. File a missing persons report." Maddox set the receiver into the cradle like it was an egg. He sat for a little while, and then lifted the receiver and called Harvey Koster at home. He listened to twelve rings. "Your party does not answer," said the operator. Koster was rarely in the Hawaii Club but Maddox called. "Mr. Koster is not here." Maddox went into the bathroom and turned the faucets to fill the tub. Who had snatched those three kids? There had to be more than one in the raid. There had to be more than one car. "Vigilantes," Maddox said, aloud. The town was coming apart. He stepped into the tub.

Maddox was slipping a tie under the collar of a fresh white shirt when he heard the doorbell. He thought it was his young gardener who usually came for his pay on Sunday, but it was someone dressed like an undertaker. Maddox thought he was collecting for missionaries. He put his hand in his pocket and saw the black and yellow convertible in front of his house. So he knew his caller's identity before Tom said, "I'm sorry to bother you, Captain."

"You weren't sorry enough to stay away," Maddox said.

"I filed the missing persons reports," Tom said. "I filed one for each of the three men who were kidnapped."

"You're kind of stuck on that word," Maddox said. "Three kids didn't come home last night. You say they were kidnapped. You don't have any witnesses, and a speeding car is your evidence. Maybe it wasn't speeding, but I'll let it stand. What's the license number? What kind of car, year, make, model, color?"

"It was still dark, Captain."

"They could be home right now," Maddox said.

"I stopped three blocks from here and called," Tom said. "They're not home." He looked at Maddox. "Their mothers are home."

This guy was cute. He didn't have a lot left to learn. "So all you can do is let the police run their own business," Maddox said.

"The officer in the missing persons bureau told me the reports aren't circulated until forty-eight hours after filing," Tom said.

"You're a lawyer, you can figure that one out," Maddox said. "About ninety-nine percent of the missing persons reported are back home within two days. Your pals could be somewhere sleeping off a drunk."

"These aren't beach boys," Tom said. "They don't drink. They weren't together. They're missing separately. Mike Yoshida was alone when he was kidnapped."

Maddox fooled with his tie to keep his hands busy, to keep from reaching for the lawyer. "Somebody saw him picked up?"

"His mother heard him," Tom said. "She didn't hear anyone else." He saw the big man reach for the door. "Captain, they're being lynched!"

"Beat it."

"You have to do *something!*"

"Here's what I'll do," Maddox said. "If you're not in your girl's car in the next thirty seconds, I'll take you downtown myself. I'll book you myself, for trespassing and disturbing the peace. I'm off Sunday but if you make me leave this house, you'll be one sorry kanaka. I'll be the arresting officer and I'll make the complaint. You won't be as lucky as your buddies. You won't make bail. You'll be up on a misdemeanor, not a felony, and you'll be on your way to the work farm for sixty days before I head for lunch tomorrow. You're using up those thirty seconds already, Counselor."

"You don't *care!*" Tom said. He turned away, starting for the convertible. Maddox watched him. The lawyer didn't know it but he was dead wrong.

In the house Maddox knotted his tie and slipped on his holster. He took his jacket off the hanger. Who had nabbed those three? Anyone on the island could have them. The whole bloody island was a suspect. Why had they skipped the halfback, Joe? The halfback was probably the only one of the four who hadn't come home. Those bloody vigilantes had dumped a real load of manure on him. The island could come unraveled over this package.

High atop a gentle slope of hills was an oblong forest. There was always a wind at the summit and the sound of branches and leaves in the wind. "Spooky," Duane had said to himself, when he had reconnoitered the hills earlier in the week.

With his cargo distributed between the two cars, Duane led the way into the hills early Sunday. There was no road into the forest so Duane knew they couldn't be followed. "Pull them up close to the trees," Duane said.

He was holding the .45 automatic, watching his three prisoners. Their backs were bare and their shirts were on the ground beneath rocks to anchor them. Their hands were tied behind their backs and each had a rope around his middle. Each prisoner was tied to a tree, facing the tree. Tying each of the three prisoners were Forrest Kinselman, Wesley Trask, and Connie. "All set," Forrest said.

"Wait," Duane said. He ran back to his car and reached through the open window to drop the .45 into the canvas bag with the other gun. He picked up the envelope the lieutenant had left in the bag. Duane raised the clasp that lay flat against the flap and took out the four white sheets of paper. "I admit I raped Hester Murdoch," Duane read. Below, under a typed line, was the name, "Joe Liliuohe."

Duane cursed him, dropping the sheet of paper into the canvas bag. He read the identical message. The name below the typed line was Harry Pohukaina. Duane read the other two sheets, one for Mike Yoshida, one for David Kwan. He ran back to the prisoners carrying the paper and the envelope.

"Want to read you something," Duane said. " 'I admit I raped Hester Murdoch.' "

"We didn't!" said David.

"All you do is sign, and . . ."

"We never touched her," David said. Duane almost punched him in the mouth.

"Who turned her face lopsided? A bee?" Duane came around the tree so David could see him. "I'm warning you. You're not in a court now. This is a different kind of court. I'm running this one. Don't pull that bilge with me."

"You're the bilge," said Harry.

"This is your last chance," Duane said. He raised the sheets of paper. "You'd better sign."

"Don't talk to him," Harry said.

"Don't look at him, David. Close your eyes," Mike said.

"You'll sign," Duane said. "I promise." He slipped the papers into the envelope and set it down with a rock atop it. When he came erect, he was facing the prisoners. Duane pushed up on his Hawaiian shirt, reaching for his belt buckle. "I gave you your chance."

All four sailors wore their Navy-issue, broad black leather

belts with metal buckles. As Duane removed his belt, the other captors removed theirs. "You," said Harry. Duane couldn't keep from smiling. He had the bastards. "I'll take David's share," Harry said.

Duane punched him in the face. "You'll both take his share!" he yelled, pulling at his belt buckle, moving back to join his shipmates. Duane stationed himself behind Harry. "I want him," he said and swung. There was a loud crack and Harry shuddered. Duane swung. "Do I have to do it all?" he yelled. Connie swung at Mike Yoshida. Duane shoved Forrest, who swung, hitting David. Wesley Trask was with Connie, taking turns behind Mike.

The prisoners' backs turned red. Blood began to ooze from their skin. Duane was sweating. His arm ached. Why didn't those three bastards sign? The bastards were crazy, taking all that punishment. They were pure crazy. David cried out, a long, soprano wail of pain. "Hold it," Duane said, waving at the sailors. They lowered their belts, gasping from their exertions. "You ready to sign?"

"Don't hit me anymore, please," David said. "Please!" he said, and screamed as the belt, like a hot iron, dug into his flesh.

"Close your goddamn eyes!" Harry said. Duane lunged at David. "Will you sign?"

"We didn't do it. Please, mister, please."

Duane stepped back and hit him again. Blood ran down David's back. Harry and Mike were covered with blood. Deep, raw valleys of mutilated skin crossed their backs. Duane swung. He was the only one swinging. He was ready to use the belt on the sailors. "Are you paralyzed?" He swung again. David screamed. Duane took the end of his belt. "Use your buckles!"

"Stop," David said. The buckle ripped into his back. David said, "Please . . ." and his legs sagged. His head dropped as he lost consciousness. Forrest Kinselman saw David hanging against the tree, saw the bare brown back red with blood, and he vomited. Dropping the belt and vomiting, he tried to run, stumbling, leaving the horror. Wesley Trask ran, and Connie followed him but at an angle, staying clear of Forrest to keep himself from vomiting. Duane was alone. He hated the bastards against the trees but he could not continue. He picked up the envelope and started toward the cars before he remembered Forrest's belt. He couldn't leave any clues. He found the belt and, gasping for breath, left the lying bastards tied to the trees. He was in a rage. After all the work and plans, there was nothing on the sheets of paper but typing. "Let's make tracks," Connie said.

Duane wanted to wrap Forrest's belt around him. He threw it at Forrest. "Do you think nobody knows what a Navy belt looks like?"

"You can't leave them," Forrest said.

"Watch me."

"They'll die here, Duane," said Wesley Trask.

"Don't use my name!"

"We have to cut them loose," Forrest said. Duane took out his knife. "Make it snappy."

Forrest backed away. "I can't look at them." Duane offered the knife to Connie, who opened the car door.

"Gutless wonders," Duane said. He tossed the envelope into the car and started for the trees.

"The rope!" said Connie. "We can't leave the rope!" Duane's heart stopped. He had bought the rope downtown. The guy would remember him. He had forgotten the rope. Those gutless wonders had saved him.

Duane cut David loose first. David slumped to the ground. Duane cut Mike Yoshida's ropes. Mike dropped, falling on his back, moaning and trying to roll. Duane raised his foot to push him over on his belly. Duane cut Harry loose. Harry went down on his knees and toppled forward. Duane bent to cut the ropes around their wrists. Holding the open knife he picked up every inch of rope beneath the trees. With his hands full, Duane ran.

"Here it comes, girls," said Harvey Koster. He was high up on a stepladder, right under the bright lights, with all the girls below. He held a sparkling star. He was beside the Christmas tree, careful of the branches and the needles. The old star was in a box on the floor beneath the stepladder. The floor was stacked with boxes full of Christmas decorations. Koster had seen the new star in a catalogue sent him from San Francisco in August. He had ordered it immediately.

Koster looked down at the eager faces. "Did you ever see anything as beautiful?" Koster and the girls always decorated for Christmas long before Christmas Day. The girls became impatient right after Thanksgiving. By the first week in December Koster had all the boxes in the large, sealed, windowless studio beyond his dressing room. The girls and he knew what was in each box because an exact inventory in Koster's handwriting was taped to every lid.

On the stepladder Koster fastened the star to the top of the tree. He was delighted with his choice. "Look, girls, look!" he said, beaming. Koster was excited by his daring. Many of the

girls expected him to follow the pattern of previous years, starting at the bottom of the tree with the familiar decorations. This
year Koster couldn't contain himself. He had been so impatient
since the arrival of the star. He had not peeked once. "Really,
Stella," he said, to the figure skater on her own rink, "you
needn't pout." Koster made his way down slowly. He looked up
at the star, thrilled with his choice. He knew Stella was angry.
He could feel her eyes boring into his back. He dreaded facing
her but he could not begin the holiday season with a rift in his
family. He approached Stella, quaking. "Won't you forgive
me?" He bent to move Debbie, careful of her skis. "Excuse me,
precious," he said, moving Debbie down the slope to the chalet.
"Stella."

Koster went to his knees beside the figure skater, head bowed.
"Have mercy, my precious." After an eternity, he raised his
head. Stella was smiling! She had forgiven him! Christmas
would be a triumph this year, Koster was positive! He arched his
neck to kiss her and whisper, "You'll be rewarded for your great
heart on Christmas morning."

He rose, brushing his hands against the gray striped butler's
apron he was wearing. He stood among the girls, beaming.
"Shall we begin?" He looked at Sybil in her riding habit astride
Thor, her very favorite jumper. "How shall we begin, Sybil?"
He nodded, beaming with pride. "The Nativity, of course."
Koster went to the boxes, directly to the Nativity. He had
wrapped it carefully in tissue paper on New Year's Day eleven
months ago. As he removed the paper he felt the arm that had
fallen from one of the wise men. Koster was about to tell the
girls he would buy another, more beautiful Nativity, when he
remembered Stella's displeasure because he had begun with the
new star. Koster was shaken. Stella would never forgive him
twice in one day.

"Look, girls, one of the wise men has lost an arm," Koster
said. He spoke directly to Stella. "No sadness, please! I'll mend
it in two shakes." Koster carried the Nativity to his tool chest,
sitting down on the stool. But he could not find glue. Koster was
well aware he could not make any excuses to Stella. "I need
some glue, girls." Sidney Akamura had a pantry full of mending
supplies.

Koster left the studio door open. Sidney Akamura never worked
on the weekend. Koster used the back stairs to the kitchen and he
was crossing it when he heard the muted doorbell at the front
door. No one came to Koster's home unless he was invited.
Koster had waited all week to be alone with the girls. He reached

behind him to untie the butler's apron. Aware that Stella was expecting another trick, Koster hurried through the house.

Maddox had never seen Koster without a suit and a tie. "I don't like busting in on you, Mr. Koster, but I figured I'd better come out. I called but you didn't answer. I called the club."

"I was in the garden earlier," Koster said, lying. "If you're here there must be trouble."

"A lot of it," Maddox said. He entered Koster's home for the first time in his life, following his benefactor into the living room. Maddox had never been anywhere more handsome. He didn't see a trace of Koster. Doris Ashley's house was a stable compared to Koster's home. Koster pointed at a chair. "Sit down, Curt."

"Three of those four fellows in the rape case are missing," Maddox said, standing.

"Missing?" Koster went to a chair and crossed his legs. "Sit down, Curt." Maddox took the chair at which Koster pointed. He leaned forward, holding his hat.

"They were picked up last night," Maddox said. He told Koster of Tom's visit. "It wasn't hit or miss. It was an organized move. They were after all four. Maybe the one they didn't get didn't *come* home last night. These four kids . . ."

"Kids?"

"One of them is twenty years old, Mr. Koster."

"They didn't behave like kids," Koster said. "Tell me how you see it, Curt."

"I think someone, more than one, grabbed these . . . people to make them confess they raped Hester Murdoch."

"It could be a false alarm," Koster said.

"It could be," Maddox said. "It could be they're hanging from trees right now, while we're sitting here."

Koster came straight up from the chair. "Good *grief!* It would take us fifty years to live that down! Washington would say they've been right about us all along. We're uncivilized! We could forget about statehood!" Koster's face became blotchy with color. He pulled at his fingers. Maddox had never seen Koster upset. "Why do you believe the worst?"

Maddox couldn't sit while the other man was standing. He rose. "Not believe, Mr. Koster," Maddox said. "I'm ready for the worst because it's what I usually see."

"So you're guessing," Koster said. "Everything you've told me is a guess."

"I do my job by guessing," Maddox said. "My insides tell me this is bad. I could be dead wrong. I sure hope I'm wrong."

"Give me another guess, Curt."

"They could show up," Maddox said. "They could be killed. They could be killed and never show up, buried somewhere or dumped into the ocean, weighted so they stay on the bottom."

Koster went to a table, lifted a lacquered box, and set it down. "What do they know in Washington?" he asked, and answered his question. "Four natives raped Hester Murdoch. A jury with natives couldn't agree on a verdict. Today three of the four are missing. If they never return, Washington could think they were afraid of a retrial. If they return, or if they're found, then you'll need to act. You told their lawyer to see the missing persons bureau. When do *they* act?"

"They wait forty-eight hours," Maddox said.

"A lot can happen in two days, Curt," Koster said. He left the table and walked toward the door but Maddox didn't move.

"It'll give the people who took them an awful big start," Maddox said. Koster didn't stop and Maddox followed him.

At the door Koster said, "You were right to come, Curt. I'll be here the rest of the day. You can call anytime." He was talking to the twelve-year-old boy he had found sleeping in his warehouse. He opened the door, dismissing the lad, watching him leave.

Koster returned to the kitchen. He took the butler's apron from the chair and suddenly began to tear at it. His face became blotchy once more as he tried to rip the apron apart. He could not. He threw it to the floor and kicked it, following the apron and kicking.

Maddox started for home but stopped less than a half mile from Koster's house. He sat with the motor running. After awhile, he drove on, but within a mile he stopped once more. He heard horses and looked up. Jay and Chloe McCutcheon were out for a ride. They were laughing. The sound of horses' hooves faded. Maddox took off his hat and set it on the seat. "You can't go around killing people," he said, aloud. At the next street he turned right instead of left, driving toward headquarters.

In the Sunday silence of the building Maddox rode the elevator to his office. Standing, he called Al Keller at home. "I don't like busting in on you."

When Keller joined him, Maddox had pictures of Harry Pohukaina, Mike Yoshida, and David Kwan on his desk. "Somebody nabbed them," Maddox said. He told Keller eight other detectives were on their way to headquarters. "Five cars ought to be able to cover this island," Maddox said.

"We'll be out in the county," Keller said. "How about asking the sheriff for help?"

"The sheriff might not be interested," Maddox said. He gave Keller the pictures. "Take a good look." Maddox stood up, unbuttoning his jacket. Everything was tight on him lately. He needed some new suits. The twelve-year-old boy had disobeyed for the first time.

Around four o'clock Sunday afternoon Senso Fujito drove out of his barn on his way to Waikiki. He was in the cab of his Model T flatbed truck, and behind him were two crates of suckling pigs for the chef of the Evening Star Hotel. Senso Fujito did not like driving, or driving alone, or driving in traffic. His oldest son was usually with him because Senso's back gave him constant discomfort. But his son had stepped on a rusty nail the day before.

Senso was a long way from home when he saw the drunken man beside the road on his right. The drunkard could hardly stand. He was naked, he didn't have a shirt. Senso swung far over to the left, directly into the opposite lane, to keep away from the drunkard, a soldier or sailor. The man staggered into the road, toward the truck. Senso would crash. The crates would fall and break, and the suckling pigs would escape. Senso would have to walk back to the farm, he would be all night on the road. The man fell.

Senso saw the other two drunkards on the ground beside the road, and finally, as he managed to escape, passing the three, saw the blood. He pushed down on the brake. When Senso came out of the truck cab, Harry Pohukaina was standing again. "Help's," he said, and dropped into the dust.

Maddox used the siren on his way to Mercy Hospital. Beside him Al Keller said, "You'll disturb the patients, Captain."

"Tough," Maddox said, but he cut the siren. "Who the hell am I mad at?" he said to himself. He saw the black and yellow convertible as soon as he reached the emergency room entrance.

Inside, Harry Pohukaina was on his belly on the table. His arms hung over the table and his hands were curled around the square metal legs, holding on to stay alive. He couldn't take anymore. They had to stop hitting him. Either they had to stop or kill him.

Frank Puana was working on Harry. Peter Monji, the orderly, was on the other side of the table, helping the doctor. The doctor had seen the three in the farmer's truck before they were carried into the emergency room. "One, two, three," the doctor said to

Peter, pointing at the guys, flat out on the truck bed with the pigs. They treated David Kwan first, and he and Mike Yoshida were already upstairs.

Maddox came through the emergency room door and stopped as though he had hit a wall. Al Keller almost walked into the captain. Keller stepped aside and said, "Holy . . . Jesus . . . Christ . . . *Holy Jesus Christ.*"

Maddox grimaced, his lips tight across his teeth. The orderly glanced at him and Frank looked up. "If they hadn't been found, they'd be dead."

"Where are the others?" Maddox asked. Frank bent over the patient. Maddox reached the orderly. On the table, the boy's back was like mud. "Tell me, kid, and be quick," Maddox said.

"They're upstairs," Peter said. "Doctor treated them first."

"Who found them?" Maddox asked.

"You're interfering with my work," Frank said.

"Shut up! You do yours and I'll do mine," Maddox said, and to Peter, "Who found them?"

"A farmer," Peter said. "A pig farmer."

Maddox gestured. "Al." Keller's stomach was churning. He came forward, watching the floor. "Tell him," Maddox said to Peter, and moved around the orderly and around the table, stopping beside Frank. He bent sideways to look at the patient who was holding on to the table legs. The kid's eyes were closed. Maddox straightened up. He talked into Frank's ear, talking low. "Stop playing prima donna. The sooner I learn things, the sooner I can start looking for them. Can he talk?"

"Are you blind? The man's not conscious!" Frank said.

Harry heard the voices far in the distance. They had stopped beating him and were leaving. "Help's." Maddox heard him and squatted, his face level with the table. The kid's eyes were open.

"I'm a cop, son," Maddox said. "I want whoever did this to you. I need your help. How many were there? Describe the car. Where did they take you? Talk as long as you can talk."

"Four," Harry said, and, "Two cars, 'n guns. Las' night. David 'n me. Mike. Tied us 'n then whipped . . ." His eyes closed. Maddox watched him and came erect, beside Frank.

"Captain," Keller said, and moved away from the table, stopping behind it near the emergency room door. Maddox pushed his hat brim with his forefinger, walking around Frank.

"Nothing!" Keller said, trying to keep his voice down. Keller didn't need to see the patient to see him. Keller saw him, saw what they had done to his back. Keller couldn't control his anger. He would have to stay away from the guys who had done this if they were picked up. "Not his name, nothing!" Keller said, raging. He had almost whacked the stupid orderly. "A pig farmer! They didn't ask him a goddamn thing!"

"They're not cops," Maddox said. "Settle down," and, quietly, "Al. Settle down."

"Yeah," Keller said. He wiped his hands. "A Jap pig farmer. Driving a Model T truck, bringing a load of pigs to town. That's it, Captain. *That's it!*"

"So we start from there," Maddox said. "Sunday. He's bringing in pigs on Sunday so it's not for the butchers. The butchers are closed. He was probably carrying suckling pigs for a luau tonight. The pits are probably burning right now. Take my car, Al. Call for help. Start with Waikiki. Check every cook in every hotel. Work your way downtown. Whoever ordered those pigs will know the farmer's name, know where he lives." Maddox opened the emergency room door. "Tell the dispatcher to send someone out for me. I'll be at headquarters." Maddox put his hand on the redhead's shoulder, moving him through the door.

Someone said, "How is he?" and when Maddox turned, he was facing their lawyer with the patient on the table between them. The lawyer didn't look like a missionary now.

Tom had left Sarah on the second floor with David Kwan's father. He had collapsed beside David's bed, and Tom and Sarah had taken him to the visitors' room. "You were right, Captain," Tom said. "They were missing but they showed up. It didn't take forty-eight hours or twenty-four hours. Here they are." Tom's arm shot out. "Here's Harry, what's left of him. David and Mike are upstairs, what's left of them! You can tear up the missing persons reports."

Maddox crossed the emergency room. "Can they talk?"

"Can they . . . ?" Tom said, and stopped. He had to get away from the big man. He couldn't be near the detective. Tom waved at Harry. "Can he talk? Why don't you look at him? You won't even look at him!" Tom whirled around, but Maddox had him.

"Where's the other one? Liliuohe?" Maddox asked. He held on to Tom's arm. "Stop wasting my time, lawyer. I'm into a criminal offense and you're obstructing justice. Do you tell me here, or do you tell me downtown?"

"He's at home!" Tom pulled his arm free but only because Maddox released him. Maddox watched the crippled lawyer leaving, dragging his foot. He was too young to be scared.

Fifteen minutes later a uniformed policeman opened the emergency room door. "Captain? Are you ready?" Maddox nodded. He followed the cop. The squad car stood parallel to the door. Maddox stopped beside it, removing his hat and reaching for his handkerchief. He wiped the sweatband. The two cops in the front seat watched him. Holding his hat, Maddox opened the front door. "Hop in the back, son," he said to the cop beside the driver. Maddox took his place. "Downtown," he said, and reached for the radio telephone beneath the dashboard.

"Maddox," he said to the dispatcher. "Joseph Liliuohe is one of those four in the Murdoch rape. He lives in Papakolea. He was booked so the desk sergeant will give you his address. Send three-two-six over there. If he isn't home, tell them to call me downtown. If he is home, tell them to stay there. If he leaves, they leave with him. Wherever he goes, they go, including the toilet. They stay until they're relieved. Starting now there's a twenty-four-hour watch on him."

The day was ending. Streetlights came up as Maddox was driven to headquarters. He had forgotten the encounter with the lawyer. He thought only of the kid on the table in the emergency room, and of the youngest one, David Kwan.

Maddox tried to focus, tried to put his mind on the lynching party. There had been four in two cars, with two guns. Guns and whips. Not whips. The wounds were too widely spaced. They had used leather. Who? *Who?* Anyone on the island. Maddox's fury embraced the entire population. He could swear only for Al Keller and himself. Maddox held his hat in his lap, turning it slowly. "Drop me off in front," Maddox said. He walked slowly, carrying his hat. The street was deserted. The long lobby was empty and dimly lit. "Place smells," Maddox said, aloud. He rode the elevator to the second floor, standing with his back arched against the rear wall of the car. His shoulders ached. He ached, all through him. Maddox felt as though he had been awake and moving for a week. "Some Sunday," he said. He would have to see those three kids in the hospital tomorrow. "Some Monday," he said.

In his office he sat down behind his desk and put on his hat. He looked at the clock over the door. It was almost seven. Some time later he leaned forward, reaching for the telephone to send someone out for coffee and a sandwich. He changed his mind, replacing the receiver.

At eight-thirty Maddox reached for the receiver once more. "Maddox," he said to the dispatcher. "Al Keller has my car. Find him and tell him to call me," Maddox said as his door opened. "Forget it." Al Keller was grinning.

"Senso Fujito," Keller said. "You were right on the nose, Captain. He was delivering to the Evening Star Hotel." Keller reached into his pocket. "He lives way out in hell and gone."

"You didn't expect him to be raising pigs on King Street, did you?" Maddox came out of the chair and Keller gave him the piece of paper with Senso Fujito's address. "Take the rest of the day off."

"How about the farmer?"

"We've been at it all day," Maddox said. "It's dark. He'll tell us where he found those guys and we'll have to wait for daylight." Maddox crossed the office with the redhead beside him. "I'll see him in the morning."

Keller stopped in the doorway. "Why don't I pick you up, Captain?"

"You lost your Sunday. Get acquainted with your kids," Maddox said. "I'll yell if I need help."

Maddox drove home, entering his house through the kitchen. He walked through it in the dark, turning up the light on the night table beside his bed. Standing, he pushed off his shoes and removed his holster, setting it beside the lamp. He emptied his pockets and then took off his clothes, making a mound beside the bed. Maddox dropped onto the unmade bed, raising his arm to press the light switch, and turning in the dark to pull the sheet over him.

When he woke, Maddox found the light switch and looked at his wristwatch. It was five minutes after four. Maddox left the bed, standing naked and arching his back. He went into the bathroom, bending and turning the taps to fill the tub. Who had whipped those guys?

Because of his terrible adventure, which he had recounted in detail to his wife, Senso Fujito overslept. His son's foot was swollen from the rusty nail so Senso was alone with the pigs. By the time he finished feeding the sows and his two boars and filling the water troughs it was almost six o'clock. He was behind already but he had to eat something before he continued. Senso was on his way to the house when he heard the car coming.

Maddox touched the car horn and saw the farmer freeze like he was caught, like he was surrounded. Maddox stopped beside him and raised his hand, showing the farmer the gold-colored police badge. Maddox smiled. "Relax. I need your help."

"I don't talk English good," Senso said.

"You talk good enough," Maddox said. He pointed at the Model T. "Show me where you found them. I'll follow you." Maddox didn't want to drive the farmer and bring him back.

Senso was afraid to say he was hungry. He was afraid to say he was late and alone because his son couldn't walk. His head bobbed up and down, and he hurried to the truck.

Maddox followed, driving in second gear. He wanted to bang the horn. He could have run faster. The farmer was probably too scared to remember. "*You* relax," he said aloud, dropping his right arm across the back of the seat as the Model T turned off the road and stopped. Maddox was at the truck cab before Senso could open the door.

They stood beside the road. "You're sure?" Maddox asked.

"Here," Senso said. He tapped the ground with his foot. "All three here." Maddox looked up. They were at the foot of a hill that sloped gradually. Maddox crossed the road. The ground fell sharply. Those kids could never have made it to the top. He hadn't noticed the farmer. "I go now."

"You go now," said Maddox. He watched the farmer, running like a girl, clambering into the cab. Maddox raised his hand to shade his eyes, looking at the hill on the other side. The Model T moved. Maddox started for his car and stopped suddenly in the middle of the road. The Model T turned right and disappeared into the hill. Maddox ran for his car. "*Sure!*" he said, aloud.

The Model T appeared, backing slowly and making an arc. Maddox stepped on the starter. The Model T stopped and came forward as Senso started back to the farm. Maddox passed the truck, looking ahead, so he didn't see Senso's grateful wave. A few feet beyond Maddox reached the break in the hill. He turned and stopped, leaving the car to walk ahead. He saw the tire tracks almost immediately.

Maddox drove slowly up into the hill. The car bucked and rocked. He reached the crest, leaving the car again, walking slowly, following the parallel rows of flattened brush. He came to the small forest. The sun disappeared. Maddox was in shadows. The land was untouched. Fallen trees, rotting and turning to sawdust, lay everywhere. "They stopped here," Maddox said. As he walked into the forest, he saw a shirt. When he picked it up, he saw another, blown against a tree by the wind. He found the third shirt on the ground beside the four trees standing in a row like poles in a fence. "Tied us," Maddox said, repeating what Harry Pohukaina had told him in the emergency room. The shirts were clean so the kids had been stripped before they were tied.

Maddox went from one tree to the other. He found the scuffed bark. Maddox squatted. The ground, barren without the sun, was damp and hard, tamped down by their shoes the day before.

Maddox straightened up and moved in a slow circle, head down, walking through the forest to the sunlight. He returned, keeping wide of his first route. Maddox searched the forest for almost two hours. He searched the area where the cars had stopped, squatting again and again to run his hands through the thick undergrowth.

"I'm nowhere," he said, rising, his shirt damp with perspiration and sticking to his back. They were running wild in town and all he had to show for it were the victims' shirts. Wiping his sweatband with his handkerchief, Maddox walked through the thick growth to his car.

Maddox came down the hill, holding onto the wheel as the car struck rocks and gullies and holes. He reached the road and turned toward Honolulu, on his way to Mercy Hospital. Those kids should be able to talk now. "Two-one-two. Two-one-two." Maddox reached for the radio telephone.

"Two-one-two," he said.

"Two-one-two," said the dispatcher in headquarters. "Report to Chief Fairly. Captain, he's been looking for you all morning."

"He found me," Maddox said, and replaced the telephone. He drove steadily toward the city. At police headquarters Maddox went directly to the chief's office.

"Is he alone?" Maddox asked. The uniformed policeman at the desk nodded and made a face. Maddox opened the door. "Hello, Len."

Leonard Fairly picked up the brass letter opener and watched Maddox come to the desk. He let Maddox stand there for a while. "You took your own sweet time," the chief said.

"I was working," Maddox said. "I'm still working. What's the beef?"

"You." The chief pointed the letter opener. "You're the beef. Maybe it's news to you, Curt, but you're not running this department. I'm running this department."

Maddox moved forward until he was against the desk, looking down at the short man in the outsized leather chair. "I'm tired, Len. I've been chasing my tail since yesterday morning."

"Maybe you ought to stop," the chief said.

"For God's sake, man, speak your piece!"

"You don't play tough with me," the chief said. He swung the letter opener as though he were pulling a sword from his scabbard. "I'm not one of your harness bulls. I'm not afraid of you," the chief said, trying to convince himself. "Where do you come off putting a squad on Joe Liliuohe?"

So the chief was finally sharing his secret. "Those cops are there to protect him," Maddox said.

"*Protect*," said Fairly. "You assign a twenty-four-hour guard, six police officers to *protect a rapist*, the head of the whole gang?"

"The jury didn't agree with you," Maddox said.

"Hester Ash . . . Murdoch agrees with me!" the chief said. "Everyone in Hawaii agrees with me. Everyone in the States agrees with me!" He was almost shouting. "Senators of the United States of America agree with me." He began to jab the letter opener into the large green blotter on his desk. "For your information there aren't any cops in the Punchbowl! There aren't any cops guarding Mr. Innocent Liliuohe! I sent them back to duty! The chief of police sent them back to duty!"

Maddox said, "Who-o-o-o-o-o," expelling air. "Double back, Len. Tell the dispatcher to send a squad over to his house."

"Not while I'm chief," Fairly said. "I'm *chief* here! I'm appointed by the mayor!" He was shouting again. "Wouldn't the mayor like to know I'm using cops to protect Joe Liliuohe! In a pig's ear!"

Maddox leaned forward, pushing his knuckles against the desk, and Fairly shrank back, and then leaped up to prove Maddox didn't scare him. "There's a lynching party loose in town," Maddox said. "They almost killed three kids yesterday."

"Too bad they didn't," Fairly said. "Would have saved the taxpayers the money for another trial." Maddox didn't move but he seemed to be advancing on the chief. The little man dropped the letter opener on the blotter. He lowered his eyes, and he said, quietly, "You can go."

Early the next morning Sarah drove Tom to the harbor, to the charter boats that lay beyond the big piers. "I'll pick you up," she said.

"I'm not sure of the time," Tom said. "You never know exactly. It depends on the kind of sea you have."

"I'll be here," Sarah said.

"You'll be tired," Tom said. "You don't need to come down."

"Yes, I do," she said. "Why are you so far away?" Tom moved across the seat, his thigh touching hers.

"Close enough?"

Sarah put her arm on his leg, her hand on the inside of his thigh. "You can't be close enough," she said, and then, low, "I feel you all the time now. You're with me all the time. Listen to me. I was never this way. I can say anything to you. I wish we could go somewhere right now. In daylight so I could see you." Her hand moved and she whispered, "Over me."

Tom wanted to kiss her. He wanted to hold her. He wanted to be lost, holding her. He could feel Sarah beside him throughout the long voyage to the big island.

When the boat reached the Princess Luahine's dock, the captain said, " 'Absolutely no visitors, absolutely no exceptions,' " reading the signs. "She's a real friendly lady."

"She doesn't like people bothering her," Tom said.

"You're bothering her," the captain said. "You must have an in with the princess, Her Highness. I heard about Her Highness. None of us folks is good enough for her." He spit. "We were good enough to boot her out of town."

"Nobody booted her," Tom said. "She left because she decided to leave." He hated the captain, who had become indistinguishable from the gang that had tortured the three innocents the day before.

"How long will it take you up there?" the captain asked.

"I can't tell you," Tom said.

"I want to start early," the captain said. The mate dropped the gangplank and Tom left the boat. "Make it snappy, huh?"

Tom stopped to look up at him. "You can leave," he said.

"You owe me some money, kid," the captain said.

"I owe you for one way," Tom said. He came back to the ramp. "I'll pay you right now. Do you want me to pay you right now?" The captain went forward. Tom walked toward the path that climbed the hill. He was near the end of the dock when he heard the captain.

"Shake a leg!" said the captain, and laughed. The mate laughed. For an instant Tom wanted to leap aboard the boat, leap upon the captain, swinging, drive him to the deck, hit him until the man was senseless. He wanted to turn on the mate then, as though the other man would stand by until Tom had disposed of the captain. He wanted to club both of them, but he never paused. He listened to the sound of his shoe scraping. The captain's jibe had only echoed a lifetime's ignominy.

At the top Tom was alone. There was no sign of the princess or Jack Manakula. He yelled. Tom heard only the rumble of the sea below. He went to the house, climbing the steps to the long porch. He saw an open book, pages down, on the cane sofa. A pair of glasses were on the book. Tom bent to read the title on the book spine. It was *Les Miserables*. He sat down on the cane sofa. He kept looking at his wristwatch.

The sound of horses brought him off the porch. There were two, far out. He raised his hand to shade his eyes, walking toward the animals. Then Tom stopped, seeing the princess. She rose like a monolith above her horse. Tom turned toward the corral. Jack Manakula was with the princess. When they stopped, Jack dismounted but the princess remained in the saddle, looking down at the young lawyer with the dragging foot. Her forehead and neck were sweaty and strands of hair waved in the wind. "Not another dime."

Tom told her everything. The princess listened, one hand over the other hand on the pommel. Jack Manakula took a sack of tobacco and a book of cigarette paper from his shirt pocket. He tried to roll a cigarette. His hands were shaking and the tobacco spilled. The paper dropped. His fingers closed over the tobacco and paper, and he threw it. He threw the slender book. He turned his back on Tom, putting his head against the saddle. Tom stopped, looking up at the princess. "Will those boys be all right?" she asked.

"Will they die? No, they won't die," Tom said. "Will they be all right? They'll *never* be all right!" He was yelling. "They were *whipped!* They were tied to trees and *whipped!* Their flesh was stripped from their backs! They're on their bellies, and they can't move! Harry bites his hand! They had to tie him up to keep him from biting himself! David screams! Every few minutes he thinks they're still whipping him! Now they'll never know who'll grab them next!"

The princess looked down at the little guy in the dark suit. She swung one big leg slowly, and lowered herself to the ground. Her face and neck were covered with perspiration. She used the back of her hand to wipe her face. "Take her, Jack," she said, and prodded the mare. The princess left the corral, moving slowly. Her head moved from side to side as she looked for Tom, who was at her right. "I thought I lost you already. No such luck."

"I came over to tell you what happened," Tom said.

"You didn't do me any favors," the princess said. "I've lived too long for another surprise from over there. I've heard enough from over there. Those swine! Those gutter rats. Filing into their churches every Sunday like they were human beings. They're not human beings. They're the droppings of humanity. Who do you think stole our land? They came from every sewer on earth."

The princess reached the steps and stopped, looking back at the corral. "Will you take the saddles off those poor animals?" she yelled.

"Maybe it's news to you," Jack yelled, "but I was only born with two hands."

"Why don't you try using them?" She wiped her face and forehead. "I've been out in the sun so long I feel like I'm turning on a spit," the princess said. She came up the steps and moved into the shade of the porch. Tom watched her pick up the book. "This man thought he had trouble," she said of Jean Valjean. "He should've been a Hawaiian." She lowered herself onto the sofa. "Sit down. You don't need permission." She watched the lawyer take a chair near her. "You said three of them. There were four."

"Joe didn't come home Saturday night," Tom said. "He was on the beach with his girl." The princess watched Jack removing a saddle.

"This Joe . . . what's his name?"

"Liliuohe. Joe Liliuohe," Tom said.

"He's the one who stopped for Doris Ashley's daughter, isn't he? The one who started all this," the princess said.

"He saved her life! He went on trial for taking her to the hospital!" Tom said.

The princess slapped her knee with the book. "You stop correcting me," she said. "You're a lawyer, you can understand what I'm saying. You find this Joe . . . I can't keep his name. You find him and send him out. I'll put him to work. He'll bunk with the other hands. Drive him to the docks, charter a boat, tell the captain I'll pay him, and send this Joe over. When the other three are able, drive them to the pier, charter a boat send them over. I'll be solving the unemployment around Papakolea." Tom stepped back as Jack reached the porch.

"They're coming up for trial," Tom said.

"They had their trial," said the princess.

"The court will think they've run away."

"You tell Phil Murray he can come over and see for himself," the princess said. "I'll pay his fare, too."

Tom faced her as though she had joined the kidnappers. "Everyone will think they left because they're guilty."

"Meanwhile they'll be in one piece," the princess said. She looked at Jack. "Say it."

"I don't need to say it," Jack said.

The princess raised one big leg and said "Ah-h-h-h-h" as she crossed it over the other leg. "I'm wrong," she said. "They can't come here. Anywhere. They have to stay. If they leave, everyone's guilty. Everyone on every island who isn't a haole." She looked at Tom. "I wish I'd never laid eyes on you. Anyway

. . . I'm giving you some homework. Tomorrow morning you visit the newspapers, English language and any language. You visit the Associated Press and the other one, the United Press. You tell them everything you told me. Next you hire a photographer. Take him to the hospital to take pictures in case the haoles decide they can't show pictures of boys who look like skinned cats because it doesn't fit with the polo. They'll want pictures on the Mainland. You mail them personally. They like all this sin on the Mainland, especially when the sinners are being punished. If the reporters need any information, you give them information." She sat back, studying Tom. "All of a sudden I've got a partner and he's a mystery man. Are you married?"

Tom saw Sarah in his head, saw her standing on the dock waving, saw her face clearly. His heart beat faster. Tom shook his head.

"How about family? How about your mother and father? Are you good to them?"

"Not good enough," Tom said, remembering instantly the money orders that had come to San Francisco every month for three years. He remembered his mother and father looking at the law school diploma when he came home, afraid to touch it. His mother kissed him as though he were a special visitor in the house. His father stayed behind the chair in the kitchen. "At least I did something," his father said.

The princess made herself stern. "Start doing better," she said. "On your way. Wait." She waved the book. "Come closer." Tom stopped in front of her. "If you want respect, first you need self-respect," the princess said. "Look like something, then you are something. You know Hansen's downtown? Men's clothes. Tomorrow morning ask for Bob Hansen. Tell him I sent you. Tell him he himself should pick you a suit." Tom shook his head. The princess glanced at Jack. "Some partner," she said, and to Tom, "You need something besides the swimming suit you're wearing. Last time you *swam* over here in that thing. Ask for Bob Hansen."

"I can't," Tom said, and stronger, "I can't!" He remembered the extra money order from his mother and father a month before his law school graduation. Tom could not take money again, ever, from anyone. "I won't," he said, and then, "Thank you."

The princess rubbed her nose. "Bend down," she said. Tom obeyed. She adjusted the knot of his tie. Then she ran her fingers over her lips and smoothed his hair. "Try and look like a lawyer, anyway,'' she said and flicked her wrist impatiently, waving him off her ranch.

"Good-bye," Tom said. "Good-bye, Mr. Manakula."

Jack touched his forehead with his forefinger as Tom crossed the porch. The princess watched him, saw him come down the steps awkwardly, saw him dragging his foot as he started for the cliff and the path to the dock. "Poor kid," Jack said.

"Shows how dumb you are!" said the princess, and whacked the arm of the sofa with the book. "He's tougher than both of us put together. He had the leg and he still won."

"For a fact," Jack said. "You want something cold?" The princess didn't answer. "Lemonade? Ice water?" Jack asked. "Talk to the wall."

The princess watched Tom until he dropped below the cliff. "I thought when I came here, I was leaving it all behind me in Honolulu," the princess said. "I thought I'd be so far away I'd be rid of it all. I'll never be rid of it. I could have moved anywhere, ten thousand miles from here, and I'd still be carrying it around with me. I've been gone more than twenty years and right here, right from this porch, I can see every street and every shack in Honolulu. I can see the young girls in the whorehouses, the whorehouses where their mothers bring them, where their mothers come Sunday morning for money for the family. I can see the girls, see them when they start and when they finish, when the madames are finished with them. They're still girls when they're finished, but they're too old for the sailors and the soldiers. Oh, Jesus, Jack, I can see everything. I see the maids, so old they're bent, coming down the beach before the sun is up, on their way to scrub, on their knees scrubbing. I can see the butlers in the houses up on Pacific Heights and Nuuana Valley and Maunalani, being charged for every jacket they use. I can see the gardeners bowing and holding their hats for every snot nose who passes. I can see Harvey Koster's plantation managers down around the Punchbowl looking for husky kids to cut the cane. There isn't a job left for us where you're not bent double every working day of your life."

Jack put his arm over the princess's shoulder. She rested her head against him. "Come on in the house," Jack said.

The princess looked up. "Now?"

"Sure, now," Jack said. "Who's to stop us?"

"I'm an old, fat lady."

"Who's being dumb now?" He raised his hand to stroke her hair. "Don't talk dumb," Jack said.

"Honest, I don't feel like it."

"I'll make you feel like it," Jack said. "Listen, I hate what he told us as much as you do."

"Would you be here if you didn't?"

"Come on, then," Jack said. "We'll be together and we'll forget things for awhile."

"Is there any hot water?" asked the princess.

"Why do you need hot water?"

"I need to clean up," the princess said. "Both of us. I need a bath."

"You don't need any bath for what we'll be doing."

"Maybe you think you don't need one," the princess said, "but I do, and if I take a bath, so will you."

"You take all the fun out of it with all these arrangements," Jack said. "Let's once do what we want to do."

The princess pushed herself up from the sofa. "You ought to learn we're not animals," she said. "We're not like the animals out there."

Jack grinned at her. "The hell we're not."

"I'm not."

"Hey, I just had an idea," Jack said. He grinned again. "Out in the barn."

"In the *where?* You're loco!"

"Come on," he said. "There's fresh hay out there."

He made her smile despite herself. "Hay itches."

"You'll forget the hay," Jack said. He moved his fingers over her hand.

"In the *hay?*"

"We'll have fun," he said, leading her away from the sofa.

"One of these days you'll drag me up on a volcano," the princess said.

"You ruined my surprise," Jack said, and put his arm around her, his hand resting on her huge buttocks.

On Thursday, four days after Duane failed to get a single signature on the typed confessions, Gerald returned from Pearl Harbor at dusk. He drove into the garage, parking beside Doris Ashley's dust-covered Pierce-Arrow town car. He turned off the engine but left the headlights burning. He came out of the garage and closed the massive door, throwing the thick bolt.

Gerald could see the glow in the windows of the bedroom on the second floor of the carriage house. "Hallelujah," he said, flatly.

He entered the carriage house, walking past the staircase into the living room. Hester was in a chair, one leg under her, reading. Gerald stopped beside the sofa, looking down at his folded blanket and pillow in the corner. "I suppose you want to be alone," Hester said.

"I am alone," Gerald said. Hester closed her book and rose. "Gerald." She waited until he lifted his head. "You hate it here. You shouldn't stay. Why do you stay?"

"I stay because I wouldn't leave you in your hour of need," Gerald said, telling her the truth. "Good night." The room became still. "Good night, Hester." He watched her walk past him, into the hall to the staircase.

Later, when he was under the blanket on the sofa, Gerald wound his alarm clock and set it to ring at six. His blue uniform was hanging from a door. When he woke, Gerald moved quickly and purposefully with the efficiency he had learned at the Academy. He left the carriage house before seven, walking in cadence to the garage. Gerald raised the garage door and went to the front of his car. The headlights were dark. He reached through the open window to turn the headlight switch, and walked back to the carriage house, stopping beside the staircase to pick up the telephone to call Doris Ashley. "I hope I didn't wake you."

Doris Ashley came out of the bed, tangled in the blankets. "Is it Hester?"

"No, no, nothing like that," Gerald said. "My car won't start. Dead battery. May I use yours?"

The fool! The stupid, incompetent fool! Unable even to maintain his car battery. "Hello," Gerald said.

"Come to the door," said Doris Ashley. "The entrance. Wait! Don't ring!" She did not want Amelia and Theresa on her hands at this hour. Doris Ashley raised the covers, dropping them at a careful angle across the bed. She intended to return. She was determined to sleep. Her nights had become sleepless. Doris Ashley put on her robe and went into the dressing room for the keys to the Pierce-Arrow.

Gerald returned to the garage from Windward. He unlocked the trunk of his car. The canvas bag lay beside his tennis racket. Gerald took the bag and got into the Pierce-Arrow. He rolled down the window to let air into the musty interior and started the big car.

He was alone on Kahala Avenue and he saw few other cars until he reached Waikiki. Traffic increased there but Gerald was at Iolani Palace before eight o'clock. He turned into the curb, stopping where he had met Duane York Saturday afternoon. Gerald knew he was early. He opened the canvas bag and examined the contents. He closed it and looked for Duane, looked everywhere, front and back and to his right and left. He checked his wristwatch. If Duane didn't come, Gerald would have to go ahead alone. He couldn't do it alone. Two men were needed. Duane wouldn't disappoint him, but something could have happened, anything could have happened. The naval engagements Gerald had studied since his days as a midshipman were *packed* with miscalculations. *Where was Duane?* Gerald twisted, turning from side to side, scouring the area. He fell back, convinced now that Duane would not appear, and saw him dead ahead, in the next block.

Duane was in uniform as they had planned. He moved with quick, short steps, and when he was closer, Gerald saw him looking constantly over his shoulder. Gerald leaned across the seat to unlock the door. "You act like you're being followed," Gerald said. Duane slammed the car door shut and set his white enlisted man's cap low on his forehead. "Just wanted to be sure I wasn't leaving tracks, Lieutenant. After last week, the place is crawling with cops. Christ, everywhere you look."

"Did you have any trouble leaving Pearl?" asked Gerald. He had called from the carriage house to say he was ill.

"I'm on liberty," Duane said. "Jenishek, you know him, the yeoman? He wrote up the liberty. So that much went okay, anyway."

"It's *all* going to be okay," Gerald said. "This operation is proceeding without a hitch. Duane?" The little man turned. "It's not too late to back off."

"Hell, no!" Duane said.

"You're positive?"

"I'd never let you down, sir," Duane said. Duane pushed his hand through the handle of the canvas bag. "This spot you picked for the . . . operation, sir. You're sure it's a good spot and all? Safe?"

"It's deserted," Gerald said. "Wooded and deserted."

"Yes, sir," Duane said, caressing the canvas bag. "Only the other spot, last week's spot, that was wooded, and . . ." Duane broke off before the lieutenant began to think he was yellow. "Battle stations!" Duane said, managing a grin. Duane stepped out on the running board and into the backseat.

"You're sure of the time?" Gerald asked.

"He's on the nose," Duane said. "Same trolley, same stop every day." Gerald had given Duane his car each morning, fabricating chores for the enlisted man, who returned to the *Bluegill* before noon chow. "We can shove off."

Gerald shifted gears and turned the big steering wheel, his arm extended in the required traffic signal as he drove away from the curb. Duane opened the canvas bag and took out one of the .45 automatics.

Two miles away Joe Liliuohe walked toward the trolley stop on his way to Mercy Hospital. He held a folded copy of the *Outpost-Dispatch* to show the guys. Their pictures were in the paper, all three of them, on their bellies in the hospital. Suddenly Joe flung the paper aside. "You must be nuts!" he said, aloud. As though they needed to be reminded. "Look at them and look at you!" he said, aloud. Joe cut through an alley.

"Turn here," Duane said, and as Gerald put his arm through the window, "No, *right!*" Gerald raised his arm, holding it parallel to the big car. "Then two blocks, and *then* left," Duane said.

Joe came out of the alley and broke into a run, just in case. He didn't want to miss it, and wait around for the next trolley.

"Another right coming up," Duane said. "The last one." The Pierce-Arrow rolled around the corner. "There's the trolley stop up ahead," Duane said as they passed Joe. Duane said, "Holy!" He said, "It's him! We just passed him!" Duane was on the edge of the seat, the .45 automatic in his hand.

Gerald's head swung around. "Where? Are you sure? Are you positive?"

"It's him!" Duane said. "Hell, I've seen him all week!" Duane pointed with the gun. "Pull in there! Back of the trolley stop!" Duane moved off the seat, squatting, raising his blouse with his left hand and shoving the big automatic into his waistband. His legs hurt. Duane set the white cap squarely on his head.

Gerald could see the man in the rearview mirror. "He's coming," Gerald said. "Here he comes."

"I don't see him," Duane said. "How close is he?" Duane's legs were killing him, squatting in the well between the seats. He came up onto the backseat. Duane opened the door, holding the door handle, set to go. The gun muzzle dug into his gut. "Where is he now? He should be here by now," Duane said, and saw him. Duane opened the door, pulling down on his blouse. "Hey, you!" There was nobody around. They were in luck.

Joe saw the sailor come out of the big car. They didn't look right together. The sailor was yelling at someone. "I said *you!*" Duane pointed at him. "I'm picking you up. Official business."

"I'm not in the Navy," Joe said. "You got the wrong man."

"Joe Liliuohe," Duane said. "I said official." He reached for Joe's arm. Joe swung, hitting Duane's open hand with his open hand, bringing all his weight into the swing, knocking Duane off balance.

"Lay off," Joe said, and for the first time saw the driver, saw her husband. They were both nuts, him and the sailor. Joe said, "What do you guys think . . . ?" and stopped. The sailor was holding a gun, a cannon.

"In the car," Duane said, and took two steps, holding the gun directly in front of him, his wrist pushing into his belly to hide the weapon. "*In* or I'll blow you apart," Duane said. He stepped behind Joe, shoving the bastard with his left hand and following him. Duane shoved him again, pushing him into the rear of the Pierce-Arrow. "Go! Go!" Duane yelled on the running board, using his left hand to grab the door, holding the gun on the bastard. Gerald released the clutch, pushing his foot down on the accelerator.

"What're you doing? What's this all about? Where are you guys taking me? This isn't official," Joe said. "You're not official. What're you trying to do?" He knew. He'd seen what they'd done to the other guys.

"Pipe down," Duane said. He raised the gun and spoke slowly. "You pipe down, understand?" He patted the barrel with his left hand. "You understand."

Joe was talking to himself. You have to do something. What? *Something!* Pretend you're sick, like you did in school. Lay back and gag, make a sound like you're gagging. If he moves, jump him. Use both hands and feet so he'll drop the gun. If he drops the gun, you can handle him. Them. You can handle them. Christ, he'll shoot me! Maybe. Maybe he won't. They didn't shoot the other guys. Stop stalling! Joe lay back in the seat. He made a gagging sound like he was throwing up. "Sick. I'm sick," Joe told Duane.

"No, you don't," Duane said. "Not in this car."

"Honest, I'm sick," Joe said.

"If you get sick, you won't be sick long. I'll promise you that," Duane said.

Gerald cocked his head, speaking over his shoulder. "Quiet! I'll tell you when you'll talk!" Gerald said.

"You heard him," Duane said.

Gerald turned, looking ahead, and saw Maddox get into his car at the curb. "Down!" Gerald shouted, dropping over the steering wheel as he passed the black sedan. "Down! Down! Get down!"

Duane used his left hand to cuff Joe. Bending, Duane yelled, "Down, he said!" Duane swung again, hitting Joe. "Down, you

sonofabitch, miserable sonofabitch!'' Duane yelled. Joe dropped
to the floorboards between the front and rear seats. Duane was
directly over and beside him, pointing the gun at his head.

Behind the wheel, Gerald lifted his head an inch, another,
another. He could see into the rearview mirror. Maddox could be
following him! Gerald turned at the corner, holding out his arm
immediately to signal for a left turn. After the turn, he put his
elbow in the window, holding up his arm to signal for a right
turn. By that time Maddox had stopped at the shoemaker to leave
a pair of white buckskins for which he needed new heels.

Gerald kept turning for more than a mile, watching the rearview
mirror constantly. He had abandoned the wooded site the instant
he saw Maddox. Gerald knew they weren't safe in the open.
They needed to be hidden. Circuitously, Gerald made his way
back to Waikiki, on his way to Diamond Head and Kahala
Avenue. ''Okay?'' Duane asked.

''Okay!'' Gerald said, his voice snapping. He couldn't take
any chances. Staying within the speed limit, Gerald drove to
Windward. One way or another he intended to complete his
mission. Nobody spoke until Gerald drove through the iron
gates. ''We're here,'' he said. ''Sit up. Watch him, Duane.''

Duane saw the mansion. Joe came up onto the rear seat and saw
the sprawling house with the enormous entrance. Gerald stopped
the car, and leaped out, pulling at the car door beside Joe. ''You,
Joe. Get out,'' Gerald said, and in a sudden spasm of rage reached
into the car to grab Joe's wrist. Duane shoved him, sliding across
the seat and following Joe out of the car. ''Inside,'' Gerald said.
Duane pushed the muzzle of the gun into Joe's ribs.

''You heard him,'' Duane said and motioned to Gerald, who
fell back behind Joe. ''What're we doin' *here?*'' Duane whispered.

''Looked like we were being followed,'' Gerald said, and
went ahead to open the towering door.

''Take him straight through into the living room,'' Gerald
said. He closed the door and followed them. The living room
was bright with sun. The glass doors facing the east, facing the
States, were opened wide and sunlight fell across the carpets.

Gerald took a chair and set it in the open, away from the
furniture. ''Sit here.''

Joe went to the chair and as Duane joined Gerald, facing their
captive, the swinging door at the far end of the room opened,
and Theresa saw the lieutenant and the two strangers. A kanaka
was in the chair, the first she had ever seen sitting in the living
room. Theresa was paralyzed until she saw the gun. She went
straight back as though she had been lassoed.

Gerald produced a folded sheet of paper and a pen. "Sign this and you can leave. You can walk out of this house. We'll let you walk out."

"Take the goddamn paper!" Duane said.

"I'll handle this," Gerald said, and to Joe, "Read it."

Joe read the single, typewritten line, " 'I admit I raped Hester Murdoch.' " He saw his typewritten name below. He looked up at them. He hadn't expected anything like this. When they grabbed him, he was sure they were taking him somewhere to kill him. When they brought him into the house, he thought they would stretch him out or tie him up and whip him like they had whipped the others. They were nuts. They were both nuts. He was with two total nuts. Gerald held out the pen. "Sign it and you can leave."

"I didn't do it!" Joe said. "We didn't do it. I swear to you, Lieutenant."

"You can't lie anymore!" Gerald said.

"I'm not *lying!*" Joe said. "It's the truth! It's always been the truth!" He was back in the nightmare.

Gerald sprang forward, lifting Joe's arm to shove the pen in his hand. *"Sign it!"* Gerald was shouting. He had to stop shouting. He had sworn to do this calmly and without any anger, or any emotion. He stepped back from the chair and took a deep breath. "No one will hurt you," Gerald said. "You have my word." He pointed at the sheet of paper.

"You're asking me to lie," Joe said. "You're asking me to send myself to prison for something I didn't do, we didn't *do. I . . . didn't . . . do . . . anything!* How many times do I have to say it, tell you? *I . . . didn't . . . do . . . anything!*" He threw the sheet of paper at Gerald, and it floated to the carpet at Joe's feet. The paper fell on his shoes, and he pulled back his legs, tossing the pen aside.

"You lousy . . . !" Duane said, and stopped as he felt the lieutenant's hand on his shoulder.

"I said I'd handle this! Don't interfere!" Christ, the lieutenant was blaming him. "That's an order." Gerald released Duane, and bent to pick up the paper and pen. He dropped both in Joe's lap. "You're going to sign this," Gerald said, matter-of-factly. He had convinced himself.

"Gerald!" Doris Ashley came through the entrance hall. When Joe saw her, he almost started bawling. She had saved him. He rose, oblivious of the pen and paper that dropped to the carpet.

Doris Ashley saw the dark face rise from her chair, *her chair.* She saw the little man with the gun. She saw her son-in-law, the idiot, the lunatic, who had invaded her home, *her home*, *Windward*, with these . . . "Get out of my house!"

Duane took one step toward Joe. "Sit down, you."

"Listen, lady," Joe said, sitting. "Lady, hurry up, lady. They kidnapped me. They grabbed me off the street. Help me, lady. Please help me."

Doris Ashley stopped, facing Gerald. "You used *my* car for this? You brought him *here?*"

"Yes, here," Gerald said. *"Yes!"* He was through taking her orders, everyone's, listening to everyone, those bastards in the Officers' Club. "I couldn't take him to the carriage house, could I? I couldn't bring him to Hester, could I?"

"Leave this house!" Mrs. Ashley said. "This minute! Leave this minute!"

"Leave this minute," Gerald said. "When I'm ready! I'll leave when I'm ready!"

"Get out!" Doris said. "*Get out!* You!" she said to Duane. "Get out of my house!" She pointed at Joe. "Take him and go!"

"Ignore her," Gerald said.

"Sorry, ma'am," Duane said.

"Shut up!" Gerald said. "I told you once, shut up! I'll do the talking! I'm in charge!" He glared at Doris Ashley. "I'm in charge!" He bent for the paper and pen, shoving them into Joe's chest. "Sign it!"

Joe knew he had no chance if he didn't talk. The lady was his only chance. She was the only one in the room, in the world, who could save him. "Lady, they want me to sign this," Joe said. He showed her the paper and pen. "They want me to say I raped her. I didn't." He shook his head. "I didn't do it. Honest to God, I didn't do it. I told the truth. Please, lady, please."

Doris knew she was dealing with a lunatic. Gerald was a lunatic. He would never set foot in Windward again. She would send Theresa and Amelia this afternoon to pack his clothes. She would hire someone to take his clothes to Pearl Harbor. No, she would personally take his clothes. She would deliver the clothes herself. Hester would file for a divorce in the morning. Doris Ashley would drive Hester to her attorney's office in the morning. No, she would summon the attorney to Windward. Preston had always conducted his business at home. "I order you to leave!"

"I order you to leave," Gerald said, and, louder, *"You* order me to leave. I order you to stay. I order you to go. I order you to sit, stand, walk, talk." He pointed. "You order me to live in the carriage house.'' Doris Ashley thought he would leap at her. ''You leave!'' he shouted, and swung around at Joe. *''Sign it!''*

''Lady, talk to him,'' Joe said. ''Please, lady.''

''Give me that gun!'' Gerald said. He put out his hand. ''Give me that *gun!''*

Duane was really worried. He said, ''Sir, listen . . .'' and stopped as Gerald pulled the .45 out of his hand. ''Sir, the safety's off!''

''If you are not out of this house immediately, I'll have you deported!'' Doris Ashley said. ''I will have the admiral deport you!''

Gerald was in front of Joe. ''You heard him,'' Gerald said. ''The safety is off. There is a round in the chamber. Your round. Sign the paper.''

''Gerald!''

''Sign the paper!''

Joe watched the gun. He couldn't take his eyes away from the gun. He said, ''Lady, do something. Lady!'' The gun was moving slowly, slowly, until the muzzle was pointed directly at him. ''Lady, please. I'll go to prison if I sign. I didn't do it, lady.''

''Sign the paper,'' Gerald said. ''You must sign the paper. There's no lady. There's no one except you and me.''

''Jesus, mister. Lieutenant. I'm telling you the truth. I swear on my mother.''

''Sign it.''

''You're asking me to do something . . .'' Joe said, and Gerald squeezed the trigger.

A massive, reverberating roar filled the room as blood, thick and red, spurted into the air. Blood erupted, cascading over the face that had disappeared, that had been shattered and shot away, covering the hair and head of the dead man, killed instantly and driven back by the force of the huge slug that had torn his face apart. The dead man was slammed into the chair by the slug and fell onto the floor with the chair, blood squirting across the carpet in rivulets, making a red octopus on the deep wool piling.

The recoil flung Gerald back. Smoke rose from the gun muzzle, drifting across the room to be caught in the sunlight, moving toward the open windows like a slow pattern of clouds across the sky.

''Oh, Christ, Lieutenant,'' Duane said. The guy was dead. The blood wouldn't stop. The blood was rolling toward Duane. ''Oh, Christ.''

The dead man's legs hung over the chair on the floor and now, slowly, slid to the carpet. One shoe was caught in the chair rung, the leg raised as blood poured out of the hole in the dead man's head.

"He . . ." Gerald said. "I told him." He moved back away from the dead man until he hit a table. He kept holding the gun, waiting for the man to pick himself up from the floor.

Doris Ashley saw her chair, broken, bent, and useless. She saw her carpet, the carpet she and Preston had designed, saw the blood soaking into the pile. She saw the dead man on the floor in her home, *in her home*. "We have to take him to a hospital," Gerald said.

"Hospital? He's dead," Duane said. "Lieutenant, he's dead."

"He's dead? He's dead?"

Mrs. Ashley looked at the imbecile, the useless imbecile. She had to save herself. She had to think. She was not thinking. "Take the gun," she said to Duane. "Take the gun."

Duane went to the lieutenant, putting his hand on the barrel of the automatic. The barrel was hot. Duane wiggled the weapon and Gerald released it. Duane set the safety.

"He's dead," Gerald said. Doris Ashley crossed the room.

"Gerald, take hold of yourself," she said. He looked through her.

"Ma'am," Duane said. "Listen, ma'am. The lieutenant will be okay, honest. I've seen other guys like this, in boot camp the first time on the range. It'll go away, ma'am." He tugged at Gerald's sleeve. "Lieutenant, we have to get rid of him. You have to help me."

"Stop!" said Doris. She could not allow these two fools to leave with the body. She could not trust them. They would involve her. They *had* involved her. A murder had been committed in Windward. "Bring me the keys of the Pierce-Arrow," she said. "Bring me the *keys!*" Duane nodded, shoving the automatic into his waistband. As Duane turned toward the entrance hall, Doris Ashley went into the kitchen. "Amelia. Theresa."

The kitchen was deserted. She went to the open door leading to the back stairs. Doris Ashley returned to the kitchen. She heard the front door open and close. Doris Ashley moved quickly, opening the pantry door. Amelia and Theresa held each other, their eyes wide with terror. "Come here." She stepped into the pantry, pulling Amelia away from Theresa, who sank to the floor. "I need towels," said Doris Ashley. "Big bath towels."

"I'm afraid," Amelia said.

"Bring me the towels. Put them on the table here." She pulled Amelia to the back stairs and pushed her.

When she returned to the living room, the little man was talking to Gerald. "Give me the keys," said Doris Ashley.

"Here you are, ma'am," Duane said.

"I take full responsibility," Gerald said.

"I'll give you towels," said Doris. "Wrap . . . him in towels. Cover him. Put him on the floor in the backseat. He'll be between you. Draw the curtains."

"Yes, ma'am."

Doris Ashley looked at her carpet. She would have to dispose of the carpet. She could not dispose of the carpet. Blood. She would set Amelia and Theresa to work. Afterward, she would arrange the furniture to cover the area. No. She would put the carpet in the attic and buy a new carpet.

"I'll tell them you had nothing to do with this," Gerald said.

"You will say nothing! *Nothing!* Do you hear me? You hear me!" Why hadn't he killed himself as well? A woman's scream rang out. Theresa! When Doris Ashley returned, she would throw Theresa into the street. She could not. Theresa would be with her for life now. Both of them would be with her for life. They were like the carpet. She could not dispose of them. She turned to Duane. "Help me with the towels."

Doris Ashley left them and went outside to open the rear door of the limousine. She returned to the entrance hall. "Pick him up, Gerald!"

"Lieutenant? Give me a hand, okay?" Duane got hold of the shoulders. "Grab his legs, okay?"

The towels hung over the body, and blood dripped as they carried it out. A towel fell. "Don't stop!" said Doris. "Don't stop!" When they passed her, she went back, picking up a corner of the towel, covered with lines of red.

The body was on the floor in the rear of the limousine. Gerald stood beside the open door. "Come on, Lieutenant," Duane said. Doris Ashley dropped the towel in the rear and shoved Gerald. "He's coming, ma'am," Duane said.

"I take full responsibility," Gerald said.

As Mrs. Ashley drove through the gates, Duane said, "What do we do now, ma'am?"

"You will dispose of the body. There is a place." Preston had sold the land for next to nothing years ago. It was worthless and had never been developed.

Three miles from Windward Kenneth Christofferson was in the police squad car, parked beneath a tree, smoking. His partner's wife was having a baby, so Kenny was alone. He had turned down the radio below the dashboard. Kenny's partner was half deaf and most of the time the dispatcher at headquarters sounded like he was in the backseat. All of a sudden Kenny saw the big car come by like a bat out of hell. Kenny swung out onto the road, hitting the siren. The big car was way ahead. Kenny would have lost it, but at the top of a hill the driver must've misjudged the turn. The car, a Pierce-Arrow the size of a steamship, ended up in the brush.

Kenny opened the glove compartment for the book of traffic tickets. He left the squad car, pulling down on the visor of his cap. There were guys in the back and as Kenny reached the Pierce, one of them crossed his legs. A towel dangled from his shoe and it was covered with blood. Kenny reached for his gun.

"Tell me everything you know," Maddox said to Kenny Christofferson while walking toward the Pierce-Arrow. The dispatcher had found Maddox at Mercy Hospital where he had, day after day, sat with the three flagellated patients, wheedling and cajoling, making them repeat their stories over and over as he waited for a piece, a shred, a speck of a clue that would put him on the trail of the men who had whipped the three.

The turn where Doris Ashley had lost control of her car was lined with police vehicles, squad cars, the wagon, the Black Maria, the morgue truck, the police laboratory van. There were cops everywhere. Listening to Kenny Christofferson, Maddox watched Gerald and the sailor, standing beside the big sedan, handcuffs over their wrists. "Put it all down on your arrest report," he said to Kenny. He saw the towels, pink with blood, covering the body in the weeds.

Maddox stopped beside the Pierce-Arrow, standing at the open rear door. He looked at the pair in handcuffs, looked carefully, starting with their shoes. There was blood on their shoes and on the sailor's uniform, and on the lieutenant's uniform. Maddox was surprised by his impulse to whack them for their stupidity. "You might as well have killed him downtown in the middle of the street, Lieutenant."

Gerald was facing Maddox but looking past him. Al Keller ran toward the car. "Captain!" He joined Maddox and whispered, "Nobody put cuffs on Doris Ashley, and when I got here, neither did I."

Maddox nodded, looking at Gerald. "I didn't expect this from you, Lieutenant," Maddox said. "They tell me the gun is a Navy issue so that means it's your gun. We'll prove it with the finger prints." Gerald was as close to attention as he could be with his handcuffed wrists between his legs. "Why did you have to kill him?'' Maddox asked. "You're a smart man, an educated man. You're a Navy officer. Why did you kill him?'' Maddox needed an answer. He needed to learn why a superior person like the lieutenant would murder. The lieutenant had thought this one out. The gun belonged at Pearl, somewhere at Pearl, probably in the submarine. So the lieutenant had taken the gun to kill Joe Liliuohe. He had known why he was taking the gun when he took it. "Why did you do it, Lieutenant?'' Maddox asked, and heard Doris Ashley.

"Don't speak to him," said Doris Ashley. She was at Maddox's right, but ignored him, talking to Gerald. "You have your rights. You are not a common criminal."

Maddox shouted, "Keller!" although the redhead was beside him. "Take them downtown! In the wagon! You ride the wagon with them! You book them! You print them! You, personally!" Maddox whirled around, facing Doris Ashley. They were close enough to kiss. "He's not common," Maddox said, "but he's a criminal. You're all criminals. You're suspects in a murder, and that's the way you'll be treated." He yelled once more. "Keller!"

Al Keller was between Gerald and Duane, holding their arms, taking them to the Black Maria. "You forgot one!" Maddox said. The redhead didn't move. Maddox took Doris Ashley's arm and brought her to Kenny. "Put her in the wagon!"

Maddox watched the procession to the Black Maria, waiting for the anger to subside. He saw the cops, spread out, stopped by his outburst, their tasks forgotten. "Show's over," Maddox said, and, louder, "Show's over!" When Kenny closed the Black Maria doors behind Doris Ashley, Maddox turned away at last.

He bent, lifting the bloody towels that covered the body. "Not much left of him," someone said. Maddox dropped the towels and straightened up, leaving the Pierce-Arrow to join Vern Kappel, the head of the police lab, at the van.

Kappel showed him the guns. "This one was still warm," Kappel said, pointing.

"How many shots?

"One. You only need one from this piece," Kappel said. "You ought to see what it did to him."

"I want the slug," Maddox said.

"First they'll have to tell you where he was killed," Kappel said.

"I know where he was killed," Maddox said. "Those aren't work farm towels they wrapped around him. Those are Doris Ashley's towels. He was killed in Windward."

Kappel stared at Maddox. He set the metal lid over the container holding the guns. "Windward?"

"You follow me," Maddox said. "I want that slug so we'd better move. I'll bring a squad."

Kappel rubbed his face. "We'll need a search warrant, Captain."

"I'll scare one up when we get back to headquarters," Maddox said. He succumbed to the anger once more, lunging forward to slam the rear door of the van. "Get in."

A church bell struck one o'clock as Maddox turned, a block from police headquarters. He was behind the lab van, which was kept in the garage at the south end of the building. Maddox wanted to avoid the reporters who would be waiting in the entrance, so he didn't see the Buick limousine with the four flags in front of headquarters.

One of the cops Maddox brought to Windward had found the .45 slug under the four brass claws of an upright lamp beside the long wall of windows. Maddox had picked up the sheet of paper from beneath the coffee table, using a handkerchief, and gave it to Vern Kappel. Maddox swung into the garage. "I admit I raped Hester Murdoch," Maddox said, aloud. Joe Liliuohe should have signed it. At least he wouldn't have to call the family. Maddox had seen the newsboys crying, "Extra!" as he drove through Waikiki. "Captain?"

Maddox left his car, waiting for Kappel, who spoke conspiratorially. "Don't forget the search warrant."

"You bet," Maddox said. He left Kappel, passing the Black Maria and reaching an unmarked door. Maddox opened it, entering a narrow corridor. There were lights in the ceiling, widely spaced and covered with steel grills ever since a prisoner had slipped away and stood on a chair in an effort to electrocute himself. Maddox stopped near the end of the corridor and opened another door. He was in an enormous room without windows. The floor and walls were concrete. A shield of thick iron bars bisected the room. The raucous, obscene shouts from a dozen or more drunks welcomed Maddox. He was in the holding cell, the tank, where prisoners were kept immediately after being booked. Maddox had come to take the lieutenant to his office. "Hey!"

The lieutenant was leaving. He and the sailor were with another Navy officer in a white uniform, and the turnkey was directly opposite Maddox, holding the door on the other side of the room. Maddox ran. "Close that door!"

He stopped the parade. The turnkey dropped his arm and the door closed. The three in Navy uniforms looked back but Maddox was with them already. Now Maddox recognized the heavy, wide-shouldered man with the prisoners. It was Commander Saunders, the All-American. "The chief's orders," said the turnkey. "He called me *himself*."

"I'm here for the prisoners," Saunders said.

"They're not your prisoners."

The turnkey squirmed. "He called *himself*, Captain."

"Hand them over," he said.

"Chief Fairly will explain," Saunders said.

"Where the hell do you think you're going?"

"Upstairs," Saunders said. "I'm going now, Captain. You can stay or you can come with us." Maddox nodded at the turnkey, who opened the door.

They left the tank, stopping beside the elevators. Maddox stayed close to Gerald, brushing against him as they moved down the corridor to the chief's office.

Maddox was last, behind the bulky commander, but he could see the admiral from the doorway. The admiral was in the center of the room, and Maddox knew immediately it was *his* room. The admiral was in charge. To his right, Doris Ashley sat alone, apart from the others. Her legs were crossed, her hands in her lap. The sight of Maddox infuriated her. She wanted to stomp on the arrogant, cruel man in the dark suit who had manhandled her earlier.

When he saw Maddox, the chief left his desk, scurrying around Saunders. "Nobody sent for you," he whispered.

Maddox didn't look at him. He spoke to the admiral. "I'm here with the prisoners."

"You've been relieved," said the admiral.

The chief looked up at Maddox. "Continue with your duties, Captain," said the chief. Maddox could see the vein bulging over the chief's eye, thick and red. "I said continue with your duties!"

"These people are *murder* suspects," Maddox said. "They're being held on suspicion of *murder*."

"I have assumed full responsibility for them," said the admiral.

"They aren't your responsibility," Maddox said. "They're ours. This isn't your reservation. It's ours."

"I'm ordering you . . ." the chief said, and the admiral interrupted him.

"You're wasting my time," said the admiral, walking to the desk. "Mrs. Ashley and these men are being taken to Pearl Harbor. They'll remain at Pearl until such times as they are required to be in court." He took his cap and gray gloves from the desk. "I'll guarantee their appearance."

"Glenn." Doris Ashley was standing, waiting for the admiral. He came to her side. "Hester can't be left alone," said Doris Ashley. "She belongs with her husband in this terrible time."

"I should have thought of it myself," said the admiral. He beckoned to the commander. "Jimmy. Call for transportation and proceed to Windward. Bring Mrs. Murdoch to my quarters. She'll be staying with us."

Gerald felt like bolting through the office. He felt like asking the police captain to handcuff him and return him to the dungeon in the basement. *Hester!* In the same *room*, the same *bed!* "We can leave, Doris," said the admiral. Gerald saw the commander walk out of the office and remembered that he lived at the bachelor officers' quarters. The commander saved him. Gerald would be in the B.O.Q. before Hester reached Pearl Harbor.

Maddox watched the chief follow the admiral and pass him, hurrying to the door like a headwaiter. The chief pledged his cooperation as they left, and then as he closed the door, turned his back to it as though he intended to stop Maddox, who hadn't moved. "This is the last time you will ever taunt me!" the chief said. The bulging vein in his forehead was like a rope. "You're through coming in here and shooting off your mouth, smart ass! You don't scare me with your Mr. Harvey Koster. He'd thank me for giving Doris Ashley to the admiral! You've been dangling Harvey Koster over my head long enough!"

Maddox said, "You little sonofabitch," as though he were giving someone the right time. The chief's mouth opened but he was dumbfounded, and when Maddox took a step toward him, he spun around to his desk like it was a bunker. Maddox came after him, pointing at the door.

"You should be with them," Maddox said. "You're as guilty as they are. Guiltier." The chief grabbed his letter opener.

"Now we'll find out who's running this department!" he said.

All the weeks, the months of frustration and impotence that had entangled him since he had heard Hester identify the four young men in Mercy Hospital, convinced she was lying, welled up in Maddox. He had been mired in defeat after defeat, and he could no longer control himself. He lunged toward the desk, and the chief, startled, stepped behind his big chair, holding it like a shield.

"Running the department, you murdering bastard!" Maddox shouted. "*You* killed that kid! Joe Liliuohe would still be alive if you hadn't pulled that tail I put on him! You set him up! You sent him out on the street naked, goddamn you!"

"You're going up on charges!" the chief said. He was almost

screaming, waving the letter opener as though Maddox had a sword. "I'm bringing charges against you!"

"Right now!" Maddox said, and hit the desk with his fist. "Right now! What're you waiting for?" He fell across the desk, raising the telephone and slamming it down in front of the chair. "You'll speak your piece and I'll speak mine! You tell the board I called you a sonofabitch, and we'll count the guys who disagree with me! Then I'll tell them I had a twenty-four-hour cover on Joe Liliuohe and you yanked it! I'll take them down to the morgue and show them what that .45 slug did to his face, what's left of his face! And then I'll go over to the *Outpost-Dispatch* and let Jeff Terwilliger in on our secret!" Maddox watched the little man who didn't move, who held on to the oversized chair. "Harvey Koster," Maddox said. "I didn't need Harvey Koster to get my badge and I don't need him or anyone else on God's green earth to keep it." Maddox buttoned his jacket. "You turd," he said, and turned away, walking to the door.

The three suspects in the murder of Joe Liliuohe were to be arraigned the next morning, Friday. At 8:00 A.M. the admiral telephoned the clerk of municipal court and told him Doris Ashley was recuperating from the shock of the previous twenty-four hours and could not leave his quarters at Pearl Harbor. Since the courts were not in session Saturday and Sunday, the admiral said his guests would appear Monday morning.

Hester was awake long before the admiral telephoned the courthouse Friday morning, the morning after Jimmy Saunders had brought her to Pearl Harbor. She had come to the door of the carriage house thinking it was Amelia or Theresa sent on some new compulsive mission by her mother. The commander had introduced himself and Hester knew, before he said, "I have bad news, Mrs. Murdoch," that something terrible had happened to Gerald.

"He's not dead," Hester said, guilty already. She could not think of him dead. She only wanted him to be gone, gone forever.

"*He's* not dead," Saunders said, and told her of the shooting. "Can I get you anything?" The girl had turned white. "Would you like to sit down?" She stood beside the staircase as though he weren't there.

Hester could see Joseph Liliuohe, see him in court sitting with the other young men, see him standing when court adjourned each day, waiting for him to turn and look at her as he did daily. She saw him now with his eyes closed and his hands folded across his belly. She could see him in the grave, in the dark in the ground. And Gerald was waiting. Her mother was waiting. "You should pack some things, Mrs. Murdoch," said the commander. He watched her climbing the stairs like he was a blind date who had appeared on prom night.

Hester set her suitcase on the bed. She went from the bed to the chest of drawers, seeing the dead man in her lingerie, on the headboard, blocking the closet. She walked back and forth like an ox tethered and moving in an endless circle around a millstone. She tried to keep the ox in her mind but the dead man came back to remind her who had killed him. Hester had killed him. She dropped clothes in the suitcase and ran to the bathroom.

Hester took the bottle of iodine from the medicine cabinet, remembering Joan of Arc with the cross at the stake. Hester removed the cap and looked at the crossed bones with the red word, POISON!, between. She tipped the bottle, watching a drop a second fall into the sink. She wanted to die. She deserved to die. Killers had to pay for their crimes. But she said, defeated, "Coward," and set the cap on the bottle.

"Mrs. Murdoch?" Saunders had followed her, worried about the girl. Hester closed the medicine cabinet and came into the bedroom. "If you're ready, let me give you a hand," Saunders said. She could not escape. She would be locked away with Gerald and with her mother at Pearl Harbor. *Bryce!*

"I'm ready," Hester said, despising herself for thinking of him. If he came to the admiral's quarters, she would remain upstairs. She would lock herself in her room.

When Jimmy Saunders, carrying Hester's suitcase, led her into the admiral's living room, Doris Ashley said, "Gerald will be staying at the bachelor officers' quarters." Hester thanked a merciful God who had taken pity on her.

Now, early Friday morning, separated from her mother by the bathroom between them, Hester dressed quietly. She carried her shoes and in the hall tiptoed past Doris Ashley's bedroom. Hester stopped at the head of the stairs, holding the railing to slip on the flat-heeled moccasins. She was almost at the door when someone said, "Miss?" A Filipino in a white shirt but without his black bowtie or his mess jacket was in the open arch of the dining room. "Breakfast?"

"Thank you," Hester said. "Later," she said, leaving before her mother could appear to stop her. Outside, she walked as though she were holding her breath, as though she were being graded for posture, looking neither to right nor left. She had stopped reviling herself. She could not check the urge within her. It was like a thirst, a need beyond comprehension, a desire that must be sated. Hester stopped the first officer she saw and asked him for directions to the submarine pens.

"Panthers," Hester said to herself, looking at the sleek black boats in the water. Crewmen were coming aboard for the day and suddenly Hester saw Joseph Liliuohe among them. He was dead. She looked away as she had in court day after day, staring at the horizon, placing Guam and Wake Island and Tahiti and the Philippines in geographic order until she dared to watch the submarines once more. To her left she saw the free and easy stride. "Hello, Bryce."

Bryce stopped and saw the submariners walking to their boats. Then he saw the woman, a thin, ordinary drone, no bigger than a jockey. She said,, "Bryce," and this time he felt as though someone had grabbed him from behind, crushing him.

Hester was at Pearl because Gerald and her mother were here. "Watch yourself, sport," Bryce said to himself. "You're glad to see her." He made himself smile and immediately stopped smiling. Gerald had *killed* a man.

"I was taking a walk," Hester said. They were both damned, damned together. They had both killed Joseph Liliuohe.

Bryce listened to her lying through her teeth. She had waylaid him. "How's Gerald?"

"He's at the bachelor officers' quarters," Hester said. "Did you get my letter?"

He wanted to throw her into the ocean. "You shouldn't have written to me, Hester. Don't . . . ." he said, and broke off. "I hope you never do it again, Hester."

She hated him. She hated herself. She despised him and despised herself because she wanted to touch him, feel his hair or arm or chest or everything in her hand. "I won't need to write," she said. "I'm here, in the admiral's quarters."

He looked at his wristwatch. "Time for me to be aboard," Bryce said. She stayed *with* him. He made himself smile again. "It's an all-male boat, Hester."

"Bryce, wait." She raised her hand to keep the sun from her eyes. "We can meet somewhere," Hester said.

"Sure. We'll be crossing paths," Bryce said.

"No, not paths," Hester said. "I want to see you. I've been alone. I'm alone. That man . . . boy was innocent. Now he's dead, and he was innocent."

"So am I!" Bryce said, and quickly, "I really have to go aboard, Hester." He turned, taking long, swift strides. Hester wanted to leap upon him. She wanted to pummel him, beat him as he had beaten her. She wanted to maim him. A short, muffled cry of despair escaped from her. She believed herself to be beyond redemption but there remained one course open to her. Hester turned and began to run.

She saw the admiral's limousine leaving as she approached his quarters. Hester came up the wooden steps and the door opened. The mess boy she had seen earlier held the door. "Breakfast now, miss?"

Hester could see into the dining room. It was empty. She hurried past him toward the stairs. "Thank you, no," she said. "No breakfast."

She closed the door to her room slowly, noiselessly, and took off her moccasins. Hester tiptoed to the bathroom, opened the door, and locked the opposite door. "Hester?" Doris Ashley's voice was faint, but Hester heard her mother's footsteps. Hester bent over the bathtub and turned both faucets, leaving the drain open. She came erect, taking a towel and wiping her hands as she crossed the bedroom for her purse. She had kept the telephone number, in a secret compartment, ever since that day, long ago, in Mercy Hospital. She knew the number. Hester had looked at it a hundred, a thousand times since that day. She looked at it again before sitting down on the bed and putting the telephone on her knees.

Hester heard the ring. This time she was ready. She could barely wait. She heard another ring. He *had* to answer! Hester was almost happy. At last she could stop detesting herself. There! He was there! "Is this Mr. Halehone?"

"Yes," Tom said.

"Mr. Halehone, the lawyer?" Hester asked. "You were the lawyer for Joseph . . . ?" and lost the telephone. Doris Ashley had the telephone and the receiver, pulling at the cord like a fisherman bringing in his dropline, hand over hand until she reached the bedroom wall. Doris Ashley was in her dressing gown and she dropped to her knees, dropping the instrument but doubled over to shield it as she pulled the cord from the wall connection.

Doris Ashley remained on her knees on the floor for a moment, panting, unable to rise after her narrow escape. Doris had asked for breakfast in her room, and she was forcing herself to eat, to keep up her strength, when she heard Hester in the bathroom. The mess boy had told her that Hester had gone out early. Now she was back and bathing. Why hadn't she bathed before dressing as Doris had taught her? Doris Ashley had knocked on the bathroom door. She had put her face to the door, calling for

Hester, and when there was no reply, when Doris heard only the water cascading as though a dam had broken, she ran into the hall and into the adjoining bedroom. Doris Ashley pushed herself to her feet. She was in total disarray, her hair unpinned, her dressing gown open and smudged and trailing. Facing Hester, she slammed the receiver into the cradle of the disconnected telephone, wrapping the rubber-coated wire around both. Mrs. Ashley would tell the Filipino Hester had tripped over the wire. She would tell them not to have it repaired. She would need to be eternally vigilant. Doris Ashley dropped to the bed beside Hester, exhausted by her ordeal. "I saved you, baby!" she said. "*Saved* you when you were lost. This is how you decided to repay me."

"They wouldn't let him live here," Sarah said. "I won't let him lie here." Tom was with her in the small, scrubbed house as she confronted her father. Sarah's mother had barricaded herself in the bedroom, sitting alone and rocking from side to side, holding Joe's shirt, which she had been ironing when she was told of his death.

"It's not our island," Sarah said to her father. "It's theirs. But it's not their ocean." She took Tom's hand. "Will you help me?"

There were no announcements. No one called the Liliuohe home. Neither the *Outpost-Dispatch* nor the *Islander* carried a story. Yet by seven o'clock Sunday morning fishermen fishing from shore far west of Honolulu began to see people walking along the beach, a man alone, or two women, or a man and a woman. Some were dressed for Sunday with shoes and socks, and some were in shabby, clean clothes, their bare feet in cheap sandals. Some carried their sandals. Some of the fishermen asked questions and joined the people, carrying their poles and bait pails with their catch in pails of sea water. Some fishermen remained for a time and then, one by one, followed the procession until there were no fishermen remaining.

When they reached the cove where Sarah and Tom had found Joe wrapped in a blanket with Becky Hanatani those who were barefoot put on their sandals. Most were strangers to each other and for a long time they stood in silence, separated by the rocks thrown on the beach by the ocean, and the only sound was the sound of the surf beating against the shore.

Others rode the trolley to the end of the line and walked to their destination. People came in cars, five and six and seven to a car, with their children, and the cars stopped for those who were walking, carrying people on the running boards. Senso

Fujito came in his flatbed truck with his wife and children, including his oldest son whose foot was still swollen. Senso stopped for people until his truck was full. Other trucks came with people sitting and standing behind the cab.

They came from everywhere, the Hawaiians from Papakolea and Kakaao, the Chinese from Liliha and Makiki, from Manoa and Nuuanu, the Japanese from Kalihi and Moiliili and Damon Tract. They were a vast and orderly horde on the warm sand, in the sun, beside the gentle Pacific. Children stood on the rocks, and all watched the sea.

Then someone farsighted watching the sea said, "There," and pointed at the specks in the distance. Someone else said, "Where?" and another said, "I can't see anything," but all those assembled moved to the water's edge, shading their eyes and searching the ocean. Soon the specks became boats, two with outriggers, slender as match sticks with five oarsmen in each, and behind them, pulled by ropes leading to each of the other craft, a scow. A simple wooden coffin with rope handles lay in the scow, and Tom and Sarah and her father and Becky Hanatani sat beside it.

On the shore young men rolled up their pants, removing shoes and socks to enter the surf, waiting to pull the boats onto the sand. The people regrouped in a wide arc, making room for the boats, and far back Maddox left his car among the other cars and trucks and walked toward the cove.

The appearance of the boats, the sight of the casket, of Sarah and her father and Becky with the lawyer, the swelling numbers of young men in the surf, occupied the assemblage so that Maddox approached unnoticed. He watched the kids in the water pulling the boats, saw the oarsmen slip over the sides to surround the scow and push it onto the sand. He moved toward the water, trying for an unobstructed view, and bumped into someone. Senso Fujito spread both arms to gather his wife and children. He recognized the policeman who had come to the farm. He whispered to his wife, and one of his children whispered to a new friend he had made on the beach. The children stared at Maddox. Other children joined the pair but their parents pulled them back. Senso and his family left Maddox, and everyone else after a quick glance, moved aside until he was alone, the single haole at the cove.

His name and identity flashed through the crowd. The boys in the water looked at him and one shouted, "Leave us alone!" A friend cautioned him but the boy yelled, "You don't belong here! This isn't Honolulu!" Another boy yelled, and a third, and the first came out of the water, headed for Maddox. One of the oarsmen followed him, and others followed both. Boys and men took their courage from the leaders and the group swelled. Maddox was facing a mob.

"You kids ought to be ashamed of yourselves," Maddox said. "This isn't a luau. You're at a funeral."

They shouted their defiance. They did not threaten. They responded out of sorrow, for Joe Liliuohe and for themselves, and out of fear, out of generations of deprivation and exploitation, out of neglect and contempt and scorn. They would not be silenced. Their voices mounted in a shrill and inflammatory cry, and because they were a mob and they had seen the casket, they became hostile and quickly vengeful.

"Let me through!" Tom said. With Sarah beside him, he pushed and elbowed his way between the solid mass that had formed an arc around Maddox, with only the sea open to him. *"Let me through!"* Tom said, over and over again, until, holding Sarah's hand, he lowered his head and dove forward. He almost fell. He was thrust from one of the mob to the other, but he would not be stopped, and he was, finally, in the front ranks, his chest heaving, facing Maddox.

Tom took a step and another, putting himself and Sarah between the rest and Maddox. Tom kept his back to the rest. He did not acknowledge their presence. He was silent, and, quickly, they became silent. "Pretty noisy bunch," Maddox said.

Sarah came close to whisper, "I don't want him here."

Tom remembered calling Maddox from the public phone in police headquarters. He remembered ringing Maddox's doorbell. He remembered, he could hear the calculated insolence in Maddox's voice, threatening to arrest him, to send him to the work farm. Tom wanted to repeat everything Maddox had said a week earlier. He couldn't. He wanted to set the mob on Maddox. They were ready; Tom knew they were ready. He couldn't. He wanted to humiliate Maddox. He couldn't. He wanted to order Maddox off the beach. He couldn't.

"Tell him to leave," Sarah whispered.

Tom said, "Sarah, we can't . . ." and she stopped him.

"If you won't tell him, I will!" Sarah said, and she was no longer whispering. Maddox heard her, everyone heard her.

"If he leaves, I leave," Tom said. He heard Sarah suck in her breath in shock and amazement. "I'll leave with him," Tom said. "I didn't ask him to come. I'm sorry he's here. But he's *here*. We don't bar people, *they* bar people. We don't keep anyone out, *they* do. We don't whip and torture and kill people, *they* do. So he stays, Sarah. Otherwise we're like them."

Maddox watched the pair. She didn't answer the lawyer. She looked at Maddox and then she took the lawyer's hand. Holding hands, they turned back to the crowd. Maddox couldn't hear the lawyer, but the crowd made a path for the pair, and as the two went past, the men and boys who had converged on him all started for the boats. Maddox was alone. He raised one leg, taking off his shoe to empty it of sand, and, wobbling, pushed his foot into it. Then he followed the others.

Tom saw Sarah's father in the scow. He saw Becky, her arm across the casket as though she were protecting Joe. Sarah's father faced the people, but he seemed to be alone with Joe. Sarah saw her father. "He's dead, too," she said.

They stopped in front of the scow, and those with them, those who had confronted Maddox, moved back to merge with the men and women and children, leaving Sarah and Tom alone. Sarah took her hand from Tom's. "It's time."

"Stay here," Tom said. He had promised Sarah he would say something. He had tried to write something, writing on his yellow legal pad, but the words he set down were wrong. Nothing he wrote fit Joe, and he had, after a few moments, put aside the legal pad.

They were waiting, silent and patient. Sarah waited. Tom didn't know where or how to begin. He said, "Joe Liliuohe . . ." and stopped, and saw Maddox reach the crowd. "Joe Liliuohe was a big, wonderful, friendly, laughing guy," Tom said, and he was, at last, answering Maddox. He was talking directly to Maddox.

"I don't mean he was always laughing," Tom said. "I mean he was always *ready* to laugh. He was ready to have fun. I had more fun, right here, with Joe, than I ever had in my life. Joe could make things better just by being there. He could make you smile when you didn't feel like smiling. It was true for everyone, kids as well as grown-ups. Everyone knew this about Joe so everyone crowded around him. He spent most of his life, his short life, in a crowd. Everyone was Joe's friend. So when he was killed, when he was taken off the street on his way to Mercy Hospital to see his friends, it wasn't only his mother and father and sister who lost Joe. Hundreds, maybe thousands, of people, lost." Tom heard Sarah weeping but he couldn't look at her. If he looked at her, he would stop. He looked at Maddox.

"Joe didn't need to die," Tom said. "He died because he lived here, on this island in this Territory. If he had lived anywhere else, he'd still be alive. And he wanted to leave. When he was arrested, when he was accused of a crime he didn't commit, he wanted to run. I made him stay." Tom swallowed. "I said, 'You're innocent! You don't need to be afraid!' So he stayed, and now he's dead." Tom swallowed again and felt Sarah touch him, felt her hand on his arm, telling him to go on.

"There are people on this island, all over the place, who believe this island is a kind of private country that belongs to them, and if anything happens, any disturbance of the peace, they solve it, with their whips and with their guns. They've had it their own way for so long they believe they own this island. And they're right. They *do* own it. They own the business in the Territory and the plantations in the Territory. What they couldn't buy, they took. They claimed it like prospectors after gold. Only prospectors stake their claims in a wilderness. Hawaii wasn't a wilderness.

"This island is a kind of miracle or would be if those people would accept the simple fact that all men are created equal," Tom said. "That's all it would take. It's the only thing missing. Right here on Oahu we've got people from just about every country on this earth living together in peace. They grow up together and marry each other, and their children grow up and marry each other. We've reached the point where in thousands of cases there *aren't* any Hawaiians, or Japanese, or Chinese, or Tahitians, or Filipinos, or Fijians, or Frenchmen, or Dutchmen, or Portuguese, or anything else. All of *these* people probably never thought of it, but they've brought the miracle to this island. We're out here, in the middle of the biggest ocean in the world, a place the size of a postage stamp, and we've made one of the wonders of the world, the *real* wonder of the world. Just by *living* with other people, with people next door and across the street, we've stopped the oldest and the worst disease in history. Men have been killing other men all through history because they've been strangers. We've stopped being strangers.

"But there's the other part of the population, the small part. It's one hundred fifty-two years since Captain Cook came here, but most of those people behave like they haven't unpacked. They haven't unlocked their front doors except for each other. They're all part of a big conspiracy. They didn't need one hundred fifty-two years to create their country. Even that isn't the real trouble. The real trouble is that deep down they believe they own us. That's why they believe Joe Liliuohe was guilty. That's why he's dead now." Tom stopped. He looked at Maddox, who hadn't moved.

"Joe loved everything but he loved the ocean best," Tom said. "So that's where he'll stay, far out. He always swam far out. Far, far out." Tom dropped his head, blinking. He said, low, "Joe," as though they were alone together, in the cove, resting before plunging back into the sea. "Joe."

Three days after Joe Liliuohe's casket was pushed off the scow more than a mile from shore, a swift, sharp drop in temperature fell along the entire Eastern Seaboard of the United States. Automobile radiators froze and long lines of cars, engines steaming, were stalled from Canada to Atlanta. The winter had been mild and gasoline stations were not prepared. Stocks of alcohol were quickly depleted. All through the night smudge pots burned between the rows of citrus from one end of Florida to the other, and in Washington snow began to fall during the night.

By eight o'clock the next morning traffic in the capital became an immovable mass. The heavy snow dropped a curtain over Washington. Trolleys and buses were jammed with people who had left their cars at home. There were automobile accidents everywhere. Hospitals filled with the injured, and police could not respond to the calls that jammed the switchboard.

"A plague has been visited upon me," said Floyd Rasmussen. "The President will cancel my appointment."

"The President of the United States does not stop functioning because of a snowfall," said Phoebe. The senator's wife sat comfortably in his office. "Sit down, Floyd. You'll exhaust yourself." Rasmussen's appointment at the White House was for three o'clock that afternoon.

"We won't be able to leave the Hill," Rasmussen said. "We won't get through."

"The President's car will get through," Phoebe said. She left the sofa against the wall to take Rasmussen's arm. "Call the White House," she said. "Tell them to send transportation for you." They reached the desk, and Phoebe lifted the telephone receiver. "He cannot cancel an appointment with someone who is being driven to the Oval Office." Rasmussen took the receiver and sat down.

As he rode down Pennsylvania Avenue in the President's limousine, the snowfall ended, and when he and the others came out of the White House, just after three-thirty, a break in the clouds let the sun escape, turning Washington into a fairyland. Rasmussen was convinced he had received a sign. He felt like Moses before the Red Sea.

With him were six other senators, Bowman of Georgia, Fox of Mississippi, Reynolds of Utah, Glanda of Illinois, Stillman of Nebraska, and Ewing of Kentucky. They were senior senators.

Rasmussen was the only junior, but he was their leader, and he was in charge.

The newspaper photographers were already at work. Rasmussen turned to Ewing, making conversation so he would not be posing. He would not be hurried today. Rasmussen had deliberately asked for an afternoon appointment, preferring the morning newspapers. When the photographers gave way to the reporters, Rasmussen stepped forward, making certain he could be heard by the radio people. The newsreel cameramen began to grind.

"I'll begin with an announcement," Rasmussen said, taking the papers out of his inner pocket. "First, let me say I am only a spokesman for the distinguished colleagues at my side. I am a spokesman for the *host* of eminent and honorable and *God-fearing* colleagues in both the Senate and the House who have joined me in this crusade to protect helpless Americans across the seas, thousands of miles from their native land."

Rasmussen raised the papers as though he were holding a torch. "I have here the names of one hundred twenty-five United States Senators and United States Representatives. They speak for the multitudes in every city and every village, in every home and farmhouse across the length and breadth of our great Republic, raising their voices in one united cry for justice. Doris Ashley, Lieutenant Gerald Murdoch, and Seaman Second Class Duane York must be set *free!* Freedom *now!*" Rasmussen paused, lowering his arm. His voice fell. "I have so informed the President."

The White House story was on the front page of the *Outpost-Dispatch* Thursday morning, beside a recent picture of Rasmussen from the newspaper's morgue. In his office Harvey Koster read every word of Rasmussen's meeting with the President. He folded the newspaper and set it on the rolltop desk. Koster sat quietly, without moving, for a long time. At last he turned his chair and set the telephone in front of him. He made several calls during the day.

He wasn't ready to talk with Doris Ashley until late in the afternoon. Harvey Koster postponed it until the following morning. The day had been wearing. There was, however, another reason for this decision. He did not like to be away from his home after dark because he could not abandon the girls after dark. His secretary made no appointments for him after four-thirty in the afternoon.

Before leaving the office, Koster dropped the *Outpost-Dispatch* into his wastebasket. Floyd Rasmussen looked up at him from the front page. The senator's visit to the White House had forced Koster to decide on Walter Bergman.

Long before 1931 Walter Bergman had become the most famous, the most easily identifiable lawyer in the United States. He was a criminal lawyer and a front-page name. Walter Bergman had been counsel for the defense in many of the most famous trials in America during the fifty-two years he had practiced law. The cases had never been ordinary, and the defendants had never been common criminals. Walter Bergman had never taken a case because he needed a client, even in the beginning, when he began in the small suite in the modest building in Chicago. The cases needed a distinguishing factor to attract him. Bergman never worked for another lawyer. After the first few years, he never lacked for clients. The clients still came to him, in the same small suite where he had started. Harvey Koster had the Chicago address in his pocket when he arrived at the admiral's quarters Friday morning.

Doris Ashley was alone. "Well, Harvey. You've come to see the prisoner."

"It's hard for me to think of you in this," Koster said. "You shouldn't be in this."

"Philip Murray doesn't have your problem," said Doris Ashley. She looked out at the wide veranda that lay beyond the low-ceilinged living room. "I'm here," she said. "I cannot return to my home. I cannot leave unless I'm under guard. Sailors with guns guard me."

"At least the admiral kept you out of jail."

"This is a jail," Doris Ashley said. "It is my jail."

"You have Hester with you." Doris Ashley looked at the middle-aged man sitting beside her. He was like someone in a long line, a supplicant hoping for alms. Doris Ashley envied him, but not for his money, or ranches, or warehouses. Harvey Koster was *free!*

"Yes, I have Hester." She left Koster, walking out onto the veranda. He followed her. "I'll be on trial for murder, Harvey."

The sun hurt Koster's eyes. "Have you thought about a lawyer, Doris?"

"I have a lawyer," said Doris Ashley. "Alton Wormser is my lawyer."

"Alton Wormser hasn't been in court for almost twenty years," Koster said. "He's never been in court for a criminal case. Philip Murray is always in court on criminal cases. It's his trade."

"No one in the islands is more respected than Alton," said Doris Ashley.

"You need someone better than Murray in a courtroom," Koster said. "Someone like Walter Bergman."

"The man from Chicago?" asked Doris Ashley. "The old man?"

"His mind isn't old," Koster said. "He's the best. His record is the best. I think you should retain him, Doris. You need him."

"I'll also have to pay him," said Doris Ashley. "He must be expensive."

"He'll probably ask for twenty-five thousand dollars," Koster said. Doris Ashley put her hand on the porch railing. The white paint glistened. The railing was damp but as clean as the tables at Windward. "Bergman can handle Philip Murray," Koster said.

"For twenty-five thousand," said Doris Ashley.

"He'll ask for his keep," Koster said. "His and his wife's."

"At the Western Sky, of course," said Doris Ashley. She remembered the presidential suite. She remembered her wedding night in the suite with Preston Ashley. She could still repeat his apologies. Doris Ashley looked out at the ocean. She had not killed the man. Gerald had killed him. Gerald's fingerprints were on the gun. She was here, imprisoned, with Windward at the mercy of Amelia and Theresa, because of Gerald. She wanted him to be punished. She wanted Gerald out of her life, and Hester's. She wanted to return to Windward with Hester. She would lock up the carriage house forever. "I have nothing to fear," said Doris Ashley.

Koster drove from Pearl Harbor to the cable office downtown. He retained Walter Bergman for the defense in the murder of Joseph Liliuohe. He guaranteed the fee. Bergman had won more acquittals than any lawyer in America. If the defendants were freed, the people in Washington would be silenced. Koster knew he was gambling, but he had no other choice.

PART 4

"Tell me the easiest, fastest way to the promenade deck," Maddox said to the purser. "Use right and left. I'm not much of a sailor." The purser gave Maddox the directions. "And I'm looking for twenty-four B," Maddox said, repeating the cabin numbers as he left the purser, his arm out and his hand touching the bulkhead. Maddox didn't like ships.

Harvey Koster had asked him to meet the *S.S. Hawaiian Queen* and take Walter Bergman ashore. Maddox was at Aloha Tower an hour before the *Queen* was eased into the pier by the tugs. Maddox had sent an extra squad car with two uniformed policemen to the tower. He gave the cops their instructions and left them. He was the first one aboard.

Maddox came onto the promenade deck and stopped at the first door. It was 36B. Holding the rail he walked along the passageway to 24B. Maddox took off his hat and knocked. He waited and knocked again, and a woman said, "What is it?"

She was in the doorway to his right, an unmarked door. Maddox figured she was in her thirties. She was slim and pale. Her skin was white, like a baby's skin. Her hair was the color of leaves in autumn, parted on the side and curling around her neck. She was in a tan dress that buttoned up the front. She wore a narrow brown belt around her waist and a white scarf around her throat. Maddox liked the way she was dressed, simple and without show. "I'm here for Walter Bergman."

She came through the doorway and Maddox saw her eyes. They were a deep green, like grass in the rain, and they were flecked with gold. Maddox had never seen eyes like the woman's. "Who are you?" she asked.

Maddox reached into his pocket and raised his hand, palm up, to show her the brass badge. "I'm with the Honolulu Police Department," Maddox said. "I came aboard to take Walter Bergman off the ship the easiest and fastest way I can." He dropped the badge into his pocket.

"I'm Mrs. Bergman," she said.

So Maddox had her story, front to back. Her clothes were nothing but a front. She was only another broad who had hooked on to a meal ticket. He felt a surge of anger, but he was angry at himself for being fooled. But he could not look away. He saw the golden flecks in her eyes and the sweep of her hair as it fell over the white skin. Maddox remembered reading that Walter Bergman was seventy-six years old, so this dame was not even half his age.

They heard a man's voice. "Lenore?"

She spoke to the door. "I'll be there in a minute," and to Maddox, "I stopped you because I try to protect him. Everyone wants to talk to him and he won't hurt anyone's feelings. He won't spare himself." She opened the door. "We won't be long. Thank you for coming."

Maddox wiped the sweatband of his hat with his handkerchief. He folded the handkerchief before stuffing it into his breast pocket. "Seventy-six years old," he said to himself. A crewman approached, almost hidden by the luggage he carried, and Maddox hugged the bulkhead to let him pass. "Will you come in, please, Captain?"

She was holding the open door. No one, ever, had noticed the word CAPTAIN above the star of the badge he carried. He took off his hat, telling himself not to look at her eyes.

Walter Bergman sat in a chair beside the bed. Maddox saw the open door flanking the bed, and he saw the cabin beyond with the other bed.

Bergman's hair was gray, a harsh gray like river ice. It was spiky and unruly. He was clean and neat, but he seemed out of place in his clothes, like a farmer who had dressed for the city. He wore a blue shirt with starched French cuffs and a starched white collar. His tie and trousers were blue. Maddox saw the blue jacket on the bed. Maddox was never impressed but he had read about Bergman, who was famous everywhere, and for that reason and because he examined everyone, he noticed Bergman's hands. They were large, oversized hands with big knuckles and thick fingers, the hands of a laborer, of a man who has been drained by the long decades of toil.

"Appreciate your courtesy, Captain," Bergman said. When he rose, Maddox was surprised by Bergman's size. He had not looked big in the chair, but he was tall, taller than Maddox, and thin. He was gaunt. He was pale like his wife, but Bergman's face was gray, and pasty. Maddox was with a sick man.

"We can start anytime you're ready," Maddox said. He saw

Bergman walk into the bed. So his eyes were bad, too. Maddox took the jacket from the bed, holding it at the shoulders.

"Much obliged," Bergman said. Maddox stepped to one side so he could see her.

"There's a gang out on the pier," Maddox said. "Honolulu is full of reporters for the trial. We can give them the slip. I've checked out a cargo hatch. My car is in front of it."

She stopped beside him, and he tried not to look at her. "We're very grateful to you, Captain," she said.

"I'll collar someone for the luggage," Maddox said.

Maddox returned with a crewman who pushed a dolly into the cabin. They followed the crewman to a freight elevator that dropped deep into the ship. When the door rose, Maddox saw his car directly ahead, guarded by the two policemen. A broad gangplank led to the pier. They could hear the ukuleles. "Lenore, listen!" Bergman said. He was like a boy when he smiled. Maddox saw her take his arm. Bergman had married a nurse. "Excuse me," Maddox said, and to the crewman, "Shake a leg." He went ahead, calling to the two cops. "Give us a hand."

The pier was thronged with the usual population on hand for arrivals and departures, friends and relatives of the passengers, and the entrepreneurs who tried to earn a living from them. Maddox could see the crowd of reporters and photographers forward. Maddox helped the cops and crewman set the luggage into the rear of the car, then gave the crewman a tip. Maddox beckoned to her and Bergman, leading them around the car and opening both doors. Maddox saw Jeff Terwilliger running toward him ahead of other reporters and photographers. "Stop them," he said to the cops, and to Bergman. "We'd better hurry." He stepped back to help her into the front seat, but she climbed into the rear beside the luggage.

"You won't see much, Lenore," Bergman said. "I wanted you to see the sights."

"Maddox!" Terwilliger was yelling but the cops blocked him. Maddox ran around the car to the driver's side. The cops were surrounded. He put his hand on the horn, driving off the pier.

Maddox could see her in a corner of the rearview mirror. She had rolled down the window and the breeze ruffled her hair. "How do you like it, Lenore?" Bergman asked.

"I've never seen anything as clean," she said.

"It's washed all the time," Maddox said. "The clouds are trapped by those hills so there's a shower almost every day."

"The smell takes me back," Bergman said. "I grew up in the

country. A month or so after the snow melted, around about early May, the ground would open. The soil was black and the wild flowers came. Everything you smelled was sweet. Are you a country boy, Captain?''

"I was born here in Honolulu," Maddox said. He was talking to her.

"A native," Bergman said. "Did you hear that, Lenore?"

"Yes, Walter." She was looking out of the open window.

Maddox drove into Kalakau Avenue. "We're coming to Waikiki," he said. She'd be gone in the next five minutes. He could see the Western Sky on his right. "There's your hotel," he said, swinging into the inside lane. The driveway curved through the hotel gardens. They drove through rhododendron and towering hibiscus set behind spectacular borders of annuals. Maddox stopped and put the POLICE sign in the window. "I'll find a bellhop," he said.

When he returned, she was helping Bergman out of the car. They thanked him and after Bergman shook hands, she extended hers. She felt like silk. Then she was gone, holding Bergman's arm. Maddox helped the bellhop. He wanted to leave.

But he didn't leave. He drove past the entrance and parked. He could use a telephone in the hotel to call headquarters.

When he came into the lobby, he saw the manager taking the Bergmans to the elevators. Maddox stopped, out of sight, until they were gone. He went to a public telephone. "Maddox. Anything?''

"Pretty quiet, Captain," said the cop on the switchboard. Maddox walked into the lobby. There was sunlight from the sea. Outside, protected by glass barriers on either end, was a large dining room. Maddox saw the white tablecloths. He saw the diners, fashionable women and well-dressed men, a million miles from the murder and the trial. He heard the clatter of flatware and the tinkling of glasses. The elegance, the serenity, the sensuous luxury was hypnotic. Maddox had never been in the hotel by choice, coming only if duty required his presence, but now he walked through the lobby, walked slowly, as though he were one of them.

Maddox stopped where the carpets met the flagstone of the dining room. The headwaiter joined him, a bundle of large menus under his arm. "How many will there be, sir?"

"I'm alone," Maddox said. He never ate lunch. She was up there somewhere. She could be right above him.

"It'll be a few minutes," said the headwaiter. "Maybe ten, maybe more." Maddox nodded. The headwaiter left him for a man and two women. The man was wearing white flannels with white shoes, and a Navy blue blazer. Maddox watched the headwaiter taking them to a table. He turned, and she was close enough to touch. He said, "Well," and stopped. He caught his breath, feeling a tight band across his chest.

"Oh, hello, Captain," she said.

"Waiting for Mr. Bergman?" All of a sudden it was the most important question he had ever asked.

"He's resting." She made a small, sad smile. "He insists on seeing his clients this afternoon."

"Well, maybe . . . I was waiting . . . would you like to have lunch?" He cursed himself for his dumbness. "You aren't here for a newspaper. I mean, would you like to have lunch together?"

"Thank you, Captain. That would be nice," she said. Maddox raised his arm to bring the headwaiter and dropped it immediately, cursing himself again. He was through using the badge for a while. She was looking out at the ocean, so he watched her.

The headwaiter returned and Maddox said, "The lady is with me. Make it two."

"I can seat you now," the headwaiter said. She followed him, and Maddox followed her. Every man she passed looked up at her.

As the headwaiter pulled out a chair, Maddox said, "Hold it." He reached for the chair opposite. "Take this one, Mrs. Bergman. You can see all the way to Diamond Head."

"You know your way around Honolulu, sir," said the headwaiter.

"A little," Maddox said, and when they were seated, "How's the view?"

"It's spectacular," she said. "Thank you, Captain."

"I'm Captain when I'm working," Maddox said. "I'm not working now. My name's Curtis. Curt." He moved a glass of water.

"All right, Curt," she said. "My name is Lenore."

"I was way ahead of you," Maddox said. "I heard your husband."

They were both silent. Lenore opened the menu. "If you want something and you don't see it, you tell me," Maddox said. "Sounds like I'm pushing. I don't like being crowded myself."

Lenore lowered the menu, smiling. The sadness was gone. The two ends of the kerchief around her throat fluttered in the wind. Maddox wanted to put a cage around them. "Pushing," Lenore said. "Crowded. I've never heard anyone speak like you."

"You and me, we live on different sides of the street," Maddox said. Lenore laughed, and Maddox grinned. "More of the same, isn't it?" She nodded, laughing, and afterward they were silent again. "Anyway, what would you like to eat?"

"A salad? A seafood salad?"

"Sounds right," Maddox said. "We'll do two of those." Maddox gestured to a waiter, ordering the salads and coffee.

The waiter returned too soon. Their lunch was over too soon. "I'll get us some more coffee," Maddox said, but Lenore shook her head. So Maddox knew they were down to the wire, and they hadn't even started.

Lenore threw back her head, closing her eyes. He saw the white curve of her neck above the kerchief. She opened her eyes, smiling. Maddox wanted to empty the place. "I want to stretch, like a cat in the sun."

"Do it," Maddox said. "You do whatever you feel like doing."

"Do you, Captain . . . Curt? Do whatever you feel like doing?"

"I don't take orders easy," Maddox said. "I suppose it's from being alone. Doing what you want becomes a habit. There's never been anyone around to give me orders."

Lenore reached for her coffee, looking down at the cup. "Are you . . . alone?"

"I'm the only Maddox on the island," he said.

She raised the cup, making a wall between them. "It must be lonely for you."

"You live with what you've got," Maddox said. He had told her too much already. "You wanted to stretch."

"It's passed," Lenore said. She lowered her coffee without drinking. Maddox knew she was on her way before she said, "Walter may need me." Maddox was on his feet ahead of her. "Thanks ever so much," Lenore said.

Her eyes were another green now. "When is your husband seeing his clients?" Maddox asked.

"He said we'd leave around three."

"You'll need one cab to take you to Pearl, and another to bring you back," Maddox said. "They can keep you waiting out there. I'll drive you."

"I can't ask . . ." Lenore began.

"You didn't," Maddox said, interrupting. "Three o'clock."

He stood until she was gone. When he sat down to wait for the check, Maddox chose her chair. He put his hand on the table, his fingers on her fork.

In his car Maddox thought of her sitting across from him. He remembered the pale pink of her fingernails when she raised her glass. He remembered her head thrown back to the sky. In his driveway at home he left the car and remembered turning twice, once on the ship, once in the entrance of the dining room, to find her beside him. "Voodoo," he said, aloud.

Maddox bathed again and shaved again. He left everything he had worn on the bed. He was back in the lobby of the Western Sky long before three o'clock. He wore a tan gabardine suit and a fresh white shirt. His holster was far back on his hip so it would be hidden by the jacket. Maddox watched the clock over the registration desk. A few minutes before three he went to the house phones. When Lenore answered, Maddox leaned against the wall. She took the breath out of him. "Hello," he said. "Ready?"

She said, "Oh, it's you. Yes, I think so. Will you hold a moment?" Maddox waited. "He'll be right down."

"How about you?"

"Walter will be with his clients."

"Pearl is a long way," Maddox said. "Here's a chance for you to see the island."

"We've just arrived," Lenore said. "I'll have plenty of time."

"Right," Maddox said. "I'll be at the elevators." He left the house phones. He should never have dug out the old gabardine. He had never liked the suit. He decided to give it to one of the young guys at headquarters. She was only being polite eating with him. Why in hell had he decided to have lunch anyway? An elevator opened and two couples came out, and behind them Maddox saw Lenore with Bergman. Maddox was out of breath again.

She had changed clothes, too, and she had a bright kerchief over her hair. Maddox figured she had brought Bergman down to deliver him. He couldn't stay mad at her. He couldn't stop looking at her. "You don't mind being saddled with Lenore for a little while, do you, Captain? A person shouldn't be cooped up in Honolulu," Bergman said.

Lenore was between them. Outside Bergman went ahead of her. "Lenore, you ride up front with the captain." She was silent. Maddox opened the car door for her, and she said, "Thank you," as though she were talking to a hackie.

Maddox stopped for a red light as rain began to fall. "Maybe we'll be lucky," he said. He pointed. "There. Up in the hills."

The rainbow, with the colors pale and almost transparent,

appeared across the hills in a shallow arch. "Look, Lenore," Bergman said. "Prettiest thing I ever saw."

"Lovely," she said. Maddox glanced at her. She sat like she was in a pew, with her purse in her lap. They were on some joy ride.

At Pearl Harbor Maddox stopped beside the Shore Patrol station. "This is Mr. Walter Bergman. He's the lawyer for the people with the admiral," Maddox said.

"Yes, sir. The admiral is expecting you, sir. They're in his quarters. Will you need an escort, sir?" Maddox shook his head, shifting grears. She hadn't moved once.

A Filipino was waiting at the foot of the broad stairs to the admiral's quarters. He was beside the car when Maddox stopped. Lenore turned as Bergman left the car. "Do you have chocolate?" So Maddox learned some of the trouble. Bergman was a diabetic.

"Soon find out," Bergman said. He began to feel in his pockets, and Lenore opened her purse. She gave him a large flat package which disappeared in Bergman's big hand. "Could've sworn I had some."

Maddox said, "Excuse me," and leaned across her. They could have been strangers in a movie house. "How much time will you need?" Maddox asked.

"Say an hour at the outside," Bergman said, and to the Filipino, "Lead the way, son."

The Filipino brought Bergman into the admiral's living room. The admiral, wearing a white uniform, was facing him. "I am Admiral Langdon." He didn't offer his hand, but Bergman did.

"Never met an admiral before," Bergman said. He saw the woman sitting alone, near the windows. He saw the two young fellows in civvies, one on each side of her, and neither of them close. She'd made a throne out of her chair.

"This trial is a disgrace," said the admiral.

"Hasn't started yet," Bergman said.

"There shouldn't be a trial," said the admiral. "Dragging Americans into a courtroom because an aboriginal got what he deserved is the real crime."

"We're a government of laws, Admiral," Bergman said. "It's what separates us from the aboriginals."

"You're a long way from the States," said the admiral, "and the distance isn't only in miles. We *live* among them. You've made a reputation. I expect you to live up to it. I expect these people to go scot-free."

"I always walk into a courtroom with that hope," Bergman

said. "I've never in my life tried a case I intended to lose. But we have a jury between us and freedom."

"That's your job!" said the admiral.

Bergman didn't understand why the admiral had to shout. "Suppose I ought to go to work," Bergman said. The admiral crossed the room with Bergman following. Standing beside Doris Ashley, the admiral introduced her.

Bergman didn't expect her to leave her throne and she didn't. He extended his hand and bowed. "This is Lieutenant Gerald Murdoch," the admiral said, "and this is Seaman Duane York." Bergman shook hands with each man and turned to the admiral.

"Admiral, I'd appreciate it if you left me alone with my clients," Bergman said.

Doris Ashley had disliked Walter Bergman on sight, and he had just proven she was right in her judgment. "This is the admiral's home," she said. "He has opened his home to us. He is my true friend, my protector. I'd be grateful if he's with me."

"Most times it would be jake with me," Bergman said. "But I've come to get acquainted. My experience is my clients and I manage better if we're alone."

"Let him do it his way, Doris," said the admiral. "I'll be in my office." He didn't look at Bergman, who followed the admiral to close the doors. Turning, he brushed his hands as he crossed the large room.

"I can't expect you people to relax, but I'd like you to try," Bergman said. "Try to remember I'm not the enemy. Until a minute ago, there were three of you. Now there are four. I'm in this. I've been in it since I was hired. I've read everything the papers have printed. Coming over I listened to the wireless. I even read the ship's newspaper every day. So I'm not new to the case. We're new to each other. I want to hear your side. Suppose you start, Lieutenant."

"Gerald acted in self-defense," said Doris Ashley. Bergman watched Gerald as if he hadn't heard her.

"There was a struggle," Gerald said. "We were struggling and the weapon discharged."

"You had a .45 caliber automatic revolver, and this man, the dead man, was struggling with you?" Bergman asked.

"He attacked Gerald," said Doris Ashley.

Bergman waited until Gerald said, "He jumped at me."

"How far away were you?" Bergman asked.

"I can't tell you, sir," Gerald said. "Everything happened too fast. He just jumped out of the chair."

"How far do you think?" Bergman asked. "How many feet

from you was your prisoner when he jumped at you and your gun?''

"I suppose about five feet," Gerald said. Bergman looked at Duane.

"What's your memory, son?"

"Yeah, about five feet," Duane said. "He came out of the chair at the lieutenant."

"Out of a chair," Bergman said. He picked up a chair and set it down facing Gerald. Bergman went to Gerald's side. He put the heel of one shoe against the toe of the other, measuring off five feet, and moved the chair until one leg touched his shoe. Bergman lowered himself into the chair. "Here I am," Bergman said. "I'm your prisoner. You're holding a gun on me. Why would I jump at a man with a gun?"

"No one can answer that question," said Doris Ashley.

"It won't keep the district attorney from asking," Bergman said. "He might ask it twelve times, once for each man in the jury box. Lieutenant? Why did your prisoner jump at you?"

"Because he was guilty!" Duane said.

"He was not found guilty," Bergman said. "The jury could not reach a decision."

"He told us he was guilty!" Duane said. The lawyer was supposed to be *helping* them.

"Did he confess, Lieutenant?"

"Damn right he did! He *confessed!*" Duane said.

"Lieutenant, did you intend to kill him after he confessed?" Bergman asked.

"Gerald is not a murderer," said Doris Ashley.

"Many men who kill are not murderers, madame," said Bergman. "They're victims, too; victims of a momentary emotion they can't control." Bergman put one hand in the other. "Did you intend to kill him?" he asked Gerald.

"No, sir. I never intended to kill him or anyone else," Gerald said.

"You say he jumped you," Bergman said. "So he must have thought you were ready to kill him." Bergman kept his eyes on Gerald. "In your struggle did he have the gun?"

"We both had it," Gerald said.

"He jumped from the chair," Bergman said. "You have the .45 caliber automatic revolver. Point it at me, Lieutenant."

"Gerald doesn't remember if he was pointing the gun," said Doris Ashley.

Bergman shifted in the chair to face Doris Ashley. "Madame, I am your attorney. I've been retained to defend you. That's why

I'm here, in this room. I'm the only lawyer in this room, so I'm the only person who knows about the law, and the courts, and trials, especially criminal procedure. I am preparing my case. I'm asking questions. When I ask you a question, I expect you to answer me." He pointed at Duane. "When I ask him a question, I expect him to answer me. When I ask the lieutenant a question, I want the answer to come from him. From now on, we'll do things my way. It's the only way we'll continue as long as I'm your lawyer. You people are charged with a capital crime. Murder is a capital crime. The penalty is death. The ultimate penalty. You're in real trouble. You need help, the best help you believe you can get. The law says you're entitled to counsel, any counsel you choose. If what you've just heard doesn't sit well with you, then maybe you ought to have another lawyer. There's a man with a car outside and he'll take me back to the hotel." Doris Ashley remained silent and Bergman shifted once more. "Were you pointing the gun at him, Lieutenant?"

"I can't tell you whether I was or not, sir," Gerald said.

"You were holding the gun, the .45 caliber automatic revolver," Bergman said. "He saw it. He saw this young fellow with you. Two against one and one holding a gun." Bergman left the chair, leaping at Gerald, hands out in front of him. Gerald's arms came up instinctively, and Bergman grabbed his right hand with both of his. He held Gerald's hand firmly. "We're struggling," Bergman said. "Struggle, Lieutenant." Bergman had Gerald's hand down low below the waist. Without warning, Bergman released him, and stepped back. He was breathing heavily and with difficulty. His face was ashen. He reached the chair and sank into it. His chest rose and fell, and the hollow, rasping sound of his breathing filled the room. After a time he pushed himself up in the chair, facing Gerald as though they were alone.

"I'm seventy-six years old, lieutenant," Bergman said. "I'm a diabetic. I have diabetes. I don't weigh any more than a handful of hay, but I kept your hand down. If you'd been holding a gun, and if it had been fired, the bullet would have gone into the admiral's floor."

"Gerald has answered honestly and truthfully," said Doris Ashley. "He is an honest person, an officer in the United States Navy."

"Why did you run, Lieutenant?"

Gerald put his hands behind his back, pulling at his fingers. "Run?"

"A policeman stopped you for speeding," Bergman said.

"Mrs. Ashley was driving, and the dead man was on the floor with you and Seaman York. You were running. Why were you running?"

"I didn't think anyone would believe me," Gerald said.

"Looks to me like we finally reached the start I asked for awhile ago," Bergman said. "You're right, Lieutenant. I don't believe you, either." He faced Doris Ashley. "I don't believe any of you. I haven't heard a word of truth in this room since the admiral left. I told you I've been reading about this case. Joe Liliuohe was killed with a single bullet from a .45 caliber automatic revolver. I've mentioned the gun about a dozen times. I had reason for repeating it. I've spent more than fifty years in court, and most of the time a gun was in court with me. I'm familiar with just about every gun made on this earth. A .45 fires the biggest bullet of any. The bullet from the gun you carried hit Joe Liliuohe on the left side of his face. The bullet went straight through, through the jaw, through the upper and lower palates, through the larynx, and out through his neck. The bullet didn't come from a gun that was fired at an angle, above or below. It came from a gun held level." Bergman raised his hand, making a gun out of his thumb and forefinger, pointing directly at Gerald. "You've been lying to me from the beginning, Lieutenant." Bergman lowered his arm, putting his hands together. "So we need to begin all over again. I hope you tell me the truth this time. I'll defend you better if I know the truth. If you keep lying, to me and to the court, you'll pay for your lies. All of you will pay."

Doris Ashley sprang up from her chair. "You're frightening us!" she said. "You've done nothing since you arrived except frighten us! You can go to your man with his car!"

"Wait a minute," Gerald said. Doris Ashley didn't hear him. Bergman started to rise.

"I have my own lawyer," she said. "My friend. He's my friend." She should never have listened to Harvey Koster. She didn't care if Harvey Koster never spoke to her again. She had never liked him. Preston had never liked him. "He'll *help* us. He isn't a bully." Bergman was on his feet.

"No!" Gerald said. He moved quickly, reaching Bergman. He was ready to hold Bergman if the lawyer tried to leave. "He's right!" Gerald said. "You're right!" he said to Bergman. "I was lying! I shot him!"

"He had it coming," Duane said. "*He* was the liar, the no-good rat!"

Gerald came at him. "Shut up!" Gerald said. "You shut up!"

He whirled around, coming at Doris Ashley. "We can't fool him! We're not with reporters or with the police! If he didn't believe me, neither will the district attorney! Neither will the jury." Gerald rubbed his mouth, standing in front of Doris Ashley, daring her to say anything. He was sick of listening to her. The room became still. Gerald returned to Bergman. "You'd probably like to sit down."

"Wouldn't mind a bit, Lieutenant. I'm pretty winded," Bergman said. He returned to his chair. Standing beside him, Gerald began to talk.

When Bergman went into the admiral's quarters with the Filipino, Maddox said, "He'll be awhile. Anything special you'd like to see?"

"My husband may need me," Lenore said. Maddox watched her, holding the door like she was trying to escape. He hadn't figured on her being scared.

"We won't be far away," Maddox said. They were a million miles apart.

"I'd rather wait," Lenore said. "You mustn't stay because of me." She opened the door.

"Hold it," Maddox said. Everything was wrong. He was losing her. "Lenore." He couldn't get her to look up. "I'm not going anywhere. I brought him out. It was my idea." She sat there like a prisoner. "I figured you'd like to see something of the place. It's nice out here by the ocean." He wanted to touch her. "I wouldn't let anything hurt you," he said.

Then she turned to him. "Did I . . . ?" she began, and stopped, and then, "I don't want to be gone long."

"You can trust me." It was a solemn vow.

As Maddox turned the ignition key, she said, "Could we walk?"

Maddox would have agreed to pogo sticks. He was out of the car and waiting at her door when she put her foot on the running board. He wanted to give her his hand but he stayed clear. He stayed clear as they crossed the parade ground. Maddox handled her as though she were a butterfly. They walked toward the jetty to which Gerald had brought Hester on their first day. "The ocean seems dangerous," Lenore said. "I've always been able to see the other side of water. Rivers. Lakes."

The jetty was deserted. They went to the far end, standing at the rail. "Doesn't look so scary here," Maddox said.

"It makes me afraid." Maddox wondered if she knew they weren't talking about the ocean.

"You're safe," he said, trying to convince her, trying not to lose her.

"I don't feel safe," Lenore said. "I've never been far from home." She wasn't talking about home, either.

"A fellow from the States told me downtown Honolulu is like anywhere else over there," Maddox said. All he heard were the small waves lapping against the jetty. She wouldn't even talk to him. "We could look at some of the ships," Maddox said. She glanced over her shoulder. Did she think Bergman was watching them?

"I'd rather not," Lenore said. "I mean . . ." she said, and stopped. "Is there always a wind?"

He unbuttoned his jacket. "Put this over your shoulders."

"No, no." She raised her hand to stop him. "Thank you, Captain."

No one, ever, had hurt Maddox as deeply. He sucked in his breath as though he had been hit hard. He said, low, "Captain. What happened to Curt? What happened?" Maddox was pleading for the first time in his life.

"I must have forgotten," she said, lying.

He knew she was lying. He knew he had lost her. He stepped back, away from the sniveler who had been begging a moment ago, revolted by his begging. "I suppose you forgot lunch, too," Maddox said. "I've spent the last twenty years with people who lose their memories. You nab them, nab them with the goods, but they can't remember a thing. Now you can remind me I don't talk English."

She was finally looking at him. He could finally see her eyes. He would be a long time forgetting her. "I remember lunch," Lenore said. "I told Walter I had lunch with Captain Maddox. You *are* Captain Maddox, someone I met today. We're strangers. I don't even know you."

"You know me," Maddox said. "You know me and I know you. We did that at lunch. There wasn't a minute, a second of that lunch when we weren't together. *Together*. So we'll forget the stranger routine. So maybe you'll tell me why you've been acting like I was poison since we left the hotel. You tried to hide upstairs. You'd still be in the hotel if he hadn't pushed. You were willing to let him go halfway across the island without you, but I had to do everything except pry you out of the car because you couldn't leave him. Ever since you came out of the elevator, you've treated me like I was a spy."

"You have no right . . ." she said, and stopped.

"Nobody has any rights," Maddox said. "I've never had any

rights. If I'd waited for my rights, I'd still be sleeping in the streets."

Maddox saw her lips quivering. She was like a kid trapped by bullies. He had done everything wrong. He was back where he had always been, all alone, eating his dumb Christmas dinner in a restaurant somewhere. "Forget that," he said. "I was shooting off my mouth. One of my bad habits."

"I'd like to go back," Lenore said.

"I figured you'd say that," Maddox said. He was beaten. "I don't blame you. All I wanted was to make this a nice afternoon for you, and all I've done is make sure it would be a mess. My mess." He had never apologized.

She said, "I think it'll be easier if I leave now."

"If that's what you want." He was through scaring her.

"You said I'm not to blame. But I feel at fault," Lenore said. "I must be at fault."

She was still with him. "You haven't done anything wrong," Maddox said.

"You were right," Lenore said. "You seem to see through me. I *was* afraid to come. The hotel was safe. I *am* afraid. You see, I'm not . . . worldly. I've lived . . . I haven't lived. I've been protected all my life."

"I wouldn't hurt you, Lenore."

She smiled like she didn't want to show she was hurting. "I knew that . . . when? On the ship? This morning seems long, long ago. I was on a holiday, a quiet holiday. Our lives are always quiet. You . . ." she said, and stopped.

"We're just two people who hit it off," Maddox said.

"I feel as though I'm spinning," Lenore said, "as though I've lost control of myself. I want to stop. I want to . . . be quiet."

Maddox was careful. She didn't seem as scared. He couldn't take any chances. "Is it better, quiet? Or safer?"

"You *can* see through me," Lenore said. "Yes, safer. I've always been safe. I can't change," she said, but Maddox didn't, couldn't, believe her. She turned her back to the sea, to them. "The admiral's house is safe." When she looked at him, Maddox wanted to grab her and disappear. "I am a married woman."

"You haven't done anything wrong," Maddox said. "You had lunch."

"And now I'm here with you." She had the guts to look right at him. "I have a husband. You're alone."

He said, carefully, "Aren't you . . . alone?" He expected her to leave him, but she looked off, and she was far, far away once more.

"We saved each other," Lenore said. "We saved each other's lives." She moved away from the rail and Maddox knew they were on the way to his car. "When I was young, I thought I was the luckiest person in the world."

She told Maddox she was an only child, and her father was Walter Bergman's law partner. They were neighbors and in the summer they shared a cottage and a boat on Lake Chippewa in Wisconsin. Her father and Bergman would come up on Friday night. "I had two sets of parents," Lenore said. "All four came to my graduations."

When she was twenty-five, in one catastrophic summer, Lenore's parents were killed in an automobile accident. She never returned to her home. Bergman and his wife took over, selling the house and furnishings. A month afterward, Bergman's wife died in her sleep.

"He wanted to die with her," Lenore said. "For a long time he wouldn't leave the house. After he went back to his office, he would call during the day as though he wanted to be sure I was still there. He always had more clients than he could handle, and gradually he became himself. It was time for me to move, to find my own place. Everyone thought I stayed to care for Walter but it was only half the story. I was afraid to leave. Walter understood."

One day Bergman asked her to accompany him to his office. He showed her a new will leaving her everything. He read, aloud, the words, "To my wife, Lenore . . ."

On the jetty Lenore stopped beside a bench facing Maddox once more. "I would have been lost without him," Lenore said. "I wasn't ready," and then, almost in a whisper, "I'm still not ready." She was telling Maddox to forget their lunch.

To Maddox she seemed completely helpless. He had never stopped for anyone, anywhere, had never opened his door to a stray, had never shared himself, not even with a pet, but he was ready to protect her for life. He had been right. She was absolutely alone. Maddox had to touch her. A gun couldn't have stopped him. He reached out for her bare arm, feeling the silky skin against his hand, feeling her everywhere, stunned by the effect on him. He heard her gasp but she did not pull away. Her head was down, and he felt her tremble, and then it passed. "Would you take off the scarf?" he asked.

He had released her, released them, and she responded gratefully, raising her hands to open the scarf and slip it over her hair. Maddox was smiling. "You're a whole lot younger without it," he said.

She smiled, tentatively, apprehensively. She said, "Curt . . ." and stopped, moving away, behind the bench, looking across the parade ground. "There's Walter."

Lenore put the scarf around her neck and knotted it, then left the jetty. She waved, but she was too far away from the car. They crossed the parade ground in silence. Maddox gave her plenty of room. She waved again. "Walter!"

Bergman was leaning against the fender. "Were you waiting long?" Lenore asked.

"Not enough to notice," Bergman said. "Did you show her the sights, Captain?"

"We were out on a jetty," Maddox said.

"You sit in the front, Walter," she said, but she was too late. Bergman was through the rear door.

"Fact is, I'd rather be back here," Bergman said. "More room to stretch."

So they were together again. Maddox could see the curve of her leg, and her thigh and her bare arm. He could see her hands together over her purse. He knew her perfume now, could place it, would be able to place it forever.

"You've been very nice to us, Captain," Bergman said. "We appreciate it. A man's first day anywhere is the hardest, whether it's kindergarten or a new case. You smoothed the way from the beginning, from over there on the pier. I don't believe that's part of your duties. I've been around a few police departments. Captains aren't chauffeurs, so it makes what you've done even nicer. We're much obliged to you."

"Glad to help," Maddox said. Bergman was chattering as they left Pearl, exclaiming over the beauties of the island. He talked steadily, asking questions of Maddox. He was still talking when Maddox stopped in front of the entrance to the Western Sky. The doorman walked toward the car but Maddox came out. He wasn't ready to lose her yet, not yet.

"I made my speech, Captain," Bergman said. "So I won't embarrass you by repeating it."

"Back there at Pearl you asked if I'd shown Mrs. Bergman the sights," Maddox said. "I'd like to show both of you around. You'll have time before the trial."

"Did you hear that, Lenore? We'll take you up on it, Captain," Bergman said.

So the day was over. Maddox took off his hat. Lenore was ready for him, her hand extended. "Thank you for everything."

Maddox felt the band across his chest again. He wanted to cover her hand with both of his. "I enjoyed it," he said.

Maddox drove to headquarters, drove slowly, his hat beside him, his right arm stretched across the seat, her part of the seat. Her perfume was still in the car. He thought of stopping at a drugstore, smelling bottles until he found hers. "Hey!" he said, aloud, astonished by his impulse.

In his office Maddox read the day's arrest reports. He walked down the corridor to the detectives' squad room to talk with Al Keller before the latter left for the day. Maddox returned to his office, raising the venetian blinds and opening the windows behind his desk. The sun was low in the west and the windows across the street were fiery red. "Pretty," Maddox said.

Night began to fall. Maddox crossed the office to turn up the lights. He came back to his desk. A breeze rattled the venetian blinds. Maddox lowered the windows. He thought of dinner and the prospect of eating alone made him frown. Why didn't he know someone who wasn't married? He'd stop somewhere on the way home. He was tired of steak and pork chops, steak and pork chops. "Seafood salad," he said, aloud, but he couldn't go back to the hotel. He was smiling. Maddox reached for the telephone. He didn't even know the number. "Maddox," he said to the cop on the police switchboard. "Put me through to the Western Sky."

"Hello." He could have picked her voice out of a mob. He leaned back in the chair, the upright telephone on his chest.

"This is Capt . . . Curt Maddox. It turns out I'm free tomorrow," he said, lying. "We could have a look at some places."

"Tomorrow," Lenore said. Maddox knew she was scared again. "I'll tell my husband."

"Put him on," Maddox said. He wasn't taking any chances. "Hello, Mr. Bergman. I was telling your wife I had a day off tomorrow. We could do some sightseeing."

Early one morning in the following week the princess emerged from her house to start the day. She was in fresh clothes and she wore worn boots that reached to her calves. Jack Manakula saw her stop and close the door, and close the screen door. Usually she came out like someone was after her. Jack was at the corral with their saddled horses. He saw her stop, looking out as though he, the horses, the corral, and the barn weren't there. "How about it?" he yelled. "Talk to the wall," he said, and then, yelling again, "You wouldn't even let me finish my coffee!" The princess had chased him away from the table and sent him out to saddle the horses so they could get going. As Jack watched her, wondering if she might be sick, she finally, slowly, moved off the porch. Jack led the horses away from the corral. As they met, the princess asked, "How can I stay here?"

They had heard about the start of the murder trial on the radio, and in the previous week a letter had come from Tom. He had enclosed newspaper clippings—wire stories from the States citing the rising support for the accused. In the Senate Floyd Rasmussen had demanded that every Hawaiian entertainer in America be fired. "We'll be lucky if they go through with the trial," Tom wrote, adding that he would be in the courtroom from the first day.

"Hurrah for our side," said the princess after she had read Tom's letter. Jack Manakula lit a match on his jeans, and as he lit the cigarette he had rolled, she said, "I ought to be there."

"To do what?"

"To *be* there, I said!" The princess waved her hand at the smoke as he exhaled.

"To do what, I said." Jack lowered his arm, holding his cigarette away from her. "Leave it alone, Lu."

Now, standing with the horses midway between the house and the corral, Jack Manakula said, "I'll get some bedrolls and some grub and we'll stay out tonight."

"Jack." He extended the reins of her horse but she didn't take them. "Jack, they're killing us now. In cold blood. If I stay, it means I don't care," the princess said. "Come in and help me pack." That afternoon she used her wireless to send Tom a message.

Tom drove to Honolulu Harbor early that morning. A ship from San Francisco had dropped anchor at Aloha Tower earlier in the morning and he could see the black funnels looming over the waterfront. Sarah had insisted on lowering the convertible top, and Tom sat in the sun looking out at Sand Island. He expected to wait—he could not risk being late.

When he heard the noon bells ringing, he left the convertible to stretch. Standing beside the car, he saw the trim white yacht slip into Kalihi Channel. He walked onto the dock and watched the boat approach. The powerful engines left a wide, white wake. Tom thought he saw a familiar figure at the rail, but he couldn't be certain. Then the yacht swung in and he could see the brightly colored patterned dress. Tom began to wave and in a moment the princess raised her arm. Two crewmen stood fore and aft, holding ropes, and as the yacht nudged the dock, they jumped off to tie her up. Tom could see the suitcases beside the princess, and hurried forward. The crewmen jumped back on deck to move a section of the rail and drop the gangplank, and Tom went aboard to greet the princess. He bent to reach for a suitcase. "Drop it," she said. "You're a lawyer, not a porter."

The crewmen could hear her. "I thought I'd help," Tom said.

"I've paid for help," the princess said. "Did you bring a taxi?" Tom pointed and she saw the convertible. "No wonder you can't afford a new suit."

The crewmen were listening. Tom turned his back on them. "It's not mine," Tom said. "It's the car . . . Joe was driving it the night . . . It's his sister's car." The princess saw the color rising in his face. She tried not to smile but failed.

"Help me off this tub." Her dress was floor-length, and she used both hands to raise it. Tom took her arm. "I said help. Get hold of me." The princess stopped at the gangplank. She didn't look at the crewmen. "Bring the luggage." She came down the gangplank like a kid scaling a fence.

Tom raised the cover of the rumble seat and the crewmen stored the luggage, filling the rear of the convertible. The princess gave them some money. "Lift the top," she told Tom. "I'm not here to be on display."

Tom raised the top and fastened it, and the princess put both hands on the car as though she were climbing into the saddle. "I hope this buggy can handle the weight."

Kalakau Avenue near the Western Sky was full of taxis bringing the San Francisco ship's passengers to the hotels in Waikiki. The driveway of the Western Sky was jammed. The princess opened the car door. "You have a bellhop unload," she said. "I never want to see you with anything in your hand but a briefcase." She moved her right leg and froze. "This thing is moving!"

Tom grabbed the emergency brake, pulling it back. He pushed down on the brake pedal. "Now stay put," the princess said, and reached out, holding the windshield with one hand and the door with the other. She left the convertible as though she were descending from a precipice. She looked back into the car at Tom. "When you come back, come back with the girl."

"She works till six," Tom said.

"I'll be awake," the princess said. Tom watched her start for the hotel entrance, the enormous long dress trailing.

In the lobby of the Western Sky the princess stopped at the end of the line of passengers from the ocean liner who waited in front of the registration desk. Those in front of her, men and women, turned their heads constantly to look at her. She ignored the gawkers. She was tired, and thought of a bath and the clean sheets on the bed above. She had hardly slept the night before.

The room clerk was too busy to notice the princess until she was almost at the desk, behind the man who was registering, a Pennsylvania physician. The doctor bent to sign the registration card, and the room clerk saw the huge woman in the wild dress. He stared at the apparition. She belonged in a street stand, jabbering away at the tourists. Why had the doorman let her in? Why had the bell captain let her come this far? "How about a bellhop?" asked the physician.

"Yes, sir." The room clerk hit the bell. "On the way, Doctor." He extended the key. "Have a pleasant stay, Doctor."

"I'd like a suite," the princess said. "I think three hundred is a corner one." Now the room clerk understood everything. She had once worked in the hotel, before his time, and had been discharged because she was crazy. She had dolled up today, happy in her crazy head, and had come downtown for a vacation.

"It's taken," said the room clerk. "Three hundred is taken."

"I don't want anything on the street side," said the princess. "I'll take one of the corner suites on the ocean."

"It's taken," said the room clerk. There was a long line behind the crazy woman. "I think you ought to leave."

"What accommodations do you have?"

"Excuse me," he said and left the desk, hurrying to the management offices behind the mail rack. To the princess's right, on the sea side of the lobby, Walter Bergman followed Lenore out of the open restaurant facing the Pacific. He stopped. "Will you look at that woman? She's like a goddess."

"She's beautiful," Lenore said.

They heard the man behind the princess say, "What's holding us up?" Princess Luahine turned to look at the man. He and his wife were wearing leis.

"I am holding you up," said the princess. "You will have to wait until I am accommodated." Bergman grinned. He saw a bald-headed man with a belly that fell over his belt striding toward the queue, and another man behind the registration desk, lifting the hinged section to reach the princess. The room clerk returned to his station. Bergman looked on in delight.

"I'm the assistant manager," said Arnold Klemeth. "I'm sorry but we're completely booked."

"The man ahead of me had no reservation," said the princess. "He was given a room."

"You're too late," Klemeth said. He gestured to the bald man. "Grogan."

Grogan, the house detective, said, "You're leaving." The princess seemed unaware of his presence.

"You heard him," said Klemeth.

Lenore saw Maddox come into the lobby. She raised her arm. He put up his hand, wigwagging, smiling. As he crossed the lobby, she saw his smile vanish. He veered abruptly, walking parallel to the line of men and women waiting to register.

The assistant manager was beside the princess, and he spoke quietly. "If you don't leave, I'll have you ejected."

"What's the problem?" asked Maddox, who knew the problem, who had known everything at first glance.

"I can handle this, Maddox," said Grogan.

"You've got other things to do," Maddox said.

"Hold it. You're not talking to some beat cop," Grogan said.

"This woman . . ." said the assistant manager, and Maddox interrupted him.

"This woman," Maddox said. "Don't you know her? Don't you recognize her? This is Princess Luahine. Give her what she wants, quick, before she has you out on the street. You won't be able to book a tent on this island."

Klemeth became pale. "I'm sorry," he said. "You didn't . . . You said three hundred. Yes, three hundred is fine. Just fine," he said, evicting, without hesitation, the Seattle couple who were somewhere in the line behind the princess and had reserved a suite before sailing. He looked out into the lobby and said, loudly, "Bell captain!" Bergman moved closer.

"Forget him," Maddox said. He pointed at the house detective. "Grogan's here. Grogan can take the luggage." Bergman grinned.

"I don't smash bags," Grogan said.

He turned away, but Maddox looked at Klemeth, who said, "Oh, no . . ." and extended his hand to the room clerk and snapped his fingers. The room clerk dropped the key into Klemeth's hand. The assistant manager said, "Excuse me, madame," squeezing past her to give Grogan the key. "Handle the lady's luggage. Escort the lady to her suite. Examine the suite and if anything is needed for the lady's comfort, report to me personally. Do you follow me, or do you want to meet me in my office?" He smiled at Princess Luahine. "It's a pleasure to serve you."

The princess ignored him. She moved aside, joining Maddox. "You haven't changed," she said. "You don't even look older. How do you stay so thin?"

"I worry a lot," Maddox said. "There's a lot to worry about. More than I expected an hour ago."

"The Territory will never make you the official greeter," said the princess.

"You could have told them who you were," Maddox said.

"Coming in here and playing those games. What if I hadn't come by? What if that lummox had thrown you out?"

"It's happened before."

"You like to think so. Why'd you come? They told me you liked it out there on the big island."

"I swore I'd never cross the water again. You made me break my promise."

"*I* made you," Maddox said.

"You and the rest. All you keepers of the peace."

"That's why they pay me," Maddox said. "To keep the peace. Now you're here, and the news will spread before sunset. That'll make keeping the peace a lot harder."

"You're a worrier," said the princess. "But you're worried about yourself. You and yours. Take a deep breath, Maddox. I'm not Napoleon."

"You're their Napoleon. You're the biggest thing they have."

"Big and fat. You're not as smart as I thought, Maddox. I'm here because I couldn't stay over there. I felt guilty. You've declared open season on us."

"You're doing it again," Maddox said. "*I've* declared?"

"You're not burying any dead," the princess said.

Maddox reached for his hat and remembered that he had deliberately left it in the car because he was meeting Lenore. "We have a homicide," Maddox said. "We have three suspects in custody. The grand jury . . ."

"They keep me up to date," said the princess, interrupting him. "I know where the suspects are in custody. I've been in the admiral's quarters, long before this admiral ever saw these islands. My great-grandfather's summer palace was on that point of land. The first admiral who came out here to help us enjoy life had an eye. He picked that point for himself. He tore down the palace—said there was too much wind blowing through it. He was right. My great-grandfather liked weather. He was a husky fellow. People said he was the best surfer in the islands. His idea of exercise was to swim out past Diamond Head and lead a ship into port. Anyway, the first admiral put up his own palace. We built it for him. They didn't have to kill us in those days. They just pointed."

Maddox knew Lenore was watching them, standing with Bergman, waiting. He had been checking the clock since waking but he had not been prepared for the princess. "I hope you have a nice stay in our city."

He left her, walking through the line of guests waiting to register. He was unnoticed. All eyes were on the big woman in the brilliant dress that swept across the tiled floor as she moved majestically toward the elevators. Maddox reached Lenore and Bergman. "Sorry to hold you up, folks."

Lenore smiled at him and said, "Hello . . . Captain." She was close enough to touch him. Maddox could see the tiny freckles made by the sun. He could see her eyes, a deeper green here within the hotel.

"Hello, Captain," Bergman said. "Say, who *is* that regal woman?"

"You're right on the mark," Maddox said. "Regal is the word. She's a princess. Was. The Princess Luahine."

Bergman turned to Lenore. "Did you hear that, Lenore? I'll say this for her, she looks the part. Doesn't she, Lenore?" Maddox saw him put his big gnarled hand on her bare arm. Bergman's starched French cuff extended from his jacket sleeve, and Maddox thought of a corpse dressed for burial.

"I suppose we should be starting," Maddox said.

"Where to today?" Bergman asked. Maddox had already shown them the city's features.

"I thought we'd drive out of town and see something of the island."

"You're heading the expedition," Bergman said. They made their way to the entrance. "Seems to me you saved the hotel people a peck of trouble, Captain."

"They're new. They didn't know her. Hawaii is civilized now, like the States."

Lenore said, "Civilized?" and Bergman chuckled.

"Haven't you noticed, Lenore? The captain has his own way of putting things." Maddox held one of the doors open for Lenore and Bergman.

"This way," Maddox said, going ahead to open both doors of his car.

"You climb in with the captain," Bergman said. "Give me a chance to stretch my legs back here."

So Maddox had her again. He could see her brown and white shoe touching the gearshift. He could see her ankle and the calf of her leg. Her hand on the back of the seat was only inches from his shoulder. "What's first on the agenda?" Bergman asked.

"I thought we'd drive out some and head for the other side of the island today."

"We'd appreciate it if you'd explain points of interest along the way," Bergman said. Bergman never stopped talking, exclaiming over every stately home, every break in the shoreline, each cluster of clouds circling a mountaintop, each bird that rose from a tree. He was enraptured by the sights and smells, chattering with the uninhibited excitement of a child.

They were riding along a ridge when Bergman leaned forward, his head in the open window. "Will you look at that beach! Lenore, there's a feast for the eyes. Say, Captain, is there a way down?"

"We can come close," Maddox said. "The road dips up ahead, and there's a dry wash we could try."

They reached the drop in the road and Maddox turned. "Reminds me of walking through the creeks back home during the summer months," Bergman said. "We'd be barefoot and never give it a second thought." Maddox stopped beside a rock thirty or more feet high and almost as wide. Bergman was the first to leave the car. He strode toward the water, his open jacket flapping.

They followed Bergman. Maddox glanced at Lenore. Her nose was beginning to turn red from exposure to the sun. He wanted to touch her nose. She made him light-headed. In front of them Bergman raised both arms as though he were an explorer signaling to his ships. He turned as they approached. "Are you in a hurry, Captain?"

"I took the afternoon off," Maddox said.

"Today's about the last chance I'll have to play hookey," Bergman said. "Can we stay a bit? Thought I'd stretch out in the sun." He took off his jacket. "Give me a few minutes, will you?" Bergman lowered himself slowly, his hand out to meet the sand. He moved the jacket and rested his head on it, closing his eyes. Maddox saw Lenore looking down at Bergman. The detective turned away and for an instant was alone, and believed he would be alone. Then he saw her shadow on the sand as she joined him. Maddox felt the tight band across his chest again.

"First time alone since the jetty," Maddox said. She was silent. He felt like he was holding his breath. "Lenore?" She did not reply. She had been in turmoil since the afternoon at Pearl Harbor. She could not dismiss him. She thought of him constantly: when she woke, when she bathed, when she read, when she faced Bergman at breakfast, when he spoke to her, when anyone spoke to her and she to anyone, when she lay in bed waiting for sleep. She prayed each excursion on which Maddox took them would be the last, yet she had to keep herself from rushing to the telephone when it rang.

They walked toward the massive rock. It seemed to Maddox that a lifetime had passed since she had spoken to him on the ship and he had turned to find her beside him. They moved into the shadow of the rock, hidden from the sea at last, and faced each other.

Maddox stared at her in wonder. She had become a part of him. He had always been alone, but his life until the moment he had seen her now seemed alien, as though all those years belonged to another man. He raised his hand to slip his fingers into her hair. "You don't need to be afraid."

She put her hand over his. Her fingers were cool and tender, like gossamer. "I'm not . . . now," she said. "I wanted this, to be alone with you." She looked at him. "Will you kiss me now?"

He came to her, opening his arms to enfold her. He saw her close her eyes and raise her head, and he bent to put his lips against her. He felt her arms drawing him to her, felt her slender body, felt her hair in his face, felt the great gift she had given him, felt anointed.

She said, "Curt," her lips touching his. "I don't know you and you've changed my life."

He wanted to respond, to tell her she was beautiful, tell her what she had done for him, what she had given him already. But he had no words. He could only smile and raise his hand to touch her nose with his forefinger. "You're starting to burn."

Maddox bent to kiss her. She sighed and pressed herself against him, and Maddox thought of taking her away, leaving Bergman on the beach.

"Lenore." Her eyes were wide, and he could hear her breathing. "Will you meet me tonight?" He could see the fear in her face. "You knew I'd ask," Maddox said. "Didn't you know?" She nodded and did not look nor move away. "I've waited," Maddox said. "I didn't want to rush you. But this is no good, we both know it's no good. Driving you around is no good. It has to be us alone. Will you meet me?"

"He . . . we've been invited to dinner. The bar here is giving an informal dinner."

"Tomorrow night," Maddox said.

"I . . ." He thought he had lost her. "What will I say?"

"It's easier if you don't say anything," Maddox said. "If you make up a story, you have to back it up with another story. We can meet late. If you're missed, if . . . someone looks for you, you were walking on the beach."

"I can't," Lenore said. Maddox wanted to sit down. He looked at her, saw her eyes, the tiny freckles, her hair rippling in the breeze. He had to remember her because he couldn't push her any longer. He was alone again, and felt a weariness that was almost paralyzing.

"We never even started," Maddox said. "We're finished before we start." Lenore put her fingers to his lips.

"No, Curt. No, no." She put her hand against his face. "I can't leave . . . at night. I wanted to ask if you could manage another afternoon." Maddox began to smile. "I can shop," Lenore said. "I can leave the hotel to do some shopping. You can tell me where I should meet you."

"Tomorrow? One o'clock?" She nodded. Maddox was so happy he felt foolish. He put his hands on her shoulders.

Lenore slipped her hands into his jacket, her fingers spread against his shirt. She was lost, she was lost.

Early the next morning Ginny Partridge made fresh coffee and left a low flame under the percolator while she took her bath. When she finished, she filled a cup and brought it into the bedroom. "Rise and shine."

Bryce saw her standing over him. "It's not my birthday," he said. "It's not *yours*." She had *some* stupid secret. Bryce took the cup and saucer and set it on the night table. "Not before I brush my teeth." He left the bed, naked, and Ginny followed him with the coffee. She could have looked at him forever.

Ginny hurried back to the bedroom. She dropped her robe on the bed and began to dress, her eyes bright with excitement. She was in front of the mirror, deciding whether to wear a belt, when she saw Bryce, a towel around him. "It's not our anniversary either," Bryce said, "so let me in on it."

She spoke to the mirror. "I'm driving you to Pearl," Ginny said, and swung around as he frowned. She had carefully waited until the last minute so he couldn't refuse. "I've got a million things to do downtown, and I need the car. I've been saving them up, Bryce." She moved toward him. "I'll take you and pick you up. I won't be late, cross my heart." She took the towel. "Sweetheart, I've been landlocked here for so long I feel like a prisoner. I'll bring you some hot coffee."

Around twelve o'clock that morning an enlisted man found Bryce in the submarine. "Message for you, Lieutenant," he said. "Report to the Officers' Club."

Bryce straightened up. "Report to whom at the Officers' Club?"

"They didn't say, sir. They just said report." Bryce reached out.

"Give me the message, sailor."

"I did, sir. This guy came over from the Officers' Club and told Ensign Watrous and Ensign Watrous said to tell you."

Bryce went forward to clean up. It couldn't be Hester. She wouldn't pull anything like the Officers' Club. Who had sent for him? "You'll soon find out, sport," he said to himself. He remembered that Ginny had the car. He would have to walk to the bloody place.

As Bryce reached the Officers' Club, hot and sticky after the long haul from the submarine pens, a car stopped and six men piled out, entering ahead of him. Bryce followed them in. The close quarters, the voices, the calls for service, were suffocating. He wanted to punch his way out. "Bryce?" He raised his head, trying to find a familiar face. *"Bryce!"* Someone clapped him on the shoulder, and he looked up at Gerald. Bryce was suddenly hollow inside. She had told Gerald, and he would, naturally, want to meet man to man.

"You're the mystery man," Bryce said, and knew, with such relief it made him weak, that he was wrong. Gerald's face was blank. "Didn't you send someone down to the *Bluegill* with a message?"

"I had a message at the B.O.Q.," Gerald said. " 'Come to the club.' I thought . . . when I saw you . . ."

"I'll settle this," Bryce said. "Come on, Gerald." Pulling Gerald behind him, Bryce stopped a Filipino waiter. "Lieutenants Murdoch and Partridge. We're expected."

"One minute, sir," said the Filipino, but Bryce had his wrist and was squeezing it.

"This minute," Bryce said, holding him and Gerald as the waiter took them to an older Filipino. "Lieutenants Murdoch and Partridge," Bryce said. "Who sent for us?"

The older man smiled. "You follow me, please." He walked into the large dining room, toward the tables at the windows. Bryce was behind the Filipino with Gerald at his left. "It's your wife," Gerald said. "It's Ginny." The Filipino looked over his shoulder, grinning.

"Mrs. Partridge, yes," he said, and over his shoulder Bryce saw Ginny at a table, her back to the window, facing another woman. He saw the book on the table beside the other woman's elbow. The bitch. The crazy, scheming bitch.

Bryce could see Ginny smiling, but she didn't look like she was having fun. The bitch had told her. Hester had arranged this whole bloody thing. She had brought them here for a showdown, to sink them all. Now the idiot at Bryce's side would come gunning for him, too. "Here are your gentlemen, Mrs. Partridge," said the Filipino, and Hester turned, holding the arms of the chair as though she was about to bolt.

"Welcome," Ginny said, still smiling. She could feel Bryce's anger all through her. He made her afraid. "Welcome, Gerald," she said, and put her hand on the chair at her left. Her hand was shaking. "Gerald, you sit here, and Bryce, here," she said, touching the chair at her left. "Well, we're all together now." Ginny dropped her arms, putting her hands under the tablecloth and pulling at her fingers. "I thought it would be nice if we all had lunch. Hester and Gerald," she said, and her voice rose over the scraping of the chairs as Bryce and Gerald sat down, "you two have been shut away alone and we've been worried about you both, haven't we, Bryce? So I thought you would like to be with someone else for a change. I made the people here promise not to say anything, and I didn't say anything. Bryce didn't have a clue, did you, Bryce? This morning I said I needed the car for errands. But I never left Pearl. I dropped Bryce and came over here to the club, and they were all so nice and helpful." Ginny's fingers ached. "I hope you're not angry with me."

No one spoke. They were a square of silence in the relaxed, hail-fellow, masculine exuberance of the club. Ginny said, "I hoped . . ." and stopped, convinced of her failure.

"You're very thoughtful," Hester said. She tried not to look at Bryce, tried to behave as though she were alone with Ginny. "It's a wonderful surprise," Hester said. Ginny didn't believe her.

"I'd like to thank both of you," Gerald said. "I would just like to say this is the first time since . . . the first time I've felt like a human being."

Hester shifted in the chair and felt Bryce's knee against hers. She moved her leg, feeling dirty, feeling marked, as though touching him branded her.

Bryce had to say something. "You haven't changed, Gerald. You're the best shipmate a man ever had." Ginny sat up, saved from her fiasco. She raised her glass of water.

"To Gerald," she said. "To safe passage and a quick return to his shipmates." Bryce had to raise his glass.

"Hear, hear," he said, waiting for the stupid bitch to pick up her glass. "Hester."

Hester said, "Oh . . . I'm sorry," and took her glass. For a long time she had thought of killing them both, herself and Bryce, so that he would never hurt anyone else. Now she made her own silent, secret toast, asking for deliverance, for freedom from the cruel and evil man at her side.

They drank to complete the toast. The water revived Ginny. She had been right to bring them all together. She was so proud Bryce had spoken up for Gerald. "Now," Ginny said. "You can order anything your heart desires, hearts desire. You needn't stay with today's special. *You're* special. *We're* special."

"Hear, hear," Bryce said.

While Bryce sat in the Officers' Club listening to Ginny cackling, Maddox was downtown, driving in second gear, looking from one side of the street to the other. He had told Lenore where he would meet her. He didn't want her standing on a corner like some tramp. She wasn't in the first block nor in the second. Maddox turned, driving around to begin again. She could be late. Bergman could be sick. Lenore could be sick.

There she was—looking into a jeweler's window on his side of the street. The world changed. He was ready to jump out of the car, leaving it in the street. Maddox passed her and parked near the corner.

Lenore hadn't seen him and was still at the jeweler's window, her purse under her arm and her hands clasped. Maddox knew no one, ever, anywhere, had been as beautiful, as . . . classy. He didn't want to startle her, so he said "Hello" as he approached.

Lenore looked up and saw him walking into the sun, smiling. She felt he would keep her safe on this perilous adventure. He seemed to be in control of the street, as though everything belonged to him, and he was sharing his domain with her, her alone. The people around them disappeared, the cars disappeared, the sounds of the day faded. Lenore saw and heard nothing as the big man in the tan suit and white shirt reached her and enveloped her in his secure, impenetrable province. He made her tremble.

"I'm not late," Maddox said. "I couldn't find you first time around."

"I was in a shop," Lenore said. "I saw a dress. They had my size but only in a color . . ." She broke off. "I don't know what I'm saying. You . . ." she said, and stopped again.

"That makes two of us," Maddox said. He stepped back, giving her room, and then helped her into the car. It was like holding a handful of feathers.

Neither spoke until Maddox left the business district and drove into the hills. Finally Lenore spoke. "You're taking me . . . us . . . somewhere."

"Yes . . . somewhere," Maddox said. They were silent again until he said, "It's a funny thing about us. We've lived awhile, we're not kids. We're starting from scratch, you and me, starting fresh." He glanced at her. "You're scared."

"No. Yes. A little," Lenore said. "It's . . . different. I don't want to leave you." She looked straight ahead. "I can't leave you. I've been away from you for twenty-four hours and it seems a lifetime. I feel as though I've aged since yesterday, since seeing you last."

"We're a pair of talkers, all right," Maddox said. "We've been talking ever since I saw you on the ship. But I haven't said anything. I haven't even started. Except for work I've never been much of a talker. Now I can't wait. I must have a million things to tell you."

"Please tell me, Curt." She touched him.

"You've got me there," Maddox said. "I don't know." They laughed together, at ease and happy until Maddox reached his street and turned, and turned again, into his driveway. She moved her hand, and Maddox felt as though she had left him.

"Where are we?" she asked, almost in a whisper.

"This is my house," Maddox said. "Lenore." He took her chin in his hand. "We can head back downtown."

"I want to be with you," Lenore said. She opened the door to leave the car.

She stood in the driveway, head down, and Maddox knew she was hiding, believing that if she saw no one, she would not be seen. They walked toward the house. "The door is open," Lenore said.

"I wanted it aired out for you," Maddox said. "I'm only here to sleep. The place is never aired out. There's nothing I'd miss," he said, answering her unspoken question. "Nothing inside." She looked up at him, her hands clasped, her eyes wide and startled, as though he had come upon her unexpectedly.

Inside, she said, "Your house is very pleasant, Curt."

"It looks like the window of a furniture store," Maddox said. "When I bought the house, I just told the furniture salesman how many rooms I had. We're still talking, aren't we? That's because we're amateurs." Maddox came to her. "Lenore," he said, and took her purse, dropping it into a chair. Their eyes met and the world fell behind. Maddox bent forward, his arms at his sides, and kissed her.

They were in it instantly. Lenore sighed, raising her arms to join him. She was mindless. She said, "Curt, Curt," and her voice, her lips against him, her body against his, inflamed him.

Holding her with one arm, Maddox put his other arm under her legs and came erect. Lenore lay in his arms, her eyes closed.

He saw the high, bright spots of color on her face, and he could feel her, hot, as he carried her through the house to his bedroom.

On the bed, Lenore pulled him down to her, her eyes wide with desire and longing, and fright and alarm. But she could not stop, would not, and when he kissed her, she was unlocked.

Maddox was unchained. For the first time in his life he was free—she had set him free!

Afterward, for a little while, Maddox could not speak. Later, when they left the bedroom, Maddox said, "There's something I need to tell you."

"Can we talk in the car?" she asked, as the fear returned.

"This won't take long, and I want to do it here," Maddox said. "There's just us here. Once we're in the car, that's gone." He cupped her face in his hand. "I love you, Lenore. I never said that to anyone. I never thought I would, never figured on it, never figured it was in the cards for me. I couldn't let you walk out of this house unless I told you."

"Now I think I can bear to say good-bye," said Lenore.

"We'll never say good-bye. Not us."

In the car they were silent again. When they reached traffic, the intrusion, the imminence of their parting, changed her. "I miss you already," Maddox said.

"I'm here, darling."

"No, you left back there a while ago," Maddox said. He stopped behind a taxi.

"I want to begin again," she said. "Go back with you."

"It wouldn't take much to turn me around. I'm almost there already. I'm about halfway to nowhere."

"Halfway to nowhere," Lenore said. "In the land of enchantment." She kissed him, and opened her door.

Maddox took her to the taxi and paid the driver. She looked at him. "Curt, give me something. Anything. Something of yours." She took the folded handkerchief from the breast pocket of his jacket, and bent to enter the taxi.

Maddox closed the door of the cab. He watched it move into traffic. He walked back to his car, and sat for a time. He wasn't ready to return to police headquarters, ready to give up Lenore. He wasn't ready for anyone else. Maddox began to smile, and turned the key to start the motor. He drove back to the jewelry store where he had seen Lenore.

Inside, he went to the window display. A man came out from behind a glass counter. "Pleasure to have you on the premises, Captain," the man said. Maddox knew he had never seen the guy.

"This jade here," Maddox said, pointing. "That number."

"Lovely," the man said, reaching into the window to take the jade necklace Maddox had chosen. "It's a lovely piece."

"Hold it up," Maddox said. The man took the necklace at either end and raised it until it lay across the knot of his necktie.

"Yeah." Maddox was happy all over again. Except for the present he gave Harvey Koster every Christmas, Maddox had never bought anything for anyone. The man took the long velvet box from the window, and Maddox followed him to a counter. "I need a card," Maddox said. "A card and an envelope. I want you to wrap that thing, put the card on top, and wrap it again and put a delivery label on the package. Can you handle that?"

"Exactly as you wish, Captain," the man said. He gave Maddox a small white envelope from which a card protruded. Maddox moved away from the man. On the card he wrote, "You can say you bought this when you were shopping today." He slipped the card into the envelope and sealed it. He made an L across the top of the envelope, waiting until the man had finished wrapping the necklace. Maddox slipped the envelope under the ribbon. "Now cover it," he said, and reached for his checkbook. "What's the damage?" The man told him and Maddox stared, holding the open checkbook.

"We can arrange credit terms, Captain. There would be no carrying charges where you're concerned."

"Too late to start that," Maddox said.

"There are other pieces less . . ."

"Not a chance," Maddox said, interrupting him. The necklace was Lenore's. It had belonged to her since Maddox had seen it.

As Maddox left the jewelry store he could feel the package in his jacket pocket. He had Lenore with him. In his car Maddox set the package on the steering wheel and printed LENORE BERGMAN on the delivery label. He drove to the Western Sky with the package in his lap.

He stopped behind the last taxi in the line at the taxi stand. The driver was asleep, the visor of his chauffeur's cap resting on his nose. Maddox pushed back the cap and shook him. When the driver awoke, Maddox had some coins in one hand and the jeweler's box in the other. Maddox gave the driver instructions. "Leave your cap." Maddox waited, his elbow on the open taxi door. She was up there, on the ocean side. He thought of walking around the hotel to the beach and throwing pebbles at her window. "You *are* a kid," he said to himself, and saw the driver returning. "Tell me what you did."

"Like you said. I went over to the bell captain's station and gave him four bits and the package. Delivery for the lady, I said. Leave it in her mailbox." Maddox gave him a dollar. He walked back to his car and drove to headquarters.

That same afternoon, in the immaculate house where he had been born and lived until he left for medical school in Seattle, Dr. Frank Puana and Mary Sue were with his mother. Norma Puana sat between her son and daughter-in-law as Mary Sue wrapped a blood pressure cuff around her left arm. "If you come to see me, why can't you bring the children?" asked Norma Puana. "Why can't I see my grandchildren?" Frank took an ophthalmoscope from his medical bag.

"We haven't been alone since they had the measles," Mary Sue said. "We finally had a few hours alone." A nurse with whom Mary Sue had trained at Mercy Hospital had agreed to stay with Eric and Jonathan. Mary Sue and Frank had driven to a favorite beach before visiting his mother.

Frank raised the ophthalmoscope. He turned up the light, looking through the instrument into his mother's left eye. The ophthalmoscope provides the physician's only nonsurgical access to a patient's blood vessels. Frank saw the bright red tracings. He saw the tiny, red, irregularly shaped spots, like microscopic flowers. He was seeing retinal hemorrhages, more than he could count. His diagnosis was instantaneous and corroborated what he had known for months. His mother was a victim of malignant hypertension. Frank examined her other eye because his training demanded it. He turned off the light as Mary Sue unwrapped the blood pressure cuff. "Frank, it's eighty over one-ten," she said, and to his mother, "You have to come stay with us."

"This is my house," said Norma Puana. "I'll die in my house."

"You're not dying!" Frank said, lying.

"I won't live forever, Frank, even if you are a doctor."

"If you'd come home with us, you'd be on a proper diet and you'd feel better," said Mary Sue.

"You have your house, I have mine," said his mother. "Two women don't belong in one house. Besides, I . . ." she said, and stopped, her face twisting in pain. She put her hands to her ears. Her hypertension had produced tinnitus, a ringing in her ears which often rose to a roar that was intolerable. "They won't stop," she said. "They play the phonograph day and night, day and night."

Frank had long since talked with the neighbor. The phonograph was a small one, kept in a bedroom by the brothers who played it. "They're careful, Frank," said the boys' mother. "They love your mother. I can't even hear it in the kitchen."

They remained with Frank's mother until the tinnitus abated but they could not budge her. In the car Mary Sue said, "I feel so terrible leaving her. Maybe we should move down here for awhile."

Frank looked at Mary Sue. Her face was pink from the hours on the beach, her blond hair combed straight back. She had changed on the beach and wore a shift that was cut low. Frank had watched her change, watched her wiping the sand from her legs. Frank remembered her in the hospital in white, wearing her cap like a crown. He had met her one night, the night of her twenty-fifth birthday, when she came into the emergency room for a patient Frank had examined. She was so friendly and chatted with such easy and genuine warmth that Frank had made up a reason for helping her and the orderly take the patient upstairs. He thought about Mary Sue the next day, and in the following week asked questions of various nurses. "That girl, Mary Sue, has she been around long?" and, "Is she from the States?" He learned a good deal about her, including her work schedule, and he managed, two weeks after she had first come into the emergency room, to be entering the hospital when she was leaving. He left a note for her that day, asking for a date.

He had the best time he could remember. Mary Sue infused him with her own high spirits, her simple delights. She made Frank feel charming, made him feel witty and gallant. She made him feel bold, and when they parted, he asked, formally, if he could see her again.

They began in the fall and that Christmas Frank gave her a brocaded robe from China. Two months later he asked her to meet his mother, and later that night, in his car, Mary Sue said, "You're leading up to something, aren't you, Frank?" He asked her to marry him that night.

Now Frank said, "You're serious about moving in with my mother, aren't you? Do you know why? Because you've never lived here. Look at the place." He was revolted by the shabby street. "Do you want the *boys* down here? Do you want them to *play* here?" The car lurched forward, dirt rising from the tires as he jammed down the gas pedal.

Frank drove around the commercial area, and east, toward Mercy Hospital. He could see Mary Sue. She sat in a corner, against the door, her head beside the open window. Her eyes were closed. She belonged in a painting. Frank swore he'd hire a painter to draw her. "It was fun out there alone," he said.

"Yum yum," she said, and sat up as though she were leaving their day behind. "I hate to think of tomorrow," Mary Sue said. "When will you sleep?"

"It's only a week," Frank said. Frank was beginning a locum tenans the next morning, relieving a Japanese physician in Moiliili. Frank had accepted the offer eagerly. They needed the money.

"All day in Moiliili and all night at the hospital," Mary Sue said. "You'll be dead."

He grinned. "And rich." Mary Sue punched him in the arm. Frank yowled as he drove past the front entrance of Mercy Hospital and turned toward the parking area and the emergency room. He had detoured on the way home to pick up the shoes he used at work. They were scuffed, dirty, and bloodstained from years of use. He did not intend to let the rabble of Moiliili ruin his one good pair of shoes.

"Don't be long, Frank," said Mary Sue. "I'm worried about the kids. This is new for them."

"In and out," Frank said. He stopped beside a pale green touring Packard sedan with a matching continental kit behind and two tires in wells in the front fender, the nickel-plate covers sparkling in the sun. It was a splendid car and Frank examined the interior as he walked past it. There were two stacks of files and papers on the front seat. Frank went into the emergency room. "Hello, Pete." The orderly greeted him as Frank went through to the doctors' dressing room beside the elevators.

Frank took his shoes out of the locker, thinking of the Packard sedan. He could see Mary Sue in it, see her driving with Eric and Jonathan beside her, both of his sons dressed like English schoolboys. He was smiling as he left the dressing room. "Frank!"

Guy Tremaine came out of the elevator. He was carrying a leather suitcase. "I'm glad I ran into you." Dr. Tremaine had one of the best practices in Honolulu. He was the only doctor on the staff who even knew Frank was alive. "It gives me a chance to say good-bye," Tremaine said. As they shook hands, Tremaine said he was giving up his practice. His wife had suffered for years from multiple sclerosis, and they were leaving for a long cruise around the world. There was a vacancy on the staff! Frank was joining the staff! Why hadn't Claude Lansing told him? Frank had to listen to Guy Tremaine. He had to say, "I'm sorry to see you go, Doctor," and stand there in the corridor. He couldn't wait—he had waited for an eternity! Claude Lansing would be leaving soon for the day!

"I hope you have a wonderful cruise, Doctor," Frank said. He pushed the elevator button and looked up. Both elevators were on three. Frank ran to the stairs.

He came out into the third-floor corridor, breathing heavily. He couldn't run. There were nurses in the corridor and visitors with patients. Frank stayed beside the wall, hurrying toward the corner suite, "I'd like to see Dr. Lansing."

Lansing's secretary studied the man in the loose shirt and the faded baggy pants who was holding filthy shoes. "I'm Dr. Puana," Frank said. He set the shoes down on the floor. The secretary didn't move. "Tell him it's Dr. Puana. Or do you want me to tell him?"

The secretary pushed back her chair and rose. She went past Frank as though he wasn't there, opening the door of Lansing's office just wide enough to slip through and closing it behind her. Frank stood in front of the door. Why hadn't Lansing told him? Frank put his ear against the door. He couldn't hear anything. He stepped back as though he were ready to jump. Where was she? The door opened. She slid out. "The doctor can't see you now."

She went back to her chair. "I'll wait," Frank said.

"He can't see you today." Frank wanted to kill her.

"Who's with him?"

"I think you'd better leave," said the secretary. She turned and rolled paper into her typewriter. Frank stood in front of the typewriter.

"Do you know who I am?"

"Yes, I know who you are," she said, "and you'd better leave. Take your shoes and leave." She began to type, but stopped because Frank was reaching for Lansing's door. She said, "You can't—" but Frank was gone.

Lansing's office was empty. She had lied. Frank could feel the blood rushing to his face. She was going to tell him the truth! He wasn't leaving until she told him the truth! Frank whirled around and heard the sound of water, and, turning slowly, saw the light from the open bathroom door. "Dr. Lansing!"

"Oh, Frank." Claude Lansing stopped in the bathroom doorway to press the light switch. He slipped the comb into his pocket. The straight alcohol he had taken with some pineapple juice moved through him. "Didn't Edna tell you? I'm on my way to a meeting."

"Guy Tremaine is leaving," Frank said. "There's a vacancy on the staff." Lansing reached his desk.

"Not exactly," Lansing said. "I meant to tell you. It's been filled."

"It's my vacancy!" Frank said. He wanted to cry. He wanted to grab the lying drunk and choke him, use both hands to choke him. "It's mine! You promised me the next vacancy!"

"Keep your voice down," Lansing said. The alcohol was like a blanket around him.

"I'll keep my voice down," Frank said. "It's down but you can hear me, can't you?" He came forward. "Can you hear me? You promised me the next vacancy."

"It couldn't be helped," Lansing said, lying. "I tried but the board . . ."

"The hell with the board!" Frank said, his voice rising as he interrupted Lansing. "The board listens to you! You're the chief of staff! You told me you'd put me on the staff!"

"I told you to keep your voice down," Lansing said. He'd had enough of the kanaka, the wog from the gutter.

"You're afraid someone will hear me?" Frank was shaking. He raised his arm to gesture, his hand shaking. "For your information *everyone* is going to hear me! You promised me the vacancy! You're going to keep your promise or everyone in this hospital will hear me! Everyone in Honolulu will hear me! I'll tell this whole town, this whole Territory about Hester Ashley or whatever her goddamn name is!"

"I think not," Lansing said. "You won't open your trap. You were the surgeon, *Dr. Puana*. The surgeon of record. I saw to that. It's your name on the surgery report."

"You liar!" Frank said. "You drunken, cheating disgrace! You're a disgrace! You're a liar and a drunk and a disgrace!"

"Would you like to see the report? Should I show you the report?" Lansing waved his arm. "Now you're leaving."

"You made me a promise!" Frank lunged forward and Lansing jumped back, standing against the wall.

"Get out of here!" Lansing said. "Get out of my office! Get out or you'll be dragged out!" He pointed at the telephone. "I'll have the police up here to drag you out! You'll stay out! You'll never set foot in this hospital! You'll never work in this hospital while I'm chief of staff!" Lansing saw the man wither. The man simply melted. Lansing felt like kicking him to send him on his way. "You're keeping me from my work," Lansing said, forgetting the board meeting he had fabricated.

As Frank entered the emergency room from the corridor, Mary Sue came through the door opposite him. "Have you seen . . . ?" she began and stopped. "Frank! What's wrong?"

Peter Monji watched the doc carrying his shoes, walking like he was at a funeral. The door bumped into Mary Sue. She reached out for Frank. He acted like she wasn't there. Holding him and pushing the door, Mary Sue led him to the car. "Frank, talk to me. You were gone so long. Sweetheart, tell me what's wrong?"

"In the car," Frank said.

"I'll drive," Mary Sue said, but Frank threw open the driver's door, throwing his shoes into the backseat.

"I can drive! I can still drive!" he said. Mary Sue walked around the car and got in beside him.

"Something terrible has happened," she said. "Please, Frank." She pushed herself against him. "Please tell me."

Frank drove out of the parking area and turned toward home. "I was with Claude Lansing," he said, and began to talk. As she listened, Mary Sue began to move her fingers into Frank's back, gently massaging him. She did not interrupt, and when Frank fell silent, she raised his hand and kissed it.

"You think I'm going to carry on," she said. "I'm not. He did us a favor, Frank. Lansing did us the biggest favor. Do you know what he did? He put us on a ship. He put you and me and Eric and Jonathan on a ship for the States. He took us out of our misery, sweetheart."

"He lied to me! He treated me like dirt!"

"He's the dirt, Frank. Lansing is the dirt," Mary Sue said. "He couldn't keep his license in the States. Delphine Lansing's money couldn't *buy* him into a hospital."

"His secretary wouldn't even let me into his office!" Frank said. "I had to bust into his office!" Mary Sue massaged his back.

"It's the last time, sweetheart," she said, promising. "Nobody will ever do anything like that to you again. They'll fight to have you on the staff at home." She became excited. "Frank, let's start packing tonight. We'll put the boys down and start tonight. We can find out about a ship. Remember, we paid the last month's rent when we signed the lease."

"Hold your horses," Frank said, becoming annoyed with her. "My locum tenans starts tomorrow."

"For a week!" Mary Sue said, turning in the seat and crossing her legs under her, facing him. "It'll give us a few more days for loose ends. Frank, it's like a sign!" she said, bubbling. "The locum tenans, I mean. It's perfect timing. We'll need the money."

"How about the car?"

"Sell it!" Mary Sue said, disposing of the car. "We'll sell it! We'll buy a new one in San Francisco! You're a doctor! They love lending money to doctors! We'll drive to Wisconsin! We'll show the boys their new country! The Grand Canyon, and Yellowstone Park. And Glacier Park and the Painted Desert, and the Petrified Forest and the Black Hills," she said, scooting across the map in all directions. "And the Dells! Frank, wait'll you see the Dells! Even in winter! We'll rent a cottage next summer! You've never had a *vacation*, Frank!"

"How about my mother?"

"Your *mother?*"

"What am I supposed to do, wave good-bye like she was some Eskimo on an ice floe?"

"We'll take her!" Mary Sue said, refusing to let anything spoil it. "We'll take her with us!"

"Listen to yourself. Do you hear what you're saying?" Frank waved wildly. "She won't leave that house!"

Mary Sue twisted, uncrossing her legs and sitting back in the seat. "Frank, we're leaving Hawaii. Today proved it. How much more proof do you need? How many more times do you need to have your face rubbed in the dirt?" She spoke carefully, distinctly, her words like hammer blows. "We're going to the States where all men are created equal. Created equal, Frank. It's in the Constitution."

"You don't hear anything I say! What do I do about my mother?"

"I said take her with us. If she won't come . . . Frank, we're four against one," Mary Sue said. "Four lives against one!"

"I'm not as cold-blooded as you are," Frank said.

"*Cold-blooded!*" Mary Sue despised him. "An hour ago I offered to move in with her, take my kids and move in!"

"I didn't mean that," Frank said. Could he do *anything* right? "I didn't mean it that way."

"Frank, I'm leaving," Mary Sue said. "The boys and I are leaving, with or without you," she said, lying. "I mean it."

"You sound like there's a plague, like we're running from a plague," he said. "You can't pick up and start a new life overnight. You can't, Mary Sue." The car swung suddenly, swerving to the right. Frank pressed down on the brake. "It's a flat." They were less than a block from home. Mary Sue opened the door.

"Well, fix it," she said. She didn't look at him. "You have to drive Kay back to her apartment," she said of the nurse who had stayed with Eric and Jonathan. Mary Sue slammed the door. She walked toward their house as though she was in peonage. Frank came out of the car and opened the trunk, bending down to pick up the jack.

"Sell it," he said, full of loathing. "You'd need a blind man to buy this junk heap."

At Pearl Harbor a few hours earlier, Bryce stepped into the road raising his arm as a Navy truck approached. There were two sailors in the cab and they were on their way to Honolulu to pick up a load of beeves for the enlisted men's messes. As the truck stopped, Bryce walked to the cab.

"Are you fellows headed for town?" Bryce asked. The door opened.

"I'll hop in back," said the sailor beside the driver. Bryce held the door and stepped up on the running board.

"Stay put," Bryce said. "We can make it." The sailors moved aside and Bryce came into the cab. He didn't speak again, so the enlisted men were silent. Bryce could see, as though it stood on the truck hood, the table beside the windows in the Officers' Club. He could see Hester, offering him the plate of celery sticks. He could see Ginny, *hear* her. She had talked all through the miserable, tortuous surprise she had arranged. That bitch! That crazy bitch, bringing him, bringing *all* of them, to the club to play Good Samaritan. He had lasted as long as he was able. "Duty calls," he had said, rising.

"I'll be with Hester," Ginny said. "Is it far for you?"

"Hop, skip, and a jump," Bryce said. Ginny raised her head so Bryce had to kiss her. He had to shake Gerald's hand, pledging his unswerving support. He had to include Hester, and when he left the club, when he was freed, he discovered that he remained imprisoned by the ordeal he had endured and thought he had left behind.

He had returned to the *Bluegill* but he could not stay aboard. He could not think about work. He could not clear his mind of the trap Ginny had sprung. Bryce told the exec he was ill and left the *Bluegill*. First Hester had been tracking him all over Pearl. Now his own wife had joined the hunting party. He did not trust himself to be with Ginny. "She'll be waiting a long time," he had said aloud as he walked away from the submarine pens and the admiral's quarters. He headed for the motor pool, where he stopped the first truck he saw.

"Next corner," Bryce said as the truck came into the downtown traffic. The driver turned into the curb. "Thanks, sailor." Bryce was on a strange street with strangers. He had picked it deliberately, having been confronted by too many familiar faces already. He crossed the street, walking aimlessly. After a few blocks, he saw a sign hanging over the sidewalk that read WE NEVER

CLOSE! Bryce stopped beneath it. The door was open and there was sawdust on the floor. "Filthy dump," Bryce said, and entered.

He thought he was in a cave. He stood for a moment and then he could see. There was a light from a gooseneck lamp beside the cash register on the bar to his right. Another light hung over two doors marked with the words LADIES and GENTS. Across the saloon and continuing along the wall opposite the bar was a right angle of booths. Someone was snoring. Bryce walked to the bar, keeping clear of the three men in the center and stopping near the cash register. The bartender approached, wiping his hands on an apron tied around his middle. He was a tall, cadaverous man with a cigarette behind his ear. "What's yours?"

"What've you got?" Bryce asked.

"Near beer," said the bartender, naming the brew with a 3.2 percent alcohol content that had appeared with Prohibition and could be legally dispensed.

"Near beer and what?"

"Near bear and near beer," said the bartender. "This isn't a speak. We're clean here."

"You bet." Bryce didn't want to hear another voice. He reached into his pocket for money. The bartender brought him an open bottle and a glass. The snoring grated on Bryce. "Noisy floor show," Bryce said.

The bartender took the money. "It's a free country, sailor," he said, as a man came out of a booth behind Bryce and crossed the saloon. The bartender pressed a key on the cash register, which opened with a bell. He set Bryce's change beside the bottle of beer as the man reached the bar and held up his forefinger and middle finger.

"Hit me," said the man. He was Bryce's height, but twice as big, a heavyweight, huge across the shoulders and chest, like a Japanese wrestler. He probably had some Japanese in him as well as everything else, Bryce thought. The man was darker than a Hawaiian, a purebred mongrel, Bryce thought. The man's shirtsleeves were rolled up and Bryce saw the tattooed snake on his right arm. He paid for the two bottles and turned toward the booths. Bryce filled his glass.

The beer was icy cold. Bryce emptied the glass and poured the rest of the bottle into it. He put both elbows on the bar and discovered that the snoring had stopped. Bryce ordered another bottle. He drank the second bottle leisurely, enjoying his solitude, his refuge made by the cool room, the quiet, the darkness around him broken only by the two circles of light. When his glass was empty, Bryce raised his arm, signaling the bartender. "Hit me," he said, and smiled for the first time that day.

He heard someone walking and then a woman went past the end of the bar at Bryce's left. She was a shapely woman, almost plump, with black hair cut short. Her breasts fluttered as she walked. She looked at Bryce as she passed him, a full look, and then she was at the LADIES door. The bartender set a bottle of beer in front of Bryce and took the empty one. Bryce filled his glass. He saw the man with the tattoo return and wait while the bartender served the three at the other end.

She looked at Bryce again as she went back to her booth. Bryce turned his back to the bar, holding his glass, and when she sat down, he followed her. He'd had enough of polite society for a bloody year. He wanted to get dirty, really dirty. "Hello." She looked him over as though he were on the auction block.

"Didn't you learn to tip your hat to a lady?"

"I don't like ladies," Bryce said, and smiled. "Or gentlemen." He leaned against the booth.

She moved an empty bottle so it was in front of her, then ran her finger slowly down the length of it. "What do you like?" she asked. Someone shoved Bryce and he felt as though he had been hit by a truck. The beer sloshed over the rim of the glass. Bryce set it down on the table, shaking his wet hands, and when he looked up, he was facing the tattooed heavyweight, who held two bottles of beer.

"You're at the wrong trough, sailor," the man said. Bryce stepped back, away from the booth.

"You could be right because I only see one pig," Bryce said. The heavyweight bent to set the two bottles on the table, and still bent, swung with his left, but Bryce wasn't there. He was behind the man and following him. As the man pivoted and raised his arm, Bryce hit him high in the face along the eye. The man wobbled, grunting in pain, and came forward, and Bryce hit him again, with his left, stepping in as he swung to bring his right hand over the jab. "Stop it!" the woman said, holding the table to push herself out of the booth. The man dove at Bryce, who shifted and, crouching, drove his fist into the belly. "Stop it!" the woman said, lunging at Bryce. He threw her against the booth, losing his cap, and as his antagonist doubled over, arms down, Bryce set himself and began to swing. The man was helpless.

"Lay off!" said the bartender, and louder, "Lay off!" Bryce didn't hear him, hear anything, see anything but the cut and bleeding heavyweight who had attacked him. The man staggered back and Bryce followed, his feet flat on the floor, perfectly balanced for leverage as he swung. The three men who had been drinking together converged on the sailor.

"Hold it," one said, and "Sailor, he's licked," said the second. The bartender came around the cash register, his apron bunched in his left hand so he wouldn't trip over it. The woman screamed.

"Stop him!" she screamed. The entrance was filling up with men from the street who stood in the doorway watching the fight.

"It's a slaughter!" someone yelled.

"Can't you stop him?" the woman screamed.

"Lay off, I said," the bartender yelled, pushing his way through the three men around the fighters. Bryce swung again, and he never saw the bartender raise his right arm, which held a blackjack—lead covered with tape. The bartender hit Bryce over the ear, grunting with the effort.

Bryce fell forward. He lay with his face in the sawdust. The woman ran across the saloon, running away, fighting the crowd gathered at the entrance. The tattooed man's legs buckled and he sank slowly to the floor, lying on his side, blood streaming from his face.

The bartender pushed the blackjack into his pocket. "Goddamn trash," he said, kicking Bryce's cap. It fell against Bryce's leg. "This is a clean place. Let 'em lay," the bartender said. "Let the law cart 'em out." He went back to the bar to call police headquarters.

"It's open," Maddox said after the knock on his door, and Al Keller came into the office. It was a few minutes after six o'clock. The redhead was unshaven and dressed like a vag, a drifter. Maddox grinned at his favorite. "You should've been an actor."

"My wife says I'm scaring the kids." He reached the desk. "I've been using a department car for that stakeout over in Pacific Heights," Keller said. Maddox had put Keller on nights after three consecutive burglaries in the swank area. "I was in the garage to pick up my car when three-sixteen called in for the wagon. Captain, we've got another hassle with another Navy officer."

Maddox forgot Lenore for the first time that day. He picked up the telephone receiver. "Maddox. Give me the dispatcher."

"A bartender had to use a sap on the guy, the Navy guy," Keller said. "He was killing the other one."

"Killing," Maddox said. "They're turning it into a hobby," and into the telephone, "First, where did you send three-sixteen?" He listened. "Call the squad and put me through to one of them." Maddox tapped the desk with his hand, and then Keller saw him hunch over the telephone, putting his fingers around the mouthpiece. "Tell me what you've got," he said, and listened. "He must've had an I.D." He looked up and said, "Al," then scribbled on the desk with his fingers. Keller pulled a small notebook with a pencil clipped to it out of his pocket. "Bryce," Maddox said, and, "Spell it. B . . . r . . . y . . . c . . . e. Bryce Partridge. Lieutenant junior grade. U.S.S. *Bluegill. Bluegill?*"

Keller stopped for an instant. The *Bluegill* was Murdoch's submarine. As he resumed writing, Maddox said, "Get a statement from the bartender. Get statements from any witnesses." The princess had been right. They were making it open season on everyone in town. He slammed the receiver into the cradle.

His chair went into the wall as he rose, and he hit the desk with his thigh as he came around it. "The wagon's on the way in," Maddox said.

In the garage in the basement with Maddox the redhead said, "Do you want me to hang around, Captain?"

"Maybe," Maddox said, and then, sharply, "No! They pay us to police Honolulu, not the U.S. Navy!" Maddox left him, walking to the ramp that led down into the garage. The light from the street was fading. Maddox came out of the garage, standing at the foot of the ramp. The glow of the headlights from Al Keller's car fell across the garage entrance, and Maddox stepped aside as the redhead drove out of headquarters to spend the night in the darkness in Pacific Heights. *"Bluegill,"* Maddox said, aloud. "Funny." He stood watching the ramp until he heard the heavy engine of the wagon, the Black Maria. Maddox walked into the building, crossing to the door leading to the tank.

The cop who was driving was alone in the cab. "One of them is a mess, Captain," he said, unlocking the rear doors of the wagon. Inside, on the bench to Maddox's right, he saw the Navy officer, handcuffed and sitting beside the other cop who rode the wagon. "Meet Bryce Partridge, Captain," said the driver. "Pretty handy with his dukes." Bryce stared ahead, looking into nowhere.

His partner prodded Bryce. "End of the road," he said. "Give me a hand with this other lug, he's still seeing stars." Maddox watched the police haul Bryce out of the wagon. He saw Bryce swaying. Maddox raised his hand, extending his forefinger and moving it across Bryce's face. Bryce's eyes followed the finger.

"Let's have a look at the loser," Maddox said. The driver climbed into the wagon.

"We'll need a hoist to drag him out," the driver said. He bent over the battered man, pulling and shoving. "Weighs a ton," he said, and managed to shove the tattooed man upright. Maddox stepped up, peering into the wagon. The man's face was raw meat. His eyes were two blue rocks. He was covered with blood. His nose was flat and discolored, broken by a single punch, and his nostrils were caked with blood. "Ever see anything like it, Captain?" asked the driver. Maddox shook his head. "I mean, I like the fights. But even in the ring, long's I've been going, this is the worst. He looks like the sailor used a knife."

Behind them the cop with Bryce said, "I'll book this one and send someone in to give you a hand."

Maddox stepped down from the wagon. "Make it aggravated assault," Maddox said. "He's going to trial. We'll put a hold on the punching bag. Phil Murray will need him in court." Maddox looked into the wagon. "He needs to be patched up. Take him out to Mercy Hospital and wait . . ." Maddox broke off, spinning around. "No!" His voice could be heard on the ramp almost a city block from the wagon. He walked toward Bryce like an executioner.

Mercy Hospital! " A ring could have done it," Doctor What's-His-Name had told Maddox in the emergency room over Hester Murdoch flat on the table. "A man's ring." Maddox stopped in front of Bryce, whose right hand was handcuffed. He took Bryce's left wrist and saw the large, crested, Academy class ring with the brass numbers 1925 rising from the stone. "I'll take him," Maddox said. The cop reached for his key.

"You want the handcuffs, Captain?"

"He's not going anywhere," Maddox said. It was a promise. As the handcuffs were removed, Bryce rubbed his right wrist. "Let's take a walk, Lieutenant."

There was a bandsaw whining in Bryce's head. His head throbbed from an echo, a measured roar that seemed to come from a distance. The garage tilted slowly and as slowly slid back to rise from the other side. The man in front of him was blurred. He seemed lopsided, and he seemed to slip out of sight as though he had stepped behind a screen. Bryce felt the man's hand on his arm, and then they were walking on the tilted floor. "Captain!"

The driver was holding Bryce's cap. "Wouldn't want the Navy saying we swiped it," the driver said. Maddox walked slowly, holding Bryce's arm and supporting him as they left the garage.

They came out of the elevator on the second floor, and Maddox stopped beside a water fountain. "Do you good." Bryce drank and started to come erect, but bent over the fountain to drink again. The cold water revived him. He could see the man, the one called Captain. The floor no longer tilted. It was a straight floor. The walls of the corridor were straight. Maddox opened the door of his office.

Inside, Maddox moved a chair, setting it directly in front of his desk. He dropped the cap on it. "Lieutenant." Maddox came around the desk, stopping at the windows. Night had fallen and he could see the streetlights through the venetian blinds. Bryce sat down, holding his cap with both hands. Maddox took his chair. "You know who I am, Lieutenant."

Bryce could see him clearly now. He was a big man, lean and fit. He looked ready. "You're a police captain."

"Captain Maddox. Curt Maddox." He leaned back in his chair, making himself comfortable as though he were chatting with a friend somewhere far from headquarters. "Do you know why I brought you up here, Lieutenant?"

"Because of the brawl."

"A brawl," Maddox said. "Not this one. I've got you cold on this one. You're off the *Bluegill*, Murdoch's submarine, aren't you? You must be pals."

"We're shipmates," Bryce said.

"You probably know his wife, being shipmates and all," Maddox said. He saw Bryce's fingers tighten on the cap, saw his knuckles turn white.

"Yes, I know her," Bryce said. "We all know each other. Why?"

"You were at the Whispering Inn the night all this started," Maddox said, guessing. "You were with the Murdochs."

"Everyone was with everyone," Bryce said. "It was a party. We were all together."

"You and the Murdochs," Maddox said. "Hester and Gerald."

"And my *wife*," Bryce said. "My wife was there. It was a welcome party for my wife."

Maddox said "Yeah," in a long sigh. "Welcome to Hawaii?"

"Yes, welcome to Hawaii," Bryce said. "Why are you asking me all these questions?" Maddox heard a truck lumbering down the street, louder and louder, and then it stopped.

"You'd been alone out here, is that it? How long were you alone, Lieutenant?"

"What's the difference? You arrested me for protecting myself," Bryce said. "I'm innocent. He swung at me."

"Sure. So there you were with the Murdochs at the Whispering Inn. And your wife. All together you said. But not all the time. Hester Murdoch left. Did you see her leave, Lieutenant?" Another truck approached and stopped. "Did you see her leave, Lieutenant?"

"You're asking me questions about something that happened a long time ago, a night last fall," Bryce said. Maddox saw him shifting his feet, wanting to run. "I can't remember what happened last fall."

"I can," Maddox said. "Did you dance with Hester Murdoch?"

"No, I didn't dance with her!"

"See, you remember not dancing with her," Maddox said. "You might remember her taking a walk. She left the party to take a walk. Was anyone with her?"

"I told you, I can't remember!"

"Search your memory, as they say."

Bryce had his fist under the cap. "You can't keep me here this way."

"I'm doing it," Maddox said. "Where were you when Hester Murdoch ducked out?"

"I told you I can't remember!" Bryce said. "Probably dancing with my wife!"

"Sure."

"It's the truth!" Bryce said. He should never have gone into the saloon. He should never have looked at that bitch, that two-bit hustler.

"That's all I hear in my work," Maddox said. "Nobody ever lies to me. You're telling me the truth. Hester Murdoch told me the truth." He opened the center drawer of his desk and took out an envelope. "But I'm still looking for the guy who put her in the hospital."

"They caught those men!" Bryce said, his voice rising. "Hester identified those men!"

"The jury didn't believe her," Maddox said. "I didn't believe her either but I had nothing to go on until tonight." He tipped the envelope as though it contained rare gems, spilling a man's white shirt button into the palm of his hand. "This didn't come from any of the shirts those kids were wearing," Maddox said. "Hold up your left hand, Lieutenant."

"I want to call a lawyer," Bryce said.

"Sure. The cop downstairs said he never saw anything like that man's face. I did," Maddox said. "Hester Murdoch, the night of the welcome party for your wife. You don't have to show me the ring," Maddox said. "I've seen it." Bryce leaped out of the chair. "You wouldn't make it to the elevator." Bryce watched him drop the shirt button into the envelope.

"I'm entitled to call a lawyer," Bryce said. Maddox rose and walked around the desk.

"She wasn't raped," Maddox said. "My guess is you and she were the real pals of the *Bluegill*. Until your wife showed up. My guess is you said good-bye at your wife's welcome home party but little Hester didn't buy it. My guess is you and she had an argument out at the Whispering Inn, and you went to work on her. You're a bad one, Lieutenant. You should be off the streets before you kill someone, you and your ring. You belong in a padded cell and I'm going to put you in it."

"You're the one who belongs in a padded cell," Bryce said.

"We'll soon find out," Maddox said. "You'll have your lawyer. He'll be right here with you. So will Hester Murdoch and her husband. And that poor bloke you almost killed today. I'll tell Gerald Murdoch he shot the wrong man, and we'll see whether he believes you and his wife, or me."

"You're trying . . ." Bryce said, and stopped as Maddox suddenly swung his fist, hitting the desk.

"I've *got* it!" Maddox said, almost shouting. "I've got it!" he said, and shook his head, berating himself for his stupidity. "It was right there in front of me! If those kids didn't rape her, they didn't knock her up!" Maddox pointed. "*You* knocked her up! It was *you!* She was at you to do something about it! Threatened to go to your wife is my guess, stop the music and make her little announcement of the blessed event!"

The approaching growl of another truck filled the office and then stopped abruptly, and Maddox heard someone in the corridor. "Captain!" He heard someone rapping on the door.

"Take a load off, Lieutenant," Maddox said, and crossed the office. When he opened the door he was facing the desk sergeant. Behind and beside him were three men in Navy uniform, Commander Saunders and two elephants wearing S.P. brassards and holding nightsticks in their hands. Each wore a web belt around his middle from which hung a holster with a .45 caliber automatic.

Three hours earlier, in the admiral's quarters at Pearl Harbor, one of his Filipinos had returned from the *Bluegill*. "Lieutenant Bryce left *Bluegill* long time back," he said.

"He knew I was waiting," Ginny said. "I told him I'd be here waiting. Hester, you heard me." Doris Ashley watched Ginny, who could not stop pinning back her hair. The woman was out of control.

"Perhaps he's with Gerald," Doris Ashley said. "Perhaps they're at the Officers' Club."

"We've called Gerald!" Ginny said. "We've *called* the Officers' Club!"

"He's a grown man," Doris Ashley said. "He hasn't disappeared." Ginny wanted to spit at her, sitting there like a school principal talking about Bryce as though he were tardy.

"He's gone!" Ginny said, and dropped a hairpin. Hester bent to pick it up.

"We could sit in my room and wait," Hester said, low.

"I have to find Bryce!" Ginny said. "He's . . ." she said and stopped, raising her hand with the pin as though she wanted to shield her eyes. *They* had him! Those three savages had him! They were taking revenge for their dead friend! They had stolen onto the base, lurking, and had leaped on Bryce as they had leaped on Hester! They would kill him, offering him up for sacrifice in a pagan rite! "I'm going to the admiral!" Ginny said.

"Here I am," said the admiral, who had been driven to his quarters from his office. Ginny ran toward him.

"My husband is missing!" Ginny was still talking, following the admiral, as he went to the telephone to order a search for Bryce. The admiral was worried about more trouble.

At police headquarters, in the corridor facing Maddox, the desk sergeant said. "This here's Commander Saunders, Captain."

"We've met," said Jimmy Saunders. Maddox moved slightly, blocking the doorway.

"You're not getting him," Maddox said. "Not this one."

"Captain, I don't want any trouble," Saunders said. "I certainly don't want any trouble with you."

"That's a load off my mind," Maddox said, "because it looked to me like we were headed in that direction."

"I'm here for Lieutenant Partridge," Saunders said. Walking toward Maddox, Bryce swore he would never raise his hands again. He promised God. He promised he would never talk to any woman except Ginny as long as he lived. He swore on his Navy oath. He swore he would never set foot in a saloon again. He would drive from home to Pearl and from Pearl home.

"Your lieutenant is charged with aggravated assault in the city of Honolulu," Maddox said.

"We'll investigate the incident," Saunders said.

"You're not taking over my beat," Maddox said. "I've finished the investigation. There's a victim over in Mercy Hospital. I've got statements from witnesses. The lieutenant is entitled to a fair trial. He's going to trial, Commander.'' He whirled around, shoving Bryce. ''Back off,'' he warned. Maddox turned to the corridor and saw the two sailors flanking Saunders raise their nightsticks. ''Tell them to back off,'' Maddox said.

''Lieutenant Partridge is an officer in the United States Navy and is under the jurisdiction of the Department of the Navy,'' Saunders said. ''Hand him over, Captain.''

Maddox pointed at the desk sergeant. ''Go downstairs and send up every cop in the building.''

''You back off,'' Saunders said.

''How'd you like me on your ship, with guns, taking the wheel away from you?'' Maddox said, and to the desk sergeant, ''If you're here ten seconds from now, you'll be on the docks tomorrow night.''

''It's out of his hands, Captain,'' Saunders said. ''It's out of your hands. And mine. I haven't taken over your beat, the admiral has. He set a six o'clock curfew for all natives in Honolulu, and it's already begun.'' He gestured at the windows. ''See for yourself.''

The desk sergeant nodded at Maddox. ''The chief called, Captain. He told the dispatcher to put it on the air, all squads.'' Maddox stepped back, closing the door and locking it. He didn't look at Bryce. Maddox went to the windows and separated the venetian blinds. Three Navy trucks were parked in front of the building and he saw a pair of Shore Patrol sailors on each side of the street. Maddox dropped his arm. He turned away, stopping beside Bryce.

''We're not finished,'' Maddox said, but he knew the man was laughing at him. Maddox unlocked the door and opened it wide, standing back from the doorway. ''Get him out of here,'' Maddox said. ''He stinks up the place.''

Maddox went back to the windows, looking into the street. He saw the commander and his two bodyguards leave headquarters with the lieutenant and enter a Navy car in front of the trucks. The car drove off. Maddox saw both pairs of S.P. converge on the intersection, where a man was padding across the street. The four dwarfed their quarry. He disappeared. Then Maddox saw him between two S.P., being led to the trucks. He slammed the venetian blinds into the window and sat down, sitting sideways to the desk, his legs apart. ''That squid,'' he said, thinking of the chief. But Maddox knew the chief was powerless. He was powerless. ''Shooting gallery,'' he said, aloud.

Maddox was tired all through him. "Go on home," he said aloud. He thought of the man being led to the Navy truck, and, unable to block the memory, saw Joe Liliuohe's casket being towed out to sea. Maddox moved as though he were in pain and reached for the telephone. His hands fell away. They had big ears on the switchboard upstairs. He rose and walked to the door, turning off the lights. He used the stairs, and in the lobby went to the public telephone.

The Shore Patrol were everywhere. As Maddox approached the Western Sky, he saw a Navy truck parked on Kalakau Avenue, and a pair of S.P. in front of the hotel. Maddox turned into the driveway and passed the line of taxis to stop beyond the entrance. He set the POLICE sign in his window and left his car. Lenore was up there, listening to Bergman. It seemed to Maddox that years had passed since that afternoon.

The lobby was cool. The lights were muted. He could see the candles on the tables in the outdoor restaurant where the late diners were sitting beside the sea. He could hear music somewhere. A woman broke into laughter, and someone said, "Marvelous! Simply marvelous!"

Maddox went to the elevators and then turned away. He could not help himself. He walked to the registration desk, stopping in front of the mail rack. The jeweler's box was gone. So she had the necklace. He thought of Lenore in front of the mirror with the necklace. He thought of her with him in his house that afternoon.

He was alone in the elevator. The corridor was deserted. He made no sound on the thick carpet. He pushed the doorbell and after a time the door opened. "You're not my idea of a gentleman caller," the princess said, and moved aside.

She was in white, a full, flowing gown. Her hair was coiled atop her head and she wore an ivory barette. The penthouse was still and fragrant, and when Maddox followed her, he saw the flowers everywhere. On a table beside a large chair, each in a slender glass vase, were several orchids. They were splendid. "Don't you ever quit?"

"We don't punch a clock," Maddox said. They faced each other and for a moment neither spoke. They had never been alone together, and yet they were intimates. They had no secrets. They were both outsiders, and they were both powerful. They were like rulers of two countries with a common boundary, distrusting each other but respectful and wary. The only instance of humanity the princess had ever found in Harvey Koster was his attachment to Maddox.

"Let's hear it," the princess said. "You wouldn't take no for an answer."

"The admiral put a six o'clock curfew on the town."

"The folks around here haven't heard about it."

"It's not for the folks around here," Maddox said. The princess looked at him as though he had persuaded the admiral to act.

"I'm not much for nightlife anyway," she said. She lowered herself into the chair beside the orchids. "Did he bring a cannon?" she asked, and didn't pause. "I remember when they broke our lease on the palace. *That* admiral showed up with a cannon. My mother said they should talk. She was the queen, it was her country, but she was willing to sit down with him. She sent a message but she didn't get an answer. The cannon was the answer. You're a crummy people, Maddox."

"I didn't set the curfew."

"The admiral didn't include you," the princess said.

"No one will pick you off the street," Maddox said. He was tired of sparring with her. "This curfew will tear the island apart. The admiral doesn't know Honolulu. Living on Pearl is like living on a ship. You can't say if, but, or maybe, to an admiral, or any officer on a ship. Honolulu isn't a ship. These people aren't sailors. The admiral would have been smarter putting them on a raft."

"They'll survive," the princess said. "They've survived this long."

"You're ducking," Maddox said. "You've been out on the big island so long it's a habit."

"Be careful, Maddox."

"Or you'll what? I tell you there's a curfew, and you give me a lesson in ancient history," Maddox said. "Wake up! The admiral has dropped a net over these people. He's telling them when they can go and when they stop. He didn't bring a cannon, but he put enough guns out there to make a sieve out of this town. You can't padlock a whole town. The older people will hold still for it, they can remember back, like you can. But how long before some kid no bigger than a pup talks some other kids into sneaking out some night? For no good reason except they're kids and the juices are running. Most of those sailors are kids and *their* juices are running. They'll be burying people in layers."

"You should run for office," the princess said. Maddox came straight at her, stopping in front of the chair.

"I didn't come up here for your wisecracks," Maddox said.

"I've heard them," he said, and louder, "I'm goddamn tired of them."

"I'm goddamn tired of you!" the princess said just as loudly. "Get back!" She waved. "Get back! I wish I were wearing stirrups." Maddox moved to one side. "Now you listen to me, Captain Curtis Maddox. You said you had to see me. I saw you. You told me we've been blessed with a curfew. Aloha."

Maddox dropped his hat on the sofa and sat down on the arm facing her. "We're just starting."

"Someone told me to stay put," the princess said. "I should've listened."

"You're the only chance we've got," Maddox said.

"I am not Miss God Almighty!" the princess said. Maddox was silent. "I never laid eyes on this admiral."

"Introduce yourself," Maddox said. "I'll drive you out to Pearl."

"Tonight?"

"Yes, tonight," Maddox said. "Now. We could be late now. Some punk could be slipping out of Papakolea or Makiki, five feet from a sailor with a gun. The sailor says, 'Stop!' but he doesn't stop, and he could be in the morgue while you and me are still arguing."

"You're giving me a headache."

"We're still arguing," Maddox said. "Listen, you can't run a place where every other person is locked up every night, even if it's your own house."

The princess said, "Same old . . ." and stopped. She put her hands on the arms of the chair, pushing and rocking so she could rise. Maddox came off the sofa and she said, "No!" heaving herself upright. Maddox picked up his hat. She was puffing. "Like getting out of a mudhole. Beat it," she said. Maddox stared at her.

"I'll drive you out," he said.

"You're not dumb," the princess said. "Don't act dumb. The admiral would boot my tail. He'll be thinking of the other admiral, too, the one who threw us out of the palace. He'll need to prove he's just as tough."

"Somebody has to move," Maddox said.

"The longer you stay, the longer my headache lasts," the princess said. Maddox looked at her, and, after a moment, turned to the door. The princess walked out on the terrace and stood facing the sea. The moon was low and bright, and the water was the color of silver. The princess hugged herself. "Cold," she said, aloud. She left the terrace and went into her bedroom. She took a white knitted shawl from a drawer and put it over her shoulders. She left the bedroom, but went back for her purse. "Forget your head if it wasn't tied to your shoulders," she said, and stopped once more, opening her purse to be certain she had money. "Full speed ahead," she said. She opened the door to the corridor and hesitated. "Oh, Jack, Jack," she said, aloud, and left the penthouse.

When the taxi stopped, the princess said, "Wait." She made her way out of the cab and paused, pulling her shawl close. "Man lives in a jungle," she said to herself. She walked slowly, a single step at a time, like a mountain climber, and, reaching the massive, deep border of hibiscus, saw the lights on both floors that were almost hidden by the thick screen of bougainvillea covering the facade of Harvey Koster's home.

The princess had not telephoned because she believed everything Maddox had told her and she could not give Harvey Koster the opportunity to avoid or postpone a meeting. She knew, as did everyone who knew him, that except for the governor's inauguration ball, Koster never accepted an evening engagement. She was puffing when she reached the entrance and found the doorbell. The princess rang and rang. She knocked, hitting the door until her hand ached. Harvey Koster was inside. He would not leave lights burning in an empty house. "Must be deaf as a doornail," she said, aloud, knocking once more but with her left hand. The princess tried to open the door. It was locked. Raising her gown, she went back to the driveway and circled the house. She saw the garage on her left, and on her right, near the rear, a narrow door Sidney Akamura had forgotten to lock that day after setting out the garbage cans for the weekly collection.

The princess came into darkness. She moved her hand along the wall and found a light switch. Steps led to the kitchen. Puffing, she said, "Harvey?"

She saw light beneath a door and opened it, entering a short hall and emerging into a sun room. Beyond it lay the living room. The princess was struck by the elegance, the pristine beauty of the house. "Harvey?"

As she walked toward the magisterial sweep of the staircase, the princess suddenly stopped, listening. She heard a sound, something musical. She continued, reaching the foot of the staircase, and stood beneath the lighted lantern that hung from the ceiling. The house was silent once more. "Harvey?"

Holding the railing, Princess Luahine started up the stairs and stopped. She heard the music again. She resumed climbing. She had to rest at the head of the stairs. She could hear the music distinctly now, sharp and almost discordant. "Harvey?"

She followed the music to an open door and stood looking into Koster's bedroom. It seemed uninhabited. The music was louder. The princess entered the bedroom and saw the glow from blazing lights at one side. She turned, facing Koster's dressing room, and beyond, the world he had created and populated.

Koster was on his knees, in his shirtsleeves, his back to the princess. He was beside a showboat, entranced by the performance of the troupe and infatuated with Margot, the leading lady. The calliope delighted him. Koster had played it constantly since the arrival of the showboat. He murmured to Margot, trying to catch her attention as she made her farewell speech to her mother, vowing to save, somehow, the plantation.

The princess didn't move. She saw the hundreds of women, each unique, around Koster. Silently, stealthily, the princess left the bedroom. She came halfway down the stairs and waited until the calliope stopped. Putting her hand to her mouth, the princess shouted, "Harvey! Harvey!" Then, clutching the rail for support and balance, she descended quickly. She unlocked the front door, and stood by it and yelled once more. "Harvey!"

Above, walking toward the head of the stairs, she saw Koster appear, buttoning his jacket. He looked like he was being invaded, she thought. She had scared him, all right. He didn't know the half of it. Koster stopped, looking down at her. *"Lu? Lu?"*

"In the flesh," said the princess. "All of it." Koster came down the stairs.

"Where did you come from? What brings you here? I didn't hear you come in. How did you get in?" His voice was high-pitched, and the words tumbled out.

"I'll start at the end," the princess said. "I got in the same way you do, Harvey. I rang the bell and when you didn't answer, I opened the door. Stop treating me like a thief."

Koster had locked the door every night since the house was built. Could he have forgotten? He couldn't have forgotten. But she was here. He had been in such a rush to see his showboat. "You surprised me, Lu."

"How about taking a load off? I'm tired," the princess said. She went ahead of him, into the living room, and took a chair. Koster followed her and sat down. "What brings me here?" the princess said. "The curfew brings me here, Harvey. You've heard about the curfew?"

"Is that why you came?" Koster crossed his legs. He could

feel himself returning to normal. "It doesn't affect you, Lu," he said.

"Oh, it affects me, Harvey," the princess said. "It affects both of us."

"Now, Lu, you and I have lived through a lot," Koster said. "We'll live through this. The curfew is a fact. It is a condition of life now, like the sea around us. We'll learn to live with the curfew the way we learned to live with the sea."

"The sea is dangerous but people can keep away from it," the princess said. "People can't keep away from the curfew."

"We must hold the status quo," Koster said.

"With guns? With sailors dragging old ladies off the street? Throwing old ladies in jail? You ought to be worried, Harvey," the princess said. "That son of yours is square in the middle of this down at headquarters, and he's worried."

Koster looked past her. The princess had always spoken of Curt Maddox as his son, and he had never dignified her with a denial. He could not stop her. No one in the Territory could touch her. "They'll obey," Koster said. "They're reasonable."

"The kids aren't reasonable," the princess said. "They didn't grow up with guns pointed at them, with your plantation managers. The kids think they're Americans."

"They are!" Koster said. "They're citizens of the Territory!" He was vehement.

"In a pig's ear!"

"You're wrong, Lu," Koster said. "We've made great progress. You've lost touch out there on the big island."

"Not altogether," the princess said. "I heard about the burial at sea, for instance."

"Terrible," Koster said. "Terrible. A real setback. That senator in Washington has hurt us. He forgets everything we've accomplished. I wish he'd come to see for himself, see what we've made of Hawaii. We're on the march, Lu. We won't always be a Territory, a stepchild. We'll be part of the Union, another star in the flag of the United States. We'll send two senator's to Washington and congressmen to the House of Representatives."

"I hope you make it, Harvey, but you'll never make it if this curfew lasts."

"We can't argue with the Navy."

"I don't argue with anyone. I ran away from here because I wouldn't argue. I decided I'd live as long as I had left to live for me, myself, and I. I made one mistake. I picked the big island instead of Alaska, or New Zealand, or . . . Timbuctoo." The princess sighed, pushing herself erect, and Koster rose.

"We must be sensible," he said. Tomorrow morning he would inquire about an alarm system for the door. If it wasn't locked by six o'clock, the alarm would sound. He would have his own curfew. "How did you get here, Lu?" he asked. "Do you need a ride?"

"The meeting isn't adjourned," the princess said. "It's almost adjourned. I'm tired. I've been going to sleep with the birds out there on the ranch. Harvèy, the curfew has to be lifted," she said, and raised her hand to keep him quiet. "I'll give you until noon. If you or someone hasn't called me by twelve o'clock, I'm moving out of the Western Sky. I'm moving to Papakolea, to Opal Nehoa's boardinghouse. I'll keep the curfew, all right, but I'll extend it. I'll order a twenty-four-hour curfew. The day after tomorrow, there won't be a maid, cook, laundress, gardener, janitor, dock walloper, or anyone else working in Honolulu. I'll shut down Honolulu, Harvey. It'll stay shut down, not until the curfew is lifted, but. for awhile *after* it's lifted, so you'll know better than to try it again." She pulled her shawl over her shoulders. "Yes, I have a ride, Harvey."

In the taxi returning to the hotel the princess said, "Dolls." She needed a bath.

At ten A.M. the next morning the admiral arrived at Iolani Palace, where Governor Martin Snelling thanked him for appearing on such short notice. The governor said he was lifting the curfew. "Matter of fact I already told the press," said the governor. "I already cabled the Territorial Delegate."

PART
5

In Washington a few minutes before noon on the day Doris Ashley, Gerald Murdoch, and Duane York went to trial for the murder of Joseph Liliuohe, Senator Floyd Rasmussen finished writing with an extravagant stroke of his pen. "Ready!"

On the sofa beside the door of the senator's office, Phoebe Rasmussen said, "Read it." She wore her gloves and overshoes. The office windows were glazed with ice and rattled constantly from the wind. The senator raised his pad.

" 'All America is depending on you to free three innocent victims of savagery and barbarism. Floyd Rasmussen. United States Senator.' "

"You are not all America, Floyd," said his wife.

"I am the country's spokesman," Rasmussen said. "Time is short." He set the telephone in front of him.

"Floyd!" Her voice was like a whip. Rasmussen's hand fell. "You are not a single voice. You have mobilized a mighty force. The names of one hundred twenty-six senators and representatives must be on the message."

"We'll be convening in a moment," Rasmussen said. He liked to be in the Senate for the invocation.

"You have the list," Phoebe said.

"My dear." He sounded as though he were begging. "I am sending a cable. Every word counts in a cable. Proper names count. It does not come under the frank. I'm paying."

"*We* are paying," Phoebe said. "We'll use the cable in our next letter to the constituents, reminding them you are the leader of a great crusade."

Rasmussen took the list of names from his desk. As he identified himself to the cable operator, Phoebe left the sofa. "Floyd!" She came to the desk. "Where are you sending it?"

"To the hotel," Rasmussen said. "To the Western Sky."

Almost four hours later, in the sun in Honolulu, the reporters and photographers were a solid mass in front of the courthouse. The admiral's driver tried frantically to keep them away from the limousine parked between the two NO PARKING standards in front of the entrance.

Behind them, alone or in twos and threes, dark-skinned and yellow-skinned men and women darted toward the lobby doors, moving almost furtively. They were Hawaiian and Chinese and Japanese, and from everywhere in the South Pacific. These were the latecomers. A solid line of people had been waiting for the courthouse to open. They had climbed the stairs to the balcony, waiting again until a bailiff unlocked the courtroom where the three defendants in the murder of Joseph Liliuohe would be tried. The men and women were orderly and compliant. They followed the bailiff's instructions. Those who came last lined the rear walls.

The selection of a jury does not ordinarily attract an audience. Those who came were not enrolled, they were not part of a planned action. Except for husbands and wives, or mothers and daughters, or fathers and sons, and those who came with a companion or two, these were all strangers to each other. They came as they had come to Joseph Liliuohe's funeral on the beach, because of a need, a compulsion they could not deny. None were challenged or molested. There were only two policemen on duty at the courthouse, one at each end of the building. Harvey Koster had talked with the chief of police. Koster did not want another visit from Princess Luahine.

The only crowd at the courthouse that morning was composed of newspapermen. The reporters had come from everywhere for the murder trial, from San Francisco and Los Angeles, from London and Milan and Berlin, from Manila and Hong Kong, from Tokyo and Sydney. Judge Geoffrey Kesselring had established a pressroom in the courthouse basement and cable lines had been brought in for direct transmission to the foreign desks of the newspapers.

As they stood at the curb, jammed together, someone said, "That's him." Photographers set shutter speeds and surrounded the taxi that stopped behind the admiral's limousine.

Someone said, "It's a dame," and Jeff Terwilliger, standing clear of the crowd, said, "His wife."

Lenore stood in the street beside the cab, her hand out. Bergman took it and left the taxi as the flashguns exploded, making sudden short puffs of light and trailing smoke. The reporters shouted questions. "Hold your horses, gents," Bergman said, and to Lenore, "No reason for you to stay."

"I'll come inside with you," she said.

"I'm too spoiled to argue." Lenore matched her step to his.

The reporters encircled them. "Slim pickings today," Bergman said. "We're starting to seat a jury."

"How long do you expect it to take?"

"You boys have been in court before," Bergman said. "It'll take as long as we need to fill those twelve seats with twelve good men and true." He answered questions until they were inside, at the foot of the stairs leading to the courtroom on the second floor. As the reporters filed past, Bergman said, "I think I can make it from here."

"Do you have chocolate?" Lenore asked. Bergman nodded.

"Enjoy yourself," he said.

"I thought I'd shop."

"Good hunting," Bergman said, holding the rail as he began to climb the stairs. Lenore waved and turned. She was trembling. She tried to walk casually, to stroll, as she crossed the lobby on her way to join Maddox.

Bergman was the last lawyer to arrive in the courtroom. As he entered, he put his arms behind his back, one hand in the other hand, and paused to look around him. To his right, behind the bar near the jury box, were men in suits and ties. They were white and brown and very dark and a few were Oriental. They were all somber and silent. These were the fifty men of the jury panel.

To the left, inside the well on the far side of the courtroom, Judge Kesselring had provided four rows of long tables and folding chairs for the reporters and artists who were covering the trial. The chairs were filling as Bergman stood at the head of the aisle.

It was the audience, the people behind the bar, that had stopped Bergman. They were orderly, they were really subdued, as though they were afraid to provoke attention, but they were not in attendance to comfort the defendants. They represented the dead man and so they were an unfriendly audience. Bergman did not like their presence.

As Bergman came down the aisle, he saw the three defendants at the defense counsel table. The two men were in blue uniforms and sat beside each other. Doris Ashley sat apart and apart from Coleman Wadsworth, who was Harvey Koster's attorney and whom he had ordered to assist Bergman.

Philip Murray and Leslie McAdams were at the prosecution table, and near the aisle in the first row, sitting behind Doris Ashley, Bergman saw the admiral, alone. Bergman unclasped his hands, and he was no longer shuffling. "Mrs. Ashley!" The admiral heard Bergman and rose, waiting at the gate.

"Look at this jury panel," the admiral said.

Bergman bent to open the gate. "Later." He left the admiral standing at the aisle and stopped beside Doris Ashley. "Where is your daughter?"

"She is not on trial," said Doris Ashley, and turned, facing the empty jury box. Bergman stepped between her and Coleman Wadsworth.

"Her husband is on trial," Bergman said. "Her husband and her mother. On trial for murder. Your daughter is the tinder that started this fire, brought her husband and you, all of you into this courtroom. Your daughter could be a widow before she's a year older. Mr. Wadsworth here and I will do our level best to prevent that, but we must have help, more help than I've ever needed. Hester Murdoch is a tragic, wounded, and scarred young woman. Our hearts go out to her. The world mourns for Hester Murdoch. I want to see her in this courtroom, every day, all day. I want the men who fill the jury box, some of whom, hopefully, will have daughters of their own, to see her every day, all day. Where is she?"

Doris Ashley was not afraid of him. She looked up at Bergman, refusing to let him browbeat her. "You are being rude and abusive to me," she said.

"Hester is at the admiral's quarters," Gerald said. Bergman swung around.

"Admiral!" He reached the rail. "I want Hester Murdoch here. *Here*," Bergman said, pointing at the first row. "She's late already. Have someone you trust escort her into this courtroom and deliver her to you. I suppose arranging transportation isn't the kind of job you ask an admiral to provide, but I'm a stranger here with a limited acquaintanceship."

"My car is downstairs," said the admiral. "I'll have the bailiff tell the driver."

"He'll be going and coming," Bergman said. "We can cut that time in half if you telephone."

"You can't let even one of those people into the jury box," the admiral said, gesturing at the fifty men of the panel.

"Shake a leg, will you, Admiral?" Bergman left him and raised both hands to smooth his hair as he approached the prosecution table. Philip Murray and Leslie McAdams came out of their chairs. Bergman extended his hand, smiling. "Counselor."

"Hello, Mr. Bergman," Murray said. He introduced McAdams.

"You look like you've just come from taking the bar exam," Bergman said.

"Not quite, sir," McAdams said.

"Maybe one day you'll try my side of the court," Bergman said.

Murray grinned. "He's here *because* you're on the other side of the court, Mr. Bergman."

"I'll watch out for him," Bergman said. He looked around. "Pretty court."

"It's a copy of one in Philadelphia, one of the oldest in America."

"Pretty, pretty," Bergman said. He returned to the defense counsel table and took a chair across from Coleman Wadsworth, who extended a typewritten list of names.

"Here are the names of the jury panel, Mr. Bergman."

"I'd appreciate it if you called me Walter," said Bergman. "Embarrasses me to have a man your age call me 'Mr.' " He was reading the names of the jury panel, glancing now and then at the men behind the rail, when the admiral returned to the courtroom. Wadsworth caught Bergman's eye and gestured. Bergman looked up and saw the admiral in the first row, standing against the rail.

"I've done my job," said the admiral. "Now you do yours." Bergman reached into his pocket and took out the envelope he had brought from the hotel. He was reading the cable from Rasmussen when Judge Kesselring entered the courtroom.

Geoffrey Kesselring was a tall, erect man. He was fifty-five years old and had become heavier in the last decade. Like his father, Kesselring's hair had turned white before he was thirty. He was the public's image of a judge. He was a native, the grandson of a German immigrant who had started as a clerk in a ship's chandler's shop. The first Kesselring was a thrifty, ambitious man. The shop was on the waterfront, and within a year the clerk began, privately, to loan money. He began with small sums, a dollar, five, ten. The loans were short term, a week or two weeks, and his rates were usurious. He was always available, especially on the Sabbath when the Saturday night revelers woke with empty pockets. The immigrant prospered, and he left the chandler to establish himself, first in a small office near the docks, and then in the financial district. When he died, he left his son, the judge's father, one of the largest discount houses in Hawaii. Kesselring and Company bought loans from lenders who could not hold the notes, extracting the same usurious fees initiated by the clerk in the waterfront.

Geoffrey Kesselring was an only child, raised in great wealth. He was enrolled in Punahou with the sons of the other men who controlled Hawaii, and when he graduated, he sailed for the

Mainland with some of his classmates to attend Harvard. He was
an excellent student, attracted by the law. In his senior year he
was accepted by Harvard Law School.

Geoffrey came home to a doting father who made him a full
partner in the firm. Kesselring and Company continued to prosper.
The young man enjoyed the privileged life of the island elite. He
became a ranking polo player. He was a dashing figure in
society.

When the war started in 1914, the Kesselrings were, like all
Hawaiian society, passionate supporters of the Allies. But there
was a perceptible change in the attitude of their friends and
business associates toward the Kesselrings, the Germans. In May
1915 a German submarine sank the *Lusitania*. There were many
Americans among the 1,198 passengers who went down with the
ship. In the United States hatred of the Germans became epidemic,
and in Hawaii patriotism was especially fervent and vengeful.
Kesselring and Company was ostracized. The judge's father
crumpled under the vicious personal attacks that accompanied
the boycott. In 1917, when America entered the war, Geoffrey
Kesselring was forced to close the firm the German immigrant
had founded in the ship's chandler's shop on the docks.

Geoffrey Kesselring was married and the father of two children and therefore not subject to the draft. He tried to enlist and
was rejected. He opened an office for the practice of law. There
were no clients. He was a pariah and at the end of his resources
when one of his Punahou classmates saved him. Harvey Koster
arranged for Kesselring to fill a vacancy on the municipal court
bench.

The new judge was determined. His abilities could not be
denied. In 1918, when the war ended and the ignoble and
unjustified prejudice abated, Kesselring received offers to join
law firms in Honolulu, but he declined them. He had chosen a
judiciary career. He rose swiftly, becoming a district court judge
before he was forty-five.

As court convened, Wadsworth leaned across the table. "He's
a stickler."

"Keep it in mind," Bergman said. The judge looked down at
him.

"Welcome, Mr. Bergman," Kesselring said. "I've known of
you and your great work all through my professional life. It is an
honor to have you in my court."

Bergman pushed himself out of the chair. "That's about as
nice a reception as I've ever had, Your Honor," Bergman said.
"Thank you. While I'm at it, I'd like to say there hasn't been a

day since I arrived when someone hasn't made me feel at home.''

"We are an island people," the judge said. "Visitors flatter us."

As Bergman lowered himself into his chair, he heard a prolonged and mounting gasp of excitement fill the courtroom. Bergman turned, and across the table Coleman Wadsworth looked back to learn the cause of the disturbance. Wadsworth rose. The admiral turned and then he rose. At the prosecution table, Philip Murray and Leslie McAdams rose, and at the four press tables chairs scraped as the newspapermen came to their feet.

Across the courtroom, in the second row with the jury panel, Theodore Okohami, a Hawaiian, came to his feet. When he rose, Bruce Tanaka, a Japanese, rose. Others in the jury panel rose, and on both sides of the aisle the benches emptied as men and women leaped up as though a barrier had been raised freeing them all. Princess Luahine had arrived.

She was magnificent. She wore a cloak of feathers, peacock and pheasant, cockatoo and parrot, reds and greens, blues and yellows and oranges, every color, deep and glowing colors, so vivid, so brilliant, the princess seemed clothed in something breathing, something alive. The cloak was regal and had belonged to kings and queens, and now was Princess Luahine's. The cloak fell to the floor and was fastened at the neck by a string of coral. To assemble the needed feathers, prepare them, and make such a cloak had taken decades. The princess had worn it last in the palace. She had never expected to wear it again, but she had known, from the time she left her ranch, that if she came to the courtroom she would be properly clothed.

There was jade in her hair and she wore a necklace of matched pearls laid before one of her ancestors by a grateful sea captain long, long ago. She was like a splendid, prehistoric bird, a god to those below, that had survived through the ages and had now descended from the sky. She was majestic, and the men and women, young and old, on either side of the aisle, who had appeared noiselessly and gathered meekly in the courtroom were transported by her presence. She was a Hawaiian princess but she was claimed by all of them. They raised their hands in welcome, in homage. They could not contain themselves. Their greetings filled the courtroom, and the judge's gavel was ignored as the princess moved slowly toward the bar with Tom following.

She was embarrassed. "Quiet down," she said, but she could not be heard. She reached for Tom. "Tell them to pipe down."

"Let's just take our places," Tom said. As they reached the

first row and Tom whispered, asking the people on the aisle to make room, the spontaneous welcome for the princess persisted.

"Bailiff!" the judge's voice pierced the tumult in the courtroom. "*Bailiff!*" Judge Kesselring had dropped the gavel and was standing up, looking out at the maelstrom the woman had made of his court. She had brazenly, willfully, invaded a court of law while it was in session, inciting a horde who were corrupting the formal, legal process of justice. Judge Kesselring wanted to leap down from the bench and begin throwing people through the doors. He was appalled by his savagery. The woman had almost corrupted him. "Empty this courtroom!" the judge told the bailiff. "Get help if you need it!"

The princess heard every word. She turned, raising both hands like a conductor and lowering them slowly as she said, "Quiet . . . down!"

"Bailiff!" She turned again to see the bailiff coming straight at the gate. Behind her, and on both sides, the audience began to subside. Some sat, but others stood lest they miss something.

"I feel awful about this, Your Honor," the princess said. "It's about the last thing I expected, or wanted." She whirled around, and this time she pointed. "Sit down and quiet down!" she said.

"Bailiff!"

The princess faced the bench once more. "You're punishing these folks for something I did," the princess said. "I'm the guilty one, they aren't. You weren't throwing anyone out until I showed up here. So if anyone has to leave, it ought to be me."

"This is not your court, madame," said the judge. "Your authority does not extend into this courtroom."

"My authority doesn't extend to the end of my nose," said the princess. "All I'm asking is that you let me pay for the damage, judge." She gestured. "You don't need the bailiff for that. I can find my way out. Stay put," she said to Tom, and started up the aisle.

"Your Honor!" Bergman was standing. He had come halfway around the world to defend three people accused of murdering a Hawaiian, and before they had a single juror in the box, their *princess* was being evicted. "Hope you'll excuse me for sticking my two cents worth in here. Maybe we're all getting off on the wrong foot this morning. Without being pro or con I'd say not one of us showed up today for the sole purpose of making trouble, of throwing a monkey wrench into the proceedings." She was halfway to the door. "I've never yet asked a judge to reverse himself, Your Honor, but I'm coming to the end of my career, and this seems like as good a time as any." Bergman smiled and looked over his shoulder. She was almost at the doors. The bailiff back there was reaching out to open the door.

"Madame!" Judge Kesselring was still standing. When the princess was facing him, he said, "You may be seated."

"Much obliged, Your Honor. I appreciate that." She started back down the aisle, and as she caught Bergman's eye, the old man bowed.

When she was seated once more beside Tom, Judge Kesselring began to instruct the jury panel. Tom saw Gerald watching the princess, and understood, in a single scalding surge of loathing and revulsion, why Sarah could not enter the courtroom. "I can't look at them," Sarah had told him, and now, fifteen feet from the man who had killed Joe, who had set out to kill him, taken a gun and an accomplice, Tom was overcome with a rage so encompassing he was made weak. Gerald's presence was, for a little while, more than Tom could accept. He was looking at Joe's killer, sitting comfortably in a chair like anyone else. Tom wanted to brand Gerald as Joe's murderer, as someone who didn't belong among men. Tom's head spun. He could not accommodate the impulses that possessed him, contradicting every moral standard he had sworn to protect when he took the oath allowing him to practice law. He lowered his head, covering his face, and felt the princess's elbow. "Straighten up, mister. This is only the beginning."

Tom dropped his hands and sat erect, looking straight ahead at the door to the judge's chambers. The princess pinched him. "Stop hiding!" she said, mad at the little snip. "You're not on trial, they are!"

Eight of the fifty men in the jury panel pushed their way toward the aisle when Judge Kesselring finished. Four had formed opinions of the case, two were civilian employees at Pearl Harbor, two were opposed to the death penalty. So there were forty-two men remaining when the judge ordered jurors 1 through 12 into the jury box. Theodore Okohami was juror number two. The judge said, "Mr. Murray."

The district attorney remained in his chair, looking past Bergman at the jury box. "What is your occupation?"

"I'm a fireman," said Oscar Sudeith, delighted to be drawing full pay and the few bucks a day for jury duty on top of it.

Murray sat back like he was in front of a fireplace. "Acceptable to the State, Your Honor."

"Mr. Bergman," said the judge. Bergman leaned forward in

his chair, one hand flat on the defense counsel table, pushing himself to his feet.

"Have to excuse me, Your Honor. I've added rheumatism to my inventory," he said, lying. "Mr. Sudeith," he said, dragging his feet to the jury box. "Are you a family man, Mr. Sudeith?"

"Eighteen years," said the fireman. "Two kids."

"Are they going to be firemen?"

"Not unless they pass a law taking women," Sudeith said, and laughed, slapping the rail of the jury box. "They're girls." Bergman looked at the bench.

"Acceptable, Your Honor."

"Mr. Murray," said the judge. The district attorney remained in his chair, waiting until Bergman was seated. Murray took the list with the names of the jury panel. He rose and, reading the list, walked past the bench and the court reporter to the jury box.

"Theodore Okohami," Murray said, reading. He lowered the list. "You're a Hawaiian, Mr. Okohami."

"Yes, sir, Hawaiian," said Okohami. "Mother and father Hawaiian. Grandmother and grandfather, too. Everybody."

"How old are you, Mr. Okohami?"

"I'm forty-one. Be forty-two in June."

"What do you do?" Murray asked. "How do you earn your living?"

"I'm a gardener. Do gardening."

"Not much money in that, is there?" Okohami looked at the judge.

"Pay my way. Always pay my way. We never ask for nothing." Bergman sat with his hands in his lap, watching the district attorney, ignoring his false symptoms of rheumatism.

Murray raised the list of names. Clipped to it was a transcript of the questions Tom had asked Warren Kamahele during the jury selection in the rape trial. He repeated as many of Tom's questions as were compatible with Theodore Okohami's age. "Have you ever been arrested?"

"No, sir, never," said Okohami. He turned to the bench. "*Never.*" Bergman looked at Coleman Wadsworth, who leaned across the table to listen. But Bergman only shook his head.

Murray was patient. He elaborated on Tom's questions. He took Theodore Okohami through complete biographies of his family and his wife's family. "You're an honest, upstanding citizen, Mr. Okohami," he said. He left the jury box. "Acceptable to the State, Your Honor," Murray said.

Bergman shifted in his chair, turning almost completely around to study the remaining thirty men of the jury panel. He saw other Hawaiians, and Japanese. He saw a Chinese and two whose racial origins he could not identify, and he saw the admiral sending him silent messages of warning. "Mr. Bergman."

"Acceptable to the defense, Your Honor," Bergman said. He leaned over the table facing Wadsworth. "We would have been stoned in the streets," Bergman said. "Let's see if we can cut our losses." He heard a stir in the courtroom and raised his head as Hester and Jimmy Saunders walked down the aisle.

The princess glanced over her shoulder and then, holding the rail with one hand and the bench with the other, turned completely around, looking directly at Hester, who seemed removed as though she had willed herself into a trance. The admiral rose to welcome her. The princess saw Bergman nudge Gerald. "Your wife is here," Bergman said. "Greet her. Kiss her. *Kiss her, man!*"

Gerald left his chair and bent over the rail to brush Hester's cheek with his lips. "Some lovebirds," the princess said.

Tom leaned toward her. "I didn't hear you," he said.

"Good." The princess turned again, grunting with the effort, and fell back. "She's their exhibit A," the princess said. "Lying little bitch."

When the judge adjourned for lunch, three jurors had been chosen. Philip Murray stopped at the rail of the well in front of the princess. "Long time no see, Philip," she said.

He grinned. "Nifty outfit you're wearing," Murray said. "Hello, Tom."

Tom returned the greeting but his voice was lost in the sound of the gate being slammed against the rail as the admiral strode into the well. Gerald and Duane were standing, and the admiral shot past them, hitting both with his shoulder and wheeling around the defense counsel table, then plunging into Theodore Okohami who was walking to the aisle along the wall of the courtroom. The admiral flung him aside as though he were throwing the Hawaiian overboard. Okohami stumbled, falling forward, grabbing the rail and managing to remain on his feet. Coleman Wadsworth came out of his chair as the admiral stopped directly in front of Bergman.

"You're a disgrace!" the admiral said. "You've lost this case before it even begins!"

"Wait a minute," Wadsworth said, reddening. *"Wait a minute!"* The admiral didn't hear him.

"You call yourself a defense lawyer!" the admiral said. He

seemed ready to strangle Bergman. "You were told to keep the natives off this jury! I warned you!"

"You can't talk to him that way!" Wadsworth said. The admiral didn't hear him. Wadsworth started to come around the table.

"You took the first one you saw!" the admiral said. He pointed at Doris Ashley. "You've dropped a rope over the heads of these people! The district attorney can stay home! You're doing his job for him!" Wadsworth reached the admiral, but Bergman waved him off.

"I'm a big boy, Counselor," Bergman said. "I fight my own battles." He stood up and pushed the end of his tie into his waistband. "You're quite a talker, Admiral."

"I haven't even started!"

"Oh, you've started," Bergman said. "Started and finished. This isn't a captain's mast. We're not out on the blue Pacific, and you're not in command. You're not an officer of the court. Mr. Wadsworth is. I am. You're not allowed in this part of the court."

"They shouldn't have let you in either," said the admiral.

"You ought to stop yelling," Bergman said. "There are about one hundred reporters over there in the bleachers. They can't hear me but they can hear you. The pen is mightier than the sword, Admiral, which may be news to you. From the way you talk, the invention of the wheel is news to you. I said you're finished. You are. If you don't get out of here lickety-split, if you ever talk to me again, if I see a flicker of recognition in your eyes, I'll have a powwow with those lads across the way, and when I'm finished, and when *they're* finished, when the people in Washington read your stand on liberty and justice for all, you'll be commanding a fleet in Nebraska. I may look as though I'm ready to meet my Maker, but don't be fooled, Admiral, I've got a surprise or two left for Him. You've got one duty in this trial. You deliver Hester Murdoch." Bergman buttoned his double-breasted jacket. "Can you point me at a good bowl of soup, Mr. Wadsworth?"

The princess, who had watched the admiral with Bergman, turned to the district attorney. "What's eating the Navy?"

Murray glanced at Tom. "I think the admiral doesn't like the color of the jury," Murray said.

"My, my," said the princess. She looked at Philip Murray as though they had just been introduced. "Maybe your old man didn't waste his money, at that," she said. Murray's father, a real estate agent, had always managed the princess's Honolulu holdings.

By the end of the first day, another juror, number 4, had been seated. The admiral sent Duane York back to Pearl Harbor with Jimmy Saunders, and Hester rode in the limousine with him and Doris Ashley. Gerald sat beside the driver. "Drop me at my office," the admiral said.

At his desk the admiral took a pad of Navy communication forms to compose a cable to the Secretary of the Navy, printing in capital letters. "HISTORY REPEATING ITSELF," he began. "ONE HAWAIIAN ALREADY ON JURY. EXPECT MORE. BERGMAN TOTAL INCOMPETENT. PREPARE FOR WORST."

The following day Bruce Tanaka was seated. He was the number-6 juror. On Friday afternoon, a few minutes before Judge Kesselring had decided to recess for the weekend, Bergman accepted juror number 12. Besides Theodore Okohami and Bruce Tanaka, there was another Hawaiian, Ben Hawane, in the second row of the jury box.

Tom left the courtroom with the princess and took her to a taxi. Then he walked to his office. Taped to his door was a yellow ruled sheet of paper. Across the top Tom had written, "BACK AT FOUR. PLEASE LEAVE MESSAGES." The rest of the sheet was clean. Tom said, "Surprise," and unlocked his office, leaving the door open. He sat at his desk until a few minutes before six. The sound of the telephone was so rare and so unexpected that Tom shuddered in surprise. "Hello," he said. He repeated himself, hoping he sounded older, more confident. *"Hello!"*

"Tom? I won't be finished until seven," Sarah said from the drugstore. "Donna is sick and . . . anyway, you don't need to wait. I might be even later. You can go home."

He was smiling into the telephone. "I go home with you."

"Are you sure?" Sarah asked and instantly whispered, "I can't talk." Tom heard the click. He began to review the day in court. Although Sarah could not attend, could not face Gerald, she asked for a full and detailed report each night. She was interested only in the proceedings, not in the principals. Tom learned quickly to omit Gerald and the rest from his account. The office became dark. Tom did not want to turn up the lights. "Save the money," he said to himself, testing the door after he had locked it. He could wait in front of the drugstore.

Sarah was waiting. He waved, and she hurried toward him. Tom forgot the barren sheet of paper on his door, forgot the empty office. She changed him. He was someone else with her, someone special, someone successful and clever, the dashing consort of the beautiful, glowing young woman who made everyone around her invisible. They said "Hello" simultaneously, astonished at being reunited after a separation of almost ten hours. Sarah took his hand, locking them together. "They seated the jury," Tom said.

He gave her a complete account of the day in court. "So the trial starts tomorrow," Tom said. "Opening arguments." He explained the procedure. They reached Sarah's convertible. "I wish you didn't have to work," Tom said.

"I've stopped wishing," Sarah said, and, defiantly, "Do you want to take a walk?" Tom was accustomed to her sudden bursts of emotion, as though she anticipated a challenge. They passed the convertible.

"Aren't you tired?" Tom asked.

"I hate to go home," Sarah said, in despair. "My mother doesn't even know I'm in the house. She's dead, too. They didn't only kill Joe, they killed her. She hates to see my car. She blames the car for everything, for starting everything."

"Maybe you should sell it and buy another car," Tom said. Sarah stopped, pulling her hand from his, whirling around as though he had betrayed her.

"I'll never sell it!" she said. "My mother is right! Joe's dead because he was in my car that night! I want to remind them! Every time they see my car they'll remember Joe was killed because he did something decent, because he couldn't leave someone who needed help. I'll never let them forget! They can't keep killing innocent people! They can't . . ." she said, and her voice broke. She turned her back to Tom, angry with herself and refusing to succumb to tears. Tom put his arm around her. "They're all to blame," Sarah said. "They should all be on trial!"

They resumed walking. Later, Tom led her into a corner restaurant and they sat on stools. Tom ordered for them. Sarah was silent, and she left most of her sandwich. "It's getting late," Tom said.

When they returned to the convertible, Sarah said, "Help me with the top."

"I'll do it," Tom said. He opened the driver's door for her. She stood beside the car as though she were lost, and then, wearily, stepped on the running board to get behind the wheel.

Tom glanced at her as they rode to Papakolea. She drove as though she were alone. "Sarah?" She did not reply, and Tom did not try again. They reached Tom's street, and Sarah turned.

"I'll pick you up in the morning," Sarah said. She stopped. The street was still, and Tom's house was dark. He leaned forward to touch her cheek with his lips. She didn't look at him.

"You kiss me like you asked permission," Sarah said. She turned, facing him, and Tom was afraid she would cry. "You can't wait to leave."

"It's not true!" Tom said. "Sarah, it's not true!"

"It is," she said, sadly. "You act like you're ashamed of . . . everything, like you're here because you don't want to hurt me." Tom took her arms, forcing her to face him.

"You're wrong!" he said. "You're dead wrong!" He brought her to him, felt her lips soft and warm and parting as he kissed her. She tried to speak, but he could not stop, not yet, not after the long, lonely weeks. Sarah clung to him, twisting and turning to be close, and when he released her, they were breathless, their eyes wide with longing. "I didn't do anything, touch you, because of Joe, because I thought you'd be angry," Tom said.

"Not with you, Tommy," she said. "Never with you."

"I thought . . ." he said, and broke off as she forced him back against the seat, kissing him. "Sarah." Her hands were inside his clothes. "Oh, *Sarah.*" She kissed him, kissed him. She could not be still.

"Where can we go?" she whispered.

"Now?" he said, and felt her hands, hot.

"Now," she said, kissing and searching. "Now, Tommy."

"The porch," he whispered. "Our porch." There was a small, screened space behind the kitchen. They left the car like burglars, pressed together, arms around each other.

"We have to be quiet," Tom whispered. He opened the screen door inch by inch, leading her, feeling her behind him. He knew every foot of the tiny porch, and took her past the table to the old, sagging sofa beside the wall.

"Tommy," she whispered. "Darling, Tommy." Holding and kissing him, she pushed her dress off her shoulder. "Here, sweetheart." Her body rose, arching to meet his.

He said, "Sarah," but could not continue. She had him.

"I want to be naked with you," Sarah whispered. "I want us to be naked."

"Not here."

"Yes. Help me and I'll help you." She was everywhere.

"We can't," he whispered unconvincingly. "Someone could come out."

"They won't. They're sleeping," she said, unbuttoning his shirt, slipping her hands inside his pants.

"We'll have to go somewhere," Tom whispered. "Do you want to go somewhere? Sarah?" It was too late. *"Sarah . . ."*

Around nine-thirty the following morning, in a guarded corridor flanking the courtroom, a bailiff led the admiral and the defendants and Hester to the door beside the jury box. When the bailiff opened the door and stepped back, the admiral said, "Once more into the abattoir." He reached for Doris Ashley's arm, but she moved aside, surprising Duane York and almost walking into him. Duane had to damn near jump to stay out of her way. She didn't even know Duane was around. The way she acted, Duane figured she didn't know anyone was around.

"I . . . I'm not ready," Doris Ashley said. The faces waiting inside, the assemblage that surrounded her in the courtroom and ogled her, that seemed to be moving like lava directly at her, had become intolerable. Waking had become intolerable, and dressing for the day. Driving from Pearl Harbor in the admiral's limousine was her daily Gethsemane, and all of this was only the preface, the overture. The reporters were always waiting to pounce, and as their voices lashed out at her, the photographers aimed their cameras like rifles. The popping flashguns were blinding.

The admiral dismissed the bailiff and sent Hester and Gerald and Duane ahead into the courtroom. "You have some time, Doris," he said. "Can I bring you anything?"

"Freedom."

"You'll be free," the admiral said. "You'll all be free." Doris Ashley was not interested in anyone else. "This country won't accept anything except your freedom." He paused. "Are you ready?"

"Give me another minute, Glenn." The admiral put his gloves into his cap and left her alone in the corridor. Doris Ashley embraced her solitude. She closed her eyes, thinking of Windward. She forced herself to see Windward, to *be* there, alone, at dusk when the wind brought the faint, musky smell of the sea into her home. Doris Ashley believed she would return to Windward, go home to stay. She believed she would be freed. She did not think of how or why her freedom would come to her, she knew only that she would be a free soul once more. She could not be sent to prison. The jury could loathe and despise her, but they could never vote to put Doris Ashley behind *bars*. Doris Ashley could not be led away to break rocks. She opened her eyes and reached for the door to the courtroom. She was ready now to let them look at their trophy for another day.

At ten o'clock when court convened, the district attorney rose to offer the opening argument for the prosecution. He crossed the well to the jury box, standing between Bergman and the twelve men he faced. "The People versus Gerald Murdoch, Duane York, and Doris Ashley, is a criminal action brought by the Territory for the single most tragic, most vicious, reprehensible and unforgivable crime in any society: murder, the deliberate taking of a person's life by another, or others," Murray began. "You are here to decide on the guilt or innocence of three defendants charged with murder in the first degree. Premeditated. *Planned* murder.

"You were instructed by Judge Kesselring, and you were questioned before being chosen to sit on this jury, so you are already familiar with some of the elements of this case. It is a repugnant case. It arouses anger and outrage. I am the district attorney of the County of Honolulu. It is my duty to prosecute wrongdoers, those who break our laws. So my work takes me, every working day, into the lower depths among the outcasts, the moral lepers of the world.

"I've been district attorney for a long time. I've seen and been with bad people, evil people. I've had a lot of experience and I believed, truly believed, there were no more surprises left for me in my work and outside my work. In the world of degradation I believed I was one of the leading experts." Murray stepped aside, standing beyond the jury box near the foreman, and looked at Doris Ashley, Gerald, and Duane York. "I was wrong," he said. "The three defendants in this case proved I was wrong. They sank to a level that makes them special. They're the new champions of inhumanity and it is my sworn duty to prosecute them. I'm here representing the People who demand these defendants get their just reward. And I won't disappoint them." Murray paused, scratching his arm as the psoriasis attacked. He needed a breather because he was astonished by his feelings for the defendants. He realized that in his attempts to convince the jury, he had convinced himself. He had to fight and overcome his fury. He could only hurt himself, his arguments, and the State's case. He had to be alert and vigilant, especially with the old, shrewd fox at the defense table in front of him. Murray looked up at the bench, needing more time. "Excuse me, Your Honor. I'm sorry to delay my argument." He moved out in front of the jury box.

"I apologize to you," Murray said to the jury. "I was hit by the fact of this hideous crime, the terrible truth of this murder. An *innocent* lad, born on this island, raised by law-abiding parents to be a law-abiding citizen, a friendly and outgoing fellow, more boy than man in his character and behavior, loving life, *starting* his life, has been killed, killed in cold blood. There is never a justification for murder. But some men have done wrong. Joseph Liliuohe *never* did anything wrong. He never harmed a single human being on this sweet earth. But they killed him.

"Joseph Liliuohe didn't die as a result of a fight or an argument, or a dispute with any of the three defendants who are on trial for his murder. Joseph Liliuohe didn't *know* the defendants. He had never *met* any of the three defendants.

"Remember that: he had never met any of the three defendants who decided to kill him," Murray said. "Think about it, gentlemen. He had never *seen* one of the defendants until the last day of his life. Joseph Liliuohe had, from a distance in this building, *glimpsed* the other two defendants. That was the extent of the relationship between the carefree, fun-loving young man whose life was snuffed out one bright sunny morning, and the persons who cold-bloodedly decided he must die. Joseph Liliuohe did not know them. They did not know him. Joseph Liliuohe was killed by *strangers!*" The district attorney turned again to face Bergman and the defendants.

"Joseph Liliuohe didn't die because he was mistaken for someone else. The defendants charged with his murder didn't kill him by mistake. They set out to kill Joseph Liliuohe. I've said the crime was premeditated and the State will prove it." Murray went past Bergman, stopping beside Gerald, and when he continued, he was speaking to Gerald.

"I've used the word *innocent*," Murray said. "The murder victim was innocent and the defendants in this case, this murder, are presumed innocent until and unless they are proven guilty. The State will prove them guilty." The district attorney slowly shook his head. "There's absolutely no question of that in my mind. The State will present witnesses and offer evidence, hard, undeniable evidence, that will leave you, the jury, with only one choice: to return a verdict of guilty of murder in the first degree." Murray walked toward the bench. "Thank you, Your Honor." At the prosecution table, Leslie McAdams pushed his chair. When the district attorney sat down, McAdams was at his left.

"Beautiful," McAdams said. "I'd like to frame it."

"See how you feel when it's over," Murray said. On the bench the judge looked down at the defense counsel table.

"Mr. Bergman," the judge said. Bergman pushed himself out of his chair, standing beside it.

"The defense would like to ask a favor of the court," Bergman said. "If Your Honor will agree, the defense would like to postpone its opening statement." Judge Kesselring never wore a wristwatch in court. He looked over his shoulder at the clock on the wall above his head.

"The court can grant your request, Mr. Bergman," the judge said. "We can recess now until two o'clock, and you can offer your opening statement when court convenes."

"Your Honor!" Bergman's voice stopped the judge, who was rising from his chair. Bergman waited until the judge was seated. "My fault, Your Honor," Bergman said. "After all these years, I should be able to make myself clear in a courtroom. I apologize to the court. What I meant by postpone is keeping my opening statement until the State has finished its case."

"Until the State has *finished?*" the judge said, but he could not be heard. Too many chairs moved and creaked as four tables with one hundred newspapermen shifted and bent over their notes, writing swiftly.

The court reporter looked up at the bench. "I'm sorry, Your Honor," he said. "I didn't hear all of it." Judge Kesselring knocked with the gavel, looking at the reporters.

"This court is not adjourned, gentlemen," the judge said, and to the court reporter, "Until the State has finished?" Bergman stood waiting. "You're making an unusual demand of the court," the judge said.

"Excuse me, Your Honor," Bergman said. "If there's one thing I couldn't do, it's to make a *demand* of the court. Couldn't and wouldn't. I meant no discourtesy or disrespect and if such is the impression I made, I beg the pardon of the court." Bergman put his hands behind his back. "I certainly agree with the court that what I'm asking is unusual. I've never heard anyone, anywhere, ask for this privilege, this change in normal practice. The court can rule against me, Your Honor. But I'd like to say, to back up this unusual request, that I'm defending three clients charged with murder, the ultimate crime with the ultimate penalty. My own feeling is that some indulgence is in order. That's my own feeling."

Across the aisle from the admiral, the princess nudged Tom. "What's he trying to do?" she whispered.

"I think he's stalling because he doesn't have anything to say." The princess scowled at Tom.

"Young Mr. Know-It-All," she said.

On the bench Judge Kesselring looked down at Bergman. "I'll respect your wishes," he said.

"I'm certainly much obliged to you, Your Honor," Bergman

said. He held the arms of his chair as he lowered himself into it. Tom was absolutely right.

"Mr. Murray," said the judge. The district attorney rose. "If we recess now for lunch, is the State prepared to begin its case when court convenes?"

"We are, Your Honor," Murray said.

At two o'clock that day Murray called his first witness, Officer Kenneth Christofferson. Kenny wore his police badge pinned to the lapel of his jacket. Murray asked him where and when he had first encountered the defendants. Kenny told the jury of chasing the speeding Pierce-Arrow until it swerved off the road. Murray's questions brought Kenny to the discovery of the body on the floor in the rear of the limousine. Murray introduced the State's exhibits A and B, the two .45 caliber Navy issue automatic revolvers he had found in Gerald's canvas bag. Murray's questions were exhaustive and his accumulation of detail seemed endless, but Bergman never rose to object. Only Judge Kesselring interrupted the district attorney to say Murray was being repetitive.

Murray showed Kenny an eight-by-ten-inch glossy photograph of Joe Liliuohe lying on the ground beside Doris Ashley's car. "Is this the body you found in the rear of the automobile?" Murray asked.

"That's it," Kenny said. Murray offered it as Exhibit C. Then he asked the witness if the occupants of the Pierce-Arrow were in the courtroom. Kenny pointed at the three defendants.

"Your witness," Murray said.

Bergman treated Kenny as though the witness were a student making his first appearance in an oratory contest. Bergman's cross-examination was brief and as Kenny left the witness box, the district attorney called Lieutenant Wylie Soames.

A Navy officer in blue dress uniform went to the witness box and was sworn in. Under Murray's questioning, Soames said he was assigned to the *Bluegill* and, among other duties, he was the gunnery officer aboard the submarine. Murray showed him the two revolvers. From their serial numbers, Soames identified them as weapons taken from the *Bluegill* armory. Bergman did not cross-examine.

As Murray rose to call his next witness, Judge Kesselring said, "I think we'll adjourn until ten A.M., counsel."

"What is your occupation?" asked Murray just after ten o'clock the next morning.

"I'm in charge of the laboratory at police headquarters," said

Vernon Kappel, the day's first witness. Murray asked him to describe his work and the extent of his duties, and while Kappel replied, crossed the well to the prosecution table. On it was an oilskin package that Murray opened. Inside was a mound of large bath towels, covered with dirt and brown stains of dried blood. Murray took one from the pile, shaking it and holding it up as though there were a clothesline over his head and he was a housewife hanging the wash to dry. He took one towel at a time, shaking each, and when he had emptied the oilskin package, carried them to the witness box. Murray offered them as Exhibit D. "Have you ever seen these towels before?"

Kappel said the towels had covered the body of Joseph Liliuohe as it had lain beside the Pierce-Arrow. Under Murray's questioning, Kappel said he had examined blood samples taken from the towels. The blood matched the blood of the dead man.

The district attorney showed Kappel the revolvers he had offered as Exhibits A and B. Kappel said fingerprints from one of the guns matched those of Lieutenant Gerald Murdoch. Murray returned to the prosecution table for a small, transparent box. From it he took a .45 caliber bullet, introducing it as Exhibit E. "Have you ever seen this before?"

Kappel said the bullet matched one fired from the .45 automatic bearing Gerald's fingerprints in the pistol range at police headquarters. Kappel was still testifying when Judge Kesselring adjourned for the day.

Jennifer Vogt, a woman in her forties, followed Kappel in the witness box. She told the district attorney she was a saleswoman at Henley & Son, a linen shop. Jennifer said Doris Ashley was a favored customer. Murray showed the witness the blood-stained towels, and Jennifer said she had sold them to Doris Ashley. Murray offered a sales slip from Henley & Son as Exhibit F. Jennifer said the handwriting was hers and the sales slip was for the towels.

When Jennifer Vogt left the witness box, Murray called Chester Preston. A prematurely bald young man with a police badge pinned to his jacket entered the witness box. Preston said he had found a .45 caliber bullet under a lamp in Windward the day Joseph Liliuohe was killed. Murray showed him Exhibit E, and Preston identified it as the bullet he had taken from under the lamp. When Murray said, "No further questions," the judge adjourned.

"We'll be here till the cows come home," Bergman said as Coleman Wadsworth reached for his briefcase. "He's subpoenaed everyone in town except the two of us."

"Mr. Bergman?" Gerald was standing beside him. As Bergman turned in his chair, Gerald said, "I guess I mean you, too, Mr. Wadsworth. You've hardly asked any *questions*." Bergman could see the color in Gerald's face. He put his big hands on the table and pushed himself erect.

"Fact is, Lieutenant, I've got hardly anything to say," Bergman took Gerald's arm. "So far, son," Bergman said. "So far."

The next morning Murray called Maddox to the witness stand. On the prosecution table beside the district attorney was a bulky object covered with a white cloth. Murray walked to the witness box holding a sheet of typewriter paper, which he offered as Exhibit G. " 'I admit I raped Hester Murdoch,' " Murray said, reading. " 'Joseph Liliuohe.' " He gave Maddox the sheet of paper. "Have you ever seen this before, Captain?"

"Yes, I've seen it," Maddox said. He said he had found it under a coffee table in Windward. Murray began a long interrogation, taking Maddox from the bluff over the sea where Doris Ashley had swerved off the road, to Windward and then to police headquarters.

Maddox was followed by Yeoman's Mate First Class Milton Penn of the *Bluegill*. At the prosecution table Murray removed a cloth covering a typewriter and asked that it be entered as Exhibit H. The sailor said the typewriter was the machine he used on the submarine. With Judge Kesselring's permission, Murray typed two lines on a sheet of paper and offered it and the confession Gerald had prepared to the witness, who said both were from the same typewriter.

The day's last witness was Dr. Arthur Doty, the coroner of Honolulu County, whom Leslie McAdams questioned to establish the time of death and the cause. Murray had rehearsed McAdams during the lunch recess. "Make him give you an anatomy lecture," Murray said. "Let the jury hear the gory details. There won't be a hung jury this time. Not when we're finished."

Around five o'clock that afternoon, Maddox left the elevator on the second floor of police headquarters behind two other cops. When they stopped to enter an office, Maddox saw Walter Bergman sitting in front of his door. Bergman grinned. "Spare a few minutes, Captain?" Maddox knew he was in trouble before he reached for his keys.

Bergman rose, holding the doorjamb for leverage. "One of your boys brought me this chair," he said. "Another bonus for getting old. I don't mind saying it's a piss poor kind of reward. Hot today, wasn't it?''

Maddox unlocked the door and let Bergman precede him. "Is this official business?" Maddox asked.

"Nothing official about it," Bergman said. Maddox pulled out two chairs from the long wooden table beside the wall.

"What's on your mind?"

"You," Bergman said. "You and I," he said, and paused. "You and I and Lenore." Bergman reached for his handkerchief and wiped his face. "Still hot. I've been waiting for you to say something, Captain."

"You came to see me."

"For a fact," Bergman said. He raised his hand and spread his fingers, holding the handkerchief at one corner as though he were a magician. "It's mine," Bergman said. "It belongs to a man. I've seen one just like it in Lenore's room back at the hotel. Doesn't belong to me. You could say I was snooping and you'd be right. I *was* snooping. What would someone as ladylike, as choosy as Lenore, be doing with that handkerchief? You take it and a ridgepole and you've got yourself a tent.'' He wiped his face.

"You gave her the jade," Bergman continued. "There wasn't the slightest doubt in my mind from the minute I laid eyes on the necklace as to what they call the place of origin. The necklace cost a lot of money. I know because I did some more snooping. Lenore wouldn't spend that kind of money on herself. It's not in her nature." Bergman ran two fingers inside his shirt collar. "Would you open the windows, please, Captain? It's awful hot in here.''

Maddox rose. The drawn venetian blinds had kept the office cool all day. He raised the blinds and the windows. "How's that?''

"Helps," Bergman said. "Hasn't been this hot since I've been here. Is this unusual?" Maddox stood beside his chair.

"I'm not the weatherman. What do you want?"

"I didn't need the handkerchief or the jade to tell me there was a mess brewing," Bergman said, as though he hadn't heard Maddox. "The evidence was there almost from the day we landed. I could see the bloom in Lenore, and it didn't come from the sun. I could hear the change in her voice. I watched her answer the telephone, listened to her on the telephone. I knew when you were calling before she said, 'Captain.' I've been watching and listening to people all my life. I know when the truth departs. As a couple of schemers, you two aren't even out of kindergarten. Lenore would leave the hotel to shop and come back with berry stains on her dress.'' Bergman's voice rose. ''I'm a country boy, Captain. I know berry stains when I see them. Damned heat,'' he said, loud. ''I'm tired of these enchanted islands.''

''I said, 'What do you want?' but you do everything except answer the question,'' Maddox said. ''I'll answer the question. You want me to stay away from Lenore.''

''There's one woman and two men,'' Bergman said. ''The woman carries one man's name and it isn't yours.''

''You must've won half your cases because it was the only way anyone could shut you up,'' Maddox said.

Bergman's face reddened. ''You're an arrogant man,'' he said. ''You believe you're above the rest of us.''

''Everyone believes that,'' Maddox said. ''How else do you make it through a day?''

Bergman hit the table with his left hand. ''Stay away from Lenore!'' he said.

''Did she send you?'' Maddox asked. If she had, Maddox had lost her.

''You'll never have her!'' Bergman said. ''She's my wife!''

''She's never been your wife,'' Maddox said. ''You own her, like you own your car or your place on the lake. Maybe you got them fair and square but you *stole* Lenore.''

''Do you think a *cop* can take her away from me? A harness bull? A deke from the boondocks? A hick flatfoot?''

''You ought to quiet down,'' Maddox said. ''This building is crawling with reporters.''

''I need her!'' Bergman shouted. ''I'm not your garden variety ga-ga waiting for a wheelchair and a lap robe!'' He yawned, opening his mouth wide, as innocently as an infant.

''She ought to leave you tonight,'' Maddox said. ''You've buried her alive. You took her life away. I gave it back to her, and you sit there telling me you're going to do it again?'' Maddox was on top of Bergman.

''You're not dealing with a hooligan,'' Bergman said, and his head fell back. Maddox saw the sweat pouring off Bergman's face and forehead. The old man's head tipped forward. ''You'll never . . .'' he said, and yawned again, and his head fell back again.

His eyes were open but Maddox knew Bergman could no longer see. His left leg slid forward, the ankle twisted, and the shoe pointed inward. Bergman's head dropped to his chest. His left arm fell over the chair. Bergman's sweating, his shouting, his uncharacteristic display of combativeness, his inexplicable yawning, his onset of apathy, his increasingly stuperous movements, were all symptoms and were all classical. Bergman had been slipping steadily, dangerously, into a diabetic coma. His body was producing too much insulin, and he was in insulin shock. His blood sugar was dangerously low, and as he slouched, helpless, in the chair, his heartbeat increased at a potentially morbid rate. Without help, informed and decisive, all these symptoms, these punishing changes in his body, would soon be lethal. Bergman would stop breathing.

For almost all of his adult life, Maddox had been with dead and dying men and women ending their lives naturally or unnaturally, violently. So he knew immediately that Bergman was close to death. Maddox knew—the knowledge was like a message on a printed placard in front of him—that in a little while, if he didn't move, or sat down and stayed in the chair, and no one appeared at the door, Bergman would be dead. All that would be left of Lenore's husband, of the man who had just told Maddox he could never have her, would be this bag of bones in his office. When Maddox went to tell Lenore, he would never have to leave her again.

All this, in every detail, flashed through Maddox's mind in an instant. Then he was running, lunging into the corridor to shout, "I need help! Fast! Fast!" He saw the first of the two cops who had been with him in the elevator come out of the office ahead. "In here!" Maddox yelled, and plunged back into his office. He bent, shoving his arms under Bergman's arms, clasping his hands together and coming erect with his burden. Maddox kicked the chair and it toppled and fell to the floor. "Grab him! Grab him!" Maddox said as the two cops ran into the room.

Maddox ran ahead, pressing the elevator button. The cops came out of the office with Bergman between them. "I said fast!" Maddox shouted. "Drag him!" He heard the elevator, and waved them forward as though he were standing at a finish line. Maddox pounded on the elevator door with his fists. "Stop this goddamn thing! Stop!" The elevator door opened, and Maddox put his back against it. There was no one inside. "Get him in here! *Get him in here!*" The cops held Bergman upright against the elevator wall. Maddox pressed the floor button. "He's going in my car. Then call Mercy Hospital. Tell them I'm on the way with Walter Bergman . . . with an old man. He's got diabetes and he passed out. He was sweating . . . and yawning and passed out." When the elevator stopped and the door opened, Maddox ran ahead to the parking area.

He drove up and over the curb, stopping parallel to the building. He leaned across the seat to open the passenger door. When the cops appeared with Bergman, carrying him between them, Maddox said, "Tell the hospital to have a stretcher outside! Come on! Come on!" He flipped the siren switch before he was into the street.

Less than five minutes later, Frank Puana parked his car near the emergency room of Mercy Hospital. He was in fresh whites, blouse and trousers, buckskin shoes and socks. He had been arriving early for days, fleeing from his home. Mary Sue had become a stranger since the night he had learned that Claude Lansing had betrayed him. Their home had become a hotel, and Mary Sue acted like she was a maid who hated the guests. Every day was the same. "Here's your breakfast," she said. "Lunch is ready." They ate in silence broken only by the mindless chatter of Eric and Jonathan. When Frank began a conversation with her, Mary Sue ended it, replying in monosyllables, leaving the table to busy herself with one task or another. Frank dreaded their meals together. He dreaded facing his night off. He played with his sons until they fell asleep of exhaustion, and when he entered their bedroom, Mary Sue's back was turned and her eyes were closed. Earlier that day Eric had pulled her lip. "Smile, Mommy." She ran out of the room, weeping.

As Frank left his car, the emergency room door opened and Peter Monji pushed a wheeled stretcher into the parking area. Another orderly followed. "Just in time, Doctor," Peter said, and told him the police were bringing an elderly diabetic in coma to the hospital.

"Get me two bottles of fifty cc. one hundred percent glucose," Frank said, welcoming, gratefully, the news of the patient. "Hook one bottle up for I.V. Send out another orderly to help with the patient."

"There's only two of us tonight, Doctor," Peter said. Frank pushed him toward the hospital.

"Hurry, hurry," he said. Peter stopped at the door, and as he squatted to push a wooden wedge under it, heard the first faint sound of the siren.

Peter had one bottle of glucose hooked to the I.V. stand on the examining table, a rubber tube dangling from it, when Frank came into the emergency room and opened the drawer of an instrument case for a packet of needles. "Do you want him on the table, Doctor?"

"No time," Frank said, as Maddox and the orderly pushed the

wheeled stretcher through the doorway. "Get an arm exposed." Maddox pushed up Bergman's shirtsleeve and jacket sleeve.

"He's ready," Maddox said. "Come on, come on, come on."

"Are you giving me orders again? Move aside!" Frank said, reaching for the rubber tube. Holding the needle in his right hand, he took Bergman's wrist with his left, twisting so the arm turned and squeezing to produce a vein. When he had a vein, Frank slipped the needle into it and the glucose began, drop by drop, to enter Bergman's bloodstream and combat and reduce the abundance of insulin that was killing him.

"Now what?" Maddox asked.

"We wait," Frank said. Maddox felt the sharp ache across his shoulders. He arched his back. Lenore was alone. She would be starting to worry. She would begin to call, looking for Bergman.

"How long do we wait?" Maddox asked. "You tell me or I'll bring Lansing down here to tell me. If he's gone, whoever is in charge upstairs will tell me.

Frank looked up from the patient, facing the bully. He had nothing more to lose. "Dr. Lansing is on the third floor," Frank said, and bent to put his fingers over the patient's wrist, closing over the pulse. "Peter, give me . . ." he said, and saw the orderly extending the stethoscope. Frank dropped the instrument over his head and listened to Bergman's heart. He pushed back an eyelid to look into Bergman's eye. "He'll be all right," Frank said. "He should stay here tonight."

Maddox looked down at Bergman on the wheeled stretcher beside the examining table. Bergman was pale. He seemed fragile, seemed . . . breakable. His forearm was an old forearm. His hand was old. His shirt collar was too big. His neck was wrinkled and the skin sagged. Bergman's face was blotchy. Maddox could see long hairs everywhere that Bergman missed when he shaved. Except for his clothes, Bergman looked like any of the aged derelicts who filled the tank at police headquarters nightly. But the wasted, spent, ravaged form whose appetites had long ago been sated, whose impulses had long ago been blunted, was actively determined to keep Maddox from having the only reward he had ever sought. "I'll be back," Maddox said. He couldn't call her, couldn't let her be alone in a taxi thinking he had spared her, thinking she would learn the truth, the dread, final truth at the hospital. Maddox used the siren all the way to the Western Sky.

The door to the Bergman penthouse, to Lenore, seemed to rush up at Maddox. He had stood at hundreds of doors, watched hundreds, thousands of faces contort in dismay and anguish as he delivered the awful announcements that were a commonplace of his work. He had never been a part of it before, and although he did not hesitate, he said, aloud, "Stop stalling," and knocked.

"Walter?" Her voice was strained with hope. Lenore opened the door wide, and Maddox heard her suck in her breath.

"He's all right, Lenore. He's fine. It's the truth," Maddox said, in a rush, all this from the corridor.

"Where is he?"

"At Mercy Hospital," Maddox said. "It was the diabetes. They're keeping him overnight." She was paralyzed. "Do you want to get your purse or something?"

Lenore seemed to come awake. She stepped back so Maddox could pass, and then closed the door. "He isn't . . . ?"

"I wouldn't lie to you," Maddox said.

"I called the courthouse," Lenore said. "He had been seen leaving, seen getting into a taxi. When I opened the door, I was sure you had volunteered to bring me the news."

"It didn't happen that way," Maddox said, and now he was stalling.

"I'll be ready in a moment," Lenore said. She left him, walking to an open door. Maddox could see part of the bed, her bed. He thought of being with her, of waking while she slept, of bringing her juice and coffee and surprises on a tray. Lenore returned with a purse. "Will you wait while I call the hospital? I want to be certain everything is . . . that there's been no change." Maddox watched her at the telephone. "This is Mrs. Bergman, Mrs. Walter Bergman." He moved away as though he had been eavesdropping. When Lenore joined Maddox, she said, "They were moving him from the emergency room."

She did not speak again until they were in the car. "Is it far?"

"Only a few minutes," Maddox said, and felt her hand on his thigh. He wanted to stop the car, wanted to bring her to him, wanted to comfort her. He felt as though he had returned safely after a long and perilous journey.

"Curt?" She paused, and then said, "I want to tell you why I'm the way I am. When I saw you, when you told me Walter was ill, I felt guilty, felt as though I'd abandoned him."

Maddox said, "It's a bad night," still stalling. But he couldn't let her walk into the hospital, into Bergman's room, and hear it there. "You haven't asked me how I came into this."

"I suppose they called you," Lenore said.

"Nobody called me." He wanted to put his hand over hers. "It started in my office."

"In your . . ." she said, and stopped.

"He got sick, passed out, in my office," Maddox said. "I took him to the hospital."

"Why did he come to your office?" Lenore asked.

"You could make a pretty good guess," Maddox said, and began to tell her. He told her everything. He omitted nothing, and when he was finished, her hand was no longer on his thigh.

"He must have known from the start, from the very beginning," Lenore said.

"I wish I could help you tonight," Maddox said. "I've been trying to think of something I could do to help you."

"How can anyone help me? He is my husband," Lenore said. "I belong at his side." Maddox glanced at her. She was talking like he was a chauffeur.

"You've done nothing wrong," Maddox said.

"Oh, Curt," she said quietly, almost unintelligibly, the way he had heard so many men confess.

"I know you haven't," Maddox said. "I know about right and wrong, Lenore. I'm an expert." Maddox felt like he was drowning. There was enough room between them for a train.

Maddox parked in the driveway in front of the hospital, and Lenore was walking toward the doors before he was out of the car. Maddox caught up with her and took her hand. She did not resist. He felt like he was with someone he had handcuffed.

In the hushed, high-ceilinged lobby, she hurried ahead of him, half-running to the nurse at the desk. When Maddox reached her, she said, "He's in three-eleven," and hurried once more, to the elevators. She pressed the button and looked at Maddox. "Please try not to be angry with me."

"Couldn't be angry," Maddox said. "Couldn't ever be angry with you."

"Curt." The elevator door opened. She said his name again, and he knew she was asking him to forgive her, knew, alone already, that he had to make it easier for her.

"It's all right," Maddox said. "It's all right, Lenore." She stepped into the elevator, and pressed the floor button. They faced each other. Then the door closed and took her away.

Maddox crossed the lobby to the nurse. "Where's three-eleven?"

"Where's . . . ? On three, of course," the nurse said, and turned to enter an office.

"Wait," Maddox said. "Wait."

"Don't raise your voice to me!"

"Point at three-eleven," Maddox said. "Can you do that without a fight?"

The nurse raised her hand. "Second from the corner," she said. Maddox walked through the lobby to his car. He drove into the street and parked across from the hospital. There were lights all the way across the third floor. Around nine o'clock the rooms began to darken. The corner room on three became dark. Maddox watched all the lights go out except in 311. He looked at his watch once. It was almost midnight. When he looked again, it was three minutes after one, and the light was burning in Bergman's room. Maddox turned the key and stepped on the starter. His house lay behind him but Maddox drove straight ahead, toward the city and police headquarters and his office. He could not go home, walk into that empty house, that empty, barren, useless house with its empty bedroom and the empty bed.

Sometime before dawn, Maddox leaned forward, crossing his arms on his desk and dropping his head on his wrists. When he woke with all the lights burning in his office, he looked up at the wall clock. It was three minutes before ten. He rose and took off his jacket, dropping it on the table as he walked to the door. He went to the bathroom and washed his face. When he returned to his office, he left the door open. The room was stale. He felt gritty. He rubbed the stubble of beard on his face. He needed a bath and clean clothes. Maddox sat down behind his desk to tell the dispatcher he'd be at home. "Captain Maddox?"

A Chinese woman was in the doorway. Maddox nodded, and watched her cross the office. She was carrying a cloth bag like they all carried everywhere. She stopped at the desk, raising the bag. "This is for you, Captain Maddox." She took a package wrapped in crumpled paper and tied awkwardly from the bag.

Maddox knew the answer before he asked the question. "Where did it come from?"

"Western Sky," said the Chinese woman. She set down the package. "I work Western Sky. Work nights."

Maddox had never seen Lenore's handwriting but he knew it was she who had written, "Captain Curtis Maddox," and, "Police Headquarters," on the card tied to the package. Maddox reached into his pocket for some coins. "Missus paid me," said the Chinese woman.

"Take it," he said. "Close the door." He looked at the package. She had sent him the jade necklace. Maddox pushed it aside, like someone who has eaten his fill.

He wondered if he would live long enough to stop seeing her face in front of him, seeing her eyes, seeing her hair blowing in the wind, her dress blowing in the wind, seeing her come toward him, waving, smiling. The telephone rang.

He fell back in the chair like a boxer sinking into the canvas. The telephone rang again. Maddox leaned forward as though he were in pain. "That's what they pay you for," he said, and raised the receiver. "Maddox."

"Call Dr. Evan Magruder," said the district attorney, and the bailiff at the rear pushed open one of the doors to the courtroom. A neat, trim man in his sixties entered and walked to the gate with quick, short steps. His gray hair was cut short. He had a gray mustache and a Van Dyke beard, trimmed to form a perfect dagger. The beard made him a rarity in 1931. Philip Murray followed Dr. Magruder to the witness box, waiting while the witness was sworn in.

In the first row the princess whispered, "Who's he?"

"He's an alienist," Tom whispered.

"They all are except us," said the princess. "Who *is* he?" The judge was watching them. Tom lowered his head, remaining silent, hoping she would be quiet.

Beside the witness box Murray said, "Doctor, tell us the distinction between an alienist and a psychiatrist."

"There is none," said Magruder. "The word alienist is a synonym for psychiatrist, and vice versa." Bergman heard the witness but couldn't see him. Murray was in the way. Bergman rose, pulling his chair along the floor.

"Like to see the players in the game, Your Honor," Bergman said. He gestured to Murray, giving him permission to continue.

"You are qualified to practice psychiatry?" asked the district attorney. Bergman took the pen out of the handkerchief pocket of his jacket.

"I am a member of the United States Psychiatric Association, a regional governor, and a past president," Magruder said. "I am a member of the International Psychiatric Institute, and the current representative of the United States to its board of trustees. I have also served as chairman of the California chapter of the American Society of Alienists." He twirled the tip of his mustache. Murray moved to his right, standing beside the witness box so that both he and Magruder were facing the defendants.

"Doctor, have you examined Lieutenant Gerald Murdoch?" Murray asked.

"I have," Magruder said.

"Tell the court where and when you examined the defendant."

"I met with Lieutenant Murdoch in the home, the quarters, of

Admiral Glenn Langdon at Pearl Harbor during the past week,"
said Magruder. "There were three meetings covering a period of
seven hours."

"Doctor, are you ever asked by another physician to see one
of his patients?" Murray asked.

"Yes, I am often called in by colleagues," Magruder said.

"How long do you need to establish a diagnosis?"

"No more than an hour," Magruder said.

"Why then did you see the defendant, Lieutenant Murdoch,
three times for a total of *seven* hours?" Murray asked.

"The defendant is on trial for murder," Magruder said. "The
deliberate taking of a life is the most abominable, the most
detestable crime one person can commit against another. The
punishment fits the crime. Much is at stake and much is asked of
me in this witness box. I was determined the conclusions I
reached would be the most thorough, the most considered I could
make."

"Tell the court your diagnosis of Lieutenant Murdoch," Murray said. Bergman took an eraser from the table, studying the
witness.

Magruder twirled the tip of his mustache. "Lieutenant Murdoch
is a reasonably normal adult who seems able to live and function
in an ordered society," Magruder said. Murray left the witness
box, walking to the defense counsel table, facing Gerald at the
other end as though they were antagonists in a duel.

"Is Lieutenant Murdoch sane?" Murray asked.

"He is sane." Murray didn't move. The courtroom became
silent, and the spectators, ill at ease, began to clear their throats
and cough. Murray kept his eyes on Gerald.

"Sane," Murray said. He left the defense counsel table,
passing the court reporter in front of the bench. "Your witness."

Bergman stayed in his chair until Murray was seated. Then he
rose, advancing in his usual shambling gait. "Doctor, you told
us you examined the defendant, Lieutenant Gerald Murdoch.
Examined. How did you examine him?"

"As I testified, by meeting with the defendant on three occasions for seven hours," Magruder said.

"I was right here listening," Bergman said. "Trouble is,
you're not answering my question. My question is, 'How did
you examine him?' "

"I questioned Lieutenant Murdoch at length," Magruder said.
"I observed him during our meetings."

"After watching and questioning him, you decided he was
fine and dandy," Bergman said.

"It is my professional opinion that Lieutenant Murdoch suffers from no emotional or psychiatric malfunction, and is in full possession of his faculties," Magruder said. Bergman left the witness box, shuffling toward the jury.

"My, my," Bergman said. "You found out all that without having to take your hands out of your pockets, in a manner of speaking."

"I was using the tools of my trade," Magruder said. Bergman stopped beside the jury foreman.

"Tools of your trade," Bergman said. "Did you use a stethoscope? Did you have a blood pressure cuff with you out there at the admiral's house? Did you check Lieutenant Murdoch's eyes, ears, nose, and throat? Did you take a blood sample? Did you X-ray him?"

"You are confusing psychiatry with physical medicine."

"Suppose you straighten me out, Doctor," Bergman said.

"Physical medicine is an exact science," Magruder said. "Psychiatry is not. We do not speak in absolutes in my profession. We cannot *see* into the patient's mind."

"Well-l-l-l-l-l-l-l," said Bergman, spreading his arms wide and then folding them across his chest. "So you're *guessing* when you make a diagnosis."

"No, sir, I am emphatically *not* guessing," Magruder said. "I reach a diagnosis based on my training, my experience, and the experience and documented findings of my colleagues in every corner of this planet."

Bergman returned to the witness box. "Tell me something, Doctor. Do you classify folks as either sane or insane?"

"In the broad sense, yes," Magruder said.

"So it's either one or the other," Bergman said. "How do you decide if someone's sane?"

"By his response, responses, to discreet questioning."

"Give us an example, would you do that?" Bergman asked.

"The most basic, of course, is the ability to distinguish between good and evil," Magruder said.

"In other words, a sane person knows what's right and what's wrong," Bergman said.

"Exactly!" said Magruder.

"Naturally, a sane person wouldn't steal," Bergman said. "Agree with me, Doctor?"

Magruder twirled his mustache. "Yes, yes," he said. "Agreed."

"How about a sane person who's starving to death and steals a loaf of bread?" Bergman asked. The princess jabbed Tom in the ribs.

"He read it, too," she said, of *Les Miserables*.

In the witness box Magruder said, "Your example takes a particular human being in a particular circumstance."

Bergman's arm shot out, pointing at Gerald. "A particular human being who was in a particular circumstance is in this courtroom charged with murder, Doctor!"

"He was not starving," said Magruder. The doctor was pleased with his response.

"Got me there," said Bergman. He raised his hands to smooth his hair. "Score one for you, Doctor. Is the difference between sane and insane clear as black and white?" The witness smiled for the first time.

"Nothing on earth *except* the colors black and white are as clear as black and white," Magruder said.

"Carrying that a step further, you're saying a person isn't completely sane or completely insane."

Across the well Murray said, "Objection. Counsel is leading the witness."

"Sustained," said the judge. "The jury will ignore counsel's last statement."

"I'll try it again," Bergman said. "You told the jury psychiatry isn't an exact science." Bergman looked at the ceiling, frowning as he pretended to concentrate. " 'We do not speak in absolutes,' " Bergman said. He looked at Magruder. "Still, you keep telling the jury here someone is sane or insane, beyond argument."

"You misunderstood me," Magruder said.

"Give me another crack at it, Doctor."

"I used the word *absolute* to define our methods, not our conclusions." Bergman rubbed his face.

"In other words, you can't tell us how a psychiatrist gets where he's going, but he knows it when he arrives," Bergman said.

Spectators and newspapermen tittered until someone could not suppress his laughter. His outburst was contagious. The courtroom resounded until the judge's gavel quickly restored silence. Immediately Bergman said, "I'm back with the starving man who stole a loaf of bread, Doctor. Along those lines, can a sane man, a man who's been sane all his life, do something insane?"

"I cannot respond to that question from a psychiatric point of view," Magruder said.

"Try this," Bergman said. "Can something turn a sane person insane for a little while?"

"Are you referring to temporary insanity?" Magruder asked.

"You tell me," Bergman said. "Can someone become temporarily insane?"

"Yes, certainly."

"While he was temporarily insane, would he be able to know the difference between good and evil?" Bergman asked.

"Naturally not," Magruder said. "He is insane."

"No more questions," Bergman said. He left the witness box, and Judge Kesselring looked at the district attorney.

"Do you have any further questions, Mr. Murray?" Murray rose, remaining beside his chair.

"I do, Your Honor," Murray said, and to the witness, "Doctor, I will ask you directly. As a trained and qualified psychiatrist, do you believe the defendant, Gerald Murdoch, could become temporarily insane?"

"I do not," said Magruder. "The answer is no."

"No further questions," Murray said.

"Mr. Bergman, do you have any further questions?" the judge asked.

"Matter of fact, I do, Your Honor," Bergman said. Standing in front of his chair, he buttoned his double-breasted jacket. He looked down, his big hands fumbling. He ran his hands over his chest and belly to smooth the jacket as he went to the jury box, stopping at the far end beside Bruce Tanaka, the last juror in the first row. "Doctor, can a fellow do something without thinking?"

"I don't follow you," Magruder said.

"Can a person do something before he knows he did it?" Bergman's voice rose slightly. "Can you follow me now?" The witness looked up at the bench.

"I cannot understand the question, Your Honor," Magruder said.

"Nor can I," said Judge Kesselring. "Will counsel try and make himself clear?"

"Hope so," Bergman said, and swung at Tanaka. The Japanese fell back, jerking his head back, falling into the juror at his right as Bergman's arm whisked past him.

Spectators gasped, and the newspapermen stared across the courtroom. Some rose to see over the heads of those in front of them. Tanaka pressed himself against the juror beside him, his left arm raised to ward off another blow. *"Mister Bergman!"* The judge was standing. The old man appeared demented. *"Bailiff!"*

The bailiff lunged forward. Bergman smiled at Tanaka. "Thanks for the help," Bergman said, and walked toward the witness box, waving at the bailiff. "Slow up, son." He patted the bailiff on the back. "You didn't think I'd hit that man, did you, Your Honor? I missed him by a country mile. I wouldn't harm a hair on his head. His or anyone else's. You can't be a defense lawyer all your life and be accused of advocating violence."

"I want an explanation of your conduct," said the judge.

"Simple," Bergman said. He leaned against the witness box. "I asked the witness if a person could do something without thinking. Your Honor asked me to make myself clear. Hope I succeeded." The judge sat down and Bergman looked at the witness.

"You succeeded in disrupting this court," the judge said.

"That's about the furthest thing from my mind," Bergman said, and to the witness, "Would you say the fellow in the jury box had time to think before he ducked?"

"You're referring to a reflex action," said Magruder.

"Done without thinking, correct?" Bergman asked, and sharply, *"Correct?"*

"It's an automatic answer, response, to a stimulus."

"Now you're the one who's not being clear," Bergman said.

"A reflex is an action, *usually* an action, responding to a signal from a nerve center." Bergman leaned into the jury box.

"Listen to the question, Doctor." Bergman became a harsh schoolmaster. "Does the fellow know he's doing whatever it is he's doing?"

"A reflex is involuntary," Magruder said.

"So the fellow I swung at didn't *know* he was ducking until he was finished doing it, is that right?" Bergman asked.

"You might say that."

"*You're* supposed to say it. You're the expert," Bergman said. "Did he know he was ducking? Yes or no?"

"No!" Bergman stepped back.

"Finally made it," Bergman said. He pushed his hands into his jacket pockets and raised them, fists clenched. He shoved both arms into the witness box and spread his fingers, palms up. He held his pen in one hand, an eraser in the other.

"If I throw the pen or the eraser at you, you'll try not to get hit, and you call whatever you do a reflex, correct?"

"Yes, that is correct," Magruder said.

"Can I get a reflex out of you without *doing* anything?" Bergman asked. "Do I have to swing at you, or throw something at you to get this reflex? Does it have to be *physical*? Can I *say* something to get a reflex?"

"Can language produce a reflex response? I would say the answer is yes," Magruder said.

"How does it work?" Bergman asked.

"If we are insulted, or angered, or made happy or unhappy by something we learn, spoken or written, our bodies respond," Magruder said. "Our hearts beat faster, our gastric juices increase, our abdominal muscles contract, other muscles produce other reactions."

"Because we hear something or read something," Bergman said. "Suppose we *see* something? A picture?"

"The response would depend on the individual," Magruder said. "On his associations, his emotional involvement with the picture."

"Suppose he saw the real thing?" Bergman asked. "Not the picture, the person. Could there be a reflex?"

"It's possible," Bergman hung over the witness box.

"Could the sight of a man produce a reflex? Yes or no?"

"Yes," said Magruder.

"Yes, one man facing another man could do something before he even knew he was doing it," Bergman said. "Correct?"

"Yes, correct." Bergman raised his hands, looking at the pen and eraser as though they had appeared by magic. He dropped them into his pockets, smiling at the witness.

"Pleasure meeting you, Doctor," Bergman said, and to the judge, "I have nothing more to ask this witness, Your Honor."

A few minutes before noon the following Monday Philip Murray stood up. "Your Honor, the State rests." Judge Kesselring looked up at the clock behind him and didn't see Bergman coming out of his chair.

"We can recess now," said the judge, "and defense counsel can begin when we return."

" 'Scuse me, Your Honor," Bergman said. "Like to ask another favor of the court. I'm a long way over my quota already but I might as well be hanged for a sheep as a lamb. If the court agrees, I'd certainly appreciate a little leeway." Bergman had no intention of facing a jury with full bellies, most of whom would be fighting to stay awake. "I've been listening to the district attorney and keeping him on the straight and narrow so long I need a little time to put my case in order."

"Will counsel be ready tomorrow?" asked Judge Kesselring.

"Tomorrow will suit me fine, Your Honor."

"I'll adjourn until ten A.M.," said the judge. Bergman was at the bar in front of Hester before the judge left the bench.

"Tomorrow's an important day, Mrs. Murdoch," Bergman said. "Could be the most important day in your husband's life.

He needs you here tomorrow. So do I. No excuses, young lady." Bergman turned to Gerald. "Don't leave Pearl Harbor without your wife, Lieutenant."

Princess Luahine was still at her place on the aisle. She had seen Bergman spring from his chair, watched him come to the rail, stand over Hester, and point at her and then at Gerald as he spoke. The princess poked Tom. "I want to see Sarah. Bring her over to the hotel for lunch."

Hester had already decided to avoid lunch, avoid her mother and the admiral and the Filipinos who hovered over her at every meal with their silent pleas that she clean her plate, as though they would be punished unless she gorged herself. Suddenly, there in the courtroom, Hester wanted to see Bryce. She could not help herself. She had not seen Bryce since Ginny's terrible surprise at the Officers' Club. Her shame was limitless. Her periodic, unannounced longing for him made her despise herself. Hester was determined to resist, and she had devised a means of combating her compulsion. First, she had to be alone, and then she remained in one place, reliving her lies and deceit, her treachery, the torture she had inflicted on the four innocent young men, the death for which she was responsible. She accepted the punishment, she welcomed it, and not until her desire for Bryce ended would her punishment end.

In the admiral's quarters Hester said, "I'm not hungry." Doris Ashley followed Hester upstairs, saying she wanted to freshen up. Doris locked the bathroom door and her bedroom to keep Hester away from the telephone.

"I wish you'd eat something, baby," Doris Ashley said. When Hester didn't answer, she left to join the admiral.

Hester stood at the windows remembering the pictures of the three boys on their bellies in the hospital. She could see their lacerated backs. She could imagine their cries for mercy as they were whipped, as their flesh was torn. She could hear their cries, and she could hear the gunshot as Gerald pulled the trigger ending Joseph Liliuohe's life. Hester wanted to scream, to beg for mercy, but she was silent. She knew she deserved to be tormented, and she stood without moving, allowing the endless procession of memories to pass before her.

At eight o'clock the next morning, Tuesday, Lenore came out of her bedroom in the penthouse of the Western Sky. She was dressed for the courtroom, since she intended to be with Bergman when he began his defense. She was in blue, with white shoes, and she carried a blue kerchief for her hair. She stopped when she saw Bergman on the sofa. "You shouldn't have waited, Walter," Lenore said. "You should have gone down to breakfast."

"No rush," Bergman said. "Fact of the matter, I'd like to eat right here today if it's all the same to you. Might have caught a little chill last night," Bergman said, lying.

"Why didn't you wake me? You should have wakened me."

"Think I'll save that for an emergency," Bergman said. "For the day I'll really need your help." He gave her a chance to digest this warning before managing a game smile.

"I'll call the house doctor," Lenore said.

"No, no, Lenore," Bergman said. "No doctors today. I'm going to court today of *all* days. I just don't feel like bucking the traffic in the restaurant. Better safe than sorry. Will you handle room service? Coffee and toast for me, thanks." Lenore went to the telephone and saw, for the first time since leaving the ship, Bergman's briefcase, which lay beside the instrument. When she left the telephone, Bergman said, "We're coming to an end over there." She turned sharply, as though a gate had clanged shut, barring her.

"You're only beginning," she said, discarding her mask, forgetting to hide.

"I might have a surprise or two," Bergman said. "Should come as a relief for them after listening to that young windbag," he said of Philip Murray, who was forty-three years old. He watched Lenore trying to recover. She moved aimlessly, finally stopping beside the glass terrace doors Bergman had closed much earlier to endorse his false claim of illness. "Can't see any reason for you to waste your time over there, Lenore." He did not intend to have the jury looking at his young wife today.

"I want to come," she said. The hours alone, the memories she could neither avoid nor erase, were torture. Lenore had suggested accompanying Bergman because she needed a refuge, a haven. The people, the voices, the panoply of the courtroom would be easier than the eternity through which she passed her days and nights.

"I'll take the thought for the deed," Bergman said. "Matter of fact you could do me a favor, do us both a favor. I've had my fill of palm trees and you probably have, too. I read where this ship, the S.S. *Lotus*, pride of the Pacific or something, is sailing a week from Saturday. Suppose I drop you off on the way to court and you can book us onto her."

Lenore felt as though her legs would give way. She put her hand against the glass doors and looked out to the flat and empty sea that seemed to beckon. "Walter, I need to talk to you."

Bergman had been waiting for days. He was ready for her. "You want to break your promise."

"*Promise?*" She came toward him. "I didn't *make* any promises."

"In the hospital you said you were coming home with me. If it isn't a promise, it's a commitment, a bargain," Bergman said. "You've never gone back on a bargain, Lenore." She stopped near the sofa. Bergman sat with his feet and knees together, his hands in his lap. Lenore thought of the aged men and women she had seen in Chicago parks waiting patiently for expected assistance, a child or grandchild.

"I said I wanted to talk to you. *Talk*, Walter. Am I violating a moral code by talking?" She was filled with guilt, and she was angry as well. He was wounded, and she hadn't even *begun*.

"This isn't the right time for it," Bergman said. "My clients need the best I've got this morning."

"I didn't choose today," Lenore said. "You forced it on me, Walter. You're sending me to the steamship office. You're setting a date. We're leaving. If we don't talk now, when will we talk? *When?*"

"We could spare ourselves the trouble," Bergman said. "We'll have enough to carry back with us and I'm not referring to the luggage." Bergman rose and went to the table. "The only reason I said yes to this case was to please you, to show you a different part of the world. I can't think of a worse mistake in my entire life." Lenore crossed the room, facing him.

"Why won't you *listen?*" she pleaded.

"I'll make the arrangements for the ship," Bergman said. He reached for the briefcase but Lenore put her hands on it.

"You're so unfair!" she said, despising herself for succumbing to her guilt and his authority.

"Unfair," Bergman said. "Beats me how you picked that particular word. You're talking to your husband. I'm talking to my wife. Up at the lake the day we were married, you promised to love, honor, and obey. We both knew the word *love* didn't include us, not the love they sing songs about. I never expected, didn't ask for the honor. When it comes to obey, I would no more give you an order to obey than walk into this ocean with weights on my legs. I didn't, don't, and never will expect anything the minister said, Lenore. All I asked the night you came to the hospital, the night Captain Maddox brought you to the hospital, is for you to remember I'm all alone." Bergman picked up his briefcase. "I remember when you were all alone, Lenore."

"You haven't had any breakfast," Lenore said. "Why must you rush away? Why must you *saturate* me with guilt?"

"Seems to me I ought to make tracks," Bergman said. "Best way to close the discussion, for both our sakes." He tapped the briefcase with his forefinger. "Remembered my chocolate, Lenore. I'll find a coffee shop somewhere around the steamship office."

She was beaten. Lenore wanted to cry out for mercy, to admit her defeat. If only he would be silent, would not parade his infirmities, would never again make her endure his endless and irrefutable lectures. She released his briefcase. "S.S. *Lotus*," she said. "You can drop me on the way to the courthouse."

When Lenore left the taxi, Bergman said, "Take me to a haberdasher," and as the driver looked back, puzzled, "A men's store."

Twelve blocks away, in Judge Geoffrey Kesselring's court, a bailiff closing the doors at the rear said, "Sorry, no more. Sorry."

Behind him, in the aisle between the first row of benches, the princess tapped the admiral on the shoulder. " 'Scuse me, Admiral." Neither had ever before spoken to the other. Beside the princess he saw the tall native woman, her face more gray then brown. The admiral thought the princess was apologizing for bumping into him, and he nodded to end the encounter, shifting in the bench. The princess tapped him again, and the admiral looked up at the huge woman with her waxen companion who seemed to cling to the princess like a patient, a madwoman, from a locked hospital, released for a few hours under guard. The admiral realized that the princess was not going away, was not taking her seat across the aisle. He was in the company of the female sex and he rose automatically, responding to more than forty years of training and discipline that had begun in his first week at the Academy. He moved back and to one side, giving Hester an unobstructed view of the princess and the other woman.

"Hate to bother you, Admiral," said Princess Luahine. "We're squeezed tighter than sardines on our side. Couldn't slip a bookmark in between us. Could you make some room over here? This lady needs a place. Half a place is more like it. She's nothing but skin and bones now. Can't get the poor soul to eat. Everybody's tried but ever since her boy was killed—" The princess stopped, slapping her temple with the heel of her hand. She watched Hester staring at her. Hester's lips parted, her eyes opened wide, and in the momentary silence she seemed to be screaming.

"Where's my head at? I didn't even introduce you," the princess said. "This here's Mrs. Liliuohe, Joe Liliuohe's mother." Hester's hands were flat on the bench, the knuckles white. "Now I forgot *her* name, her first name. Elizabeth! It's Elizabeth Liliuohe, Joe Liliuohe's mother." The princess hugged the stick of a woman, holding her close. "This here's Admiral Glenn Langdon, honey. He'll help you, won't you, Admiral?" The princess didn't wait for an answer. She moved Elizabeth Liliuohe into the first row, into the admiral who had to arch his back and push against the rail, unable to reply, to comment, to resist the tidal wave of a woman who was engulfing him. "You can sit," said the princess to Elizabeth Liliuohe, pushing her down onto the bench beside Hester. "Don't be afraid." The princess pointed. "I'll be right here across the aisle. Sarah's here." To the Admiral, Princess Luahine explained, "Sarah is Joe's sister, the dead man's sister." The princess heaved herself erect. She stood for a little while, waiting for her breath to come normally. To the admiral's left, at the defense counsel table, the princess faced Doris Ashley, who was watching her, watching Hester beside Elizabeth Liliuohe. "Much obliged, Admiral," said the princess. She was finished.

She had begun the day before, during lunch at the outdoor restaurant facing the sea beyond the lobby of the Western Sky. The princess sat between Tom and Sarah, whom he had brought from the drugstore after Judge Kesselring adjourned. "I'm only allowed forty-five minutes," Sarah said.

"I only need one," said the princess. "I want your mother in court tomorrow."

"In *court?*" Sarah looked at Tom as though they were conspirators, sharing a secret she was being forced to divulge. Then Sarah turned to the princess. "My mother hasn't been out of the house since Joe . . . since he was killed."

"Tomorrow is the day," said the princess. Sarah leaned forward, her elbows on the table, her fingertips touching.

"She didn't come to Joe's *funeral*," Sarah said. "She wouldn't leave the house for her own son's *funeral*."

"Anyway," said the princess, and pointed at Sarah as the waiter appeared. "She gets the club sandwich. Serve her first; she's only got so much time," and to Sarah, "You bring her to the courthouse, you and Tom."

"*Bring* her?" Sarah didn't see the waiter or the club sandwich. She stared at the princess whose breasts rose and fell as she tried, and failed, to subdue herself. The princess's arm rose, big as a ham, and she hit the table with her fist.

"Stop playing echo!" the princess said. She saw Tom wince and look in both directions at the other diners. "If the climate doesn't agree with you, leave, mister!"

Tom put his hands on his thighs, squeezing. He told himself what the princess had done, starting with the bail bond money. "Sarah hasn't said anything to make you mad at her."

The princess said, quietly, "Ah-h-h-h-h-h-h," in an extended, mournful sigh of self-pity. She needed Jack Manakula. She could yell until she was hoarse at Jack. The princess put her hand over Sarah's. "Eat your lunch, sweetheart."

Sarah raised a triangle of sandwich from her plate, then set it down. "My mother won't even come outside to hang the wash," Sarah said. "If I'm not home, my father hangs the wash." The princess shook her head sympathetically. She couldn't wait for the girl to vamoose.

When Sarah finally said, "I really have to go or I'll be late," and reached for her purse on the empty chair, Tom rose. "I'm sorry," Sarah said. "I wish I could have helped, but nothing can make her leave the house."

"Don't worry your pretty head," said the princess. She pointed her fork at Tom. "Come back and keep me company while I finish this whale," she said. As Tom followed Sarah, the princess waved the fork at the waiter. She had eaten too much anyway. "Check."

Tom walked to Sarah's convertible with her. He returned to the Western Sky, coming around the rim of the driveway, and as he reached the steps leading to the hotel he saw the princess emerge from the lobby. "I wasn't very hungry," she said, crooking her finger at the doorman. "Taxi."

"I may as well go to my office," Tom said. Sometimes he really had to control himself when he was with her. He could have ridden back with Sarah and walked from the drugstore. The princess tugged at his coat sleeve.

"You better keep me company," she said, holding him as she came down the steps. To the left the doorman was on the running board of a taxi approaching the hotel entrance. "I need a guide," the princess said. "This town has changed so much I might as well be on the moon." The taxi stopped and the doorman stepped off the running board and opened the rear door. The princess reached for the taxi with both hands. "Slip him two bits, Tom," she said.

Tom handed the doorman a quarter and walked around the rear of the cab to enter from the other side. "Punchbowl," the princess told the driver, and to Tom, "I suppose you know where we're going."

"Mrs. Liliuohe," Tom said. "Sarah told you—"

"Yeah," interrupted the princess. "Give the driver the address." She twisted from side to side on the seat, trying to make herself comfortable. Then she leaned forward to roll down the window. "Look at them, Tommy." She gesturing at the women behind the small flower stands who were braiding orchids into necklaces. "Orchids and mops," she said. "That's our legacy from the white man's ships. Do you blame me for hauling my butt out of this town?"

Tom did not reply. He had become familiar with her moods. He knew when she wanted a dialogue and when she wanted silence. For a long time the princess, too, was silent. Suddenly she began to hit the door with her open hand, slowly, rhythmically. Looking straight ahead, she said, "Doris Ashley came into court with the United States Navy on her side. She's got Harvey Koster on her side. I happen to know who paid for Walter Bergman to hightail it halfway around the world. And ever since the first day of this trial, that little bitch has been sitting up front on display for the gentlemen of the jury. They might have been listening to Phil Murray but they were *seeing* Hester Anne Ashley Murdoch. Well, it's time *we* played a card. Walter Bergman comes to bat tomorrow and we ought to have a little something working for our side. How much farther?"

"We'll be there soon," Tom said.

"Thanks for nothing." The driver reached the Punchbowl and the princess looked from side to side as they left the city's commercial area and rode through the streets where the Hawaiians were clustered. "At least they're not cooking outside anymore," the princess said.

"Yes, they are," Tom said, and pointed.

"Where in the godforsaken hell do these Liliuohe people live?" asked the princess, yelling, raging at the poverty around her.

"Two more blocks," Tom said. When the taxi stopped, the princess looked at the darkened house with the drawn shades. It appeared deserted, abandoned.

"Looks like a tomb at that," the princess said. Then she said, "Everybody in town thinks I'm the second coming of Christ so I might as well admit it. Tom, go in and tell her the Princess Luahine is out here. You tell her the Princess Luahine came all the way up here to see her."

Tom said, "She won't . . ." and stopped because the princess wouldn't listen. He left the cab and walked around it, stopping beside the princess's door. He said, "She's as dead as Joe."

" 'Bye," said the Princess. Tom turned away from the taxi and walked toward the lifeless house. The princess watched his dragging foot raising dust. She wondered if some doctor somewhere in the States could do something. Then, remembering that the boy had been in the States for three years, in law school in California, she realized he must have asked one hundred doctors. The princess sniffed and wrinkled her nose. He was a good boy. They needed him in the Territory. They needed one thousand like him. She cupped her mouth with her hand. "Get the lead out!" yelled Princess Luahine.

Tom walked to the side of the house and up the path where Sarah parked her convertible. He reached the empty and parallel clothesline and walked between it and the path until he disappeared.

The princess was hunched forward, her head on a line with the open taxi window, staring at the house into which, somewhere at the rear, Tom had vanished. She heard nothing, saw nothing. She felt as though days had passed. "Excuse me, ma'am . . . I mean, Princess," said the driver. "Okay if I smoke?"

She watched the house. "Sure, sure," the princess said, thinking of Jack rolling his cigarettes, sitting beside her with the smoke curling around them. "Light up," she said, welcoming the smoke. Where was *Tom?* "He's been gone an awful long time, hasn't he?"

"Guess I wasn't keeping track," said the driver, who was in no rush with the meter ticking beside him. "Want me to . . . ?"

"No!" said the princess, watching the house, rubbing one hand in the other, beginning to perspire in the close confines of the taxi. What was he *doing* in there? She moved back, and as she fell against the seat, she saw the front door of the house open and saw Tom.

"Ma'am . . . *Princess*," said the driver.

She said, "Yeah," low, as though she might be heard. Tom was in the doorway. The princess wriggled forward on the seat and saw him come out of the house. She saw him turn, and was convinced he was turning to close the door, was convinced he had failed, *she* had failed. She said, "Boob," meaning herself, and saw the shadow, the wraith, appear from the house. The woman was tall, extraordinarily tall for a Hawaiian woman, and when she stopped, bewildered, on the threshold, lost even here, in her own home, the princess wanted to help. She reached for the door handle but dropped her hand. "Ruin everything," she said to herself.

Standing in the doorway of her home, Elizabeth Liliuohe said, "You told me the Princess Luahine is here."

"She *is* here," Tom said. "In the taxi." He wanted to yell at the princess. Why didn't she come out?

Elizabeth Liliuohe shrank back. "You and Sarah are playing tricks," she said. Tom took her arm, holding on to her.

"We wouldn't do that, Mrs. Liliuohe," Tom said. "It's the princess." He moved her over the threshold. "I wouldn't lie to you." He was moving her, slowly, slowly, hesitating between steps to keep her from bolting, to keep her with him.

In the taxi the driver shoved his cigarette into the ashtray, snuffed it out, and reached behind him to open the door. "Stay put!" said the princess.

"I thought I'd help—"

"You're helping," the princess said, watching Tom with the poor, sad beanpole. "Come on, lady," said the princess. She was coming. "Don't stop now," the princess said. She was on the way for sure now. Tom had her and they were on the way. The princess could see Elizabeth Liliuohe's face now. The woman was starving. She was skin and bones. The princess wanted to hug the poor woman, but she had to wait, she had to wait. Not until Tom had brought Elizabeth Liliuohe to the taxi did the princess open the rear door and hoist herself out of the backseat. "Hello, honey," she said, spreading her arms wide. Since Joe Liliuohe's mother had come out of her house once, the princess was confident she would come out twice. "I need a big favor," said the princess. "Tomorrow."

The next morning, in the Western Sky, the princess was awake in her penthouse before Lenore or Walter Bergman were awake in theirs. Her mind was busy instantly, and though she had hours to squander, she called for coffee and left the bed. She could never lie quietly when something needed doing, however far ahead. She opened the penthouse door and left it open so the room service waiter wouldn't disturb her.

She was in the lobby by eight o'clock, in a chair with the *Outpost-Dispatch*, looking at a three-column picture of Bergman on the front page. MURDER DEFENSE BEGINS read the banner below the nameplate. The princess folded the newspaper and dropped it into the wastebasket beside her. "Baloney," she said, grunting as she came out of the chair.

The princess was waiting in front of the hotel when the convertible turned into the driveway. She started for the car and was squinting in its path when she saw that three figures were in it. Sarah was driving and when the car stopped, Tom came out of the convertible. "I'll hop in the rumble seat," he said. The princess smiled at Elizabeth Liliuohe, sitting beside Sarah.

"You look real nice," the princess said. "Just pray I make it up there with you. Climbing into this buggy is like getting on a Ferris wheel." She put one hand on Tom's shoulder for leverage, grabbing the convertible with the other, and stepped up on the running board. As she dropped down beside Elizabeth Liliuohe, the princess smiled at the bewildered creature. "Now I know where Sarah gets her looks." She had only one way to gentle anything that might spook, and she talked all the way to the courthouse. She didn't know they were in front of the building until Sarah said, "Tommy will take you home, Ma. I'll see you after work." Tom opened the door beside the princess.

"Whoa . . ." said the princess, putting her hand over Sarah's hand on the gearshift. "You're coming with us."

"I can't." Sarah shook her head.

"I told you—" Tom said.

"Butt out!" said the princess, and to Sarah, "We need you in there today."

"I can't look at them," Sarah said.

"I'm tired of 'can't,' " the princess said. "Forget that word. I'm not asking you to throw yourself in front of a train. All you do is sit on a bench in a room. If I can and your mother can, so can you. Tell your boss, whozis, to dock you a day's wages. You're working for me today." The princess reached for Tom. "Here's how we'll do it."

So the princess and Elizabeth Liliuohe left the convertible while Sarah and Tom drove off to park it. All four entered the courthouse together but the princess and Elizabeth remained on the balcony above the lobby as Sarah and Tom and the public quickly began to fill the courtroom. The princess held onto Elizabeth Liliuohe, talking constantly, gently, softly, watching the doors and vowing to kick Tom's behind up to his shoulders until he showed up at last. He said, "Hurry," and the princess was right behind him, her arm around Elizabeth Liliuohe as if she were carrying a mannequin. As they entered the courtroom and passed the bailiff, he spread his arms to close the doors.

Now, while Bergman was being driven to a men's store on King Street, the princess took her place beside Sarah and Tom, across the aisle from the admiral and Elizabeth. The princess leaned forward to smile across the aisle, wriggling her fingers at Elizabeth Liliuohe. "Looks like a cardboard cutout," the princess said to herself. She tried to make herself comfortable. Her strategem was complete.

The admiral sat in the bench like a plebe at the mess table, elbows tucked in and hands between his legs. He looked at the woman beside him. "Do you have enough room?" She didn't turn. She didn't answer. Her eyes were open but the admiral felt as though she didn't see anything.

Elizabeth Liliuohe was far away and all by herself, remembering Joe's appetite. He could eat for two, for three. She always cooked extra for Joe. She always sat at the table with Joe when he ate. She liked to watch Joe eat. He always said she was the best cook. She couldn't cook anymore. Joe was dead. She couldn't go into the kitchen. She couldn't sit down at the table if Joe wasn't coming.

Hester could feel Joseph Liliuohe's mother squeezed against her, against her knee and thigh and hip and arm, like manacles, like rails impaling her. Joseph Liliuohe's mother was so thin Hester could feel her bones. Hester tried to push herself clear of Joseph Liliuohe's mother but there was no room. Joseph's mother had come to remind Hester *he* was a skeleton, a skeleton at the bottom of the ocean, in a casket instead of the convertible filled with young men who had helped her. Joseph Liliuohe had helped her first. He had carried her into the convertible, and for his charity, for the mercy he had shown her, Hester had killed him. She had sent Joseph Liliuohe on the road to his death.

Doris Ashley saw Hester raise her purse until it covered her face. She could not see Hester biting her lip behind the purse, digging deep to hurt herself, to bleed, to pay for having killed Joseph Liliuohe.

Doris Ashley had heard the princess identify the woman beside Hester. Doris Ashley rose and, from the other side of the defense counsel table, Gerald watched her walking to the bar. He saw the admiral rising. Doris came close so no one could hear. "Please take Hester back to Pearl," Doris Ashley whispered.

"*Impossible!*" said the admiral, trying to whisper. "You heard Bergman yesterday. He personally ordered Hester to be here today."

"The man's *mother* is next to her," said Doris Ashley, whispering. "His *mother!* Hester is frail. She's weak. Her system can't stand up under such shocks. Her nervous system. Please take her away, Glenn."

"Bergman is starting his case today," said the admiral. "He's fighting for your life, for your lives. His orders are for Hester to be present."

"Lower your voice," said Doris Ashley. "They can hear us. For the love of God, do what I ask!" she said, as the door beside the bench opened and Judge Kesselring entered his courtroom.

"All rise," said the bailiff near the bench. The admiral patted Doris Ashley's shoulder.

"Stop worrying about Hester," said the admiral.

Eleven minutes later Bergman arrived at the courthouse wearing the raincoat he had just bought, buttoned to his neck. He carried the umbrella he had bought, and in his other hand, his briefcase.

Inside the courtroom Judge Kesselring looked at the clock on the wall behind him. "Mr. Wadsworth, are you prepared to open for the defense?" Coleman Wadsworth rose.

"I am not, Your Honor," Wadsworth said. "When court adjourned yesterday, Mr. Bergman specifically mentioned his opening statement here this morning." The judge looked out at the courtroom. It was jammed. He had allowed the public to stand at the rear and they were lined up from wall to wall. The low babble of voices, the audible whispering, the constant movement as men and women shifted in their places, made it impossible to hear the knock on the door.

The judge said, "In that case I'll recess . . ." and broke off as the bailiff opened the rear doors to the courtroom and Bergman entered. "Awfully sorry, Your Honor."

As he came down the aisle, Bergman stopped and coughed, lowering his head. "Had a bad night," Bergman said. He reached the gate. "Must've picked up a cold. I thought of calling in sick, but didn't want to hold up the proceedings, Your Honor." Bergman shifted the umbrella from one hand to the other so he could open the gate, moving sideways like he was squeezing through a turnstile. Coleman Wadsworth left his chair.

"Let me help you," Wadsworth said, extending his hands, but Bergman turned slightly and coughed once more, bending under the strain until the spasm passed. He cleared his throat.

"Worst part of it's over," he said, moving around Wadsworth. Bergman did not want any interference with his arrival, nor did he intend to share it with anyone. He stopped beside the empty chair in front of Gerald and set the briefcase and umbrella on the defense counsel table. Bergman pulled himself out of the raincoat as though it were a rope.

"Be with you in a minute, Your Honor," Bergman said. He dropped the raincoat on the table and opened his briefcase. He took out a yellow legal pad, holding it close to his eyes, studying the blank page. Satisfied, he dropped the pad into the briefcase and moved his chair, standing behind it. He was on schedule. Bergman had concentrated so completely on his appearance in the courtroom that he had seen no one as he came through the doors except Judge Kesselring and Coleman Wadsworth. He was ready.

"Your Honor, back when the district attorney finished his opening statement, I asked the court for a favor," Bergman began. "I said I'd like to postpone mine and Your Honor was nice enough to grant me my wish. In a way, I'd still like to postpone it," Bergman said, and raised his voice to speak above the reaction of the courtroom. "Combine might be a better word," Bergman said. "You might say I'm combining my opening statement with my closing argument." This time Bergman did not ask the court's indulgence.

He paused, giving his audience time to subside. While it is the prosecution, the State, that begins a criminal action in court, as does the plaintiff in a civil suit, the defense leads the final arguments, the summations.

"Is counsel saying he will not call any witnesses?" asked the judge. No defendant can be forced to testify against himself and Bergman had never considered putting any of his clients into the witness box. Exposing them to the district attorney's cross-examination would be crucial, perhaps fatal.

"Seems to me the State has called enough for both of us, Your Honor," Bergman said, holding on to the chair, his shoulders bent, head lowered as though he were weighed down by his responsibilities, as though he did not hear the laughter he had provoked.

Bergman did not see Hester trying to free herself, trying to get away from Joseph Liliuohe's mother, to move her body clear of Elizabeth Liliuohe's body. Doris Ashley saw her, watching Hester from the defense counsel table as she twisted and turned, pushing, *pushing*, into the man on her right. Hester could not escape the skeleton thrust against her, jabbing her, digging into her. Hester could feel the woman's bones piercing her flesh. She could not endure it. Hester looked at the woman who stared ahead, like someone blind, like someone dead. "Please excuse me. I have to leave."

In the laughter Bergman provoked, Elizabeth Liliuohe didn't hear her. "I have to leave," Hester said, louder. Doris Ashley saw the admiral lean forward and turn to face Hester.

"You were told to be in court today," the admiral said.

"I can't stay," Hester said. Doris Ashley tried to hear and could not.

"You're staying," the admiral said. "This is the most important day of your husband's life. You're staying where you are."

The judge's gavel silenced the courtroom. "Will you proceed, Mr. Bergman?"

"Yes, sir." Bergman left his chair and walked the few feet to the jury box. "Gentlemen, every trial is a mystery because nobody knows how it will end. I've spent most of my life in a courtroom and I've never once since the day I first faced a jury had the first clue to what the verdict would be. Can't work any other way. You twelve men sitting here are the reason we've got a criminal justice system that guarantees everyone a fair trial. For almost all of you, it's the first time you've been asked to decide whether someone is guilty of murder.

"Our law says a person accused of a crime must be tried before a jury of his peers," Bergman said. "That's you, all twelve of you. I've been watching you men since this trial began. You're the defendants' peers, no question about it. There's not a murderer in the jury box, and there isn't a murderer in this courtroom, either."

Bergman turned, leaving the jury as if he were in pain, and made his way to the witness box. He stopped in front of it and put his elbow on the rail. "I know I'm right," Bergman said. "I'm going to prove it, gentlemen, prove . . ." he said, and stopped as he saw Hester and the woman beside Hester. Bergman's elbow slipped off the witness box rail. Who was the woman with a face like a death mask between Hester and the admiral? ". . . to prove there isn't a murderer in this courtroom," Bergman said.

"Few minutes back I said I wasn't calling any witnesses," Bergman continued, watching Hester and the woman, who seemed lost, like some aged incompetent robbed of her mind by the ravages of senility. "I said the State had called enough for both of us. People laughed at that but they were wrong," Bergman said. "It wasn't funny. The district attorney was only trying to do his job. He showed you the gun that shot Joseph Liliuohe. He showed you the bullet from the gun. He showed you the towels that covered the dead man."

Hester began to shiver. She could feel every word Bergman uttered as though they were arrows. At the witness box Bergman said, "He had an expert tell you whose fingerprints were on the gun. He even brought a picture of Joseph Liliuohe into this courtroom. The only thing the district attorney didn't do, because he couldn't do it, is bring a killer into this courtroom." Bergman spread his arms wide and then clapped his hands with each word as he said, "There . . . is . . . no . . . killer . . . in . . . this . . . courtroom."

Bergman dropped his arms, reaching behind him to hold the rail of the witness box. "Seems to me everything in this case sort of depends on what you gentlemen decide about one defendant, Gerald Murdoch." Bergman had known Gerald was the key to the fate of his three clients from his first day in Honolulu, from his first meeting with them in the admiral's quarters. "In a way I'm going to introduce him to you," Bergman announced.

He left the witness box, returning to the defense counsel table. "Hope you'll bear with me while I refresh my memory, Your Honor," Bergman said. "Used to be able to keep things like this in my head." He opened the briefcase, bent over to remove the legal pad, and looked across the table at Coleman Wadsworth. "Who's sitting with Hester Murdoch?"

Wadsworth glanced over his shoulder, and Doris Ashley said, "It is Joseph Liliuohe's mother."

Bergman said, "*Mother-r-r-r-r-r?*" as though he were dying. "Who—?"

"The princess," interrupted Doris, answering him. Bergman came erect holding the yellow legal pad. He saw the princess in the aisle in the first row, looking straight at him. Bergman had depended on Hester. He had planned to deliver most of his argument to Hester, standing at the bar facing her, drawing the jury's attention to the tragic young woman, but the princess had outfoxed him. She had made Hester a liability. Bergman studied the empty page until he knew how he would proceed. When he dropped the legal pad into the briefcase, and lowered the lid, Bergman moved to his left, to Gerald's side, making a wall between Hester and the jury, hiding her and the woman beside her.

"I'd say Gerald Murdoch, Lieutenant Gerald Murdoch, United States Navy, is just about the cream of the crop," Bergman said. "Here's a young fellow without a spot on his name. To start with, there's his life's work. He's been doing it, too, wherever his country sends him, and his record there doesn't have a spot on it, either. That says something to me. It says Lieutenant Gerald Murdoch is a man who does his job, obeys orders, gets along with people, accepts them and is accepted by them. He's well liked. None of this makes him a saint but on the other hand he's a long way from being the town clown, as we used to say back home." Bergman put his arm across Gerald's shoulders.

"If anyone a few months back had asked Gerald Murdoch if he liked Hawaii, I suppose the Lieutenant would have said he was the luckiest man in the world," Bergman continued. "It was right here in Honolulu that he met a young, innocent, radiant young woman. They fell in love and were married. They were supposed to live happily ever after. Gerald Murdoch certainly expected to live happily ever after. He had a brand-new wife. He was stationed out here in Hawaii where the sun is always shining and the wind is always soft. I suppose, young people being what they are, these two were thinking of starting a family."

Hunched forward, digging her fingernails into her purse, feeling Joseph Liliuohe's mother digging into her, unable to escape, Hester said, to herself, "Please stop," over and over and over. She begged Bergman, she pleaded with him, she wanted to crawl on her knees, entreating him to be silent, but she was trapped, she was imprisoned, unable to raise her hands and close her ears to Bergman's lies.

"Starting a family," Bergman repeated. "Turns out someone threw a monkey wrench into those plans. Fact is that the only time in her life Gerald Murdoch's wife was pregnant she couldn't be sure whom the father might have been. Fact is that one day Gerald Murdoch was sitting on top of the world, and the next day he was looking through the gates of hell from the inside. Now there's no denying an awful lot of people suffer through an act of God. Well, I can tell you gentlemen of the jury it wasn't an act of God that dropped Gerald Murdoch down into the deep black hole of misery. It was an act of the devil. It was the devil's work," Bergman said, just as Hester screamed.

"No-o-o-o-o-o-o!" Hester screamed, standing at the bar, her hat sliding down across her shoulders, dropping into Elizabeth Liliuohe's knees and, unnoticed, falling to the floor. "No-o-o-o-o-o!" Hester screamed, shaking her head, twisting from side to side, side to side, harder, harder, faster, faster, like a child reaching the peak of a tantrum.

"*No!*" she screamed, her head jerking convulsively as she tried to rid herself of the lies inside, the picture of Joseph Liliuohe in his coffin beneath the ocean. "They didn't do it!" Hester cried. "They didn't do it! They're innocent!"

Doris Ashley was out of her chair lunging toward Hester, but Bergman was ahead of her. Gerald was out of his chair behind Bergman, and the admiral was on his feet, trying to get past Elizabeth Liliuohe to reach Hester. "They're innocent!"

Everyone was standing except Elizabeth Liliuohe, everyone was talking. Judge Kesselring was standing and pounding his gavel. Both bailiffs, front and back, were heading for Hester. Those men and women who had been standing at the rear were coming down the aisle, and far to the right, newspapermen were climbing on their chairs so they could see. "They're innocent!"

Bergman forgot his assumed frailty and infirmities. He reached Hester first and threw his arms around her like a tackler, yelling, "Of course they're innocent!" Smothering her he yelled, "Of course they're innocent!" He knew everything, and he pressed Hester against him, hurting her as her legs slammed into the rail while he shoved her face into his chest to silence her. Doris Ashley pulled at Bergman.

"Give her to me!" Doris Ashley demanded. "Give her to me!"

She was shouting and the judge was shouting from the bench. "Order!" He pounded the gavel. "Bailiff! *Bailiffs!*" He pounded the gavel. "Get help! Order!"

Holding onto Hester, Bergman spoke directly into Doris Ashley's ear. "Muffle her!" he said. "Can you do it? Shove a handkerchief down her throat, or your fist, or your arm, but *shut . . . her . . . up!*"

The admiral was there then, in front of Elizabeth Liliuohe. "Help me, Glenn!" said Doris Ashley. "Help us!"

The bailiffs were there then, one in the first row behind the admiral, the other with Bergman, who kept Hester quiet. The bailiffs were giving orders, unnoticed and ignored. Gerald was there, beside Bergman, who thrust Hester into Doris Ashley and stepped straight back, hitting the bailiff and lurching past him, swinging around, his jacket swirling like a muleta as he headed for the bench. "Recess!" Bergman shouted, to drown out Hester. "Recess, Your Honor! Will you call a recess, Your Honor?"

The admiral had Hester. Doris Ashley had her. Both held on to Hester, moving her past Elizabeth Liliuohe, toward the aisle, toward the princess, who was standing in the aisle, watching the procession as though she were supervising the branding at a roundup on the big island.

Doris Ashley was holding Hester's head down. Mrs. Ashley's fingers were spread across Hester's face, over her mouth.

"This court is in recess for fifteen minutes!" said Judge Kesselring, and louder, "Bailiff, clear the aisle!" and, louder, "Clear the aisle!"

Bergman was at the gate, opening it and waiting, watching Hester between the admiral and Doris Ashley. "Make it snappy, Admiral," Bergman said. They had to get the girl out before she broke free and started expanding her confession. Bergman stayed beside Doris Ashley, staying close. "Keep her quiet, madame. You must keep her quiet."

Watching the procession crossing the well, watching Gerald join them and then go ahead to open the door beside the jury box, the princess said, to nobody, "Should've done it a long time ago." She turned, leaning against the bench to look down at Sarah. "Go and keep your mother company." As Sarah crossed the aisle, the princess let herself down onto the bench and crooked her finger at Tom. "Does anyone know whom that girl had in mind?"

"This is a court of law," Tom said. "It weighs evidence. You heard a hysterical outburst."

"Sure," said the princess. "Since you're so cute, did Hester Ashley . . . *Murdoch* hurt us?" For the first time since she had seen him, soaking wet and desperate, the princess watched Tom's lips curl into a slight, almost an apologetic smile.

"No," Tom said. "She didn't hurt us."

In the corridor flanking the courtroom, Bergman opened the door of the empty jury room. "In here," he said, and stood aside for the admiral and Doris Ashley, who had Hester between them. As they entered, Bergman put his arm across the doorway, stopping Gerald. "You know your way around here, Lieutenant," Bergman said. "Suppose you bring up the admiral's driver." Gerald looked into the jury room and Bergman reached for the door. "Move along, Lieutenant."

In the jury room Bergman closed the door behind him. The admiral was at the long table surrounded by the twelve empty chairs, and to Bergman's left, in the corner behind the foreman's chair, he saw Doris Ashley holding Hester close. They were like fugitives cornered after a desperate chase. Bergman understood immediately that Doris Ashley was putting herself between Hester and the rest of the world. He joined the admiral, watching Hester. She seemed exhausted, docile, but Bergman had seen docile people run amok.

"I'm the guilty party here," Bergman said. "I forced this young lady to be in court. I wish there was some way to undo the damage I've inflicted on you, Mrs. Murdoch. Saying I'm sorry doesn't ease your pain, they're just words." Bergman wasn't certain she heard him.

"Glenn, take us back to Pearl," said Doris Ashley, as though Bergman wasn't in the room.

"I've sent Lieutenant Murdoch for the admiral's driver," Bergman said. "Your ordeal has ended, Mrs. Murdoch. For you the trial is over. You'll be on your way in two shakes."

"I'll take you back, child. I won't desert you," said Doris

Ashley, who knew now she could never leave Hester alone again, could never trust her. "I'll be with you."

"Not for awhile," Bergman said. "You're due back in court." Doris Ashley despised him. She loathed and despised him. She wanted to order him from the room.

"This is a private matter. You are intruding on a private matter."

"Can't be helped," Bergman said. "You're forgetting the facts, madame." He pointed at the wall. "There's a trial going on in there and you're a defendant. The judge didn't adjourn. He called a recess. He'll be back in fifteen minutes and so will you unless you want to be arrested."

"My daughter needs me!" said Doris Ashley. She could not let Hester *loose!* Hester could start running through the streets, shouting like a newsboy. Doris Ashley looked at the admiral. "Glenn, help me."

"You heard him, Doris," said the admiral. "You're a defendant."

Doris left Hester to join the admiral. She raised her head. "In her condition she might . . . do anything." There was a knock on the door. Doris lunged at Hester, arms out to enfold her once more. "I can't abandon my child!" Bergman was walking toward the door. "Wait!" Doris Ashley said. "Wait!" She felt the admiral's hand on her arm.

"No harm will come to Hester," said the admiral, tired of taking orders from this woman. "She'll be safe."

As Bergman opened the door, the admiral joined his driver in the corridor. "Take Mrs. Murdoch to my quarters and don't stop en route," the admiral said. "No stops," he said. "She's not to leave my quarters, and she's not to be left alone. When you've relayed my orders, return to the courthouse." The admiral looked into the jury room. "Hester."

"Mother is with you, baby," said Doris Ashley. Hester didn't look back. She didn't pause. She didn't speak. She left the jury room, walking beside the sailor in the blue uniform. He said, "Guess you know the way, ma'am."

In the limousine the driver said, to himself, "Don't stop," repeating the admiral's orders. The driver knew the admiral like a book. He had to deliver this dame pronto. He could see her in the rearview mirror, all by her lonesome behind him.

But Hester was not alone. Joseph Liliuohe was with her. And Elizabeth Liliuohe was still with her, prodding Hester, demanding retribution, demanding payment for the loss of her son. The driver stopped sharply as a traffic light changed, and Hester was thrown forward, and then back into the seat. "Sorry, ma'am."

If only she had been killed, Hester thought, instantly killed, as Joseph Liliuohe had died. The traffic light changed and the limousine proceeded. Hester knew she would never be spared. She would be punished every day of her life for the rest of her life.

The driver never stopped at the S.P. station at the entrance to Pearl, even without the admiral. They knew the limousine. Besides, he wanted to dump his passenger, and because he was anxious to deliver Hester, the driver took a shortcut, coming around headquarters and the post office to turn at the base hospital. As the limousine passed the entrance, Hester saw ambulatory patients in pajamas and robes in the sun, saw other patients in wheelchairs, each with a nurse in white behind a wheelchair. She saw nurses together, capes over their shoulders, walking into the hospital. She saw a nurse in a window. She saw a nurse on the lawn, surrounded by patients who listened as she read to them. As she *read* to them! Hester wanted to fling open the door. She wanted to leap from the limousine and join them. She had been rescued! She had found her salvation, the only liberation available to her. She would enter nurse's training! She would become a nurse! Somewhere in Windward or in the carriage house were all the papers she had once accumulated. She would find them. She would spend her life caring for people, for everyone. Hester's eyes filled with tears. She had been spared!

In the courtroom, Judge Kesselring said, "Please proceed, Mr. Bergman."

"Do my best, Your Honor." Bergman came out of his chair, leaving the defense counsel table. "I'll need some help," he said. "I was talking about the gates of hell. Maybe the stenographer could refresh my memory."

" 'Fact is,' " said the stenographer, reading his transcript, " 'that one day Gerald Murdoch was sitting on top of the world, and the next day he was looking through the gates of hell from the inside. Now there's no denying an awful lot of people suffer through an act of God. Well, I can tell you gentlemen of the jury it wasn't an act of God that dropped Gerald Murdoch down into the deep black hole of misery. It was an act of the devil. It was the devil's work.' "

"Much obliged," Bergman said. "Devil's work," he said, turning to the jury. Bergman had heard the judge instruct the jury to disregard Hester's outburst, but the warning was meaningless.

"Gerald Murdoch was a bridegroom. His wife was a bride.

They were newlyweds," Bergman said. "These newlyweds sat here in this same courthouse letting everyone on earth peek into their lives, their souls. The distinguished members of the press handled that job. And when it was all over, Gerald Murdoch was back where he had started, behind the gates of hell." Bergman shuffled across the well to reach the bailiff who sat beside the bench. Bergman took the Bible from the bailiff's table. Holding the Bible and facing the jury box, Bergman said, "Strictly speaking, I can't say I know Gerald Murdoch like he was my own son. I never had a son. But I'll tell you this," he continued, one hand under the Bible and the other hand flat atop it, "Gerald Murdoch is everything I'd want in a son, so help me God!" He dropped the Bible on the bailiff's table. "Thanks."

Bergman returned to the jury box. "I started out here today by admitting the district attorney did a whale of a job in this trial," Bergman said. "He didn't stop with the gun, and the bullet, and the fingerprints, and the rest of the list you heard me recite. He brought a doctor, a psychiatrist, an alienist, we call them, over from the Mainland to tell you gentlemen Gerald Murdoch wasn't crazy." Bergman turned to look across the courtroom at Philip Murray sitting at the prosecution table. "I could've saved the State the money. Gerald Murdoch isn't crazy," Bergman said. "The district attorney was probably waiting for me to show up here with an alienist of my own. It usually works out that way." Bergman turned back to the jury box.

"Well, I'll tell you why I didn't bring over my alienist, someone I'd hired," Bergman said. "I've been in a whole lot of courtrooms and heard a whole herd of alienists." Bergman held up his hand and as he continued began raising his fingers. "One alienist, one opinion," he said. "Two alienists, two different opinions. Three alienists, three different opinions, and on, and on, and on, and *on*." Bergman walked to the defense counsel table to examine his barren legal pad again.

"Now we come to the day Joseph Liliuohe died," Bergman said, "the day Gerald Murdoch faced him. Here's something else I'll swear to: Gerald Murdoch, Lieutenant Gerald Murdoch of the United States Navy, the officer without a single blemish on his record, didn't look for Joseph Liliuohe because he intended to end that man's life. Gerald Murdoch had suffered so long, his *wife* had suffered so long, that he had reached the point where he was forced to face this man, Joseph Liliuohe. Gerald Murdoch had to clear the air of any doubts the world had about his wife, her sworn testimony, her good name. He had to hear the truth. He brought along the confession, something else the district attorney showed you gentlemen of the jury.

"Well, Gerald Murdoch heard the truth. He heard Joseph Liliuohe confess," Bergman said. In the first row, sitting between the admiral and her mother, Sarah listened to the liar. She watched the liar. She watched Gerald Murdoch who had murdered Joe. Sarah wanted to kill Gerald Murdoch and knew she could not. She wanted to run him down, set a trap and drive over him as he crossed the street, and knew she could not. She could only hate him.

"When Gerald Murdoch had the truth at last," Bergman said, "he had been punished so wickedly, wounded so deeply, seen his innocent young wife who would never be young again suffer so long, that something deep inside of him crumpled. Gerald Murdoch was a man without a rudder, and when Joseph Liliuohe died, it wasn't Gerald Murdoch who was responsible. It was someone who had been pushed beyond his limits." Bergman moved away from the defense counsel table and walked to the witness box.

"Little while back I said I agreed one hundred percent with Dr. Evan Magruder, the district attorney's alienist who testified that Gerald Murdoch wasn't crazy. The doctor and I agreed on something else," Bergman said. "You gentlemen heard us. We agreed that a man could do something *without knowing* he was doing it. Well, Gerald Murdoch didn't know Joseph Liliuohe was going to die when he did. Gerald Murdoch doesn't *remember*. *He does not remember.*" Bergman left the witness box, passing his chair at the defense counsel table and stopping beside Gerald. Bergman put his hand on Gerald's shoulder.

"I'd like you gentlemen to think of the kind of life Gerald Murdoch has had since the night he found his wife in Mercy Hospital," Bergman said. "I can't ask you to put yourselves in his place. I pray to God Almighty no man here, no man anywhere, inherits such agony. You gentlemen of the jury can spare Gerald Murdoch more suffering. You can put an end to his suffering." Bergman looked down at Gerald. "We could sew this man in a cocoon for the rest of his life and he would still have suffered more than any single human being I've ever known. Gerald Murdoch has been punished enough. You people should come back into this courtroom after you've listened to the district attorney and me and send Gerald Murdoch through those doors." Bergman raised his arm, pointing at the rear.

He left the witness box, returning to his chair. "I want to apologize to each and every one of you gentlemen for keeping you waiting this morning,'' he said. ''It sure wasn't my intent or desire, and I hope you'll remember it was Gerald Murdoch's lawyer and not Gerald Murdoch who was the guilty party, the only guilty party here.''

When court convened after the lunch recess, Philip Murray summed up for the State. He had prepared his final argument in detail, working with Leslie McAdams, and he had rehearsed it, delivering it to his wife, and incorporating her comments into his outline. Murray spoke from notes on a yellow legal pad he consulted frequently. The district attorney was factual and concise. He outlined the case he had presented, citing the witnesses who had testified and the evidence he had introduced. He did not cajole the jury; he did not harangue. He was neither obsequious nor demanding. He departed from his prepared argument in only one respect. Murray addressed a substantial portion of his summation to the murdered man's mother and sister, Elizabeth and Sarah Liliuohe, turning to the jury again and again to repeat his theme.

''You must judge this case on the *evidence* and *only* the evidence,'' Murray said.

As the district attorney returned to the prosecution table, Judge Kesselring said he would instruct the jury the following day.

In front of the courthouse the admiral's driver saw the gang inside heading for the street, and he left the limousine, pulling down on his blouse and adjusting his cap. As soon as he spotted the admiral, the driver opened the rear door.

He didn't hear a word out of his passengers all the way through town. They rode like they were tongue-tied. They were into Pearl and the driver was on his way to the bachelor officers' quarters to drop off the lieutenant when the admiral said, ''Proceed directly to my quarters.'' When the limousine stopped, facing the sun low in the west, the admiral said, ''Lieutenant. York. Come inside.''

''Yes, sir,'' Gerald said, so Duane, beside the driver in the front seat, said, ''Yes, sir,'' as crisply and correctly. He didn't know what to figure. The only enlisted men who ever saw the inside of the admiral's quarters worked for him. Duane got out, standing against the fender, waiting. All he could do was stick close to the lieutenant.

Mrs. Ashley didn't understand why Glenn was inviting Gerald and the sailor inside, and she didn't care. She only cared about reaching Hester.

One of the admiral's Filipinos came out of the house and stood beside the open door. The admiral took Doris Ashley's arm as they reached the wooden steps to the veranda. "Each day is the worst until the next day," she said. She preceded him into the house. "Excuse me, Glenn. I must go to Hester."

"Wait!" said the admiral, and when she didn't stop, he said, "Doris!" She paused near the stairs. The admiral turned to the Filipino. "Is Mrs. Murdoch comfortable?"

"Yes, comfortable."

"Good." The admiral extended his arm toward his living room. "Come in, Doris." He gestured at Gerald and Duane, sending them ahead.

Doris Ashley had endured all she could bear. Hester had threatened her life in the courtroom. She had to stop Hester. "My daughter needs me." She started for the stairs and found the admiral in front of her, as though she were one of his sailors. "Are you forbidding me to see my own child?"

"You'll see her soon enough." He didn't move. Doris Ashley was blocked. He was humiliating her. She looked over her shoulder but Gerald and the sailor were gone.

"What do you *want?*"

"We'll talk in there," said the admiral. He reached for her but she stepped aside.

"I don't recognize you, Glenn," Doris Ashley said. "Is this Glenn Langdon, my *friend?* My protector?"

"I've proven it from the day this ugly affair began," the admiral said. "You're wasting time, Doris." He was tired of her mulish behavior. "Go into the living room with the others."

She pulled her coat over her left shoulder. "You're taking me somewhere against my will," she said. "By force. Is that your idea of a friend and protector?" He didn't answer, and Doris Ashley turned away and walked toward the admiral's living room. He followed her, pausing in the doorway. Gerald and Duane were beside the Buddhist priest on its pedestal, and Doris Ashley went to the other side of the room, stopping near the admiral's console radio in its Empire cabinet.

The admiral closed the double doors and stopped behind a large leather chair, his own favorite. "Doris." She stared at him in silence. He left the chair and stood in the center of the living room, facing them. "You all heard Hester today," the admiral said. "She started something but she wasn't allowed to finish. What was she trying to say?" The admiral waited. "*Who* is innocent?" He waited. "She said, 'They're innocent. They didn't do it.' Didn't do what?" the admiral asked. The admiral knew he would get nothing from Doris Ashley, so he watched the two men. "Lieutenant?"

"Sir, I don't know," Gerald said. He was at attention, his cap in his right hand against his knee.

"They didn't do it," the admiral said. "The dead man, the murdered man was killed in Windward. He was found in the Ashley motorcar covered with Ashley bath towels. Who are *they?*"

"I'm sorry, sir, I don't know," Gerald said, at attention.

"York?" Duane was at attention, facing the admiral but looking past him, trying not to see him.

"Sir, I don't know, sir," Duane said.

"You heard Mrs. Murdoch today," said the admiral. " 'They didn't do it.' Who, York? Who?"

"Sir, I swear I haven't got any idea," Duane said. The admiral seemed to be advancing, coming across the room at him. "It's like the lieutenant said, sir. I don't know, either."

The admiral looked at Doris Ashley, who faced him like an enemy commander, defeated but still defiant. "Doris, can you unravel the mystery?"

"I could have answered your question without being forced in here. There is no mystery. Anyone with eyes in his head can see that. Hester was pushed too far, pushed beyond the limit, her limits. She was punished too long, month after month, and today she cracked. She lost touch with reality, with the real world. She's in another world now, a private, dangerous world. I'm afraid to leave her alone. You've kept me from her, and I must go to her."

"I'll save you the trouble," said the admiral, who didn't believe a word he had heard. He went to a door behind the sofa and opened it. "Bring Mrs. Murdoch down here," he said, loud, so the Filipino in the kitchen could hear him.

"I forbid it!" said Doris Ashley, springing forward. Gerald saw her become someone else. She wasn't Doris Ashley any longer. "I forbid it!" The admiral closed the door and turned to her. She stopped. "You have no right!" Doris Ashley said. Her throat burned and her face was aflame. "Hester has suffered enough! You mustn't torment her!"

"I tried to spare her," said the admiral. "I brought you all in here to spare her, but you told me nothing."

Doris Ashley and the admiral were face to face. She raised both arms, her hands doubled into fists. "There is nothing to tell! Hester has lost touch!" She swung around, lunging at Gerald. "Stop him! What kind of a man are you? Protect your wife!"

Gerald was at attention in front of an *admiral*, in the admiral's *quarters*, Admiral *Langdon*, commanding the entire Fourteenth *Naval* District. Yet he said, "Sir, excuse me . . ." and paused. He cleared his throat. "If the admiral could postpone this," Gerald said, and was interrupted.

"It's *been* postponed," said the admiral, and looked at the lad, the young officer whose life had been twisted inside out. "I'm sorry, son."

"We are not your prisoners!" said Doris Ashley. "I'm taking Hester away with me! We're leaving!"

She started for the double doors, but the admiral said, "Then you'll go to jail," and she stopped, facing the doors. "You're here with me instead of being in jail. You're on trial for murder."

Doris Ashley closed her eyes. Her voice was husky, was almost a whisper. "How can you be so cruel?"

"If I am, it's not deliberate," said the admiral. "I'm one of you, Doris. I've been one of you from the beginning. I told the authorities I would vouch for you. I committed myself. I believe in you, believe you were the real victims in this tragedy. I've almost abandoned the duties of my command to be with you in court, to show everyone my position, my feelings." The admiral crossed the room to join Doris Ashley but she stood as though she were alone. "If something has been kept from me, I must hear it. After all these months at your side, you can't keep secrets from me." The double doors opened.

"Mrs. Murdoch," said the Filipino who had guarded Hester since her return from the courthouse. Doris Ashley hurried toward Hester as she came past the mess boy.

"Don't be frightened, baby," said Doris. "I'll protect you." She opened her arms to enfold Hester, who moved aside, who left Doris Ashley behind.

While Hester had been in her bedroom in the admiral's quarters she had been aware of the Filipino in the hallway. She had taken a book from the night table but had held it in her lap unopened. When the Filipino on guard announced lunch, she told him she was not hungry. Later he brought her tea and cookies on a tray, but it was still in her room untouched. She did not want food. She was tired but did not want to sleep. Hester felt free and *clean*, as though she had emerged from some odious, foul pit where she had been locked away. She had sat watching the sea and the gulls, *understanding* the gulls in their exuberant freedom. Nothing that might happen to her, ever, could be as a horrible as the eternity since she had first begun to lie. "I'm not frightened," she said, and when the admiral repeated what she had cried out in the courtroom, when he asked her who was innocent, Hester calmly said, "They all are. Were. All four were innocent, especially Joseph Liliuohe."

Doris Ashley backed away. She stumbled but nobody moved. They were watching Hester, and as Doris regained her balance, the admiral said, flatly, "Innocent." The single word was like a thunderclap.

"They saved me," Hester said. "They brought me to the hospital. Then my mother came." She didn't look at Doris Ashley. "My mother took charge. My mother said I would ruin her if I told the truth. So I lied."

"Don't lie here," said the admiral.

"No," Hester said, and as she continued, Doris Ashley sank into a chair, sitting sideways, bent and suddenly old. She sat with her back to the others in the living room.

While he listened, Duane got dizzier and dizzier. He could feel a bad taste coming up in his mouth. He could feel his gut twisting. He could see the three guys tied to the three trees. He could see their *backs*, see the blood oozing. Everything around Duane began to spin, around and around and around, and in the center, right square in the middle, ten times bigger than he really was, Duane could see Forrest Kinselman dropping his belt and vomiting, running and vomiting. Holding both hands against his mouth, head down, Duane staggered out of the living room and across the entrance hall. He hit the door with his shoulder, shoving it, trying not to fall, to stay on his feet, and found the doorknob. He half-slid across the veranda to the wooden steps. He tripped on the wooden steps, and fell and rolled down the steps as he began to retch, unable any longer to delay the eruption.

As Hester spoke, the admiral began to pace the floor. He could not be still. He went from one end of the living room to the other, back and forth, back and forth, passing Doris Ashley, passing Hester and Gerald.

Hester fell silent and stood with her hands clasped in front of her, fingers laced, like a student facing classmates and parents, about to offer a declamation. Hester had come to the end, she had emptied herself. The admiral stopped beside the large, illuminated globe near his writing table. "Go on, Hester."

"I've told you everything," Hester said.

"Everything except the beginning," said the admiral. He started to cross the room. "The beginning. Those four men took you to the hospital because you were beaten. Who beat you?" The admiral reached her. "Who beat you, Hester?"

"Bryce Partridge," she said. Hester realized she had not

thought of Bryce, neither in the courtroom when she tried to tell the judge nor in the jury room afterward nor here in the admiral's quarters, alone in her bedroom with the Filipino beside the open door. She had *forgotten* Bryce. And remembering him now, wanted to forget him, quickly, quickly. He was someone in the distance now.

"Who?" The admiral was talking to her.

"Bryce Partridge," Hester said. "Lieutenant Bryce Partridge. He beat me. He was my lover. It was his baby."

Hester heard a sound like someone gagging, and saw Gerald. He was coming toward her, walking as if he were in formation. He marched past her out of the living room as the admiral said, so slowly he seemed to be spelling, "Lieutenant . . . Byrce . . . Partridge."

The admiral looked over Hester's shoulder at Doris Ashley, huddled in the chair. He seemed to have forgotten Hester, and when she said, "I'd like to return to my room," he nodded, then started for Doris Ashley. He stopped beside her, looking down at Doris Ashley as though he were discovering a stain on his rug.

"You've used me," said the admiral. "You've used us all, the people of this island, all the islands, the people of the United States, the government of the United States. You're the worst criminal, Doris, the arch-criminal."

His bitter, relentless denunciation brought Doris Ashley out of her chair. She was no longer the wilted figure who had listened to Hester. She left *that* Doris Ashley behind. She was not afraid of Glenn Langdon. Doris Ashley had seen admirals come and go. She faced him squarely. "I had no choice."

"The truth is always a choice!" said the admiral.

"Don't lecture me!" she said as though she were chastising a maid. "My daughter was in a hospital, at death's door in a hospital! Her life was at stake! Her reputation! Her *future!* You accuse me while Bryce Partridge roams free. He's the truly guilty one, the monster of this tragedy. He forced me to . . . act."

"Criminals are like cowards," the admiral said. "Every one of them has an excuse, whether he lives in the gutter or in Windward."

No one had ever spoken to Doris Ashley with such venomous dislike. She could feel his contempt and could not escape it. She was trapped here, with the admiral, until her nightmare ended. "I am a mother. I acted as a mother." She vowed to repay him.

"An innocent man is dead!"

"An innocent man pulled the trigger!" Doris Ashley said. She needed Gerald for the moment. "Gerald is a hero. Newspapers all over America say he is a hero. Senators stand in front of the White House and praise him. You cannot tarnish a hero, Glenn. You *especially* cannot. You've been at Gerald's side from the first day. If you change, if you *try*, I'll swear *you* are the liar. I'll match you, Glenn, word for word, in the newspapers or in court, or in Washington.''

The admiral's honesty, his candor, which had saved and sustained him ever since his first independent days as a midshipman, had just been stolen from him. He found it impossible at that moment to remain in the same room with Doris Ashley. "Who spawned the likes of you?" he said, leaving her.

The admiral's driver just managed to beat him to the door of the limousine. The driver stood at attention, watching the sun beginning to slide down into the Pacific. Cripes, they were *pouring* out of the admiral's quarters. Lieutenant Murdoch had come past the limousine like he was being taken to a firing squad.

Doris Ashley heard the admiral slam the door as he left. She crossed the living room and as she reached the entrance hall, she heard one of the Filipinos say, "Madame have tea?"

She did not see him. She did not look for him, nor reply. She reached the stairs and held the banister as she climbed to the second floor. Doris Ashley was convinced she would survive, would triumph, despite any obstacles.

Hester sat on her bed, legs dangling, facing the open door. Stunned by her discovery that she had lived an entire day without thinking of Bryce, she realized she could not summon his face from memory. She could remember *him*, his quick, lithe figure, but only in movement, only in the distance. Bryce was receding. Hester could see him fading while she tried to recall his features, his persona. She was rid of Bryce and left only with Joseph Liliuohe in his casket in the sea. "I'm here, baby," said Doris Ashley. "I'm here with you."

Doris Ashley sat down on the bed beside Hester. "I forgive you," she said, lying. She could no longer deny the truth, hide from the truth. Hester was feeble. She looked sane, looked like any other young woman, sitting on the bed holding one of her books. It was all a pose, a facade, a masquerade. Doris Ashley realized Hester was retarded. She needed a book like a baby needed a rattle; the books were Hester's rattles. Doris Ashley's daughter, her flesh and blood, was not like other persons. Something in Preston Lord Ashley's makeup, some weakness, had been transmitted to his daughter. Hester could not deal with life by herself. Doris Ashley knew she must help Hester with each day, but she also knew she would never be alone. She kissed Hester's forehead. "We'll have dinner here in my room, baby."

Doris Ashley needed a bath. She needed to remove her clothes. A bath would revive her. She would be able to prepare herself for the following day. First and foremost, Doris knew she was safe. Gerald and the sailor would keep their lips sealed forevermore. They would remain silent to save their own necks. Glenn was powerless. Doris Ashley had sealed *his* lips. An admiral could not defy the American people, defy senators of the United States of America. In her bedroom Doris Ashley removed her coat. She carried her cigarettes and an ashtray into the bathroom. She would soak in the tub and smoke a cigarette.

Leaving the admiral's quarters, Gerald passed enlisted men and officers. He stopped for vehicles crossing his path, and saw no one and nothing. He heard nothing, neither voices, nor car horns, nor car engines, and yet there was a steady roar in his head and all through him, growing louder and louder and never reaching a crescendo. There was a vise around him, and although it tightened with every step he took, although he could hardly breathe, his cadence neither broke nor faltered. His posture, stride, bearing were flawless. But Gerald believed he was a traitor. He believed he had betrayed the Navy and his country. He believed he was not worthy of the uniform he wore. Everything Hester had said, every word she had spoken in the admiral's quarters, seemed to have been directed at Gerald. He had condoned the flogging of innocent men, and he had killed an innocent man. Only a few moments had passed since Gerald had plunged out of the admiral's quarters, neither seeing nor hearing the driver who had greeted him, but Gerald was already an outcast. Gerald believed he did not belong with decent people. He believed he had lost that right with the explosion of the .45 automatic in Windward. Gerald believed he was damned.

He could see the submarine pens ahead and soon, the *Bluegill*, indistinguishable from her sisters except to those who served aboard her. In the waning daylight, turned scarlet by the setting sun, Gerald could see a work party on her deck aft of the conning tower, but he saw other men leaving the boat, and he knew he might be late, knew he might need to return the following day.

Those leaving the *Bluegill*, officers and enlisted men, greeted Gerald, and to these, the shipmates he had disgraced by his presence among them, he responded. He tried to remember his early months on the submarine, his proud and carefree days and nights of duty in port and at sea, but he could not. And the roar in his head, the din, increased. Gerald came aboard.

Bryce Partridge was in the wardroom, alone, with a final cup of coffee. He had not been in the Officers' Club since the day of his fight in the saloon, since being rescued from police headquarters. The other officers were still including him in their daily drinking plans although he declined daily. He could not take a chance on drinking, on the lock he had put on his fists. He was the last officer except the duty officer to leave the boat now. He waited until the others were out of sight and sound before emerging from the submarine for the drive home. Bryce heard footsteps and looked up from his mug. "Gerald!" Bryce sprang up. "For Pete's sake!" Bryce was delighted to see him. If Gerald was here, on the *Bluegill*, not in court, and not in the bachelor officers' quarters, he was, for some unaccountable reason, free! "Gerald!"

Bryce flipped himself around the table, right hand extended. Gerald's arms were at his sides but Bryce grabbed his hand and raised it. Bryce grabbed Gerald's arm with his left hand, holding on in genuine affection. "Are you back? Is it over?" Bryce asked.

Gerald stepped away. "I'd like to see you alone," he said, and Bryce knew, instantly and beyond doubt, there was trouble, all the trouble he had successfully evaded since the night outside the Whispering Inn. Bryce moved clear, moving back, back, out of arm's length, until the table was between them.

"We're alone," Bryce said.

"I'd like to see you off the boat," Gerald said. Bryce didn't move. "Now."

Bryce watched him. He examined Gerald's uniform, chest and hips. Gerald could be carrying a gun again. He was damn fool enough to do it again. "What's the problem?"

"We can talk off the boat," Gerald said. "You're free. You can leave. You're not the duty officer. Tim Cannon has the duty tonight."

"Sure, but give a fellow a clue," Bryce said. "How about a cup . . . ?"

"No!" Gerald said, interrupting, and, louder, "The *Bluegill* is not involved! I've thrown enough mud at the *Bluegill!*"

"On my way," Bryce said. He shouldn't have argued. He didn't want a cheering section to gather, attracted by Gerald's stridency. Bryce wanted to be a long way from the *Bluegill*, from anyone. "I'll just grab my blouse and cap, old sport."

Gerald turned and left the wardroom. He made his way to the

ladder and waited there until Bryce appeared. "Lead on," Bryce said, making a smile, hoping to keep Gerald quiet until they were a long way away from an audience. Directly behind on the ladder, Bryce brushed Gerald's ribs and hips with his hand. "Sorry." At least Gerald wasn't carrying a gun.

As they made their way through the submarine, Bryce tried to convince himself he was wrong, that Gerald had learned nothing. Gerald had always been a funny duck, too damned noble for the kind of world they lived in, for *any* world. Gerald was too damned straight, too honest, too sincere, too full of . . . rules. He loved the rules. Maybe Gerald had said it all in the wardroom. He really wanted to see Bryce alone, away from eavesdroppers. Maybe Gerald only wanted to talk, to empty his gut after all the days in the goldfish bowl downtown.

They reached the deck and Bryce was beside Gerald as they stepped off the boat onto the pier. "My car's a good place, sport," Bryce said, making another smile.

He and Gerald left the pier shoulder to shoulder, two young officers, slim and erect, moving in the flawless rhythm four years at the Naval Academy had made automatic. Only half the sun remained above the ocean, turning the water bloody from the horizon to the beaches. Bryce could not be near the sea without responding to it. He was ready to cast off, at any hour and in any turn of weather. Now, at sunset, the air above the surface seemed to shimmer with the vivid red of the water. "Wouldn't it be lovely to be sailing into that?" When Gerald neither acknowledged him nor turned to the ocean, Bryce gave up all hope of being saved from a face-off. His car seemed to rush up in front of him. Bryce stopped in back of the trunk, stepping away from Gerald. "We're all alone now, sport."

"This time you're with me instead of my wife," Gerald said. So Bryce had the whole dirty bundle dumped in front of him at last. "This time you can beat me up instead of Hester," Gerald said. Gerald took off his cap and set it on the trunk of the car. He remembered his humiliation in the Officers' Club, his rescue by Bryce, but Gerald had to do *something*. He couldn't challenge Bryce to a duel. He couldn't pick up another gun and kill *another* man, not even Bryce Partridge. "My friend, Bryce Partridge," Gerald said, aloud.

"I was your friend," Bryce said. "Am your friend. It's the truth, Gerald."

"It was *your* baby!" Gerald said, unbuttoning his jacket. "You swine! *Cad!* You cad!" He flung the jacket onto the trunk of the car, shouting, "You sonofabitch!" Gerald sprang forward and swung, but Bryce wasn't there.

"You said talk. Stick to talking," Bryce said. Gerald lunged forward, swinging, but Bryce was gone, out of arm's reach. "Cut it out!"

Gerald whirled around, arms raised. He saw Bryce and swung, swinging with both arms at nothing because Bryce was behind him. "For the good Christ's sake, Gerald, belay!" Bryce said, pleading.

"What kind of a man are you? You can only whip women!" Gerald shouted, and rushed Bryce, swinging. Bryce bent back from his hips and down, bobbing his head down and away from the wild, amateur punch, and as Gerald went past him, carried past by his own momentum, Bryce extended his left foot, tripping him.

Gerald buckled, falling, arms out, hitting the dirt with his hands and knees. He was jarred by the fall. "I told you to stop it," Bryce said. Gerald came up on his knees. "You're not proving anything," Bryce said. "Get up and I'll drive you back to the B.O.Q." Gerald tried to tackle him but Bryce stepped aside, and Gerald went into the ground with his shoulder, lying spread-eagled as the powerful searchlight found them.

The searchlight was blinding. Bryce raised his arm to shield his eyes as the searchlight moved in on them and he heard the car approaching.

The car was a Navy vehicle assigned to the Shore Patrol, and the searchlight, changing dusk into daylight, was mounted beside the driver's window. Gerald came up from the ground, head down to avoid the searchlight, as they heard a man shout, "Hold it, Partridge!" The beam swung past them, focusing on Bryce's car, and they saw the officer come out of the Navy vehicle. They saw the three fat stripes on his shoulder boards, which brought them to attention, and then Jimmy Saunders was standing between them. "Can't keep your hands to yourself, can you?"

"Sir, I . . ." Bryce said before Saunders interrupted.

"There's a gym on this base with a boxing ring but I never see you around," Saunders said. "You could get all the action you wanted, Lieutenant. I'll guarantee you the action myself. No rank, tough guy. Just you and me," said the All-American.

"Sir, I wouldn't have hit him," Bryce said.

"He never hit me, sir," Gerald said. "He never swung at me, sir. I did all the swinging." Saunders loathed the sight of both.

"You've been confined to quarters, Lieutenant," Saunders said to Gerald. "You're on trial for murder! Now what the goddamn hell else are you looking for?" His arm shot out, pointing at the Navy vehicle he had commandeered. "Get in there!"

Gerald took the jacket of his dress uniform and his cap and opened the rear door of the car. "Get in, Partridge," Saunders said.

"This is my car here, sir," Bryce said.

"The front seat where I can keep an eye on you," Saunders said. "You and your busy fists."

Saunders drove to the bachelor officers' quarters. "I'm sorry, sir," Gerald said. He opened the rear door. Saunders shifted gears. Gerald emerged and the car was moving before the door closed. Gerald put on his cap and opened his jacket to shove his arm into the sleeve. His hands were dirty and the skin was torn from his fall. He tugged at his shirt cuffs automatically to expose them beyond the sleeves of the blouse. Gerald heard voices and darted into the shadows. He pressed against the building as three men came out of the bachelor officers' quarters. When they were gone, when there was silence, Gerald hurried into the building and through the corridors to his room. He locked the door and stood in the darkness, hoping to obliterate the ignominy of his failed encounter with Bryce, hoping to eliminate the scalding knowledge of Hester's confession. Gerald could erase nothing from his consciousness. In the darkness he could see Hester and Bryce entwined, naked bodies thrashing. He could see in endless procession the four young men Hester had accused, and he could see, pressing down on him, Joseph Liliuohe, standing in Windward as Gerald pulled the trigger.

Gerald groaned and groped for the light switch. He dropped his cap and fell onto the bed, lying on his back, his eyes open, dazed by all the days to come.

Jimmy Saunders drove from the bachelor officers' quarters to the admiral's headquarters. The building had emptied and the offices were dark. Saunders turned the ignition key. "All out."

Bryce didn't move. "What is this, Commander? Am I under arrest?"

Saunders held his open door. "Inside, Partridge."

"I'm entitled to some answers, Commander," Bryce said. "I haven't done anything. I haven't broken Navy regulations. I didn't even defend myself when Lieutenant Murdoch attacked me." Saunders left the car and came around it, opening Bryce's door.

"The admiral wants to see you," Saunders said. Bryce had never been as afraid. Fear flowed through him, leaving him physically exhausted. For a moment he was immobilized. Only Saunder's goading saved him. "On your way, tough guy."

Bryce wanted to sink his fist into the commander's fat gut, hit him directly under the heart where the mound of blubber lay. The impulse countered, for a little while, the paralyzing fear in which Bryce had been entangled. He opened the car door, hurling imprecations at himself, exhorting himself to *think*, to *think!*

The admiral had sent for him, for a submarine lieutenant of whose existence he would normally be unaware. So the admiral knew what Gerald knew. Hester was living in the admiral's quarters. The bitch had deep-sixed him in front of an audience. Why now? Why *now?* She had kept her mouth shut since September. Something had started her talking! Why had she spilled everything now? "Belay!" Bryce said to himself. He was wasting time. He saw two shore patrolmen inside headquarters. One unlocked the door and both came to attention as Bryce and Saunders entered.

They crossed the lobby to the dimly lit stairs. Think, man, *think!* Bryce would deny everything. It was Hester's word against his, a looney bird's accusation. Everyone knew the bitch was looney. On the second floor Bryce saw the swath of light from an open door ahead. Relax, he thought, then, You're crazy. I'm heading for the *admiral*. You can't *quit*. When did I ever quit?

In the admiral's outer office his chief yeoman was working at a typewriter. Saunders led Bryce to a door and knocked. Bryce heard the admiral. Saunders opened the door. The admiral was behind his desk. "Help me," Bryce said to himself, beseeching God as he came to attention in front of the admiral.

"Partridge, Bryce, sir," he said, saluting. The admiral kept him at attention.

"You're retiring, Partridge," said the admiral. "The chief is typing your retirement papers."

Bryce felt the wind go out of him, all in a rush, whoosh, leaving him breathless, leaving him empty. He said, his voice cracking, "Retire?" as though the word were foreign.

"You're leaving the Navy," said the admiral. "You're terminating your association with the service."

Bryce heard but didn't believe him, couldn't believe him. "No, sir," Bryce said, and, louder, "No, sir. Excuse me, sir, pardon me, I'm not retiring, sir. I didn't put in for retirement."

"I did it for you."

The admiral was torturing him. "I don't want to retire, sir," Bryce said. Holy Jesus Christ, what were they trying to do to him? *Retire?* Holy Jesus Christ! "I never want to retire, sir," Bryce said. "I mean . . . ever since my appointment, my appointment to the Academy, sir. Before I even *saw* the Academy, I belonged to the Navy, sir." He wanted to climb over the desk and scream into the admiral's ear. "I was born for the Navy, sir." Bryce turned to Saunders, begging for help. "I can't retire!" The commander looked like he was holding a noose.

"You're on the way," said the admiral.

Bryce wanted to put his fist into the old buzzard's face, sitting there like God Almighty, telling him his life was over. His life wasn't over! "Why would I retire? On what grounds?"

"Hester Murdoch has told the truth," said the admiral.

"She's a liar!" Bryce forgot that he was at attention. He lunged at the desk. "She's a liar!"

The admiral came out of his chair. "You didn't hear what she had to say." Suddenly there wasn't a sound. The silence was complete until the admiral said, "You cur. I've seen the scum of the earth, but you're beneath them all. If I could, I'd string you up myself." There was a knock on the door. The chief yeoman entered, carrying a sheaf of papers. He set the papers on the desk and turned away. Bryce watched him as though he were leading an escape. As the door closed, Bryce stepped away from the desk.

"I won't do it!" Bryce said. "You can't make me do it! You're not the ultimate authority! I'll go to the chief of Naval Operations! I'll go to the secretary! I'm not retiring!"

The admiral raised the papers the chief yeoman had delivered. He held them with one hand and pulled out several sheets of carbon paper with the other. "You can't keep me here!" Bryce said.

"Try leaving," said the admiral. He reached for the pen in the pen holder set into marble.

"I told you I won't resign!" Bryce said. "I'll *never* resign! I want a court-martial!"

"Your crimes aren't against the Navy," said the admiral.

"All right!" Bryce said. "Damn right!" Bryce said. "That's why I won't retire."

The admiral threw down the pen and pointed at Bryce. "I've had enough from you!" he said. "You should pay for what you did to Hester and that civilian, you bloodthirsty swine. I'm not sending you to the police because I'm trapped," the admiral said, candid as always. "We're all trapped by this trial!"

"I'm not!" Bryce said, darting through the opening the admiral had provided. "I'm not," he said to Saunders. "I'll tell

Captain Maddox the rest of the story. He'll hear the truth about Hester and her rape."

"You're rotten all the way through," said the admiral. "You think you have me. No, mister, I have you. You can go to Maddox, to him and to jail. You won't need to retire. You'll be dishonorably discharged." The admiral sat down. "You're free to leave."

Bryce leaped at the desk and held on with both hands as though clutching the gunwales of a sinking boat. "Admiral! Sir!" Bryce came to attention. He was pouring sweat. The sweat formed a film over his eyes. He wanted to wipe his eyes, wipe his face, but he was battling for survival. "Reduce me in rank, sir. Please. I'll start over. Put me at the bottom of the ensign list, sir. I'll work and live in a way that will make you proud of me, make the Navy proud of me. You'll see, sir. I'll prove it to you, Admiral."

Without an instant's pause the admiral said, "You can stay in the islands, or you can return to the United States. If you choose to return, the Navy will transport your wife and you, and your personal possessions, including one automobile, to the Mainland." The admiral picked up the pen and extended it. "Sign all five copies, name, rank, and serial number."

Bryce wiped his face. His hand came away wet. He reached for his handkerchief, pressing it between both hands. The admiral was holding out the pen. Bryce rubbed his hands into the handkerchief. He could see nothing but the pen, neither the admiral nor the admiral's hand. As he bent to sign the first copy of his resignation from the United States Navy, the room seemed to darken, and Bryce knew that so long as he lived, the darkness would remain.

In the jury room the next morning, Wednesday morning, the bailiff had barely closed the door when a man said, "Let's not make the same mistake the guys did in the other trial. If they had sent that S.O.B. to prison where he belonged, we wouldn't be here. The lieutenant wouldn't have been put through all this misery. His poor wife. Her poor mother. I've got a *daughter* at home!"

Theodore Okohami, the last man to enter the jury room, didn't know who had spoken. He was still near the door, no one was sitting, and there was a cluster around the end of the table. He heard Oscar Sudeith, the foreman, say, "Hold it! Let's hold it, okay?" The foreman had the gavel the bailiff had given him.

"We need some order here. We shouldn't rush into anything. First, everybody sit down, okay?"

A broomstick of a man with a big adam's apple pointed at the foreman. "Don't give me any orders, friend," the man said. Theodore Okohami recognized the voice he had heard earlier. Donald Cedarholm. He was an iceman, stooped from carrying blocks of ice into stores and homes, into cellars and up two and three flights of stairs. His hair was cut so close his head seemed to be shaved.

"Let's just sit down," said the foreman. "Everyone take a chair." Donald Cedarholm pulled out a chair in the center of the table. Standing beside it, he rapped a round can of chewing tobacco with his knuckles before raising the lid to take a wad with his thumb and forefinger and shove it behind his lower lip. "We have to make it look good," Cedarholm said. "We can't go barreling back. The place probably hasn't emptied out yet." Cedarholm grinned, his lower lip protruding. He looked like a skull. "It would be funny to see their faces."

Bruce Tanaka, who was almost sixty, took Okohami's arm. "Here are two chairs," he said. They went to the other end of the table to sit with Ben Hawane.

On the other side, Cedarholm turned to the foreman. "Get going!"

"The first thing I want to say is I'm not an expert," the foreman said. "I've never been through this before, never been on a jury."

"You can count, can't you? Soon's you count twelve hands we're finished," said Cedarholm.

"It's not all that easy," said the foreman. "You heard the judge. He . . ."

"*He?*" said Cedarholm, interrupting. "*He* isn't here! *He* doesn't vote!"

Okohami turned to Bruce Tanaka, whispering, "Why is he so mad?" Tanaka put his fingers to his lips.

"We have to follow the rules," said the foreman.

"The rules are *we decide*," Cedarholm said. He looked from side to side.

"For a fact," said the man at his left.

"Still and all," said the foreman. "You heard the judge same as me."

Cedarholm dropped his right arm across the table and pointed his forefinger at the foreman. "You had your say, now I'll have mine. I'm not thumbing my nose at the American people and the

Congress of the United States. The American people say send the lady and the two guys home.''

"You read that in the newspaper," someone said, and another, "You saw that in the papers." Someone else said, "We weren't supposed to read the papers."

Cedarholm smiled the skull smile. "You don't snitch on me, I don't snitch on you. I'm an American and I'm doing what my country wants."

"The judge said we have to go by the evidence," said the foreman. "He said it was our duty."

"I heard that speech," Cedarholm said. "All the lieutenant did was pay back that S.O.B. for what he did to the lieutenant's wife. He raped the lieutenant's wife!"

"Oh, no," said Okohami, surprised by the sound of his voice. Cedarholm looked at the far end of the table.

"Oh, *yes*," he said. "He raped her. He admitted it." Now Theodore Okohami knew he would speak.

"Lieutenant Murdoch told his lawyer Joseph Liliuohe did it. Joseph Liliuohe never said he did."

"Whose word you gonna take?" asked Cedarholm. He swung his arm as though he were hitting someone. "You don't even belong on a jury," said the iceman. "You don't even belong in this courthouse, any of you. That's the whole trouble around here."

"We belong the same as you," said Okohami. Bruce Tanaka was tugging at his arm.

"We don't go around raping women!" the iceman shouted.

"Try and keep your voice down," said the foreman.

"Nobody of us rapes anyone," said Okohami. He pushed Bruce Tanaka's hand away. Cedarholm moved back his chair.

"So you're calling an officer in the United States Navy a liar," he said.

"Joseph Liliuohe never swore he raped somebody," said Okohami.

Cedarholm exploded, leaping up. He flung his chair aside and took huge strides to reach the far end of the table. The foreman pounded the gavel, asking for order. Theodore Okohami wanted to run but didn't know where to run. He wanted to crawl under the table but was filled with disgust at his impulse. He saw the big broomstick with the big arms coming, but he couldn't move. He was paralyzed.

"You stop!" said Bruce Tanaka. "You're not in an alley." He came out of his chair to face Cedarholm. He was small and almost twice the iceman's age. "Stay away! You stay away!"

"Butt out," said Cedarholm.

"I'm calling the bailiff!" said the foreman. Cedarholm raised Bruce Tanaka's chair and threw it aside. He reached for Bruce Tanaka to throw him aside, but the small man grabbed the iceman's arm with both hands, like a terrier leaping into the air after a stick. With Bruce Tanaka holding on, Cedarholm swung his arm, flinging the small man into the wall. The foreman ran to the door.

Bruce Tanaka hit the wall with his arms wide apart. He was helpless. Cedarholm's right hand, which had lifted tons and tons of ice, curled into a fist and he swung in a wide arc, hitting Tanaka along the jaw. The blow sent Tanaka careening to his right into the corner of the room, where he began to slide to the floor like something spilled.

"Why did you hit him?" asked a juror. "You didn't have to hit him," said another. "You've killed him!" said another.

"I didn't kill anybody," said Cedarholm, and was confronted by Okohami, who was afraid he would faint with fear.

"You're like the lieutenant," said Okohami. A juror pulled him back.

"Stay away from him," said a juror. "Keep away!" said another. Okohami didn't listen to them.

"You're the same," he said. "You think a man is grass under your feet." Ben Hawane was kneeling beside Tanaka, holding a handkerchief.

"He needs a doctor," said Ben Hawane.

"We're not grass under your feet," said Okohami as the bailiff came through the door. He saw the men standing together on one side of the table, saw the tall guy with the shaved head, and beyond, he could see blood. It was the handkerchief Ben Hawane held to Tanaka's face.

"Give me some room!" said the bailiff, his arms out. The bailiff reached the end of the table and squatted in front of Tanaka. He saw the crooked face and the handkerchief filled with blood, saw the blood spurting from the slashed skin and the shattered bone. "Holy . . ." he said. "Get an ambulance!" he said to the foreman. "Run! Someone go for a bailiff . . . No! Someone see if the judge is still in his chambers, still here! Run! Run!" The bailiff looked around. "Who's the slugger?"

No one spoke. Cedarholm bent to pick up Bruce Tanaka's chair and Theodore Okohami said, "He's the one." Okohami pointed. "He did it." The bailiff studied Cedarholm as though the iceman were a recruit.

"Don't tell me it was self-defense," the bailiff said. "You're bigger than three of him. You'd better say your prayers, buster. So far it's only assault. Start moving and keep your hands where I can see them. You're under arrest." The bailiff stepped back against the wall, waving at Cedarholm and following the iceman. Ahead, Judge Kesselring, in shirtsleeves, came through the door. The foreman and another bailiff followed.

Judge Kesselring went directly to the corner, to Bruce Tanaka. "Good God!" The judge swung around, advancing on Cedarholm. Geoffrey Kesselring had to control himself. He was ready to hit the juror. He wanted to hit the juror. "Why did you do it?" the judge asked, talking to control himself. Cedarholm pointed at Okohami.

"He started all this," Cedarholm said, and heard the room crackle and resound with astonished and outraged rebuttal.

"Take him into court, bailiff," the judge said. "He's under arrest. I'll arraign him. He's being held for trial. Get a public defender in here. There'll be no bail for this man." He turned to the other bailiff. "Get the first two alternates up here immediately to complete the jury." He looked at the men standing around the table. "Remain here. You are not excused."

Theodore Okohami stayed beside the inert, crumpled form lying in the corner like a broken and discarded toy. The color of blood made Okohami dizzy, made his head swim, but he dropped to the floor. He couldn't abandon Bruce Tanaka, let him lie there alone. "They want to kill us all," he said.

Several hours later, in the day's lonely and evocative twilight, Maddox drove into the hills toward his house. He drove slowly. He had left police headquarters on his way to dinner somewhere, somewhere small and quiet, and changed his mind before he was out of the parking lot. He couldn't sit through a full dinner. Maddox decided he would find something at home. He stopped for a red light. The thought of once more opening a can, of emptying it into a plate, of standing in the kitchen eating, gulping down the food to be done with it, made him grimace. Maddox decided to bathe, dress in easy clothes, and come back down for dinner. The prospect was appealing for a few minutes and then was discarded. Maddox resolved to take a vacation. He would take a month. He would travel around the States. No, not the States; not with Lenore in the States. He would go to China. China and Japan. Maddox abandoned the vacation. What could he see over there that he hadn't seen in Honolulu? He had lived with Chinese and Japanese all his life. Maddox took off his hat and dropped his arm across the top of the seat, remembering, instantly, Lenore beside him. He remembered her head in his shoulder, and for a moment he would have sworn the car was filled with the odor of her perfume. He made a sound, low and guttural, primeval, really, a sound of suffering that could not be contained. Maddox pressed his foot down on the accelerator. He was in a rush to reach his home, as though by leaving the car, he could leave everything behind him.

Maddox turned into his driveway. He left his hat on the seat and walked toward his dark house, the only dark house in the block. He opened the door wide as he did whenever he returned and stopped dead on the threshold in the dark. He could smell her perfume again. Maddox was shaken. Something was wrong with him. He felt for the light switch, turned up the lights, and then reached out behind him, pawing the air for the door. He was looking at Lenore, in a chair fifteen feet away.

She wore the tan dress with buttons up the front that she had been wearing at their first meeting on the ship and later at lunch. She wore the same white scarf around her neck. A sweater, a beige cardigan, was over her shoulders. Her hair was held back by a tortoiseshell band. She was more beautiful than he remembered. She took his breath away. "Don't be angry."

"Coming in, I recognized your perfume," Maddox said. "In an empty house. I thought I was over the edge." He remained in the entrance.

"I remembered you didn't lock your door," Lenore said. "I wanted to surprise you."

"You surprised me," Maddox said. He took off his jacket and carried it into the room, his hand brushing his gun in the holster. He threw his jacket onto a chair and fumbled with the holster in his haste to remove it. The exposed weapon infuriated him.

"You are angry," Lenore said. "I've made a horrible mistake, haven't I?"

Maddox dropped into the chair and shoved the holster into the jacket pocket. "You said good-bye, Lenore, or the maid from the Western Sky did it for you. So what is this? Hello?"

She tried to smile. She hoped she was smiling. She hoped he would think her brave and be proud of her. "Yes, Curt. Hello."

"You mean it's not you and him," Maddox said. "It's you and me now?" He knew the answer before he spoke. She played with the sleeve of her sweater.

"I had to see you," Lenore said.

"Had to," Maddox said. "I've heard those words more times than I can count. People in handcuffs or in jail. They *had* to do whatever it was they did." His voice rose. "Nobody *has* to do anything but eat and sleep. Everything else is a choice." Maddox looked away. "Oh, Christ." He couldn't handle her, handle himself with her "You have to go, Lenore," he said, to the wall. "I'm turning mean, and I'll turn meaner."

"Not you, Curt," she said.

"Yes, me," Maddox said. *"Me!"* He swung around. "What did you tell him? I know what you told him," Maddox said. "You told him the truth. What does he care? What's a night out to him? He won, didn't he, Lenore? He won."

Lenore rose, pulling the sweater over her shoulders, and when she looked at Maddox he saw her eyes glistening with tears. He saw her turn her head, defeated and helpless as he was defeated and helpless. She was all alone and he could no longer resist. He came out of his chair to enfold her and bring her damp, flushed face to his.

Lenore felt his arms around her. She felt his face against hers, felt the familiar, the longed-for rough skin against her skin. She kissed him, his shirt and chest and shoulder and neck, demanding admittance. She said, "I love you," her lips against his, tasting her own tears. She raised her hands, holding his face to part his lips with hers, to be inside him.

He said, low, "Wait," and Lenore said, "I can't. I can't." She was wild. He could feel her pulling at his shirt, at his trousers. She made him wild, and he began to unbutton her dress. It fell away from her shoulders, and she helped, dropping the straps of her brassiere. She said, "Here, darling," freeing herself, and as Maddox bent, she reached to find him.

He carried her, as he had the first time, feeling her lips and her tongue. She could not stop, she could not wait. They fell to the bed together, pulling at their clothes until, his body bare, Maddox was over her, and Lenore's legs opened and her hips moved to take him into her.

Later, Maddox propped himself on one elbow to look down at her, and although he smiled, he made her afraid.

"You can't do this again," Maddox said.

"I was waiting for you to say it," Lenore said. "Waiting and dreading the moment. I can't do this again. I promise. I'll give you my word. I've never broken my word."

"We always mean things when we say them."

"You can trust me," she said. "I had to come tonight. I had to see you once more. We never said good-bye. This is good-bye." She watched him. "Please talk to me."

"I've never seen anyone like you in my life," Maddox said. "Anyone as beautiful."

"You're beautiful," Lenore said.

"Sure."

"Yes," she said. She came to him, her body curved into his. "I've memorized you, Curt. I can see you now, wherever I am. I think of you wherever I am. I try to imagine you when you were young, when you were a little boy. Were you a happy little boy? Did you have a dog? Were you an explorer, you and your dog? Did your playmates look up to you? Were you the chief, the leader, taking the rest into adventure?" He did not reply, and Lenore shifted, to look up at him. "Have I said something wrong?"

Maddox kissed her hair. He held her, stroking her hair, and after a time he told her of himself, of his mother, of the closet where he was shut away when she had a patron in the room, of the other whores. He told her everything, what he had told no other person, ever, not even Harvey Koster. "Sounds just like Horatio Alger, doesn't it?" Lenore's eyes were glistening again. "Hey, none of that!" Maddox said. "Anyway, I wanted to tell you and never had the chance, never *thought* I would have the chance, the right time and the right place all at once. But here you are, tonight anyway, so now you can leave with the whole story."

She could feel him beside her, naked bodies together, but he was gone already. She would be alone forever. "You want me to go," she said.

"No, Lenore. I want to put up bars, lock us in here and glue us together," Maddox said. "But you're going, so we're only fooling ourselves now."

When they were dressed, they left the bedroom without speaking. Lenore stopped. "My sweater," she said, and Maddox bent for it and dropped it over her shoulder. "I came in a taxi," she said. "Will you call one for me?"

"This time I will," Maddox said. "It's too tough watching you walk into the hotel on your way . . . on your way. It's just too tough, Lenore."

"Don't hate me."

"Couldn't do that, Lenore," Maddox said. He had to end this. "Forget the taxi. Take my car. Leave the keys in it. I'll have someone come for it in the morning." He went to the door ahead of her.

They walked to the car and Maddox opened the door and stepped back so she could get in. "I'll roll up the window," he said. She looked up.

"Will you kiss me?" Maddox leaned into his car and touched

her lips with his. Lenore raised her hand but she was too late. He was out of reach and the door was closing between them. Maddox stood beside his car. She seemed a million miles away.

Two minutes less than forty-eight hours after the bailiff had led the jury into the jury room, Oscar Sudeith, the foreman, whose hand was in the air, watched the other eleven hands in the air. "I'll tell the bailiff."

Maddox had the news before Judge Kesselring was told, before anyone except the jury and two bailiffs knew there was a verdict. When the bailiff whom the foreman had summoned came out of the jury room on his way to the judge's chambers, he nodded at a colleague in the corridor. "They're ready." The other man stepped into an office to telephone police headquarters.

"They're coming in, Captain."

"Much obliged," Maddox said, and called Harvey Koster.

"You'll be in the courtroom, won't you, Curt?" Koster asked, although it was not a question.

"I'm looking at a desk full of work down here, Mr. Koster," Maddox said, lying.

"I've been counting on you to tell me the verdict," Koster said.

"Sure," Maddox said. "I'll call you from the courtroom, Mr. Koster." Maddox pushed away the telephone. If he was lucky, maybe she wouldn't be there.

In Waikiki, in the Western Sky, Tom was with the princess, waiting, when the telephone rang. She said, "Hello," and listened. "Thanks, Phil," she said to the district attorney, who had promised to call her. She looked at Tom. "I wish it was *Good* Friday, good for us, not them," she said of the defendants. "Help me with my costume."

"Sarah wants to come," Tom said.

"She might not like what she hears," the princess said.

"She wants to hear the verdict herself," Tom said.

The princess gestured impatiently. "Get a move on!" Tom telephoned Sarah at the drugstore and told her they would meet in front of the courthouse.

As Maddox turned into the alley flanking the courthouse, he saw a few people, mostly men, standing in front of the building, away from the entrance. They stood apart from each other and clear of the admiral's limousine between the NO PARKING standards. When Maddox stopped, parallel to the side doors of the courthouse, two Japanese passed his car. The Japanese had learned of the verdict from the daughter of one who worked with Sarah in the drugstore. Another man, a Hawaiian in front of the building, had been told by a bellhop at the Western Sky who had seen Bergman and Lenore leave the hotel and had followed them, listening to their conversation. Another Hawaiian was the brother of a janitor at the *Outpost-Dispatch* who had overheard Jeff Terwilliger tell the city editor there was a verdict as he rushed out. Each of those told someone, and each person who was told repeated the news.

Maddox had remained in police headquarters as long as he could. He left his car and used the stairs at the rear to reach the second floor. The balcony was almost empty and the courtroom doors were locked. He knocked. It would be over fast. He would be in and out in no time. The door opened slightly, held by a bailiff. "Hello, Wes," Maddox said, and slipped through into the courtroom.

Maddox was in a crowd. Spectators were jammed against the doors. The walls at the rear were lined with men and women. Maddox had to come up on his toes to see the jury box, and as he did, Lenore looked back for the thousandth time. They were together again, and Maddox wanted to disappear, to flee, as though by leaving he could free himself. Lenore raised her hand, removing the pale green silk scarf from her hair.

She felt as though she would never stop weeping for him. Yet she did not regret coming to the courthouse. She had insisted on accompanying Bergman. Seeing Maddox once more would make it easier to remember him, his face and his hair, his hands, his hands on her. "All rise!"

Judge Kesselring reached his chair on the bench as the bailiff finished. "I will caution all present to conduct yourselves with proper respect for the court and for the principals in this case." He looked at the reporters. "I am aware of deadlines and sympathetic to your problems," the judge said. "Nevertheless, I cannot allow the proceedings of the court to be disrupted, and I expect all of you to maintain decorum and restraint."

"Jesus Christ," said Duane York, sitting beside Gerald. "Jesus Christ, why doesn't he stop talking?" Duane couldn't keep his hands still.

"Gentlemen of the jury, have you reached a verdict?"

Oscar Sudeith, the foreman, rose from the first chair of the first row in the jury box. Sarah, sitting between the princess and Tom, made herself look at the foreman. She felt like she was choking. "We have, Your Honor."

"The defendants will rise," said the judge. Gerald shot up from his chair, standing at attention, and Duane came to attention because he followed the lieutenant's lead. Doris Ashley rose, holding her gloves in her right hand and trying to keep her head high, to face them all. Bergman held onto the table to push himself to his feet. "What is your verdict?"

"We find the defendants guilty of manslaughter in the first degree," said the foreman.

Tom said, *"Manslaughter!"* glaring at the foreman.

Maddox pushed his way out of the courtroom, and in the well Philip Murray turned his back to the bench, facing Leslie McAdams. "They're going to prison," Murray said, so he didn't see Doris Ashley begin to sway.

A black shroud dropped over Doris Ashley. She felt herself sinking. The floor slipped away and her purse fell from her hand with her gloves as her legs buckled. Duane grabbed her but couldn't hold on. Coleman Wadsworth got her with both arms around Doris Ashley's middle, but he was off balance and was losing her as Duane tried again, his hands under her arms, pulling her up against him. Between them, Wadsworth and Duane managed to get Doris Ashley into her chair. The bailiff filled a glass of water, and as he crossed the well, Duane picked up her purse and gloves.

Doris stirred. She opened her eyes. The bailiff held out the water. Now Doris Ashley knew she had fainted. Everyone had seen her make this spectacle. She felt as though she were stark naked. She took the glass to be rid of the gawking bailiff. But they were all gawking. She could feel them behind her. The judge watched her drink. "Are you feeling better, Mrs. Ashley?" She drank the water, but she didn't look at the judge nor reply.

"Mrs. Ashley has recovered, Your Honor," Bergman said. When the judge had thanked the jury, Bergman said, "Like to approach the bench, Your Honor. Like to have the district attorney there, too, if you don't mind." Murray had to wait for Bergman. "Your Honor, these defendants aren't your run-of-the-mill felons. Doris Ashley is a woman at the top of the heap, anywhere in the world. They've been through a lot and the worst is yet to come. I hope you don't keep them in the dark too long. It'll be a Christian act to sentence them as soon as possible. I wanted the district attorney to hear this because I'm hoping he'll second the motion."

"I do, Your Honor," Murray said. "Please think of this as a request from both of us."

Judge Kesselring looked at his calendar. "I'll set sentencing for the twelfth at ten A.M.," he said. "Thursday, a week from yesterday." He watched Bergman and Murray return to their chairs. "The defendants are ordered to appear at ten A.M. March twelfth, when sentence will be imposed. This court is adjourned."

As the reporters spilled out from the four tables at one end of the courtroom, the admiral came through the gate alone and passed Doris Ashley as though she were not there. "I'd like to leave the crowd behind," the admiral said. He stopped and looked over his shoulder at Gerald, who stood beside his chair. "Lieutenant!" The admiral's voice crackled, and Gerald snapped to attention. The admiral gestured and Gerald followed, behind Doris Ashley and Duane.

Behind them, Bergman led Lenore to the door flanking the jury box. "Can't face those reporters again," Bergman said, lying. He had seen Maddox at the rear of the courtroom. Bergman did not intend to see him twice. "Discovered a shortcut," Bergman said.

As Lenore emerged from the side doors of the courthouse, she was facing Maddox's car. She looked in both directions for Maddox. Behind her Bergman said, "We can find us a taxi back here," gesturing at the rear of the courthouse. "The sooner the better," he said, moving past Maddox's car, which he, too, had recognized.

Lenore had only a few seconds. She saw Bergman walking away from her. She had to join him. She would never see the car again, see Maddox again. She had to do something. Bergman might stop, he might turn. The car windows were down. Despite her turmoil, Lenore dropped her scarf into the car and turned away. "I'm coming."

Only the princess and Sarah and Tom remained in the courtroom, and only the princess remained seated. "Well, Tom, how do you feel?"

"I've been thinking of the others," Tom said, "about Harry and Mike Yoshida, and David. They'll be coming back for another trial."

"Can't you postpone that for one day? Concentrate on what happened here," the princess said.

"I hate what happened here!" Sarah said. "They killed Joe! They should be killed! They should be locked up for life! Instead they're guilty of manslaughter! In a few years they'll be out of prison!"

"Take what you can get," the princess said. "I wish someone would tell me how I'm supposed to feel."

"How would you feel if the jury had decided they were innocent?" Tom asked.

"I'd be hopping mad," the princess said. "That's easy, because it's easy to be mad. Does that mean I'm supposed to be happy? I don't feel happy."

"They're not free," Tom said. "They won't be walking out into the sun like Bergman thought they would." The princess looked at Tom, who was sitting on the bar.

"How long since I first saw you? Standing there with Jack, looking like a drowned rat. Looking crazy, is what I really thought," the princess said. "I wish I'd never listened to you. My whole life has been turned upside-down since you showed up at the ranch." She raised her arms. "Help me out of here. I need to line up a boat for next Thursday. I can't wait to leave this town."

Sarah and Tom each took one of the Princess's hands and the big woman came to her feet. They followed her out of the courtroom to the head of the stairs leading to the lobby.

The princess put her hand on the railing. "At my place I can walk straight up a mountain," she said. "Over here I'm afraid of coming down these dumb stairs."

"Take my arm," Sarah said.

"Then we'd both land on our ears," the princess said. "Just stand clear. If I wasn't wearing this bird cage, I'd come down on my bottom the way I used to at the palace." She waved them on. "Vamoose!"

Sarah and Tom waited at the foot of the stairs. Clutching the rail, the princess descended, a step at a time. When she joined them, she said, "I feel like I did a whole day's work." None of them saw the two lines of faces on either side of the entrance, and as the three came out of the courthouse, the princess stopped. "What is this?"

The few men Maddox had noticed on his arrival had become a vast crowd, a throng. He had seen them as he came down the stairs from the courtroom to call Harvey Koster, and because he had been worried about a disturbance when the defendants appeared with the admiral, Lenore had been able to leave her scarf in his car. Maddox was still in front of the courthouse, beside a NO PARKING standard, waiting with the crowd for the princess.

They lined the entrance from the doors to the sidewalk. They filled the sidewalk to the corner on the right, to the alley, and beyond the alley. They were across the street waiting. They were everywhere.

They watched the princess come through the doors. They were silent. They allowed her to reach the sidewalk, and then, slowly, hesitantly, like parishioners approaching a revered prelate, the men and women, and the children some had brought, surrounded the princess and Sarah and Tom. A woman took the princess's hand and tried to kiss it. The princess pulled her hand away. "Don't ever do that!" she said, and then, shaking her head, repeated, "Don't ever do that." A man reached the princess and he removed his cap and moved aside. The princess was very embarrassed. She held on to Sarah. "It's a good thing I didn't bring my checkbook," she whispered. "I'd be broke trying to buy us out of here." Another man stepped in front of them, bent down, and stood up holding up his son.

"This is the Princess Luahine," the man said, and lowered the boy to the sidewalk. He moved aside and another took his place, a woman holding an aged woman's arm.

"I think we should all go home now," said the princess. "Let's all go home." Holding on to Sarah and with Tom beside her, the princess took a step into the crowd. The crowd moved back and parted. A path opened and immediately closed behind them. The princess saw Maddox. "Are you on vacation?" Maddox shook his head. "Give us a hand," she said. Maddox shook his head.

Princess Luahine looked at the men and women around her. "We're only going to the car," she said. Nobody left. "Sarah, where's your car?"

"Around the corner and down a block," Sarah said. They reached the corner and turned, and nobody left. They walked to the end of the block and stopped, waiting for the light. Everybody waited.

"There's our car across the street," the princess said. When the light changed and the princess started to cross the street, everybody crossed the street. The convertible was surrounded.

"They don't want to leave you," Tom whispered.

"How did you become so smart so young?" The princess turned. "All right, we'll have a parade. We won, didn't we? Sarah, I'm walking back to the hotel. If I can make it."

"I'm coming with you," Sarah said.

"You too," said the princess, holding on to Tom. "If I'd known this was coming, I'd have hired a band," and, louder, "We're walking! Hup, hup, hup!" Men and women moved aside, making a path for the three, and walking beside and behind them. Nobody pushed. Nobody tried to get ahead. With the princess between Sarah and Tom, the long, quiet, peaceful procession began to wind through Honolulu streets on the way to Waikiki. In the distance they could hear the first cries of "Extra! Extra!" as the newsboys appeared with the newspaper that carried the jury's verdict.

* * *

Monday morning, three days after the defendants had been found guilty of manslaughter in the first degree, and three days before they were to be sentenced, the admiral's limousine stopped in front of Iolani Palace. Unlike the admiral's last appearance at the palace, when the governor had ended the curfew, he had not been summoned. The admiral had called early that morning for an appointment. "Now," the admiral told the governor. "I'm leaving now."

Of the entire male population of Honolulu, Governor Martin Snelling was the man most influenced by Harvey Koster. The governor was diligent and devoted to the performance of his duties. He was a bear for work. He was the first governor of the Territory to eat regularly from the prison kitchens to check the food. He was the first to read and initial, personally, every contract let by the Territory. Since he was himself an accountant, he was the first governor to hire independent auditors to examine records of revenues and disbursements in the Territory. His appearances in the islands were constant and unannounced and included weekend sorties. Martin Snelling dressed like Harvey Koster. He often quoted his idol and he was aware, from the time he learned of his succession to the palace, that he could never have taken office without the endorsement of Harvey Koster.

The governor never kept anyone waiting. When the admiral telephoned Monday morning, the governor immediately canceled the appointment he had made for that hour. He was in the doorway when the admiral, alone, entered his secretary's office. "Please come in, sir."

Governor Snelling followed him across the spacious office with the broad windows where a king had slept. "I've cleared my desk for you, Admiral."

"My advice is to keep it clean," the admiral said. "As of now, you're on tactical alert." The governor couldn't sit down, since the admiral hadn't.

"What's your problem?" the governor asked.

"I wish it *was* mine," the admiral said. "But it's your problem. It falls in your command." He reached into his jacket pocket. "I'm disobeying orders but it won't be the last time." The admiral dropped a long official Navy envelope on the desk. "Read it!" The governor slipped on his glasses and picked up the envelope, which was open. He removed the Navy communiqué.

"COMFOURTEEN FROM SECNAV. SECRET. REPEAT SECRET. READ AND DESTROY.

PERSECUTION OF THREE AMERICAN NATIONALS MUST END. NATION IN UPROAR. FREEDOM SOONEST DEMANDS HIGHER AUTHORITY.''

As the governor lowered the cable, the admiral took it from him. ''I've memorized the contents, in case your mind needs prompting,'' the admiral said, crumpling the communiqué. He picked up a metal candy dish on the governor's desk and held it upside down, making a mound of the caramels. He set it down and dropped the paper ball into it as he took a box of matches from his jacket pocket. The admiral struck a match, cupping the flame with his hand and setting fire to the secret signal he had received at dawn that morning. ''Read and destroy,'' the admiral said. He blew out the match. ''Now I'm obeying orders. Any questions?''

The governor disliked erasers. In his years as an accountant he had corrected his mistakes by beginning over with a fresh page in the ledger. He disliked all disorder, and the pile of caramels on his desk unsettled him. The black, dissolving ashes in his candy dish made him anxious. The admiral's high-handed manner, barging in to set fires in his office, upset the governor. ''I can read English, Admiral.''

''Freedom soonest,'' said the admiral, quoting the Secretary of the Navy. ''*Freedom soonest*. You only have five days to set a battle plan. I'm delivering them to the Courthouse at ten A.M. Thursday for sentencing.''

''Thanks for coming to see me,'' said the governor. The admiral didn't move.

''Mister, you're in trouble. You're the senior officer in this Territory so you're the man responsible,'' the admiral said. ''You're not dealing with me now, lifting a curfew. '*Higher authority*,' '' the admiral said, quoting from the cable. ''The Secretary of the Navy is a member of the President's Cabinet. He's pretty high himself. You don't need a diagram to decide who's higher. The President of the United States. The President of the United States is telling you he wants freedom for those people.'' The admiral put the matchbox into his pocket. ''I've already cabled the Secretary informing him I was meeting with the governor of the Territory.''

The governor did not escort his guest to the door. He remained beside his desk. When he was alone, Martin Snelling bent for the wastebasket, emptying the candy dish of ashes. He unwrapped a caramel. ''The President,'' he whispered. The governor felt surrounded, felt besieged. Doris Ashley and her daughter and her daughter's husband were not part of his job. He had ended the admiral's curfew only to please Harvey Koster.

"*I'm* innocent," he said, aloud. Suddenly the entire dirty bundle, which had been far removed from the palace, had been spilled across his desk like his candy. Swallowing what remained of the caramel, the governor telephoned Harvey Koster himself, ignoring the secretary who usually made his calls.

"I'll be there at five," Harvey Koster said.

PART

6

M A D D O X was lost. He was awake, but he couldn't see and he couldn't remember, couldn't think, direct his mind. The telephone saved him; the sound was like a siren. He was breathing heavily from some dream that was completely gone. Maddox rolled over in bed, turning up the lamp on the night table. "Maddox."

"I had to call now, Curt," said Harvey Koster. "I couldn't take a chance on losing you, on missing you." Maddox swung his legs over the bed, sitting up.

"Are you all right, Mr. Koster?"

"Yes, yes. Curt, you're the only one I can trust, the only one I *would* trust," Koster said. "I'm leaving for my office. I'll wait there for you."

"Can you give me a clue, Mr. Koster?"

"Not over the telephone," Koster said. "I'd appreciate it if you came straight over without stopping anywhere."

Maddox dropped the receiver into the cradle. He felt as though he weighed a thousand pounds. He was logy, body and mind. He leaned forward, naked, peering at the clock on the night table. It was a few minutes before six. He had been awake at three o'clock, moving from his bed to the living room and back to his bed and back to the living room, and always with Lenore before him. Whatever in him had planned and hoped, had reached for tomorrow, would leave when Lenore left. He was like a dray horse now, plodding slowly, obediently, through the day's rounds, answering Harvey Koster's commands. Harvey Koster was on his way to the warehouse on the waterfront. Maddox left the bed and the bedroom to shave and bathe. "I'm done for," he said to himself.

Almost four hours later, just before ten A.M. that day, Thursday, the admiral stepped out of his limousine in front of the courthouse. He turned to help Doris Ashley from the car, but did not speak to her. The photographers were already at work photographing her and Gerald and Duane York. Doris Ashley heard the reporters'

questions as from a distance, the words indistinct. The courthouse seemed blurred. The admiral took her arm, but he did not
look at her, merely helping her through the newspapermen to the
bailiff waiting at the doors to escort them to the unused stairs
into the courtroom. Except for the reporters and photographers,
the entrance was deserted. There was no sign of the crowd that
had come to learn the jury's verdict. The trial was over.

Duane stayed beside Gerald. He hurt all over like he was back
in boot camp being run ragged. Duane couldn't even remember
if he'd really slept at all. He felt like he was heading for his own
graveyard. "What d'ya think he'll say, Lieutenant? The judge?"

Gerald was silent. Duane looked at him. "Lieutenant?" Duane
touched him. "Sir?" Gerald turned but didn't say anything, and
Duane had the spookiest feeling that the lieutenant didn't really
hear him.

Ahead of them Doris Ashley was walking to her death. She
was ending her life, her *life*. In the next few minutes, someone
else would be in control, some sadistic matron with keys jan-
gling from her hip.

When Tom took his place in the front row of the courtroom,
the district attorney left the prosecution table and walked to the
bar. "The princess better get a move on or she'll miss the
show," Murray said.

"She won't be here," Tom said. "She sprained her ankle."
Coming into the restaurant from the lobby of the Western Sky
the day before, the Princess had taken a misstep, and would have
fallen if she had not lurched into the headwaiter. She had been
helped upstairs to the penthouse.

"Too bad she couldn't be here at the end," Murray said.

"She *was* here at the end," Tom said. "They're guilty.
They're going to prison."

"Amen," Murray said. He hit the bar with his fist. "Amen,"
he said. He straightened up, looking out at the courtroom, and
saw Maddox enter and remain at the doors at the head of the
aisle. Murray returned to the prosecution table. "She sprained
her ankle," he told Leslie McAdams.

At exactly ten, Judge Kesselring entered the courtroom. He
carried several file folders with the notes he had made during the
trial. "All rise."

Standing at the defense counsel table with the defendants and
Coleman Wadsworth, Bergman watched the judge. When the
judge took his place and the courtroom was seated, Bergman remained standing as though he intended to address the court. He

was looking at an uncompromising and inviolate man. Bergman lowered himself into his chair. He was very worried.

Judge Kesselring opened a file folder and removed a sheaf of paper. He studied it for a moment, and then he said, "The taking of a life is the most terrible act in the human experience. The death of one person at the hands of another remains the cardinal crime against humanity. For if one man is killed, then all men are endangered. In the civilized world there are two sets of circumstances under which men *legally* kill men. War is the first. The second occurs in those systems of government that rule that execution is the ultimate penalty for a person convicted of a crime." The judge looked at the defendants. "In every other instance the taking of a life is unlawful and must be punished.

"Evidence offered by the State has been conclusive," the judge said. "Each witness presented by the district attorney added to the mosaic linking the defendants inexorably to the crime for which they have been found guilty.

"The defendants can thank the jury for the leniency given them. It is an undeserved gift, unwarranted when confronted by the evidence in this case. But the opinion of the court carries no weight in our system of justice. The defendants were found guilty of manslaughter in the first degree by a jury of their peers. I am sworn to honor the verdict brought to me and to base the sentence I impose upon that verdict. The defendants will rise."

Duane York was shaking so badly he could hardly stand. He was afraid he'd keel over like the old lady when the jury had pronounced them guilty. Duane glanced at the lieutenant. The lieutenant looked like a ghost, like someone stuffed into a set of dress blues.

"Gerald Murdoch," said the judge, and paused. "For the crime of manslaughter in the first degree I sentence you to ten years in the Territorial Prison without recommendation for parole." Standing beside Gerald, Bergman put his hands behind his back. He had lost badly.

Gerald didn't move. Nothing of him moved. He never blinked. He seemed to be alone in the courtroom; he seemed frozen.

"Doris Ashley and Duane York, you have been found guilty of manslaughter in the first degree," said the judge. "Your part in the death of Joseph Liliuohe is not one iota less horrific than Gerald Murdoch's. Duane York, you went willingly with Lieutenant Murdoch. You willingly kidnapped Joseph Liliuohe. You were beside the victim when he was killed, and you made no effort to avert his death. I sentence you to ten years in the

Territorial Prison without recommendation for parole." Duane rubbed his eyes. Jesus Christ, prison! Ten years in *prison!* All his years in the Navy shot out from under him, bang. He'd be D.D., dishonorably discharged. Jesus Christ!

"Doris Ashley," said the judge. "I have sent many criminals to prison. I cannot recall a single defendant whose presence at the bar was so shocking, so unexpected. You are, were, a leader of the community. This city looked up to you, was proud of you, of your late husband, of the example you set. All this has ended. You have ended it by betraying us, all of us. For the crime of manslaughter in the first degree I sentence you to ten years in the Women's House of Detention without recommendation for parole." Maddox moved into the center aisle.

"The prisoners are remanded to the custody of the sheriff, who will deliver them to the appropriate places of confinement to begin serving their sentences. Bailiff." The judge swung the gavel. "Court is adjourned."

Tom was on his way. He had to call Sarah. He had to call the princess. The newspapermen were on their way. Over one hundred reporters were fanning out from the far end of the courtroom, running up the aisle along the wall and through the almost empty rows of benches. The few spectators were in the center aisle, some ahead of Tom, some at his side. Maddox had to push his way through them, using his hands as though he held a paddle. The judge was leaving the bench. "Your honor!" Maddox threw back the gate, and behind him Tom reached the doors and was engulfed immediately in the increasing numbers of reporters fighting their way to the telephones in the basement.

"Your Honor!" Maddox said, loudly, and to the bailiff, who was at the defense counsel table for the prisoners, "Stay put!" Maddox grabbed the bailiff's arm. "Stay put, I said!" Maddox raised his other hand and waved an envelope at the bench. "Your Honor! *Judge!*" Bergman had seen Maddox come through the gate like he was breaking down a door. Bergman saw the white envelope arcing over Maddox's head. So it wasn't over.

Judge Kesselring held the file folders, looking down at the big man. "This is for you, Judge," Maddox said, releasing the bailiff and going to the bench. Maddox came up on his toes, his arm over his head, the envelope in his fingertips. The district attorney stood beside the prosecution table, holding his briefcase.

"What the hell *is* this?" asked Leslie McAdams, watching the bench. Murray didn't reply. He saw the judge take a folded sheet of paper from the envelope. By that time the admiral was in the well with the defendants.

On the bench, the judge folded the sheet of paper and pushed it back into the envelope. "I have an executive order from the governor," the judge said. "He directs me to deliver the prisoners to the bearer."

Philip Murray swung around, facing the prisoners as though he were about to attack them. "This smells awful," said Leslie McAdams. Murray set down his briefcase and began to scratch his arm.

"The governor is waiting, folks," Maddox said.

"Move out, mister," said the admiral. Maddox went to the gate, holding it open. The admiral was beside and a little behind Doris Ashley. Gerald and Duane York were behind them. Maddox saw Bergman shake hands with Coleman Wadsworth, and he saw the district attorney standing at the prosecution table watching the procession. Maddox followed the procession, so he didn't see Walter Bergman hurrying after him.

They were alone on the stairs and in the lobby. They were alone when they left the building. The photographers were waiting at the rear, in front of the doors used to transport prisoners to and from the courthouse. Maddox's car was in front of the admiral's limousine, and he saw the driver emerge to open the rear door. Maddox reached it ahead of the others, and turning, saw Bergman leaving the courthouse. Maddox pointed. "There's my car, folks."

"Stand aside," said the admiral.

"You heard the executive order," Maddox said. "Deliver the prisoners to the bearer. I'm the bearer."

"Then you can lead us, or follow," said the admiral. "These people are in my charge. They've been in my charge ever since this foul matter began. Get away from my car!" he said as Bergman reached them.

"Now, Admiral. Captain," Bergman said, quietly, like a wise teacher standing between schoolroom combatants. "You gents are forgetting Mrs. Ashley and these two fellows. Their lives are hanging in the balance while you men are fighting over transportation. Doesn't seem fair, does it?" Maddox stepped away from the open limousine door. "I'll come along, Admiral," Bergman said, "If it's all the same to you."

"There's no room in my car," the admiral said. "Ride with him." Maddox pushed Duane York toward his car.

"You're with me," Maddox said, and to the admiral, "Now you've got room." He turned, walking into Duane. "In the back."

The governor was ready by ten o'clock. He looked at himself

in the mirror. The double-breasted suit hid most of his belly. Martin Snelling swore he'd lose at least twenty-five pounds before he was sworn in for his second term. He went to his desk, moving his chair until it was centered, only to remember he would be standing. He couldn't sit with women around. The governor crossed his office and opened the door. "I want to be told when they arrive, when the car arrives," he said. He returned to his desk, poured himself some water, and took the vial of digitalis tablets from his pocket. He had to be careful. He decided to work until they arrived. Work always relaxed him. He was reviewing the proposed budget submitted by the University of Hawaii when his secretary opened the door. "They're here."

"Announce them," the governor said. He remained at his desk. He wanted a caramel but he remembered his vow to lose twenty-five pounds. He closed the budget and set it aside. He took his prepared statement from the center drawer and set it on the desk in front of him. When the secretary saw Doris Ashley with the admiral, she said, "I'll tell the governor."

The governor left his desk, crossing his office as if he were laying a wreath. He opened the door wide. "Thank you, Captain," he said to Maddox, and looked at Doris Ashley. "Will you come in, please?" She led the others. The governor saw an old man in a rumpled brown suit who said, "Walter Bergman, Governor. Counsel for the defense." When the sailor, who was last, passed him, the governor closed the door.

In the secretary's office Maddox said, "I need a phone by myself. Where is it?" Harvey Koster had asked him to call as soon as he had delivered them to the palace.

The governor returned to his desk. They were all standing in front of it. He had memorized his speech. "I've followed the progress of this case from the first day of your trial," he said.

"Excuse me, Governor," Bergman said. "Hope you won't take offense, but these folks have been through an awful lot for an awfully long time. If you could jump straight into whatever it is you've brought them here to do, they'd certainly appreciate it."

The old man stopped the governor cold. He had no choice. The governor picked up the paper on his desk. He had intended to read it in full after his speech. Anyway, the newspapers would print it. "Everything you're waiting to hear is at the very end," the governor said. "I therefore commute your sentence, each and all of you, to one hour." The governor looked at the clock over the door. "In less than ninety seconds you'll be free," he said, and left his chair to shake hands with them.

Duane York jumped up and down, clapping his hands, hooting, hitting the tops of chairs, slapping his thighs, laughing, screeching, chortling. He stopped once to put two fingers in his mouth and produce a piercing whistle. Duane had his arm over his head, swinging his cap like a cowboy with a lariat until he fell, panting, into a chair, legs extended, giggling spasmodically.

Doris Ashley didn't see Bergman shake hands with the governor. She turned away from the rest. She went to the windows to be alone. She was going home, home to Windward. She was taking Hester home. They would be in Windward, behind the gates, *safe* behind the gates before lunch. They would be safe *forever*. Doris Ashley raised her head. She was free! *Free!* Nothing and no one, anywhere, ever, man or woman, would dare even *approach* her without permission. She saw Gerald, standing alone to the left of the sailor who was making a spectacle of himself. Doris Ashley would never again be forced to look at Gerald Murdoch, the ass, the fool and the ass, who had flung her into a living hell for so long. He would never spend another night within the gates of Windward. She had already banished him.

Gerald stood motionless, facing the governor as though he were still in the courtroom, still listening to Judge Kesselring sentence him to prison. Gerald seemed frozen, hypnotized.

The admiral watched the sailor, who was behaving like an organ grinder's monkey. He saw Doris Ashley, the organ grinder, who had deceived them all, deceived everyone, an entire country. The admiral wanted to leave them all behind and empty his mind of the lot.

Bergman remained beside the governor's desk, watching them. He had seen hate and loathing throughout his career. He was almost never surprised, but these people were of another species. They were not confederates who had fallen out and turned against each other. Bergman remembered Hester with her husband. Those two, Doris Ashley, and the admiral despised one another with a rapacity even Bergman had not encountered. "I guess it's more than ninety seconds," Duane said. He came out of the chair and looked at the lieutenant, who was all by himself somewhere. Duane went to the governor.

"Thanks very much, sir," Duane said. "Thanks from the bottom of my heart. I'll never forget what you just did, sir, never."

"I must tell Hester," said Doris Ashley, starting to cross the office. "I'm ready to leave," she said to the admiral, as though he were working for her.

Bergman left the governor's desk, smoothing his hair with his hands as he walked toward Doris Ashley. "We've forgotten one item on the agenda, folks," Bergman said.

"I wish to leave," said Doris Ashley. "I have not seen my home in eighty-seven days."

"There's an old saying about shooting the courier," Bergman continued, "the fellow who brings the bad news. Still, it needs to be said, and you need to hear it, Mrs. Ashley, bitter as it is. You're in a rush to be under your own roof, and I can't blame you. Fact is, none of you should go home, not here in Honolulu, not ever again." The office was silent. "I can't blame any of you for letting it slip your mind but there's another trial staring you in the face. Your daughter's rape, madame. Somewhere in this town are three young fellows living under a cloud. They'll want the cloud lifted, that's only human nature."

"I refuse to be dragged into another trial," said Doris Ashley.

"Way things work, you won't be consulted," Bergman said. "Not too many hours from now what the governor did here will be public property. Everyone will know you people are free as the breeze. Might make it hard to seat another jury who would decide those three boys are guilty of raping Mrs. Murdoch. They've claimed they didn't all along. The jury's verdict would mean they were telling the truth. It would mean Mrs. Murdoch was . . . mistaken. If they didn't do this deed she accused them of doing, who did? The police would be asking themselves that question, and then they'd ask a lot of people, starting with Mrs. Murdoch, and you, Lieutenant, and you, Mrs. Ashley. Way I remember from reading the transcripts, you were the first one to make the rape announcement. You're the one who started the ball rolling. This fellow, Captain Maddox, would begin all over again. In a way the second jury in the second trial would make a fool out of him. No man likes to wear that label. Captain Maddox has crossed my path since I've been in this dreamland. He strikes me as being a pretty persistent fellow. From the looks of him I'd say he could turn out to be a regular part of your lives for as long as it took him to dig up the truth." Bergman took a bar of milk chocolate from his pocket and began to fold back the wrapping.

"That's what I meant about not going home," Bergman said. "If I were in your shoes, any of you, I'd leave Honolulu. I'd leave Hawaii. All of you. Mrs. Ashley. You, Lieutenant, you and your wife. You, too, York. Get out while you can. Stay out." Bergman broke off a piece of chocolate.

Doris Ashley stopped beside the governor. "Thank you for giving me back my life," she said.

"Thank you, sir," Gerald said. The governor extended his hand, and Gerald shifted his cap from his right to his left hand.

"Good luck," said the governor, and, louder, "Good luck to all of you."

Bergman, eating his chocolate, followed them out of the governor's office. He stopped beside the secretary. "Can you fetch me a taxi, young lady? I'd be in your debt," he said. He went to the windows, and in a moment saw the group come out of the palace. They walked toward the admiral's limousine like four strangers.

Duane had been copping peeks at the lieutenant ever since they had come out of the governor's office. Jesus Christ, the lieutenant was *free* but he didn't act like it. Maybe he couldn't get used to the idea yet. Maybe the lieutenant couldn't believe it yet. Duane waited outside the limousine until the other three were in before he opened the front door to join the driver.

It was the first time out of the jillion times Duane had been in the limousine that he enjoyed the ride. The sun was warm and the sky was clear, and to Duane the day seemed to sparkle. Duane could have ridden along for the rest of the day, although he wasn't sure about the gang with him. The limousine was like the inside of a tomb. Duane could see them all in the rearview mirror. Doris Ashley was between the admiral and the lieutenant. It was like looking at a waxworks.

They were at Pearl one hell of a lot sooner than Duane wanted to be back on the base. "Take me to my headquarters," the admiral said to the driver. When the limousine stopped, the admiral said, "Stay where you are. Deliver the others and remain at my quarters. Mrs. Ashley and Hester are leaving. You'll drive them." The admiral left the limousine without looking at or speaking to Doris Ashley.

The admiral's departure released Gerald. He was no longer restrained by any authority. As the limousine moved forward, he shifted to the edge of the seat. Gerald was against the door, as far from Doris as he could get, but it was not far enough. Gerald's chest filled. He was consumed with rage. He felt as though he would explode. Gerald could not bear Doris Ashley's presence. "Stop!"

The driver said, "Sir, I'll drop Mrs. Ashley and then—" Gerald jabbed him.

"Stop, I said! Stop the car!" He was ready to go over the seat for the emergency brake. "Let me out of this car!" Although the limousine was moving, Gerald opened the door.

"Yes, sir," the driver said. This guy was really nutty and had proved it once already. "Yes, sir." They were a good mile from the bachelor officers' quarters.

Gerald put his foot on the running board and as the limousine stopped he stepped off, swinging the door without looking back. He could hear Doris Ashley in the governor's office, "I must tell Hester." He watched the limousine, saw Doris Ashley's head in the rear window. He wanted to pelt the car with rocks. As he began to walk, he was shaking with fury. An endless mass of linked memories tumbled through his mind: Hester and her betrayals; Hester and Bryce; Hester accusing the four young men with Doris Ashley beside her; Doris Ashley lying, swearing under oath; Hester swearing, pointing at Joseph Liliuohe and the three others in the courtroom; Hester with Bryce's baby inside her all those months in the carriage house, in the same bedroom, saying, "Good night, Gerald," and turning her back on him. Anger coursed through Gerald, wave after wave of hatred. His face filled with color as the detestation for Hester and Doris Ashley mounted. Gerald marched toward the bachelor officers' quarters seething, seeing no one but the mother and daughter who had turned his life into a cesspool. He never wanted to lay eyes on them as long as he lived.

At the admiral's quarters Doris Ashley came out of the limousine and stopped beside the driver, who held the door open. "I'll be leaving within the hour," she said. It was a vow. Nothing on earth could keep Doris Ashley here in the house of that disreputable, cruel, and insulting man. "Within the hour." She left the limousine, already on her way to Windward.

Doris Ashley came into the entrance hall and could no longer check herself. "Hester!" Her voice carried through the house. Doris Ashley was glowing. "Hester!" She started for the stairs and saw her daughter on the veranda. Doris Ashley darted through the living room. "Baby!"

Hester closed the book she had been reading, her forefinger between the pages. Doris Ashley raised her arms in triumph. "Baby, we're free! We're free!" She came out on the veranda, arms above her head, reaching Hester to embrace her. "We're going home to Windward!" Doris Ashley wanted to dance. "We're free!"

Hester slipped out of her mother's arms. "I'm not," Hester said, looking out at the sea, at Joseph Liliuohe somewhere on the bottom. She was linked to Joseph Liliuohe forever. She could never be free. She could endure only if she began, quickly, to atone. "I'm not," she said, to Joseph Liliuohe. She walked toward the entrance.

Doris Ashley caught up with Hester, stopping her. Hester did not resist. "You are, baby," Doris Ashley said. "We both are. It's behind us now. We'll put everything behind us." Doris Ashley put her arm around Hester. "Give us time, child. In a little while this . . . nightmare will begin to fade away, to drop away, to evaporate. We'll begin fresh. We'll begin again. We've been given a new start."

Doris Ashley took Hester inside and up the stairs. "We must pack," Doris Ashley said. At Windward she would make Hester her first priority. Hester's happiness would consume her every waking day. Hester would change at Windward. Doris Ashley made a solemn vow.

In his dress blues in the sun, Gerald was sweating when he reached the bachelor officers' quarters. He flung open the door and strode down the corridor to his room. Gerald slammed the door shut and locked it, and turning, threw his white cap in the chair. It fell to the floor and Gerald let it lay. He pulled off his jacket and threw it on the bed. He got out of his uniform as though he were in a race, flinging shirt, trousers, underwear in a heap on the bed. Clothes were hanging over the mattress and trailing to the floor. He pushed off his black shoes and removed his socks.

He took fresh underwear from the chest of drawers and in the closet removed a pair of white duck trousers and a Hawaiian shirt with short sleeves from hangers. He bent for his white buck shoes. He was ready in minutes.

Gerald's wallet was in a drawer. He counted his money. He had several hundred dollars in cash. Although he had been removed from duty, he had continued to draw pay and allowances. Since his confinement in the bachelor officers' quarters, his expenses had been minimal. He couldn't spend his money. He paid for his meals but the Navy did not operate its kitchens for profit. Gerald started for the door, stuffing the wallet into his pocket, ignoring the litter he had made on the floor and the bed.

He went down the corridor to the lounge, deserted except for an ensign with a broken right arm in a cast in a sling who was bent over the radio. Gerald sat down at the writing table, taking stationery from a drawer. There was a pen in the gutter of the base of the lamp and Gerald dipped the nib into the inkwell on the blotter. Leaning forward, Gerald wrote rapidly, putting down what he had already composed.

He filled a single sheet of paper. Gerald folded the paper and slipped it into an envelope and sealed the envelope. Across it Gerald wrote *Admiral Glenn Langdon*.

Carrying the envelope in his hand, Gerald left the bachelor officers' quarters and walked across the base to the Pearl Harbor post office. Inside, he dropped the envelope into the guard mail hopper, which was emptied throughout the day and delivered on the base. When Gerald came out of the post office, the sun was directly overhead, and he could feel it on his head and across his shoulders. Gerald walked past headquarters on his way to the bus station.

The bus was almost empty. Gerald sat beside the window across the aisle from the driver. The bus came into the city without stopping. After another mile, Gerald pulled the cord over his head, and when the bus stopped, he began walking toward the ocean. After awhile, he saw the charter boat signs.

He passed the big boats, each with its captain aboard. Owners called to him but Gerald neither acknowledged them nor paused. Then, far ahead, he saw a runabout, perhaps eighteen feet, swing into a dock. Gerald walked faster.

There was a shack beside the dock and a sign over the dock that read, HAPPY HOLIDAYS. Below were the words *William "Billy" Finch, Prop*.

Finch was a short man in his sixties with a silvery mustache. He wore a yachting cap and a yellow shirt with "Billy" sewn across the breast pocket and HAPPY HOLIDAYS sewn across his back. Finch saw the young cake-eater approaching, all spiffed up, ready for a joyride so he could tell his pals in the States all about it. Finch reached into the shack for a clipboard. "Name your pleasure, friend."

"I'd like to rent a boat," Gerald said.

"I'm your man," Finch said, stepping onto his dock, leading Gerald. "Little scenic cruise? All by your lonesome, friend?" Finch spread his arms. "We've got them in all shapes and sizes as the madams say."

Gerald stopped beside a trim launch. She was a twenty-two-foot boat with an inboard motor and a small cabin forward. "Couldn't do better," Finch said. "I suppose you've had some experience, friend?"

"Yes, I have," Gerald said. He stepped aboard. "How much is it?" Finch quoted a figure and when he saw Gerald's billfold cursed himself. "Plus the deposit," Finch said. Gerald paid him and turned, examining the launch. The wheel came out of the instrument panel set into the cabin wall on the starboard side of the boat. There was a high seat beside the wheel. "Key . . . starter . . . compass," Finch said, gesturing at the instrument panel that lay behind a windshield. He folded Gerald's money and put it into his pocket. Finch touched the throttle, which protruded from the side of the launch at Gerald's right. "Forward and reverse," Finch said. "You've got a twenty-five-horse engine here. It'll give you ten knots if you ask for it." Finch pointed with the clipboard. "Life jackets in the cabin but you've got a beautiful day and this boat's A-one. Hey," Finch extended the clipboard. In his annoyance with himself for not clipping the dude on the rental, he had forgotten. "Need your John Henry."

Gerald scribbled his name, making it indecipherable. Finch walked forward to drop the bow line and Gerald turned the key and pressed the starter switch. The engine caught immediately, low and rumbling, with the gurgling sound of marine motors. As Finch cast off the stern line, Gerald turned the wheel, moving the throttle forward slowly. Finch cupped his mouth with his hand, shouting, but Gerald could no longer hear the man in the yellow shirt, or anyone. He had stopped listening.

Gerald took the boat through the harbor and out into the open ocean. As he moved away from the shore, the sea became stronger. The boat began to ride the waves. Gerald looked back to find a familiar bearing and then he turned the boat, running parallel to the shore. He could remember every detail in the newspaper accounts of Joseph Liliuohe's funeral. Gerald steered a course for the cove where Joe and Tom had played and swam, and from which Joe had been buried.

The metallic taste in Gerald's mouth became more bitter. The sea breeze was brisk and his shirt billowed in the wind. He was chilled by the wind despite the sun. A spray rose, falling over the windshield that curved around the cabin wall, and Gerald could feel the salt water and taste it. He left Honolulu behind and soon he was alone. Since he knew he could not escape, Gerald tried not to be afraid.

He was at the cove long before he expected. He wanted to protest, cry out, "Too soon! Too soon!" but stifled the impulse, forcing himself to look at the shore, to imagine the throng that had gathered to honor Joseph Liliuohe. When Gerald was on a line with the cove, he turned the wheel hard to port. A moment later he turned again, to starboard, looking over his shoulder. The cove was behind him. Gerald sailed toward the horizon. He was more than five miles south of the beach from which Sarah had chosen to bury Joe.

Gerald slid off the seat, standing at the wheel and holding it steady. He sailed on, trying not to think, to proceed as though he were executing an order from a superior officer. He was in choppy seas, sailing into whitecaps. The launch rode the whitecaps, dropping into troughs with thuds that rattled the boat. Gerald had long since lost sight of land and now the gulls were gone and he was alone in the ocean.

Holding the wheel with his left hand, Gerald inched backward, moving toward the stern. When his fingers slid off the wheel, Gerald pivoted, crouching to open the doors of the wooden engine housing. He could feel the boat turning to starboard. Gerald fell to his knees, reaching down, down behind the engine for the drain plug. The plug came up easily, and holding it, Gerald rose, arms out for balance in the lurching boat. He lunged for the wheel. Gerald righted the boat and threw the drain plug far out into the sea.

Now, holding the wheel with one hand, he opened the cabin door. He saw the mound of life jackets but couldn't reach them. Gerald released the wheel and plunged into the cabin, flinging out the jackets like a dog digging for his bone. He backed out of the cabin, rising and grabbing the wheel with one hand, bending to throw the life jackets overboard with the other hand. When they were gone, floating in the wake of the boat, Gerald pushed the throttle to full forward. The bow rose out of the water as the engine responded.

For a time Gerald sailed due west. His eyes stung from the salt in the constant spray flung against and over the windshield. His shirt was wet and clammy across his shoulders. His hands were cold. He made a fist of his right hand and blew into the curve made by his thumb and forefinger. He remembered a schoolyard game in which each participant hit the top of one fist with the bottom of the other but he could not evoke either the rules or the goal of the innocent contest. He said, aloud, "Choosing up sides, I guess," and turned the key. The engine stopped.

So long as the boat moved, the open drain was no danger to Gerald. The hole in the bottom served as a bailer, allowing water to run out of the boat. Now, as the boat began to wallow, riding broadside to the waves, it was immediately vulnerable.

Gerald became terrified. He clutched the wheel as though it would save him. He could barely breathe. He leaned against the seat for support. As he rested, he heard a sound and looked down. A layer of water covered the entire deck and rolled back toward the stern, eddying around the motor housing. The sea was rising through the open drain. The bilge was full to overflowing. Gerald shut his eyes but could not keep them closed. He tried not to hear the water on the deck. He tried to believe the *Bluegill* was coming to take him aboard. Then Gerald felt the water seeping through his shoes, and, as the bow plunged into a trough, felt the water sloshing over his ankles. The boat was sinking, the boat was sinking!

Gerald wanted to cry out for help. He looked from side to side for a sign of the life jackets. He had to plug the drain hole! He had to stop the water! The water was rising! Gerald began to shiver. He shook with terror, but he did not restart the engine. He was on his way to join Joseph Liliuohe.

At Pearl Harbor two hours later, Duane York sat in a chair tilted against the wall of the room to which he had been confined since the day of Joseph Liliuohe's murder. He was smoking. Duane wore his black shoes and socks, and his white cap, but he was in his underwear with a glass ashtray on his belly. Mostly Duane held the burning cigarette as though he had forgotten it, allowing long ashes to form. Then, in the nick of time, he would tap the cigarette against the rim of the ashtray and take a deep, deep sustained drag, filling his lungs before letting smoke emerge from his mouth and nostrils.

The closet door was open and the closet was empty. The chest of drawers facing the foot of the bed was empty. Duane had packed immediately. His duffel bag, jammed, lay on the bed. His open ditty bag was beside it. Duane's uniform, folded blouse and pants, was on the bed. He had stripped the bed and folded the sheets and pillowcase. He was leaving the room as clean as he had found it. If it was one thing on Christ's earth Duane never wanted, ever again, it was trouble, on or off the base. No one was ever putting Duane York on report again if he could help it.

When Duane had finished packing and stripping the bed, when he was free to go, free as the breeze, he had reached for the pack of cigarettes and lighted up. He went to the window, smoking, watching gulls circling and diving near a commissary. He turned away, taking the ashtray off the night table and pulling out the wooden chair. All of a sudden Duane didn't want to see anyone, hear anyone, or talk to anyone.

If he never saw another courtroom or judge it would be too soon to suit Duane. He could hardly remember back when all he had to worry about was standing reveille and reporting to duty aboard the *Bluegill*. Yeah, and making his pay stretch until payday. He always failed but he always had the lieutenant to touch for a few bucks.

Duane tried not to think of the lieutenant, or of old man

Bergman, or of what the old man had said about heading for the States because of the new trial. It always took Duane straight back to the night in the admiral's quarters when the lieutenant's wife made her speech. Christ! Duane doused his cigarette, leaning forward so the front legs of the chair would hit the floor. Anyway, Duane was in the clear. The lieutenant was the only person in the whole world who could hook up Duane to that miserable Saturday night and the Sunday in the woods, and Duane trusted the lieutenant more than he trusted himself. Duane knew he never had to worry about that miserable weekend. He was in the clear.

He just hated thinking of those three guys. Right away he remembered the three of them tied to the trees. They hadn't done a damn thing wrong. All *four* hadn't done a damned thing wrong. Whenever Duane thought of the three, Joseph Liliuohe came into it. Duane could see Joseph Liliuohe like he could see the guys when he cut them loose from the trees. Christ! Duane rose, setting the glass ashtray down on the chair. He walked to the bed and reached for another cigarette and matches.

Duane and the lieutenant were really as innocent as those four guys. The lieutenant's wife and her witch of a mother were really to blame. Hell, they were to blame for everything. He remembered Lieutenant Partridge. Whenever Duane thought of Lieutenant Partridge he waned to spit. Good riddance!

He returned to his chair, picking up the ashtray and making himself comfortable. Duane pushed back and the chair tilted, resting against the wall. He slipped the heels of his shoes over the lower rung of the chair. Best thing he could do was start over again like nothing had happened. Maybe some good would come out of it. Maybe it would stop some other guys in Honolulu who might be thinking of going after an officer's wife one night, going after any woman.

Duane had to forget everything since the night he had borrowed the lieutenant's car at the Whispering Inn. He had to start right now. Duane decided he'd put on civvies in a little while and go off the base. He'd go downtown, pick out a real nice restaurant and have himself the biggest T-bone steak in the joint. Duane tapped the cigarette against the edge of the ashtray and as he raised his hand to take a drag, someone knocked on the door. "It's open." Duane figured it was a reception committee, shipmates off the *Bluegill*. But Commander Saunders came through the door.

Duane jumped out of the chair, standing at attention, knowing he looked goddamn stupid with the ashtray in one hand and the cigarette in the other. " 'Scuse me, sir. I was only . . ." he said, and stopped. Christ, he was in his *underwear* and here was a three-striper, dressed like he was reviewing a parade. " 'Scuse me," Duane said. He jammed the cigarette into the ashtray, set it down, and jumped back to attention. He remembered he was wearing his cap. Christ, he really looked stupid.

"Stand easy," Saunders said.

"Yes, sir. Thank you, sir," Duane said. He pointed at his uniform on the bed. "Just give me two shakes and I'll be dressed."

"Sure." Saunders turned, closing the door, and stood in front of it while Duane pulled on his pants and took his blouse off the bed, forgetting his goddamn cap and knocking it off as he shoved his arms through the sleeves. Duane bent to pick up his cap, cursing himself. He was worse than a stupid recruit. What the hell was the commander doing here anyway? The admiral's *aide*. Duane was finally ready, standing easy in front of the bed, facing the commander with his legs apart, his hands clasped behind him, holding his cap.

"Yes, sir. Did you want me?" The commander stayed right there at the door. Christ, he was *huge*.

"Have you seen Lieutenant Murdoch?"

"The lieutenant? Sure. Yes, sir," Duane said. "We came back to Pearl together."

"Have you seen him since you came back?"

"No, sir, I haven't," Duane said.

"Have you heard from him?" Saunders asked.

"No, sir, I haven't," Duane said. "I haven't heard from anyone. I've been right here, sir, sitting right here."

"Any idea where I could find him?"

"No, sir, I don't," Duane said. " 'Scuse me, sir, is something wrong? With the lieutenant, I mean."

"I need some information," Saunders said. "Maybe you can help me, York."

"I'll sure try, sir," Duane said.

"Who was with you when you tied those three lads to trees and whipped them?"

Duane got so scared he thought he would pass out. His whole insides turned over. He felt like he didn't weigh anything, like he was floating. "York?"

Duane said, "Sir . . ." and stopped because he couldn't catch his breath. He said, "I . . . " and stopped again.

"You and who else?" Saunders asked.

"Sir, I . . ." Duane said, and shook his head. "I didn't . . ." he said, shaking his head. "You've got it wrong, sir."

"How many of you were there?" Saunders asked, standing at the door.

"Sir, honest," Duane said. "I swear. Sir, I swear. I swear on my mother. May God strike me dead, sir, right here where I stand."

"God," Saunders said.

"That's right, sir," Duane said. "May God Almighty strike me dead if I'm lying to you. I don't know anything about any whipping, that whipping, sir."

"You're positive, aren't you, York?"

"Yes, sir," Duane said, nodding. "It's a mistake, sir. You're . . . somebody's making a mistake. I admit I was with the lieutenant when he . . . that morning at Windward. I was with him right from the start, from the minute we picked up Joseph Liliuohe. *I* picked him up, sir. It was me who jumped out of the car. I did that, yes, sir," Duane said, talking a mile a minute, trying not to keel over, he was so scared. "This here's something else," he said, shaking his head once more. "*Kidnapping. Whipping.* It's a mistake, sir, Commander." He saw the commander reach into his pocket for an envelope. He could see the open flap of the envelope. The commander took out a sheet of paper and unfolded it.

" 'I hereby absolve Duane York and the others of any and all responsibilities in the kidnapping and flogging of David Kwan, Michael Yoshida, and Harry Pohukaina,' " said Saunders, reading from Gerald's letter to the admiral. " 'Neither Duane York nor any of the others are guilty of this act and should not be held liable for the consequences, either from civilian legal sources, or from the Department of the Navy,' " Saunders said, continuing to read. " 'I, the undersigned, conceived and executed the abduction of the three individuals named above. Duane York and the others followed my orders. They are as innocent as the victims.' " Saunders looked up at Duane. "Signed, Gerald Murdoch, Lieutenant, j.g., U.S.N.," Saunders said.

Duane thought he would bust out bawling. The lieutenant must've gone crazy. He was loco. "Sir, I don't mean any disrespect, sir," Duane said. "I don't believe it, sir. I don't believe the lieutenant wrote that, sir. No, sir." Duane was afraid he would wet his pants.

"He wrote it," Saunders said, folding Gerald's letter. "He sent it to the admiral." Saunders slipped the letter into the envelope.

"Sir . . . Commander . . . Someone's making a big mistake here," Duane said.

"The others," Saunders said. *"The others.* I want their names."

"Sir, you're wrong," Duane said. "I swear you're wrong, sir. Listen . . ." he said, and stopped, because he could not go on, he could not find words.

"You've got ten seconds," Saunders said.

"Sir, wait," Duane said. "Sir, listen." Duane was ready to fall down on his knees. He was ready to do anything. "Sir, Lieutenant Murdoch, he's . . . 'Scuse me, sir, he must've gone crazy. Something must've happened to him, the trial and all, sir. Everything he said . . . I mean, nothing he said in that letter is true, sir. There ain't, isn't, one word in it that's true, sir. Lieutenant Murdoch knows that better than anybody, *would* if he wasn't crazy, sir." Duane saw the commander step away from the door. "Sir, it's not true!" The commander seemed to get bigger every step he took. "It's not *true!*" The commander seemed to blot out the light in the room. Duane moved back and felt the bed against his legs. The commander was right on top of him. Duane raised his arms, elbows bent in front of him, hiding his face with his fists.

Saunders slapped away Duane's arms, raising his right hand over his shoulder and swinging, putting his entire body into the blow as he hit Duane with the back of his hand.

The blow made a dull thud, driving Duane sideways to his left. He hit the foot of the bed and spun into the chest of drawers, caroming off and slamming into the wall. Duane cried out. There was a ringing in his ears and in his head. He could feel the pain inside his mouth. He could see the commander coming, and he turned, crying, trying to hide, but the commander shoved his hand into Duane's chest, propping him up against the wall. "You've got ten seconds."

"Sir, I'm innocent!"

"Eight."

"I didn't do it!" Duane said. "I never came near those guys!"

"Five," Saunders said. "Four . . . three . . ."

"Forrest Kinselman," Duane said. His head fell forward, and he spoke to the floor. "Wesley Trask. Conrad Hensel."

"All from the *Bluegill?*" Saunders asked.

"Yes, sir," Duane said. Saunders released him, crossing the room and opening the door. The two shore patrolmen whom Saunders had left in the corridor came to attention.

"Forrest Kinselman, Wesley Trask, Conrad Hensel," said

Saunders. He repeated the names, pausing after each vowel, as one of the shore patrolmen wrote on a small pad.

Moments earlier, in headquarters, the admiral had given Saunders the letter from Gerald. When Saunders finished reading it, the admiral had sunk into a chair. He had become an aged man.

"Partridge," said the admiral. "Murdoch. Now York and the others. How many others?" He looked up at his aide and rose. "Jimmy, I've disgraced my command."

"No, sir," Saunders said, and, louder, "No, sir! You haven't sir. You've stood up for your men, sir, your officers and men, and they've stabbed you in the back. *They've* disgraced us, sir, disgraced the Navy. We'll clean this up, Admiral," Saunders said. He pushed Gerald's letter into his pocket. "We'll fumigate this base fast."

Now, in the doorway of Duane's room, Saunders watched the two shore patrolmen leave to pick up the three vermin, and then turned to the fourth.

"Put on your cap," Saunders told Duane. "It's the last time you'll wear it or the uniform. You're out of the Navy, you scum. D.D."

Much earlier, around lunchtime that same day, the princess lay on a chaise beside the open doors to the penthouse terrace in her bedroom in the Western Sky. She was oblivious to the billowing curtains that the breeze from the sea filled and transformed into sails. Her feet were bare and the right ankle, swollen and discolored, was bound with an elastic bandage. There was a telephone on the floor and a thick cane lay against the chaise. Tom stood in the doorway to the terrace, his mind a jumble, seeing Sarah, frightened and bursting into the kitchen that Sunday morning when it all began; seeing Joe and the other three in police headquarters; seeing Joe in the morgue and trying to keep Sarah away from what he had seen.

"I should have more sense," the princess said. "I'm twice as old." She reached for the cane. "I said to come on up and we'll celebrate. Thomas. *Thomas!*"

He turned away from the sea. "How about some lunch? I'll have them send us a feast," she said.

"I'm not very hungry."

"I am, and I'm tired of eating alone." She pointed the cane at him. "Listen to me, boy. The show is over. We have to live our lives. I've got a ranch, and you've got an office. A law office.

And a girl. Think of something tasty. I'll order it for you." The telephone rang.

The district attorney was in his office in the courthouse, alone. "It's Phil Murray," he said.

"You did good, Philip," she said. "Come on out to the big island and I'll roast something."

"Yeah." The goddamn psoriasis was killing him. "Look, I figured you might as well hear it from me. The governor commuted their sentences."

"Say it again. In plain English."

"They're free!" Murray said. "They're free!" The princess raised the cane and swung, hitting the floor as though a snake lay coiled and about to strike. She listened to Murray without speaking again.

Tom saw the princess slip the telephone receiver into the cradle and let the cane fall to the floor. She did not look up. "That was Phil Murray," she said, and told him.

"Free?" Tom's voice was an ascending howl of anguish and rage. He came toward the princess and was trapped by the flying curtains. For a moment he was helpless, arms flailing as he tried to escape, giving way to a rage that was blinding. He fought his way out. The princess, who held the telephone on her belly, lay motionless. She was an intruder, she had violated his private despair. Tom could not face her, face anyone. He had to run and remembered, as though it was the ultimate defeat, that he could never run. Dragging his foot, he left the bedroom as the princess called to him, ordering him to stay.

In the corridor he stopped beside a fire extinguisher on the wall, his chest heaving as though he had been chased and had miraculously escaped. But he had not escaped. They were free! Tom heard footsteps and looked up to see a young couple, their arms around each other. They stopped at the elevators. Tom followed them, pulling at his shirt cuffs, entering the elevator behind the pair and pushing himself into a corner. The ride to the lobby was interminable. The elevator was filled with voices, light and cheerful, as visitors to the islands made and discarded plans for the day and evening. There was no word of the trial, of the defendants, of their crime, of the sentence imposed on them by Judge Kesselring. Tom wanted to scream for silence so he could tell them of the governor's treachery, tell them murder was free in Hawaii.

He was the last one out of the elevator. The lobby was a kaleidoscope of colors and voices. To Tom they were all traitors, all enemies, all part of the vast, omnipotent conspiracy. He felt invisible to these revelers, to whom the governor's reprieve was an expected and welcome climax to an unfortunate incident. He despised them. They were all guilty.

He reached the entrance, made his way past the taxis and the cars in the motor crescent in front of the hotel, into Kalakau Avenue, and realized that while his flight had ended, he had no destination. He could not face Sarah, could not tell her they had been cheated. He thought of returning to the courthouse, but he couldn't join Philip Murray, couldn't add his voice to the meaningless epithets hurled at the governor. Tom couldn't go home, could not face his father and mother, could not listen to their futile protests over the governor's treachery. He could not roam the streets, and it was the overpowering need to be alone, totally, the need to hide, that led him to his office.

He came up the steep flight of steps, feeling a great weariness all through him. He stopped at the head of the stairs and took his keys from his pocket. The sheet of yellow lined paper with the words, BACK AT FOUR. LEAVE MESSAGES, barren as always, infuriated him. Tom's arm shot out, pulled the paper from the door. "What messages?" he said. He entered his office, shutting out the world at last, and closed the door, locking and testing it. He dropped into his chair. There was a heavy, stale smell in the office. The faint sounds of traffic below seemed miles off. Tom was alone at last.

At the first ring of the telephone Tom knew Sarah was calling, knew the princess had told her. There were four rings before the phone became quiet once more. He felt sleepy. He thought of stretching out on the desk or on the sisal rug his mother had brought for the floor. He sat back, closing his eyes, and was completely alert and in torment.

Later, as he heard footsteps, Tom knew Sarah was on her way. He heard her heels on the landing before she knocked. "Tom?" She knocked again. "Tommy? If you're there, let me in. Please, Tommy." She remained at the door for a long time before leaving. He listened to her footsteps fading, contemptuous of himself for his behavior. He sprang up, rushing to the windows and raising the curtains. He had to blink in the hard sunshine as he tried to open the window. It didn't budge. He unlocked it and pushed up. She was gone.

The office was bright with sunlight, and he could see the walls of dust rising from the floor. He decided to clean his desk and opened a drawer but closed it without even looking for the dust cloths his mother had provided. He didn't need a clean office.

No one was retaining Thomas Halehone. "Lawyer," he said, aloud, his voice hollow with surrender.

He did not speak again. The phone remained silent. No one else climbed the stairs. There was only the sound of an occasional car horn until he heard the newsboys. Tom went back to the open window and listened to the cries of, "They're free!" and, "Governor commutes judge's sentence!" and, "Doris Ashley and Murdoch freed by governor!" As a newsboy came down the middle of the street, weaving between the cars, Tom could read the giant headline across the front page. "GOVERNOR FREES MURDER TRIO!" said the banner in the *Outpost-Dispatch*. Tom remained at the windows as though forced to pay penance, watching the newsboy until he could no longer be seen or heard. The telephone rang until he was ready to pull the wires out of the wall. When it stopped, he sat down once more, and, mercifully, fell asleep.

An insistent knocking woke him. The sun was gone and there were shadows in the office. "Sarah!" Tom was overcome with gratitude. He sprang up as though he had recovered from a long fever, and, approaching the door to apologize, heard a child. "Mommy, where are we?"

There was another knock. "Mr. Halehone? Are you there, Mr. Halehone?" asked a woman. Tom heard the child say, "Mommy," and the woman, "Shshshshshshsh." Tom straightened his tie and opened the door.

There were two children with the woman, and Tom could see, even in the diminishing light, the strain in her face. She had one of the children, a boy with blond hair like her hair, in her arms. The other boy was pushing against her leg for safety in the strange place. "I'm Mary Sue Puana," she said. "Dr. Puana's wife. Dr. Puana? From Mercy *Hospital?*"

"In the *emergency* room?" Tom asked, and Mary Sue nodded.

"Can I come in?" Tom discovered he was blocking the doorway. He moved aside and Mary Sue said, "Eric," and reached for him, putting her hand on his tousled black hair and moving him ahead of her. Tom closed the door and swung around.

"These chairs are kind of dusty," Tom said. "No, they *are* dusty." He opened the desk drawer for the dust cloths and bent over the chairs beside the desk, wiping the seats and then the backs of each. "I haven't been here much," he said. "I haven't been here at all, really. Neither has anyone else."

"Eric, you sit there. These are my children. This is Eric. He's almost six. This is Jonathan. He'll be two years old on the Fourth of July," she said. "Ha, ha."

So Tom finally had a client. But he didn't want her to retain him. She had brought her boys, so she must have decided to divorce Dr. Puana. Tom didn't know anything about divorce. He didn't know whom to recommend. "Is this a legal matter?"

"Is this a legal matter? Oh, it's legal, all right," Mary Sue said. She moved Jonathan, setting him in her lap. "Lying is legal, isn't it? Under oath? Isn't that what you call perjury, lying on the witness stand?"

"Perjury, yes," Tom said. He had the dust cloths in his hand. Tom dropped them into the drawer and pushed it shut. He felt a knot in his belly, high up, under his ribs. Tom pulled his chair away from the desk and sat down to face Mary Sue. "Why did you come here, Mrs. Puana?"

"You can call me Mary Sue," she said. "In fact, I want you to call me Mary Sue. I'm one of you now. So are my children, my sons." She kissed Jonathan's hair. "Jonathan is one of you, and so is Eric. Frank . . . I can thank my husband. It didn't have to be this way. We could have gone home, to my home in the States. I begged him to leave. He promised he would but . . . he didn't."

Tom didn't want to rush her, didn't want to upset her. But he couldn't keep quiet. She had said *perjury*, and Tom had heard lies, been immersed in lies, trapped by lies, for so long he could not let her continue her autobiography. "You are talking about perjury."

"Perjury," said Mary Sue. "Yes, perjury. Today did it. The final straw. First I heard on the radio they were sentenced to ten years. It didn't sound like much for murder, but at least they were going to prison. They were going to pay for their crimes. The next thing I heard the governor pardoned them."

"Commuted their sentence," Tom said.

"They're free!" Mary Sue said. "Kids came down the block yelling, 'Extra! They're free!' I was doing the ironing and I thought, 'After everything they did, they can go anywhere, but I can't.' I thought, " 'I'm the one in prison.' "

"I want to go home," Eric said. Mary Sue put her arm around him, pulling him close.

"Pretty soon, sweetie," she said. She looked at Tom and spoke as though they were in church. "I'm scaring him," Mary Sue said. "I'm a nurse, was, I should know better, and I'm scaring my own child."

Tom gave her a minute. "Mrs. Puana? Mary Sue," he said, and slowly, quietly, "Who committed perjury?"

"They all did," Mary Sue said. "Hester Ashley. She lied on the witness stand. Doris Ashley lied on the witness stand. Claude Lansing, *Dr.* Claude Lansing, lied. Frank, the gutless wonder, lied." Tom's heart was pounding. He was shaking, his hands were trembling. He was afraid to stop her but he had to make notes.

"Let me get a pad and a pen, Mrs. . . . Mary Sue," Tom said, leaning back and pulling at the desk drawer, nearly pulling it out of the desk. Christ!

"Go ahead," said Mary Sue. She bent over Eric. "I won't be long, honey." Tom had a legal-size pad and a pen, and was writing fast. "Tell me when you're ready."

Tom nodded, writing. "Ready," he said.

"Hester Murdoch said she was raped by those four kids, and six weeks later, when her period was thirty-two days late—you can check the dates—she was back in Mercy for a D. and C. Dilation and curettage. I'll spell it," said Mary Sue, and did. "The newspaper said it was because of the rape, six weeks after the rape." Mary Sue stopped, and Tom stopped writing and looked up at her. "She was really twelve weeks into term, twelve weeks pregnant. She was three months pregnant." Tom forgot the pad.

"Can you prove it?" Tom asked.

"Frank did it," Mary Sue said. "Claude Lansing set it up, but he's too drunk to slice bread. He scrubbed in and stood beside Frank. He told Frank he was the surgeon of record, but he even lied about that. He watched Frank and then he went back to his office and told the newspaper the lies. Seven to eight weeks!"

Tom threw the legal pad and pen on his desk as he came out of the chair. "Why didn't your husband go to the police? Why didn't he go to the district attorney? He could have told *me!* He could have told *anyone!*" Mary Sue looked straight at Tom.

"He didn't," she said.

"None of this would have happened!" Tom said. "He could have stopped it! Stopped everything! Joe would still be *alive!*"

Mary Sue shifted Jonathan and took Eric's hand. "We're going home now, sweetie," she said. "Why do you think I came?"

"I'm going to subpoena you *and* your husband," Tom said. "I'm going to subpoena all of you!"

"I'm ready," Mary Sue said. "Open the door, please." Tom obeyed and as she left he was already on his way to the telephone, forgetting his limp. He felt like yelling, like sticking his head out of the window and yelling. He had to tell Philip Murray! Tom had a town full of perjurers to subpoena! Philip Murray wouldn't believe what he heard. Tom would make him believe it. He had Mary Sue. The district attorney didn't answer.

Tom assumed he had been given a wrong number. He tried again. There was no answer. He was about to call the operator and ask for help when he noticed the soft glow of the street lamps on his windows. Tom looked at his wristwatch. The courthouse had been closed for two hours.

Tom called information and asked for Philip Murray's home telephone number. There was no listing for Philip Murray. Tom asked for Leslie McAdams. "He's had a hell of a time," McAdams said. "Can't it wait?"

"I need his number," Tom said. "I need it." He bent over the desk to put it down beside the notes he had made.

There was no answer. Tom went to the windows and stood for a time like someone beginning to relax after a long day. Then, as though an alarm had sounded, he reached up to close the window he had opened earlier. He came back to his desk and removed the pages with his notes from the legal pad and stuffed them into his jacket pocket, his movements hurried and almost frantic. He left his office and clattered recklessly down the stairs. He had to tell Sarah. He had to tell the princess. He had to be at the courthouse when it opened, *before* it opened. How would he ever be able to make it until tomorrow morning?

Friday morning, the next morning, Sarah and Tom left Papakolea early. "Last night I wished the doctor's wife hadn't come to your office," Sarah said. "I thought everything was finished, the governor finished it."

"We're just *starting!*" Tom said as though Sarah had challenged him, as though she were an adversary. The high spirits, the elation approaching euphoria that Mary Sue's appearance had provoked, was replaced by an urgency that could not be denied. The governor's commutation, the knowledge that Gerald Murdoch and Doris Ashley and Duane York were *free*, had to be countered. The governor had won over justice. Tom could not accept the defeat. If Sarah's car had broken down, he would have crawled to the courthouse.

"We've never had a day to ourselves, a single day from morning to night alone," Sarah said.

"We will," Tom said, automatically. He looked at her. "We will, Sarah." She was silent, driving as though he wasn't there.

When she stopped in front of the courthouse, Tom smiled at her. "Don't be so sad."

"They ruined our lives!" Sarah said, her voice a shrill cry of grief.

He said, "Sarah . . ." taking her hand, but she pulled free, holding the streering wheel and looking ahead. Tom left the car and stood at the curb watching the saucy black and yellow convertible until it turned the corner. He was alone as he came up the broad entrance, and over and over again as he walked to the doors he heard Sarah. "They ruined our lives! They ruined our lives! They ruined our lives!" Tom walked to the district attorney's office like an assassin.

He arrived ahead of the secretaries. He turned up the lights and went to a desk for a telephone. He had memorized Philip Murray's home number. There was no answer. As Tom waited, listening to ring after ring, the district attorney came through the door. "I was just calling you," Tom said, moving between the desks to reach Murray. "I've been calling since yesterday. Your phone must be out of order."

"We weren't home," Murray said. "We were on the boat." Murray's sloop was his great love. "I was all set to shove off for the weekend when my wife got a toothache. I wouldn't be here otherwise. I dropped her off at the dentist." Tom followed Murray into his office. "That spineless toad," he said of the governor. Murray fell back in his chair. "What's eating you, anyway?"

"You have to set a date for retrial in the Hester Murdoch case," Tom said.

"Yeah, yeah," Murray said. "I will." Tom stepped back and made room for Murray to pass.

"Go ahead."

"Go *ahead?*" Murray sat up. "It's not twenty-four hours since I left court! I can't see straight!"

"All I'm asking for is a date," Tom said.

"What in the pluperfect hell is the big rush?"

"I've got new evidence," Tom said. While the State is required, on motion, to provide the defense in a criminal action with a complete inventory of evidence, a procedure known as discovery, the reverse is not true. The defense does not share its case.

"Fine, fine. Hold on to it," Murray said. Tom didn't move.

"Put it on the docket," Tom said.

Murray pushed back his chair. He thought of the sloop tied up, the food he had bought for the weekend in his refrigerator at home. "Look . . . Counselor . . . Let me catch my breath,"

Murray said. "Why the goddamn rush? Why does it have to be today?"

"Because of what the governor did *yesterday*," Tom said. He was hanging over the district attorney. "He said you can kill any of us and walk out free. Not only free but a hero. Gerald Murdoch is a *hero!* Have you seen the papers? The stories from the States? They're talking about Murdoch like he was Lindbergh! They don't believe we're human! They come over here and sit in the sand on Waikiki and eat the suckling pig and go home to tell their friends about the jungle! That's why the retrial has to go on the docket today! Today!"

Philip Murray rubbed his eyes. "My wife's toothache," he said, coming out of the chair. Tom followed him out of the office. "I'll call you."

"I'll wait right here," Tom said. He leaned against an unoccupied desk, facing the door. The district attorney was gone for almost thirty minutes. As he returned, Tom came away from the desk.

"April twentieth," Murray said. "Neil Ostergren's court."

"Thanks," Tom said. He was in a hurry. "Thanks," he said, passing Murray.

Tom used the stairs to the basement. The temporary press room in the corridor was almost deserted. Telephone repairmen were removing the instruments that had been installed for the murder trial. The long tables were being dismantled. Here and there reporters using portable typewriters were at work on wrap-up stories for their newspapers' Sunday editions. Tom saw the beat men from the *Outpost-Dispatch* and the *Islander* who were assigned to the courthouse. He told them the date for the retrial. Neither moved.

"There's important new evidence," Tom said. The reporter from the *Islander* took out a pack of cigarettes and turned away. "Okay, I'll tell the Associated Press," Tom said. The reporter took the unlighted cigarette out of his mouth.

"Hey, hold it," he said. "What kind of evidence?"

"*Medical*," Tom said. "*Medical* evidence. And evidence of perjury. *Perjury!*" Tom said. The reporter pulled a sheaf of copy paper out of his pocket and the man from the *Outpost-Dispatch* said, "Go ahead."

"It'll all come out at the trial," Tom said. He hurried back to the stairs.

In his office Tom called the Associated Press and then the United Press. He called the foreign language newspapers. He called every radio station in Honolulu. He was perspiring. Tom looked up. He hadn't opened the windows. He left his desk, and when he was standing in the welcome breeze, he took the sheets of notes he had made the day before from his pockets. Turning his back to the sun, Tom read again what he had written while Mary Sue had sat in his office the day before. Tom decided she would be his first witness.

About one o'clock that day, Doris Ashley returned to her bedroom. She had a slight headache. Doris was still in her peignoir, still luxuriating in the discovery of her freedom. The arrival at Windward, finding it intact and serene, had made her profligate with her emotions. She and Hester had dined from trays on the terrace, and long after Hester was asleep in her own bedroom beside the master suite, Doris Ashley had roamed through the house. That morning, waking early, careful not to disturb Hester, she had hurried downstairs to discover it afresh.

She had been almost euphoric, safe and secure once more. Then, just before nine o'clock, Amelia had answered the telephone. "He says, 'Commander Saunders.' "

Doris Ashley never wanted to hear from or of the Navy as long as she lived. "Hello."

"Mrs. Ashley, this is Commander Saunders. Is Lieutenant Murdoch there?" Doris Ashley could trace her headache to the telephone call.

"Lieutenant Murdoch no longer resides at Windward." Doris Ashley said.

"Excuse me, madame," Saunders said. "We're trying to find Lieutenant Murdoch. He could have come for his car, for his clothes."

"He is not here," Doris Ashley said. She replaced the receiver. "Theresa!" When the kitchen door swung open, Doris said, "No more calls." Later today she would take Theresa and Amelia to the carriage house where they would pack Gerald's belongings and remove every trace of him.

Doris Ashley closed the door of her bedroom and went to her bed. She lifted the lid of her cigarette box but replaced it. A cigarette would exacerbate her headache. Doris Ashley shut her eyes, intent on blotting out the world, and heard a car in the driveway. No one she knew would dare arrive at Windward without calling first. She heard, faintly, the doorbell. Amelia and Theresa had been ordered to turn away anyone who appeared, from tradesmen to reporters. In a moment there was a single, quick knock and then Theresa's face was in the doorway. "Admiral here."

Doris Ashley rose from the bed as though she had been yanked out of it. "I told you . . . !" she said, and became speechless with rage.

"I told *him*," said Theresa, her head bobbing up and down.

"Send him away!" said Doris Ashley. "Close the door! Lock the door!"

"He's inside," said Theresa. "He says, very important." Doris Ashley seemed about to strike the short, pudgy woman in uniform, but she didn't move. When she raised her hand to close the bedroom door, she didn't see Theresa. She saw the courthouse where she had been, she truly believed, imprisoned for week after week. She saw, she *heard*, Judge Kesselring pronouncing sentence. Doris Ashley crossed the bedroom, her rage giving way to apprehension. She had never flinched, not even before her father in the Bronx apartment she had hated. Doris Ashley did not flinch now.

She took two aspirins and in her dressing room selected her clothes for the encounter. She did not hurry, and when she was at the head of the stairs, she stopped for a moment and remembered the sight of the detective, Maddox, below, waiting to tell her Hester was in Mercy Hospital. She remembered riding to the hospital with the detective, and she remembered Hester's mutilated face and her daughter's confession. Doris Ashley had not faltered during that first catastrophic night, nor once since. She reached for the banister. Nothing could be worse.

When Doris Ashley reached the foot of the stairs, she was ready. She was in *her* quarters now, not his. At Windward she was in command. She entered the living room and saw the admiral beside the long mahogany table flanking the Chinese screens. "I'm not accustomed to uninvited guests."

The admiral watched her still trying to play the empress. She wasn't worth the reward he had brought. Late that morning the admiral had heard from the Coast Guard commandant in Honolulu. One of his cutters, alerted by Billy Finch, whose boat Gerald had chartered, had found two life preservers far out to sea. "The owner claims he didn't realize it was Murdoch until the boat was overdue," said the commandant.

The admiral sent for his aide. "You can stop looking for Murdoch," the admiral told Saunders, and repeated his conversation with the commandant. "That leaves the enlisted man . . . Hensel. Any sign of him?"

The previous afternoon, after Duane had told Saunders everything, the Shore Patrol had picked up Forrest Kinselman and Wesley Trask. But Conrad Hensel had left Pearl Harbor on a weekend liberty. So Saunders had locked Duane and the other two in separate cells in the brig. He had posted a heavy guard, leaving orders that the three were to be kept apart, fed in their cells, and accompanied individually to the head. Jimmy Saunders didn't want word of their confinement reaching Conrad Hensel. Saunders wanted Hensel reporting back from liberty by reveille Monday. "No, sir, not yet," Saunders said. He intended to personally deliver the four scum to police headquarters.

"Tell me when Hensel appears," the admiral said.

"Yes, sir," Saunders said. "Sir, there's more. It's the rape case. Their lawyer says he has new evidence." Saunders had heard of the retrial from a radio news report.

"Jimmy, it's time for me to do my own fumigating," said the admiral.

In Windward, as Doris Ashley reached the mahogany table, the admiral said, "This isn't a social call. Let's not waste energy fencing. I've learned of more trouble, but I don't intend to wait for it."

All the resolutions she had made while she dressed, all the courage she had summoned at the head of the stairs, deserted Doris Ashley. "Tell me. Tell me quickly."

She had not mentioned Murdoch so the admiral knew she had heard nothing. It made his task easier. "I've sent one of your women to fetch Hester," the admiral said.

"Tell me now," said Doris Ashley. "*Now!*"

"I should have listened to Walter Bergman in the governor's office yesterday," the admiral said. "He finally made sense. Bergman warned us about a new trial. It begins April twentieth. Their lawyer has important medical evidence. He claims he has evidence of perjury. He sounds like he knows everything. I followed that boy's tactics for weeks during Hester's trial. He isn't bluffing. He certainly isn't coming back into court to put the defendants in jail. The defendants are his clients, his friends. You'll go to jail. You and Hester. And the senators in Washington and the President will have another cause to rile them up. This island will become a battleground. We can't wait for April twentieth. You won't be here April twentieth. You won't be here tomorrow night."

"Won't—"

"Listen to the rest," he said. "You and Hester are sailing tomorrow on the S.S. *Lotus*." The admiral had personally booked the two adjoining cabins. The admiral had sealed off Pearl Harbor, land and sea, before leaving for Windward. Navy launches, carrying searchlights for the night, patrolled the approaches to

Pearl. Any vehicle owned by an officer or enlisted man would be searched before entering. No civilian was to be permitted until Saunders personally came to the Shore Patrol station at the base entrance and approved the man or woman. "You can spend the night in my quarters," the admiral said. Once they were at Pearl, completely secured from intrusion, he would tell them about poor Murdoch.

"In your quarters," Doris Ashley said. "I am never leaving Windward again."

"Their lawyer asked for the retrial," the admiral said. "He told the reporters. He had the medical evidence, the evidence of perjury."

Doris Ashley opened her arms wide. "Look around you," she said. "You've traveled. You've sailed the seven seas. This is *Windward!* You tell me to leave *Windward* because of some one-legged sewer rat?"

The admiral knew and no one else, not even Jimmy Saunders, knew that Doris Ashley was sailing for the Mainland within twenty-four hours, willingly or not. If she pushed him, the admiral would send Jimmy Saunders with enough men to carry her out. She would be under guard until the S.S. *Lotus* dropped the pilot beyond Diamond Head the next day. The admiral had decided there would be no more cables from SECNAV, no more headlines with threats from Senator Floyd Rasmussen and his cutthroats in Washington. The admiral was never spending another day on his butt on a hard bench in a Honolulu courtoom. If Doris Ashley raised enough hell over her departure, if SECNAV challenged him, the admiral had decided to resign. The thought of being out of uniform was intolerable but he could no longer exercise a command that was dominated by civilians. "Oh, Hester. Hello," he said, as she entered from the kitchen. "You're wondering why I sent for you." The admiral repeated everything he had told Doris Ashley.

"I suppose I should pack," Hester said. She turned away but Doris Ashley took her arm, stopping her.

"I forbid it!" said Doris Ashley. "We are not packing! We are not leaving Windward!"

"You have no choice," said the admiral. "Leave now, or leave after the retrial. You're free now. You won't be when that lawyer is finished." The admiral was ready to call for Jimmy Saunders and the S.P. but he saw Doris Ashley's arm fall, saw her release Hester. "Take only what you need for the voyage," said the admiral. "Everything else can be sent."

"What I'll need for the voyage," Hester said. She crossed the living room to the kitchen and crossed the kitchen to the outside door. Hester came down the steps and bent double, far below the kitchen windows. She remained doubled up until she was almost at the crescent driveway in front of Windward. The admiral's driver was stretched out in the front seat of the limousine, his head against the window. Hester stayed behind the car, on the grass. As she reached the open gates leading into Kahala Avenue, she began to run. She could not sail away with her mother, remain with her mother. She could not be a nurse in the States. She had to deliver her penance here, in Hawaii.

In the living room the admiral said, "The sooner you're at Pearl, the better. You're safe there."

Doris Ashley could not give up. "If Hester leaves, there can't be a trial," she said, choosing Windward.

"They'll still have you," said the admiral. "That lawyer will be twice as hard on you. You won't last under his battering." Doris Ashley turned away, running away, but the admiral stayed with her, following her to the terrace.

Doris Ashley spoke to the sea. "You're telling me to come away with you, to sail away tomorrow. My mind cannot accept it. What will become of me when I *know* I'll never again see Windward?" Doris Ashley turned to the admiral. "Kill me and end my misery."

"I'll call your maids. They can help you pack." Neither he nor Doris Ashley had used the other's name.

Almost two hours later, in police headquarters, Maddox returned from a late and solitary lunch and heard his phone ringing as he reached the door of his office. "The chief wants to see you, Captain," said the uniformed policeman who was Leonard Fairly's secretary. "Right away."

Maddox dropped his hat on his desk. He had not been in the chief's office since the day of Joseph Liliuohe's murder when Leonard Fairly had surrendered Doris Ashley and the lieutenant and the sailor to Commander Saunders. He had seen the chief twice, once in the garage and once in the lobby, but Fairly had turned away both times.

The chief sat at his desk. He looked up but he did not greet Maddox, who stopped behind a chair, resting his elbows on the back. Maddox would have waited silently until morning. "We've got a serious problem," the chief said. "Hester Murdoch is missing." Maddox was suddenly very tired. He came around the chair and sat down.

"Her again," Maddox said. "When did she turn up missing?"

"Around lunchtime," said the chief. "Around one o'clock."

"She could have taken a walk," Maddox said. "She could have fallen asleep in the woods or on a beach. She could be locked in her room because she wants to be alone. She's been living in a crowd since last fall. She's also a little cracked in the head."

"She's missing," the chief said. "Drop whatever it is you're doing and find her. Time is important here."

Maddox didn't move. "What happened to the missing persons bureau? Why didn't you put them on it?"

"Because I'm putting *you* on it," said the chief. He picked up his letter opener. "I'm ordering you to find her. And keep it to yourself. This is confidential." Maddox crossed his legs.

"Hester Murdoch is gone. I'm supposed to dig her up, fast. All hush-hush. You ought to let me in on the secret."

"I told you she's gone," the chief said. He pointed the letter opener at Maddox. "You're wasting time."

"One of us is," Maddox said, and raised his hand wearily as though he intended to pull a handkerchief from his sleeve. "You haven't told me anything."

"I've told you she's missing!" said the chief. "I've told you to find her! Are you going to obey?"

Maddox leaned forward like an exhausted athlete on a bench in the locker room. He rose as slowly. "Instead of making this another showdown, do yourself a favor," Maddox said. "If I walk out of here now, I'll be driving around town watching the people on the street. Hester Murdoch is gone. One reason could be the new trial I read about a little while ago. But it's set for April twentieth, a long way away. So there's more. You know more. Somebody told you she was missing. Why? Somebody told you time is important? Why? Why is it confidential?" Maddox paused. "Do I get the story?" Maddox paused once more. "Suit yourself," he said, and turned, buttoning his jacket.

"All right, yes," said the chief, and, louder, "Yes, I said." Maddox stopped at the corner of the desk. "The admiral called." He repeated everything he had learned from the admiral.

"Sailing tomorrow," Maddox said. The chief rose, pushing his chair back to come around the desk.

"No one must know. I swore to the admiral. What you just heard can't leave this office."

"I'll need some help," Maddox said. "At least one."

For a moment the chief was silent, and then he capitulated. "Who?"

"Al Keller," Maddox said.

"Do you trust him?" Maddox looked across the desk.

"He's the only man in the department I *do* trust," Maddox said.

He was in his office, standing over the long wooden table with his hands on an open street map, when Keller appeared. Maddox had told him to get out of uniform, and the redhead was wearing the cast-off clothes he had used for the stakeout in Pacific Heights. "What've you got, Captain?"

"Hester Ashley," Maddox said. "She's on the loose."

"Running away from the retrial?" Keller asked.

Maddox grinned. "You'll never make chief," he said. "You're not dumb enough." He straightened up, arching his back. "You better hear the rest of it," Maddox said. When Maddox finished, he folded the map in half. "I'll take everything to the Punchbowl. You handle what's west of it. We'll cover every hotel, boarding-house, flop joint in town. Take your own car. If she does check in somewhere, she'll use another name and she'll pay a lot. So you'll have to convince the guy or the woman to level with you. Convince them. If you find her, you keep her. If it takes handcuffs, use handcuffs. Bring her back here." He rapped the table with his knuckles. "Right here."

As Keller left, Maddox took off his jacket. He dropped it on the table and went to his desk. Maddox opened the telephone book. He didn't expect to hear any lies after he identified himself. Maddox began with the Western Sky. She was just dumb enough to show up there. "Arnold Klemeth," Maddox said, and when he had the assistant manager, he said. "Do this yourself and don't waste my time with questions. I'm looking for Hester Ashley Murdoch. She could've checked in anytime after twelve o'clock noon."

"I'll call you back," Klemeth said.

"I have to know now," Maddox said. "Get a move on." Waiting, he turned the page of the telephone book, writing down the numbers of other Waikiki hotels.

"Maddox? No dice," Klemeth said. "No woman alone checked in today, all day."

"Right. Much obliged."

"Maddox? No woman checked in," Klemeth said, "but there's one checking out. I figured you'd like to know in case you wanted to say aloha. The Bergmans are leaving tomorrow. The old man told me they'd be . . ."

Maddox didn't hear the rest. He lowered the receiver and Klemeth's voice became a garbled, faint monotone. Maddox said, "Thanks," into the mouthpiece and hung up. He seemed frozen. Looking at the telephone numbers he had copied, he saw only Lenore. He raised his head and saw her. She was everywhere. Her face was everywhere. He could see clearly. He could hear her. She said, "Curt, Curt," softly, bringing him closer, closer still. Maddox leaped up, swinging around his desk and crossing the office as though he were under attack. He came out into the corridor and walked to the water fountain opposite the stairwell. But he did not drink. He put his hand against the cool wall to steady himself. He said, low, "Oh, Jesus," and then looked in both directions, certain he had been seen. He was alone. Maddox walked back into his office.

He remained at his desk, hunched over the telephone as though it was a life preserver, until he had called every hotel in the eastern half of Honolulu. Maddox looked at the clock. It was after five. He rose and stretched and went to the table against the wall to look down at the street map. Where was she?

Maddox returned to his desk. He called every hospital in Honolulu. He called the harbor master to ask if any drownings had been reported. He called the sheriff's office on the chance a deputy had found Hester somewhere in the county beyond the city limits. Forty-five minutes later he pushed the telephone aside, trying not to think of Lenore as he waited for Al Keller. The redhead phoned a few minutes before six o'clock. "I haven't had any luck, Captain. Anything else you want me to do?"

"Yeah, but I don't know what it is," Maddox said. "Come on in." Maddox went back to the street map. He glanced at it, shook his head, and left the office, returning to the water fountain. This time he bent to drink.

In his office Maddox sat parallel to his desk, staring at the wall. He heard the door open and turned as Keller came into the office. "Captain, this sounds crazy, but have you called missing persons?"

"The woman's people want it kept quiet," Maddox said. "The chief told me to stay away from the bureau." He arched his neck, feeling the ache across his shoulders. "Any ideas?"

Keller raised his hands and dropped them. "If it was a man, I'd have some kind of a chance," he said. Maddox tapped his fingers on the desk.

"We're nowhere," he said, and came out of his chair, moving. "Al, we're going to the movies."

In Maddox's car he said, "If there's a balcony, we'll start in the balcony. She could see men walking up and down the aisles and run for it. This is a good time. Dinnertime. The movies must be almost empty."

He parked directly in front of a theater and put the sign in the window. Keller waited for Maddox to come around the car, and they walked past the ticket booth to the lobby. Maddox raised his hand, showing the man at the door his badge. "Is there a balcony?"

"No, sir, it's just one floor. Are you after someone? Do you think he's in here?"

"Just keep doing what you're doing," Maddox said, beckoning to Keller. Two doors led to the auditorium, one at each end of the lobby. "We'll start together," Maddox said, leaving the redhead.

Inside, Maddox stayed at the door, waiting for his eyes to adjust to the darkness. On his left, across the wide center section of seats, Maddox saw Keller walking slowly down the aisle. Maddox moved forward, looking from side to side.

Keller reached the first row and, starting back, saw Maddox. Keller moved more slowly, staying abreast of Maddox as they came up the aisles. They left the auditorium and Keller turned to the street. "Al." Maddox crossed the lobby. "Let's take another look," Maddox said. "We'll switch."

Now, with his eyes accustomed to the darkness, Maddox began immediately. Keller kept pace on the other side of the center section. They reached the first row together, pygmies before the Brobdingnagian figures on the screen, turning to start back toward the lobby. Maddox was almost at the door when he brushed against someone. A woman's arm hung over the seat on the aisle. She sat sideways, her head hidden under her other arm. She was asleep. Maddox leaned forward. "Hello, Hester."

She woke refreshed. She did not resist. She heard the man say, "I'm Captain Maddox." In the theater, watching the players' antics in a collegiate farce, Hester discovered she did not need to run. If she could not escape from her mother in Honolulu, she would wait until the ship docked in America, wherever it docked. She would leave her mother on the pier, ask directions to the nearest hospital and start walking. While the scattered audience laughed at the outrageous comedy, Hester wept with gratitude and then, exhausted, fell asleep.

It was almost eight o'clock when Maddox turned into the parking lot at headquarters. "See you in the morning, Captain," Keller said. He started for his car.

"Al." The redhead stopped, turning. Maddox was in the light in front of the doors to headquarters. Keller came toward him. The captain looked awful tired.

"Do you want something, Captain?" Keller waited. "I'm in no rush." He waited. "Captain?"

"Put in for overtime," Maddox said. The redhead couldn't help him. Maddox pushed one of the doors, coming into the harsh headquarters smell. Nobody could help him because nobody was in it with him. Wherever he went from here, he went alone.

In his office, Maddox called the chief at home, telling him Hester had been delivered to the admiral. When he finished, Maddox pushed his hat back on his head. "Show's over," he said, aloud, as though he hoped to convince himself.

He remained in his chair watching the door as though on it or beyond, in the corridor, was something of profound or critical importance that he and only he could understand. "Then head for home!" he said, aloud, angry and merciless with himself. He raised his hands, dropping them on the arms of the chair like someone who has made a decision, but he didn't move. He sat facing the door for almost three hours.

It seemed to Maddox that he remembered every day of his life. He remembered when Harvey Koster had found him in the warehouse and the first time he had heard someone say he was Harvey Koster's son. Harvey Koster knew whose son Maddox was. Koster knew and now Lenore knew. Maddox was the whore's son, the hooker's son. He had been an outcast long before he ran away from his mother. He was a haole, all right, living in the haole's world, but Maddox had never lied to himself. "You never really made it anywhere," he said, aloud.

Then Maddox opened the telephone book. He turned thick sections of pages and then paused to turn a single page and a second. Maddox bent over the small type, moving his left hand down the column of names. He stopped, forefinger on the column, and with his right hand copied a number. Maddox closed the telephone book as he rose. Suddenly he was in a rush.

Maddox rode down to the darkened lobby and went to the public telephone. He dropped a nickel into the slot, and he didn't look at the number he had copied. He remembered the number. He heard a ring, he heard another. The phone rang five times before Maddox heard a sleepy, "Hello." He waited to be sure. *"Hello?"*

"This is Maddox. I'm coming by. I'm in headquarters and I'm leaving now. Put on some clothes and mosey along in about ten minutes." Maddox replaced the receiver. He took a deep breath, and another, then exhaled and said, "Yeah . . ." When he left the telephone and walked toward the parking lot and his car, Maddox was, deliberately and dangerously, leaving his old life behind.

He drove toward the Punchbowl. When he reached Papakolea, he stopped at a corner, leaning out of the window to read the street sign. Maddox was not sure of his bearings, and he turned left, guessing. He stopped at the next corner and now he was on familiar ground. Maddox turned left once more, and two blocks beyond, turned right, touching the brake. Almost all the houses were dark and the street was dark. As he approached the intersection, Maddox saw the lawyer appear in the headlights, facing the car. Maddox crossed the intersection and stopped and darkened the headlights.

Maddox pushed back his hat. He had never, even as a child, a castaway on the streets and in the alleys, made friends with one of them. He had never sat at a table with one. He had never spoken, except professionally, to a cop or a suspect, with a Hawaiian or any of the others. Maddox bought his clothes from haoles. His doctor and dentist were haoles. A haole cut his hair. Maddox's car was cared for by haoles, but as the lawyer came abreast of the small sedan, Maddox leaned across the seat and opened the door. "Get in."

When Maddox fell back behind the wheel, Tom Halehone was standing in the dirt road beside the open door, standing clear of the car.

The sight of Maddox, of the black, unmarked, and ominous sedan, the scalding memories the big man provoked, revolted Tom. Maddox was like some powerful and malevolent creature waiting to destroy anyone who came within reach. Tom hated him and himself for the fear he could not suppress. "Why did you call? Why did you come?" Tom's voice rose. "I suppose you think *we* killed Gerald Murdoch? I suppose you've got a *new* witness, someone who saw four guys come out of the water and chop a hole in his boat!" First in the *Islander* and later in the early edition of the *Outpost-Dispatch*, Tom had read the news of Gerald's disappearance again and again.

"You're making too much noise," Maddox said. "Get in."

"Tell me why you came."

"If you don't . . . no," Maddox said. He hadn't come to fight with the kid. Maddox was in Papakolea because of something between himself and himself, something he could no longer ignore, forget, submerge, or contain; something he could no longer accommodate; something he had to resolve, resolve now, tonight, here. Maddox would have followed the lawyer up a telephone pole. He took off his hat and pushed himself across the seat, leaving the car. The lawyer was wearing sandals and old cotton pants, narrow as bandages, and a scivvy shirt. He was an awful skinny kid. He looked like nothing at all. ''You picked yourself some partner,'' Maddox said to himself, and, aloud, ''You know about Murdoch. There's some things you don't know. You're losing Doris Ashley. She and Hester are heading for San Francisco tomorrow on the *Lotus*.''

''They *can't!*'' Tom said, in a piercing cry of outrage, as Maddox delivered the ultimate threat of defeat. ''They *can't!*'' he said, as though his protest, here in the darkened streets, would stop the exodus.

''They're as good as halfway to the States already,'' Maddox said. ''The admiral took over when he heard about the trial date. He's got them at Pearl. Altogether there's fifteen or sixteen hours left to stop them. I'm not sure you *can* stop them, not alone.''

''I'll subpoena both of them!'' Tom said. ''Doris Ashley and Hester Murdoch.''

''So you'll need a judge. I know a few,'' Maddox said. For the first time in his thirty-six years, Maddox was offering his hand to one of them. ''Better start early.''

Tom said, ''Okay,'' and turned away. Maddox watched him for a moment, and then walked around the rear of the car, going to the driver's side. The kid was out of the light, somewhere in the shadows. Maddox opened the car door. ''Captain!''

Maddox looked ahead, peering into the darkness. ''Captain, wait!'' He heard Tom and then he saw him. The boy with the limp who could never run was running, and when he reached the car, although he had covered less than fifty feet, Tom Halehone had come as far as Maddox. ''Thanks.''

Maddox studied the lawyer. He was really the runt of the litter. But Maddox remembered him in municipal court skinning Phil Murray and having bail reduced for the four kids Hester Murdoch had identified. Maddox had been told why the princess had posted the bail. Maddox had watched the lawyer in court during Hester's rape trial. This kid, this Tom Halehone, was the reason Maddox was standing in Papakolea. There was a line running down the middle of the island, down the middle of the Territory, like a boundary separating two countries, and it had to be removed. Maddox believed that if it wasn't removed, a lot more people than Joseph Liliuohe and Gerald Murdoch would be dead. And he believed the change would never come unless someone like this kid in the scivvy shirt had some help. This kid was worth ten of Martin Snelling, and if he had some help, he could end up in Iolani Palace one day. "Thanks, Captain," Tom said.

Maddox looked straight at him, and Tom felt as though he were being pushed back into a corner. "Don't let me down," Maddox said. Tom knew the captain was talking about a lot more than the next day. The captain was talking about the rest of Tom's life.

Lenore woke in the dark Saturday morning. She left her bed immediately, turning up all the lights and the light in the bathroom. She ran the tub and while it filled set her luggage on the bed and opened the suitcase. Lenore bathed quickly and, when she was in her robe, emptied the medicine cabinet in the bathroom, tightening caps and stoppers before setting bottles and tubes into her cosmetic case. She saw daylight through the corners of the drapes and pushed them back to open the doors of her terrace. The rising sun was hidden but the surface of the sea was tipped fiery red.

She turned away, unable to stand idle, to leave her mind idle. Lenore went to her chest of drawers, choosing jewelry for the day, slipping on a ring and selecting a necklace. She loosened her robe and opened the door of the closet. Lenore reached for a dress, but her arm fell. She had worn the dress when she was with Curt. She reached for another, but she had worn this one during a second rendezvous. She reached for a third, determined, until she pulled it out of the closet and, in the light from the terrace, recognized it as Curt's favorite. Lenore turned, blindly, crumpling the dress against her breasts and falling into a chair as she began to sob. She did not hear the first, soft knock. "Lenore?"

She saw the door open and sprang from the chair. "Wait!" She rushed into the bathroom, slipping the dress hanger over a hook. Lenore ran cold water, bathing her face, and when she emerged to admit Walter Bergman, she believed she was safely masked.

"I noticed the light under your door so I didn't think I'd be waking you," said Bergman, who saw, at first glance, that Lenore had been weeping. He was fully dressed. "I'm ready," Bergman said. "Ready to go. Rarin' to go, as they say. We can check out soon's you're ready, Lenore. Sooner the better."

"This morning?" She wasn't ready, she wasn't ready! "I'm not packed!"

"I'll have them send someone up to help," Bergman said, and quickly, "I'm rushing you for a reason. Two reasons. First, I'd feel better if I could give the reporters the slip today. There's a reward in it. The captain of the *Lotus* sent a message asking us to lunch," Bergman said, lying. Bergman had seen the captain on Thursday. Bergman told the captain he intended to board the ship early, and talked about lunch until he was invited. Bergman put his hands behind him. "This isn't the county fair we sat through coming over," he said. "We'll be alone with the captain in his cabin unless I miss my guess. Seemed to me you'd like the notion."

Lenore could not reply. She was uncomfortable and guilty. Facing her in the doorway of her bedroom was someone she had known since memory began, someone she had seen nearly every day of her life except during her college years. The man in the doorway had been her other father, and then her husband. He was her husband. Lenore knew they were leaving the hotel together, boarding the ship together, sailing away from Honolulu, from Curt, together, going home to the same home. Lenore knew she would care for him as she had cared for him. She would come when he called, do what he asked, but she had discovered, with no warning, now in the hotel they were leaving, that she had nothing to say to him. Lenore backed away as though a stranger had appeared before her, managing to nod, acknowledging the date with the captain of the *Lotus*, as she closed the door.

Bergman welcomed the closed door. He went to the telephone in his bedroom and called the registration desk. He told the clerk to send a chambermaid for his wife, and asked for room service. Bergman ordered a varied breakfast from which Lenore could choose. He did not intend to sit beside her for an hour or more in the dining room where Maddox could decide to have his Saturday breakfast.

"SECNAV FROM COMFOURTEEN. RETRIAL EMPTY THREAT. PRINCIPALS STATEBOUND UNRETURN ABOARD S.S. LOTUS. LANGDON."

In his office at Pearl Harbor the admiral read the cable he had printed in capital letters. He slipped it into his desk drawer. He intended to hold it until the *Lotus* dropped the pilot. The admiral intended to leave the ship with the pilot. The admiral left his desk, returning with a map, and as he set it down there was a knock on his door. He crossed his office, feeling a whole lot younger than he had the day before. "Hello, Jimmy."

Like the admiral, Jimmy Saunders was in a fresh white uniform and he wore a bleached web belt with a holster carrying a .45 automatic. "I haven't given you much rest, Jimmy."

"I'm glad I could help, sir," Saunders said. "It'll all be over by the end of the day."

"That's why you're here. We'll make damned sure it's over by the end of the day. You and I are plotting every move from the time we leave Pearl until the ship sails." He led Saunders to his desk. The commander saw the large map, in color, of Oahu. "I want to hoist anchor by nine o'clock."

"We're ready, sir," Saunders said. "My men will be out of chow by seven. The convoy can roll five minutes later."

"Your convoy will roll but you won't be aboard," said the admiral. "You'll be with me. We'll be with the two passengers in my launch. *We're* putting them aboard the *Lotus*, you and I. They can board from the sea. I won't let them out on the streets of this island. They've as good as left Honolulu." The admiral took a pencil with a thick, soft point and bent over the map on his desk. He put a large X across Aloha Tower. He put another in the sea at Pearl Harbor and drew an arc connecting the two Xs. "How many launches did you have on patrol last night, Jimmy?"

"I still have them, sir. Eight."

"They'll escort us," said the admiral. "There'll be no hitch in this operation.

Tom rushed out of his bedroom, barefoot and in shorts. He was certain he had overslept. He had been awake for hours after Maddox drove off the night before, thrust into a whirlpool by the captain's disclosure. They were getting away! They had killed Joe, and they had branded the others for life, but they would be gone forever unless he could block their escape. He had to stop them! Tom took his briefcase, hoping he wouldn't wake his parents as he felt his way through the darkened house to the kitchen. At the table he set down the names of all the judges he could remember. He brought the telephone book to the table and copied the numbers of those judges who were listed. He did not remember falling asleep, and when he woke, he was certain the ship was gone. "What time is it?"

"Early," said his mother. Tom's father had long since left for the beach with his fishing pole and bait pail. "Not even eight o'clock. It's Saturday. Go back to sleep." Tom hurried into his bedroom, pulling on his pants. Carrying his briefcase, he returned to the kitchen. His mother began to smile. "Did a client come?" she asked, using the word she had carefully repeated over and over until it was part of her vocabulary.

Tom shook his head. He brought another chair to the telephone and set the briefcase on it to use as a desk. "I don't have a client," Tom said. "It's—" he said, and broke off. Tom saw her turn away as though he had slapped her. "Ma." He ran after her as she crossed the kitchen. "Ma!" Tom took her arm, making her face him.

"I shouldn't bother you," she said. He wanted to plead for forgiveness.

"It's about the new trial," Tom said. There was no time! He was wasting time! "I'll tell you later," he promised. "Tonight or tomorrow." Tom kissed her on the cheek and felt her hands on his arms, unable to keep away from him.

"When your father's here, too," she said. "He likes to listen, too."

Tom went back to the telephone and called Judge Neil Ostergren, who would be presiding over the retrial. There was no answer. So Tom's best hope was forfeited at the outset. Tom gave the operator the home number of Judge Samuel Walker. "Who's calling, please?" asked the judge's wife. Tom identified himself. "He's camping on Maui," she told Tom. "He'll be gone a week." As Tom replaced the receiver, the telephone rang.

"Any luck?" Maddox asked. He was sitting on his bed, fully dressed, wearing everything including his holster with his gun.

"I've just started," Tom said.

"I've just finished," Maddox said. "Forget these guys," he said, and gave Tom the names of the judges he had called, beginning before seven o'clock and waking several. Maddox rose with the telephone and stood over the night table, looking down at the instrument in his hand as though he were interrogating a suspect. "Take my number," Maddox said, and repeated it. "I'll be here waiting."

Maddox sat down on the bed. For a little while he held the telephone and then he set it on the night table. He looked at the clock beside the telephone, and then at his wristwatch. He left the bedroom, walking through the house to the front door. He hurried across the lawn to the rolled the copy of the *Outpost-Dispatch* in his driveway. He returned to the house and began to pace, slapping the rolled newspaper against his thigh and listening for the ring of the telephone. He could not stop looking at his wrist watch.

In Papakolea Tom tried another judge. That judge refused to issue subpoenas. The next man refused. Tom watched the clock. He called another judge. Tom had two names left when Sarah hurried in. "Your line's been busy for an hour!"

Tom's mother had seen the convertible, and she came into the kitchen. "Sarah! You look so pretty!"

"I'm on the telephone!" Tom said, as though they, too, had enlisted in the conspiracy against him. It was almost nine o'clock! Tom called one of the last two judges on his list, and as Sarah listened, she crossed the kitchen to his side.

When that judge refused to issue subpoenas, Sarah knew everything. "They can't leave! How do you know they're leaving?"

Tom told her, quickly, of his meeting with Maddox the night before. Sarah watched Tom as though he had crossed the enemy lines.

"Captain Maddox!" she cried. "*Maddox!*" She was enraged. "Have you forgotten . . . ?" she said, but Tom rose, interrupting.

"I haven't forgotten *anything*, Sarah," he said, hoping to placate her.

"He's one of *them!*"

"Not since last night," Tom said. "Sarah." Tom reached for her. He had one more judge on his list.

"Why should Captain Maddox *care?*" Sarah demanded.

"He does," Tom said. "He came here because he *does* care." Tom sat down to telephone the last judge whose name and number he had included the night before. Sarah heard Tom pleading and saw him lower his head slowly as though he were under a great weight. She saw him replace the receiver and drop the legal pad into the briefcase. "I thought I could stop them," Tom said. When Tom came erect, she wanted to hold him. "I'd better get dressed," he said, but remained standing between the two chairs. "I have to call Captain Maddox," he said, and sat down once more. Tom looked up at Sarah. "I needed one guy. One guy who wasn't afraid of the governor and Doris Ashley and Harvey Koster and the rest."

Tom could not give up. He telephoned Philip Murray. There was no answer at Murray's house. Tom called Leslie McAdams, who said the district attorney and his wife were at sea on their sloop. "Didn't anyone ever teach you to relax?" McAdams asked.

"Hester Murdoch is sailing today!" Tom said. "She's going for good!" Tom said. "She and her mother. I'm losing my case because I can't get one, single, solitary, independent member of the bench in this whole town with the guts to respect the oath he took!"

"Those bastards," McAdams said. "Meet me at the courthouse. Those bastards."

Tom set down the telephone and, full of hope once more, turned to Sarah. "Will you drive me downtown?" He ran out of the kitchen past his mother, and stopped, whirling around. "Captain Maddox!"

When he heard the telephone, Maddox tossed the rolled newspaper on the sofa, running. He was in his bedroom as the first ring ended. "It's Tom Halehone."

"Good or bad?" Maddox asked.

"I'm meeting Leslie McAdams at the courthouse," Tom said. "He'll help me."

"Yeah . . ."

"Captain?"

"I'm here," Maddox said. "I'll call you at the courthouse." He turned off the lamp on the night table and went from the bathroom to the kitchen, switching off lights. Maddox went from room to room, slowly, as though he were looking for something, and paused to take his hat from the top of a chair in the living room. Outside, he stopped beside his car, opening the door and rolling down the window before entering. He backed out of his driveway and stopped, pulling down the brim of his hat to keep out the sun. "Get lucky," he said, admonishing both Tom and Leslie McAdams. "Get lucky."

It was almost nine-thirty when Sarah and Tom reached the courthouse. She followed him out of the convertible. "You'll be late for work," Tom said.

"I want to be with you today," Sarah said. Tom took her hand and they hurried through the alley to the side doors.

Leslie McAdams was alone in the district attorney's office, standing beside a secretary's desk. "Here's the list of every judge in the county," he said. "Check off those you've called and we'll split the rest. Hi," he said to Sarah.

Sitting at adjoining desks, Tom and McAdams began phoning judges on the bench of every court in Honolulu. Some did not answer. Some were not at home and their wives or children took the urgent, the desperate messages. Of those who came to the telephone, some were blunt, some offered elaborate excuses, but all refused to issue subpoenas. It was almost eleven o'clock when Leslie McAdams said, "Give up." He raised the paper with the names of the judges, studying it as though he held a rare and priceless manuscript, an antiquity. "If someone had told me I couldn't find a man in this town to issue a writ, I would have fought him," McAdams said. He flung aside the paper and as it fluttered to the floor he pointed at Tom. "Did you call Judge Kesselring?"

"No answer," Tom said. Leslie McAdams bent for the paper and as he found Geoffrey Kesselring's home number, a telephone rang. The telephone was on a secretary's desk near the door. All three ran and Sarah won, raising the receiver and extending it to Tom. "Any luck?" Maddox asked.

"We're going to try Judge Kesselring again," and to Sarah and McAdams, low, "Captain Maddox."

"What did he say the first time?" Maddox asked.

"He wasn't home."

"I'll wait," Maddox said. He was using a public telephone on a wall in a restaurant. The kitchen was open and the odors from the ovens and the ranges were hypnotic.

The operator said, "Your time is up. Signal when through," and then Tom said, "There's no answer."

"Yeah . . . Stay put," Maddox said. "Stay right there in the courthouse." He didn't want the kid or anyone with him making more conversation, taking more time. Maddox put another nickel in the slot, obeying the operator, and left the restaurant. He was on Kalakau Avenue, one block from Western Sky. "Didn't I know it?"

He made an illegal U turn and when he straightened his car he saw the Western Sky on his right, saw through it into the penthouse where Lenore and Bergman were packing, or finished and waiting for the bellhop, or following the bellhop out of the suite, or into the elevator, or out of it and into the lobby and across the lobby, heading for the ship, for the States, leaving forever. Maddox said something unintelligible, low and in despair, and turned into the curved hotel driveway past the waiting line of taxis. He stopped in the center of the broad stairs. He heard the taxi horn behind him and saw the hotel's doorman in his uniform coming down the steps, waving. Maddox put the police sign in the window. The doorman pointed. "There's plenty of room over there!"

"Touch this car and I'll come after you." He came up the steps to the lobby. Lenore could be coming through the doors. What was he supposed to say?

Maddox made it to the lobby. She wasn't in the lobby. He made it to the elevators. So all he had left was the penthouse floor. Maddox came out of the elevator. He didn't need to stop but he stopped. He didn't need to turn, but he turned, and as he did, reached for his hat as the penthouse door opened. Nobody had ever made him run, and he lowered his arm, holding his hat, as a chambermaid came out of Lenore's penthouse loaded with bed linens. "They checked out right after breakfast," she said.

Maddox turned, in a hurry now. He went to the opposite end of the corridor, stopping at the door of the other penthouse on the sea side of the hotel. He knocked, forgetting the doorbell, and when he dropped his hand, he could hear the princess. "It's open."

She was lying on the sofa in the living room of the penthouse with the telephone on the floor beside her and the cane next to her. She saw Maddox come through the door. "I should've kept it locked."

"I've come through locked doors," Maddox said, crossing the living room.

"Last time you had the common decency to call," the princess said, remembering his appearance on the night the admiral had established the curfew.

"You would've said no," Maddox said.

"I still say no, whatever it is." Maddox didn't move. "Beat it," the princess said. "You won."

"Same old song," Maddox said. "*I* won," he said, and louder, "I'm not here to trade punches with you. Can you walk?"

"I didn't fly out of bed," the princess said. "Go away, Maddox. I'm tired of you. You and everyone else in this town. I want to go home where I belong."

"I need your help," Maddox said. "*We* need your help. Me and Tom Halehone," he said. The princess raised the cane, holding it with both hands, studying Maddox.

"You and Tom," she said, and Maddox knew she was calling him a liar.

"Listen," he said, and told her everything from the moment the chief had ordered him to find Hester. Maddox spoke steadily, without pause. "We need two subpoenas," he said. "We need them fast."

"What makes you think I can do it?"

"There's nobody left," Maddox said. "Maybe you can't, and if you can't, Doris Ashley and that doxy daughter of hers sail away into the sunset."

"It's a new one," the princess said. "Nobody ever asked me for a subpoena." Maddox wanted to pull her off the sofa.

"We're running out of time!"

The princess swung her good leg off the sofa, and, using the cane for leverage, sat upright. "Don't be too sure, Maddox."

Maddox stepped aside to come around the coffee table. "Let me give you a hand." The princess raised the cane, stopping him.

"Why don't you go down and have a cab waiting?"

Maddox put his hand in his pocket and then raised it, showing her the badge. "Cabs don't have this."

"You might not like where we're going," the princess said. Maddox pushed the cane aside.

"There's a ship out there getting ready to haul anchor!" he said, loud.

The princess reached for the telephone on the floor and set it on her knees. She looked up at Maddox. "I warned you," she said, and watching Maddox, gave the hotal operator a number.

Maddox's fingers closed around his badge. He could feel the ragged configuration of the metal in his hand. "Harvey, I'm coming to see you. You'll find out when I get there," the princess said into the telephone. She set it on the floor, looking up at Maddox. "Now you can give me a hand."

In his house Harvey Koster went from the telephone across the dark polished floors to the staircase, moving through his home with quick short steps like a tiny beach bird skittering across the sand. He hurried up the stairs almost hidden by the railing, hurried through his bedroom to press the wall beside the mirror in his dressing room. As the mirror swung open and the ceiling burst into light, Koster stepped through the doorway, safe among his lovelies. They set up such a clamor, each demanding his personal, his undivided attention, that he was forced to protest. "Please! Please quiet down!" They persisted, however, until Koster realized it was Saturday and they had waited all week for their holiday. They were incorrigible, and in the end Koster became stern and spoke sharply. "This is *not* your party," he said, and as the uproar assailed him, clapped his hands. He could not be heard above the clamor of voices. Koster took drastic action. He turned off the lights and turned them up again. "Are we ready to be sensible?" he asked. "I should hope so. You'll have your party. *You shall have your party*. Later. Now I need your help. I've come for your help," Koster said, and sat down on his stool to think calmly, to find a reason for the telepone call from the princess. He was still searching when the alarm he had installed after the princess's last visit reverberated through the house. Koster rose from the stool. "I'll tell you everything!" he promised, and waited in the dressing room until the mirror was in place. The alarm sounded again as he came down the stairs. "Hello, Lu."

"Hello, Harvey," said the princess, leaning on the cane and holding the doorjamb with her other hand. Koster saw her bare foot. "I sprained my ankle." In the living room the princess waved her cane at the furniture. "Bring me something hard to sit on," she said. "You'd need a hoist and derrick to pull me out of this stuff." Koster left and returned carrying a dining room chair with a high wooden back. "Pretty chair," said the princess. She let herself down. "Pretty house. *Beautiful* house, Harvey. Did you do all this? Choose this stuff yourself?"

"It's my home," Koster said.

"Check and double check," said the princess. "Captain and crew, that's you. Harvey Koster doesn't like partners. You've always done your own picking, except for that son of yours. You didn't figure on Curt Maddox, did you?"

"Why are you here, Lu?"

"You've read or heard about the new Hester Murdoch trial," the princess said. Koster was silent. He had known there was trouble since her call. The new trial was like another plague. They were being eaten alive by the trials. They were being devoured. Everything they had worked to achieve, everything they had accomplished, was being destroyed, ploughed under, obliterated by these free shows in the courthouse. "Harvey?"

"Are you involved?" Koster asked.

"You're a little late with that question," the princess said. "You also know the answer. I've been in it since I made bail for those four kids. That's before the sailor killed one. *Yes-s-s-s*, I'm involved," she said, and told Koster what the admiral had done.

Koster tried but could not mask the relief, the joy her news had brought him. His pleasure was fleeting, however. The princess had not left the Western Sky in bare feet carrying a cane to make him happy. He was silent.

"You can't start celebrating yet," the princess said. "They haven't sailed yet. Tide isn't in yet. Why don't you ask me why I'm here?"

In his head Koster could see the water line creeping up the beaches. "Would you like a cup of tea, Lu?"

"While the tide rises," the princess said. "You're cute, Harvey, but we've warmed up. Let's play ball. Those folks are sailing today unless they're served with subpoenas. If they sail then, they'll be on the lam April twentieth, they'll be fugitives." The princess raised her cane, pointing it at Koster. "I'm here for the subpoenas, Harvey."

"Me? You're asking me . . . ? You want me to . . . ?" Koster's voice cracked, and he stopped. The princess's declaration was so unexpected, so shocking, so incomprehensible, that Koster became dumbfounded.

"That's right, Harvey," said the princess. "I want you to get me those subpoenas."

"Lu, Lu," Koster said, and stopped. He wrung his hands, trying, *trying* to understand, understand *her*. "Why do you come to me? Why do you come to *me?*"

"You're the only man, woman, or child in Honolulu, hell, in the Pacific, who can do it," said the princess.

"Do it! Do it!" said Koster, unable still to recover from his incredulity. "Do I look like a judge?"

"You know them all," the princess said. She pointed the cane at the telephone. "Call one."

Now, finally, blessedly, Koster could think once more, could digest her impossible demand, could dissect and confront the reason for her presence and its catastrophic consequences. "You know them all, too, Lu," Koster said. "You're not a stranger although you like to say you are."

"Sure I know them," said the princess. "A slew of them, anyway. But none of them owes me anything, and there's always *somebody* who owes you."

Koster was silent. Why had she chosen *him?* She knew he would be counting the seconds until the ship sailed, until the curse that had covered the entire Territory all these months was lifted at last. "You're talking about the law, Lu," Koster said. "We can't interfere with the law."

"You're watching the clock, Harvey," the princess said. "You're waiting for high tide. Don't. A judge issues subpoenas. What I'm asking for isn't interference."

"Lu . . ." Koster said, letting her name slide through the room. He came closer. "We've had enough publicity to last us a lifetime. Two lifetimes. It needs to be ended, Lu. We need to be finished with it, to lift the cloud that descended on us last September."

"Harvey, I—"

"You love these islands," Koster said, interrrupting the princess. "You never need to prove that to me, Lu, and I never need to prove it to you. Listen to me, Lu. Trust me. I know what's best for us, for all of us, for your people, too."

"My people," said the princess. "You're back to *that* swill." She pointed the cane at the telephone. "Call someone."

"It's Saturday," Koster said.

"That's why I'm here instead of the courthouse."

"I wouldn't know where to begin," Koster said. "Why would a judge listen to me?"

"Harvey, I've got to have those subpoenas," the princess said. "You've got to get them me those subpoenas."

"I've tried to make you understand," Koster said. He'd had enough of the princess. "I wish you could see this matter the way I see it." He took a step toward the door.

"Meanwhile the clock is ticking," said the princess. She extended the cane, holding it in Koster's path like a barrier at a turnpike. "Get me those subpoenas, Harvey."

"I've tried to be helpful!" Koster said, and meant it. "I've tried to explain to you! I've let you into my home, welcomed you into my home! Now I've had enough! I've had enough, even from you! I want Doris Ashley and Hester out of Honolulu! Good riddance! Doris Ashley is sailing! Hester is sailing!"

"Do yourself a favor," said the princess. "The biggest favor of your life. A little while back you said, 'Trust me.' Turn it around. Trust *me*, Harvey. Get me the subpoenas."

"Never!" Koster was angry. "Never!"

"You made me do it," the princess said, low. She looked up at the sallow man in his splendid house. "You remember the night of the curfew, Harvey, the night I came to see you. I didn't come through the front door. The front door was locked. I came in through the side door, and found out why you didn't hear the doorbell, Harvey. The steamboat music. You and your dolls were listening to the steamboat music. I climbed the stairs and saw you and your girls. Then I came down and started to yell."

For Harvey Koster the room became black. He couldn't see. He was spinning. He was falling in the black room. He was falling fast, like a rock falling, down, down, down, down, in a hole far, far below, forever below. He couldn't stop. He was lost. He would never return.

The princess saw Harvey Koster change right in front of her. He turned into a crazy man. He didn't even look the same. His face became red, bright red, like the setting sun. His eyes were popping. She thought he would drop. He looked like he was sinking, like he would sink and melt on the polished wood floor. She was ready to push herself erect and save him when he screamed. "Bitch!" Koster screamed. "Dirty bitch!" His voice sounded like a baby crying. "Dirty spying bitch!" he screamed. Koster sprang at the princess, and she raised the cane to protect herself, but he stopped, fists clenched. "Fucker!" he screamed. "Fucker, fucker, fucker!" jumping up and down as the words came, arms pumping as though he were pounding a drum with his fists. Suddenly he whirled around, running fast, on an angle across the room to throw himself onto the sofa. Face down he began to cry, to sob, his body heaving with the force of his convulsions. His voice was like a bellows, rising and falling with each sob, growing in intensity until the room seemed to echo. Koster's sobbing reached a peak, his body thrashing on the sofa, and the princess, alarmed, came to her feet, and started slowly to cross the living room. Then his cries began to subside. His voice fell. He lay still. The princess heard only the steady, "Uh . . . uh . . . uh . . . uh . . ." as Koster fought for breath, and when she was beside him, he was quiet. "Harvey?"

She saw him sit up like someone who has awakened from a nap. He was in the center of the sofa, his hands in his lap. His face was wet with tears but Koster seemed not to be aware of it. To the princess he looked no bigger than a chick but she felt, suddenly, in danger. "Nobody will believe you," Koster said.

"We'll soon find out if you're right. I'm heading for a printer. I'll have handbills printed up, *today*, with the story of your harem. I'll hire every kid in Honolulu to pass them out on every corner in town. I'll hire airplanes to scatter them over the island, over all the islands. The skies will be dark over the archipelago. I wonder if that was our word. You not only stole the islands, you took away the language." The princess took a step and said, "Ow-w-w-w-w!" as the pain shot up from her ankle, but she kept going.

Behind her Koster said, "Wait." The princess stopped and turned to see him leave the sofa, staying wide of her as he went to the telephone. Her leg throbbed but she remained standing, hunched over the cane. She had to finish now. Koster and his dolls and his home were noxious. She wanted to be gone. She could see Koster at the telephone and hear him, but his voice was too low; she could not make out a word. When he left the telephone, the princess could read nothing in his face. If he had failed, he was safe. No one would ever learn of his pathetic playhouse, certainly not Curt Maddox, not even Jack Manakula. "Judge Geoffrey Kesselring," Koster said. "He's at the Palama Stables. He's expecting you." The horses were Geoffrey Kesselring's enduring passion, and all that remained of his string of polo ponies that had vanished with his father's fortune was the single jumper he kept for his weekend riding. Koster had known where to find Kesselring, and he had known he would not need to remind the judge how his classmate at Panahou received his appointment to the bench.

Koster went past the princess and waited beside the closed front door. He did not open it until she reached him. The princess said, "Well, Harvey . . ." and broke off. She felt herself in danger once more, and she was right.

"Don't come back," Koster said. He had already decided that

if the princess spoke of his girls to anyone, anywhere, he would have her killed. He would hire whom he needed to hire and send the man to the big island.

He remained in his doorway, listening to the tap, tap, tap of her cane. The sound ended, and he waited to hear an automobile engine, to hear a car leave. Harvey Koster wanted no other surprises. No sound reached him, and after awhile, leaving the door ajar, Koster came out of his house, brushing against the giant hibiscus to remain hidden. As Koster approached the end of the border, he heard the princess say, "Well, you got what you asked for," and then, pushing back against the hibiscus, saw Maddox helping her into his car. The world became black once more and Koster reached out, grasping the thick limbs of the aged hibiscus for support. He heard the engine, heard the car moving, the gears changing, heard the sound of the motor fade and disappear before he began to make his way back to the open door, to the girls who were all that remained to him now.

In the car with the princess beside him, Maddox took the radio telephone from beneath the dashboard. He pressed the talk button and said, "Maddox. Ring Phil . . . ring the D.A.'s office in the courthouse. Ask for Tom. When you've got him, hook me in." Maddox knew that after what he had done since the previous night, he would never again have any secrets from the dispatcher or anyone else.

He held the radio telephone and drove with one hand until Tom said. "Captain Maddox?"

"Judge Kesselring. He's at—"

"You got them!" Tom cried. He was yelling.

"Hot *damn!*" yelled Leslie McAdams.

"He *got* them?" Sarah said, and began to clap her hands. In the car Maddox said, "Listen!" and then shouted, "*Listen!* Kesselring is at the Palama Stables. Have you got a car?"

"Yes, sure, yes!"

"*Listen!* Meet me at the pier," Maddox said. The kid would need help. "Wait! *Listen!*" Maddox had to tell him now, right now. "I didn't get those subpoenas. Your pal, the princess, got them. Okay? The Palama Stables. Okay?"

Maddox replaced the radio telephone. The princess studied him. "What is all this? Curt Maddox," she said, "did you have a vision or something?"

"You heard me," Maddox said. "We're all pals now."

"You're nobody's pal," said the princess.

Maddox was tired of her tongue. Her telephone call to Harvey Koster, the ride to Koster's home, the helpless, imprisoned eternity in his car, had depleted Maddox. As they reached the intersection, Maddox spun the steering wheel to the right as though he were being chased. He fell into the princess, shoving her into the door as he turned the wheel hard to the left, and as she rocked from side to side in the careening car, Maddox said, "Neither are you," and flipped the siren switch to shut her up.

The S.S. *Lotus* was prettied for a party. She was all white and the white glistened. The *Lotus* had come out of drydock before sailing to Honolulu, and she was resplendent. She carried two stacks, bright red with a single black stripe around each, and from these, fore and aft, the ship's pennants flew in the wind. She was a dashing ship, lean and trim. She had been from the start a favorite of her architect, and at his board he became infatuated with his lady. He swore she would be a nonpareil. He wanted a ship with an unequalled flair, and he could not let her go. His clients had to take the drawings away from him. He fretted over her from the day he saw her keel laid and yet, when she came off the ways, he knew he had created a queen. The *Lotus* was a beauty.

She remained a beauty. She was a good luck ship. Passengers wrote strange tales to the line offices in San Francisco. An incurable miraculously regained her health. A man facing economic disaster arrived in port to learn an inexplicable swing in the market had saved him. A British ambassador, on his way home to a disgraceful end, left the ship to discover his dispatches had been vindicated and he was en route to London for a knighthood.

She was a romantic ship from the day she sailed on her maiden voyage. People always fell in love aboard the *Lotus*, and each of her three masters married couples who had been strangers when they embarked.

Her appearance was always an event and even now, as she was about to sail, her pier was active and bustling. Jimmy Saunders had sent one hundred officers and men of the Shore Patrol to the *Lotus*. They were like an honor guard, standing in formation on either side of the gangplank. They all wore S.P. brassards and carried nightsticks and each officer wore a sidearm.

The ship's orchestra, dressed in bright colors and wearing leis, was grouped on the pier in front of the gangplank. Beside it was a chest-high table on which lay the deck plans with the cabin diagrams of the *Lotus* and the bookings for the voyage. As the passengers arrived and produced their tickets, the pursers checked their names on the manifest. Two Navy lieutenants examined every person who came aboard.

Maddox cut the siren when he reached the Western Sky to deliver the princess, but he turned it up once more as he swung out of the hotel driveway. Hearing it, the two cops assigned to the pier for the sailing cleared the entrance. They were beside his car when Maddox emerged. "What's the problem, Captain?"

"Just sightseeing," Maddox said. He left them, walking toward the hullabaloo. The ship was ready to go so Lenore was up there somewhere. She could be at the rail somewhere. She could be watching the orchestra. Maddox saw the white Navy uniforms lined up. He saw the two Navy lieutenants. The admiral wasn't taking any chances. Maddox made it all the way to the gangplank without looking up, and then he heard a woman's laughter, and he lost. He raised his head. She wasn't there. Maddox took off his hat and wiped the sweatband with his handkerchief, remembering Bergman in his office showing him the one Lenore had taken. Bergman had won it all.

The orchestra finished a tune and followed their conductor aboard the ship. Men and women selling flowers and souvenirs began to collect their wares, storing them in cartons and folding display cases that lay on collapsible stands. One vendor offered Maddox a tray of fruit at a bargain. Then the ship's stacks sounded for the first time, a deafening roar that engulfed the pier, sweeping down and through it like a cyclonic wind. Even the Shore Patrol broke ranks momentarily, startled by the sudden sustained boom announcing the ship's departure. The pier was emptying. The sellers of orchid leis and corsages, of flags and photographs, of embroidered pillows and sport shirts and sandals, were leaving in a steady procession, carrying their merchandise. Maddox could not help himself. He looked up at the ship again, high up, seeing the boats covered with canvas slung along the boat deck. She wasn't there. Nearby, Maddox heard someone say, "I think that's him." Maddox saw one of the Navy lieutenants at the gangplank pointing, and heard his companion say, "Must be. The commander said he had a limp." Maddox turned. Tom and the girl were headed for the gangplank. So Maddox had the girl besides. He hadn't figured on the girl.

The girl took the kid's arm to whisper something. Tom said something but Maddox was too far away; he couldn't hear it. He heard one of the lieutenants. "The commander sent down one hundred men for *him?*"

Now Maddox could see both kids clearly. They were scared but they kept coming. One lieutenant turned to the pursers. "We'll handle this." The other lieutenant joined him. They were directly in front of the gangplank, and as Sarah and Tom drew near, one said. "Too late. You can wave good-bye." Maddox put two fingers in his mouth and whistled. It could be heard in the street. He moved to his right and stopped beside Sarah.

"On your way," said the same lieutenant who had told them to wave. "All of you," he said. Maddox saw the two cops running. He didn't even know their names. Maddox turned to the two Navy lieutenants, grinning at them. "I should've introduced myself," he said, as though all three were standing at a bar, and held up his hand palm out so they could see the gold-colored badge. "You fellows are worrying yourselves into a sweat. I'll take care of these kids." The uniformed policemen ran up. "Stand by," Maddox said. He had to keep talking, keep moving. Those one hundred lunks could throw all five of them into the drink. Maddox came around Sarah and Tom to the table, facing the pursers. "I want some stateroom numbers," Maddox said. "Let me see that book of yours," he said, and had it, turning it around so he could read.

One of the Navy lieutenants said, "Now wait a minute, Captain. We've got our orders." Maddox flipped the pages, and when he turned, he was grinning again.

"Sure," Maddox said. He moved in between the lawyer and the girl, taking each by the arm. "This is police work," Maddox said, affably, and to the two cops, "If they try and stop me, arrest them." He became stern. "No rough stuff!"

Each cop went for a Navy lieutenant. "You heard the Captain," one cop said as they moved their arms in a breast stroke, clearing the gangplank. Maddox was right behind them, holding Tom and Sarah.

"You're a lawyer," Maddox said. "You should've had enough sense to bring a marshal."

"It's Saturday," Tom said. "I couldn't find one."

"Yeah," Maddox said. "I've been lucky all day." Maddox saw a crewman ahead. "Hold it!" They left the gangplank, coming aboard. "Where's A Deck? Cabins thirty-nine and forty-one. Use right and left so I can understand you," Maddox said. The crewman gave him instructions. Maddox pushed his hat back on his head. "Come on, lawyer. Let's get your pigeons," he said to Tom, and wondered, suddenly, if the princess had told Koster the name of her chauffeur.

They walked along the deck to a ladder and Maddox went first. Below he said, "This way," leading them to a passageway. It was worse than a pier, a hodgepodge of passengers, visitors, crewmen, stewards with trays of food and drinks high above their heads, and luggage everywhere. They walked single file to the end, where Maddox turned right. He stopped after a few feet. To the left was a passageway running parallel to the first. Maddox read the numbers on a plate screwed to the bulkhead. "Almost home," he said. He turned and was facing Commander Saunders.

Jimmy Saunders had men with him, all wearing webbed belts with holsters with guns. There were so many Maddox could not see past them. "You shouldn't have come aboard, Captain," Saunders said. "Turn around. Take him with you. Take him and the girl with you."

Maddox never paused. Tom looked at Sarah. She was pale, watching Saunders. "Stay here," Tom said. She followed Maddox. Ahead, Saunders took one step, stopping in front of his men. "End of the road, Captain."

Maddox pointed. "Here's thirty-nine," he said. "There's forty-one. This man is here to serve some subpoenas."

"No one enters those staterooms," Saunders said.

"Same old song," Maddox said. "Still doing everyone's job for him."

The captain didn't know it, but he was right. If Maddox and he had been alone, Saunders would have told him about Murdoch's letter, about the three enlisted men he was holding in the brig, waiting for Hensel so he could deliver all four to police headquarters. "Leave the ship," Saunders said. "Take them and leave the ship, Captain."

"The subpoenas," Maddox said.

"You're not going in there," Saunders said.

"You could be wrong," Maddox said. "This time you could be wrong. You're standing in the city of Honolulu. This pier is in the city limits. I'm a police officer. This man with me is an officer of the court in the county of Honolulu," Maddox said. "This time there's no chief of police around to let you do his job for him! You got me, Commander, not the chief of police!"

"You won't get through," Saunders said.

"You and me have been coming head to head for a long time," Maddox said. "You've been stealing people from me ever since I laid eyes on you. I told you, we're alone this time and you're interfering with justice. So whatever I do, I'll be doing to uphold the law. You'll be breaking the law. This man is going to serve those subpoenas. You can try and stop it, but you'll need to stop me first. It'll take more than an All-American, Commander. It'll take a gun. Think about that and think about this. You'll be playing with your life for a tart who isn't worth a bottle of soda pop. You can die for that tart. If you die, I'd have to get through a hearing but I would have killed you in the line of duty. If you win, it's murder. It's *murder!*" Maddox said, louder. "You can't kill a cop and walk away from it, not even out here. Besides, the governor can't turn every killer loose."

"I've got my orders," Saunders said.

"*Your* orders!" Maddox was shouting. "*Your* goddamn orders! Carrry out your goddamn orders where you belong! Your goddamn admiral has pushed us around long enough!" The ship's stacks sounded again, deep and throaty here in the passageway.

Maddox's arm shot out and when he could be heard, he said, "I'm going in there! Me and these kids are going in there." He glanced at the kids. "Stay behind me, up against me." He reached out, pawing the air, pushing the girl so he was hiding her. Watching Saunders, he came forward. He kept coming, and after a few steps, Maddox knew the commander had quit. Maddox went past Saunders, feeling the girl bumping him as he reached forty-one. He went into the door with his right shoulder, slamming it back against the bulkhead, leaping aside to grab Tom and swing him into the cabin. Holding Tom, Sarah stumbled and almost fell. Ahead of them, Maddox saw the admiral. He followed the girl into the cabin and saw Doris Ashley sitting alone in a corner.

The cabin became galvanized; it erupted. The admiral roared "Jimmy!" and lunged toward the passageway, bulling through Sarah and Tom. Doris Ashley leaped up. Saunders entered, his bulk seeming to fill the suddenly crowded cabin, and Maddox was turning every which way and shouting.

"Where's the girl? Hester Murdoch? Hester Anne Ashley Murdoch!" Maddox shouted, making the name into a curse. *He* had finally erupted, after keeping himself down ever since last night, ever since the start, really, and now he had to finish it, finish everything.

Behind him Saunders said, "There would have been another killing, sir."

"Why are they here?" asked the admiral. Maddox started for Doris Ashley. "You learned that much, didn't you? Why are they here?"

Doris Ashley was utterly and totally alone. She had been removed from Windward and now she was being delivered to the hands of the detective and the little beast with the limp. She heard Maddox say, "You'll find out pretty quick, admiral." The detective was coming after *her*. Doris Ashley pushed herself into the corner, along the cabin wall behind a chair. "Where's your daughter?" Maddox asked, and, shouting once more, "Do I have to dig her up again?"

Tom said, "Captain . . ." and Maddox looked away. Hester stood in the hatch connecting thirty-nine and forty-one.

"Yeah," Maddox said. "Gang's all here." Less than a minute had passed since he had burst into the cabin. Maddox nudged Tom. "Get a move on."

Reaching into his pocket, Tom said, "I have subpoenas for Hester Anne Ashley Murdoch and for Doris Ashley." He displayed the two folded documents. "I hold legal instruments of the Superior Court of the County of Honolulu that place you under the jurisdiction of the court. You are being ordered to appear in courtroom twenty-two of the Courthouse of the County of Honolulu at ten A.M. April twentieth, 1931, Number three-two-six-three, People versus David Kwan, Michael Yoshida, and Harry Pohukaina."

"You've had your trial," said the admiral. He'd been bullied long enough. "Those men are free men. Consider that before you act."

"They're innocent!" Tom said, as though he intended to serve the admiral as well. "I intend to prove their innocence!"

Maddox remembered the two spaced blasts from the ship's stacks. "Finish it off, Tom," he said, calling the lawyer by his name for the first time.

Tom moved away from the admiral. "Doris Ashley, I hereby . . ." he said, and Sarah cried, "No!"

She beat Tom to Doris Ashley, standing between them, her arms spread wide. "No!" Sarah cried. "No, Tommy, no!" She saw Maddox coming.

Tom looked at her in stupefaction, her arms out, protecting Doris Ashley. First he thought Sarah had been paid, that Doris Ashley had paid her. Tom knew that was insane. He thought Sarah had collapsed inside, had lost her reason. He said, carefully, talking to someone temporarily deranged, "Sarah, I have to serve these subpoenas."

She said, "You can't! I won't let you!" and caught him unaware, lunging forward to grab the folded documents, but she ran into Maddox. Sarah began to swing both arms, hitting Maddox with fists, wrists, forearms, until he put his arm around her middle and lifted her off her feet.

"Settle down," Maddox said, calmly, as he had to ten thousand nuts on ten thousand days and nights, in uniform and in plainclothes. "Settle down and we'll talk," he said. He looked at Sarah, giving her his word. "We'll talk."

Sarah's arms fell and her body slumped. She looked around her like someone who had acted on impulse and badly. But she faced them all without shame, and turning, spoke to Doris Ashley.

"I don't want them here!" Sarah said.

"Sarah, they're going to trial!" Tom said. He had the subpoenas out of reach.

"Why? Joe's dead!" Sarah said.

"Why?" Tom repeated. *"Because* Joe's dead! Because they accused innocent men whom they knew were innocent! Because they perjured themselves under oath! They're going to prison! This time they're going to prison! They must go to prison!"

"Why?" Sarah cried. "What will it prove?" She pushed her hair back from her forehead. "Tommy, I don't want them here! They don't belong here anyway! They never belonged here! They only came to steal. They're still stealing." Sarah stepped away, facing Doris Ashley. "She's *running*. Let her run. Let them both run. Everyone will know they ran."

"Everyone *you're* talking about will cheer," Maddox said. He could have pulled the subpoenas out of Tom's hand and served them himself, but the girl had to get things straightened out in her head. She was with Tom, and if she couldn't see this his way, Maddox had picked the wrong guy.

"They'll cheer," Maddox repeated. "They've been making their own law ever since the first ships put into port the first time. You'll never stop them unless you *stop* them." He pointed at Doris Ashley. "You have to convince them it's over, that they're finished making the rules, or changing the rules, or forgetting them, or spitting at them.

"They spit on *us!*" Sarah cried.

"Only if they leave!" Tom said. "Can't you understand that, Sarah? If we let them go, they're heroes . . . heroines! If Gerald Murdoch was here now and you let him go, people would be waiting on the dock in San Francisco to give him a medal!"

"Listen," Maddox said. He wanted to pick her up and shake some sense into the girl. "Your brother was murdered, and after the D.A. proved it, after they were convicted, they were on the street in an hour. An *hour!* The next guy who kills somebody's brother will probably break that record unless you put an end to it. *You.* Tom. Me. They can't keep thumbing their noses at the law. They can't. That's why these people have to go to jail. Doris Ashley has to go to jail. Her daughter has to go to jail."

Sarah said, "Joe . . . Tommy . . ." She moved back, and Maddox, nodded, praising her. He jabbed the lawyer in the ribs.

"Let's go, let's go," Maddox said.

"Doris Ashley," Tom said, and gave her a subpoena. "Hester Anne Ashley Murdoch," he said, and gave her a subpoena. Tom repeated the instructions from Judge Kesselring.

Doris Ashley held the subpoena as though it were infected. She felt infected. She shuddered, feeling her skin crawl *Prison!* She was being sent to *prison!* She would be in a *cell!* Doris Ashley saw the bathroom, saw the inhabitants of the bathroom, the flotsam, the refuse, the untouchables of the world. Doris Ashley moaned. Only Hester could save her. They would be together. They would share the cell, counting the days until they could return to Windward. Doris Ashley reached out for Hester who wasn't there.

Hester was with the detective, with Maddox. She had her suitcase and she clutched her subpoena, her freedom, the freedom Tom Halehone had given her. "Can I go now?"

"Hester!" cried Doris Ashley.

"You're on your own until April twentieth," Maddox said.

"Hester!" Doris Ashley reached out for her, but Hester jumped back, bumping into the admiral.

"I'm not coming with you," Hester said, free at last, free forever. "You can't send anyone to find me and bring me back. I'm never coming back. You heard Captain Maddox. I'm on my own." Preston Lord Ashley had left his daughter more money than she could ever remember.

"You can't leave me," said Doris Ashley. Hester was leaving. "Hester! *Baby! Please!* Baby, please! Please don't *leave* me!" Hester never looked back.

Tom Halehone had rescued her. Prison was only a way station. Hester knew her destination at last, her haven, her true home. It had been waiting for her since she had looked at Joseph Liliuohe from her bed in Mercy Hospital and sent him to die. Hester was already embarked on her journey, her final journey. No one would turn her away at Molokai. Since she, too, was a leper, she would learn to care for the other lepers.

In the stateroom Doris Ashley staggered and fell back into the chair. She said, whimpering, "Hester," as though she were alone in the dark calling for help. She sat like a derelict, like someone lost and without power of comprehension. In the crowded stateroom Doris Ashley was utterly and irrevocably isolated. Her defeat was absolute.

"Dismiss your men, Jimmy," said the admiral. He gestured at Maddox. "They're in command here."

"Uh, uh," Maddox shook his head. "You brought her, admiral.

You take her back.'' He looked at the wreck in the chair, remembering that she had refused to ride in the front seat of his car with him. Maddox turned and went past Saunders as he left the cabin.

Sarah and Tom caught up with Maddox in the passageway. "You'll probably end up in a lot of trouble," Tom said.

"Yeah. You two can find your way off this tub without me," Maddox said. He had one more stop.

Maddox hailed the first crewman he saw. "I need the promenade deck." The crewman gave him instructions and Maddox climbed a ladder. He made a turn and was at the foot of another. Maddox was at the bottom of a skyscraper. He went up and up. His thighs ached. He refused to pause and rest. He began to breathe with difficulty and when he saw the words *promenade deck* above him, he was flushed and shaking inside, and it was from something besides his exertions. He entered a passageway, turned into another, and stopped to read the metal plate with the stateroom numbers. He had reached the end and despite the interminable climb, it seemed to have come too soon.

He stopped at 103. He had two choices, 103 or 105. He wet his lips. "Do it," he said, and knocked on 105. He raised his hand to knock again, and the door opened. "Hello, Lenore."

Maddox knew, irremediably, he was sunk forever. He would never forget her. He would never stop wanting her, aching for her, longing to have her with him, beside him, near him, waiting for him, there to welcome him. He would never see another woman without turning away because she wasn't Lenore. He would never hear a woman laugh without missing Lenore. He would mourn her every day of his life for the rest of his life. What would he do all the rest of his life?

"Hello, Curt." She was doomed. She felt truncated, as though part of her was being cut away. She had found, and lost, everything of value in her life, all in a flash, in a few short spinning weeks. She had come alive here on this island with Curt, and now it was being taken from her. She had been rewarded only to be punished for having come upon the reward. She was dazed by her loss. All that mattered to her, the hopes and dreams, the radiance of her days with Curt, was disappearing with him. She felt old, shriveled and cold. She would always be cold now.

"I brought something of yours," Maddox said. He reached into his inside jacket pocket for the pale green scarf she had dropped into his car in the alley beside the courthouse. "You must have forgotten it," Maddox said.

"I suppose, yes," Lenore said. Both knew the truth and both knew he had not made the journey to return a woman's scarf she had chosen from scores of others on a Chicago counter.

"I keep saying good-bye to you," Maddox said. "I've been doing it ever since that night at the hospital. It doesn't work, Lenore. You won't go away."

She said, murmuring, "Nor will you." Her voice electrified him.

"Don't go. Don't go, Lenore." He could not lose her. "Don't leave, Lenore." He watched her, looking into her eyes, looking for help, looking for hope. "You belong here with me," Maddox said. His throat was tight and hurt. "Wherever you are, you belong with *me*. You can cross six oceans, and you won't have moved an inch, you'll still be right here and I'll still be right there, only we won't be together. So you have to stay, Lenore. You have to stay."

"I thought that was you," Bergman said, coming down the passageway. Maddox felt as though someone had put a dagger into his back. Lenore's fingers brushed his as she took the scarf, and then Bergman was with them, in front of 103. "Coming around the corner I said, 'There's a fellow who's the spitting image of Captain Maddox.' Come all the way over here to say good-bye, Captain?"

"Nope." The word hung in the air.

"Don't imagine we'll ever meet again, Captain," Bergman said. "Best of luck to you." Maddox looked at him.

"I'm not finished here," Maddox said. Nobody moved. Nobody spoke. Then Maddox reached out to open the door of 103. "This one's yours, isn't it?"

"You're running out of time," Bergman said. He went into the stateroom but didn't close the door. "You heard him, Lenore," Maddox said. "We're running out of time, you and me. There's all the time in the world ahead of us but not here, not on this ship." He took her hands; they were like ice. "Come on, Lenore!" Maddox said. "You don't owe him! He owes you!"

"Lenore?" Bergman's voice was weak and strained. Lenore moved her hands away from Maddox's.

"This is our last chance," Maddox said. "I told you once nobody gets two, but we beat the odds, you and me. It's you and me, Lenore! You belong to me! We proved that right from the start!"

"Curt . . . I . . ."

"Not I!" he said. *"We! We!"*

"Lenore." Bergman's voice was faint. Maddox extended his hand.

"Hold on to me," Maddox said. "Forget your clothes. They're his clothes. Leave it all. We'll start from scratch. We'll be brandnew."

"Not like this," Lenore said. Maddox's arm fell.

"There's no other way," Maddox said. "There never will be."

"You don't understand," Lenore said. "He deserves . . ."

"*We* deserve!" Maddox said, interrupting. "He's had his run! It's our turn!"

She said, "Curt . . . darling . . . I must talk to him, tell him."

"Lenore?" Bergman's voice seemed to be fading.

She said, "Help me, Curt. You've always helped me. You've always been my savior, my true friend. Leave me alone with him."

"Don't let him sink us," Maddox said. "He'll try anything, pull anything. Run if you have to. Start running and keep running."

Lenore looked at him and they were together again as they had been from the first. She put her fingers to her lips, and then to his lips, and turned. "Yes, Walter."

Maddox was alone again. He took a step, another, another, listening for her, seeing her in his head, running, joining him so they could run together. He came out on the promenade deck, high above the pier. Walking toward him was a steward holding a cord from which hung a metal disc, and in the other hand a stick, like a drumstick. One end was a ball covered in felt, and as the steward approached, he struck the disc with the ball. Bong-g-g-g-g-g-g! A hollow, resonant, melodic sound carried along the deck and then the steward said, "The ship is sailing! The ship is sailing!"

Maddox reached the ladder and looked back. He saw only the steward. Bong-g-g-g-g-g-g!

Maddox went down to the sports deck. A man and a woman were at the rail, their arms around each other, kissing. Maddox went past them and past two priests who were busy talking and pretending to ignore the lovers. Maddox reached another ladder and a boy of about eight or nine ran into him and fell. Behind him the boy's mother rushed forward, glaring at Maddox. "Can't you watch where you're going?"

Her son scrambled to his feet and ran. Maddox came down the ladder and turned.

Bong-g-g-g-g-g-g! "The ship is sailing! The ship is sailing!"

Maddox went from the main deck to another ladder and

halfway down saw the admiral walking with Doris Ashley. Saunders was with them and a steward with a dolly with the luggage. Maddox wanted to slow up. He wanted to start back, all the way back to Lenore. He wanted to pick her up and carry her off the ship. Maddox came out on A deck, moving steadily down to the pier. Ahead of him was a steward with a gong.

Bong-g-g-g-g-g-g! "The ship is sailing! The ship is sailing!"

Maddox was sweating. He walked beside the rail, his head raised for the breeze from the sea. He came to another ladder. A lady carrying a Pomeranian was coming up. Maddox stepped aside. The lady reached the top. "It's always nice to meet a gentleman," she said. Maddox went past her, clattering down the ladder. His chest hurt.

He was at the gangplank. The pursers were carrying the high table aboard.

Bong-g-g-g-g-g-g! "The ship is sailing! The ship is sailing!"

The gangplank was clear. Maddox came down the pier and turned. He couldn't see her. "Captain?"

Maddox turned around as though he had been ambushed. The two uniformed cops were facing him. "Everything okay, Captain?" Maddox nodded. "Anything we can do for you?"

"No, no." Maddox turned. He was in front of the gangplank. He didn't see her. Maddox spread his arms, holding the handrails of the gangplank. The ship's stacks sounded, a long, sustained, thunderous bellow. Maddox searched the decks. "Lenore!"

The pier became quiet. Where was she? "Lenore!"

Bong-g-g-g-g-g-g! "The ship is sailing! The ship is sailing!"

"Lenore!" She had to hurry. The clock was running out. "Lenore!" Maddox's lips made a word. "Please."

Bong-g-g-g-g-g-g! "The ship is sailing! The ship is sailing!"

"Lenore!" If she was coming, she had to come now. *Now!* "Lenore!"

Bong-g-g-g-g-g-g! "The ship is sailing! The ship is sailing!" She had to come now. Maddox was spread out, holding the handrails as though someone was trying to move the gangplank. On the pier men approached the bow and stern lines. *"Lenore!"* Maddox was shouting.

"Lenore!"